Immortal Wife

BOOKS BY
IRVING STONE

IMMORTAL WIFE (*Jessie Benton Fremont*)

LUST FOR LIFE (*Vincent Van Gogh*)

SAILOR ON HORSEBACK (*Jack London*)

THEY ALSO RAN (*Defeated Presidential Candidates*)

CLARENCE DARROW FOR THE DEFENSE

FALSE WITNESS

PAGEANT OF YOUTH

DEAR THEO
(*Autobiography of Van Gogh from His Letters*)

Immortal Wife

THE BIOGRAPHICAL NOVEL OF

JESSIE BENTON FREMONT

By IRVING STONE

THE SUN DIAL PRESS

Garden City   New York

The Books

For

JEAN

in whom I found my Jessie

BOOK ONE

Dawn Comes Early

SHE SWEPT into the reception room of Miss English's Academy, her hazel eyes bright with anger, the rustle of her taffeta gown raised from a crisp whisper to a cry by the vigor of her movements. Looking neither to right nor left Jessie Benton stormed up to her father and said in a low voice:

"I won't stay in this school another day. I'm going home with you tonight!"

Without trying to rise, her father asked, "What has happened?"

"I had Harriet Williams elected May Queen. She's the prettiest girl in the school, and the best dancer. But at breakfast this morning Miss English announced that we had to have a different queen."

Thomas Benton gazed into his daughter's enormous eyes.

"I trust you accepted the decision philosophically?"

She threw back her head with a spirited gesture of denial.

"I jumped to my feet and cried, 'This decision is unjust and unfair. The first choice of Harriet was honestly made!' "

"What happened then?"

"Miss English called me to the head of the dining room, put her hand on my forehead and said, 'Miss Jessie, you seem feverish. Please report to the infirmary.' "

Tom Benton chuckled at the mimicked severity of his daughter's voice. "How was the hot senna tea?"

"Dreadful, thank you. They kept me in solitary all day. But I used the time to good advantage, planning a mutiny. On May Day all the girls will complain of a headache, and we'll be sent to bed with senna tea. The tea won't be half so bitter as watching that other queen try to dance. They only appointed her because she's a Fitzhugh, and Harriet's father is a government clerk . . ."

"Jessie dear," broke in her father, "Mother didn't feel well enough to come to the musicale, so I've brought a friend. May I present Lieutenant John Charles Fremont?"

A young man in army uniform who had been standing a few steps behind Tom Benton's chair came forward into the light of the candelabrum. The red wine of Jessie's anger, which she had been storing since breakfast, drained from her mind as suddenly as if someone had pulled the stopper of a vat. Her first thought was, At last I've met a man who is better-looking than my cousin Preston. I'm glad I wasn't too mad to wear my new pink candy-stripe with the rose sash instead of the dotted muslin with the blue.

She extended her hand, and instantly it was clasped in his. The young man had not moved with abruptness, nor was he now gripping her hand tightly; but here was a hand and a grasp that matched her own. She sensed what it was about a handshake that made it more than an empty social gesture: this brief embrace of the flesh.

The presentiment passed. She heard her father speaking to her.

". . . May Queen was supposed to be the best student in the school. Was Harriet at the top of her class?"

Only with the greatest reluctance could she bring herself back to the discussion. This morning seemed far away and long ago. In her dislike of the school she had seized upon the injustice to Harriet as a means of escape.

"No," she conceded, "Harriet was at the top of the mulberry tree more often than at the top of her class. We can climb into the tree from the window of my room, and the teachers can't hear us talking and laughing."

"You were vulnerable," pronounced Senator Thomas Hart Benton in his most pontifical tone; "when you decided that you were going to have Harriet elected, you should have managed her studies as well as shepherded her votes. Isn't it true, Lieutenant Fremont," he continued, "that in politics as well as war we must never permit ourselves to be vulnerable?"

"True," murmured the lieutenant, "in war, politics and love. But not always easy to live up to."

Jessie gazed at the young man admiringly. She thought, He outflanked Father neatly.

"As for that May Day uprising," her father went on, "mutiny is dangerous business; a little of it goes a long way."

Jessie turned to Lieutenant Fremont a cameo face, the delicate oval accentuated by the long brown hair parted in the center and combed over the temples to conceal all of the ear except the tip of the lobe. For so slender a face, her mouth was startlingly full and red-lipped, high-lighted by the smooth creamy texture of her skin. When she was thinking fast the color pounded into her cheeks, just as now, when she murmured:

"My father is really not qualified to preach that sermon, Lieutenant Fremont; he brought me up on stories of how he and Andrew Jackson mutinied against the War Department."

Her father made a ducking gesture of pleased acceptance of defeat; their years of close association had taught Jessie how to pull the sting out of any impending parental rebuke.

"However, I'll give up the idea," she agreed. "It wouldn't do any good, anyway: Harriet's mother took her out of school this afternoon. Come, gentlemen, let us go into the auditorium; the music will start any moment."

She sat between her father and the lieutenant while her older sister Eliza opened the program with a faithful but uninspired playing of a Bach fugue. There were perhaps a hundred guests in the assembly room; the small stage was lighted by guarded footlight candles, and the deep blue draperies were pulled over the side rows of windows to blot out the early February dusk. Because of her tale about Harriet they had come in late and were seated in a far corner on a button-back chaise. She was glad it had happened that way, for it gave her a chance to study John Fremont's face in the semidarkness.

She was astonished to see that he was a little man, certainly not much bigger than she, for their shoulders came to precisely the same height against the green silk of the sofa; their eyes too were on a level.

Why, he's small, she thought. Exactly my size, and I'm only five feet two. How odd I didn't notice that when we were standing. He doesn't have the feel of a little man.

She turned to look at her father, who towered above her, an enormous fellow with a big-boned frame, shoulders that sloped sharply as did her own, but heavy and powerful from years of outdoor living.

She was not greatly interested in music, and particularly not in this fugue which Eliza had been dinning into her ears for a solid week. Her eyes wandered over the backs of her schoolmates, seated between their parents. She had not wanted to come to Miss English's Academy in Georgetown, a suburb of Washington. She remembered the scene with her father when he had first told her that she must attend.

"What can I learn there that will be of as much value as studying at home?" she had demanded. "What will I find to read in their juvenile textbooks after I've been over most of the world's literature with you?

Who is going to help you with your reports and speeches, who is going to calm you when you stomp up and down this room crying out at the stupidity of your opponents? By the Eternal, Tom Benton, I am not going to that girls' finishing school."

"Yes, you are, Jessie," he had said, his head down, eyes averted. "If it were ever to happen that anyone should accuse you of lacking in manners or grace or anything you can get at that school, I would never forgive myself. I'm afraid that you have become old before your time by associating with me so much. Mother accuses me of robbing you of your childhood."

"But that's not true," she had exclaimed, hurt at her mother's blindness. "I've had a magnificent childhood with you: we went quail hunting each autumn in the country, and lunched on biscuits and apples while you read to me the stories your friend Audubon wrote; we spent whole weeks in the saddle riding through Missouri while you campaigned; we . . ."

"Mother says you're undisciplined. She thinks you need classroom work; she says you need to learn to play girls' games."

"But damme, Father," she had answered, "I don't want to play games. And will you tell me why I need classroom discipline when every time we went out on a picnic you would make me take my copy of Homer's *Odyssey* and read from it in Greek? If I'm not better educated than any girl you will find at Miss English's Academy, I'll eat the twenty volumes of your *British State Trials*."

Her father had not even listened to her.

"I know my duty, Jessie, and I'm a hard man to divert."

Later that evening she had come back to his library and stood before him on the thick rug, her eyes red and swollen, her brown hair cut off at the shoulders.

"What in heaven's name have you done to yourself, Jessie?" her father had cried in anguish.

"I've cut off my hair so I'll be ugly," she announced through her tears; "now I won't need any classrooms or discipline, or to go out in society. Father, all I want to do is stay here and be your companion."

Tom Benton had remained firm. "I can't take the responsibility for anything lacking in your life. You are fourteen years old, you are already late in entering. Now stop the sniveling and go out with your mother and Eliza and order some new clothes."

As she had turned to leave the room he had called, "Maybe the school will only be half as bad as it sounds. I promise to save all of my important speeches for when you will be home on week ends."

That was two years ago; her hair had grown long again, but her dislike for the school had persisted.

Eliza finished her number, acknowledged the polite applause. Jessie looked to John Fremont, waiting for him to project himself, create the impression which the hundreds of men who crossed the threshold of the Benton home in Washington had sooner or later set out to create. The young lieutenant returned her gaze with friendly interest, but said nothing.

Words always had been beautiful to Jessie Ann Benton, but as she sat in the comfortably poised silence, feeling keenly the presence of the Army officer beside her, she sensed that words were not the sole measure of communication, nor perhaps even the best. John Fremont did not speak; yet some inward ear, hitherto unsuspected, heard him speaking to her.

"What branch of the service are you in, Lieutenant Fremont?" she asked.

"The Topographical Corps. I'm working with Mr. Nicollet and Mr. Hassler on the map of the Minnesota country."

"Nicollet and Hassler? Why, they are two of Father's closest friends."

"That's how I met Senator Benton. He came to Mr. Hassler's house, where I am plotting the material we gathered on our expedition to the upper Missouri."

"Were you on that expedition with Nicollet?" she demanded excitedly.

"Yes, I've been his assistant for four years now; most of that time we've spent in the northern wilderness, in the Indian country."

An exclamation came from Jessie's full lips.

"Is it true, Miss Benton," asked the lieutenant, "that your father has never been west of Missouri? I can hardly believe it: he knows more about the West than any man I've met."

Jessie was warmed by the tribute to her father; she felt a companionable glow come over her.

"He has never been west of Missouri, but his mind has lived in those regions ever since he was a boy. His closest friends are the explorers and hunters who outfit in St. Louis and work their way to the Rockies; they stay at our home in St. Louis when they return from their expeditions." She made a half-turn to include her father in the conversation. "Father had it all planned for me to be a son. I was to be trained for the Army, join the Topographical Corps, and explore the West. Isn't that so, Father?"

"Something of the sort," he grumbled.

A string quartet began to play, and they again fell silent. At the intermission Thomas Benton introduced Lieutenant Fremont to Eliza. While Eliza and the lieutenant exchanged greetings, Senator Benton suggested to Jessie that they take a turn about the garden. Though it was only seven o'clock they found the air cool and sharp as they walked along the gravel path between Miss English's rows of trimmed hedges.

"Do you think Eliza will like Lieutenant Fremont?" asked Tom Benton.

"He's tremendously exciting," Jessie replied, her wide-set hazel eyes flashing.

Tom glanced quickly at his daughter.

"I asked if you thought Eliza would like him, not if you liked him. Young ladies who are still two months short of being seventeen aren't supposed to find strange men exciting."

Jessie looked amusedly at her father in the darkness.

"Would you mind citing your authority for that statement, Senator?" she asked, mimicking the tone which he reserved for his opponents on the floor of the United States Senate.

When they came back into the auditorium Jessie's eyes quickly caught the wiry figure of Lieutenant Fremont silhouetted against the blue draperies. He seemed surcharged with energy, yet he had the sensitive face of the intellectual. He's terribly young to be so close to the top of his profession, she thought.

As her sister and Lieutenant Fremont joined them, she felt a wave of resentment at her own romantic foolishness. Now I am behaving like a sixteen-year-old, she said to herself. If I can't do any better than this, Father is right to keep me in a girls' school.

She raised her sloping shoulders, tensed her diaphragm, concentrated on the group of ballads being sung. The music was diverting, her shoulders slowly slipped, and she sat relaxed. As the song reached a crescendo she had a feeling that the young man was speaking to her. She glanced about at him; his lips were quiet.

"Yes?" she asked softly.

His voice, deep for so small a person, said, ". . . nothing important; just that—I've been watching . . . your pearl earrings . . . gleam in the candlelight. The lights and shadows were keeping rhythm with the music."

Jessie lifted her hand to where the rich brown hair was combed tightly over her ear, took his finger and touched it lightly to the tiny circle of white lobe which she left exposed. Then she laughed, her laughter leaping forward; his laughter came forth strong, meeting her halfway, mingling with hers, seizing it. Happily the music had reached its climax, and no one heard them; but Jessie heard, and she asked herself in wonderment: What does this mean?

2

SHE SAT BEFORE THE MIRROR of her dressing table, alternately gazing at her reflection and out the window at the back garden. This was the moment for which she had been waiting since her father had announced casually, after the Wednesday evening musicale, that she would meet Lieutenant Fremont again at dinner on Sunday. The intervening days had passed in stops and rushes; with Harriet gone from school, and the young lieutenant having pre-empted her place in Jessie's mind, Miss English's Academy for Young Ladies seemed more childish than ever.

Her father's friends and associates who habituated the Benton drawing room called her the prettiest girl in Washington; at Cherry Grove, her mother's home in Virginia, the family would put her on exhibition every summer when she visited, turning her about slowly, commenting on her lithe figure, the deep brown hair, the magnificently soft and sensitive hazel eyes and the delicacy of her face, which they declared to be in the genteel tradition of the McDowells.

Jessie had never been impressed by these comments; she had taken for granted that she was an attractive girl, as were all the girls about her; it was part of being young to be pretty.

Now for the first time as she scrutinized herself with what she insisted was objective detachment, she realized that her family and friends had been flattering her. Her eyes were too large and wide-spaced for so slender an oval. I'm all eyes, she thought, like a cat at night. The rest of my face drowns in them. No, not my nose; unfortunately I've got Father's nose. He has always loved his long Roman nose because it makes him look like a senator, but I don't want to be a senator, and I have no use for it. And if nature meant for me to have slender cheeks, why wasn't the design carried through? Why do I have a chin that looks like Senator Benton's when he's got it stuck out pugnaciously demanding free land for the settlers of the West?

Her interest in her own face passed abruptly as she swung about on the low dressing-table stool and tried to conjure up instead the face of Lieutenant John Charles Fremont. A feeling of disappointment came over her: she could not remember what the man looked like. How can this be? she asked herself. How is it possible that I cannot remember what color his eyes are, or the shape of his mouth, or how he combs his hair?

Hearing the sound of a carriage drawing up to the front entrance, she quickly adjusted the coral collar and cuffs on her white spencer blouse, grateful for the sheen of color with which they brushed the pallor of her skin. I wouldn't want him to think me delicate, she mused as she rose, pushed back a strand of hair which insisted upon wandering down over her brow, and seized a coral lace handkerchief from her bureau drawer. As she passed the door of her mother's bedroom she stopped for a moment to look in.

Elizabeth Benton was stretched out on a satin-covered chaise; her black hair was streaked with gray, her once beautiful face deeply lined. Though she was only forty-seven, twelve years younger than her husband, she always had seemed to Jessie to be incomparably older, perhaps because she had spent most of her waking hours on this chaise, not bedridden, but with both her body and spirit immobile. Mrs. Benton had made it understood that her bedroom was her sanctuary, that no one might enter without permission. The floor was covered with a deep rose carpeting, the curtains were of fine lace encrusted with small medallions, two fragile gilt chairs stood before the windows, and next to the small bed was a tilt-top table with pink roses painted on its mahogany surface. It was all very elaborate and delicate, unlike the rest of this house which had been built by a wealthy English merchant and had been both designed and furnished in the most massive masculine taste. It was as unlike the rest of the house, the girl thought, as Elizabeth McDowell Benton was unlike Thomas Hart Benton . . . or Jessie Ann Benton.

As her mother beckoned, Jessie walked quickly to her side, smoothed the quilted chaise robe. "How are you feeling?" she asked.

"Fairly well, thank you."

"You're not coming down to dinner?"

"No . . . o, I'm comfortable here. Maylee will bring my tray. Father told me everyone who was coming; there will be an interminable argument, Jessie. I'm just not up to it; you know how ill the noise makes me."

Jessie knew that her mother was suffering from some intermittent ailment, but its source was obscure to her. No doctors came to the house; Mrs. Benton took no medicines or treatments; no symptoms ever were described. Yet several years before she had stepped down from active management of the household, leaving it in the hands of the trained servants she had brought with her from Cherry Grove. She now joined the family for dinner only on those rare occasions when there were no guests present. She seemed to her young daughter to take part in no active life whatever, for she did not read, her hands lay idle, she had abandoned her circle of women friends, and no serious matter could be discussed in her presence.

Yet it had not always been so: Jessie could remember when her mother had sat with them before the bright winter fire, her father at one side reading one of an endless succession of books, Mrs. Benton sitting at a smaller table opposite her husband, knitting or embroidering; Jessie and her sisters and brother working at their lessons at a heavy, square desk under the front windows.

Even now, during their yearly vacations at her mother's home in Virginia, where both Elizabeth McDowell and Jessie Benton had been born, the illness seemed to vanish, the lines in her mother's face to recede, her vigor return, so that she appeared again the happy woman whom Jessie remembered from her childhood.

As she went to the windows and drew the blinds, then put a few drops of fresh eau de cologne on her mother's lace handkerchief, these early memories of her mother were pleasant to recall, even though there never had been a complete love or understanding between them. It had been largely her own fault, Jessie knew: she had loved her father and the work he had trained her to do so devotedly that she had been unable to hide her preference. And always in her mind there had been a resentment that her mother did not work with her father, that she did not assist him in formulating his plans, help him write his speeches and articles, did not discuss with him the unendingly exciting issues and causes of the contemporary world.

Though her father never had said anything to her, though she was given daily, even hourly evidence of how utterly Tom Benton was devoted to his Elizabeth, Jessie felt that he missed her sorely in his work. It was only by the implications of the philosophy on which he had raised his second daughter that she had come to understand this:

"Don't be content to be a housewife; don't be content to think only of manners and charm and dilettantish conversation; don't be content to have your mind and personality obliterated by your husband. Prepare yourself, develop your thinking powers, grow accustomed to conflict and the clash of ideas. Then when you grow up you will be able to make a contribution to the society in which you live, you will never weaken in the face of personal warfare."

Jessie wished her mother a pleasant dinner, then hurried on down the stairs. She paused on the threshold of the drawing room to listen to the relaxed hum of Sunday afternoon conversation, while her eyes roamed the room to identify their friends. Sitting in the bow of the window overlooking C Street, and framed by floor-length curtains of starched white lace, she saw her father and Senators Linn and Crittenden, his fellow battlers for western expansion, dressed in the conventional white waistcoat, black coat with square-stubbed tails, and black trousers which fitted tightly over their Wellington boots. Sprawled before them on a velvet love seat with curlicue arms were their two most savage opponents in the House, bantering the senators on the legislation they had blocked the week before.

At the back of the room Jessie saw her large, rather plain-faced sister Eliza playing softly on the piano. It had not surprised her that Eliza had been uninterested in the young lieutenant from the Topographical Corps. Eliza was quiet, slow-spoken and inclined to be literal-minded. She had inherited her father's rawboned physique and heavy features. If she were a man she would have been a lawyer, for she liked the precise and methodical thinking of the legal mind. Eliza had been ill during most of her childhood; she was not strong and she greatly feared the ravages of personal emotion. Jessie had thought at first that Eliza had no feelings, until she had learned that her sister was avoiding personal involvement in order to spare her limited strength.

Leaning against the piano was Mrs. Linn, dressed in a new white India muslin redingote lined with a pale blue silk. She was telling Mrs. Crittenden and Mrs. King, the Bentons' next-door neighbor, about the glass-blowing exhibition she had seen at the circus the day before. Seated in the far corner at a round, marble-topped table, and sipping sherry, was Nicholas Nicollet, the greatest scientist of exploration and map-making in America. He was describing to Colonel J. J. Abert, head of the Topographical Corps, and Colonel Stephen Watts Kearny, one of the oldest and dearest friends of the Benton family, a new invention of a rubber boat which the next expedition could use for shooting the rapids of the Des Moines River.

Skimming quickly over the familiar surface of these faces and conversations, Jessie's eyes sought the tall rectangular mirror over the massive fireplace, in which she saw reflected three faces: that of Samuel Morse in his shiny black clothes, sallow and ill with the ravages of disappointment; Anne Royall, a bony, sharp-featured woman in her seventies, dressed in a stiff calico gown wrapped around the waist with a cord and tassel; and Lieutenant John Charles Fremont, in his blue army uniform with shining gold braid. The first feminist to invade Washington, Mrs. Royall was talking passionately about an article in her magazine, *Paul Pry*, while Samuel Morse stood unhearing, chewing his own bitter thoughts, and the lieutenant, in a most unmilitary manner, was trying to ward off the avalanche of words by gazing head down at the carpet and following a leaf pattern with the toe of his boot.

A quickening ran through Jessie. Now, before he sees me, she thought, before I get too close to him, I'll take a long, careful look. She gazed steadfastly at the reflection in the mirror, but the harder she looked the faster her breath came and the more blurred became the vision. It's like those first daguerreotypes Sam Morse made, she told herself; they catch an imprint, but faintly, through a haze.

Her eyes went first to his hair, which she saw with a start was parted in the center. Just like mine, she exclaimed to herself. It was black, and with a twinge of envy she noted its soft wave as it came a little forward on his high brow before sweeping backwards over the top of his ears. His black eyebrows slanted angularly downward at the corner of his eyes; his dark eyes were grave, sympathetic, his bone-ridged nose short and slender, his black mustache as straight as his stiffly pressed uniform.

Yet even as she enumerated to herself his separate features she realized that no such physical description could engrave an ineradicable picture of Lieutenant Fremont on her mind: for the look of the man was something over and above the component parts of the features with which he confronted the world. There appeared to be promise behind that slow, enigmatic smile: he radiated an aura of confidence.

Samuel Morse had begun to tell a story in a low hoarse tone, and as Lieutenant Fremont listened to the inventor with an expression of interest and sympathy, Jessie perceived that until she came to grips with this young man, until she understood the spirit which motivated him, she never could have a clear perception of what he looked like. She recalled how radically she had had to change her estimate of many of the men she had met through her father's work; some of those whom she had thought handsome had proved to be men of small souls, grasping, fickle, without the stamina to do a job that was so necessary in a full man. As their characters unfolded she had come to think of them as unattractive, while others, whose noses or eyelids curved in queer patterns, had grown not only increasingly attractive with the passage of the years but as beautiful in her mind as their qualities of integrity and devotion.

She was aware of how acutely Lieutenant Fremont stimulated her; there could be no escape from that realization. Would he continue to remain handsome and exciting as she traveled the mysterious road to knowledge of him? Or would he become dull-looking, perhaps downright ugly?

As though conscious that he was being studied, Lieutenant Fremont threw up his head sharply. In the mirror their eyes met. He smiled a boyish smile. Quickly she went forward to greet him.

3

ONLY THE SUNDAY BEFORE, Jessie had heard their good friend James Buchanan characterize the Benton dining table as a place where lost causes mingled with unborn causes, and no one could tell them apart. As she waited for Joshaam, half of a pair of handsome Negro twins, to swing open the heavy wooden doors leading to the dining room, she reflected on what a considerable portion of American history had been rehearsed across its long mahogany table since her father had been elected senator from the state of Missouri and moved from St. Louis to Washington City in 1821. Every president since Madison: James Monroe, John Quincy Adams, Andrew Jackson, Martin Van Buren and William H. Harrison, had tucked his boots under this table and eaten heartily, along with the majority of cabinet officers and ambassadors, the changing panorama of congressmen, army officers, explorers and trappers of the western wilderness.

The doors opened, she stepped inside for a quick inspection before summoning the guests. It was a pleasant room, with paneled mahogany walls, high ceiling and tall windows, a simple Federal fireplace, its frame set flat into the wall, the mantel a narrow, tailored shelf. Her roving eyes took in the shining chandelier, hanging by its four highly polished chains, the deep burgundy rug with its border outlined in squares, the portraits of Thomas Benton's mother and father on the broad wall over the serpentine-front buffet, and the lovely portrait of Elizabeth McDowell Benton, painted many years before by Samuel Morse.

The table was covered with a damask cloth; in the center were the twisted candlesticks Elizabeth McDowell had brought with her from Cherry Grove, and on either side exquisite crystal cut-glass stands filled with fruits and flowers. At both ends of the table a monster salmon rested on waves of clear jelly, while at each place there was a cold broiled lobster, and before it metal cups of bubbling butter and rum over tiny charcoal braziers.

Satisfied that everything was as her father would wish it, she sent Joshaam to announce that dinner was served. She had arranged to have Lieutenant Fremont at her right, and in recompense to the remainder of the guests for what she considered a pre-empting of the most desirable dinner partner, she put Anne Royall on her left. When they were all seated, Jessie counted noses and saw that there were twenty-two at the table.

She poured the hot butter and rum over her lobster, then turned to her newest guest and asked, "Do you like to argue while you eat, Lieutenant?"

"Not unless the food is poor."

"Then I suggest that you enjoy the first three courses, for that is the extent of Father's indulgence. By the time the roast comes in, you won't be able to hear yourself think."

It was her task to guide the early conversation, to keep it entertaining, to see that the table did not break into circles of private discussion. Long practice had taught her the technique: she led Anne Royall into telling the story of how the editor of the Washington *Globe* had called her a petticoat editor, and how she had replied that a petticoat patriot was better than a trouserloon traitor. Having caught a snatch of Mrs. Crittenden's story in the drawing room about the production of *Richard III* at the National Theatre, she cued the lady into telling how the actor, Mr. Hackett, had handed out a program in which he attacked every other actor's interpretation of Richard. Mrs. King excoriated Congress for being too stingy to appropriate money to have the main streets of Washington City paved, or the lamps turned on at night.

"Why, only last week," she exclaimed, "poor Mrs. Spingarn, all dressed up in her new lace-cuffed evening gown, tried to walk to the National Theatre to hear the great Celeste, and fell headlong into a tremendous mudhole on B Street."

There was a deep-toned Chinese gong fastened to the right leg of the table, and by giving it a backward kick with the heel of her pump Jessie was able to summon the servants when she wanted them. While the twins padded about the table in their short black coats and trousers rolled above the ankles, replacing the lobster dishes with blue Wedgwood plates for the cold salmon, and then deep dishes for the oyster stew, Jessie encouraged Samuel Morse to tell what he knew of the stinginess of the Congress. Morse, his gloom unrelieved, portrayed the obtuseness of the committee to which he had demonstrated his telegraph: the congressmen had refused him the small appropriation necessary to build an experimental line to Baltimore.

But when the sides of rare roast beef were brought in, flanked by kidney pies, Jessie saw her father, who had hardly touched his food up to this point, cut himself generous helpings and then promptly launch into an argument with the congressmen from New England on the need to explore the country between Illinois, Missouri and the Rockies, so that one day the United States would extend from ocean to ocean. To the New Englanders this was the sheerest lunacy, and they had not the slightest hesitancy in telling their host so.

As the clamor at the table rose, Jessie laid down her knife and fork and sat back in her chair.

"Appetite gone, Miss Jessie?" asked John Fremont.

"Father eats best when he is arguing the hardest. I'm just the opposite: I can't eat when there is strong argument about. Father never expresses himself better than when in the midst of a heavy dinner . . ."

"I've been noticing," he remarked, glancing up the table at Senator Benton with amused admiration.

". . . though you would imagine he has not the slightest idea of what he is eating when he is thinking so hard. Once I teased him by asking how he enjoyed the mallards and frozen pudding. He replied, 'We haven't had duck since Tuesday, and the frozen pudding was last Sunday.' "

John laughed. "I guess that chided you."

"Indeed it did. Later tonight he will call me into the library, sit me down at my desk and dictate a whole speech for the Senate tomorrow, based on the material he is formulating right now with his mouth apparently full of candied yam."

"I've heard that the senator has the finest private library in Washington. Will you show it to me sometime?"

Jessie eyed her father's guests, then thought how pleasant it would be to have Lieutenant Fremont alone for a few moments. There was nothing she wanted to say to him that could not be heard by the others, yet she knew that their relationship would change subtly if their words could be flavored with privacy.

"When the others go to the drawing room for coffee," she said, "we can slip upstairs."

Before bringing in the pastries, Josheem and Joshaam removed the damask cloth, revealing a second one equally fresh and lovely; and then when the fruits and sweets were ready to be passed, they took off this second cloth, to leave the silver candlesticks, cut glass and crystal gleaming on the highly polished mahogany surface.

At last she suggested that her guests retire to the drawing room for coffee. She stood aside while her father, his arms linked through those of Mrs. Linn and Mrs. Crittenden, escorted the two ladies across the hall. When everyone had left the room, she murmured to Lieutenant Fremont:

"No one will miss us if we go upstairs for a few moments."

She entered the open door of the library, motioning for him to stand beside her. The lamps had been lighted, the Venetian blinds closed; the room had a feeling of warm evening intimacy. It was a large room, running the full width of the house, with a row of windows overlooking C Street and the open fields beyond; small windows were spaced intermittently along the walls of shelves freighted with books of every color, age and nationality, with full sets of Shakespeare, Racine, Molière, Voltaire. Along the east wall was a long oak table almost completely covered with maps and atlases. In front of the fireplace, facing each other, were two great leather chairs, and alongside of them two tables which could be swung around to form writing desks. Scattered about were comfortable chairs to drop into for the length of a paragraph or a page; a well-worn rocker with curlicue arms stood beneath Tom Benton's beloved *British State Trials,* and an Empire armchair before the Duncan Phyfe table with its chessboard by the front windows.

Seeing the library suddenly through a stranger's eyes, it became new and fresh to her, bringing back sharply her years of comradeship with her father.

"What a beautiful room!" Lieutenant Fremont murmured, so softly that she hardly heard.

He seemed no longer conscious of her presence, going to the tight-packed shelves and pulling down the rare and beautiful volumes with the touch of tenderness native to the man who loves books.

"Lieutenant Fremont, your eyes light at the sight of a beautiful book the way other men's do when they see a pretty girl!"

He flashed her an eager smile.

"Must they be mutually exclusive tastes, Miss Jessie?" he asked shyly.

She laughed, then picked up a copy of Henry Schoolcraft's *Expedition to the Upper Mississippi.* "Do you know this book? Father taught me to read from it. I think he did it purposely, so that an interest in exploration would come as natural to me as reading itself."

John Fremont was nodding his small dark head approvingly.

"I didn't know that men were constantly exploring the frontier until I was almost nineteen." He opened the copy of the *Journals.* "I stumbled onto this book the first day I went to work at the Apprentices' Library in Charleston. It was like a new world to me. Until that time I hadn't the faintest notion of what I wanted to do with my life. I read all night, and when dawn came I knew what I was going to be. I spent the next six months devouring the books you have here: General William Ashley, Jedediah Smith, Zebulon Pike, John Jacob Astor, Lewis Cass."

Jessie indicated the two chairs by the fireplace. "Here, take my chair, I'll take Father's."

She sat facing him as she had for so many years sat facing her father. "This library, and the chair in which you are sitting, were my schoolroom. Father taught me to read when I was four, and to draw and trace the maps of the United States when I was five. Before I knew that Paris was the capital of France, I knew there was a great river which flowed from the Salt Lake to the Pacific Ocean."

"Which there may not be!" he exclaimed almost sternly. "Yes, I know that Jedediah Smith reported it, but Mr. Nicollet and I have gone over the reports of the topography of the country, and we can't find any possible route for a river from Salt Lake to the Pacific."

"And one day you will prove it," she added quietly.

He looked at her, both pleased and surprised.

"How did you know?"

"You would have a hard time concealing the fact that you are an explorer."

"I was not as fortunate as you, Miss Jessie," he continued, aroused; "I had no father to go to school to. I went to Charleston College for a couple of years, took languages and mathematics, which interested me, but I could never see any purpose behind my studies."

She followed his quick gestures as he told her of his childhood, of his

father, an itinerant French teacher and painter who had died while his
son was a small boy; of his mother's struggles to support her three children; of his friendship with Joel Poinsett, who had secured him his first
job as an instructor in mathematics on the American warship *Natchez*,
which sailed to Rio de Janeiro and Buenos Aires. His voice was low and
musical and caused an excited tremor to run through her. Her mind
caught the overtones of his early struggles and the joy in finding himself
as he related his work on the survey for the proposed route of the Louisville, Cincinnati and Charleston railroad, and later as civilian assistant
to Captain Williams of the United States Topographical Corps in surveying the Cherokee country.

She had rarely had any desire to talk about herself, but now she found
the idea pleasurable.

"There isn't a great deal to tell," she started self-consciously. "My
greatest happiness has always been working with Father. Before he sent
me to that dreadful school, I used to sit in the chair where you are now,
with that table across my knees, and write down his speeches for the
Senate, while he paced the floor and dove into books for the references
he wanted. When I was six I began to walk with Father up to the Capitol
every morning where he would stake me out in the Congressional Library.
Old Mr. Meehan would bring me Mr. Audubon's books on birds, or a
collection of prints from the Louvre Gallery, and other books of old
French engravings. When I grew tired of looking at the books I would go
out onto the broad, recessed gallery and look at the wonderful view of the
Potomac and the green hills opposite. By the time I was eight, Father
decided I was old enough to listen to the Senate debates."

She walked to the oaken table with its profusion of maps, the bright
reds, greens and yellows of the colored plates lending a touch of gaiety to
the room. Her voice was serious.

"I think Father would forget that I was a girl, for he wanted to teach
me everything there was to know about exploration and travel and the
country of the unsettled West. He taught me Spanish so that I could read
the reports of Cortez, Balboa, Magellan and De Soto. It was because he
so desperately needed a companion in his work."

Reaching out to her with eagerness, John Fremont exclaimed, "I too
studied Spanish in order to read Coronado and Cortez. Like you, I also
know the geography of the wilderness far better than I do New York or
Boston. Your father wanted you to be a son and to go into the Topographical Corps; from the first day I set out with Captain Williams on the
railroad survey, I was determined that I would become an officer of the
Topographical Corps, and explore the Far West for the government.
While you were sitting in this library, I was in those very forests and

mountains and prairies you were reading about, drawing maps, collecting botanical specimens, shooting the stars."

As he paused, Jessie turned her face full toward him, her eyes ablaze.

"Actually, Lieutenant Fremont, we were together out there in the wilderness!"

Then she blushed fiercely.

4

SHE WAS SITTING AT HER DESK in the small, characterless bedroom allotted to her at Miss English's Academy when she heard the throaty voice of a colored mammy singing a plodding spiritual; it was the song that announced the presence of the washerwoman below. All laundry was delivered up the side of the building by means of a rope and pulley attached to each of the window sills; Jessie never could figure why, except that it saved tracking through the schoolhouse. She left the desk, a fragile one designed to hold only light books and light thoughts, and walked to the open window where she could watch the woman tie the rope through the cross-handles of the basket and slowly haul it up to the rhythm of her song.

Leaning over the sill to take in her own basket, she was surprised to see a piece of writing paper resting on top of the crisply ironed clothes. She read, "I couldn't seem to wait until next Sunday. Isn't there some place we can talk? J.C.F."

Once again she looked out the window. This time she saw John Fremont standing beside the mulberry tree.

"Hello," she said, "this is a surprise."

"Can you come down?"

"No, but you can come up."

"Up?"

He gazed in bewilderment.

"Yes, up the mulberry tree. I'll come out from here and meet you in the top branch. That is, if you're not afraid of ripping those lovely blue breeches."

His delighted laughter drifted up to her as she watched him catch a high branch and swing himself onto it. She gathered her skirts tightly about her and climbed over the window sill onto a crisscross of sturdy limbs which formed a platform beneath her. She had no sooner seated herself than John Fremont's head appeared through the green leaves; with quick, graceful movements he was seated beside her. He had left his hat on the ground, and his hair was tousled from pushing upward through the foliage. They overlooked the rolling lawns of the school and the dark green forests along the Potomac. Sitting in the tree swinging her legs through the branches, Jessie Benton would have had difficulty convincing anyone she was almost seventeen.

"Isn't this a mild case of mutiny, Lieutenant Fremont," she asked, her eyes sparkling, "interfering with the curriculum of a girls' school? And how does it happen that the Army lets you wander around loose of a Wednesday afternoon?"

He smiled broadly.

"Messieurs Nicollet and Hassler held a conference over me at lunch today and decided that I had an acute attack of spring fever. That was the only way they could figure why I should be drawing girls' faces on my maps, instead of mountains and rivers."

"But it seems perfectly normal for a young man to draw girls' faces," she answered. "Haven't you ever done that before?"

"Oh, yes, but not for a number of years. Not since I was suspended from Charleston College."

To herself she said, I'm not going to like this, but it will be better to hear it now than later. Aloud she asked, "Who was the girl, Lieutenant Fremont?"

His dark eyes became serious. "Cecilia. She was the oldest daughter of a Creole family that escaped to Charleston in the midst of the San Domingo massacres. I grew up with her brothers; when we were sixteen, Cecilia and I decided we were in love."

"And were you?" she interrupted.

He hesitated for a moment, then said softly, "It wouldn't be right to disavow Cecilia; yes, I loved her as a boy loves his first sweetheart. She was beautiful with flashing eyes and a magnificent smile."

Completely jealous, Jessie struggled with herself not to ask, Was she prettier than I? She said instead, "But why did being in love cause you to be suspended from school?"

"I'm an impetuous man, Miss Jessie . . ."

". . . or you wouldn't be at the top of a mulberry tree at three o'clock . . ."

". . . and I just couldn't stay in the classrooms when there were green hills covered with wild flowers, and a boat to take out into the harbor to fish and swim from in secluded lagoons. And that was why I was never graduated. You see, Miss Jessie, I'm not one to take love lightly. When I fall in love, I throw over everything for it."

"I think I approve of that, Lieutenant. I have never been in love, but I should feel much the same way about it." She hesitated, embarrassed, then deciding to brave it through, added quickly, "Speaking of love, I had the most exciting news this morning: my friend Harriet Williams is going to marry Count Bodisco, the Russian minister."

"Count Bodisco?" he asked, with a puzzled, almost pained expression. "Isn't he the pretentious one who drives to his Embassy every day in a snow-white barouche drawn by four black horses?"

"Yes, I suppose he is pretentious, but in a kindly sort of way that does no one any harm. He's just trying to maintain the dignity of the Russian aristocracy in what some of the other ambassadors call a mudhole capital."

"But," he exclaimed angrily, "he's an old man. He must be past sixty!"

"Just sixty. And Harriet is just sixteen. But he is so terribly kind, the Count Bodisco. He has been most generous to her parents, who are having a difficult time with their large family. The count is going to educate the children and see that they have a brilliant future. Just think, Lieutenant, last week Harriet wasn't good enough to be the May Queen at this school, and in a couple of weeks she will be Countess Alexander de la Bodisco, cousin to the Czar, with a state wedding and President Harrison giving away the bride."

He did not reply. Not a muscle of his face twitched, but she felt a withdrawing, as though he were sorry he had come out to the school today, as though the spirit of the man had flown from the mulberry tree back to the workroom of the Hassler home. When he spoke his voice had a metallic edge.

"You seem to approve all this, Miss Benton."

She put a finger lightly as a falling leaf on his sleeve. "I would not want it for myself, Lieutenant Fremont," she said quietly. "But do you think it fair of us to judge Harriet Williams? The count is an entirely charming and cultivated man, one whom everyone respects. I know that Harriet likes him and is grateful to him. She's being generous, Lieutenant; don't you think that we might be equally generous to her?"

He picked up the finger resting on his sleeve and kissed it. "Forgive me, Miss Jessie; it was boorish of me, but I turned cold when I thought that you . . . might approve—that is you yourself . . ."

"No, Lieutenant, not I myself. I will marry a young man, one whom I can love with all my heart. A man at the very beginning of his career, who has an uphill fight to attain the ends he wants, and who will let our marriage be a partnership in the fullest sense of the term."

He did not answer, looking instead toward the west where the sun was setting behind an early spring heat haze which streaked the sky with flaming horizontal stripes ranging from light rose to deep purple. Jessie's eyes followed his gaze; they sat quietly in their bower taking in the beauty of the spring sunset and the fragrance of the budding foliage about them. She was the first to speak.

"Lieutenant, would you come to Harriet's wedding? I am sure it will be very gay."

"But I don't know Count Bodisco . . ."

"I was in the middle of a letter to Harriet when your note came up in the basket. Won't you let me ask her to have the count invite you? There will be a ball after the wedding supper. Do you like to dance, Lieutenant Fremont?"

On the day of the wedding Jessie was the center of attention in the Benton household, for this was to be her first state affair. She enjoyed the dressing up enormously, surrounded by her mother, two younger sisters and Maylee, who had raised her. Her gown of white figured satin with blonde lace about the neck and sleeves had been built by Mrs. Abbott, the fashionable mantua maker from London.

In midafternoon she entered the family carriage with her father and mother, who had stirred herself to make this effort for the sake of Harriet's family and social position. It was a gentle day, the air soft and intoxicating. The road for a mile before Bodisco's estate was swarming with carriages, for the entire Diplomatic Corps was there, as well as the upper circle of army and navy officers, with General Winfield Scott leading the procession of magnificent uniforms; the president and his Cabinet attended, as well as most of the older members of Congress and the Supreme Court.

Jessie was ushered to the bridesroom on the second floor where she found Harriet in a paroxysm of gaiety. She was a lighthearted, vivacious child who got the most fun from everything.

"Darling," she cried to Jessie, "here's a pearl ring the count wants you to have."

She ran to the window, peeped through the blinds. "Jessie, look at this carriage with the satin rosettes on the horses. It must be the French ambassador. I'm so excited, I haven't been able to eat for three days. The count says I can't have anything until the wedding supper."

Jessie smiled quietly; a feeling of release from anxiety came over her; Harriet would love every minute of her marriage: the jewels, the gowns, the coaches, the travel, state dinners and balls and ceremonies. She would take the happiness from her own bubbling nature, from the excitement of passing events and her family's well-being, and she would never stop long enough to tell herself that her husband was old and ugly.

Soon the bridal party was shepherded down a back stairway to the drawing room, which faced the loggia. The doors were thrown open and the seated guests watched the ceremony performed. Jessie scanned the room in a flash, her eyes finding Lieutenant Fremont, handsome in his

full-dress uniform, a smile on his face. During the elaborate dinner she
felt miles away from him, for he was more than halfway down the long
table. But later when the orchestra began to play behind its screen of
palms in the ballroom, and she had danced the first waltz with James
Buchanan, and a Bohemian polka with Count Bodisco, she was free to
join him on the open piazza overlooking the capital.

The music of the soft-stringed instruments floated out to them from the
ballroom, where a large number of couples were already dancing, their
jewelry and gold braid and lace glittering under a thousand lighted
candles. Jessie, her cheeks flushed with the day's excitement, smiled in
the growing darkness as the lieutenant slipped his arm under the frill of
lace which fell over her elbow and murmured, "You may have come here
for the wedding ceremony, but I came to dance with you."

They stepped onto the dance floor; for a moment they stood unmoving,
tense, questioning, as though the beginning of this dance might be the
start of something which they themselves might never be able or willing
to stop. For Jessie it was a moment out of time, indistinct, yet caught forever. Then she was in his arms whirling about to the strains of Johann
Strauss's *Brillante Vienne*.

For the first time since sitting next to him at the musicale she realized
that he was a little man; she had never before danced with someone so
short, so slender-limbed and -torsoed. At first it seemed strange, almost
unpleasant, this not being able to look up to a man, to feel his bigness
towering over you, his width and breadth making you seem small and
delicate. With a start she recoiled at the emptiness of her quantitative
evaluation.

Her thoughts and her feelings raced on, their impact so overpowering
that she became frightened, began suddenly to feel faint. She was glad
when the music stopped and they made their way to the end of the ballroom where she sank into a deep chair.

As suddenly and incomprehensively as weakness had come, there came
anger over her, and a touch of awe. Who is he, she asked, this strange man
who can do these things to me? A few weeks ago I had never heard of
him, and now I can hardly stand on my own feet! It wasn't like this
before: I thought about him, I pictured his face, and listened to the
music of his voice; I liked him because he was the handsomest man I had
ever seen, and because he also had a wistful quality; it seemed miraculous
that he loved the books I loved, that he had decided to make a career of
exploration and the settling of the West just as my father had, and I too,
in my own small way. All these things seemed delightful and coincidental
and exciting; but there was no wild force inside me to tell my knees that
they couldn't sustain me!

5

ON A WARM SUNDAY MORNING early in March, after they had attended
services at the Presbyterian church, Jessie and her father set out for
Hassler's house, where Nicollet and Hassler had planned a conference to
provide the senator with live ammunition with which to bombard the
Senate into authorizing a series of expeditions to open the western wilderness. Tom Benton was a prodigious walker. His long, shambling legs carried him along at so fast a clip that Jessie had to do double time at his
side to keep up with him. But it had always been so. Her father had never
slowed his pace to suit the size, age or gait of his growing daughter. From
the very beginning he had treated her as an adult, speaking to her with
the same vocabulary and intensity as he did to his constituents in St. Louis
or his confreres on the floor of the Senate. Jessie had groped slowly, many
times painfully, toward understanding; but with the passage of the years
the ideas he stood for became clearer and more firmly entrenched in her
mind. The child born to Elizabeth Benton after Jessie had been a boy,
but he had died, binding Tom Benton in his grief still closer to Jessie. By
the time her brother Randolph had been born it had been too late to
break her father's attachment to his most promising daughter, in whose
mind and spirit he had found the desired reproduction of his own.

James Buchanan had remarked that Jessie was the square root of Tom
Benton. Both father and daughter were delighted with the characteriza-
tion; and both knew it to be true. Listening to Jessie talk about western
expansionism, the need for a national road from St. Louis to Santa Fe,
the listener could close his eyes and see Thomas Hart Benton before him,
his tone, his vocabulary, his rolling out of incisive phrases.

Yet no one had ever dreamed of calling Jessie Benton an echo of her
father. She had a mind of her own, and a good one; it just so happened
that, coming from the frontier of St. Louis, having been raised with the
hunters, trappers, guides, fur dealers and merchants who saw before them
the great unexplored stretches of land where lay fortunes, she too had
become convinced that the United States was now only a small fragment
of what it must become. She even used terms like "manifest destiny,"
which sounded pompous in the mouth of a young girl, but Tom Benton
had been preaching manifest destiny since she was five; since she was
eight she had been listening to him battle for it on the floor of the Senate,
seen him work with his companions in the library of the Benton home; she
had read or had had read to her all those facts of history and biography
which Tom Benton believed proved his case that no young nation can

stand still, that it must conquer the wilderness which lies about it, that it must make of its physical flesh an organic unity. In the many speeches that she had written down for him in his library, and in the comments she had come to make during their discussions, she had even gone beyond Tom Benton in her thinking, for being younger by a generation she dared more by a generation.

As they walked along briskly in the spring sunshine, Jessie's mind went back to the earliest recollections of her childhood. Her first vivid memory was from the age of three; in 1828 her father had campaigned like a hurricane for the election of Andrew Jackson, his old commander and friend. For months she had heard the cry of "Hurrah for Jackson!" One morning she and Eliza went into the library dressed in their velvet pelisses and bonnets, prepared to take a walk around Lafayette Square with their father. Tom had been working that morning on a blistering attack on the isolationists of New England, who were not only content to have America stay as it was with twenty states, but were grimly determined that there must be no more territory acquired, neither in the South, the West, nor the Midwest, since it would upset the political balance in Congress, and weaken their influence over the control of national affairs. The week before Senator Foote had spoken for New England when he advocated that all public lands be removed from the market except those already owned by settlers, that the borders and boundaries of the United States be frozen forever at their existing latitudes.

Jessie and Eliza had found themselves alone in the library; they sat quietly in a chair for a few moments, then seeing the sheets of writing paper spread about, had gotten a box of crayons and begun to draw designs around Senator Benton's writing. A few minutes later when their father came into the room and saw what they had done, he demanded roughly, "Who did this?" Eliza burst into tears, but Jessie looked up, her face streaked with crayon, and announced:

"A little girl that says hurrah for Jackson!"

Tom gazed at his daughter incredulously for a moment, then burst into laughter. "Jessie, you're a chip off the old block; you know how to wriggle out of tight places."

Picking up his sheets of manuscript he had inspected the damage, let out a hearty exclamation as his eyes traced the twisting lines of her blue crayon. He read aloud, "The West is my country, not his. I know it; he does not. It is an injury to the human race to preserve the magnificent valley of the Mississippi for the haunts of wild beasts instead of making it the abode of liberty and civilization, an asylum for the oppressed of all nations."

Hassler's house was on Capitol Hill, overlooking the Potomac; they turned north past the Coast Survey building where Hassler directed the country's geodetic surveys, and continued up Pennsylvania Avenue. Nicholas Nicollet, looking old and ill from the remnants of jungle fever, led them up to the second floor of the rambling house and into a large front room which was entirely bare of furniture. Two long boards mounted on horses were covered with a profusion of maps, papers, charts, notes, journals, atlases, logarithms, tracing paper, crayons. As Jessie stepped into the room she caught a picture: Lieutenant John Charles Fremont on a high stool leaning over the table, a heavy drawing pencil in his right hand, the widespread fingers of his left hand holding down the pages of a journal; his shirt sleeves rolled high, his plain army shirt open at the throat, his dark hair rumpled and falling slightly over his brow, his face filled with the intensity of the man who is devoted to the job on hand.

"He was only twenty-four when I took him with me," Nicollet had told her; "he had had some training under Captain Williams on the two earlier expeditions, but he was really only a beginner in the craft of living harmoniously with the wilderness. Yet he sopped up training and experience like an impassioned one."

Looking intently at him as he sat concentrating on his work, synthesizing rough, hand-drawn maps, notes jotted down beside campfires, checking them against the published notes and maps of the wilderness they had explored, Jessie had the feeling that here was a first-rate man. A flutter at the pit of her stomach told her so, and told her in a way different from the way his hand had grasped hers that first evening at the Georgetown school; different from the way his laughter had engulfed and possessed hers; different from her feeling in the library when he had held her father's books and talked of them; different from that night at the Bodisco wedding; different from all these, something quite apart from them and over and above them. Here was a man who would be admired and respected by his associates, who would go forward in his work, a man who would have the substance and solidity of the job to which his life would be bent, who would make a valuable and permanent contribution to his times.

She stepped into the room, followed by her father and Nicollet. John looked up swiftly, disturbedly; then, seeing her, leaped off his stool and came forward to bid her welcome.

Tom Benton hurried to the big map in the making, ran his finger over the sections in which he was most interested.

"Yes, yes," he said, "that's what we need . . . but I am disappointed, it all comes so . . . so slowly."

Jessie watched Lieutenant Fremont as he turned to her father to say in a patient tone, "Yes, it is slow work, Senator, for we must achieve the utmost precision. The tiniest error on this map may mean danger to caravans expecting water or provision at a designated spot . . ."

"True, true," Tom murmured, "but our time is so short: England is scheming to take over the Pacific coast. This whole vast area has to be cut open with roads, dotted with forts and farm settlements. We've got to push expeditions through to the Columbia River Valley so that it can be settled by Americans."

"I agree, Senator Benton," John replied, his face aglow. "We must push our expeditions through every mile of the wilderness. But we cannot expose unprotected immigrant trains to hostile Indians and deserts and snow-covered mountain ranges until we can assure them that these maps are accurate."

Jessie felt a hand on her shoulder. She turned to find Nicollet beaming at his protégé.

"He is right, the young lieutenant," he whispered. "Think of it, Miss Jessie, in that tremendous map of the Missouri for which he himself gathered most of the material, and which he drew entirely by himself, he made only two small errors in calculation. That is good workmanship."

Watching her father and John Fremont with their heads together she saw how they stimulated each other. Yes, she thought, as she gazed at his tapering fingers which were sketching rapidly even while he talked: good workmanship. Only good men can turn out good work. Most of the young men I know are lighthearted; they seem inconsequential compared to a man like this. I could never love anyone who was not a good workman, who was not as devoted to that work as he was to me.

6

KNOWING THAT LIEUTENANT FREMONT had been invited, Jessie had asked Maylee to prepare a specially delicious dinner, but this time her warning to him to stay clear of the argument was to no avail; he had regretfully to lay down his knife and fork when Tom Benton called on him to persuade two newspaper editors, a cabinet officer and several congressmen that the land between the Mississippi and the Rockies was fertile and good for homesteading.

The first warmth of impending summer was in the drawing room, a hint of the intense heat that soon would settle over Washington City. Jessie had put on a cool gown of lawn. After the demitasse she suggested to John that they go into the back garden for a breath of air. Scarlet trumpet vines covered the high, enclosing walls. Just outside the porch they passed a small, improvised shed with two wooden barrels suspended over its top. At John's inquiring glance Jessie explained, "That's Father's shower bath. He takes it icy cold at dawn and sunset, part of his old army regime; he says he enjoys it, but Father loves hardship. I sometimes think he likes it for its own sake."

"Quite so!" exclaimed the lieutenant understandingly. "I enjoy the hardship of the trail and the danger of the unknown for its own sake. Frankly, the only hardship I find painful is that of being obliged to live in a big city, with crowds of people."

"Really, Lieutenant?" she asked, a trifle archly. "I've recently heard reports that you are one of the gayest young men in the capital, that never a dance takes place but you're still there at three o'clock in the morning."

He blushed.

"Ah well, Miss Jessie, I'm young, only twenty-eight. There are times when I like pretty girls and music, and if I must live in civilization to complete my work I might as well have the most fun of it. But give me a stampeding buffalo herd, a three-day forced march across the desert, our canteens empty; give me a prairie of blue wild flowers that no white man's eyes ever gazed upon before; or an unknown, unnamed river stream rushing by in the night while I lie on the ground and gaze up at stars."

Her ear caught the poetry of his words, mitigating the jealousy she had felt when thinking of him as part of the capital's society from which, because of her youth, she was still excluded. They walked along the hedge-lined path to the summerhouse. It was shaded by tall sycamores and much of it was covered by a deep green ivy. They sat side by side on the hard white bench, the air filled with the fragrance of honeysuckle, and chatted lightly about the people at the dinner table.

"I'm not greatly interested in politics," he commented absently. "I can hardly wait for the day when I can start out again on a new expedition."

"Father always said that politics and science make uncongenial bedfellows, but how is there any escape from it? You can do nothing without the help and authorization of Congress, and you can do nothing with Congress unless you do play mighty smart politics."

He nodded agreement with the well-turned argument, then leaned back against the latticework, his face set, his eyes serious. The coolness of the arbor seemed to magnify his detachment. She was hurt and baffled by his need for escape. Despite his openness and candor she had a sense of being unable to come into contact with the core of him. Her first reaction in the darkened music room of Miss English's school had been that there was in his character something mysterious, something submerged. This feeling of elusiveness, of withdrawal behind the poise and lovability frightened her.

She turned a little to face him. "Whatever happened to Cecilia?"

"I don't know," he answered. "I left Charleston and she stayed there. Why do you ask?"

"Because I'm interested in love, and it suddenly strikes me that I don't know a blessed thing about it."

"I'm afraid you've come to the wrong man," he grinned. "I don't know much about the subject myself. A topographer who spends most of his time in the wilderness doesn't get much chance at love."

They smiled, conscious of each other, of the sharp smell of the night earth, the scent of late spring. The words were all gone. They moved close. Their hands touched, her hair touched his lips as she leaned her head on his shoulder.

Suddenly she looked up to see her father and Nicollet standing on the path. Nicollet smiled, murmured something to Thomas Benton. Her father stiffened. There was a hostile pause, then he came to the door of the summerhouse and announced in a cold voice:

"Jessie, come into the house."

She rose and, with John Fremont at her side, trailed her father and Nicollet up the garden path. In the light of the foyer she saw that her father's face had frozen, that Nicollet was apologetic. Ignoring Lieutenant Fremont's presence, Tom Benton said, "Jessie, will you excuse yourself, please? It is growing late."

In the strained silence the unspoken words of these four leaped out to each other and clashed and were withdrawn. Lieutenant Fremont spoke out in a small voice. "I too must excuse myself. Thank you for your hospitality, Senator Benton, and for your excellent dinner."

He bowed formally, took his hat from a corner stand and left the house.

Tom Benton and his daughter stood gazing at each other. Nicollet murmured his adieus and left.

Jessie trailed her father up the stairs to the library, watching his broad, angry back. After he had slumped far down in his chair, his hand covering his face, she asked softly, "What have I done?"

He looked at her, his face seeming haggard and old.

"Jessie," he said, "I'm stunned."

"What is it that you feel so strongly about?" she queried.

"That is a silly and evasive question," he replied harshly. "You were so obvious that even Nicollet commented on it. I've been so absorbed in my work that I failed to notice . . ."

Her voice too became firm. "I've done nothing but enjoy Lieutenant Fremont's company. You've done as much yourself. What is it you are accusing me of?"

"Of falling in love with him," he shot back.

There it is, she thought, out in the open at last. I have never let myself think it, and now Father has put it into words.

"You may be right," she answered quietly. "I had not let that word come into my consciousness. I knew that Lieutenant Fremont was the most delightful and sympathetic young man I had ever met. But you never approved of romantic novels, and there is very little in the literature of exploration to tell a young girl when she is in love. Now that you face me with it, I think I am in love with him."

With a tight voice Tom Benton pronounced, "Lieutenant Fremont will not come to this house any more; he will not be invited; and you will not see him again."

"But why are you punishing him?" she demanded.

"He has made you fall in love with him."

"Made me!" Her face was as taut and pale as his. "Have I no mind of my own? Really, Father, that's unworthy of the years of training you have given me; you know that I am not a weak or silly child . . ."

"Nevertheless he is not coming here any more. You will not see him! It's far too advantageous a marriage to tempt the young lieutenant with."

"Lieutenant Fremont is no adventurer. He is one of the most talented and promising men in Washington. You said so yourself."

"Perhaps. But he is not so promising that he can't see the benefits of a marriage to Senator Benton's daughter."

Jessie's eyes flashed her indignation. She walked to the window, put aside the draperies and stared out over the dark green fields.

"So you think you have produced a daughter so unattractive and so unstimulating that the lieutenant could not fall in love with me for my own sake?"

Tom Benton said more quietly, "Forgive me, my dear, I did not mean to disparage your charms or your worth." But the coldness did not leave his voice. "Jessie, it is my job to protect you. You are too young to know . . ."

"Senator," she said deliberately, "that's the worst piece of sophistry you've ever been guilty of: Did you think I was too young at four to learn how to read, or too young at five to spend my days in the Congressional Library, too young at seven to go on hunting and camping trips with you, too young at eight to watch you from the Senate galleries, to read these heavy, serious books with you; too young at ten to begin writing down your speeches, too young at fourteen to become your adviser and confidante, to walk the streets of Washington at night while you were thrashing out your problems, using me as a sounding board? And now suddenly you thrust a calendar in my face, tell me that I am undeveloped, not quite seventeen, a child who doesn't know what she is doing."

She did not pause to give him an opportunity to answer, but pursued her advantage ruthlessly, even as Tom Benton did when his own desires were at stake.

"I've never questioned your judgment; when you praised me for some good work I had done, I worked ten times harder to earn more praise, until you have said that you'd soon be going to school to me. And now, at the first turn of events that displeases you, you become heavy-handed, the outraged father laying down the law."

Tom eyed her calmly. "That was quite a speech, Jessie; perhaps you should be the senator from Missouri."

She walked quickly to her father's side, her manner conciliatory.

"I don't want to be the senator from Missouri; I want to be the daughter of the senator. You know how much I love you, Father; we have never had to talk about that. You've led me gently by the hand through all these happy years; you can't suddenly put a ring through my nose on the pretext that it's for my own good."

"What has Lieutenant Fremont said to you?"

"Nothing . . . not with his lips anyway. Perhaps I've been reading his mind, but that kind of evidence isn't admissible in a court of law, is it?"

"I am not amused."

"Lieutenant Fremont has been very circumspect," she continued. "You are forcing issues, Father, and it has never been your tactic to bludgeon your way through delicate situations."

"I've taught you too well," he moaned.

"Come now, Tom," she chided. "You gave me weapons with which to fight; did you think I was not going to use them whenever my happiness was threatened?"

"Your happiness! But this is fantastic, Jessie! It is the first time you have had a romantic attachment, and you talk to me about your happiness! Lieutenant Fremont simply will not be invited to this house any more."

They stood in silence staring at each other, two pairs of brooding eyes, as alike as a reflection in a gold-backed mirror. Their wills met too, their stubbornness. Then Jessie turned and went to her room.

Maylee was waiting for her with a tray of food. "You must be starved, child," said the old colored woman, "I seed your plate when it come out the kitchen. You never even mussed it round."

"Thank you, Maylee, but I'm not hungry."

The woman looked at her in blank astonishment.

"You ain't hungry! What's the matter with you, child, you sick?"

"Father would say so."

"What you catch? You want I bring you some hot senna tea?"

Jessie smiled wryly.

"Thank you, no, Maylee, senna tea never cures anything, much less what I've got."

7

IF NOT FOR THE PRESENCE of Grandmother McDowell, who had arrived for her annual spring visit with the Bentons, the following weeks would have been unendurable for Jessie. Both at school and at home she suffered the agonizing experience of having Lieutenant Fremont's face fade from her mind. Though she was unhappy at being separated from him she did not despair, for she felt certain that the forces which had brought them together were too strong to be broken because Thomas Hart Benton thought her too young for love. She had wanted to talk to her father about Lieutenant Fremont, to show him that his arbitrary method was having the opposite effect to what he desired. If he would let him come to dinner again on Sundays, she would promise to keep the conversation in hand, to behave casually.

But on her second week end at home she was unable to discuss the subject with him, for he was preparing to make a speech in the Senate which he estimated would consume seven hours, and was maintaining an absolute silence for several days so that his voice would hold out. Jessie decided that she would wait until the day after his speech, giving him the night to rest, before pleading for a frank discussion. When she joined him in the library the following morning, and found him still suffering from the rawness of his throat, she had only compassion for him. She resolved to be patient.

The separation had been the more painful because there was no one in the Benton home with whom she could talk about John Fremont. That was why she had been happy to see Grandmother McDowell again.

Grandmother McDowell had been born in Cherry Grove, Virginia, eighty years before. She had lived through the Indian Wars and the War of the Revolution; on her forehead she carried a scar caused by an Indian's knife thrown at her in her childhood, an Indian in the British service. She called this scar King George's Mark. When Grandmother was ill or troubled or her children or grandchildren were in difficulty the scar seemed to grow larger; when she was feeling well and the family prospered it receded to almost unnoticeable proportions. Grandmother McDowell's growing old had proved an anomaly: instead of becoming thin in her advancing age, she had grown pleasingly plump; instead of becoming cantankerous because of her slowed gait and accumulated ills, she grew increasingly mellow; instead of growing fatigued with the love affairs and marriages of her children, grandchildren, nieces and nephews, she maintained a keen zest in seeing each of them in turn go through the process. Jessie had not needed to say more than a few sentences about Lieutenant Fremont before Grandmother McDowell had nodded her head and commented:

"So it has come to my Jessie at last. I was getting worried about you; by the time I was your age I already had a daughter."

The death of President William H. Harrison only one month after his inauguration furnished Jessie with her first opportunity to see John. The funeral cortege was to make its way up Pennsylvania Avenue to the Capitol; since the Benton home was a block off the main street, and the members of the family would not be able to watch the procession from their own windows, Tom Benton had announced to Grandmother McDowell that she might view the cortege from Mr. Hassler's house on Capitol Hill. To Jessie's sharply interrogating look he replied, "Mr. Hassler made the offer today when I met him in Colonel Abert's office. Yes, you may accompany your grandmother."

The morning of the funeral dawned cold and rainy. Though Grandmother McDowell wore a black silk dress with a wadded black cape, Jessie's mother permitted her to wear a dress and coat of dark green velvet. Tom Benton dropped his daughter and mother-in-law outside the Hassler house, then hurried on to the Senate for the official ceremonies. When the front door was opened by Lieutenant Fremont dressed in his full regimentals, Jessie exclaimed:

"Lieutenant, why aren't you with your regiment?"

"I developed a cold. The doctor at the armory did not consider it wise for me to march in this rain."

They stood smiling at each other, an eager smile. Then Jessie turned to her grandmother.

"This is the young lieutenant I have been telling you about."

"I'm glad to meet you, young man. I must confess I came more to see you than to get a better view of the funeral. At my age one is not overly partial to funerals."

"But Grandmother," Jessie exclaimed, "you couldn't have known that Lieutenant Fremont would be here. He was supposed to be marching with his regiment."

"Do tell!" murmured Grandmother McDowell.

John bent over to kiss the old woman's hand, then led them up to the second-floor workroom which had been cleared of its tables and working paraphernalia. He had placed potted azaleas on the window sills and there were many vases filled with geraniums and roses. A bright fire was burning in the fireplace, the cedar wood giving off a pungent fragrance.

Before the fireplace a low table had been set for tea; comfortable chairs had been placed in front of the windows overlooking Pennsylvania Avenue. Jessie watched John as he received Colonel Abert's wife and Mrs. Crittenden, who also had been invited to this vantage spot. She sat at the big windows with the other women listening to stories about William Henry Harrison, but John was standing behind her chair and her head was spinning; the feeling that ran between them was strong and certain.

In the distance could be heard faintly the dirge of the funeral march; in another moment six white horses could be seen pulling the plumed hearse which was carrying the body of President Harrison up the slope of Capitol Hill. As two more women were ushered into the room, Jessie quickly rose to offer her chair, and John led her to the fireplace. Here they sat opposite each other over the tea table gazing into the yellow-red flames. The women assembled at the windows had their eyes on the solemn scene below; Jessie could not have felt their privacy more complete had they been alone.

"I've been to the Senate twice while Senator Benton was speaking," he said. "I hoped I might catch a glimpse of you there."

"But I am still attending Miss English's Academy."

"I knew our separation was only temporary. I knew that nothing could keep us apart, not even—forgive me—Senator Benton."

Jessie did not speak; she could not have uttered a word if her life had been at stake. He took her hand between his.

"Miss Jessie, perhaps a funeral procession is not the best possible background to speak of love, but I am so full of the subject that I am afraid I would find any moment and any background a good one."

"Always the impetuous one," she murmured.

"You have a way of reading my eyes," he said. "I think you've read what I feel for you."

"No," she mocked gently, "when it comes to love, I'm illiterate. Or so Father thinks."

"Do you know the first thing I said to Mr. Nicollet when I returned from the musicale at Georgetown? I said, 'I have fallen in love at first sight.' When you stormed into the reception room, indignant because an injustice had been done to your friend, I knew at once that something important was happening to me; when you laughed and your laughter enveloped me with its warmth I knew that the rest of my life would be barren unless I could be with you always. My one thought was how and where I might meet Miss Jessie again. I love you," he said very quietly. "I loved you from that very first instant. I think you love me too."

Her eyes glowed.

"Surely you too believe that it's all part of a design, that if we searched the world, both of us, spent years looking for the one man or woman who would be our most perfect mate . . ."

"Yes, I believe that," she replied softly.

"Mr. Benton is telling the truth when he says I am a penniless lieutenant with only modest prospects . . ."

"Modest prospects! You have the most brilliant prospects of any young man in America: you will do great things . . ."

"We will do them together, Jessie."

She withdrew her hand from his, sat up stiffly in her chair, her slight body rigid.

"You are serious about that?" she demanded. "I must warn you, I can't live without work to do. I could not marry a man who would not let me work by his side as an equal and his partner. Call me Anne Royall if you will, my mother has done that a hundred times, but I am not a feminist, you will never hear me cry for equal rights for women. I believe that the greatest job a woman can do in the world is to be a good wife, but I believe that to be a good wife a woman must stand shoulder to shoulder and brain to brain alongside her husband." Her voice faltered. "I simply must have a man who will have faith in my judgment, who will make me his confidante, who will not try to exclude me because I am a woman, tell me to go out into society and amuse myself."

She relaxed in her chair, but her hazel eyes were still intense.

"I will never embarrass you, John Fremont; I want no credit or limelight or public acclaim; I will never stalk the street with a bundle of causes in my hand so that my friends will duck down side alleys when they see me coming. But I want to help you, I want to make my own small contribution to your work, I want to extend your reach by just a little bit, that little bit of which I am capable."

She cast down her eyes and sat laving her small hands as though in anguish.

"There, I've said it all. I hope it hasn't repulsed you, that you will not think it unwomanly of me."

She looked up at him. His eyes were closed, his twenty-eight-year-old face had lines in it, his forehead was furrowed.

"I hope I'm not being romantic about this," she said. "I know that from the viewpoint of the outside world it is an unwanted task. I know that most men prefer an amusing and charming wife who will bear their children and manage their houses and be there when they come home from a day's or a year's work. It is a full-time task to bear children and raise them and watch after the health of the family and keep the home beautiful and peaceful so that they can grow up to be fine human beings. It is enough for any one woman. But can you understand, Lieutenant,

that it is not enough for me? I am my father's daughter; if I were a man
I would be deep in a profession already. Since I am a woman I must work
through my husband, and so I must find a husband who will let me
achieve this ambition, who will allow me to become as indispensable in
his work as in his life."

The slowly dying dirge of the funeral procession could be heard in the
room; several of the women at the window were weeping quietly. Lieutenant Fremont had started to speak.

"I love you, Jessie," he was saying. "I would not want an Anne Royall,
but your radiance and charm dissipate my fears. Jessie, I will always love
you, of that you may be sure. I may make other mistakes, I may fail you
in other things, I may never come up to your full expectations, but I will
always love you."

A flicker of tender amusement came into her eyes, and she was glad to
feel her spirit lighten; she did not want this sacred moment which she
would never forget, no matter how old she grew, to be too deadly in
earnest.

"Spoken as a true French poet, Monsieur Fremont," she said with a
twinkle.

"I will confess I have been writing verse to you. Bad verse, Miss Jessie,
astonishingly bad verse, considering how deep a love it sprang from."

"I am not marrying you as a poet, Lieutenant Fremont, and I will not
hold your bad verses against you."

With one of those lightning changes to which she had not yet grown
accustomed, his eyes clouded.

"You really ought not to accept me, you know," he said sternly. "I am
suspect in this affair. You can see how it would be a marriage of con-
venience: being Senator Benton's son-in-law would be of tremendous help
to me in my career; the senator would use his influence in the Congress
and the War Department to get me promoted quickly, put in command
of expeditions . . ."

Jessie answered with mock seriousness:

"Yes, of course, but then you realize, Lieutenant Fremont, that I am
too young to know what I am doing."

"Quite! At sixteen you are an irresponsible child."

". . . it will be several years yet before I will be old enough to make
up my mind."

His dark mood had vanished.

"Since you are not marrying me as a poet," he asked eagerly, "when
can I expect that you will marry me as a second lieutenant in the Topographical Corps?"

"That is the one answer I don't know. You must promise me to keep this secret until I can talk with Father."

"Will we have to wait long? You will forgive me if I appear impatient."

"We won't have to wait as long as he waited: Mother kept refusing him for six years. She said, 'I'll never marry a redhead, an army man or a Democrat.' Father replied, 'I can't change the color of my hair and I can never be anything but a Democrat, but I will get out of the Army: I only went into it to lick the British.' Let us allow circumstances to precipitate the right moment for telling him."

"I will keep our engagement a secret," he smiled; "what a beautiful word, engagement. My darling Jessie, now we are engaged to be married, and all our lives we will be engaged, engaged in valuable work, engaged in being happy and loving each other."

The funeral procession had passed out of view. Lieutenant Fremont threw another log on the fire, brought the chairs from the windows and made his guests comfortable. The air had grown warmer; the rain was beautiful as it slanted angularly over Pennsylvania Avenue. He disappeared for a moment, returning with a tray of ices, French *gateaux* and a Russian samovar. He chatted happily as he poured the tea.

Heavens, thought Jessie, is my happiness that apparent too? If it is, our secret will be all over Washington within an hour.

"How was the funeral cortege?" she asked her grandmother.

"I would say that it served its purpose," Grandmother McDowell replied.

8

THE NEXT MORNING she awoke and burst into song, then realized that she might as well tell her father everything that had happened as go into his presence unable to contain her happiness. She put on a blue flannel robe, combed her hair, tied it on top of her head with a ribbon and went downstairs.

She had no sooner joined the family at the breakfast table than Josheem and Joshaam came in, each carrying two potted azalea plants. Tom Benton looked at the card which accompanied them, failing to note that it had been addressed to Mrs. Benton. He laid down his knife and fork, pushed aside the cutlet he had been vigorously dispatching and stared at his daughter.

"Was Lieutenant Fremont at home yesterday, by any chance?"

"Yes," admitted Jessie, "he was."

"Why wasn't he marching in the procession?"

"He had a cold."

"Did you know when you went to Hassler's that Lieutenant Fremont would be there?"

"No, Father, I don't enjoy second sight. But to be quite honest with you, I did hope . . ."

"I don't like this kind of deception, Jessie, even when it seems so innocent on the surface. I forbade you to see Lieutenant Fremont, and you have disregarded my wishes."

The rest of the family had silently finished breakfast and slipped out of the room. Jessie and her father were alone.

"Will you kindly tell me what took place at Hassler's yesterday? For it is apparent that something did take place."

She was unwilling to tell a deliberate lie. Since she saw that she must expose her hand, she played it the bold way.

"I'll let you in on a secret, Father, if you promise not to tell anyone.'

"A secret from whom?"

"From you, darling. I am engaged to Lieutenant John Charles Fremont!"

When Thomas Benton's anger was red hot he could get off the most profane diatribes to be heard in Washington; but when his anger was icy he held his emotion in leash and chose his words fastidiously.

"So you are engaged! Without my knowledge, without my consent, and against my express orders that you were not to see Lieutenant Fremont."

She could think of no reply, but only hung her head.

"Do you think your life is going to end that you must rush precipitately into clandestine arrangements? What has happened to your sense of perspective, Jessie?"

She realized with a shock that this was her first major difference with her father. She didn't like it, she didn't want to create a change in their relationship, but neither could she avoid this scene. Should her father gather that she was heavyhearted at quarreling with him, he would bludgeon her emotionally until she gave in. She had to keep the contest in the mood in which she could best and most effectively oppose him.

Pushing aside the plate before her, she stretched out her arms across the table.

"If I felt that my marriage to Lieutenant Fremont would separate me from you, Father, or in any way hurt you, I would do what you ask: I would give him up. I would give up whoever it might be, without your asking. But John Fremont is the fulfillment of your own ambitions. He will explore and conquer the wilderness. He will open the West, create the empire you have been tracing on maps and have had me tracing since I was five."

Joshaam padded in with a ham steak, grits baked in a casserole with orange honey, and a silver pitcher of chocolate. Jessie let him put the food down, then pushed her chair back from the table. Her young face was sober.

"Tom Benton, you should be the one pleading for this marriage, and I should be the one holding out: for I know what your dreams and plans will do to him, I know of the hardships and ever present dangers that will face him; I know of the long and bitter separations which your collaboration will bring about. It's a hard and painful future to think about, Father, but I rush out to meet it with open and loving arms."

"The first thing I know, you'll be telling me you are marrying him for my sake." After a pause, he cried, "Jessie, would you really set yourself up against my wishes? Would you oppose me in anything so critical?"

"If I let you deprive me of the most important thing in my life, Papa, my love for you might turn to hatred. I want you to protect and counsel me, but in the end it must be I and not you who determine my life. Surely you can see the justice of that?"

Thomas Benton alone had taught her to respect logic instead of people, to form her opinions on the basis of fact, and then stand by them through hell and high water. But Tom Benton shouted in his rage:

"And who is this sixteen-year-old that dares to defy her father?"

"A little girl who cries, 'Hurrah for Jackson!' "

His anger was caught up, stopped short by the summoning of their past.

Jessie drew her chair to the table, helped herself to the breakfast. She spoke quietly.

"All I can say, Tom Benton, is that you underestimate yourself. If I am a misguided fool and romantic idiot at seventeen, then your efforts and work are wasted, and I shall still be a fool at twenty-seven or sixty-seven. Let us say instead that I matured early owing to the fact that my father was a maturing influence, owing to the fact that his intensive education had a sobering influence on me. Perhaps if during those years I had been thinking about nothing but pretty manners and conquering the hearts of young men, instead of wildernesses, lost rivers and hostile Indian tribes, I would not have found it only natural to fall in love with the one man who I think is going to do more to open that West than anyone alive today."

Her voice carried a touch of bitterness. "Perhaps you should have let me have a normal childhood of dolls and games and giggling. Perhaps that would have been better for me."

Tom passed a heavy hand over his eyes.

"Jessie, my dear, have I really robbed you of your childhood? Your mother . . ."

With a tinkling laugh she dropped her fork, ran around the table and sat herself on her father's lap.

"For heaven's sake, Papa, don't let me take you in with my ridiculous feminine logic. By this time tomorrow you would know I had tricked you out of your opposition. You gave me the most wonderful and exciting childhood any girl ever had. All I'm trying to say is that I don't feel like a child, that you didn't leave much for the finishing school to finish. That it is possible for some people to live more and learn more and enjoy and suffer more, within the passage of time, than others."

"Yes, of course."

But when he looked up at her with hurt eyes, she realized that he was not thinking along with her; that he was feeling the impending loss not only of his favorite daughter, but as he himself often had told her, of his favorite human being. Intuitively she understood by imagining what her world would be like with Thomas Hart Benton gone out of it. She stroked his hot brow.

"You don't understand, child," he groaned; "a man needs time to prepare in his mind for changes as important as this. In the back of my head there was always the idea that when you fell in love and wanted to marry, I would be ready for it. It wouldn't descend upon me when I was unprepared."

"But, Father, we have no control over when we will meet the person we love: it might be at fifteen or fifty—or never. Would it be better to wait until I was eighteen or nineteen or twenty, when your mind would be prepared, and marry someone with whom you had little in common, than to marry a bit earlier than you had anticipated, and make a perfect marriage?"

She walked to the window and stood leaning against the sill, the sun warming her back.

"Whenever I have thought of marriage, it was to a man whose work I could be excited about. I have always believed that the woman who is excluded from a man's work has no contact with the best part of her husband's life. Where could I find anyone better suited to me than Lieutenant Fremont?"

Her father grunted, "Jessie, you have too many answers."

9

THOMAS BENTON'S REPLY to the potted azaleas arrived a few days later in the form of Nicholas Nicollet, looking very old and muttering to himself, "There has been devil's work down there." To Jessie he reported, "They are taking him away from our map making; they are sending him on a survey of the Des Moines River in Iowa territory. Your father persuaded Secretary of War Poinsett to send him out immediately."

Half a dozen thoughts sprang simultaneously to Jessie's mind.

"On another expedition! But surely not without you?"

"I have work to do here, Miss Jessie. Besides, the lieutenant knows the Iowa territory; he will not need me."

She flushed with pride.

"In charge of the expedition! That is a promotion, is it not?"

"Most certainly; and it is the position for which I have been training him these four years." The full circle of wrinkles radiating out from the old man's eyes made his dark pupils look like water at the bottom of a well. "But I cannot spare him now; I need him to finish the maps; the original drawings are his . . ."

She was doing her best to listen to Nicollet, but there were insistent voices in her ears.

Why has this happened exactly at this moment? Will it be dangerous? Who is responsible for it? How am I to pass the months without him?

"He will be gone six months," Nicollet continued. "Do not mistake me, Jessie, it is a work that needs doing. But it comes suddenly; and I am so grieved that I cannot go . . ."

Tears came to her eyes.

"We can wait for him six months, you and I, for it will be the beginning of important things for him. He will do his work well, and when Father's plans for the great expeditions to the Rockies and to the Oregon country are approved in Congress, Lieutenant John C. Fremont will be the man they will turn to for leadership."

Nicollet rose. "Ah, it is good to be young, for then you are master of time." He embraced her gently.

She did not mention Nicollet's visit to her father. One thought kept whirling about in her mind: Will I see him before he leaves?

During dinner there was a sharp knocking of the door clapper. Joshaam came in and whispered something to Mr. Benton. He flushed, left the table. A moment later the twin returned for Jessie. When she reached the hallway she saw Lieutenant Fremont, his military hat under one arm.

"I leave tonight for St. Louis," he said. "I have asked your father's permission to say good-by to you."

She could not speak, but stood there, all eyes. Looking up quickly she saw John too was all eyes. The yearning of two people in love and about to be separated filled the little hallway. Thomas Benton could endure it no longer.

"Very well," he said not unkindly, "at the end of a year, if you two feel as you do now, I will give my consent to your marriage."

He turned to John with his hand extended, "Good luck to you, and do a good job."

"That I will, sir," he grinned, as Jessie stood by, happy and proud of him. "I thank you for this opportunity to head my own expedition, and I assure you that I will bring back material which will make future and longer expeditions inevitable."

"I could almost permit myself to envy your summer out of doors," said Tom, "sleeping under the stars, shooting your own food, plunging at dawn into a mountain stream. It is a healthy life, Lieutenant."

"Very healthy, sir," John agreed with a twinkle in his eye, "but not likely to cure my particular ailment."

Tom Benton chuckled silently, then walked into the dining room and closed the door behind him. Jessie and John were alone.

During the long months of separation she would try to remember the moment that followed. She did not know what look had been exchanged, or what word had been said; she did not know who had moved first, or what the signal had been that united them in their first embrace. Suddenly she was in his arms and her lips were on his. There was no breath in her body or thought in her head, for his arms crushed her against him; his mouth covering hers was speaking not words, words that could be obscure or retracted, but the vitalizing kiss which could tell to both whether this mating was a lie or an ultimate truth.

The following morning her father called her into the library to tell her that she no longer had to attend Miss English's Academy.

"Thank you, darling, it is good of you to understand. Will you drive to Georgetown with me this morning and help me make a formal exit?"

She packed her possessions in her school bedroom quickly, then joined her father, who was making his apologies to Miss English. Miss English commented, "Miss Jessie is intelligent, Senator, but she lacks the docility of the model student. Moreover she has had the objectionable manner of seeming to take our assignments under consideration, to be accepted or disregarded by some standard of her own."

Jessie and her father exchanged a glance. Miss English understood the quick look, for she added:

"In a man this trait might be a praiseworthy attribute. But not in a young woman. It can only lead to trouble and heartbreak. I'm afraid Miss Jessie has strange ideas about a woman's place in modern society."

Turning to Jessie, she continued, "If you take nothing else from your two years at my school, Miss Jessie Benton, I hope you will remember that we tried to teach you to be a fine lady: to be quiet, to remember that fine manners are the most important thing in a woman's life, that without them she loses all charm and beauty; and that there is nothing more obnoxious than a pushing, self-assertive woman who refuses to remain within the sphere of her own influence: her home and her children. Senator Benton, I trust you will not allow your daughter to become a pioneer in this radical feminist movement; it can bring her nothing but unhappiness."

With the barest twitching of his lips, he replied, "It is true, Miss English, the life of a pioneer is a hard one; in my own modest way I have tried to do a little pioneering too; you are right in saying that the path is stony." Turning to his daughter he concluded, "Please remember what we have said here, Jessie; and when you get all through ignoring our strictures, don't say we didn't tell you so."

10

JESSIE HAD EXPECTED to spend the next months working with her father, but word came from Cherry Grove that one of her young cousins was about to be married. Her mother decided that they would go south for the wedding. She could not help but see that her parents were delighted with the opportuneness of the trip, that they hoped the excitement of travel and gaiety of the wedding party might dissipate her memories of Lieutenant Fremont.

Her father escorted them onto the narrow river steamboat which would carry them down the Potomac to Fredericksburg, while Joshaam loaded their strapped and bulging bags up a rear gangplank. After the farewells had been said, Jessie and her mother stood in the prow and watched the little boat cut a clean swath through the placid blue water.

As their boat drew away from Washington City, as the miles began to intervene, Jessie noted that her mother seemed to grow younger; her eyes cleared, a little color came to her pallid cheeks, she stood up straighter. When she began to talk to her daughter about her childhood at Cherry Grove, about its beauties and peacefulness, it seemed to Jessie that a full ten years dropped from her mother's shoulders, that she once again was the beautiful woman she remembered from her childhood.

She was glad to be taking this trip with her mother, for her romance with John had seemed to separate them even farther. Though she loved her mother, Jessie deeply resented the fact that Elizabeth Benton was no longer interested in her husband's campaigns and battles, did not flush with gratification at the news that Senator Benton had won a victory for the national road or the gold bullion theory; that she did not suffer when he was attacked, or sit up nights working with him, giving him the best efforts of her heart and head to assure him of victory.

From aunts, uncles and former admirers, and particularly from Grandmother McDowell, she learned that her mother had been a soft-spoken, genteel southern girl, the favorite of Cherry Grove. Her room had been the sunniest of the large estate, her dressing table adorned with silver candelabra, her four-poster piled high with feather beds. She had a sweet, small voice and entertained her suitors with the popular ballads of the day, accompanying herself prettily at the pianoforte.

Jessie had at first been amused by the stories of how her mother, for six years and on six separate occasions, had rejected her father's proposal of marriage; but slowly this amusement had turned to indignation. In the small places of her heart she wondered why her mother had rejected Thomas Hart Benton when he was a young lawyer from St. Louis, but accepted him when he was the first senator from Missouri and started on an important career. She could not understand how one could not love a man or woman for six years, and then suddenly decide one loved him enough to marry him. For her, as for Thomas Benton, there could be no long line of suitors, no long line of years of doubts or hesitations, no wavering allegiance for man or cause.

Her father had met her mother at the home of her uncle, Governor James Preston of Virginia. It was on one of the many occasions when she drove to Richmond accompanied by her own maid and manservant in her English coach, painted a brilliant yellow and lined with scarlet morocco. He had fallen in love instantly; the following morning had declared himself. As she gazed at her mother now, at the face from which youth and beauty and serenity had fled, Jessie recalled her telling the story of how she had thought Tom Benton a boring young man who had fallen in love in a bovine fashion, and who suffered by comparison with her entourage of handsome Virginia cavaliers. At the time, Elizabeth McDowell, member of one of America's oldest and most important families, seemed to have all the advantages over Tom Benton: wealth, social position, beauty, breeding. Yes, Jessie thought, Mother had all the advantages, except one: intellect. She had been courted by one of the best minds in America, and yet for six years she kept saying:

"Papa and Mama admire and respect you; I respect you, but I have decided I can never marry you."

Nor, having her choice of the cream of southern aristocracy, had she accepted one of the Virginia blades. Elizabeth McDowell was having too good a time to select any one man and settle down. She liked the courting too well, the being surrounded by flattering males; she enjoyed the parties and the balls and the gaiety and complete lack of responsibility. Yet when she had married Senator Benton and come to Washington with him, she had become a thoughtful wife and mother; no one could doubt that she loved Tom Benton.

Suddenly her mother turned to her with unwonted intensity:

"Jessie, your cousin, Preston Johnson, will be at the wedding. You always said he was the handsomest man you ever met. Preston is a darling, he could give you such a pleasurable life. He comes into his inheritance of Blue Ridge Farm when he is twenty-one; it's every bit as beautiful as Cherry Grove. You could have such a fine life there, so free from the turmoil of Washington."

Jessie gazed at her mother incredulously.

"Are you suggesting that I marry cousin Preston?" she asked.

"You could love him, Jessie, very easily."

Mrs. Benton leaned against the curved railing of the prow. "Oh, Jessie, darling, I want to save you from what I've been through. Please believe me, my little girl, there is peace and tranquillity in Virginia. You can live a life of ease and charm. You don't have to fight and struggle and be called names, and have your private life spread over the vile newspapers. You don't have to be part of that pushing, grasping crowd of opportunists who always are trying to throw someone over, who use any means to get ahead."

"Then you never have liked Washington?"

"I have hated it more bitterly than anyone could know. I was brought up in peaceful country, I knew nothing of wars and vendettas; I came out of the amiability of Cherry Grove and I was deposited into a cesspool of politics. In Virginia, at least among the Whigs, it was a gentleman's game. But since that dreadful day of Andrew Jackson's inaugural, when the mob broke into the White House, pushed the invited guests around, tore my lovely white gown . . . all politics is like that: the uninvited, unwashed, pushing around their superiors, ripping handmade lace gowns and handmade traditions."

She turned from her daughter, her excitement gone, gazed down into the white foam of water. "Do you think I liked it when my husband was called names, addressed as Old Rhinoceros Hide?"

"But Mother," exclaimed Jessie, "there is nothing bad about that. The name calling and abuse have never hurt Father, he took them in his stride. How much worse it would be for him if he lived under a king or a tyrant and neither he nor his opponents could speak their mind."

"But what about me?" wailed Mrs. Benton. "There is nothing I loathe in this world more than controversy. I could not come down to dinner without finding a group of your father's henchmen or opponents ready to thrash out their differences over the dinner table; for years if I went to a party there was no room for dancing or conversation or laughter, but only for argument and quarreling and plans about how to beat a person or a party into line. Wherever we went, wherever we traveled, the quarrels and the differences, the constant strife and sordid bickerings of public life followed us . . ."

". . . because they were part of Father's work."

"Jessie," her mother pleaded, "please try to understand. I do not criticize your father's work, nor do I mean to minimize its importance. I am only trying to say that that life could never be for me. I like quiet, pleasant, amusing people, people without troubles or conflicts, the easygoing kind who would hurt no one, like those I knew in Cherry Grove. Jessie, I want to save you from what I have gone through: I should have married one of those charming boys who had a plantation near to ours; then I could have continued the kind of life that I was raised for, that I knew and loved. I knew this when I was young, that was why I refused your father for six years. I love your father; he will be the first to tell you that I have been a faithful and loving wife, but I knew all the time that his way of life could never be mine. Wherever he went he carried with him turbulence; I never wanted these things, I detest them as vulgar, as destructive of the real and permanent values. I tried hard; in the early years I went everywhere with your father, I listened to his dreams, tried to share his defeats, but always it was against my nature and always it sickened me . . . until I could no longer face these people, I could no longer stomach their eternal vehemence. It made me ill, Jessie, as ill as though I had contracted a disease."

"I understand," said Jessie gently. "I'm sorry, Mother, terribly sorry."

"But that is not the reason I have told you this," said her mother softly. "I vowed that I would go to my death without telling anyone, because I would never want Tom Benton to think that he had hurt me. I have broken my resolve for you, Jessie. My darling, I know that something has come between us; I know that in the last few years I have not been with you enough, that I have withdrawn from your life and problems . . ."

"I have been all right, Mother; I have been happy and well."

". . . but now I must urge you, I must do everything that a mother can do for her daughter to save her."

Jessie gazed at the gentle green hills.

"Save me from what?"

"From Lieutenant Fremont! Don't misunderstand me, Jessie, I like the young man, but he is dynamic and pushing—like your father! He always will be striving and battling his way uphill, spreading about him with a vast club, as Tom Benton has; for that reason he will have enemies, he will never be free of them. You will live with wrangling and dissension, the interminable struggle mixed into the very food you eat. That is not good for a woman. It destroys that inner spirit which must give her a sense of relaxation and security if she is to live happily and raise her children."

She took Jessie's hand in hers and held it tightly.

"That is why I urge you to think seriously about your cousin Preston: he comes from the best family in Virginia; he is wealthy and secure, he has no ambition except the very proper ambition that his plantation be run well and prosperously; he is full of laughter and he loves all the little things. How beautifully you could live with him, Jessie; what a serene life you could enjoy."

Seeing that her mother looked faint, Jessie insisted upon helping her to their tiny cabin, where she made her comfortable on the combination berth-bed and wiped her brow with cologne. At first she thought her mother would sleep, but she felt Elizabeth's eyes following her every move, silently demanding an answer. She sat on the edge of the bed and stroked her mother's thin white arm.

"Mother, do you think Father could have lived without this constant conflict which has been so unpalatable to you?"

"No," replied Mrs. Benton, "what was the breath of life to him was poison to me."

"You have often said that I am Father's daughter; then you will understand, dear, that I too am ambitious, and I am not afraid of conflict. I understand and accept the turmoil of politics because I have grown up with it. Like you, I cannot eat dinner with arguments going on about me. But one can eat at any time, and it only sometimes happens that one can be with robust minds. I like Father's way of life, Mother; it comes as natural to me as it does to him. I would find it difficult to settle at Blue Ridge Farm, to spend my time in riding and dancing and hunting. I would die under that way of life. It would poison me as the turbulence of the life in Washington has poisoned you."

Mrs. Benton's tired, faded eyes looked at her daughter without comprehension.

"Jessie, you are so like me, your face is like mine, your figure is delicate like mine, it will not take all this hammering, it will sicken you, wither you . . ."

"You are wrong, Mother, you will see that you are wrong. I love John

Fremont and I feel that he will leave his mark on history. I want to be part of that struggle and contribution."

". . . it would be so easy for you to love cousin Preston," her mother persisted. "He's handsome, charming . . ."

They were met at the wharf at Fredericksburg by the high-swung yellow family coach which the children had long since nicknamed the Pumpkin. Jessie clambered onto the hard leather seat beside her mother. After a few moments of bumpy riding she perceived that Elizabeth Benton had not yet given up the attempt to influence her.

"I can't tell you how it grieves me, Jessie, because I see nothing of the Cherry Grove tradition in you, but only your Father's tradition of a brawling, squawling frontier. I did not love your Father less because he became embroiled in those uncouth quarrels, but it created barriers between us. It is hard to separate a man from his work, Jessie, and when his work is a dirty one, when he brings in the vulgar trappings of his job with him, then one's whole way of life is disrupted."

"The best of a man is in his work," announced Jessie, categorically.

"Your father taught you that."

"Does that make it any the less true?"

Tears rolled down Elizabeth Benton's cheeks; but this time she made no effort to gather her daughter to her.

"My poor baby, how I pity you! How much misery and suffering you are rushing out to embrace."

As the tall oaks of Cherry Grove loomed into sight, Elizabeth Benton made a futile, fluttering gesture with her slender white hands which admitted defeat.

"I came into your father's life too late to change him, nor would it have been decent, or even sensible, to try. But you are so young . . . No one listens to me; everyone goes his cocksure way."

11

CHERRY GROVE HAD BEEN PAID in grant to Jessie's great-grandfather by the King of England in return for his military services in the colonies. It had been built in the manner of the Arlington Colonial, with the pillared portico and stately white wings, the great drawing room and dining room on either side of the lofty, spacious hall.

They were escorted into the house by Colonel McDowell, her uncle with the florid face and long silken mustaches. In addition to her grandmother McDowell and Eliza, who had returned with her in the spring, Jessie found herself exclaimed over and embraced by thirty-five aunts, uncles and cousins, the complete gathering of the clan: there were still-English cousins from Smithfield, the aunt from Richmond who had descended from Patrick Henry, the uncles from Abington who owned the salt works there; Uncle McDowell, whom the family claimed to be the most profound scholar in all Virginia, their cousin, the Reverend Robert Breckinridge, who was known all over the South for his fire and eloquence in the pulpit.

And her cousin, Preston Johnson, was there, home on his first vacation from West Point. He seized upon the opportunity in the crowded hallway to join in the embraces and kiss her enthusiastically. Preston was a tall, blond, blue-eyed boy, one of the most daring and skillful riders in Virginia. He was Jessie's second cousin. She had no sooner been ushered into the drawing room than the aunts and uncles insisted that she stand side by side with Preston so that they could exclaim over how amazingly she looked like Preston's mother and comment, in soft but audible undertones, what a beautiful couple they made.

While the elders collected in the library each morning for what she considered to be an endless recounting of family history, Jessie and her cousins escaped by going horseback riding in the hills. Preston was an incorrigible tease who kept them laughing.

"But Preston, have you no ambition beyond having fun?" she asked one morning.

She saw him grow sober and mature for the first time in the years she had known him, and for the last time until they would bring home his shrapnel-torn body from the plains of Cherubusco.

"I pity people with ambition," he said, measuring his words carefully. "They tear themselves apart so; and everyone around them, too. They never have any pleasure or peace; ambition feeds on itself; the greater the accomplishment, the greater the appetite. No, thank you, Jessie, no ambition for me; I want to live graciously; ambition is for the upstarts, for those who hope to leave off where I begin."

Jessie liked her young cousin better because he had revealed something of himself. At the same time she knew how wide was the bridge that separated them.

At dusk she wandered alone through the oak-lined park. The cherry trees were in rampant bloom, the maples and sycamores were in flower. While her serious attachments always had been for Washington City and Grandmother Benton's home in St. Louis, the spacious beauty of Cherry Grove never failed to awaken a nostalgia in her. While walking through the stately grounds, crossing the large stretches of lawn and gardens with square-boxed hedges, she understood a little the startling revelation her mother had made. Her mother had called her headstrong. Could it be

that her dream of marriage as a joint career for husband and wife was
an impossible one? That her love for the man who not only inflamed her
senses, but whose work she considered important and valuable, was misplaced? She thought of her cousin Preston and of how different she felt
when she was in the company of John Fremont, who served as a heady
stimulant, who excited her to her deepest thinking and sharpest expression.

A woman had to work through a man; she must choose a good vessel
into which to pour herself.

When she returned to the house she found her grandmother sitting
quietly in the library with a book on her lap.

"Come here, child," she called.

Jessie sank onto the soft blue rug with her feet tucked beneath her and
looked up at her grandmother.

"I shall make your wedding here at Cherry Grove," she said. "I will
live that long, though I am getting very old and tired." She stroked Jessie's head gently. "It is you who make me realize how indestructible
things are: my mother came here as a young bride a hundred years ago,
in 1743. Her life was rich, but it was also full of hardships. She carried
her scars from the Indian wars, just as I do: her first child was killed in a
night raid. You will have your battles too, Jessie, after you marry that
young man of yours; and you will carry scars, but you will carry them
the way my mother did, like medals bestowed for bravery."

12

FOUR MONTHS HAD PASSED, and there were two more months of days in
which, for the first time in her life, she found herself avoiding the company of her father. Her sister was the only one with whom she could
talk about John, and talking about him somehow filled the hours of
waiting.

She was reading in the family's small upstairs sitting room the evening Joshaam entered and announced that Lieutenant Fremont wished to
pay his respects. No one moved: her mother looked hard at her multi-
colored afghan; Thomas Benton glared at his young son as though he
were responsible for Lieutenant Fremont's not having been permanently
lost among the Sioux; Jessie gazed at her father, her face hot and her
heart cold with anxiety. Only Eliza seemed able to do the natural thing;
she rose, went downstairs and returned with Lieutenant Fremont in tow.
Jessie wanted to rise when she saw him in the doorway, his face bronzed,
his hair long, making him look like the Indians among whom he had
spent the summer.

Still unable to rise or speak, Jessie thought Mrs. Crittenden was right when she said he was the handsomest officer ever to walk the streets of Washington.

It seemed to her as though a very long time passed in awkward silence, but actually it was only a moment before Thomas Benton remembered his manners, clasped the young lieutenant firmly by the hand and welcomed him home. John presented the girls with gifts of Indian jewelry, young Randolph with a tomahawk. For Mrs. Benton, Jessie, and Eliza he had brought handsomely carved turquoise necklaces, and for Tom Benton a picturesque Indian pipe of peace. Jessie sat stiffly in her chair while Randolph demanded stories of the Indians. Then Tom Benton said, "I would like to hear something of your findings; suppose we go into the library where I have my maps."

Up to this moment Jessie had exchanged no word with her betrothed. She had not been invited into the library with the two men, but she knew that no matter what Senator Benton said later, she would go in with them.

The library was cool and dark, the heavy Venetian blinds having been closed all day against the hot sun. As her father lighted his astral lamp Jessie stood awkwardly on one foot, her eyes on John, wanting to be in his arms. But as Tom Benton moved about the room laying out his own rough charts she could feel his disapproval, the lack of understanding in the way he held his head.

She stood with her back to the worktable watching John as he bent over his maps, listening as he answered her father's questions in a deep voice. She watched his eyes, the glow of excitement on his dark face; though the fingers of his left hand gripped hers under the table, crushing them, she knew that he had forgotten her presence, that he was living again those hours of exploration. And she was not jealous.

But when Tom Benton went to put away his papers, they turned to each other; not knowing how they had overcome their restraint before him, or their reluctance in the face of his hunched-up disapproval, they were in each other's arms. In the distance they heard a voice; it was Senator Benton.

". . . very well, you love each other; I am not blind. But you still have six months to wait . . ."

Somewhere in the process of walking out of the library, going down the stairs and bidding him good night, always with her father at her elbow, she managed to murmur, "Tomorrow afternoon at Mrs. Crittenden's. Three o'clock."

The next afternoon she rang the doorbell of the senator from Kentucky. Mrs. Crittenden had always been fond of Jessie Benton; in addition she was a woman who liked to gather the world and its troubles to her.

"He's here, my dear," she said. "I sent him out to the garden; it's cool and quiet there and you can be alone. Really, I envy you, Jessie: that man grows more exciting every time he comes back from an expedition. If I were you I'd marry him fast."

Her teeth chattering, Jessie could only reply, "By the Eternal, Mrs. Crittenden, I'm trying! If only something could convince Father . . . The next six months sound to me like six decades; I'm certain I'll never survive them."

"You'll survive them," replied Mrs. Crittenden, "but you'll be on the point of death at least a hundred times."

Jessie tried to smile in response to the little joke.

"I think Father is planning to have him sent on another expedition before the six months are up. This time he may send him away for a year, or even two. Oh, he can do it, never fear," she said swiftly as Mrs. Crittenden appeared to protest, "he can persuade Secretary Poinsett again; there is endless work to be done. But not now, Mrs. Crittenden, not until we're married. I can't let Father send him away again!"

"No," agreed Mrs. Crittenden slowly, "I don't think you should."

She put her arm around Jessie's slender shoulders and walked with her out to the garden. "Do exactly as you think best, Jessie, though heaven knows I have interfered with my own children enough."

As she saw John Fremont sitting placidly in a low wicker chair, waiting for her, Jessie knew that she would do nothing, that she could not make herself bold. She would have to wait until he spoke his mind.

They sat in a shaded swing and talked about the past six months; she told him of the wedding festivities at Cherry Grove, of the riding and hunting on the estate, the talk of the elders about how many colonial and American governors they had contributed; of the death of Grandmother McDowell just two days after the ceremony.

The next afternoon when she met him at Mrs. Crittenden's, she saw that he was nervous and ill at ease.

"Let's take a walk," he announced brusquely. "I want to talk to you."

It was a crisp fall day, one of the few times in the year that one could take a real walk in Washington, for the early rains had been sufficient to settle the dust, but not heavy enough to create vast mud puddles. He struck out along the rough cobblestones of F Street, then lifted her over a rail fence, crossed a grazing field and a number of ditches and once again lifted her over a stile to come to the Navy Yard, where Christ Church stood in the center of a cluster of small cottages. From here they turned east past the city workhouse and the congressional cemetery. She was glad she had worn her walking dress of rose satin, for its long skirt puffed out with hoops swished back and forth rhythmically as she kept up with the lieutenant's pace. She buttoned her Brussels-lace gloves, then grasped his arm firmly to keep from tripping on the rough ground outside the Navy Barracks.

As they swept along she glanced at his profile and noted uneasily that his skin seemed darker than she had known it; his features heavier; she wondered if something was upsetting him. She enjoyed striding by his side, the feel of her shoulder touching his lightly. Then slowly their harmony was broken: he slowed his pace, in an instant he had stopped without giving her warning, his figure stiffened. He whirled about to block her passage, a look of resolution on his face, the charm and surety gone, so that she almost did not recognize the man who stood confronting her. Nor did she recognize his voice when he finally spoke, for it was hoarse and off key.

"I've waited—yes, I know it's almost too late . . . but please believe me, Jessie, it wasn't because I wanted to . . . to . . . conceal . . ."

"What is it, my darling?" she asked softly.

"I simply could not, Jessie, I dared not leave it for you to find out by yourself . . . later by accident . . . and then have it be something you would hold against me, because I did not tell you the full truth."

Jessie took his arm. "Let's walk over past Duff Green Row; it will be easier for you to talk."

They started out again, but his pace was slow, almost dragging.

"Jessie, I couldn't let you marry me until I told you . . ."

He was silent for another moment, then stopped dead in his tracks and said in a flat tone, "I never told you about my mother, did I?"

They were in front of the large brick building where Congress had held its first meetings. The air was utterly still.

"Only that she had a difficult time supporting her three children after your father died."

"Yes. Well. My mother's maiden name was Anne Beverley Whiting. Her father was Colonel Thomas Whiting, who was a large landowner in Virginia and one of the leaders in the House of Burgesses. My mother was the youngest of twelve children; the family was prosperous, but when her father died her mother married a man who dissipated the entire estate. Her mother died soon after, and my mother was brought up by a married sister."

He paced back and forth, talking faster.

"She never spoke about those days much; she was kept almost as a slave in her sister's house. My mother was a beautiful young girl—I will show you her picture one day. When she was only seventeen an elderly man by the name of John Pryor began courting her; he had fought under Washington, was wealthy, owned the biggest livery stable in Virginia, and the Haymarket Gardens. He was past sixty, but he wanted my mother. John Pryor offered security, a place in Richmond society, an escape from my aunt's household. She married him when she was only seventeen, and she spent twelve unhappy years with him."

Jessie took her eyes from his harassed face; she glanced down at her shoes, idly noting that the patent leather about the toe was hopelessly scuffed. Free from her observing eyes, John increased the tempo of his short staccato steps, and his story gained momentum.

"When my mother was twenty-seven she met a young schoolteacher in Richmond by the name of Charles Frémon. My father—he became . . . my father had been a Royalist during the French Revolution and had fled to San Domingo during one of the uprisings. His ship was captured by the English, he was made a prisoner in the West Indies for several years. Finally he was released and came on to Virginia where he made a living teaching French and painting frescos. Here my mother met him, and they fell in love."

He stopped short and whirled about to confront her.

"Jessie, they could not endure to be without each other. For a year they found happiness in Richmond, and then John Pryor learned about it. He told my mother that he would kill Charles Frémon and that everyone in Virginia would not only approve his act but would help him if necessary. The next morning my mother and Frémon were gone from Richmond."

He stopped, announced, "Let us turn back!" took her roughly by the shoulder and began walking impetuously in the direction from which they had come.

"John Pryor went to the Virginia legislature and asked for a divorce from my mother. My mother knew about this."

They circled the buildings of a brickworks, watching its blazing kiln. "Did my mother and father have a marriege ceremony performed? My mother said they did. But she never showed me the wedding certificate. It would have made little difference, in any event, for the Virginia legislature had turned down John Pryor's request, and he never did secure a divorce. I was born in Savannah on January 21, 1813. So . . . you see, I was . . . yes, I am . . ."

Jessie stood looking at him, feeling the deepest sympathy she had ever known.

"I am . . . an illegitimate child, Jessie. I can try to forget it or pretend it doesn't matter, I can tell myself that my mother did have a ceremony performed, that John Pryor's appeal to the Virginia legislature was as good as a divorce, but when I am all through I still come up against the cold fact of my illegitimacy."

John Fremont appeared to shrink until she seemed taller than he and had to look down into his eyes. She spoke out quickly.

"It has hurt you, it has made you bitter, I can see that; but surely you do not blame your mother?"

"No, no," he said fiercely, "I have always been happy that she found love and had the courage to take it."

"Then I must ask you, has all this made any difference to you?"

"No . . . o," he replied hesitantly, as though realizing that he was telling only a fraction of the truth, "except that it has made me more determined to make good, to show them that Anne Beverley Whiting's son is as good as the rest of them."

"Then why must you torment yourself so?"

"Because I'm afraid," he whispered.

"Afraid? You, who live in the face of imminent death every moment you are in the wilderness?"

"I live in terror . . . of the day when someone . . . will call me a . . . bastard!"

Jessie thought, There, it is out: it is better for him to have said it; now perhaps it won't fester in the dark places of his mind.

"You are the finest man I have ever known," she murmured softly, "as fine and wonderful as my own father. I love you completely. It wasn't necessary to tell me this, it's not of the slightest importance, and I know how much it cost you in the telling."

". . . the most painful . . . difficult . . . moment of my life."

"Be comforted, John; we will never discuss it again." She wrapped her long cashmere shawl tighter around her shoulders. "Come, let us go to Mrs. Crittenden's. A cup of hot tea will be good for both of us."

"One thing more, Jessie: I want you to know what has precipitated this. It was the stories you told me of Cherry Grove and the McDowell family that goes back two hundred years in American history. Imagine how outraged your family at Cherry Grove would be if they learned that a McDowell had married a bas . . . an illegitimate child. For they will find out, Jessie; far too many people in the South know, not to tell them. Behind your back they'll say, 'Are the children of an illegitimate man illegitimate?'"

Again she tried to reassure him, more by her manner than her words, for she knew that he had already told himself all the possible answers.

"My dear, you have made your own way and established a place for yourself; your ability and your reputation are growing, nothing can harm you . . ."

"Jessie, your position is impregnable: no one can ever challenge it. You could never know how this insecurity can poison a man, though he puts on a bold and charming front. Oh Jessie, if you could only know how I've wanted to belong, to be invulnerable, so that no one could possibly point out any difference! How I've wanted to belong to the majority, not to a despised minority; how I've wanted to have the security of knowing that I am thinking what everyone else is thinking . . ."

They walked on awkwardly, past the Old Glasshouse where some of the country's best glass was made. About a hundred men and boys were working in the big shop. Jessie and John watched them for a few moments, then wandered through their settlement of freshly painted cottages with wide verandas, covered by vines and shaded by tall trees.

So his strength was born of weakness, thought Jessie. Her father too would not have had to become a reckless and courageous fighter, but would have been a simple and ordinary man, like all other ordinary men, if he had not been a consumptive, if he had not been on the very verge of death. Adversity had made Tom Benton strong, as it had John Fremont.

She told him of Tom Benton's father, who had died of consumption while the children were still young, of how her father's three sisters had died of consumption, and within another year, two of his brothers. Then Tom had studied law in Nashville, been admitted to the Bar and elected to the Tennessee legislature. When war broke out in 1812 he had volunteered and become a colonel under Andrew Jackson. Going home to say farewell to his mother, he had had to admit to her that he too was in the early stages of the disease, for he had a fever, was coughing, and she could tell from his thin, racked frame that he had been having sleepless nights. The pioneer woman saw that her last and most promising child would be taken from her.

"This is the end of all my hope," she had cried. "Tom, stay home, let me put you to bed, let me take care of you."

"No, Mother," he had replied, "with this disease we have no chance. If I'm doomed, then it is better to give the last few months of my life fighting for my country."

Tom Benton had joined his regiment and made his way south to meet the British. But he had not given himself up to death. An iconoclast by nature, with a mind open to any radical thought that seemed to make sense, he had recalled that he felt best when he was outdoors in the sunshine, when he was subjecting his body to rigors which everyone told him would be fatal. He bathed at dawn and sunset in cold streams, rubbed down his body with coarse towels, stripped off his clothes when there was even a moment's time to stretch out naked in the sun; he foreswore alcohol and tobacco, made Herculean efforts to find eggs and milk to drink every day; and instead of pampering his sick body he had pushed it beyond its outermost limits on forced marches. By the end of the summer he had put on twenty pounds of hard flesh.

"Fear did that for my father," she said. "That fear has never abated, never for a day of his life, and consequently he has never given up his discipline. All this not only saved his life, but made a fighter of him. Think of how valuable a man he has become through that courage; think of the great work he has done, how he has stood up against his enemies and never given up to despair. Fear is good, my dear, it made a strong man of my father. It can make a great man of you."

Gratefully John murmured, "You are kind, Jessie; there are no walls that close in your understanding."

Jessie smiled wistfully. "I too have used weakness to build with. I was afraid that I might not measure up, that being a woman I would find myself weak, my mind unable to grasp the real issues and struggles of the day. That is why I studied and worked so hard, because I didn't want to fail, because I didn't want my father or my husband to feel that I didn't have the brains or the courage or the training to serve as his companion."

Some of the darkness receded from John's face, a little warmth came into his eyes, his figure seemed to regain its height. And Jessie felt her own blood sing through her veins. She stopped at the edge of the marsh along which they had been wandering, locked her arms around him, her open palms pressing his back tightly, and kissed him full on the mouth, a kiss of love and faith and affirmation, so strong, so indelible that all other words died in his throat.

13

THE CRISP WIND OF AUTUMN was flurrying the leaves from the sycamores and poplars when Jessie and John, together with Mr. Nicollet and Mrs. Crittenden, met at an appointed hour at the home of the Presbyterian minister whose church Jessie attended.

Her fear that Senator Benton would have John sent off again was heightened by the sense of insecurity from which the lieutenant suffered and which imperiled their relationship. He had commented to her, "Confidence is the greatest gift that one human being can give to another." What greater token of confidence could she bestow upon him than immediate marriage?

They found the minister in his study, a tall white-haired man with a lean, esthetic face and an enormous mouth, reputed to be the largest in the contemporary service of the Lord. He looked at the unannounced assemblage and asked, none too cordially, "What can I do for you?"

It was Mrs. Crittenden who answered without hesitation, "Jessie Benton and Lieutenant Fremont wish to be married. Since Miss Jessie is a member of your congregation, we have naturally come to you to perform the ceremony."

"Ah, splendid, splendid," murmured the clergyman, his mouth smiling, but his eyes glancing swiftly and uncertainly from person to person. "And when can we expect your mother and father, Miss Jessie?"

"You can't," replied Nicollet shortly; "they're not coming."

"Not coming!" exclaimed the clergyman. "But I don't understand. Surely they will want to be at Miss Jessie's wedding . . . ?"

"They would and they wouldn't," replied Jessie. "You see, sir, this is a secret—er—marriage, that is, Father doesn't exactly . . . he wants us to wait another six months."

"You mean your mother and your father don't know about this?"

"No, sir."

Pulling himself up to his full six feet the clergyman closed his lips so tightly his mouth appeared almost small.

"Did you really think I would incur the wrath of Senator Benton? Did you imagine that I would perform a secret ceremony knowing that the senator disapproved? Have you all taken leave of your senses?"

There was a dull pause before he continued, "I will not expose your secret, Miss Jessie. Come back with your mother and father, and it would be my great happiness to marry you to Lieutenant Fremont. Good day to you all."

A little stunned and very much disconcerted, the would-be wedding party trudged down the front stairs of the minister's house.

"What do we do now?" asked Lieutenant Fremont.

"We try another clergyman," replied Mrs. Crittenden; "whom do you recommend, Mr. Nicollet?"

"Let's try that new Methodist minister; he seems to have gumption."

The Methodist minister had discretion. He asked very politely, "Are you not a Presbyterian, Miss Benton? Why do you not go to your Presbyterian clergyman?"

"We've been," replied Jessie.

"And?"

"He won't marry us unless my mother and father are along."

"That sounds like uncommonly good sense," observed the minister with a twinkle in his eye. "Never let it be said that a Methodist rushed in where a Presbyterian feared to tread."

Once again the wedding party trooped out of the house. They tried the Lutheran minister, who was rehearsing his choir in a little wooden church. The Lutheran must have read defeatism in their faces, for he replied, "Quite unthinkable; however, if you are of the same opinion to-morrow, I will come to your home, Miss Benton, and perform the ceremony."

They had started out in high spirits and high hopes; now they stood in the brisk October sunshine looking at each other guiltily.

"Well," drawled Nicollet, "better luck next time; come along, Lieutenant, if you can't be married, you might as well go back to work."

Jessie walked Mrs. Crittenden home and then continued wearily onward to her own house. First she had been bewildered, then hurt, but now she was mad. What has the world come to, she asked herself, when a young couple in love can't get married? Surely there must be some way . . . ?

There was, but she spent three agonizing days before the answer turned up. Mrs. Crittenden arrived on the afternoon of October 19 for a visit with Mrs. Benton. She asked Mrs. Benton if Jessie might spend the night with her, as she was giving a party for her young niece. There could be but one purpose to this proposal: Jessie packed an overnight bag, jumped into Mrs. Crittenden's carriage as though the world had been reborn.

"It's all arranged," said Mrs. Crittenden. "I went yesterday to Father Van Horseigh, the Catholic priest, and persuaded him to perform the marriage. He is coming this afternoon. I've already sent word to Lieutenant Fremont. Nicollet and Hassler will be there, Harriet Bodisco, and several other of your young friends. I have pledged them to secrecy."

When they arrived at the Crittenden home they found Lieutenant Fremont waiting. He was wearing his full-dress uniform, the same one in which he had proposed to her eight months before. Jessie was presented to Father Van Horseigh, a plump little Dutch priest with a moonlike face, a shock of red hair and a bubbling gift of laughter. Though Jessie and John Fremont were Protestants, they saw no reason why they should not be married by a Catholic priest: Jessie had been raised with the French of Catholic St. Louis; John had been taken by Nicollet for a vacation to St. Mary's College at the Sulpician Seminary in Baltimore after their second expedition.

The service was short and simple. Only once did Jessie Benton's determination almost fail her, and the tears well up behind her eyes: where were the beauties of Cherry Grove, the hundreds of friends and relatives who would gather; where was the magnificent Paris gown of blonde lace over satin, where the mahogany dining table laden with wines and wondrous foods, and the bridecake embedded in a wreath of ivy and geranium leaves cut from the candied rind of watermelon; where were the linens and cambrics, the muslins and lace, every stitch of delicate needlework sewn by friends and relatives? She would be the first of Cherry Grove to be married in "paid-for" sewing. Where were the saddle horses and barouches and London carriages gathered at the hitching shed, and all the countryside of Virginia alive and glowing because Miss Jessie Ann Benton was being married?

As a tear rolled down her cheek, Jessie Benton paralleled the traditional words the priest was speaking with her own prayer: I give up the traditions of Cherry Grove, I give up the Empire gown, I give up the lovingly sewed linens, I give up the bridecake; I can give up everything so long as I have you, John Fremont.

She came up from the depths of her thinking to find a quiet in the room; the ceremony was over, she had not even heard herself and John pronounced man and wife; nor had she need of the corroboration.

Mrs. Crittenden served a wedding supper, after which the servants offered claret, cheeses, fruits, candies, and as a grand climax a silver platter of ice cream which Jessie saw had been made with the expensive vanilla bean. There was the music of a violin, guitar and accordion, but Jessie left her food untouched and danced only a little, for her head felt feverish and her feet uncertain. At ten o'clock Mrs. Crittenden beckoned to John and herself and walked them out into the cold of the garden.

"Attention, my children," she said, "I will be responsible to Tom Benton only for the marriage ceremony. Kiss your bride good night, Lieutenant Fremont, for you are returning home to your bachelor quarters."

And so Jessie walked up the Benton steps the following morning, trembling with joy because she was Mrs. John Charles Fremont, and trembling at the thought of her father's rage when he should learn what had happened. Each day she and her husband saw each other for a few moments, but never alone, always there were Nicollet or Mrs. Crittenden, who played chaperon far more ardently than she had before the ceremony. Occasionally too Tom Benton found it awkward to exclude from his house the rising young star of the western expeditions.

The oval mirror on Jessie's dressing table told her that she was becoming peaked and hollow-eyed. It was growing increasingly difficult for her to stand looking at John, talking politely and restrainedly of impersonal things. Eliza knew of the marriage and urged her sister to reveal it. Nicollet also urged it. He was eager for them to get on with their normal life and work. "I'm growing older and more ill every hour, *mes enfants,*" he would say, "it won't be long before I'll be studying celestial maps. Before I go, I would like to see this affair settled."

When at last John pleaded, "I have never liked this secrecy. We have been precipitous but not criminal. Let me go to the senator and explain," Jessie said firmly: "We will explain tomorrow morning. I will ask the senator for an early interview."

A little more than a month after their marriage ceremony, Jessie led John to the upstairs library. Tom Benton was sunk in his chair, his high domelike forehead creased with four deep lines, his mouth and chin set grimly, his gray eyes tired. They stood before him.

"We are married, Father," said Jessie in a low tone. "The ceremony was performed on October nineteenth."

She was frightened. She wanted the two men to be friends. Could her father understand that she did not love him the less because she had acquired a husband?

A bellow came up from the depths of Tom Benton's chair; the outburst was directed at John Fremont.

"Get out of my house and never cross this door again! Jessie shall stay here."

Quietly, and without hesitation, Jessie linked her arm through her husband's. Her voice was calm and clear.

"Father, do you remember Ruth's pledge from the Bible? 'Whither thou goest, I will go . . .' "

Tom Benton rose slowly and towered above them. He would give in, but in his own peculiar way. Her hope was that it would not be too peculiar for her husband's understanding.

"Go collect your belongings and return at once to the house," he ordered the lieutenant, his tone suggestive of the colonel commanding a subaltern.

There was a stillness in the room. It was broken by a brusque knock on the door. Two newspaper reporters stood on the threshold.

"Senator Benton," said the man from the *National Intelligencer,* "we hear there is news about Miss Jessie."

Tom Benton glared at the man, then growled, "Yes. I have the pleasure of announcing the marriage of my daughter, Jessie Ann Benton, to Lieutenant John Charles Fremont."

The reporter from the New York *Globe* grinned. "Isn't that an unusual way of putting it, Senator? Families generally announce the marriage of the man to their daughter."

Tom Benton looked sharply at his daughter, then said, unsmilingly, "If ever I saw a woman do her damnedest to get married to a man, it's my daughter Jessie. But if you print that I'll sue you for libel. Good day, gentlemen."

BOOK TWO

A Woman Waits

SHE LAY QUIETLY in her high bed, the air cold from the window above 'he garden, the quilt tucked under her chin. In a few hours it would be New Year's Day. Lieutenant and Mrs. John Charles Fremont had been invited by President John Tyler to a reception at the White House.

It was now two o'clock in the morning; her husband lay sleeping peacefully beside her. It amused her to see that this man who held himself so erect while in public now lay curled up like a child, all need for defense vanished. She thought, Who but a wife can know all about a man, see him and feel him whole, understand his sudden flights and equally sudden withdrawals?

They had talked for a long time with the darkness of the bedroom like a sheltering canopy, and only an occasional burst of laughter from some incongruous idea broke the silence. She liked these hours the best, the comradely periods when she could lie with a protecting arm about her, nestled against the man she loved.

From her earliest days she had wanted to create a fine marriage. She had been born with the idea, but it also had been nurtured by her father, who had talked to her about the "great marriage," which would be the highest aim she could achieve, of equal importance with the children she would bear. Marriage was to be her proving ground, the combined art and science with which she could most truly express herself. It would be different from the fragmentary unions she saw about her; it would show that in the accomplishing two human beings could reach their completest fulfillment. Her father had told her how valuable her mother's judgment had been to him; of how tremendous his loss had been when she was taken ill. Jessie sometimes watched her mother and father together in the hope of catching a glimpse of their early relationship; she was heartbroken to see how little was left. In the arrogance of her youth she was certain that she would be equal to the task in which her mother had failed.

As she gazed at her husband's dark face on the pillow, pushed a lock of hair off his brow, she was overcome by a sense of elation that she had found not only the top man in the profession into which she had felt she must marry, but also a man who excited her now every moment she was with him. She might have married a man whom she admired but never loved with this sense of ardency; or she might have loved and married a doctor, an architect, a lawyer, and thus robbed the second half of her dual personality of its ambition.

She had never allowed anyone to know she was thinking these thoughts, for they would have accused her of being an Anne Royall. But as she ran a fingertip along the faint lines in her husband's forehead, down the small-boned nose, and across the warm lips, there was joined to her feeling of elation a sense of awe that she could have been so fortunate as to find one of those exceedingly rare men who would permit his wife to work by his side. She had never assumed marriage to be a relationship from which she would take, but rather a relationship to which she could give.

She was delighted with what marriage had done for John. Before this he had been a homeless one, a man without a family. Now the Benton loyalty and confidence had reached out to envelop him; their marriage seemed to dissipate the last fragment of uncertainty at the back of his eyes.

They had spent their honeymoon in the big house on C Street; their blue-tinted bedroom and sitting room faced south, overlooking the garden, and was flooded with gentle winter sunshine. The family disturbed them not at all; Maylee or one of her twins served breakfast in their rooms; the children stayed out of the garden as much as possible. She had let their friends in Washington City know that they did not want to be entertained by formal dinners or receptions. Her only visitor was the Countess Bodisco, who dropped in frequently with a box of imported Russian or French candy under her arm, amusing chatter on her lips.

"I laugh," said Harriet, "when I remember what one of my uncles told my father. I eavesdropped and heard him say, 'Don't let Harriet marry that old man; he can never give her a complete married life.' My dear, I'll wager that within five minutes of the time the count first closed that bedroom door behind him, I was *enceinte*. That old Russian has me down to skin and bones."

Jessie glanced at Harriet's tall figure, which was filling out rapidly.

"You seem to be thriving under it," she retorted.

She took pleasure in murmuring to herself: my husband. There was nothing possessive in the phrase except in the sense that she belonged; since John Fremont was now her husband, she belonged to him as his wife. Because of her Anne Royall idea of equal work and equal responsibility she found it difficult to call her sweet and lovable husband Mister Fremont. Her mother still called her father Mister Benton after all these years. In public Jessie referred to her husband as Lieutenant Fremont; when they were alone she called him John.

Tonight they had enjoyed several hours of talk before he had at last dropped off to sleep in the middle of a sentence, the room in friendly darkness, the bed soft beneath them, the air cool and spiked with the scent of night-blooming jasmine. At the height of their physical union she had felt that there was no further enigma, no possible withholding. But once it was over, though their love was as great in its ebbing peacefulness, the connecting rod had been snapped like a brittle twig; and dimly she perceived that this probing, onrushing fever of understanding could not be constant or sustained: that it must ebb and flow, that it must now be hard and strong and compulsive within her, and now recede, be withdrawn entirely, be extinguished as a light is extinguished, leaving her abandoned, and yet exhilarated at having even for so short a climax possessed him whole.

Perhaps that is what marriage means, she thought, the spending of a lifetime trying to understand your mate, trying to evolve the mysteries of character which even he may not suspect are there. Perhaps that's what success in a marriage means: not the establishment of a place in society, not the acquiring of a fortune, no, not even the creating of children; but the full understanding of another human soul, the most difficult and at the same time the most beautiful task of all.

2

When lieutenant and mrs. john fremont reached the White House shortly after noon on January 1, 1842, Pennsylvania Avenue was jammed with private carriages, public hacks, broad-beamed omnibuses and a hundred horses tethered to hitching posts. Hassler had urged them to use his imported English carriage for the New Year's call. The carriage was famous up and down the Atlantic seaboard as Hassler's Ark, for he had had it built large enough to house his sleeping and cooking equipment, his scientific instruments, books and journals. Jessie made a last critical appraisal of her dark blue velvet gown with its full straight skirt over narrow hoops, the close-fitting bodice outlined at the neck and sleeves with frills of Mechlin lace. In her strapped slippers she stepped lightly to the ground, leaned on her husband's arm, took an approving glance at his blue-and-gold dress uniform, then gave an adjusting hitch to her blue velvet cape. As they reached the front door she turned to her husband with an inquiring glance which asked, Am I all right? John touched the white lobe of ear which she had not covered with her tightly drawn hair and said:

"What lovely pearl earrings you wear, Madame."

They passed the Marine Band which was playing in the vestibule and were welcomed by Senators Linn and Crittenden. Linn exclaimed:

"My dears, you are positively radiant. I know you are going to captivate President Tyler."

"Captivate him thirty thousand dollars' worth," said Senator Crittenden. "If he'll sponsor the bill in Congress, we'll get that appropriation, and you'll be off for South Pass."

"We'll do our best," promised Jessie.

The senators escorted them into the reception room and presented them to President Tyler: high-domed and hollow-cheeked, with a bony nose which curved sharply in an outward arc and seemed to be a continuation of the outward curve of his high forehead. It was the arresting, characterful face of the incorrigibly independent man.

As a former senator from Virginia, President John Tyler had long known the Bentons. He congratulated the young couple upon their marriage, then said to Lieutenant Fremont, "Young man, I understand that you are aching to get off into the wilderness on an expedition."

"That's right, Mr. President," John replied.

"I have reason to believe you won't be disappointed," said President Tyler, "though if I were in your place, just married to Miss Jessie, nothing could persuade me to leave Washington."

"But I plan to wait for him, Mr. President," she replied, smiling.

President John Tyler's lean, hard-bitten face became serious; he said in a low tone: "We need detail maps of all the country from St. Louis to the Rockies so our immigrant trains will settle there. But see that you don't go west of the Rockies, young man; we already have more than a hundred Americans in Oregon; if many more of our settlers reach the Columbia, there will be danger of a war with England."

On a cold gray morning in mid-January they walked up to the Senate Building with Thomas Hart Benton: this was the day for which the expansionists had been working for twenty years. A bill was before the Senate to appropriate thirty thousand dollars for an expedition "intended to acquaint the government with the nature of the rivers and country between the frontiers of Missouri and the base of the Rocky Mountains, and especially to examine the character, and ascertain the latitude and longitude of the South Pass, the great crossing place to these mountains on the way to Oregon."

Jessie sat in the first row of the visitors' gallery watching the scene in the red-plush amphitheater below them. Both she and John knew that on the passage of this appropriation rested their future, for Nicollet was certain to be named to command the expedition and he in turn would name Lieutenant Fremont as his second in command. They waited breathlessly while the roll was called; when the last senator had voted aye and the expedition was authorized, husband and wife turned to each other with happy eyes.

That evening there was a party at the Benton home to celebrate the victory. Jessie, who had been talking with Colonel Abert and Colonel Stephen Watts Kearny about how jubilantly this news would be received in St. Louis and the Southwest, saw Nicholas Nicollet beckoning to her.

"Put on a wrap, my child," he said, "I want to talk to you."

As they walked down the garden path Nicollet commented, "It was here I first saw you sitting with Lieutenant Fremont. I said to your father, 'How beautiful is young love.' And because of my congenital Gallic romanticism, I got poor John banished from the house."

"If you hadn't precipitated that crisis," laughed Jessie, "we might not yet have been married."

They sat side by side on the garden bench. Nicollet said, "Miss Jessie, I have something to tell you."

For an instant the words stopped revolving in her mind. "But surely you are taking Lieutenant Fremont as your second in command?"

"No, Jessie. He will be the commander of the expedition. I am not going, I am too ill."

"But that's not possible," she exclaimed, her sympathy for the white-faced old man overcoming her first flash of joy. "This is the most important expedition sent out by the federal government since Lewis and Clark, an expedition for which you have been working for twenty years!"

"I am an old man," said Nicollet doggedly, "I have done my job. To-morrow morning I shall inform Colonel Abert that I am unable to command the expedition and that I nominate my successor, Lieutenant Fremont."

By the next afternoon all Washington rang with the news that Nicholas Nicollet had retired, that Lieutenant John Fremont was to head the expedition to South Pass.

The months that followed were the gayest of Jessie's life. Countess Bodisco gave a glittery ball in their honor for the Diplomatic Corps in her Georgetown home. Nancy Polk collected the young people of Washington City for a dinner and dance. Senators Linn and King gave dinners at which astonishingly large groups of the Congress came to be wined and dined and tell Lieutenant Fremont, on a full stomach, how to map the barren West. Samuel Morse gave a masquerade ball to which everyone came dressed as either a painter or one of his subjects; Anne Royall had a tea for the feminists of Washington with Jessie as her guest of honor. Colonel Abert entertained at Army Headquarters for the Topographical Corps, Stephen Kearny gave them a dinner at the Metropolitan Hotel, to which he invited the high-ranking army officials. James Buchanan bought out the house of the National Theatre, inviting Jessie's friends to a performance of *The Conscript, or the Maiden's Vow*. To climax the whirling, happy weeks, President John Tyler entertained them at an informal dinner in the White House.

But if there was a round of parties, there also was work to be done. John had his expedition to assemble, his equipment to purchase. In addition it appeared that half of America wanted to help map the South Pass. Mail poured into the Benton home from every hamlet in the country, from every walk of life, from men young and old, asking if they might go along; they came in person to the house on C Street bearing letters of introduction; and with them came the inventors with new instruments and weapons, the manufacturers with products they wanted to sell.

Almost without either of them noticing it, Jessie slipped into the role of secretary. Each morning she rose at six, had chocolate in her sitting room, answered the basket of mail which had accumulated the day before; each afternoon she set aside an hour to talk to the eager ones who came knocking at the front door. In the late afternoon when John returned from the Topographical Office she wrote down the notes and outlines he had been formulating during the day. In early March she rode with him to the Baltimore & Ohio station to see him off to New York where he would spend two weeks buying equipment. He returned excited by several new inventions he had discovered there, chief among them a collapsible rubber boat which Nicollet had had a hand in conceiving.

"We'd better take it out on an open porch to unwrap it," he told the family. "The manufacturer in New York said the chemicals might smell bad."

When the oilcloth paper was unwrapped on the open loggia they were enveloped in an overpowering stench which quickly spread through the house. Jessie turned green. When she was able to walk, Maylee said:

"The lieutenant want you in your sittin' parlor, honey. From the look of him I think he know."

While Joshaam and Josheem heated two big shovels in the kitchen stove, filled them with coffee beans and walked through the house, letting the burning coffee dissipate the noxious odors, Maylee helped her to the doorway of her bedroom, gave her shoulder a reassuring pat. Jessie saw her husband half leaning against, half sitting on a window sill. There was a perplexed and at the same time chiding look in his eyes.

"Confound it, John," she said, "I've been looking for a delicate way to tell you. But you would bring home that newfangled rubber boat. During the weeks you were gone I had so much fun figuring out picturesque ways of revealing . . . We would be sitting by a fire, and suddenly you would notice that I was crocheting baby things . . ."

He crossed the room, picked her up and kissed her. Then with stumbling fervor he told her of his hunger for a son, this disinherited one who had lived without the security of a family name. He had changed his father's name of Frémon to the anglicized Fremont, yet he knew that no matter what the change or what the form, the name was not legally his. But if he spent a lifetime establishing it, passed it on to a son, the process of carrying forward would also carry back to the very moment when he himself had taken it.

Hosts of friends and well-wishers jammed the Benton house on the afternoon before he was to leave. At three o'clock Jessie served tea and little cakes to a hundred guests. By five o'clock, when dinner was ready, some fifty of them remained. After dinner there was laughter and storytelling, and Jessie's heart was full; it seemed that everybody in the world loved and admired her husband and was confident of his success.

By ten o'clock the last of the guests had gone. Jessie made her way to their bedroom. She was tired, yet these were the hours she had looked forward to; the last moments when she could have her husband to herself, taste the last kiss, hear the last word of love.

"You wouldn't want me to stay, to have someone else head the expedition?" he asked.

She bolted upright in the bed, her tears dried miraculously.

"Heavens, no. If that happened, I would cry ten times louder and a hundred times longer."

In the darkness she felt rather than saw him smile.

"Ah, my dear," she murmured, "you are being tactful with me. Well, never mind, it worked. I always thought I would make a good wife; at least I always wanted to: that was my ambition, just as yours was to be an explorer and topographer. I thought of marriage as a career, the way a man does. I'll shed a few tears, but it's part of my job to send you out into the wilderness and to represent you in Washington while you are gone; make you divisible into two, half of you on the trail and the other half here."

"That's quite a speech, Senator," he mocked gently.

"Wasn't it? But you would be astonished how much better it made me feel. And now you really must go to sleep, my darling, you have a hard day tomorrow, getting started."

He took her at her word; almost in a flash she felt his rhythmical breathing and knew he was asleep. For an instant she was hurt: this was their last night together, when they should have talked until dawn of their plans and their child, and yet at her first suggestion he had fallen into a sound sleep. Then she remembered that it must be well past midnight, and he had been up since five that morning. For just one moment longer she let the warmth and breathing of his body reassure her, then she too was sunk in deep slumber.

3

THE NEXT EVENING she was sitting in the library before the fire when her father returned to tell her that John had gotten off successfully. He dropped into his chair and said matter-of-factly:

"Jessie, I've let my work pile up. Do you think you will feel well enough in the morning to help me?"

"Help you? Of course I'll feel well enough."

"Good!" he exclaimed brusquely. "I need a copy of the Treaty of 1818; the one which establishes our joint sovereignty with England over the Oregon country."

"Yes, Papa."

She rose from her chair, sank to the red carpet at his feet and leaned her head against his knee.

"So many times when I've had little problems you sat in this chair opposite me and blew them into thin air. You're sure you're not giving me this work just to take my mind off . . . ?"

"Yes, of course I am," he replied harshly to conceal his feelings. "Work is good for you. But at the same time I need the results of that work. Surely there is nothing wrong in combining your needs with mine."

"Always the able tactician," she exclaimed. "It is good to know that you need me: I need to be needed just now."

"It will be a sad day for you, my dear, when you no longer need to be needed. Come along now, it's time for bed."

She left word for Maylee to bring her breakfast at five-thirty and got quickly into bed, though she was sure she would lie awake all night thinking of John, visualizing his trip to Baltimore on the slow, smoke-filled train. That thought was the last she had until there was a knock on the door and Maylee brought in a silver pitcher of chocolate, two croissants, a pat of butter and a tiny glass dish of blackberry jam.

By five minutes to six she entered the library, thinking to surprise her father by being there before him, but Tom Benton had arisen an hour earlier than usual; he had set up her movable desk in front of her deep chair. There were six new Perry-point steel pens and fifty sheets of satin-finish foolscap on the desk, lighted by her father's own candelabrum invention which he used for early morning work: four spermaceti candles burning on a square of white blotting paper which reflected the light. She slipped into her chair silently.

In his youth someone had told Thomas Hart Benton that he looked like a Roman senator. Jessie had never been able to figure out whether Tom had become a senator because he looked like one, or that he looked like one because he had made himself so completely the apotheosis of the senator. He had a long bony nose which started at the very level of his bold eyebrows, but where it passed his wide-set hazel eyes the skin was curiously wrinkled. He had a great head, and his brow was so high that his face seemed to jut backward. He carried it at an aggressive angle, his chin stuck up in the air as though the whole of him were ready to spring into intellectual action on the slightest provocation. His cheekbones were high and strong, but his mouth was small in proportion to the nose and chin. He wore his sideburns low, almost to his upper lip line, and brushed forward; it was a stubborn face, not handsome but attractive, showing the strain of warfare.

"I didn't follow orders last night, Jessie," he said. "I lay awake for an hour or so evolving a plan: no one has put together the story of American exploration . . ."

"Lewis and Clark and Pike and Cass all wrote about their expeditions . . ."

"Yes! Each man has told of his own adventures, but their journals are technical. I think the American people would enjoy the story, Jessie, if you could put it together."

Her eyes shone with excitement.

"You know, Papa, this fits in with a curious idea I have. When John showed me his provisional maps, trying to give me an idea of how many miles his party would cover each day, I thought I might set up a duplicate map, drawing to scale all the country between St. Louis and South Pass. We know what day he expects to leave St. Louis; I could start him off on that date, drawing a line for the extent of ground he might cover in that day, then put a red dot where they would camp for the night and build their fires."

Her father was nodding his head, so she took courage to continue.

"I had thought I would read the available accounts of what the country is like for each day's march: what wild life is there, what kind of animals they will be shooting for their food. I would draw my map to show the plains and forests and rivers and mountains, and dotted through the map, I would paint in what I imagined the country looked like, with a small field of wild flowers, a patch of pine forests, a few buffaloes roaming across a plain . . ."

"You've set quite a task for yourself," said her father, amused.

"But don't you see, Father," she cried passionately, "in that way he never leaves me, I'll never be alone, I'll be with him on the trail every hour."

Her father left for the Senate. There was a split second in which the sudden loneliness of living through the next six months without her husband seemed to press down on her heart and cut off the breath at her throat. She made a deliberate gesture to throw off the hysteria, sat down quickly in her chair and bent over the pile of papers which her father had left on her desk. At first she could see no word of the writing that lay before her, then she perceived that he had written her a note. It read:

Jessie, my dear, I wanted to leave you this one line from Marcus Aurelius. "Be not disturbed about the future, for if you ever come to it, you will have the same reason for your guide which preserves you at present."

She unbuttoned the top of her tight-sleeved robe, folded her father's note, pinned it securely to her petticoat, buttoned up the robe again with lightning fingers, and plunged into her work.

4

NICOLLET AND HASSLER thought it little more than an amusing idea, but they indulged her. They set up a rectangle of thin wood, four feet high by nine feet long, covering it with large sheets of white paper. For several days the two old men showed her how to reduce to scale and organize the outlines of the big map.

Joshaam and Josheem carried the map down Capitol Hill the next morning, installing it in the library, where her father had made space for it on the back wall. At four-thirty Nicollet and Hassler arrived in the Ark, making their way quickly up to the library. Jessie had estimated how many days it would take her husband to reach South Pass, plotting her map into these fifty-five daily vertical divisions. She had then ruled a

sharp black line horizontally across the center of the map, dividing it into
the journey out and the journey back. Toward the end of the trip home
she put a small symbol which only she would understand; somewhere
around that time her first child would be born.

Hassler took some notes out of his black coat and began to sketch in
part of the terrain of the Colorado. Nicollet said, "You're using Major
Long's map for that material, and you know perfectly well Long has been
discredited as a scientific observer."

"This material is not out of Long," exclaimed Hassler heatedly; "I put
it together myself from trappers' reports."

Her map began to cause interest in Washington. General Winfield
Scott, who had gone out to Detroit to fight the Blackhawk Wars, insisted
upon putting down everything he knew about the territory around the
Great Lakes, while General Lewis Cass, the first governor of Michigan
Territory, came in a few nights later to sketch in the country between
Detroit and Chicago, a trail over which he had been the first white man
to pass. Colonel Kearny, who had planned several of his military expeditions into the Southwest on the porch of Senator Benton's St. Louis home,
did a water-color sketch of that terrain. A professor of botany from
Harvard suggested some of the wild life. Colonel Abert, who fancied
himself as an astronomer, came to dinner and could hardly finish his
chocolate mousse in his impatience to draw in the heavenly bodies.

Each morning she joined her father in the library until it was time for
him to walk up to the Senate. The bookcase at her right elbow was now
filled with some thirty-four volumes, in addition to copies of the official
reports made to the United States government in the form of House and
Senate executive documents. On the bottom shelf she assembled the notes
her father had written in his large, bold, almost undecipherable script on
the wide porch of their St. Louis home during the many years when the
French, Spanish, Mexican and American hunters, trappers, traders and
merchants had come back from their voyages to Mexico and the Pacific
coast.

Starting with the date of 1836, when she had been twelve years of age,
the reports were in her own handwriting, for Tom Benton had hated to
write while he was listening, had turned the job over to her as soon as he
had thought her handwriting legible. At first she had written furiously,
trying to get down every last syllable, but slowly she found her own mind
editing more and more these alfresco discussions. Each had a kernel of
fresh and applicable material, but much of them was pointless repetition.

One day her father asked her for the material on the Santa Fe Trail,
read her extract of a five-hour conversation, and said to his daughter:

"Well thought out, Jessie. This will save me endless work." He looked at her curiously out of the corner of his eye and over one shoulder. "Jessie, I always thought I would make a great educator. Now I am convinced of it."

"Of course it doesn't hurt you to have good material to work with, does it, Senator?"

"Tush, tush, child," he said, "never let yourself get bitten by the virus of conceit." He took her in his arms. "Look what an old fool it's made of your father."

Both in St. Louis and in Washington she had continued her practice of sharp editing. The intensity of this training had an inevitable but almost tragic result: she soon began to edit Thomas Hart Benton.

In the early years she had thought everything her father said to be God-given and perfect; but as she listened to his comrades and opponents on the floor of the Senate, to Clay, Hayne, Webster and Calhoun, she perceived that her father had limitations: he was sometimes repetitious where a straight attack would have been more effective, he leaned too heavily on Marcus Aurelius, the Caesars and Plutarch, sometimes favored the high-flown phrase where simplicity would have won the day. At first when he dictated to her she would simply leave out a word or a phrase; later, she condensed paragraphs, eliminating the weaknesses and redundancies.

A fierce storm raged when Tom Benton learned what his daughter had been doing. For several days he had not talked to her . . . not until she had secured the *Congressional Record*, copied on one piece of paper what Tom Benton had said in the Senate, and on an opposite piece what he had actually dictated to her. After much persuasion and a few tears she succeeded in getting him to look at the two papers side by side. She watched his face as he sat huddled in his deep chair studying the sheets, knowing that her future was at stake; that he must approve what she had done or she would never be able to work with him again.

At length he had raised his head, his face still flushed.

"By the Eternal, Jessie," he exclaimed, "you had no right to do this. It is the damnedest piece of presumption I ever heard of . . . but having done it, I am glad to see you did it so well!"

5

SHE WAS AT HER DESK in the library every morning from eight until eleven. After luncheon she would take a long slow walk through Washington with her sister Eliza, Harriet Bodisco or Nancy Polk. She called for her father at the Senate building at four and walked him home for dinner.

In the evening she busied herself making baby clothes, crocheting their thread edgings, cutting out sacques and nightgowns to be given to the Negro seamstress.

She was stimulated to learn from her reading that American exploration of the West had begun just a decade before her father settled in St. Louis in 1815, that the West had been opened to migration at almost precisely the hour of her own birth: by the discovery of a pass over the Rockies which brought the Oregon Trail into being.

When the United States made the Louisiana Purchase in 1803, doubling the extent of its territory, no man knew more than the tiniest fraction of what had been bought for the fifteen million dollars. For this reason President Jefferson had sent out Meriwether Lewis and William Clark to traverse the country and map a possible trail. Lewis and Clark had been the first white men to cross the Continental Divide of the Rocky Mountains, had made their way down the west slopes of the Rockies into the Columbia River country. They had no sooner returned to Washington in 1806 with their report than the government sent Zebulon Pike to explore that part of the Louisiana Purchase which ran southwest of St. Louis. Pike made his way to Mexico, establishing the Santa Fe Trail, which quickly became a well-traveled route for traders and trappers.

By 1811 John Jacob Astor's hunters and trappers had begun crossing the Rockies through Idaho, and by 1814 the trappers of the Northwest Company and the Hudson's Bay Company were crossing the Rockies every year. They built up a tremendous lore about the wilderness in their rovings to find better furs, yet they were largely uneducated frontiersmen who drew no maps and wrote no journals; consequently their knowledge was of little value to the thousands of families in the East who were eager and poised for western migration, but unwilling to strike out without accurate descriptions of the country.

Then General William Ashley had founded the Rocky Mountains Fur Company and persuaded such frontiersmen as Andrew Henry, James Bridger and Jedediah Smith to join with him. It was a fateful moment in western exploration: for in their wide-swinging movements in search of game, Jim Bridger discovered Salt Lake in 1823, and within a year South Pass had been discovered. When Jessie was only one year old, Jedediah Smith had discovered the Humboldt, followed that stream to the Sierra Nevadas, which he crossed into the Sacramento Valley. Yet neither Ashley nor Smith nor Fitzpatrick nor Henry had made their discoveries available to the American public; the information had been elicited only by the efforts of men like Senator Benton, who had asked that the material be submitted in reports to the Congress.

Then about 1832 the government began sending out army surveyors to map specific localities for railroad sites and Indian relocations. Among the most important of these were the two expeditions under Captain Williams, and the two under Nicholas Nicollet, in all four of which Lieutenant John Fremont had participated. Prior to these four expeditions the maps that had been drawn had been fragmentary and often erroneous; now Lieutenant Fremont was to draw the first scientific and comprehensive map of the region between St. Louis and South Pass. He would not be exploring in the way that Lewis and Clark, Pike, Cass and Schoolcraft had been exploring, for his avowed job was that of pathmarker rather than pathfinder. Yet before he had left he had told his wife:

"I want to do some exploring before this expedition is over; I want to traverse some new ground that no one ever reported on."

"Will there be time for that?" she had asked.

"I most urgently hope so; after all of our topographical work has been done I should still have several weeks for exploration. I want to show them that I can blaze new trails as well as map old ones."

"Yes," she had agreed, "you must do that if you can; then the War Department will give you more latitude on future expeditions."

The days passed, and the nights; the feeling of life inside her grew more insistent and pushed itself outward as she grew bigger in body and heavier in step. She never mentioned to anyone how achingly she missed her husband during these months while her child grew within her. Already the baby gave her companionship, even in those dark hours after she had gone to bed, for those were the hours in which she missed John most, in which she longed to clasp her hand in his, to feel his arms about her, protecting her from the deep-lying anxieties of impending childbirth. She passed many sleepless hours in repeating the child's name, John Charles Fremont, for she was positive that it would be a son, a son whom they would raise to be an explorer.

As important to her as the company of her child was the delightful game which half of official Washington was playing on her giant map. Not only did Nicollet and Hassler come in three or four times a week to protest that in her enthusiasm for her husband's abilities she was letting him make far too rapid progress each day, but everyone joked with her about it. She laughed when Samuel Morse said:

"What a wife you are, Jessie; your hapless husband can't even escape your surveillance by going into the wilderness." Or when James Buchanan commented, "Those are pretty large campfires; you are keeping the lieutenant warm, Jessie, only I hope you don't start forest fires," she would be moved to answer:

"Never you mind, James Buchanan, some day cities will spring up on the sites of Lieutenant Fremont's campfires."

During the months of preparation for the expedition, Mrs. Benton had joined in the family life more than she had in several years; she had even seemed to take a sense of pride in the fact that her son-in-law was to command the expedition. Then Jessie noticed that her mother's resurgence of strength was ebbing. One evening she was horrified to perceive that one half of her mother's face was pulling against the other, that the corner of her right eye and right temple arched upward, while the left corner of her mouth and lower cheek were pulling downward. When she went to her mother's bedroom to say good night she saw some of this pulling and twisting reflected in the terror of her mother's eyes.

The following morning Maylee could not awaken Mrs. Benton. She ran screaming for Senator Benton. Joshaam hurried for the doctor, who came at once and stumblingly informed Tom Benton that his wife had had a paralytic stroke. Thomas Benton stood as though clubbed, his eyes bloodshot, his big face sagging.

The three days that followed were an agony to Jessie. Her father never left her mother's bedside, trying to rub life back into her white, motionless hands, speaking to her, kissing her lips. On the evening of the third day Jessie entered the dark and forsaken library, saw her father facing the front windows, weeping silently. She went to him and put her arm about him; after a moment he quieted.

"Jessie, you can't know what it's like . . . not to be able to fight back. It's like being hit in the dark: you don't know who your adversary is—you don't know where to turn, what to say or do. I've never felt helpless before, but now . . ."

The words and the look of her father were cut deep in her memory.

The next morning Mrs. Benton's eyes fluttered open; she lay without moving. Then she achieved a little smile, a smile which told her family that her life would be spared. Eliza took over the management of the household; Jessie remained most of the day with her mother, sometimes reading to her from the Bible. On the tenth day Mrs. Benton indicated that she wanted to talk to her daughter. Jessie waited for several moments before Mrs. Benton could summon her strength.

". . . not your father's fault . . . I couldn't . . . enjoy . . . not father's fault . . ."

She rested for several moments, closed her eyes, then opened them again. "I was . . . ill . . . you must not . . . blame your father . . . Remember, Jessie, not . . . his fault."

Her head down, tears swimming in her eyes, Jessie realized that the only words her mother had striven to achieve since her stroke was an attempt to eradicate from her daughter's mind any reproach or bitterness that might have been left from their discussions on the trip to Cherry Grove.

And she began to realize how far she had to go on the long uphill road to becoming a good wife.

6

SHE WAS WELL INTO HER NINTH MONTH when word came that John and his party had returned safely to St. Louis.

"I hope the lieutenant gets here in time for the birth of your baby," her father commented.

"He will."

"How can you be so sure?"

"Because I'm going to wait," she replied doggedly.

It was the twenty-eighth of October when John bounded up the front stairs of the Benton home, his black hair falling over the collar of his uniform. After he had been welcomed by the family, had gone to Mrs. Benton's room to kiss her cheek and let her know that he was happy she was better without intimating that she had ever been ill, Jessie led him to their sitting room where they sat down together in the roomy armchair by the fireplace.

"I'm sorry I'm so bumpy, darling. It would be nice to be ravishingly beautiful for your return."

"If you hadn't been so ravishing before I left, you wouldn't be so bumpy now. Don't be worried, I can wait for our second honeymoon."

She got a comb, brush and scissors, called him to sit on the edge of the bed and then knelt behind him. She wrapped a towel around his shoulders, brushed out the long hair. After she had cut off as much as she dared, she stood in front of him saying: "There, now you're my beautiful lieutenant once again," and kissed him gently. He pulled her down on the bed beside him.

"You look hungry," she said, running her fingers over his sunken cheeks. "We'll have to fatten you up with terrapin and sides of roast beef."

"You just want to make me as fat as you."

The next day she slept late, able to rest with a tranquillity she had not known in the months he had been away. She opened her eyes to find the fall sunlight flooding high in the room and her husband gone from her side. She found him in the library, stretched out on his stomach with a pencil and crayons in his hand, working on her big map, which he had taken down from the wall. He looked up, aware of her presence.

"When I first walked in here and saw that map on the wall," he said, "I thought I had taken leave of my senses. I don't know how long I stood in front of it before I realized it was your work."

"Mine," laughed Jessie, "and everyone else's in Washington: Nicollet, Hassler, Colonel Abert, General Clark, Colonel Kearny, General Scott, Senators Benton, Linn, Crittenden, King, that botanist friend of yours at Harvard, and half the amateur astronomers in the capital."

He led her back to the map and drew up a chair for her.

"You've made a lot of errors: you pushed our party ahead much too fast, you didn't give us a fraction of the time we needed in the Rockies; you've left out dozens of small ranges, canyons and streams that you couldn't possibly know about. But look how close your line runs to mine."

Jessie pointed with her finger to a campfire on the Big Sandy.

"That was the night I missed you most. Since I couldn't be there, I made you comfortable: I put you alongside of a cool river so that you could have a swim after the day's march; with plenty of game at hand . . ."

Joshaam padded in with a broad grin, his short black trousers rolled just below the knee. He set up a table and served John's favorite dishes: grilled lamb chops with creamed potatoes, a fluffy egg soufflé, cornbread with blackberry jam, a large pot of coffee with thick cream. When her husband had loaded his pipe with fresh tobacco Jessie said:

"You are going to have to tell all the stories of your expedition; by this afternoon the house will be crowded. But I would like to hear the first story and the best."

He was silent for a moment. "You remember how we agreed that I should try to do some exploring after we had South Pass mapped?"

"Yes."

"Well, we struggled up the Sweetwater Valley, and on August eighth reached South Pass. It was such a broad opening, and we reached it by such a gradual ascent, that I had difficulty in fixing the precise point of the Continental Divide. There was no gorge. Instead we found a wide sandy road which followed a slow and regular grade to the summit, about seven thousand feet above sea level. We continued up to the headwaters of the Green River and followed this to the Colorado. Then there rose up before us the greatest sight I have ever seen: the Wind River chain of mountains tumbling backward pile upon pile, with their icy caps glittering in the bright light of the August day."

"Has anyone recorded any material on the Wind River chain?"

He sprang from his chair and began pacing back and forth.

"Darling, what do you think I found? The highest point in the central Rockies! I scaled a peak that no one has ever seen before, let alone reached the summit! You remember that flag I had made in New York with the pipe of peace in the eagle's mouth to show the Indians we were friendly?"

"Of course I remember."

"I took five of my companions with me. It was a rough ascent, with the five of us riding beneath a nearly perpendicular wall of granite. We could look straight up three thousand feet to endless lines of broken, jagged cones. We left our horses and climbed hand over hand up this wall. After we got up about a thousand feet we found three little lakes of emerald lying in a chasm below us. At one point I had to work my way across a vertical precipice by clinging to the crevices. I sprang upon the summit, but if I had gone another half-foot I would have fallen into an immense snow field five hundred feet below. For I was on the very edge of a sheer icy precipice."

Her eyes reflected his excitement.

"Jessie, it was magnificent: a bright and sunny day, to the west a vast shining network of lakes and streams, on the east the deep, forested trough of the Wind River Valley with the faint gleam of streams which flow into the Yellowstone and down to the Missouri. To the far northwest we could pick out the snowy peaks of the Three Tetons which mark the sources of the Snake and the Columbia. I fixed a ramrod in the gneiss, unfurled our flag and planted it on the summit."

"That is a lovely story," she murmured.

The welcome-home party that had gathered by five in the afternoon was much like the farewell party except that it was more hilarious. Everyone wanted stories. Colonel Kearny, in his usual blunt manner, got in the first demand:

"We heard reports that the Sioux, Blackfeet and Cheyennes had combined and might block your route from Laramie to South Pass. Did you have any trouble with them?"

John stood with his back to the fireplace. Jessie sat watching her husband, thinking how handsome he looked.

"We reached Fort Laramie just as Jim Bridger came in from the North Platt trail with a company of traders. He told us about the Sioux and Blackfeet being done up in war paint and spoiling for a fight. The traders and the Indians at the fort advised us to wait for a few weeks until the raids were over and the Indians had gone home, but that didn't sound like a wise idea to me."

"We're having trouble enough with them now," grunted the colonel. "If they ever get the idea they could keep us out of their country simply by putting on war paint . . ."

"That's exactly the way I figured it, Colonel Kearny: one of the purposes of this reconnaissance was to find the best spots for the Army to establish forts; but no amount of forts would be any protection against Indians who had succeeded in frightening us."

General Winfield Scott wanted to be shown exactly where on the map John recommended that army forts be built; the western senators wanted to know about the nature of the soil, whether there was water available, how much of the land was tillable and how large a population it could support; several eastern congressmen demanded to know whether farm and laboring families really could take covered wagons over the South Pass.

The party lasted late, almost too late; Jessie did not know whether it was the joy of having her husband home again or the excitement of the party, but before dawn her first child was born. When the doctor told her she had a daughter she burst into angry tears. She had failed her husband; had not fulfilled her part of the relationship. She knew how keenly disappointed he would be. When he entered the room she could not meet his eyes.

"No, don't console me," she said. "If you try to turn me off with platitudes, I shall never forgive you."

John had already had two hours in which to become reconciled. He wore a too bright smile as he came to the side of her bed.

"Very well, no platitudes; but might I suggest two thoughts: at eighteen you are not exactly too old to bear more children; nor has six months in the wilderness slaked my desire to sire them."

A tiny gleam appeared in her tired eyes.

"Neatly put, Lieutenant. Now go away and let me sleep."

She slept straight through until noon of the following day. When she awakened and had been washed, her hair combed and tied with a pink velvet ribbon, her husband came in holding a cloth bundle bunched under his left arm.

"Darling, you remember the flag I told you I planted on Fremont's Peak?"

Jessie's eyes said yes, wonderingly.

"It's a little faded now, and the wind whipped a few holes in it; but it's the first American flag to be raised on the highest peak of the Rocky Mountains. I brought it back for you, my dear."

He shook out the flag and laid it across her bed. Jessie was touched. "Always the romantic poet," she whispered, holding out her arms for the embrace which her disappointment of the night before had denied her.

7

AT THE END OF TWO WEEKS she could be carried to a chaise in their living room, which was directly in the path of the early winter sun, and here John would entertain her with stories from the trail. She listened to his narrative to see how it fitted into the history of exploration, and what contribution Lieutenant Fremont might be able to make to the tradition of Rogers and Clark, Pike, Ashley, Smith, Cass, Long or Captain Bonneville.

During the succeeding days he unrolled a panorama of his voyage in a kind of continuous serial, a portion of it related in bed, portions over the breakfast table, portions in his pajamas walking up and down the bedroom, in his underwear as he shaved, in his rough dungarees and faded khaki shirt sorting specimens on the floor, in his blue-and-gold uniform waiting to go to an appointment with a War Department official.

She watched him ford the Kansas River a hundred miles from its mouth, trying out Nicollet's India-rubber boat on the swollen yellow current. She advanced with him into hostile Indian country where powder was distributed to each of the men in the early morning; she met up with a party of immigrants going to the Columbia, who gave them mail to be taken back to the States; she crossed the Big Vermilion and encamped on the Big Blue, where antelope overran the hills and Amorpha bent beneath the weight of its purple clusters; she traveled on the fresh traces of Oregon immigrants, which relieved the loneliness of the road; she found the earth more sandy as she traveled westward, with rain coming at night and thousands of mosquitoes biting hungrily; she went thirsty for two days because the creeks at Big Trees were inexplicably dry, but when she reached the Little Blue she and the men and horses together all drank and bathed in the clear cool stream; she mounted guard every night but safely reached the Platte, where the party divided at the forks, Kit Carson leading half the men over the regular Oregon Trail to Fort Laramie while her husband took the other party by way of Fort Saint Vrain. There were the dramatic hours at Fort Laramie when Jim Bridger told of the Sioux, Blackfeet and Cheyennes combining on the warpath, and the determination to push forward in the face of the danger, the long ascent up Sweetwater Valley, and then at last the great day on August 8 when the party mounted South Pass, making maps and sketches and voluminous notes to document the trail for future immigrants to Oregon.

Jessie asked her husband if he had any objections to her reading his journal. She was delighted by much of his poetry and imagery, but she soon saw that the diary consisted of brilliant fragments. Lieutenant Fremont had reported faithfully and picturesquely what he had seen, but he had set up no organizational plan which would have enabled him to fit all the parts into a design. His journal was much like the raw material published by Lewis and Clark, by Cass or Schoolcraft. As such it would be read by scientists, explorers and students, but not by the general public. In order to accomplish the most good for western migration, Lieutenant Fremont's report must be vastly more readable than its predecessors; it must include everything of beauty and fact from his notes, and yet somehow in the process of transcription become literature.

She knew she must exercise the utmost tact, find a subtle method of leading him to conclusions about what his written report to Congress must be. When she was up and around again she showed him the work she had been doing on the history of exploration; in the process of telling him about it she was able to make many of her points as to why former accounts of expeditions had not been widely read.

John appeared interested, yet he gave no indication of whether he would do any part of the job she suggested. She set up a desk for him in their sitting room, laying out pens and pencils and foolscap; she arranged for quiet and privacy. She kissed him, said, "Good luck, my dear, I know your report will come out well," and closed the door behind her.

At dinner she found him in an unhappy state of mind; he had not been able to put one word on paper. She comforted him by saying that the first page was harder than the next ninety-nine put together, that the story would come with a rush once he had started. At the end of the second day she found their sitting room a mass of crumpled papers, the ink spilled over the desk, her husband so grouchy she could not talk to him. When she knocked lightly at dinnertime of the third day, she found him in the midst of a nosebleed. She stretched him out on the floor, washed his face and put cool cloths on his brow.

"I just can't understand it, Jessie," he growled; "when I tell you stories of what happened on the trip I am stimulated and excited, the words flow and the scenes are vivid in my mind. But once I sit down to write on paper, the words become cold and dead."

Jessie had a moment of panic in which she demanded of herself, What have I done? Have I imposed such pressure on him, have I put the report in such a light that he can no longer work with it?

The panic passed; she said quietly to her husband, while holding a cold towel over his face, "Perhaps it is just the mechanics of writing that disturb you. Perhaps your mind works too fast for your fingers to record what you are thinking."

"No, I think it's something your presence does to me, Jessie: you stimulate me so that I think and talk swiftly; everything comes alive in the air between us."

With her pulse bumping in her throat she asked, "Then perhaps, my dear, I could serve as your amanuensis? You tell me the stories just the way you did before, and I'll write them down for you."

She had been uneasy at making the suggestion; she shuddered lest he think she was trying to intrude, gain a voice and an importance through collaborating with him. He jumped up from the floor, threw his arms about her and began dancing her around in circles.

"Jessie, my love, I've been sitting here in misery for three days wondering how long it would take you to offer your services. Confound it, I've been lonely in here; you gave me such complete privacy I felt like a hermit locked in a cell."

It was on New Year's Day of 1843, just a year after they had gone to President Tyler's reception, that she sat down at the desk in her sitting room, with John agitatedly walking the floor behind her. Her father had protested her going to work so soon after the birth of her child.

"But Father, I feel entirely well. This report to Congress is as important to you as it is to John; the better we make it, the more ammunition it gives you."

"That's entirely true," he agreed, unsmiling; "if this report comes out well, a second expedition, this time as far as California, may be authorized. It's only that I feel you need another month or two . . ."

She found that her husband needed her help in organizing his material; she rejected a number of dullish starts and got him off to a beginning which would not only excite the reader but pull him out of his chair and send him on the trail across the swollen Kansas River. In the first rush of his enthusiasm she was unable to write down everything, so she selected the most germane of what he said and let the rest go. She began joining bits of narrative together while he talked, shaping a sentence a little more roundly than he had, using a more explicit or precise word when he stumbled.

"Let me see what you've done."

When he had finished reading, he commented, "No man is fool enough not to enjoy being made to look his best."

And so their story grew, sometimes at the rate of five finished pages a day. She had heard these stories before; she had retold them to herself, frequently in her own terse and direct language. When she found his prose too flowery or poetic, she related the episode with something of her own lean style and pacing. This last experiment she was frankly frightened to tell him about. She remembered the violent scene when her father had discovered that she was not only editing him but had had the presumption to be collaborating in his speeches for the Senate.

When she went into the sitting room the next morning she found her husband reading their previous day's work. He had a strained, somewhat puzzled expression on his face.

"Jessie, when did I say this sentence? I don't remember it."

She gulped, replied, "You didn't say it. Shall we tear up these sheets and do this section over again?"

He walked to the window overlooking the garden. She stayed awkwardly by the desk, unable to guess what was going on in her husband's mind. After what seemed an interminable length of time, he came back to the desk, expressionless, and asked:

"May I read those pages again?"

She handed him the five clipped pages. When he had finished reading, he returned them to her.

"It was only the strangeness of those sentences that bothered me the first time over." After a pause he continued, "I agreed the day I proposed to you that our marriage was to be a collaboration. Each of us has fractional talents. If you have the fraction that is missing from mine, then how fortunate I am."

Jessie sat down weakly.

They labored for three months to complete the hundred-page report. During the last few weeks she worked alone, revising and rewriting. They both agreed that Tom Benton must be the first to see the manuscript.

"It's good," her father declared when he had finished; "it will not only start a wave of immigration to Oregon, but we'll have no trouble getting an appropriation for a second expedition."

Three days later her father returned from the Senate with good news: Congress had been highly pleased with both the report and the map, had ordered a thousand extra copies to be printed, the major newspapers of the country were asking for permission to reprint. The second expedition had been ordered, the money appropriated, and Lieutenant Fremont was once again to command. They would all leave for St. Louis within the month, Tom Benton to mend his political fences and prepare for the coming election; John to assemble his expedition; Jessie to live in the Benton home while he was away.

These were happy days for her: her baby girl, whom they had named Lily, was growing strong and pretty; it seemed as though everyone in the country were talking about Lieutenant Fremont, his expedition, his report and map. He was praised in the press, the pulpit, the schools. The War Department and the Topographical Corps assured him that he had made an important contribution.

Lieutenant Fremont wore his new honors with modesty and decorum. And Jessie Fremont sat quietly in the background, glowing with love and pride, utterly content.

8

THE MANY SUITCASES, trunks and boxes were taken down to the Baltimore & Ohio station the evening before. The next morning Jessie, her mother, her father, her husband, Maylee with little Lily in her arms, and Randolph and the two younger girls, took the hard-benched, smoky cars to Baltimore, a trip which consumed much of the day. They passed the night at an inn on the waterfront, where their baggage could be transferred to the steamboat at dawn. The passage to Philadelphia was cool and pleasant. They spent a night and a day in Philadelphia before making connection with the mail coach, which bumped and jostled them up the length of the Susquehanna Valley to Harrisburg. There were canal boats plying between Harrisburg and Pittsburgh, but there was no regular schedule and they considered themselves fortunate to catch one on the second night. The high-pressure steamboats which operated between Pittsburgh and Cincinnati were among the fastest and most luxurious traveling inland in America. Jessie and John mingled with the passengers, listening to the conversation. There were hunters and trappers in their leather garments and coonskin caps; land speculators carrying sacks of gold and headed for the new townships in Illinois and Iowa; the ever present group of surveyors heading west to lay out new villages and roads; traveling salesmen from Louisville and Cincinnati with their boxes of wares; adventurous Englishmen taking their resources into the wilderness to get in on the ground floor; congenital frontiersmen moving west for a third or fourth time; merchants from the East with their wives and children, seeking independence in still another new world; and most conspicuous in noise and excitement, Irishmen and Germans just over from the old country, looking forward to the frontier as eagerly as to paradise.

The trip took between two and three weeks, according to one's luck and the connections. But Jessie was in no hurry. She had her husband with her and was greatly enjoying these days of his company, unharassed by work or demands on his time. She knew every foot of the road: she had first made the passage when she was ten months old, had been thrown out of a coach at the age of three, had stopped at nearly every inn and private home along the way in the fourteen round trips she had made in her nineteen years.

They crossed the Mississippi from Cairo on the bright and sparkling spring morning of May 16, the busiest period in St. Louis' life, with the roustabouts thronging the riverbanks, the Mississippi churned by steam-boats, vessels and scows moored to the rough wooden docks, the levee crowded with Negro boat hands chanting rhythmically as they loaded up.

Tom Benton insisted upon driving the party up Main Street to see if the new rock pavements were still smooth, and to rejoice at the sight of new buildings. They passed the mansion of Colonel Auguste Couteau, fronting on Main Street, protected by a ten-foot-high, two-foot-thick stone wall with portholes through which to shoot Indians in case of attack. As their carriage continued along the locust-lined street they saw the few whitewashed aristocratic houses in St. Louis, the magnificent Cathedral and Bishop's Garden. After that, on the way out to the Benton home, there was little but alleys and a confusion of mean houses, for St. Louis had grown by accretion, everyone building how and where he pleased.

Jessie remarked how fast the city was growing: it was the great and last metropolis of the West, the fitting-out and jumping-off place for Mexico, California, Oregon and Canada and the vast stretches of wilderness that lay between. Gazing out of the carriage she saw the colorful, dramatic and heterogeneous scene on which she had been raised: hunters and trappers in the garb they wore on the trail; friendly Indians in their native costumes; adventurous and restless ones from every country in Europe, still wearing their native clothing and speaking their native tongue. There was always a sense of excitement pervading the air, for St. Louis was not a place where people stayed, but a spot where they outfitted and prepared to jump off into adventure. To her it was as though the city were the last outpost of civilization into which the whole world poured, eager to get away from that civilization, to plunge into the vastness of the unknown, only sometimes realizing that it was this very stream of plungers who must inevitably push civilization farther and farther west until it had eaten up the wilderness and all of America would be settled and civilized.

Tom Benton had built his home so far out of the business district of St. Louis, some twenty years before, that he was still on the outskirts and enjoyed a measure of quiet and privacy. When he had arrived in 1817 with four hundred dollars in his pocket he had invested three hundred dollars of it in ten acres of land just outside the tiny village. Two years later, so swiftly had the traffic in the Mississippi border port grown, so many had been the armed caravans of merchants which had assembled, so countless the number of traders, trappers and voyagers of the American Fur Company who had been outfitted, that Tom Benton began selling his land for two thousand dollars an acre.

The Benton home was shaded by acacias with their clusters of vanilla-scented blooms; built in the prevailing Creole fashion, there was a central courtyard paved with flagging, and a line of locust trees making a delicate green screen for the wide galleries which ran the length of the house on both sides. The floors were of black walnut, brilliantly waxed. Tom Benton had built to the south of the wharf and business district, on a slight rise overlooking the wide muddy torrent of the Mississippi.

Jessie settled herself in the south bedroom which looked out on what remained of Tom Benton's pear orchard and was furnished with the light cherrywood bed, bureaus and chairs which he had bought from the early French immigrants. Though there was the ever present knowledge that her husband would leave in a week or two, she felt happier that she would pass the time here in St. Louis where everyone was interested in western expansion, where one talked of little else; where any stranger she might stop on the street would be able to tell her approximately how far Lieutenant Fremont had progressed and why it was so important for him to find an easier crossing of the Rockies. In Washington she had enabled herself to be with him during the six months of the first expedition by keeping detailed maps; here in St. Louis she would need no artificial stimulus to keep her abreast. Within St. Louis lived every race, religion and philosophy to be found in the world; and if, she thought, it is one's fate to stay at home and wait for one's husband, then surely the best spot to wait is where all the world has assembled and where one ate, breathed, slept and dreamed expedition.

The only thing missing from her return was Grandmother Benton, who had died five years before. Grandmother Benton's welcome on their trips to St. Louis almost never varied. An invalid in her eighties, Anne Benton put on her best black dress and waited in her rooms at the end of the lower gallery to greet her son and his family. The first moments of greeting had always perplexed Jessie, for despite her father's being so happy at coming home, there were tears in his eyes when he bent to kiss Grandmother. When it came her own turn to greet the silent old lady sitting on the couch, she trembled as the white fingers motioned to her to draw near and she felt the touch of dry lips upon her cheek.

There seemed to be no valid reason why Anne Gooch Benton should have left her established home in Hillsborough, North Carolina in 1798, where she was surrounded by relatives and friends, where life was safe and secure. But Mrs. Benton, after her young husband's death, had packed her belongings, children and slaves into a series of wagons and taken the long, dangerous, four-hundred-mile trail through the Carolina mountains and the dark pine needle forests to Nashville. Her husband had been given a large grant of land in Tennessee years before, worthless and uninhabitable land at the time the King of England had granted it, and still overrun by hostile Indians. Here she had set up the Widow Benton Settlement, built her own log cabin, a church, school and general store. Widow Benton offered seven years of free rent to the settlers who came along the trail, after which she either sold or leased the land to the established families at moderate rates.

Anne Benton had wanted and deliberately chosen the wilderness; this urge for the rough-hewn, the just-being-born, the pioneer opportunity had been buried deep in Tom Benton. The tiny outpost of St. Louis, settled by the French people he liked and felt so comfortable with, was in the process of germination. He abandoned his law practice in Nashville, struck out for St. Louis. Though he could speak little of their language, the French settlers liked and trusted him. A few other Americans were beginning to come in and settle, and Tom Benton had become the liaison between the two national groups. By the end of the year he had been appointed to the school board, was contributing political articles to the *Missouri Enquirer,* was named as one of the editors, crusading for immediate exploration of the wilderness in order to "place these vast lands forever under the domination of our people."

By 1820 he was in prosperous circumstances; he had built himself a big house, brought his mother to St. Louis. He was active and important in making Missouri a state, was elected to the first legislature, helped to draw its first constitution, and then been elected one of the state's two first senators. He found Washington City a wretched scattering of houses alongside a river and surrounded by marshes; most of the congressmen left their families behind them, lived in third-rate boardinghouses and escaped the capital at the earliest opportunity with little but curses for its dampness, malaria and miserable life. But Tom Benton had seen in Washington a city just being born, and he had loved it; he had brought his wife and children to Washington, declared it to be his second home, rented the best house he could find until he was able to buy one. He urged his fellow congressmen to bring their families with them so that they could set up schools and churches and develop Washington.

Jessie's days in St. Louis were full, for she now was secretary to both her father and her husband, and nothing could have persuaded her to give up any part of the work. The sun rose over the Mississippi at five in the morning; though she had closed the shutters tight, John was awake at the first touch of light. Within a half-hour he had dressed, breakfasted, and left the house. At six o'clock Jessie and her father had their light breakfast out of doors, on the long gallery of the parlor floor. This gallery was also Tom Benton's office, where he set up a settee, table and what he called a colony of chairs, for by six-thirty visitors began to arrive to get the latest news from Washington and to discuss the ever-growing problems of Missouri. She kept a record of these morning meetings so that her father would have his notes when he returned to Washington in the fall. At eleven o'clock her husband would return, his organizing for the day completed, and after their lunch would dictate to her on the setup of the expedition: the names of the sixty-odd hunters and trappers who were going with him; the one-dollar-a-day wage which each was to receive, the hundred dollars a month for Kit Carson, an unheard-of sum. but one which he defended on the grounds that Kit Carson had no equal in America. There were the lists of materials that had been bought and how much they had cost, the scientific implements which were needed for a complete record of the journey: the compasses, telescopes, sextants, chronometers, barometers.

Dinner was at five, after which their many friends and cousins came in for music, dancing and laughter, for St. Louis was a lighthearted town in the French tradition, with a fiddle in every house.

Then all too soon her double stint came to an end; her father left for a barnstorming trip of the state, and John prepared to leave for Kaw's Landing, where the expedition would receive its final integration, the horses fattened and the long journey to Oregon begun. Several days before he was to leave he asked his wife:

"Could you invite Colonel Kearny to dinner? I have some special business I want to talk over with him alone."

"I'll arrange it."

Colonel Stephen Watts Kearny, commandant of the Jefferson Barracks just outside St. Louis, came to dinner on the intensely hot afternoon of June first. He was a hard-bitten soldier, with sandy hair, sandy of face as well as voice. He had distinguished himself in the War of 1812. He was fearless, never a brilliant strategist but an inexhaustible plodder who wore out rather than outsmarted his opponents. He had the blunt, ungraceful manner of the man who has spent the past thirty years in the wilderness and in army encampments.

After much pleasant talk, John asked, "Colonel Kearny, do you suppose it would be possible for you to lend me a cannon for the expedition?"

His guest took the cigar out of his mouth.

"A cannon! What ever do you want a cannon for?"

"I expect serious trouble with the Indians; their prestige fell last year when they failed to make an attack on us while on the warpath. I understand they are out for revenge."

"I see."

"Besides," John continued, "I think it about time we demonstrated that the Army can move its heavy equipment across the continent . . ."

"But you are not commanding an army expedition," interposed Colonel Kearny, "you are a scientific expedition. The sight of that cannon might lead the Indians, yes, and the English and Spanish also, to imagine that we are sending an army of conquest across the plains."

"All this with one small cannon, Colonel? My main reason is to show that we can take a heavy cannon across the new pass in the Rockies which I hope to find. If we can move a cannon over it, then the immigrant trains will know they can get their wagons over it."

"But in the heavy snows? Lieutenant, you would never make it. You'll beat out your strength trying to pull it over the mountains."

"You are doubtless right, Colonel," replied John, "but I should like a chance to try. Can you spare me a cannon? I promise to bring it back to Jefferson Barracks at the end of a year."

Colonel Kearny was silent for a few moments, puffing on his cigar.

"Very well, since you seem so keen on it. I don't anticipate that we will need it here in Missouri during the next year."

Three days later Jessie once again bade good-by to her husband. There were no tears this time. After his work was done of plotting the trail to Oregon, and finding a new pass over the Rockies which would be easier to traverse than South Pass, he was to drop down with his party into California, be careful not to alarm or antagonize the Mexican government, assure the local governors from Mexico City that this was purely a scientific expedition, but at the same time survey the ground, talk to the Americans who had ranches there, become acquainted with the Californios and get some idea of the military strength of the Mexican garrisons, learn what would be needed to enable California to fall into American hands: for no one could doubt any longer that Mexico was going to lose both Texas and California. The western people were grimly determined that the English must not own California.

"I want to go with you to California on the next expedition," said Jessie. "I want to settle there."

"But I doubt if there are half a dozen American women in the entire state."

"I wouldn't mind if I were the first," she answered. "In fact I would like it. We already have a Bentonville in the family. Now it's our turn to start a Fremontville."

John laughed. "I'm sure I can make Sutter's Fort, and that will give me a chance to investigate the Sacramento Valley. From what I hear it's fertile land. I'll prospect around, see if I can find the exactly right spot for Fremontville. If I do, I'll stake it out."

"Excellent," said Jessie, "and as soon as California becomes a state, you will be sent to Washington as its first senator."

9

SHE SET UP A RIGOROUS PROGRAM which she hoped would leave her little
time to be lonely. She awakened at six, went into the nursery for a play
with Lily. At seven she took coffee and rolls up to her mother. At eight
she went into the kitchen with Maylee to plan the day's marketing and
menus, then talked to old Gabriel about the work that needed doing
around the grounds. Having established a routine for the house, she
organized a schedule of intellectual activity: four hours of reading every
day, one in Spanish and one in French to keep her hand in, two hours of
reading and notetaking in her father's books on history.

She had almost a year to endure without her husband. The first of the
fifty-two weeks passed quickly enough, for she found a kind of pleasure
in establishing her discipline.

At the end of the twelfth day the mail boat arrived. Gabriel brought
her an official-looking letter from the War Department addressed to Lieutenant John C. Fremont. Having been instructed by her husband to open
all mail in order that she might be able to take care of whatever business
arose, Jessie put aside her sewing basket, inserted a long ivory opener
under the flap and slit the top of the envelope. She read:

LIEUTENANT JOHN C. FREMONT
U. S. Army Topographical Corps
St. Louis, Missouri

SIR:

*You are herewith ordered to turn over your expedition to your second
in command, and to repair at once to Washington. An explanation is required of why you have taken a twelve-pound howitzer cannon on a
peaceful, scientific survey.*

*Another officer of the Topographical Corps will be dispatched to take
charge of the expedition.*

COLONEL J. J. ABERT

Her trembling fingers dropped the paper. Lieutenant Fremont recalled to Washington? But that was impossible! The party must leave
Kaw's Landing within a few days if they were to get over the Rockies
before snow fell. Another officer in command! How could another officer
take over John's hand-picked party? He had organized every last detail
of the expedition, he had the journey laid out with scientific precision:
the reorganizing would take weeks, half the men would leave, it would

become a haphazard, poorly integrated party which would accomplish only the smallest fraction of what was desired.

Then the paralyzing thought came to her: What would happen to her husband? Would they penalize him at the Topographical Corps in Washington, give him a routine job behind a desk, send him to some obscure fort? This second expedition, which was intended to go all the way to Oregon, was the most important since President Jefferson had sent Lewis and Clark to traverse the continent. If successful, John could go on to ever greater accomplishment. But if he were pushed aside now there would be no more expeditions for him, another man would take over, someone with only the smallest fraction of his genius for the wilderness.

She concealed the order at the bottom of her Martha Washington sewing basket, then went into the courtyard and stood with her face in the hot sun. I've been too much a part of the whole plan, she thought, to put it in peril now. I simply cannot fail John and his men; I can't fail my father and the westerners who have worked so many years for these expeditions. I've got to save this expedition! But how?

She knew that a duplicate of the War Department letter would be on the mail boat, which would deliver it to Kaw's Landing. Once John received his letter he would have no choice but to abandon the expedition and leave for Washington.

The answer came to her almost immediately: the duplicate must not reach him! The expedition must start on the trail without his learning that his command had been revoked!

She sent Gabriel to summon the French-Canadian DeRosier, to whom John had granted permission to remain an extra two weeks in St. Louis because of his wife's illness. DeRosier came within the half-hour, a tall, black-eyed trapper who had spent the better part of his life in the wilderness.

"DeRosier, I have an urgent message which must reach Lieutenant Fremont at once."

"I will take it, madame."

"How long will you need to get ready?"

"The time to get my horse."

"You know the country between here and Kaw's Landing?"

"Like my beard in the mirror."

"Can you get there before the mail boat?"

"But certainly, Madame Fremont. I know how to cut off the bends in the river. I can save the time the mail boat will lose lying at anchor by night on account of the river fogs."

"Good! I am relying on you, DeRosier. This message must reach Lieutenant Fremont before the mail boat gets there. Is that clear?"

"Perfectly, madame. May I suggest taking my brother along? Two horses travel together better, and my brother will bring back a letter from Lieutenant Fremont."

"An excellent idea. It will take me only a moment to write the message."

She went to her father's table on the enclosed porch where there were pen, ink and paper. Without hesitation she wrote:

My dearest: Do not delay another day. Trust me, and start at once.

She sealed the envelope, handed it to DeRosier. Unsmiling he said, "Have no uneasiness, madame. The message will be delivered in time."

"God bless you," said Jessie.

She went back to her father's table and sat down, the starch gone out of her. She could feel little but the devitalizing fear that something might happen to DeRosier on the ride to Kaw's Landing, that the duplicate order from the Topographical Corps would reach John before her note could get there.

The day hours and the night hours merged into each other in a sleepless confusion of hope and anxiety. Would her husband trust her judgment? Would he start on the trail at once, even though the party were not quite ready? Or would he dismiss her note as a hysterical outburst to which women were prone? This was the first real test of whether or not John Fremont had meant what he said when he had promised to accept her as full partner, with faith in her judgment.

She did not know how many days had passed, three, four, when DeRosier's brother came galloping up to the Benton house at top speed, slid off his horse and pounded on the front door. He took a now soiled and sweat-stained letter from his buckskin jacket. Handing it to her he said:

"Lieutenant Fremont sends this message to you, madame. I brought it as fast as my horse would travel."

"Thank you, DeRosier; you and your brother have been wonderfully kind."

She tore open the message and read:

Good-by. I trust, and go.

Standing in the doorway, feeling weak but triumphant, the thought flashed into her mind: There is no need for anyone to know about this! The DeRosiers will never talk. We will simply let the War Department think that the letter reached Kaw's Landing too late.

She rejected the idea summarily; she was not afraid of her act or ashamed of it. Picking up the same pen with which she had written to her husband, she wrote a letter to Colonel Abert explaining what she had done; outlining the reasons why a cannon was needed to get through the Blackfeet country; why it would have been a tragic mistake either to recall Lieutenant Fremont at that moment and abandon the expedition or to put his picked body of men under the line-and-rule control of another officer. She ended by saying that she was entirely willing to stand for investigation and trial upon her return to Washington, but that she felt the results of this second expedition would be so gratifying to Colonel Abert and the Topographical Corps that her conduct would be vindicated.

She wrote in full blood and full confidence, but once Gabriel had taken the letter to the post, her courage abandoned her and she threw herself face down on her bed. That her husband would approve of her decision, she had no doubt. But what of her father? Tom Benton was a rigid disciplinarian. By what outrageous presumption did a nineteen-year-old girl rebel against the United States government? She was certain that she had been right, yet she was equally certain that if her father condemned her she could never endure the year of separation from her husband.

Early the next morning Colonel Stephen Kearny arrived, his face as bilious yellow as his eyeballs.

"I have just received a letter from the War Department," he said in a cold tone, "reproving me for having given Lieutenant Fremont a howitzer for his expedition. The affair is my fault; I did not stand firm in dissuading the lieutenant. I do not like being rebuked by the War Department, Jessie, but I will not be selfish enough to think only of my own humiliation; I'm sorry that Lieutenant Fremont has been recalled to Washington."

"He is not going back to Washington, Colonel Kearny," said Jessie, in a small but firm voice.

"Not going . . . ? My letter informed me that he has been ordered back."

"That order will never reach him. He started on the trail several days ago."

"I don't understand, Jessie. One copy of the letter must have reached you, since you know what is going on. Lieutenant Fremont was not scheduled to leave Kaw's Landing for another week. The mail boat would have been there by now with a duplicate copy of the order."

"That is why I had to act quickly, Colonel Kearny," she replied. "When the message from the Topographical Corps reached me, I sent a note to Lieutenant Fremont asking him to break camp at once. I gave no reasons. Yesterday afternoon I received a message that he had started on the trail."

She watched the blood come into the colonel's eyes, turning the yellowish fields to a vein-ribbed red. At the same time his lips became pale and bloodless. His voice too, when he spoke, was without warmth.

"And you had no thought that this action would fall upon my shoulders! That I will not only be condemned for lending Lieutenant Fremont the howitzer, but in the event its presence causes trouble with the Indians, the English or the Mexicans, I will be held to blame for the consequences."

"There will be no consequences; Lieutenant Fremont will use the cannon only in the event that he is attacked."

"That is not for you to say!" shouted Colonel Kearny. "We are on the verge of war with both Mexico and England. How can we explain away an army howitzer, under the command of an army officer, being taken into disputed territory? I tell you, Jessie, this affair can precipitate a war. What a fool I was to have let a rash and impetuous officer talk me into such an act of folly!"

She saw that his fears were genuine, not only for himself but for the country as well. When she spoke her voice was conciliatory.

"I'm truly sorry, Colonel Kearny, not that Lieutenant Fremont took a cannon with him, for that will protect his party against the marauding Indians. Nor am I sorry that I intercepted the command for Lieutenant Fremont to return to Washington. But I am deeply regretful over the trouble we have caused you. You have always been our good and dear friend; when I intercepted the order, I had no realization of how deeply you would be involved. I have already written to Colonel Abert telling him what I have done and taking the full responsibility. I will write again this very day and further assure him that the taking of the cannon was Lieutenant Fremont's responsibility and not yours, and that he will stand up to the consequences of any act of his."

Colonel Kearny's rigid figure softened a little.

"Ah, Jessie," he said with quiet exasperation, "you are mature in so many ways, and yet fundamentally such a child. Do you really think that a letter from you to the War Department can absolve me from responsibility if Lieutenant Fremont gets into trouble? And have you no comprehension of the terrible thing you have done in suppressing orders?"

"It was a question of comparative values, Colonel. I could either see the expedition destroyed, all of my husband's and my father's work wiped out; or I could take matters into my own hands. I met the situation as I saw right."

"Jessie, let us sit down. I must talk to you as a friend who knew your father many years before you were born. You know that I have your best interests at heart; that is why I must try to make you understand."

They sat side by side and there were a few moments of silence. Then Colonel Kearny began speaking in the plain language of the soldier.

"Jessie, there is no one who can disobey the War Department or his superior officer, no matter how right he may think himself or how completely wrong he may think the command."

"Under ordinary circumstances that would be true . . ."

"It is true under all circumstances. An army will fall apart without complete discipline, particularly a citizens' army. Mutiny breeds chaos; this is true not merely of the army but of the whole democratic government."

When Colonel Kearny used the harsh word, mutiny, Jessie was profoundly shocked, shocked to think that what she had done could be called mutiny. When her scattered thoughts came into focus she explained that what she had done had been only good common sense, carried out in the best interests of the expedition, the Army and the government.

"Then you demand the right to define mutiny according to your own terms?" queried the colonel. "Don't you realize that everyone accused of mutiny swears that it wasn't mutiny at all, but conduct justifiable under the circumstances?" He shook his head sadly. "No, I suppose women don't understand things like that. There isn't a man in the world who would approve of what you have done, Jessie."

"Lieutenant Fremont will approve."

"Then so much the worse for Lieutenant Fremont. If you were a man you would understand exactly what I mean. But don't think your being a woman constitutes your justification. I know of no other woman who would approve of your conduct."

She nodded her head in denial.

"I think there are many women who would have done for their husbands exactly what I did—if similar circumstances had arisen."

"Then I can only say that for everyone's sake I am glad wives are kept out of men's business. If all women were permitted to create the kind of chaos your temperament creates, the work that men do would soon stop. Anne Royall would probably call you a modern woman, but in my opinion an interfering woman is a retrogression and not an advance."

He paused for a moment, looking at her steadily.

"Jessie, many times our superior officers are wrong and mistaken; many times our elected officers are wrong and mistaken. But we do more damage by mutinying against them than we possibly can by carrying out a bad order. We have set up our own form of government; without the discipline of obedience which we have imposed upon ourselves we cannot sustain our way of life."

He rose, picked up his hat, put it under his left armpit and added, before leaving: "I regret this entire affair. I regret it even though I am as deeply interested in the expedition and in western expansion as you, Senator Benton or Lieutenant Fremont. I say that Colonel Abert was wrong in recalling Lieutenant Fremont. I say that the expedition would have failed without him in command; I say that the cause of western expansion would have been retarded. Yet in the light of all these things, I still regret most bitterly that you saw fit to set yourself up against established authority. For your sake I hope Colonel Abert will decide to do nothing. Good day, Jessie."

The interval before Senator Benton's return to St. Louis was the worst of all. She was positive she was right, that one cannot always obey blindly, that every rule must be broken under exceptional circumstances. And yet she knew that Colonel Kearny would answer, "Every man thinks his own case constitutes exceptional circumstances."

Her father returned several days later. Unable to contain herself for one moment longer than necessary, she blurted out the story without giving him even a chance to wash or rest after his long journey from the interior of Missouri. She watched his face while she talked, seeking some sign that he would approve her conduct. But Tom Benton's face was set. When she had finished telling everything Colonel Kearny had said, he sat uncertainly for a moment. Jessie was stricken with terror, for she saw that he was not instantly going to proclaim his agreement.

"I wish . . . I wish you had waited, Jessie, consulted me . . ."

"But there was no time, Father, it was a matter of hours, even minutes. I had no way of knowing whether DeRosier could beat the mail boat. It was a gamble, and I did not know until his brother came back . . ."

"Yes, yes!" he exclaimed, pulling himself up to his feet. "You did the right thing! Confound those idiots in Washington. Can't they understand that it's a dastardly mistake to break up an expedition that's about to start, with the whole country waiting eagerly for its results? Can't they understand that you don't just pull off a commanding officer and stick anybody in his place, that exploring is a difficult and complicated business? What would have happened to the English fleet if Lord Nelson hadn't held up his blind eye to the telescope when his admiral was issuing a stupid order? What would happen to the human brain and human soul if we never used our own judgment, if we behaved like machines even when we were facing destruction? That's the confounded military mind, Jessie; all it can understand is obedience and more obedience and never mind if you get killed for it."

"Then you don't feel that I have committed a mutinous act?"

"Most certainly not! You have done us all the greatest possible service. Colonel Abert will be the first to agree when the expedition returns triumphantly. A little mutiny goes a long way, but that little is the sometime genius of democracy. I mutinied against the War Department once myself; it was at the end of March 1813, when I was a colonel under General Andrew Jackson. We had moved our little army to Natchez when we received an order from the War Department to disband our troops then and there. When General Jackson showed me the dispatch, I advised him to disobey it. I said, 'This is dated February 6. The Secretary of War expected it to reach you before we were so far from home. We are now a full five hundred miles from Nashville. This is General Jackson's army. It should be marched home under Jackson. We can appeal to Governor Wilkinson for money to transport the sick, and treat with the merchants here for stores.' Our little insurrection saved the health and loyalty of the Tennessee army, so that when General Jackson went back into the field his troops fought with him in the battle of New Orleans and helped win the War of 1812.

"Get me ink and paper, Jessie, I'm going to write to Colonel Abert and take responsibility for the affair. You are to put it out of your mind, for you only acted as my agent; had I been here I would have done the exact same thing."

When her father had finished his letter, Jessie asked quietly: "What is the worst they can do to us?"

Tom Benton reread his letter without answering.

"Father, I asked you a question. What is the worst that the Army can do to Lieutenant Fremont?"

Without looking up, he said disinterestedly:

"They will do nothing. When John returns to Washington, and the second report is published, the Topographical Corps will thank you . . ."

"I want to face the last-ditch consequences of what I have done, so that I may be prepared. What is the worst they can do to my husband?"

Tom Benton gazed at his daughter, studied her delicate but resolute face, and in her eyes read that there was no use deluding her.

"Court-martial. Dismissal from the service."

10

SHE LAY IN HER ROOM off the shaded courtyard in air that was soft with perfume and which should have lulled her to sleep. But she tossed all night, convinced that her husband would be court-martialed and dismissed, that she had ruined his life, that he would be unable to forgive her and would cease loving her; that she had destroyed their marriage, that a woman should never mix in her husband's work but should remain aloof so that, even though the family suffered if the man were unsuccessful, it could never be the wife's fault: the husband could not hold it against their marriage relationship.

When she rose at dawn she expected to find herself pale and haggard-eyed. When she looked into the mirror she could find no trace of the night's unrest, except that her clear and soft skin was marred by a slight swelling under the left corner of her mouth.

She made no attempt to re-establish the discipline that had served as a connecting link for the hours before the fateful letter had arrived from Washington. Instead she drifted through the days, making no plans, never thinking past the moment at hand, watching over her mother and Lily. The days weren't so bad: there were several hours of work in the morning with her father, there were people in the house discussing trade and politics and exploration. But at night she would lie awake in her high four-posted French bed longing for her husband, for the chance to tell him what she had done, to know that he would condone her action.

One afternoon she took a walk along the Mississippi to the outskirts of the town, where in a wide meadow a number of immigrant caravans were resting and making their final preparations. Wagonmakers and vendors of oxen, mules and horses were selling their wares, representatives from the grocers, clothiers and gunmakers were displaying their goods. She was attracted to the large letters DELAWARE painted in bright blue on the canvas top of a prairie schooner. Seated on an overturned tub near the wagon was a young woman about her own age, nursing her baby. Her laughing blue eyes peeped up at Jessie from a pink-ruffled sunbonnet.

"I have a little girl just about your baby's age," said Jessie. "Won't you tell me its name."

"John, named for his father."

"My husband's name is John, too."

"Well, now, that's a coincidence, ain't it? Are you going to Oregon, too?"

"No. . . .That is, not yet."

"But it ain't dangerous no more. Look, I'll show you the map we got, it was drawn by that military officer."

The young woman climbed up onto the seat of her wagon and took a much-thumbed paper from an inside pocket of the canvas.

"You see here, it shows where there's plenty of grass for the horses and where we must stock up with water, and just how we get over the mountains at the pass. And the Indians ain't so bad if all the families stay together and fight together."

"I wouldn't be afraid," said Jessie. "My father taught me how to shoot a gun."

Stirred by the yearning in Jessie's voice, the young woman's eyes became serious.

"Wouldn't you and your folks like to come along? There are three wagons of us. Did you know you can get a whole section of good land to yourselves and save your children from a life of wages?"

Jessie was crying. Impulsively the woman seized her hand.

"Tell you what I'll do," she said. "Give me your name and address and when I get out to Oregon I'll write you a letter, all about the trail and how you can make it best. Next year maybe you could get your own wagon and join us out there. My name's Mary Algood. What's your'n?"

The long summer passed with no word from John. She was not worried about his welfare, yet always lurking at the base of her brain was the dagger of fear; it took only one small accident such as a rubber boat overturning on the Platte; one moment of relaxed vigil at night; one Indian arrow . . . All these images she managed to keep locked away during the active hours of the day, but the night weighed on her like a soggy blanket, and the hours from dark to dawn were a hundred times longer than those from dawn to dusk.

In the fall her father returned to Washington for the opening of Congress. It was a difficult parting for both of them.

"I know how endless it is for you," he said, "this waiting and uncertainty. But I beg of you not to grieve. Don't fight the hours, go along with them. Soon you will possess all those that have passed, and Lieutenant Fremont will be back."

As she moved slowly against time, she came upon the duality of her love for John and the duality of her own personality. She was the woman who loved him as a man, but also the wife who loved him as a partner in marriage. It was the wife who sent him forth on these long and hazardous expeditions, the wife who was ambitious, not for herself or for her husband, but for their marriage. It was the wife who was strong to the point of steel, who could endure privation and hardship; and it was the wife who frequently made the woman suffer, the woman who had no ambition whatever except to be with the husband she loved. She had made her important decisions as a wife who believed that marriage was the highest goal between a man and a woman, that to it everything had to be subjugated; but when the loneliness overwhelmed her she became convinced that the only imperative between a man and a woman was their

love. It was their love which must be sustained, even at the expense of
their marriage collaboration; and at such times she would have recalled
him gladly to her arms, let the expedition and their career be forgotten.

Her father came home for Christmas. There had been no letter from
John in all these six months, yet coupled with her uneasiness was a sense
of elation that half of the year of separation was already gone. Tom
Benton insisted that they have gaiety, so he borrowed a custom from
St. Louis' German population and put up a Christmas tree for Lily. A
few of their closest friends and cousins were invited to share the roast
goose and plum pudding and to exchange gifts before the roaring log
fire. Jessie was particularly pleased by her father's present, the three-
volume set of Prescott's *Conquest of Mexico* which had been published
only a few weeks before in New York.

When her father returned to Washington in the middle of January,
she said to him in a far happier mood than she had been in when he had
left that fall:

"Lieutenant Fremont must have been in California for some time now.
I'm sure he'll be leaving very shortly and will come home by the southern
route. I expect him by the end of March at the latest."

For an instant she thought she saw a cloud pass over his eyes, but he
answered, "Captain Sutter will provision him in the Sacramento Valley,
and that will make his trip home by the southern route a comparatively
easy one."

It was not long after her father's departure that she began to notice a
change in the attitude of the people around her. Her cousins and friends
had shown her many kindnesses, yet their manner had been casual: after
all, Lieutenant Fremont was off on a glorious mission, no man knew better
how to command an expedition and bring it back safely, and while the
year of separation was necessarily hard, it was a fate many wives shared.
By the beginning of February she saw that her cousins were going out of
their way to shower tenderness upon her, that some of her father's friends
were coming to the house rather more often than they had, bringing little
gifts, chatting animatedly.

She asked herself, Why are they so solicitous of me? What has happened
to make them change their attitude? She searched the newspapers line by
line for some communication from the Pacific coast, sent to Washington
and New York for the major journals. She asked indirect questions, but
her cousins and friends veered away from them. Unable to bear the added
burden she went to her cousins, the Brants, and begged them to tell her
what they knew that she didn't know. She saw the same withdrawal in her
cousins' eyes that she had seen in her father's: they put her off with comforting speeches, and she felt trapped in a conspiracy of kindness.

That afternoon when she returned home she saw the reflection of her face in the rectangular mirror over the fireplace as she passed the downstairs parlor. Something drew her to the glass. During the months of the fall, whenever her anxieties would come to a momentary crisis, she had noticed that the little swelling under the corner of her mouth would come forth; when she had pushed the fears to the back of her mind, the blemish gradually disappeared. Now as she gazed into the mirror she saw that it had come out again, this time larger than before.

It's my King George's Mark, she thought, like Grandmother Mc-Dowell's mark on her forehead.

From the labyrinth of her brain a thought shot forth: *They think my husband is dead!* There could no longer be any doubt about it: even her father had known there was bad news when he had been home for Christmas. Nor did she imagine that these people were making up a story from whole cloth; somewhere, somehow, a report had come out of the West that Lieutenant Fremont was in trouble. But where had it come from? And how could she find out what it was?

If John were dead, then for her all the world was dead. She remembered the story of Grandmother Benton: she had been only thirty when her husband died. Young Tom was not allowed to see his mother for three months. When he had seen her last she had been a lovely, blue-eyed woman; when he was taken in to her again he found in place of the vivacious young woman he had known a thin white-haired old lady.

No one knew better than Jessie that the Bentons loved only once.

At last she cornered an old trapper who had not the guile to deceive her. He told her that a report had come out of Oregon that Lieutenant Fremont, after reaching the Columbia with his party intact, had then made the hazardous crossing from the Columbia to the Truckee River just east of the Sierras. Here he had disregarded the advice of the Indians that the Sierras were impassable, had plunged into the ice and snow, been enveloped by blizzards, and vanished completely. No word had come out of California of his arrival at Captain Sutter's, and so much time had passed in the interval that it would have been impossible for him not to have perished.

Having been separated from her husband for ten months, Jessie had imagined that she had learned all there was to know about the anatomy of loneliness. She imagined that loneliness had a traceable pattern, that once she had met the worst of it, she would recognize her old enemy when he arose the next time, and would have the technique with which to combat it. But she found that loneliness was a Hydra-headed monster who never appeared twice in the same shape or form; that it was an unslayable enemy who thrust himself upward in unexpected places and at unexpected times, just when one was beginning to feel some small measure of security. It could emerge in the middle of a page of print and make a superb piece of prose suddenly unendurable; it could burst forth when one was washing one's face or combing one's hair, and the brush would fall out of the hand and the soap drop into the basin and one's reflection in the mirror stare back like a lifeless mask; it could get into one's mouth while one was talking, and the words would die and the teeth would clench, and the lips would be bitten; it could crawl into bed at night when one lay half awake, half asleep, and bring with it the most excruciating torture of all, making of this one small bed a wide and empty world with no man to love, no husband to embrace, no arms to lock one safely against the darkness and the fatality of life.

Yet this kind of loneliness was endurable because the loved one would return; the first embrace of meeting would obliterate the wretched hours. But if the loved one is never to return?

For four days she went with little food or drink or sleep, walking through her duties with her feelings numbed. She did not accept the fact of John's death any more than she was able to repudiate it. She knew that if there was any man who could get through the Sierras in the face of blizzards, it was he. But if no human being could get through, what then?

Toward dawn of the fifth day, as she lay rigid on her bed, the cycle of anxiety broke; she fell into a sound sleep. When she awakened at noon she leaped out of bed, bathed, brushed and combed her long hair, donned a close-fitting blue silk dress which she had made almost daringly short in front, exposing her ankle, in order to get some comfort in walking the rough cobblestones of St. Louis. After luncheon she spent an hour with Lily, then put on a matching jockey cap of blue silk and set out for the Brants. To her cousins she said:

"You can stop your worrying. Lieutenant Fremont and his party are safe."

They betrayed their past concern when several of them exclaimed at once:

"Oh, Jessie, how wonderful, we are so happy for you, we are so relieved! When did the news come? How did he manage to survive in the mountains under those horrible conditions?"

"There has been no news. I have received no letter. I simply know that my husband is safe. Nothing could possibly persuade me otherwise. Lieutenant Fremont will be home in a very few weeks."

Her cousins were shocked. When she saw the frightened expression in their eyes, she smiled and said:

"No, my dears, I have not gone out of my mind. What I know, I know.

It is almost a year now since Lieutenant Fremont left on his expedition. He will soon be back in St. Louis."

11

SHE THREW HERSELF into a happy fever of preparation for his return. Though the first of March was a little early for spring cleaning she turned the house upside down and had everything scrubbed, whitewashed, painted and waxed. Then she planned new outfits for herself and Lily, spending hours cutting out dresses and embroidering on them. She set a place each night at the table for John, and when the rest of the family had finis..... dinner, his setting was transferred to a small table by the fire. His food was left on the kitchen stove where it could be heated on short notice.

"A man must not feel unexpected," she said.

A log fire was kept burning brightly in the downstairs parlor, which she replenished just before she went to sleep. However, sleep was the last of her desires; she stayed up until midnight studying and perfecting her Spanish, which she felt would be a great asset when she returned to California with her husband. She then placed her reading lamp on a table by the window that faced toward town, a light which he must see from far off as he came down the riverbank to the Benton home. It was not that she thought he needed light to guide his steps, this man who had just crossed an uncharted continent, but only that it would stand for the light in her heart and for her great and burning desire for him to be back. She knew that he would understand.

Occasionally she would fall asleep in her chair by the fire, but she would awake with a start thinking she heard footsteps outside, those short, swift, staccato footsteps which distinguished him from every other man in the world just as surely as did his voice or his appearance. Some time after midnight she would go to bed and lie there certain that he would return before morning, catching only snatches of troubled, conscious sleep. By dawn she was up again to put away the lamp, to remove the setting from the table by the fireplace, to face another day of waiting, sustaining herself on faith and devotion, feeding off them because no other food was digestible.

March passed, and then April. Still there was no word from John. The population of St. Louis was positive that he and his party had perished in the snows of the Sierras. When her cousins learned that she was setting a place at the table for him each night, saving his food and lighting a lamp to guide his footsteps, they became concerned for her sanity.

She grew thinner and frailer. By June, one year from the day he had left, she was down to ninety pounds, her skin pulled taut over the bones, her eyes enormous and staring in her hollow-cheeked face, the King George's Mark flaming red below the corner of her mouth.

There was something about going into the second year of separation which broke down her discipline. She ceased reading altogether, almost ceased thinking. There were no longer any divisions in her mind between night and day, nor among the weeks or months. The heat of summer sapped her last strength as she drifted through the days of July and early August. It was five months since she had told her cousins that John was alive and well; she realized that by now she was the only one in the United States who thought so.

In the early morning of August seventh when she had fallen into that curious state she had known so many months of being a little asleep and yet terribly awake, she heard the sound of excited voices below her in the hallway. She jumped out of bed, put on a robe and ran downstairs. Maylee was talking to Gabriel, who was either excited or trembling with fear. She heard him say:

"I hear pebbles against my window . . . the coachhouse . . . I look out. There Lieutenant Fremont. He ask can I let him in without I wake the family?"

Jessie confronted the old man.

"You say you saw Lieutenant Fremont? What time was it? Why didn't you bring him to me?"

"It must be three o'clock, Miss Jessie. He say he wait till morning, he don't want to wake nobody, he walk downtown till dawn."

Then she heard the sound for which her ears had been attuned for fourteen months; footsteps running up the front stairs; a sharp knock at the door, and John was in the hallway, had brushed past Gabriel and held her half fainting in his arms. He carried her to one of the larger chairs, sat down with her, covered her trembling face with kisses.

Word spread around town almost as fast as though a cannon had been fired. Friends began thronging into the Benton house. By eight in the morning it had turned into a full-scale reception, with people laughing and crying and everybody talking at once.

Jessie's happiness returned in a great rush. The waiting was over now, all the uncertainty gone. Beside her sat her husband, thinner than she, his cheeks sunken, his skin gray and blotched with stubble, his face engraved with heavy lines of fatigue, his eyes a little wild, his clothes threadbare. But here he sat beside her, his bony tired arm about her tired shoulder, his exhausted voice against her unhearing ear, his dry, cracked lips against her hollowed cheek. She knew that neither of them was beautiful to look at, but ah, how beautiful the world, how beautiful to be together again!

At noon the milling throng of friends departed.

"My poor darling," said Jessie, "you have no luck: when you came home from your first expedition I was big with child; and now I am as skinny as a starved cat."

"You never looked more beautiful," he replied, kissing her full on the mouth. The kindness broke the back of her resolve to be calm; she began blubbering like a child, and he had to hold her against him so hard that there was almost no breath left in her body.

Later she said, "I must tell you why I sent that message to Kaw's Landing. I hope you will approve of what I did, but if you do not approve, you must tell me so quite honestly so that I may use it as a guide for future conduct."

"If you told me to go, I knew there was sufficient reason to go," he said. "What happened?"

"A letter arrived from the Topographical Department calling you to Washington to explain the presence of a cannon on a peaceful expedition."

"A recall. But that would have meant . . ."

" . . . another officer was being sent to take your place."

"Take my place!" He reared up like a balky horse, his face a dull, brick red. "It's that West Point clique! They're jealous of what I've accomplished."

"Then I did right to suppress the order?"

"Right!" He shouted at her as though she were the entire West Point aristocracy. "You would have been a fool if you hadn't. You saved the day for all of us."

"Good! What happened to the cannon? Was it valuable? Were you able to bring it back?"

"Yes and no: it staved off one major Indian attack; we could have survived it, but it might have cost us several men. We pulled that cannon from Kaw's Landing fifteen hundred miles to the Dalles on the Columbia, then another four hundred miles through the snow and icy passes going south from Oregon to the east side of the Rockies. We even got it halfway across the Sierras; there we lost it in snowdrifts twelve feet high. We were hard pressed to save our own lives, and the cannon had to be abandoned."

"I'm sorry you couldn't have brought it back to the Jefferson Barracks. But since it saved you from an attack you have justified its presence to both Colonel Abert and Colonel Kearny."

"Wait until they see our maps and reports, Jessie; we'll both be vindicated."

It was then she asked, "What happened in the Sierras? Why did the report get out that you and your party had perished? Did you have terrible hardships? Were you in serious danger?"

He rubbed his feet up and down on the cool wood floor. He had left her side, had gone back to the Sierras and the blinding snows.

"Hardships? Yes. Danger? Yes. Death? No. Only the weak die on the trail. Only those whose will power succumbs to a stronger force. I crossed the Sierras in midwinter, Jessie, when the Indians who had lived there all their lives said it was impossible. I am the first man to traverse the Sierras in winter. I found a pass over a fourteen-thousand-foot wall of ice when we were all nine-tenths dead and everyone except Carson and myself had abandoned hope. I forced that crossing, Jessie, right where my calculation told me it must be. And once we were over, we dropped straight down into the Sacramento Valley and Sutter's Fort. I found a straight route and a new pass to California; one day it will be as widely used as the Oregon Trail. If war comes with Mexico, we will take California by the Army moving in over the trail I blazed."

His voice rang with exultation. "Jessie, it was the greatest experience of my life! I was defeated; the Sierras had whipped me; it was impossible for humans to get through . . . we were only shadows of men, almost too weak to move; the snow lay so deep neither man nor horse could struggle forward; we were too blinded to see, too cold to feel, too hungry to move our legs. Never has a party been closer to death and destruction."

He paced up and down the room. "That's when a man lives at his height, when he is beaten, when all the world knows he's beaten, when he hasn't the slimmest chance, and yet he pushes through, he defeats and surmounts all the obstacles, when he is stronger than nature, when he is the strongest force on earth. For, Jessie, I found that pass! I found it without food or strength or eyesight or arms or legs. I crawled up over ten thousand feet and found our pass and went back and got the rest of the party and dragged them up with me, men and horses, both. Ah Jessie, such moments, such triumphs are vouchsafed but a few times in a man's life."

And Jessie, sitting there, intensely proud of his accomplishment, found her heart wrung in pity; pity for this unfortunate creature who must make himself a king because in his own mind he was not a whole man. In the icy passes of the Sierras the last could be first, John Fremont had vindicated himself: by making himself the conqueror of nature he had conquered his own illegitimacy. If only he could live forever in these icy passes, she thought, overcoming insurmountable obstacles, making impossible conquests, then always he would be a king, the fear and uncertainty

would vanish, the enigma of John Charles Fremont would be solved and
vanquished.

12

THE NEXT TWO WEEKS were delightful ones. Lingering over their late
breakfast, Jessie heard her husband say in a ruminative voice:

"The man who has a good wife is a king; she sweetens every hour.
There can be no real happiness or success in life for the man with a
poorish wife, and there can be no genuine failure for the man with a good
wife. What a stroke of pure genius I had when I recognized you, Jessie.
I shall always think well of myself for that magnificent flash of wisdom."

She chuckled at the oblique compliment.

"And what about me?" she asked. "Don't I get any credit for recog,
nizing you?"

"A relatively minor accomplishment, compared to mine. Do you know
wherein the true greatness of your accomplishment lies?"

"Do tell me."

"In the fact that, search my memory as I will, I can find no scars on
our marriage. I know that I have sometimes been difficult and unreason-
able, that you are hard pressed not to become angry with me or lose
patience. But you have been so unfailingly kind, you have kept our relationship so sympathetic and serene that, when I want to quarrel with
you, my mind can find no dark spots around which to fester. I can't even
conjure up a quarrel with you in my imagination. That is a great accomplishment, Jessie, and all the credit must go to you."

"A mere nothing," she mocked, to conceal her emotion. "All you need
is love, and it's as easy as falling off a precipice."

At the end of two weeks they had completed their arrangements to
leave for Washington. They took the steamboat to Wheeling, where they
rented a carriage and drove the rest of the way along the now completed
national road to Washington. It was good to be home again in Washington, but the crush of people was so great in the Benton house that it
proved impossible for them to get to work on their report. At the beginning of October, when she was looking well and fresh again, she found a
vacant two-storied cottage just a block away. She took John to see it,
showing him through excitedly.

"Look, darling, we can have complete privacy here, for no one need
know it is our workshop. We can turn these two upstairs rooms into
writing rooms and give the downstairs quarters to Preuss and John
Hubbard for their maps. Does it look good to you?"

"Rent it at once," he replied. "I'll move over our notes and journals
first thing in the morning."

John and her father rose at dawn, had their showers, coffee and rolls at six, and John left for his cottage. Jessie was not allowed to appear until nine. From nine until one she worked with him on the report. Then Maylee would arrive with little Lily under one arm and a luncheon basket under the other and tell them stories of the baby while they ate cold chicken on cornbread and munched fresh fruit. After lunch Maylee would place Lily in the basket and take her back home, while the Fremonts went for a half-hour's walk along the Potomac before returning to the workshop.

John had done an even better job on his journals than he had on the previous expedition. There was a magnificent wealth of scientific observation, vivid descriptions of the trail, the mountains, the rivers and the forests; and of the greatest importance to her, the rich and natural poetry of his mind when, sitting by his campfire late at night, he had written unrestrainedly of everything he had seen and experienced. There was no hesitation in their collaboration now; each knew his own role and was respectful of the contribution of the other. She took the utmost pains to preserve the color and flavor and beauty of his rough notes, the sharp pungency of the stories he told, content to contribute form and organization, to burn out the dross and to leave John's work appearing at its best.

They labored for five months on the report, the most concentrated piece of work she had ever done. She knew her contribution to this document to be a modest one, and for that reason she felt secure in believing that it was to be one of the great books of exploration; here were descriptions of forest and mountain ranges, of sunrises over icy blue crags which had not been surpassed for beauty in any literature she knew; here was an entirely new fund of material about the Indians and their way of life; here were studies of the souls of men enduring excruciating agonies, bending under the burden but always snapping back; here was a fluid technique of exploration which utilized everything known to the minds of explorers, yet went beyond all precedent of daring ingenuity and resourcefulness in the face of hardships which staggered the imagination; here was a wealth of observation on botany, geology, the nature of mountain and snow and forest which had not been surpassed for scientific meticulousness or for the brilliance of poetic observation.

Colonel Kearny came to Washington on army business and was invited to dinner by Tom Benton. A blunt and earnest man, he was not one to allow a fractured relationship to limp along without splint or bandage. He found a moment alone with Jessie, saying to her in his slightly rough voice, "Do not mistake me, Miss Jessie, I am tremendously happy for your sake that everything has worked out so well. I am putting the entire incident out of my mind."

The following evening she and John were invited to Colonel Abert's home as guests of honor at a dinner for the officers of the Topographical Corps. She was slow and uncertain in her dressing; John urged her to hurry several times, but she could not seem to complete her coiffure.

"What are you fretting about?" he asked.

"I'm afraid. Colonel Abert's home is almost the last one in Washington I care to go into."

"Colonel Abert is a subtle man; he's not like Colonel Kearny. He will never mention that obstructed order, any more than he ever answered your letter."

"Nevertheless I'm nervous," she replied, "so nervous that I can't get this confounded part straight in the middle of my hair."

"Then leave it crooked. I don't want to be late."

But when she got to Colonel Abert's home, still a little pale, and without words to carry her over the difficult moment of meeting, the colonel welcomed her with warmth and charm, seated her at his right and was more delightful than she had ever known him. She couldn't touch the delicious bouillabaisse for fear that his charm was only a front, that the colonel would take the first opportunity to reprove her; but by the time the mallards and suckling pig arrived she saw that her little uprising had been forgiven.

The frequent meetings which took place in the Benton home showed Jessie and John that to official Washington the most interesting part of his trip was his brief sojourn in California: for war with Mexico over the annexation of Texas seemed to be growing closer every day, and nearly everyone in Washington was resolved that California must not fall into British hands. Senator Benton, as chairman of the Military Affairs Committee, had been receiving disquieting news.

"That magnificent coast and its harbors are going to fall into British hands like ripe fruit off a tree," he exclaimed. "The Mexican government has granted them thousands of acres in a huge tract, and the British are sending in a whole colony of Irish families. If that colony gets established, California will be lost to us."

No one in the capital had been in California except John, and his opinion was eagerly sought. There was material which Jessie had not been able to write into the report, for Mexico was still considered a friendly nation, but he had sketched for her the outlines of his findings: Mexico City's only interest in this vast country appeared to be the taxes it could extract; no Mexican colonizing was going on; the Mexican government kept a small army in California, inadequately equipped and officered. There were almost a hundred fast-shooting Americans in California, none of whom liked the Mexican rule and nearly all of whom would fight to join the United States.

"An army officer with a hundred men under him could capture California," said Lieutenant Fremont, "only they have to be there at the right moment."

When they had finished the report on February 20, just a year after he had crossed the Sierras, Jessie asked anxiously:

"Will Congress order a thousand extra copies to be printed again? That was such a tremendous help last time."

"I hardly think so, Jessie."

"Why not? This report is far superior to the last, and all the material from South Pass to the Pacific coast is new . . ."

"But it stretched to three hundred pages; Congress may find it too long and boring."

Before she could answer she saw that he had been teasing her. On March 3, 1845, the day before President James K. Polk was to be inaugurated, John came home flushed with pleasure.

"What do you think?" he exclaimed. "The Senate passed a resolution ordering five thousand extra copies of our report."

"Five thousand," exclaimed Jessie, "why, that's magnificent!"

"Only half as magnificent as what finally happened: James Buchanan praised me to the skies and carried a motion that the number be increased to ten thousand copies. And here, my dear, read what Secretary Buchanan said about your husband. I'm too modest to tell you."

Jessie made a mocking grimace, then read aloud Buchanan's statement to the Senate of John's progress: "He is a young gentleman of extraordinary merit, great energy and ability to serve his country. Lieutenant Fremont deserves encouragement." Hiding her pleasure under a little joke, she said, "I never found that you needed encouragement; you just sort of reach out and grab everything you want."

The next day Jessie did her hair in the new Polish fashion with a braid of nine strands, a small bunch of flowers and leaves hanging from the coil at the back, and on top of her head a small black muslin cap. Her new gown was black moire, with the bodice opening over a chemisette of white muslin. Her silk paletot wrap was trimmed with black lace and caught around the waist with a broad ribbon.

"I think I look uncommonly handsome," she remarked to her husband.

"Why do you always get dressed up in your best clothes and look so gorgeous when we go out?" he countered. "Why don't you get dressed up like that for me when we stay home?"

"You're supposed to love me for my spiritual values, dear, not for my new clothes."

"But even your spiritual values show up to better advantage in a black moire gown."

Driving up Pennsylvania Avenue, Jessie asked, "Do you remember the last reception we came to? We were newly married and President Tyler gave us the first clue that an expedition might be ordered."

"I hope that established a precedent for inaugurals," he replied. "I would like President Polk to give me an intimation today that he favors a third expedition to California."

"I'm sure he will, dear," she murmured. "Who could resist you when you look so beautiful in your new uniform?"

"True. But I'm afraid I don't stimulate the president quite as much as I do my wife."

They were welcomed on the reception line by Nancy Polk, Jessie's long-time friend. After the formalities were over, President Polk summoned them and, surrounded by a group of army officers and Cabinet members, asked Lieutenant Fremont for stories of the West. He chose a number of short and dramatic incidents which seemed to capture the president's imagination. Encouraged by his success, he became emboldened to say, "Mr. President, the entire Pacific coast could be of the utmost value to the United States. Geographically it belongs to us; there will be a continuous conflict if two or three nations own land on the Pacific."

Polk's face lost its interested expression; knowing that he faced four years of being importuned, he said, not unkindly, "Lieutenant Fremont, you suffer from two afflictions under which I labored not so long ago: youth and impulsiveness. I expect you will outgrow them both; in the meanwhile please accept my warmest congratulations on the accomplishments of your second expedition."

Lieutenant and Mrs. Fremont found themselves dismissed. On the way home in their carriage they were a little glum together.

"The precedent fell on its face," mourned John. "Mr. Polk has no intention of backing a third expedition."

"Maybe he just needs a little time. I do wish we could have told all this to Nancy. She is open to new ideas, and she would have known how to convince the president."

It was no surprise to Jessie that when Congress released the second report, Lieutenant Fremont became the popular hero of America. The newspapers reprinted substantial excerpts, featuring his picture on the front page. Several publishing houses rushed the book into print, and it sold like wildfire, in England almost as widely as in the United States. Honors poured in from scientific societies in England and Europe. General Winfield Scott, founder of America's professional army, six foot four of military brilliance, came to the Benton home with an official-looking document in his hand to announce to the delighted family in his most ceremonial fashion that President Polk had breveted John captain for "gallant and highly meritorious services in two expeditions commanded by himself."

Such popularity had not been seen in the capital since army generals had won important military victories in the War of 1812. Sermons were preached on the morals of the expedition, school children had parts of the report read to them in the classrooms; everywhere in the United States, on small farms, in crossroad stores, in hotels and bars and clubs, on the sidewalks of great cities people gathered to talk about the second Fremont report, to feel in their blood the stir of the westward movement, of the desire to experience these great adventures, to see these beautiful sights, to farm this new and rich land, to win property in this vast new country, to be once again movers, doers, breakers of trails, settlers, pioneers of new states as well as new lands: to be their own man.

And Jessie Benton Fremont was content; she had known her man the moment she had seen him; she had recognized him for the strength and greatness that were in him; she had helped him beat his road through the mountains; she had strengthened his sinews and extended his reach, made him a little bigger by lending that little talent which had been hers to contribute.

These were the things of which she had dreamed when her mind had turned to marriage.

13

THE ARGUMENT IN WASHINGTON over the possibility of war with Mexico because of the annexation of Texas waged warmer every day. Much of it centered in the home of Chairman Benton, of the Senate Military Affairs Committee, and his son-in-law, Captain Fremont. Senator Benton was averse to war with Mexico, felt that Texas and the Southwest, including California, should be bought at a fair figure, just as the vast Louisiana Purchase had been made from France. There was neither ethics nor justice in forcing Mexico to sell, and even though this attitude of purchase was comparatively new on the international scene, Tom Benton realized that his government was on the difficult side of the situation. Mexico had no use for the land; it was a hang-over from the Spanish days, and there was little likelihood that the country could become prosperous or settled while being ruled from Mexico City. Nevertheless, it legally belonged to Mexico.

Captain Fremont, thinking as a military man, was more opportunistic in his attitude. He didn't care how the United States got California— by purchase, occupation, seizure, or even pure theft.

"My ethics may be a little obscure," he admitted to Jessie, "but my eye-sight is perfect. I have been to California. I know that geographically it belongs to the United States. I should like to help in its acquisition. I can't shed any tears over the Mexicans; aside from the revenues they extract, they are as interested in California as we are in the moon."

One evening when she was browsing through a copy of the *United Science Journal,* published in London, she found a passage which con-siderably startled her. She exclaimed, "Father, John, listen to this:

"'There is no doubt that we, the English, have three powerful rivals in France, Russia, and the United States, but of these three the Americans are the most important on account of their origin, their courage, and their even greater enterprise and activity than our own. They have raw ma-terial, workingmen, and sufficient merchant navy to arm as men-of-war when called upon to do so.'"

Senator Benton, who had disliked the British profoundly since the War of 1812, snatched up the newspaper, put on a hat and coat and walked to Senator Calhoun's house. Calhoun felt confirmed in his suspicion that England intended to wage war against the United States for the acquisi-tion, first of Oregon, then of California. The two men marched militantly to Secretary of Navy George Bancroft's house. The next morning Secre-tary Bancroft had a long session with President Polk. Within a very few days the third expedition to the West had been authorized, the War De-partment had set aside fifty thousand dollars for its prosecution, and Cap-tain Fremont had been named as commander.

The following days of confidential meetings were exciting for Jessie, but before long a tinge of uneasiness crept into her thoughts: everyone wanted to acquire California and would prefer to buy it at a reasonable figure, yet it was obvious that no one wanted to let it go by default to England if it couldn't be bought. Men spoke of how valuable and im-portant California was, how it was manifest destiny that it belong to the United States; everyone was certain that Mexico would not sell or nego-tiate; everyone seemed to know that California would have to be seized if the United States were not to lose the territory to England. Yet no one would admit he thought this, no one was willing to be quoted to that effect, no one wanted to be held responsible for outlaw conduct or go down in the historic record as an instigator of an international theft.

Many of Captain Fremont's superior army officers, many cabinet members, senators and congressmen assured him how happy they were that a scientific expedition was on its way to California; they agreed that it would be propitious to have an army officer present in the event that war should break; yet no one would lay out a definite course of conduct or give him specific authorization.

"Everybody knows what they would like you to do," said Jessie, "but no one is willing to take the responsibility for it."

"It's not difficult to understand," replied John. "We are still at peace with Mexico; no representative of our government can go on record as sponsoring aggression. That would make the United States government responsible for his acts. But I am not an official representative of the government. I am just a captain in the Topographical Corps. Anything I may do, aside from exploring, I do on my own responsibility. If I embarrass my government, they can disavow me."

"I do wish that you could get some kind of written authorization."

"It's not possible in such a delicate situation. It may be that Mexico will sell us California; it may be that the Americans out there will revolt and set up an independent republic, the way they did in Texas; it may be that the time is not yet ripe for annexation. In any of these instances it would be dangerous for me to have authorization to do anything but explore and make maps of the Pacific coast."

She planned to remain in the capital during her husband's absence, for the situation had changed so rapidly that Washington City rather than St. Louis would now be the hub of activity for the West. She knew that this separation would be the longest of all, that her husband would have to remain on the Pacific coast until the climax of events could release him. How long would he be away? A year, two years, three years! She had hoped to go with him the next time he went to California; instead she faced a staggering separation. Her only reassurance was that this would, probably be the last time he would go west without her. They had agreed that he was to invest their savings in the most beautiful ranch he could find between Monterey and San Francisco. California would be an American state within a few years, and the Fremonts would be among its first settlers.

They spent their last evening together in their upstairs sitting room after a jolly family dinner at which Mrs. Benton had been the only one to break down and show how bad she felt about his leaving. To everyone's amazement, Eliza had asked permission to invite a young lawyer she had met recently, a tall, spindly, blond chap, quiet and dry-spoken.

The preparations for the expedition had gone smoothly, except that Preuss, the magnificent map maker, had had to withdraw because his wife had issued him an ultimatum: "Choose between your home and family and your instinct to wander."

While Jessie sat sewing a waterproof pocket on the side of John's canvas-and-leather jacket, in which he was to keep his valuable papers dry, her husband cried:

"Darling, how can I leave you here? I was gone for fourteen months last time; this time I will be gone longer. The days when I am with you go so fast, but when I am away from you they drag so terribly."

A tear splashed on the leather pocket.

"There," she said, "your jacket has been christened. Now it will bring you good luck." She ran her fingers through his short black hair. "It was good of you to say that, even though in its strictest sense it isn't true; you live at the height of excitement when you are on the trail. Your job is to go, my job is to let you go cheerfully."

"Confound it, Jessie, would you mind looking a little sad so that my ego can be inflated?"

"Like your India-rubber boat? You wouldn't want me to be a Mrs. Preuss. I decided long ago that you would tire of a pining wife. My dear, I don't want you to tire of me, I want you to love me all our long lives together."

When she awakened the next morning she saw Maylee's grinning black face before her, holding a copy of the *Union* for her to see. In the center of the front page was a large picture of Captain Fremont.

"How wonderful, Maylee, to be greeted by my husband's face when I cannot be greeted by his voice. Would you like to hear what they say?

" 'Captain Fremont has gone upon his third expedition, determined upon a complete military and scientific exploration of all the vast unknown region between the Rocky Mountains and the Pacific Ocean, and between the Oregon River and the Gulf of California. This expedition is expected to continue nearly two years, and its successful result is looked to with the highest degree of interest by all the friends of science in America and Europe. His life is a pattern and his success an encouragement to young men of America who aspire to honorable distinction by their own meritorious exertions.' "

She hardly had had time to adjust herself to his absence when Secretary of State James Buchanan dropped in unannounced, gratefully accepted her invitation to a cup of tea, and asked if he might speak to her privately. She led him to the library, closed the door behind them. James Buchanan had come to Washington to enter the House at the same time that Tom Benton had arrived to enter the Senate; thus Jessie had known him all her life. He was a good-looking man with an open face, almost round eyes, and what women thought an amorous mouth. He was a lonely man who had endured tragedy in his youth: the girl to whom he was devoted with the single-purposeness of his nature had become angry with him over a bit of gossip. Without giving him a chance to explain, she had terminated their engagement and boarded a train to visit some relatives in New York. She died while en route; he never was able to learn whether it had been a natural death, an accident, or suicide: nor had he ever ceased reproaching himself for not having prevented her from leaving. After the loss of his first love he had never loved again or married, though many women had tried to invade his bachelorhood.

James Buchanan never pretended to be brilliant, but he was conscientious and painstaking. A man of quiet charm who had developed an iron-clad system of logic from his studies of the law, he had been respected as minister to Russia, his constituents in Pennsylvania had declared him to be a valuable senator. He lived an impeccable private life, taking pleasure from work well done; he was a man who loathed force, crudity, irregularity. If some people thought him too meticulous, too encased in an unassailable shell of formal manners, too spinsterish, these qualifications had enabled him for some twenty-five years to render valuable service to his state and his country.

Jessie noticed a curious thing about him: the front half of his full underlip, the exposed half, was always dry, apparently covered by a fine white powder. Anyone looking at him would think him to be a dry and powdery man. Yet when he opened his mouth to speak, the inner half of his lip was revealed to be red and moist and alive. This was the paradox of James Buchanan: inwardly he lived a rich intellectual and spiritual life; the side which he exposed to public view he allowed to appear dry and dead.

While she had been ruminating about his life and career, he had begun to speak.

". . . difficult to understand how a woman of her family background and breeding . . . I refused to believe it for some time until I felt obliged to make a test. There can be no doubt of it, Mrs. Greenhow is a spy, in the pay of the British government."

If the accusation had not come from the secretary of state himself, Jessie would have refused to believe it.

"Mrs. Greenhow a spy! Why, her family is one of the best in Washington!"

"We must spend our time not in trying to understand the lady's motives, but in undoing the harm she has accomplished. Do I remember rightly that your Spanish is good?"

"Quite good. Father brought me up with the language."

Secretary Buchanan placed his tongue tentatively on the dry half of his lip, moistening the white powder before speaking.

"You know how delicate our situation is with Mexico. I have private and confidential reports coming in every day. I never learned to read Spanish, and since the revelation about Mrs. Greenhow, I feel that I dare not trust anyone in my own office. Would you translate these confidential reports for me? Would you survey the Spanish newspapers and magazines and write me a report every few days on the tone and temper of the Mexican press?"

"Mr. Buchanan, I thank you with all my heart for this opportunity, and you may be sure that I will do a good job."

"Of that I am certain, Miss Jessie. You realize, of course, no part of the information you gather from the confidential reports may be passed on to your father. As secretary of state I am an officer of the executive branch of the government, while your father, as the chairman of the Senate Military Affairs Committee, is an officer of the legislative branch. While there can be no conflict between us over the national interest, there is sometimes a struggle between the executive and the legislative over the powers of government."

"I understand, Mr. Secretary. No word of my information will reach Senator Benton."

"Good! And now the last stricture: your husband is en route to the Pacific coast. There are certain people in our government who would be willing to encourage him to use force in taking California. To this attitude I am unalterably opposed. I shall have to ask that no part of your information be transmitted to Captain Fremont. I would be violating the function of my office if he were to secure advance and confidential information which might precipitate him into a conflict with the Mexicans."

"You will see, Mr. Secretary, that all American women are not irresponsible."

Secretary Buchanan rose, bowed stiffly.

"Thank you for the cup of tea, Miss Jessie. A page will bring you a pouch early tomorrow morning. Here is a key to the lock; never allow anyone in the room while you are working, and never leave the room without returning the papers to the pouch."

"Very good, sir."

He shook her hand, then bade her good day.

14

IN HER FIRST BATCH of confidential papers from Mexico, Jessie learned that the Mexican government was negotiating with Great Britain to intercede in the event of hostilities with the United States. The trouble had arisen over Texas: when the United States annexed Texas, the Mexican government broke off diplomatic relations. When Texas accepted the American offer of annexation, Mexico reorganized its army. President Polk was preparing to send Joseph Slidell to Mexico City as minister, with an offer of forty million dollars for the peaceful purchase of Texas, when news of Mexico's war preparations flooded Washington. Since the

United States and England still were quarreling over the Oregon territory, Jessie concluded from the dispatches that in the event of a war between England and the United States over Oregon, England would seize California with her Navy, having made an advance agreement with Mexico to do so.

When she went to Secretary Buchanan's office the next day to show him her synopsis of the news, he was distressed. He said:

"Mexico wants to go to war over Texas; England seems to want to go to war over Oregon; the United States seems to want to go to war over California. President Polk fears that the British will accept no compromise on the Oregon boundary, but I am convinced that they will. I am also convinced that Mexico will accept a cash settlement for Texas and California, since they have no legitimate use for them. When our minister goes to Mexico City, I am going to suggest that he offer twenty-five million dollars for California and New Mexico."

"Yes, Mr. Secretary, but the tone of the Mexican press indicates that they would not consider any price a fair one because they feel they are being forced to sell. Unless there is a sharp change of attitude, our minister may not even be received."

"Miss Jessie, I am determined to avert war with both England and Mexico; if either war comes about, I shall feel that I have failed in my office."

She rose, assured him that she would keep the information flowing to him, and returned home.

Her days were so crammed with duties and obligations that she found little time for pining. In addition to her work for Secretary Buchanan and her father, she managed the household and played hostess for unceasing dinner parties: one for Sam Houston, who had served under her father in the War of 1812, and who had just arrived in Washington as the first senator from Texas; one for Commander Robert S. Stockton of the United States warship *Princeton,* who was about to leave for California and would unquestionably see Captain Fremont when he got there; one for Secretary of the Navy George Bancroft, a dynamo of energy and a lion of courage, handsome, rugged-faced, virile and militant, young but already famous for his histories of the United States, the leader of the forces in Washington who were determined that all the Southwest, including California, must become American, even if it meant a bloody war with Mexico; one for John L. Stevens, author of the travel books on Arabia and Palestine which Jessie had read as a child; her own dinner party in honor of Samuel Morse, who at long last had been given a small appropriation by Congress, and from a Senate room had sent a message to Baltimore on the first thirty miles of telegraph line.

Her deepest gratification of the passing weeks was watching Eliza fall in love. She had been alarmed over her twenty-three-year-old sister, for it seemed that Eliza would never care to marry. Jessie watched her sister and William Carey Jones together at the Benton dinner table; they took each other casually, without personal interest. When the young lawyer asked Tom Benton's permission to marry Eliza, Jessie understood that that had been their manner of falling in love.

One afternoon at the beginning of November, Secretary of the Navy George Bancroft sent a message asking if he might come to tea. Jessie put on a wide-skirted silk dress that made her look rather like a petunia blossom. When George Bancroft arrived she led him to her sitting room, which was filled with the pleasant fragrances of potted rose geraniums, burning sassafras wood, Chinese tea and spice cake.

George Bancroft was as informal a man as James Buchanan was meticulous. He refused her invitation to a deep lounge chair, taking instead a hard seat, whirled it around so that he was sitting on it backwards, his elbows resting on the back while he looked at her over his own folded arms and half-clenched fists, studying her with magnificently alert wide-set blue eyes. He did not speak for several moments. Jessie took in the black hair combed back straight over his head, the sideburns chopped off toward the top of his ears, the long bony, curved, unbeautiful nose with hollows just above the nostrils; his uneven but rugged and eloquent mouth: a rough-hewn face, muscular, powerful, direct, the face of a man with a driving will and intellect.

She poured him a cup of tea, then lay back in her chaise against a nest of lace pillows, tired from the long day of work but curious about what he might want of her.

"You have been doing some translating for Secretary Buchanan," he said, after downing three slices of spice cake. "I only tell you that I know because it means we can go forward from this moment without discussing the background of the Mexican situation."

"Very well, Mr. Secretary."

"Miss Jessie, the British think they are going to capture California with their warships. They're mistaken; they can capture the ports, but they can't move those ships into the interior."

"Yes," agreed Jessie, not knowing what he was leading up to.

"But what holds true for the British warships holds equally true for ours: warships cannot take possession of a country. We need soldiers in California."

This time Jessie did not even bother to answer yes. She just sat up a little straighter on her chaise, waiting for Bancroft to declare himself.

"From the advice I have from Consul Larkin at Monterey and certain commanders of our ships that have put in at Monterey and San Francisco, I am certain that we would not need a large force to take California. But we are faced with a dilemma, Miss Jessie: we cannot send troops into the territory of a country with whom we are not at war. And if we don't send in troops before they declare war, we are going to lose California."

Again she did not interrupt, but rather said to herself: He knows as well as I do that Captain Fremont will soon be on the Pacific coast. He is an army officer. He has sixty well-armed men with him, men who are unquestionably willing and ready to fight.

"Things are touch and go, Miss Jessie. President Polk is right in saying that we cannot steal into another man's orchard, but if the fruit is ripe and is about to fall to the ground, where it will either be stolen or rot, why is it unethical to be standing under the bough with our hands open?"

"It is only unethical if all opportunism is unethical."

"Which is not necessarily true. As you know, I am a historian; I have watched the progress of our nation as it has unfolded year by year. I have always been in agreement with your father that this country must and shall extend to the Pacific Ocean. It would be criminal stupidity on our part to allow California and the Southwest to fall into the hands of a European nation, or even to lie dead and unused by Mexico. That is against our national character; that is against our national interests; and I am passionately convinced that it is against the entire flow of history. Do you agree with me?"

"I would not be Senator Benton's daughter if I did not," said Jessie.

"Good," exclaimed Secretary Bancroft, "then we understand each other."

"Yes," she replied, not knowing what it was that she was supposed to understand. The secretary of the navy had not come to her house to discuss a historical theory. Bancroft seemed to be waiting for her to make the next move. Seeing that she was not going to say anything, he began again, this time in a more tentative tone of voice.

"At first I thought President Polk was in error in not taking a more militant stand in California, for he is as eager to have California as I am, but as president of a peace-loving country his hands are tied. I have sent several of our ships of war to lie off Mexico and California ports to be on hand if anything happens, but beyond that point there is nothing I myself can do; as a cabinet officer my hands too are tied."

Knitting her brows Jessie thought, He is trying to lead me to a conclusion without involving himself in it.

"Without official authorization," he continued, "nothing can be done in California." He was talking fast now. "That is, unless unofficial action is taken for which the government cannot be held responsible. If, for

example, we had someone in California who could act swiftly and decisively at the right moment, Mexico would have no opportunity to call
for British protection, and England could not take possession. What we
desperately need, Mrs. Fremont, is what we will call for the moment an
irresponsible man, someone whom we can honestly repudiate if things do
not turn out well."

"I see your dilemma," said Jessie softly, and to herself, even more softly,
she said, And I also see mine. He has just called me Mrs. Fremont for the
first time; Mrs. Fremont has a husband by the name of Captain Fremont
who at this very moment must be dropping down the Sierras into the
Sacramento Valley with a well-trained party. Captain Fremont is an
unofficial representative of the United States, not of the government or
the Army, but of the scientific Topographical Corps. His rank and his
reputation will win him support in California if he should need it, and yet
as an "unofficial" of the government he could readily be repudiated.

Aloud she said: "A few moments ago you said to me, 'We understand
each other.' I answered yes, but frankly I did not. Now I think I do. What
is it precisely that you would like me to do?"

George Bancroft jumped up from his chair and began striding energetically about the room, picking up objects and laying them down, moving
the lighter pieces of furniture around, raising the Venetian blinds, then
lowering them again. Watching him, half amused, half frightened, Jessie
poured herself a cup of tea and thought, I have put my finger on a sore
spot. He can't tell me what he wants me to do. He has reached the climax
of this scene and he quite frankly does not know where to go from here.
But I can outsit him even if he wrecks the whole room.

After a few moments he came back to her chaise, dropped down beside
her with a hard thud.

"Let me see if I can explain to you the kind of man we need in California: he must be willing to act on his own initiative, without orders. He
must be willing to be an opportunist; what the outside world might call
an adventurer. He must be hotheaded, impulsive, quick to action. He
must be a man who is not afraid to face the consequences of rashness,
failure and international censure."

"In other words," murmured Jessie, "he must have a fast trigger finger
and a stout heart."

"Ah, Mrs. Fremont, a far stouter heart than you will be able to imagine.
I am willing to take the responsibility of causing a war, but I will take
that responsibility as secretary of the navy. The man who starts the war
with Mexico in California, or seizes that country without a war, can
expect no backing and no authorization. We would have to have his resignation in our pocket, dated considerably prior to any conceivable action,

so that we could publish it if we thought it expedient to do so. If it became necessary for the United States government to save face, he would be thoroughly excoriated. The press would tear his reputation to shreds. He would become an entirely discredited man. If he were a naval officer, I as secretary of the navy would be obliged to call for his court-martial. He might never again be trusted, given a responsible position; his life and career could easily be smashed."

"That also I can understand," said Jessie slowly.

"It is tragic that we have no such man in California. Yet even if we had I could send him no written orders or authorization, nor could anyone else in the government. If at some future date he were to find it necessary to vindicate himself and were to try to present evidence, such as, let us say, this conversation, I would be obliged to deny that it ever took place. For obviously it never did take place, Mrs. Fremont; I have just come here to talk with you and unburden my mind."

He smiled warmly.

"And now I must bid you good night. It was extremely good of you to listen to my long harangue. Frankly, I have been quite jealous of Secretary Buchanan, and now I feel that in some small measure I have evened the score. Speaking of Secretary Buchanan, it is hardly necessary for me to tell you that he would agree with nothing I have intimated this evening. The secretary of state is a meticulous man, as indeed the secretary of state ought to be. The secretary of the navy is a man of action, even though he has been a historian; and a man of action is what the secretary of the navy needs to be. Good night, Mrs. Fremont; please don't trouble to take me down."

For several hours Jessie lay on the chaise dissecting Secretary Bancroft's statement of the problem. Though he had never once mentioned Captain Fremont's name, it was clear he had been talking about her husband all the time; there was no other army officer within two thousand miles of California, and no naval officer could possibly act without implicating his government. Secretary Bancroft wanted Captain Fremont to seize California for the United States when the proper moment arose; but he would give him no authorization, he would refuse to stand by him if the seizure miscarried; he might find it necessary to deny that any such plan for Captain Fremont had ever entered his mind. His description of the type of man needed in California, while not altogether complimentary, she had to admit was a fairly accurate description of her husband: impulsive, quick to action—like herself, something of an adventurer, more mindful of today's job than tomorrow's consequences.

Would Captain Fremont take this terrible risk? Would he put his career and future in danger? Would he stand the chance of having his government declare him an unscrupulous adventurer, cashier him from the service? Would he gamble his years of scientific training, his skill as an explorer and topographer, on one turn of the wheel?

Almost as important, Jessie knew, was the question of whether she could allow him to face these hazards. What would happen to him if he were to be retired from the Army in disgrace, with no one to back him or stand by him, his former work thrown into deep shadow? What would happen to the character and spirit and the pride of John Fremont if all the world thought him a disreputable man, one whom his government had been forced to repudiate? Could he stand up under such a blow? Could he carry such a burden, this man who had a canker of uncertainty already eating at his vitals, who had to make himself greater than all men in order to feel the equal of the least of them? Would not such a fate destroy him? Could he go through life content to know that he had done a service for his government, a service to which he had been directed, though only his president, his secretary of the navy, and his wife knew that he had been acting under orders?

Her heart beat wildly. What would happen to their life together, to their love, their marriage?

She was not able to answer for herself how well her husband could endure the consequences of failure, but she knew for a certainty that nothing could prevent him from taking the gamble. He was not afraid of the word adventurer; the thought of failure would never enter his mind; when the time came to seize California, he would lead his men to victory and take over the conquered state.

He would be willing to take the risk. She too was not only willing, but eager. History was on the march, and she wanted John to play an important role. Here was his chance; more accurately, since she was ambitious for him, here was their chance.

15

JESSIE WONDERED what she was supposed to do. What action had Secretary Bancroft meant for her to take?

She was not left long in doubt. The following morning Marine Lieutenant Archibald H. Gillespie came to the Benton home to announce that he was leaving for California on the warship *Cyane*. He was carrying dispatches from the president, the State Department, and the secretary of the navy. He understood that Captain Fremont would be in or near Monterey about the time he would reach the Pacific coast. Would Mrs. Fremont care to send a letter to Captain Fremont in his charge? He could assure her it would be delivered safely.

She sought out her father and quickly gave him the gist of what had happened, without repeating Secretary Bancroft's words. Did he think Captain Fremont justified in using force against the Mexican Army and the Californios? Was he convinced this action would be in the best interests of the United States? Was it a gamble she could advise her husband to take? She waited impatiently while Tom turned his thoughts over. When he finally spoke it was in a tone from which he had consciously removed all emotion.

"Our people have moved from the Atlantic coast westward, ever westward," he said. "The movement will grow a hundred times stronger and swifter in the next few years because of Captain Fremont's expeditions, reports and maps. There is nothing that can stop this flood of immigration to new and rich and free lands. Our people will overrun them in the next few years, and what happened in Texas is certain to happen all over the West, spontaneously, without any help or even any encouragement from our government."

"That's an interesting generality, Father," she insisted.

"My dear," said Senator Benton softly, "I am eager to instruct Captain Fremont to go ahead with the conquest of California. But I must also protect you. You understand what this entails, perhaps another year of separation . . ."

"I understand," she replied firmly.

She must give John the signal for action. Everything he had said to her before he left indicated that he was willing to take these risks; they had agreed that the main purpose of the expedition was for him to be on hand in the event of war so that he and his party could take over California. They had even arranged a code for confidential communication. There could be no reason for him to have changed his mind.

She seated herself at her desk, fondled the long quill of her pen, smoothed her hand over the cool surface of the foolscap. For whom was she doing this? For John, because it was what he most wanted to do regardless of the risk involved? For Tom, because it would fulfill his lifetime ambition? For herself, because she was ambitious as a woman and wanted important things to come to her through her husband: power, prestige, prominence?

It was impossible to separate their interests, but as John's dark face and eager eyes glowed back from the paper before her, she knew that she would be doing it for her husband, who would never cease to reproach her if she failed to send him the word; for her husband, whom she must encourage to seize every important opportunity. As a woman in love she could only urge him to come home; he had done the work that had been assigned to him; he could return to make his maps, write the third report which would open the highway to California. But as his wife she would not be faithful to their marriage if she did anything less than help him achieve the full potential of his opportunity.

As always when she had her full strength, the wife dominated the woman in her. The marriage was more important than her momentary happiness.

She wrote most of the night, telling her husband stories of Lily and of the family, of Eliza's coming marriage, of the dinner parties and the politics that had been discussed, all the things that a husband who has been away from home for half a year wants to hear. She spoke of her love for him and how much she missed him, how resolutely she was carrying on in the full confidence that his work would be well done.

Using their code of reference to things in their past, she gave him a picture of the official status of American and Mexican relations, picking her way carefully among the bones of fact, for her original promise to Secretary Buchanan had been that she would reveal nothing of a confidential nature which might impel her husband to action. Then she told him that when the time came he must act, that he must not feel limited by lack of official authorization. She gave no explanation for this sentiment, any more than she had given it two years before when she had sent with DeRosier the order, "Do not delay another day. Trust me, and start at once." She knew that her husband's answer would be the equivalent of, "I trust, and go."

Lieutenant Gillespie came for the letter early the next morning, assured her that he would tell Captain Fremont how well the family appeared. She watched him until he turned the corner of C Street and disappeared up Pennsylvania Avenue; then she knew the die was cast, that before many months Captain Fremont would be involved in action of far-reaching consequences.

Christmas passed quietly; she had decorated a tree in the upstairs sitting room for Lily. When there was an occasional hour of fatigue or shapeless anxiety she would peer into the mirror to see if her King George's Mark had returned, but could find no trace of it, and so she knew that her mind was at peace.

When news reached her it was sudden and dynamic. Picking up the morning edition of the *Union*, she learned that Captain Fremont had set himself up against the Mexican Army. The Mexicans had been suspicious of him and his party of sixty men, but they had given him temporary permission to remain in California. Toward the end of February Captain Fremont had broken camp and moved, not back to Oregon and American territory as he had promised, but south, deeper into Mexican country.

Within a couple of days a Mexican cavalry officer had dashed into Captain Fremont's camp with a dispatch from General Castro ordering the party out of California immediately, assuring them if they did not depart they would be arrested and forcibly expelled by the Mexican Army.

Captain Fremont had known that the Mexicans were within their legal rights, that actually he was an intruder on their soil. However, he had spent several months making friends with the Americans in California and sizing up the strength of the Mexican arms. He had come to the conclusion that if he accepted General Castro's order and departed hastily under the threat of expulsion, he would forfeit the respect and confidence of the Americans in California, all of whom would also have lost caste by his retreat.

Captain Fremont had decided that the historic moment had arrived. He moved his party to a natural fort on top of a peak overlooking the Santa Clara Valley; here he cut a tall slender tree and raised the first American flag in California. For three days he and his men had stood ready to defend their fort and their dignity. In the *Union* Jessie read her husband's letter to Consul Larkin:

From the heights where we are encamped, Hawk's Peak, we can see with the glass, troops mustering at St. John's. I would write you at length if I did not fear my letter would be intercepted. We have in no wise done wrong to any of the people, and if we are hemmed in and assaulted, we will die every man of us under the flag of his country.

She began to feel nervous spasms in her stomach as she read that toward evening of the second day a body of Mexican cavalry had come within a few hundred yards of the fort, that the Americans had waited in the thicket with their fingers on their triggers, ready to fire the first shots of the Mexican war. However, the Mexican cavalry had not attacked. At the end of the third day, convinced that they never would attack and confident that he had established his position and authority among the American settlers, Captain Fremont had withdrawn his party and moved slowly into Oregon.

The next morning when she went to Secretary Buchanan's office she found him looking harassed and pale.

"We should never have allowed Captain Fremont to go to the Pacific coast at such a delicate time," he said. "He has committed what amounts to a declaration of war on Mexico. He acted outside the pale of all legal and international rights. If his conduct starts a war with Mexico, he will have to take the full responsibility for it; he had no orders, no authorization . . . he has put the State Department in an embarrassing and painful position."

Jessie shriveled. All she could whisper faintly was, "Isn't it true that President Polk has ordered General Zachary Taylor into the disputed territory around Texas, that he is now only a few miles from the Rio Grande?"

"Yes, but . . ."

"I myself translated the dispatch for you which said that the Mexicans would consider this a declaration of war. The president's action is far more likely to begin the war with Mexico than Captain Fremont's resist-ance in California to what he called an insulting order."

"It is not Captain Fremont's prerogative to decide when the United States has been insulted. That is the privilege of the State Department!" He stopped abruptly, his round, doll-like eyes softened. "I am sorry, my dear Jessie: I did not mean to punish you for your husband's conduct; I know you are not responsible for what he does three thousand miles away. I think you will forgive me when I tell you that I am distraught, on the verge of resigning. I see war coming; everyone around me is doing his best to force this war on Mexico when I know it is a detestable thing to do and will create the first black blotch on American history. Thank you for coming. I shall communicate with you in a few days."

She walked over to Secretary Bancroft's office. Here she found an en-tirely different atmosphere, for Secretary Bancroft was delighted with the progress of events.

"Yes, yes, I read the *Union* article," he exclaimed. "I am glad Captain Fremont stood up to them. It was premature, it was indiscreet, and I assure you that I would not have had the courage to behave as he did without governmental orders in my pocket. Your husband is an impulsive man, Mrs. Fremont, perhaps even a little too impulsive; but it is a quality for which I greatly admire him. His three-day rebellion will teach the Mexicans that we are not in a docile frame of mind."

"Do you think that Captain Fremont's action will cause a war?"

"No, the war will start over Texas, and I am the one who must take the responsibility for that. If you want to know what the administration thinks about the California episode, I have just been informed that Presi-dent Polk has promoted your husband to the rank of lieutenant colonel."

News from the West began to reach her more frequently. She watched the conquest of California unfold day by day, fitting the pieces of the story together from the American newspapers, the Mexican newspapers, the confidential dispatches to Secretary Buchanan, and the information which came to Senator Benton as chairman of the Military Affairs Committee. Because she had access to these combined sources of information, and because she saw much of this material before anyone else, she knew that she was keeping closer to the conflict in California than anyone east of the Sierras. This gave her a sense of being by her husband's side day by day.

Encouraged by Colonel Fremont, who was working behind the scenes, on June 14, 1846, the Americans in California staged the Bear Flag uprising and declared California a republic. When the settlers had their first battle with the Mexicans at San Raphael, Colonel Fremont stepped into command, but not before he had written out his resignation from the Army and dispatched it to Senator Benton to be published in the event his action embarrassed the government. He then captured San Francisco on July 4, formed the California Battalion of some three hundred men and, upon learning that war with Mexico had been declared some two months before, that fighting was going on in Texas and Mexico, seized all of central California. On July 10 Commodore Sloat of the United States Navy occupied Monterey, and Colonel Fremont moved his battalion in. Commodore Stockton, replacing the irresolute Commodore Sloat, swore Lieutenant Colonel Fremont and his battalion into the Navy and transported them to San Diego in the *Cyane*. From San Diego Colonel Fremont moved his men north toward Los Angeles, where a Mexican division was reported to be encamped, and rejoined Commodore Stockton near San Pedro. On August 13 they occupied Los Angeles without firing a shot or without encountering the Mexican Army. Stockton sent Colonel Fremont north to recruit another battalion and to command northern California. During his absence the Mexican Army defeated the small American garrison and recaptured Los Angeles.

There were several uneasy weeks while the Americans continued to be defeated in southern California, but Jessie was encouraged by the fact that John had been able to organize a strong army which was marching south, and that their old friend Colonel, now Brigadier General, Stephen Watts Kearny had left Santa Fe with three hundred volunteers, en route for southern California. By January 9, 1847, the Americans had once again taken Los Angeles. Colonel Fremont accepted the surrender of the Mexican general Pico, gave him generous terms, and the war was over in California.

Now assured of her husband's safety, Jessie was further delighted to learn that Commodore Stockton had named Colonel Fremont the first civil governor of California. Reports began to come through in the press of the generosity and efficiency of his rule, and everywhere people spoke with enthusiasm of the young colonel who was doing such a good job. From the notes and drawings which John had sent east after reaching California, cartographer Preuss had drawn a superb map of the compara-

tively safe route to California which he had just established. When Senator Benton presented the map to the Senate, he delivered a eulogy on
Colonel Fremont which made Jessie, sitting in her accustomed seat in
the gallery, swell with pride.

In the middle of February, some twenty-one months after John had
left Washington, she wrote a letter to her cousin Sarah Brant. In it she
tried to explain the innumerable devices, fill-ins and fortitudes which she
had used to somehow pass the time, explaining also the sense of being
only fractionally alive when one cannot hear the voice of a loved one,
touch his hand, see a look of understanding flash into his eyes. She ended
on a cheerful note which looked toward the future:

*I feel that the honor to Colonel Fremont is but honor due for the ardu-
ous labors he has performed and for his conspicuous bravery, and it is
little enough reward for his incalculable scientific contributions to his
country. It is difficult, indeed, dear cousin, for me to express my own
happiness. Its warmth and light have driven all the chill and dark fore-
boding from my heart. My happiness gives me renewed strength and
patience.*

Exactly a week later, when she was working at her desk in her sitting
room, Josheem brought in a page from the State Department with a
packet of Spanish letters.

"If you will return at five this afternoon," she told the page, "I will
have the material ready for you."

She was skimming a long letter from Monterey which dealt largely
with land grants when she suddenly sat bolt upright in her chair. The
letter told of a quarrel which had arisen between Commodore Stockton
of the Navy and General Kearny of the Army over the command and
control of California. The letter ended with a sentence which the writer
included as of only mild interest:

"Colonel Fremont has been removed as commandant of California."

16

SHE WAITED WITH IMPATIENCE until Senator Benton returned at four
o'clock. She expected that when she read the translation to him he would
be as dumbfounded as she had been. Instead she saw her father flush, his
eyes become watery. In a terrifying moment she thought, He knows
about this; then it must be worse than it appears in this dispatch.

After a moment he said, "I heard of it in St. Louis when I was there
last month."

"Why didn't you tell me?"

"I had hoped the trouble would blow over, Jessie. I had hoped that it was just a passing quarrel between General Kearny and Commodore Stockton."

"Has it blown over?"

"No."

She began pacing the room nervously.

"But what could possibly have happened? According to the reports John was doing a good job as governor. Why did they suddenly become dissatisfied?"

"It was not a question of his performance; your husband got himself caught in a contest between the Army and Navy for authority over California. Commodore Stockton had orders to take and hold California and to set up a civil administration. When the Mexicans surrendered, Commodore Stockton appointed Colonel Fremont as the governor. But General Kearny also had orders from Washington to assume the governorship of California, should he conquer and take possession of the country."

"But wouldn't Commodore Stockton's orders be considered the valid ones, since the fighting was practically over by the time General Kearny got there?"

"Kearny fought one battle, a battle which he lost, by the way. However, the problem revolves about the question of who had the latest orders from Washington, Kearny or Stockton."

"Who did?"

"We're not certain yet. In any event, General Kearny demanded that Colonel Fremont acknowledge him to be the commander in chief of California. John and his men were still serving under Stockton as part of the Navy, and so he declined to acknowledge Kearny's authority. Kearny then moved his headquarters to Monterey, where he set up a civil government and declared Colonel Fremont to be deposed as governor, with no further authority."

"Why can't President Polk put an end to this squabble?" she asked with a heavy heart. "The Army and Navy belong to the same government, don't they?"

Once again her father's manner was evasive. He had been honest with his daughter for so many years that he found the transition difficult.

"I have already spoken to the president."

"Yes?"

"He wants the men in California to settle this dispute among themselves."

"Do you think they will?"

"There is certainly nothing in the argument that can't be settled."

Her peace shattered, Jessie impatiently edged through the weeks that followed, waiting for some word of how her husband was faring in the conflict. Her only momentary diversion was Eliza's marriage; Eliza had been so helpful during her own troubled courtship that she was happy to be able to stage a beautiful wedding for her older sister in the drawing room of the Benton home. Eliza wanted the affair to be a quiet one, but before the imperative lists were completed Jessie saw that she must of necessity invite some two hundred people. The dinner which followed the ceremony was elaborate, for Jessie tried to duplicate for her sister the magnificent wedding dinner served at Cherry Grove. The preparations, the excitement, the visits to the dressmaker, the planning of the ceremony and dinner occupied her time for almost three weeks; she was glad to be so exhausted by the end of the day that she could fall into a troubled sleep.

She saw her sister and new brother-in-law off for a trip to New York, then bade good-by to her father, who was going to St. Louis on political business. At the front door he said to her:

"Be of good courage, and take care of your health."

"I'll do my best, Father, but it is this groping in the dark that has upset me. If only I could know what is going on out there . . ."

Thomas Benton had a saying that good news travels on the swiftest horse, but bad news rides the lightning. Jessie had not long to wait before the almost comfortable silence surrounding the events in California was split open. Her cousin Sarah sent her an anonymous letter published in the St. Louis *Republican* which mercilessly flayed Colonel Fremont for the part he had played in the conquest of California, challenged his motives, his character and his conduct, accused him of dictatorial methods, willful insubordination, usurpation of authority, and conduct detrimental to the welfare of the Army.

This then was what George Bancroft had intimated; the Army was in process of disavowing Colonel Fremont! John had waged war successfully and conquered central California . . . but without authorization.

The following day a similar clipping arrived from a friend who had cut it from the New York *Courier and Enquirer.* When practically the identical article arrived from the New Orleans *Picayune,* it became obvious to her that the indictments all had been written by the same hand. She now knew that the quarrel had not been settled in California, that affairs were growing worse. She sat down to write a letter to her father telling him what was contained in the articles, when Maylee knocked sharply on her sitting-room door and said:

"A packet just come from the colonel, Miss Jessie."

Without rising, she held out her hand for the letter, tore it open and was plunged into the reading before Maylee could close the door behind her. An enclosed dispatch to President Polk fell to the floor while she quickly scanned the opening paragraphs of affection, her eyes racing ahead to get to John's statement of his trouble, his assurance that every· thing was working out well. He warned her to be prepared for a severe attack in the eastern papers, for Lieutenant Emory, General Kearny's dispatch bearer to Washington, had left for the capital, and it was being rumored in California that he had been sent to undermine John's position.

She sat reading his description of how California had been in American hands before General Kearny arrived on the scene; during the final battles with the Mexicans, General Kearny had acknowledged that Commodore Stockton was commander of all American forces in California. However, after John had signed the peace treaty with General Pico at Cahuenga Rancho, and Commodore Stockton had set him up as governor of California, General Kearny had established his own headquarters on the Plaza in Los Angeles, proclaimed himself commander of all forces in California, ordered both Commodore Stockton and John to step down, to issue no more orders or appointments without his sanction. Commodore Stockton refused to accept General Kearny's authority; John also refused to be deposed. He had gone to General Kearny's headquarters the next morning to tell him that until the Army and Navy had adjusted their difficulties in California, and the supreme authority had been established by word from Washington, he would take his orders from Commodore Stockton and retain his position as governor of California. The scene had been a bitter and violent one. General Kearny had then moved his troops to Monterey. John was still governor in southern California, but there was no one to sustain his authority.

She did not close her eyes all night, but lay awake in the candlelight reading and rereading the letter from John, almost memorizing the words of love. In her mind she formulated the best method of approach to President Polk; perhaps from him she could get a written authorization for Colonel Fremont to remain as governor of California.

Visitors were not permitted at the White House until one o'clock, so she had ample time in which to make the most meticulous toilet. She donned a green cashmere gown, spent a long while brushing her hair, and on top of it, at a saucy angle, she perked a green corded hat.

President Polk received her promptly at one o'clock with assurances of his pleasure in seeing her. He broke the seal on Colonel Fremont's dispatch and read it quickly. As Jessie saw him lift his eyes from the last word, she asked with a rush of emotion:

"Mr. President, doesn't Colonel Fremont's course seem reasonable under the circumstances?"

There was no doubt in her mind that he would reply at once, "Entirely reasonable, Mrs. Fremont; I shall send a dispatch which will clear up the situation and leave Colonel Fremont in command as civil governor."

But no word came from President Polk. He dropped into a chair, glanced at the letter again and then looked up at her with a noncommittal expression.

"The misunderstanding may be settled by now, Miss Jessie. In that case, there would be no need for any of us to take sides."

She saw that the President had terminated the interview. A feeling of frustration arose, then a calm seized her.

"Mr. President, I do not expect you to side against General Kearny. I only beg you to assure me that Colonel Fremont will not be victimized by the quarrel between the Army and Navy. General Kearny is threatening to relieve him of command of his California Battalion."

"Miss Jessie, I think we can do that much to put your mind at ease," replied the president, slowly. "I will send a dispatch giving Colonel Fremont the right to remain on duty in California or to join his original regiment of mounted rifles in Mexico if he prefers."

"Thank you, Mr. President. That is the fair and equitable thing to do."

President Polk smiled slightly at the thought of Jessie assuring the President of the United States that he was doing the fair and equitable thing. He then shook her hand, sent his compliments to her father and walked with her to the door of the reception room.

17

THERE WAS LITTLE she could do now but sit back and wait. A few days later her father returned from St. Louis and asked her to take a walk with him along the Potomac.

"I am sorry that I must be the one to break this to you, Jessie, yet as your father I suppose it is best. Things in California have come to a most unfortunate pass."

Jessie stopped. She turned to confront her father, who loomed big before her. Even in her anxiety she had time to notice how old he was looking: his thinning hair was completely silver, his eyes had a tired and commiserating expression, the flesh wrinkles at the bridge of his nose seemed tightly lined.

"General Kearny ordered John to bring his archives from Los Angeles to Monterey. Colonel Fremont took a wild horseback ride up to Monterey where a most unfortunate scene took place. General Kearny revealed the latest order giving him command, and Colonel Fremont went back to Los Angeles, followed by several of Kearny's officers, all of them antagonistic to your husband. There were quarrels and recriminations until finally . . ."

"Yes?"

One corner of Tom Benton's mouth fell loose, as it always did when he labored under heavy personal emotion.

"Colonel Fremont has been relieved of his command. He was ordered back to Washington."

A thin smile came over her tired face.

"Then he is coming home! At least I shall see him again. We will be able to work this out together, all of us."

Her father took her arm and began walking along the riverbank. Jessie tried to watch his eyes, but he was turned so she could not see him too closely.

". . . you don't understand, my dear: Colonel Fremont . . . is coming back to Washington . . . under arrest."

Jessie got home as quickly as possible, refused dinner and went straight to bed, lying as still and lifeless as a corpse. John coming home under arrest! After all his accomplishments, after all the magnificent promise for the future, he was being dragged across the continent like a prisoner, in disgrace!

George Bancroft had intimated that if the capture of California were successful, anything her husband might have been required to do would be forgotten. California was in American hands, war had been waged officially with Mexico, and there had been no international scandal. Then why were they visiting upon him the punishment which had been promised only if he failed and embarrassed his government?

She began to thrash about in the bed, turning, twisting, matching with her movements the turnings and twistings of her mind as she sought some way out of the hopeless trap. Why had John quarreled with General Kearny? Was it because he had started the war in California without authorization? Or was there something more personal involved? She pulled the covers up over her head and burst into weeping, giving vent to all of the fears and misgivings of the past months, months during which she had maintained her self-control with an iron discipline.

Suddenly she found herself picked up, the blanket over her head, and miraculously was sitting on her father's lap.

"Here, drink this," he said. "It is warm milk and rum. Do you know what time it is, child? Two in the morning. I went down into the kitchen and warmed the milk; drink this now. It will put you to sleep."

"And may I ask what you were doing until two in the morning?"

"You may ask. I was writing a stiff letter to President Polk, summarizing the case and demanding an investigation. I assure you there is nothing to worry about, Jessie. We will bring all the facts to the light, and when we have done so, Colonel Fremont will be vindicated."

"Thank you, Father. This warm milk and rum has made me drowsy. I think I can fall asleep now."

She spent the intervening weeks, before John could reach Washington, in a state of suspension, giving in neither to despair nor sanguinary hope. She knew that she and her husband faced a difficult time. She knew that they could not come out of the contest unscathed. She knew that the coming months would demand the most of their faith in themselves and their loyalty to each other.

At the end of August the long vigil was ended. She was sitting in the bow of the drawing-room windows watching out over C Street when she saw a carriage turn Pennsylvania Avenue on two wheels and dash up to the Benton home. Out sprang a young man in a faded blue army uniform. He turned and spoke to the driver about his luggage, giving Jessie time to run through the hall, fling open the door, and welcome home her husband after two years and three months of absence. Unashamedly in the open doorway she clung to him, wet his beard with her tears, kissing him many, many times.

But even at this first numb moment of joy she perceived that her husband was not responding. She took his hand and led him to the drawing room, then stood gazing at him. Her heart sank: this was only the shell of the man whom she had sent forth with such high hopes more than two years before. It was not merely that he was cadaverously thin, his hair long and unkempt; his eyes were those of a stranger, of a man desperately ill. The John Fremont she had sent away on his third expedition was a man of charm, of grace and poise, a man who knew his world and not only loved it but commanded it. This gray-haired and sunken-cheeked person before her stood awkwardly, his arms not seeming to fit into their sockets, his torso twisted at an ugly angle, his legs slumped within the discolored trousers, his face at war with itself, the mouth taut, awry, the features twisted. It was difficult to remember that this was the indestructible body and spirit that had forced a passage in the winter-locked Sierras where no other man could have survived; that this was the powerful yet quiet and graceful one who was beloved by Kit Carson and the frontiersmen of America.

For this man who stood before her was no leader, no strong one; this was a man profoundly hurt, caught at his most vulnerable spot, disorganized, frightened, unbeautiful and ineffective. His skin, his manner, his whole expression was bleak. Jessie remembered the night when John Fremont had put himself through the agony of revealing his illegitimacy to the woman he loved. Then, too, he had been awkward and disjointed. She could tell by every discordant line and knot of him that he felt humiliated, defeated. Above all, he was angrily and bitterly ashamed.

She brought him a drink, ran her fingers through his long, shaggy hair, smoothed the whorls of black beard with the gentlest touch of her finger-tips; she kissed the bloodless lips and then buried her head on his shoulder and lay quietly.

She did not let him see that she was alarmed. Her task was to bring him back to himself, to revive his courage, his faith. It was a moment in their marriage that she must handle with sensitivity and tenderness; if she succeeded now she could serve at his side to the end of his days. What happened later was of little importance: he must be made whole and well again. If she could do that they could triumph over their difficulties.

She sensed that he was frightened of her reception, afraid that she might censure or condemn him, believe him to have been hotheaded, blundering, stupid. She knew that this would have been the worst blow of all to him, and from his withdrawal, his refusal to come to her, she saw that he had already built up his defenses of cynicism and indifference.

There had been no word from him, or any caress; he had not told her how happy he was to see her or how much he loved her. He was too bitterly unhappy to think in such terms.

"Why has General Kearny done this to us?" she asked. "What is the meaning behind it all?"

John did not reply to her question, but began talking disjointedly.

". . . refused to let me join my regiment in Mexico . . . didn't let me get my notes or journals in San Francisco . . . any of my scientific instruments or specimens that I collected for two years . . . had plans to arrest me for six months, but didn't give me five minutes' warning . . . made me trail behind him across the Sierras and Rockies like a servile Indian or a common criminal . . . heaped indignities . . . degraded me in front of my own men . . . deprived me of the privileges of my rank . . ."

"But now that you are back in Washington, what does General Kearny plan to do?"

John bolted to his feet and thrust his head upward belligerently.

"Court-martial."

"Court-martial! But on what charge?"

"Mutiny!"

Her breathing stopped. Her mind flashed back to the scene with Colonel Kearny four years before. At last her chickens had come home to roost. This court-martial was the logical culmination of the long line of events that had transpired since that fateful moment in St. Louis when she had torn open an order from the War Department and concealed it in her sewing basket.

BOOK THREE

Court-Martial

SHE DID NOT WANT ANYONE to see her husband while he was in his present condition, yet there were few places they could go where Colonel Fremont would not be recognized. She thought of Francis Preston Blair's estate, Silver Spring, which lay just outside the District of Columbia, but she had no desire to go there if the Blair family were present. While John was resting she sent Josheem by horseback to Silver Spring with a note. He returned later that evening with a letter from Mr. Blair saying that by a happy coincidence he and his family were leaving for St. Louis the following day, and he would be delighted to have her spend as much time at Silver Spring as she liked.

She now had the more difficult task of convincing her husband that for a short time at least he should step outside the arena, let the battle wait. She could tell by his every nervous gesture and intonation that he was spoiling for a fight; she also knew him well enough to realize that he would be least effective if he ventured forth now.

After a quiet dinner in their apartment she waited for a suitable moment and then said:

"Darling, the good book of matrimony preaches that when a husband and wife have been separated for twenty-seven months, they have a right to demand a honeymoon."

He was not amused by her oblique approach. He looked up sternly, muttering:

"Honeymoon! At a time like this? How can you even think, Jessie . . . We have a whole case to prepare . . ."

"I'm looking forward to working with you, John, but please, not just yet. Doesn't love have any rights?"

"There is a time for love, and there is a time for . . ."

"Why aren't you entitled to a couple of weeks' vacation after you have been in harness for two and a half years? Even the government wouldn't begrudge you that, hardhearted as it may be. You're so tired and worn, sweetheart; two weeks of rest and you would feel like a different man."

"I don't want to feel like a different man, I'm satisfied with the old one. Besides, I'm not tired and I'm not worn, I'm just determined to . . ."

She rested her head on her arms.

"Very well, if you insist on my telling the truth: I'm the one who is worn. I was brave when you came home from the other expeditions. I didn't cry on your shoulder or fill your ears with how much I had suffered or how tired I was. Now did I?"

"No, you've always been brave."

"But I don't feel brave right this moment. I feel exhausted after the long months of waiting for you. By the Eternal, if I don't have you to myself for a few days I just can't face the long ordeal. I know that it's weak of me, and that I shouldn't add my burdens to yours . . ."

His expression lightened.

"But what do you propose? Where could we go?"

"Francis Preston Blair has offered us refuge at Silver Spring. We won't tell anyone where we are going, and we'll have complete seclusion. It will be wonderful to become acquainted all over again."

Since Josheem had carried the note to Silver Spring the day before, they let him drive them in the carriage the next morning, warning him that he was to tell no one where he had been.

They rode through rows of tall pines, chestnuts and oaks, then crossed a stone bridge and drew up on a triangular roadway before a rambling house with a wide front porch. The servant who carried in their bags and made them comfortable in the guest suite assured them that they would have privacy.

Jessie did not wait for their suitcases to be unpacked but urged John to take her for a long walk through the estate. Francis Preston Blair had supported Van Buren for the presidency, arriving in Washington in 1836 with a family of three sons and a daughter. He founded the *Globe,* which became one of the outstanding newspapers in the country, rapidly becoming rich on its proceeds and on the benefits of governmental printing contracts. With his first affluence he had bought the wooded acres of Silver Spring.

Jessie and her husband walked past the Acorn summerhouse and vegetable gardens, turned down the Lovers' Walk which followed the stream almost to the Potomac, then entered the forest where the hot August sun was blocked out. They relaxed in the cool green darkness. They walked for almost three hours, resting frequently in the bowers and grottoes which Francis Blair had built along his many gravel-lined trails.

Determined as she was not to think about their troubles until she had nursed her husband back to balance, there was a complication she could not drive out of her mind; the War Department had decreed that the trial must be held at Fortress Monroe, an island off the coast of Virginia. John would be held almost incommunicado; it would be difficult to find a lawyer who would be able to isolate himself on the island for several months; in all likelihood the proceedings would be secret, and newspapermen barred from the fortress; there would be no way for the Fremonts to present their case to the public. Tom Benton was working with all his might to get the trial transferred to Washington. Time enough to tell her husband about Fortress Monroe, from which even she would be excluded, if the senator's efforts failed. When Josheem brought a letter from her father she scanned it eagerly for news of the removal of the trial to Washington, but there was none.

I have a full view of the whole case, Kearny's as well as yours, and I am perfectly at ease. Your husband will be justified and exalted; his persecutors will be covered with shame and confusion. The process through which the colonel has gone is bitter; but it will have its sweet. You both will realize the truth of what Lord Palmerston said to Van Buren when he was rejected by the Senate: "It is an advantage to a public man to be, in the course of his life, the subject of an outrage."

They had complete quiet, yet Jessie perceived that the beauty of Silver Spring, its air of seclusion and peacefulness, was lost upon John. His spirit was in turmoil and he did not know where he was. She talked to him quietly, trying to analyze not the case itself nor the troubles in California, but his feeling about them; for she had to know what he was thinking in order to work with him. He was torn by humiliation and rage, but above all she saw that his attitude was dominated by the idea that he was being persecuted.

"They never wanted me," he muttered. "They were after me all the time, that West Point clique. They were just waiting for the best hour to strike. They let me get so far, and only so far, and then they conspired to knock me down. I told you before we were married that they would never give me any permanent peace, but only a truce. I signed more than half a million dollars' worth of notes in California for horses and supplies, but General Kearny laughed at the people who trusted my signature, told them my notes were practically worthless. It is a conspiracy to keep me from returning to California. We'll never be able to live on that beautiful Santa Cruz ranch I bought with our savings."

While he recounted the indignities that had been heaped upon him she slowly understood that these slights had come to have more importance for him than the basic dispute in California. When she saw how ill he was in his mind she cried to herself, What have they done to him? How am I going to save him from them and from himself? How can I bring him back to health so that no matter what the outcome of the court-martial he will be strong and resolute in the face of it?

She thought shrewdly that everything that happens in a marriage, both for good and evil, is not only implicit but actually revealed in the court-ship. There were no surprises in marriage, only the working out of every-thing one has dimly perceived during the process of becoming acquainted. If she had stopped to analyze things then she could have predicted not only the nature of her happiness but the outlines of her troubles as well.

She approached the rebuilding of her husband scientifically. She had never had any intention of being an amateur wife, for she had little en-joyment of amateur talent; she had meant to be a professional wife; one who used the same degree of skill as any serious practitioner of an art or science. Her problems up to this moment had been comparatively simple: to sustain herself while her husband was on his long voyages; to protect his interests in Washington while he was away; to help him turn out the reports which were so important in spreading knowledge of his work and of the West. The serious element now was the one that lay submerged and ever ready to spring: his obsession with his own illegitimacy and the danger it created because of the sense of insecurity it bred within him.

She spent sleepless hours during the long nights wondering what method she could best use to elicit the full story from him without causing a continuous uproar or protracting his bitterness as he relived the events. They were nerve-racking days, for no word or gesture could be accidental, spontaneous. Each step had to be planned, integrated, tested; any slip could tear down hours of work. She needed art in handling the situation, all the art that ever a wife needed, all the accumulated skill that wives the world over have needed to help their husbands. If the task seemed difficult, exhausting, she knew that it was not unselfishness on her part, but intelligent self-interest. Everything that happened to John must of necessity happen to her; when two people marry they cease to be purely themselves but step into a new and expanded character, the character of their marriage. It was not possible for either of them to do a misguided act without injuring the creation, the third being, which resulted from their having put their lives together: the child that was born of the mating of their temperaments before any child could be born of the mating of their loins.

It was too early for her to think logically about the facts; she went along with John emotionally, agreeing with his attitudes, accepting what he said as the truth, asking only those questions which would lead to the further sustaining of his position, using no method of analysis with which to achieve perspective. For she conceived it to be her function not to earn an acquittal of the charges, but to put her husband in a frame of mind to acquit himself to advantage in the courtroom, to appear at his best before the nation during the trial. For herself, she had not time yet to decide whether she was to believe only what he told her, or to hold her sympathies for her husband while keeping her mind open. What had been done in California had been done; although the action there could be interpreted in different ways, none of it could be changed. For the moment she could do a better job as a wife, acting as a complete partisan on her husband's side. As a wife she could only influence the result by working to keep her husband balanced, his poise unshatterable, his attitude toward the proceedings respectful but penetrating; later perhaps she could be the strategist seeking to set up the best possible case for her client.

In her sympathy for the man she loved she could not do otherwise.

She used every art and guile known to the heart of woman to nurse him to health. As they rode Francis Blair's spirited horses through the forests she challenged him to race with her, complimented him on how beautifully he sat the horse. Sitting before the warmth and bright red flames of the fireplace she played up the hours and episodes he had enjoyed most in their years together, in which he had appeared to the best advantage, filled him with her pride in his accomplishments. She showed him the accumulation of honors that had come to him while he was away: the Founder's Medal of the National Geographical Society of London, the gold medal from Baron Humboldt, awarded by the Prussian government for his contribution to science: read him articles from such magazines as the *Southern Literary Messenger*, the *Electric Review* and the *Democratic Review*, in which it was declared that the name of John Fremont was immortalized, that his accomplishments were greater than those of Lewis and Clark, that he should be compensated as they had, with large land grants and double pay. She turned the pages of her scrapbook in which she had pasted the stories of his achievements from the newspapers and magazines of Britain and Europe. She concurred with his motives even when she was not able to follow his reasoning. She played the temptress, wearing her loveliest gowns, using her most delicate perfumes, shamelessly arousing his sexual love for her, the love that always had been such a strong and potent force between them.

There were moments when she thought she was making headway, when a flash of humor would illuminate his remarks, but these successes were momentary and all too soon he slipped back into the pattern of his illness: his overstatement of his own importance, his conviction that everything he had done was right, that he couldn't possibly have made even one mistake during the harrowing circumstances; his lack of sympathy or tolerance for his opponents while decrying their lack of sympathy and tolerance for him; his discounting of his own impetuousness, his irritability with restraint, his tendency to act on his own.

When everything looked hopeless because, no matter how subtly she tried, she could not set his perspective straight, she indulged in a melodramatic scene in which she wept bitterly, showed herself to be weak and frightened. She did not have to pretend, for deep in her heart she felt weak and frightened.

Ashamed at last, realizing something of the agony he was putting her through, he wrapped his arms around her, kissed her tears upward along her cheeks, drying his lips in the hair of her temples.

"Don't cry, dear," he murmured, "it's not that bad. We'll work it out, we'll defeat them, now don't you worry about it."

One evening toward the end of the second week, knowing that they had only a few more hours on what she called their happy island surrounded by a sea of troubles, they had the horses saddled and rode over to Miss English's Academy. It was a full moonlit night, the countryside bathed in a white and powdery fluorescence. They tied the horses to the mulberry tree and stood holding hands while they gazed up at her window.

"Do you remember how you hid your first letter in the wash basket?"

"I remember."

"What would you have done if Mammy hadn't come along at just the right moment with that bundle of wash?"

"I would have wrapped the note around a rock and thrown it through your window. I was an irrepressible youth, Miss Jessie; I should have pursued you and thrown rocks through your window until you were eighty."

"How nice. Just think of all the time I was smart enough not to waste. Do you think you could climb up this mulberry tree without tearing your lovely breeches?"

Without waiting for an answer she pulled herself up into the tree, climbed quickly among the familiar branches and then sat in the nook where she and John had first talked. It was only an instant before she saw his head appear between the branches. The moonlight on his hair made it seem silvery; instead of being projected back to their first meeting, she saw how he would look thirty years hence when his hair and beard would be white. He pulled himself up and sat beside her.

"I have had exciting news this morning, Lieutenant Fremont: my roommate Harriet Williams is going to be married to Count Bodisco. Would you come to the wedding?"

"I'm not likely to receive an invitation."

"I was just writing to Harriet when your note arrived in the wash basket. I'll ask Harriet to have the count send you an invitation. Do you like to dance, Lieutenant Fremont?"

He put his arm about her and lifted her half out of the juncture of the limbs, until she was lying against his chest, her cheek on his, the corners of their mouths touching.

"Ah, Jessie," he whispered, "a good marriage is truly a miracle."

2

ON THE DAY her father was due back from St. Louis, Jessie donned one of her new house gowns which she wore high at the throat, finished with a small flat collar of lace, and went down to the drawing room to await his arrival. The hours passed and Senator Benton did not come home. Finally she saw him striding down C Street from Pennsylvania Avenue, his big frame swinging along quickly and confidently. She could tell by his manner that he bore good tidings. The first thing he said as he gave her a bearlike hug was:

"I've been to the War Department. The trial has been transferred to the Arsenal Building in Washington. I showed them what the public would think if they dragged a man all the way from the Pacific Ocean to a secret trial in the Atlantic Ocean. Now I'll be able to attend the trial myself."

A surge of relief swept over her. She kissed her father's cheek, commented on the fact that he needed a shave, and then said, "So far so good. Now there's just one more thing we need to do."

"What is that?"

"Have the court-martial stopped altogether. Colonel Fremont was acting under secret orders from President Polk: why else should Captain Montgomery of the S.S. *Portsmouth* have provided him with money, munitions and medical supplies to start the war in California, and Consuls Larkin and Leidesdorff help him to organize the campaign? If the president can't reveal these secret orders, then at least let him tell everybody involved to let bygones be bygones."

"No, no, Jessie," cried Tom Benton. "It's too late now to try to hush up the affair. Too many of General Kearny's officers have been writing articles in the newspapers attacking John. If we withdraw, everyone will say we're guilty. We want this court-martial; the best way to prove the colonel's innocence and justify him is a public trial here in Washington. We'll use it as an open forum to tell the whole world of his accomplishments. You will see, Jessie, he will emerge as a greater man than ever. The administration will back us . . ."

"Even if he were to win," she replied quietly, "I still wouldn't think it was the wise thing to do. Father, won't you go to President Polk and ask him to call off the trial?"

Her father looked at her long and hard, then replied: "I can't do that, Jessie, but if your husband wants to, that is another affair. From all Colonel Fremont has said, I don't think anything in the world could keep him from fighting this case in the open."

"I might be able to persuade him," she replied. "Is there no one who can intercede to stop this court-martial without anybody losing face?"

"Yes, General Kearny. He is the only one. If he would withdraw his charges . . ."

"Then if you'll excuse me, Father, I will dress at once and go to see him. Somebody must stop this dreadful quarrel."

She walked to the office which General Kearny occupied in the War Department on his trips to Washington, feeling as gray and barren as the grayish cubicle into which she entered. One look at the general's ill and aging face showed her that he too was suffering deeply. He rose from his chair, stiffly, no sign of recognition or friendliness coming over his sand-worn face, the eyes small and dull. She closed the door behind her and leaned against the hand which still gripped the knob.

"General Kearny, no matter what has happened or will happen, I want you to know that I regret this entire affair bitterly."

He made no reply; she felt that he was probing her intent and would make no move until he was sure of its nature.

"There have been mistakes made," she continued in a tight tone. "I have come to ask you not to multiply those errors into misfortunes for all of us."

After a painful pause he spoke:

"Then you can see that Colonel Fremont made serious mistakes."

"I grant that, General. The only ones who don't make mistakes in life are those who do nothing."

"Am I to understand that Colonel Fremont is prepared to make public apologies?"

Jessie flinched. She made her way uncertainly to a hard wooden chair, sat on its very edge. "I don't know, General Kearny; I am here without his knowledge."

"Then why did you come?"

"To ask you to put an end to this conflict. Nothing can come of it but grief for all of us."

"There will be no grief for me, Miss Jessie: I am the commanding officer whose orders have been thwarted. Your husband caused me untold difficulty in California. Now it is his turn to suffer."

She rose from the sharp edge of the chair, went close to him.

"He has already suffered; more than you could possibly imagine. This court-martial will be tragic for him, but it will be equally tragic for you and everyone concerned."

"There you are wrong; I have nothing to conceal; no discredit can possibly fall upon me."

"Please forgive me, General, if I am so presumptuous as to contradict you: I know the nature of the charges that will be hurled, both by you against my husband and by my husband against you."

In spite of her sincerity, General Kearny was offended.

"If you are so sure he is right and I am wrong, then why have you come to me?"

"Because I am convinced that in a case like this, even though everybody may be right and nobody wrong, everyone must lose and no one can win."

"Have you seen the case against Colonel Fremont? Do you know how completely we can crush him? Or have you been listening only to your husband's version?"

"I have been listening to my husband's version; I am prejudiced in his favor, but that prejudice has not blinded me. I know how right you were, and—forgive me—how wrong, no, not wrong, but intolerant you were. I also know how wrong Colonel Fremont was; no, not wrong, but rash and impetuous. But he is a younger man; because of your friendship for our family you could have been like a father to him. Senator Benton and I could have expected that much of you."

"My obligations to the Army come first, Mrs. Fremont. We play no favorites and allow no infractions for the sake of friendship."

"But surely you are exaggerating the importance of Colonel Fremont and his conduct."

"I know your father is outraged with me, Miss Jessie; and please believe that I have loved you almost like a daughter. I am deeply regretful of the pain I must inflict on you. But Colonel Fremont insulted me in the presence of other officers; he refused to obey my orders and quarreled with my representatives. Mutiny is a habit of mind with Colonel Fremont. If I let this mutiny go by I will so have undermined my position that I will never again be able to command. I owe it to myself and my long career to punish this conduct. Colonel Fremont must not be allowed to get away with this second mutiny successfully, or he will establish a precedent which will injure the morale of the Army."

"Second mutiny? What was the first . . . ?"

"When he left Kaw's Landing after having received the order to report back to Washington."

Jessie paled, began to feel faint.

"But that was my doing, General Kearny. My husband never knew that order had been sent out, not until I told him about it upon his return."

"Forgive me for being brutal," replied General Kearny with the devastating plainness of a sandstorm sweeping across the desert, "but I don't believe you. I think he is the one who received the order and arranged this scheme with you to avoid its implications."

She stumbled back onto her chair.

"How can you say that to me, when you have been a friend of the Benton family for forty years? When you have known me since the day I was born?"

"That is the very reason I say it. The Bentons have always been passionate partisans, putting the cause above the truth. I know that you would lie to defend your husband, Jessie: I know there is nothing in the world you wouldn't do to protect him. I don't speak critically when I say that you lie; it is a kind of compliment; every man's wife should lie to protect her husband. But that is no reason for me to be deceived. Your husband is a confirmed mutineer. The sooner we get him out of the Army, the better."

"Very well, then," said Jessie, hardly recognizing the metallic tone of the voice she somehow managed to project. "I am a liar and my husband is a congenital mutineer. Even so, must all the world hear our charges and countercharges? It will hurt the administration, it will hurt our government, it will hurt our army."

"I shall insist upon the court-martial," he replied hoarsely, "because I will allow no one to do this to me at the end of my career."

"Then I can answer with equal truth that you must not do this to yourself at the end of your long career! The bitterness of the trial, the accusations will make you enemies and obscure what you have done for your country."

"I will take my chances," he replied. "I would consider myself derelict in duty if I failed to prosecute this case."

There was an awkward silence. Finally Jessie pleaded, "Why must you revenge yourself on him because of me? I was responsible for Colonel Fremont's leaving with your cannon, against orders. If not for that trouble you would never have thought of him as a mutineer. You would have been more patient and kindly with him in California, forgiven his brashness and concealed his refusal to obey. But because of what I did in St. Louis you were already set in your mind to think of him as rebellious. I am the one who is responsible for your state of mind. And if my husband is retired from the Army in disgrace it will be my fault. Would you make me responsible for destroying my own husband? I cannot believe that of you. Submit your report to the War Department; let the War Department take whatever disciplinary action it sees fit; but don't make this a matter of public scandal. Give me time to reason with Colonel Fremont and I promise that sooner or later he will see what mistakes he made and will come to you with his apologies."

General Kearny turned from her and stared unseeing at the blank gray wall. When he turned back his eyes were as blank and gray as the walls at which he had been looking.

"I ordered Colonel Fremont to come to Monterey and bring his archives; this, after four months in which he kept himself in command in southern California against my direct and explicit orders. He came into my headquarters at Monterey unkempt and disheveled after a four-hundred-mile dash on horseback, still having disobeyed my orders and not having brought his records. Colonel Mason was with me. Your husband demanded that I dismiss Colonel Mason from our presence, so that he could talk to me privately. When I refused, he shouted, 'Did you bring him to spy upon me?' Please believe me, Mrs. Fremont, I know of no equivalent of that scene in all army history. Later, when I sent Colonel Mason to Los Angeles to take over Colonel Fremont's command, your husband had the effrontery to challenge his commanding officer to a duel! He was so arrogant and contemptuous of my command that he refused to return to me the two howitzers I had brought across the desert from Santa Fe, and which the Mexicans turned over to him when they surrendered. This is chaos, Mrs. Fremont. Can't you understand that? How could I do anything else but put him under arrest?"

Jessie dug her short nails into her palms. Now both of the mutinies of the Fremont family centered around howitzers; for it was obvious from General Kearny's critical attitude and tone of voice that he had been more deeply offended by Colonel Fremont's refusal to return the cannon than by anything else in their conflict.

"He was overwrought from the months of conquest. If he had been ill in his body you would have seen that he got the best medical care, you would have nursed him with your own hands. But he was tired in his mind, and for that kind of sickness you have neither understanding nor sympathy."

She rose from the chair, toyed with her gloves. "General Kearny, why must you be so cold and hardhearted? Why must you try to destroy Colonel Fremont? And me? Why should you want to injure the cause of western expansion, to hurt my father? You cannot harm people whom you love and not maim yourself along with them."

"If I had been afraid of mortal combat, Miss Jessie, I should never have become a soldier."

"But this is something infinitely worse than death: the same tar with which you will cover my husband will cover you."

"My conscience would no more permit me to withdraw from this battle than it would have to withdraw from a battle against the British, the Mexicans or the Indians. There are fundamental issues involved here, issues more important than any one person or group of persons. Good day, Mrs. Fremont."

After leaving General Kearny's office Jessie wandered slowly through the streets of Washington. An hour later she found herself in the Navy Yard and sat down on the wooden stairs of the barracks to let her head clear. Then she picked herself up wearily and trudged homeward, asking Maylee to heat her some water for a hot bath. While sitting in the big iron tub, her knees drawn up under her chin, she utilized the quiet and relaxation to review the morning.

Yes, John had overstepped himself, his attitude toward General Kearny appeared inexcusable; but she would not try to post-guess him. To herself she said: Living in the security and comfort of my Washington home, able to exercise the most beautiful hindsight, I could easily say that he should have done so and so. But in the heat of the excitement, with the future still an unwritten document, called on to make split-second decisions, what he did must have seemed right for him to do at that particular moment and under that particular set of circumstances. It is easy enough to have good judgment after all the facts are in, but a soldier is not a philosopher, he is a man of action. I am not going to be a blind and adoring wife, but I certainly shall not sit in Olympian calm and decide that I would have done it differently or better.

As the steam from the hot water rose about her head and enveloped her in its mist she thought, We both have incipient mutiny in our blood: I rebelled against the head of my school and her choice of a May Day Queen, leading my cohorts into the infirmary rather than letting them participate. Seven years later I mutinied against the War Department. My husband rebelled against discipline and was expelled from school because as a romantic youth he preferred to roam the hills with his sweetheart. Twelve years later he too mutinied against the War Department. We are too much alike; we double each other's weaknesses. He should have married a different kind of woman, one who would never have interfered . . . who would have been a better balance wheel . . .

In her own feeling of guilt she was not able to look too deeply into her husband's guilt. She remembered her father saying, "A little mutiny goes a long way." Yes, too frequent mutiny would ruin not only the American Army, but the American form of government which, resting upon the consent and co-operation of the governed, must also have the absolute obedience of the governed. It was very well for Vice-Admiral Nelson to raise his blind eye to the spyglass when his inadequate commanding officer was giving a stupid and disastrous command, but what would happen if every one of the thirty million Americans constituted himself a Lord Nelson, raising his blind eye to orders from Washington? A co-operative government could survive mistakes and blunders in particular events, but not consistent disobedience. The government was the parent, the particular affair on hand the child; if one child be lost, the fruitful parents can create more children; but if the child destroy the parent, the family is destroyed.

Thus she came to feel that although her revolt had been justified in everything John had accomplished, in the gathering of the scientific data and the further opening of the West, actually he had not been indispensable: someone else would have gathered the data; the historical forces, of which he was only an instrument, would have opened the West. She had struck a great blow for her husband and his work, but when a blow is struck for someone, it must be struck against someone as well. That someone had been the American form of government, for which her grandmother McDowell had carried a scar on her forehead all her life.

3

ELIZA AND WILLIAM CAREY JONES came in for dinner that night. That they were happy together Jessie knew from little hints that Eliza had let drop; but there was nothing in the undemonstrative manner of either to indicate that there had been any change in their lives. Jessie managed to keep the conversation away from the trial during dinner, but when they had adjourned to the drawing room for coffee, Thomas Benton launched into a legal analysis of Colonel Fremont's course in California, intermingled with a tirade against General Kearny.

Jessie found her eyes glued to William Jones's face. He rarely indicated what he was thinking, yet she felt that he disapproved of what was being said. She had been so preoccupied with her own troubles that she had paid little attention to her new brother-in-law, but now she found herself studying him intently. He was tall and slender, with cool green eyes, a turned-up nose, a shock of blond hair which stood up straight, and an ascetic, almost beardless face. He had a quiet and reserved manner of speaking: she admired his calm, unhurried, unemotional nature; she herself could never aspire to this type of temperament, yet she knew its worth. Mr. Jones's position in this family difficulty was not yet clear; she had not discussed the case with him, nor had he volunteered any opinions. She knew that he could be valuable to their cause, not only because he would remain quiet and logical in the face of her husband's and father's hurricanes, but also because he was a student of international law. John Fremont and Tom Benton would fight in terms of personal conflict, but in the courtroom the issues would have to be tried according to the legal imperatives. Her husband was no lawyer; her father had not practiced law for some twenty years.

Later in the evening, while Eliza went up to visit with her mother, Jessie created an opportunity to talk with her brother-in-law. She did not know whether she could speak to him frankly, for although he was now a member of the family, he had given no indication of affection for anyone beside Eliza. For all she knew he might be entirely disinterested in the dispute.

"Forgive me if I try to read your thoughts," she said, "but it did seem to me that while Father was discussing the case, something in the back of your mind was disagreeing."

After a moment of expressionless but not unfriendly silence, he replied, "There is an old saying that in a lawsuit nobody wins except the lawyers."

"And in this instance not even the lawyers can win! I feel that Colonel Fremont was right in what he did, that his conduct can be justified because of the complicated circumstances. However, I must tell you that my heart sinks at the very thought of a public squabble."

"I must agree with you, Jessie. Things will be said in a spirit of vindictiveness and revenge which will be impossible to expunge from the historic record."

"But do you see any way of stopping the trial? I've already been refused by Father and General Kearny."

William Jones glanced at the other end of the room where John and Tom had their heads together.

"I'm afraid we have to go through with it, Jessie."

"We?"

"Yes. I want to offer my services. I don't know that I can be of any great help, but I should be happy and honored if you will permit me to serve as co-counsel."

The welling up of her emotion was cut short by the matter-of-fact manner in which her brother-in-law had made his offer, an offer which would cost him months of hard work and neglect of his own practice. She was nonplussed to see that a man could make a considerable sacrifice in the same casual manner in which he would offer to bring her a demitasse.

"It is extremely kind of you," she said quietly. "My husband and father and I are all so emotional, we fly off the handle so easily. Won't you please try to hold us down? If only you will stay calm and logical, we will always have a solid legal base. Please don't pay us the compliment of sharing in our vices."

"I will be as I am, Jessie," he remarked. "I cannot be otherwise."

Senator Benton secured a second and last concession from the War Department, the postponement of the trial for another month so that Colonel Fremont might gather his witnesses from the frontiers.

Jessie was interested to watch the trial fought in miniature before the hearing opened: their army friends, who had been visiting the house for years, stayed away; naval officers with whom the Bentons had had only moderate contact became most friendly, called on the slightest provocation to assure Colonel Fremont that he had been entirely right in supporting the navy command in California. When Jessie went to the War Department to secure copies of papers needed for the defense, she was treated politely but coolly and given no assistance. At the office of the secretary of the navy she was received with warmth; the entire staff aided her not only in locating documents but in organizing and copying them. It was extreme bad fortune that Secretary of the Navy Bancroft had been sent abroad as minister to England. George Bancroft should have been in Washington to defend them, though she realized that he would have been able to do little: he had warned her that anything John might attempt in California would be his own gamble, that he would be obliged to deny that he had given encouragement to a campaign against the Mexicans; and in any event, the Army would vehemently have denied that any order from the secretary of the navy constituted a valid defense for an army officer.

The library of the Benton home was set up as a workshop. Jessie and her father used their regular tables in front of the fire, while her husband and brother-in-law spread their papers over the map table. The lawyer spent his day making a detailed study of the records of all court-martials held in America up to that time; Jessie spent her hours in the Library of Congress securing data, her mind going back to the years when she had been "pastured" there by her father while he attended the Senate.

For her the most interesting period of the day was the evening, when they assembled in the library to instruct each other on their findings. John was concentrating on only one aspect of the trial: the fact that Commodore Stockton was the legal and rightful commander in California between January and May 1847; Tom Benton was concentrating on his legal authority for the conquest and governing of California; William Jones was concentrating on the trial framework and the laws of evidence. Jessie's task was to write the letters that had to go out to witnesses, to extract and copy the orders which each man wanted to include in his working brief, to reconcile the coldly legalistic approach of her brother-in-law with her father's hotheaded denunciation of General Kearny and every last one of his witnesses; and to somehow keep her husband's faith and confidence running strong and logical so that together they could build a foolproof case.

She awakened early on the morning of the trial, November 2, 1847, and ran quickly to the window to see what kind of a day she was to have. The sun was already up, bright but not hot; there was the crisp crackle of autumn in the air. She had slept little the night before, but over their light breakfast she assured her husband that she had slept the sleep of confidence. She kissed him good-by with a firm embrace, saying, "Everything is going to come out all right."

"There is not the slightest doubt of it in my mind," he replied, but she could see that he was sorely troubled.

The men left early in Hassler's Ark to round up the defense witnesses. Court was not to open until noon. Jessie sat before her dressing table anxious that she emerge from her preparations looking serene and confident. She had several obstacles to overcome: there were bluish rings under her eyes, her temples were a greenish white, and her King George's Mark was hard and prominent. She bathed her eyes with warm and then cold water, massaged her face for a long time to bring back some blood and color, then sat quietly brushing her hair. At ten-thirty she put on a warm, wine-colored dress with hat and shoes of the same color. While she was engrossed in her thoughts there was a light knock on the door, and Eliza came in. She had on a black gown. Jessie gazed at her sister for a moment.

"Eliza, my dear, this isn't an occasion for mourning."

"Then you don't approve of my black?"

"No, please put on your new dress, the lovely navy one."

At a little after eleven General Dix's spacious carriage arrived with Dix's two daughters, who had offered to take the Benton sisters to the Arsenal. They drove down C Street to Pennsylvania Avenue and then turned left. Since this was the calling hour in Washington there were many carriages abroad, some of them on their way to the Arsenal, others en route to friends' homes. Jessie saw a number of their family acquaintances walking, and she returned their bows with a series of forced smiles; with the hand that was out of sight she clung to Eliza.

"Your fingers are ice cold and trembling, Jessie. Here's the turn toward the Arsenal, you had better put on your gloves."

The Arsenal was a huge rambling wooden building painted a faded mustard color. As Jessie alighted she saw a large crowd of spectators gathered on either side of the entrance. A murmur went up as she stepped out of her carriage, one which she felt was sympathetic. This told her even better than had the friendly tone of the press for the past few days that the sympathies of the people were with Colonel Fremont.

The trial chamber was not overly large except that it had a high-domed ceiling with windows up toward the roof. There was room for only two hundred spectators, and guards were already barring the doors because every seat was occupied. Clasping Eliza's arm, Jessie walked down the center aisle with every pair of eyes fastened upon her. She took her seat in the front row of spectators just behind the railed enclosure inside of which, at a long mahogany table to the left, sat her husband, her father and her brother-in-law, and on the opposite side the prosecuting attorney and his assistants. Since there was to be no jury at this trial, a duplicate jury box had been built on the left side of the enclosure, and here sat Kit Carson, Alexander Godey, and a large number of John's California Battalion and associates in California who had come to testify. In the opposite box near the prosecutor sat a bolt-upright array of army officers banked silently behind their commanding officer, General Stephen Watts Kearny. In the front row across from Jessie was the phalange of newspaper reporters come to report what the *Union* called "the most dramatic army trial since General Wilkinson's, thirty years before."

The sympathy of those in the courtroom heartened her. Then the thirteen judges, comprised of generals, colonels, majors, a captain, filed in, their uniforms resplendent with gold braid. They took their seats on the high judges' bench which ran almost the full width of the courtroom, their position ranging downward from the general to the captain. The court was called to order, the preliminary ceremonials dispensed with and then, while she listened to the terrifying quiet of the courtroom, the charges were read against her husband. The critical hour of their lifetime had struck.

4

SHE STUDIED HER HUSBAND ANXIOUSLY when the court demanded whether he had any objection to the judges. She had persuaded him to buy a new uniform for the trial and he appeared to her to be as trim and handsome as ever, with his flashing eyes and quick, expressive face, albeit more mature-looking because of his rapidly graying hair and the lines in his face. But most important she saw that he was poised and balanced for the long ordeal.

According to the rule of court-martial the defense attorneys could never address the court; they could work up the legal points, but Colonel Fremont alone could speak in the courtroom; he alone could read the arguments and papers that had been prepared during the arduous nights of work; he alone could cross-examine witnesses, make protests to the court. This was a hardship, for it not only obliged the defendant to function in a field in which he was not trained, but also put upon him the burden of appearing before the court with the legalistic phlegm of the lawyer who has only a single decision at stake.

She watched her husband rise and read in a clear, charged voice the paper on which they had worked the night before.

"Mr. President: In preferring the usual request to be allowed counsel in this case, I wish to state that it is no part of my intention to make a defense on any legal or technical point, but only to have friendly assistance in bringing out the merits of the case. With this view, no objection will be made to the relevancy or legality of any question proposed by the prosecution or the court; nor to any question which goes to show my motives, either by words or acts; nor to the authenticity of any evidence, written or printed, which I know or believe to be authentic. In this way I hope to facilitate the progress of the trial, and enable the court the sooner to obey the feelings which call them to a very different service. I name as the counsel allowed me the two friends who accompany me, Thomas H. Benton and William Carey Jones."

She flashed him an approving nod as he half turned to her while sitting down, but her heart was racing when the judge advocate rose to open his case by reading a letter from Colonel Fremont to General Kearny of the United States Army.

To Brig. Gen. S. W. Kearny, *United States Army*
Sir:

I have the honor to be in receipt of your favor of last night, in which I am directed to suspend the execution of orders which, in my capacity of military commandant of this territory, I had received from Commodore Stockton, governor and commander-in-chief in California. I avail myself of an early hour this morning to make such a reply as the brief time allowed for reflection will enable me.

I found Commodore Stockton in possession of the country, exercising the functions of military commandant and civil governor, as early as July of last year; and shortly thereafter I received from him the commission of military commandant, the duties of which I immediately entered upon, and have continued to exercise to the present moment. I found also, on my arrival at this place some three or four days since, Commodore Stockton still exercising the functions of civil and military governor, with the same apparent deference to his rank on the part of all officers, including yourself, as he maintained and required when he assumed in July last. I learned, also, in conversation with you, that, on the march from San Diego, recently, to this place, you entered upon and discharged duties implying an acknowledgment on your part of supremacy to Commodore Stockton.

I feel myself, therefore, with great deference to your professional and personal character, constrained to say that, until you and Commodore Stockton adjust between yourselves the question of rank, where I respectfully think the difficulty belongs, I shall have to report and receive orders, as heretofore, from the Commodore.

With considerations of high regard, I am your obedient servant,

J. C. FREMONT, *Lt. Col. U.S.A.*
Military Commandant of the Territory of California.

As simple and respectful as the letter sounded she felt with a quick flash that herein lay the crux of the case which the Army would present, the focal point around which the conflict and confusion would center: the court would decide who had been the legal commander of California! If it were Commodore Stockton, then Colonel Fremont would be declared innocent of the charges. If it were General Kearny, then he was guilty of disobeying the orders of the army officer. All of the thousands of words that would be spilled in this courtroom, many of them in anger, even more in hot blood, would revolve about this one point.

The prosecutor proceeded to charge Colonel Fremont with twenty-two "specifications" of mutiny, disobedience of lawful command and conduct to the prejudice of military discipline. For four solid hours she heard the case against her husband pile up until the prosecution had presented the most formidable body of charges brought against an officer since the trial of Aaron Burr for treason. As an ominous and crushing rehearsal for all that was to follow during the three feverish months of claims and counterclaims, accusations and counteraccusations, the judge advocate drove spikes into her consciousness by accusing her husband of: breaking his word to the Mexican authorities, cruelly and shamefully abusing the native Californios and antagonizing them against the American government; taking their horses and provisions and paying for them not in cash but in promissory notes; leading a body of well-armed troops into a country on the pretext of scientific survey and rising in arms against that country because it had ordered him out of its boundaries; instigating the American settlers to rise against their Mexican governors, declaring war against California in a series of surprise attacks, assuming full authority over northern California and the supplies and ammunitions of American battleships in San Francisco Harbor without written authority to do so; granting peace terms to the Mexicans without conferring with a superior in command. He had refused to return the two howitzers captured from General Kearny at San Pascual; refused to acknowledge the authority of General Kearny, giving orders to recruit more troops for his California Battalion after the general had commanded him to cease; he had tried to make a bargain with General Kearny for the governorship of California, had turned against him only when his demands were refused, instructing his civil officers in California to regard General Kearny's orders as obsolete. He had used insulting conduct to General Kearny before staff officers, illegally purchased supplies for his troops after having been suspended by General Kearny, illegally carried on a civil government and proclaimed himself to be governor.

By the time the court adjourned at four o'clock she was exhausted and numb with fear. How were they ever going to overthrow this tremendous body of accusation? What could they possibly do in the ensuing days to upset the dreadful charges, free John from them in the minds of the nation?

Official Washington suspected that there had been secret orders sent to Colonel Fremont, yet it would be as impossible to bring them up during this court-martial in vindication of her husband as it was to make them public at the time they had been sent to him through Lieutenant Gillespie. The trial could only be bathed in a fog of innuendo: while ostensibly trying Colonel Fremont for mutiny against General Kearny, the Army actually would be prosecuting him for presenting the United States Army as an implement of conquest. Since in their effort to clear the Army for the historic record they could call to trial neither Secretary Bancroft and the United States Navy nor the president and those of his cabinet members who had sponsored the forcible pre-empting of California, they would visit upon Colonel Fremont the full strength of their outraged wrath, build up the strongest personal case they could expound against him, disown him, convict him on the only charges they dared make public.

Jessie could not touch her dinner. She noticed that only Eliza and her husband were eating theirs. After she had successfully downed a cup of hot black coffee, she broke the silence by asking:

"Why have they the right to convict a man before he is tried? Why is it just practice to throw up this terrifying screen of accusations before we can enter a defense?"

"Don't you worry about our defense," boomed Tom Benton, angrily pushing away his plate. "If you think their list of fabrications against us is terrifying, wait until you hear what we will do to them."

Jessie turned an anxious face to William Jones, who was dispatching the last of his baked ham and sweet potatoes. He continued uninterrupted until his plate was clean, then wiped the corner of his mouth meticulously with his napkin, pushed back his chair, crossed one long bony knee over the other and spoke in a quiet voice.

"It is entirely proper procedure. We cannot enter a defense until the case against us has been stated. Furthermore, from their point of view, all twenty-two of the specifications are rightfully lodged. If we grant the premise that Colonel Fremont was legally bound to obey General Kearny's order of January 17, then every move he made for the next ninety days was illegal."

"But he was not obliged to obey General Kearny," cried Jessie, her emotion, like her stomach, rising into her throat. "Commodore Stockton refused to allow him to resign from the Navy."

"Quite so," murmured Jones. "I was merely stating the case for the opposition. Now let us look at our case: if the colonel was right in obeying the orders of Commodore Stockton because he had been sworn into the Navy, then everything he did between January 17 and May 8, when he was permitted to see General Kearny's new and conclusive orders from Washington, was not only right and legal, but necessary to the fulfillment of his duties as governor. He would have been derelict in his duty had he done less. That is our case. We will be given every opportunity to present it."

While Jessie tried to quiet her feelings with a second cup of coffee, Tom Benton rose heavily from his chair and boomed:

"If the worst comes to the worst, who is the Army convicting here? Certainly not Colonel Fremont! They will be convicting the Navy, trying to chastise the Navy with a backhand slap at an army officer."

"They're not going to convict us," cried Jessie. "Every last charge in that dreadful bill of particulars happened before Kearny received his conclusive orders from Washington in May . . ."

William Jones, who had lighted a cigar and risen from the table, came to her side.

"Easy does it. We can only fight this case on the facts, not on our hypotheses of what lies behind those facts. I believe in our case."

She looked up at him with tears of gratitude in her eyes.

"Of course we believe in our case," said Tom Benton. "But we've got to make the world see it the way we see it. Come now, let us go to work. We can convince no one by merely reassuring ourselves."

"Please, not yet, Father," begged Eliza. "It's too soon after dinner. Come into the drawing room for an hour and let me play for you. Jessie, it will do you good to sing a few ballads."

"Eliza is right," announced her husband; "we should all rest for an hour and talk of other things."

Jessie saw that John and her father resented this cool good sense, that they wanted to go upstairs and plunge into work immediately, not because they were short of time and couldn't get everything done, but because it was intolerable to their impatient natures to be kept away even momentarily from a refutation of the charges. Nevertheless she knew that her sister was right, and she walked across the hall into the drawing room with an arm tucked under her husband's arm.

At eight o'clock they went up to the library to begin work. The wooden-pegged map table which had always stood by the bookshelves was brought to the center of the room and an astral lamp placed at each end. Here the notes from the day's proceedings were spread out, as well as the documents in John's possession and the copies of official papers which they had made during the day. Jessie and John sat facing the wall, Tom Benton and William Jones opposite. At midnight they had their paper completed, a statement which exonerated John on every charge made against him that day by the judge advocate.

Now, suddenly, they were hungry.

"We didn't have any dinner," exclaimed Jessie; "at least we didn't eat any. All I can remember is that wonderful chocolate cake. Come along, we'll ransack the kitchen; there should have been some ham left over, and I'll make a fresh pot of coffee."

"I feel considerably better," announced her father. "I feel like an avenging angel who has demolished the forces of evil."

Jessie glanced eagerly at her husband to see if he too were feeling the upsurge of emotion which had engulfed them.

"We have stated our case," he said heartily, "and we've stated it mighty well."

"Easy does it," cautioned William Jones, lighting his second cigar of the evening, now that he again had a few moments to relax. "We must beware of overoptimism, just as we had to beware of overpessimism at the dinner table."

"Oh come, William," cried Jessie, amused that she had used her brother-in-law's Christian name for the first time; "it's after midnight and we're all tired and hungry and exultant. For a few moments let's not be cautious, let's be confident and happy. Let's talk about that long row of gold braid that sits up on that bench: did you ever see so many gorgeous uniforms? They looked as though they were about to decide the strategy of Lundy's Lane or Waterloo."

"No," protested her father good-humoredly, "let's not be prejudiced against the court. I think we will get a fair trial."

"I'm sure of it," she cried, feeling carefree for the first time in days. "We're also going to get a fair amount of ham. Look, Maylee baked an extra one. John, you make the coffee; William, slice a French bread; Father, how about a little brandy to celebrate the successful conclusion of our first day's work?"

He returned with a bottle of brandy. When the glasses had been filled, Tom Benton raised his in a toasting gesture and said, "To us."

"Yes, to us," murmured Jessie. Going to her husband, she kissed him and said: "And to you, my dear."

5

THE FOLLOWING DAYS were bad ones: General Kearny, Lieutenant Emory and Colonel Cooke occupied the stand and built up detail by detail the edifice against Colonel Fremont. It was clear to Jessie that her husband had been headstrong, yet this process of unclothing a man in public seemed to her a vicious and senseless one. As the trial progressed it was apparent how his difficulties had pyramided; the moves he had made over a period of three months resulted from his first decision to conquer California for the United States and command as governor, and inevitably had to follow. Judged individually, without reference to the original reasoning which had prompted them, the acts looked hasty, misguided, rash and quarrelsome; anyone picking up a newspaper and reading a given set of charges made by General Kearny, Lieutenant Emory or Colonel Cooke would convict Colonel Fremont on the very face of things. Yet once the original premise was granted these acts followed logically; anyone reading the full story would see that Colonel Fremont's actions had to be judged as sequences rather than a group of isolated incidents.

In all fairness to General Kearny, she perceived that the same was true of him: anyone reading a single day's accusations against him would have had to pass severe judgment on him: he had been domineering, officious. He had arrived in California after indiscreetly sending back two thirds of his Mormon Battalion, had been defeated at San Pascual, had his two howitzers captured by the Mexicans, had to be rescued from annihilation by Commodore Stockton; he had played a subsidiary part in the last battles against the Mexicans in California; he knew that Commodore Stockton had orders from Washington to set up a civil government and had named Colonel Fremont as governor; despite this he had behaved like a martinet in brushing aside the commodore's accomplishments, Colonel Fremont's almost bloodless conquest of the territory and successful civil rule, and had suddenly decided that he would be the sole commander. Yet his conduct in relation to Colonel Fremont was inevitable if one granted the rightness of his original premise: that he had the latest order from Washington to rule California, that in refusing to accept his authority Colonel Fremont had committed an act of mutiny.

She spent a good deal of her time watching the faces of the judges to see how they were reacting; she stole quick glances at the spectators who thronged in each day at noon to enjoy this dramatic conflict between two famous men; she devoured the newspapers, cutting out the favorable articles to show to her husband, but feeling depressed at the condemnatory ones, which she destroyed before he could stumble across them.

On the morning of the twelfth day the judge advocate summoned General Kearny to the stand; Jessie saw that his leathery face was sallow. She thought how ill he looked, and had a moment of sympathy for this aging warrior who had chosen to fight in a court-martial instead of on a battleground. This sympathy was dispelled when he accused Colonel Fremont of destroying important papers. Jessie was glad to see her husband jump to his feet to protest. General Kearny apologized, said that he hadn't meant to use the word destroy, but in his first accusation the accuser had set the tone of the trial. General Kearny told of how he had led his troops across more than one thousand miles of desert, faced by hostile Indians, hunger and thirst, how he had played an important part in subduing California. Jessie extracted pencil and paper from her black handbag and began jotting down questions. After dinner she found that her husband, father and brother-in-law had engaged in the same process; for four hours they sat in the library framing a cross-examination which would lay bare a truer picture. When they went to bed that night she said to her husband:

"I can sleep easily for the first time since this trial opened, for I think General Kearny has exposed himself."

She had found that trouble and love were not amiable companions: from the moment they had left Silver Spring and plunged into the work of the trial, she and John had not been husband and wife, or even sweethearts, but business partners immersed in difficulties which threatened their association. Tonight because she genuinely felt the confidence she had been pretending, because he too felt hopeful, they could be lovers once again.

The next morning, refreshed and bright-eyed, they left the house a half-hour earlier and walked in the cool and invigorating air to the Arsenal. There were a few people standing outside the entrance, with its wide wooden overhang, and some of them spoke in a friendly tone.

"Good luck to you, Colonel. Don't be afeared of them, Mrs. Fremont, they can't hurt you."

The *Union* that morning had stated that Colonel Fremont would cross-examine General Kearny; there were whole periods of the California story to be gone over, hundreds of people would testify and a thousand documents be introduced, but everyone in Washington knew that this was the critical moment of the trial, when the two adversaries would come face to face. It was still a half-hour early when Jessie and John entered the courtroom, but every seat was taken. There was a hum of conversation, and quick looks were flashed at them as they walked down the aisle, an uncommonly handsome couple: twenty-three-year-old Jessie in a sea-green redingote with a brown velvet bonnet which matched her hair, her slender cheeks brushed with color from the walk in the sharp winter air, her eyes glistening from the confidence in which the people of the courtroom engulfed them, her mouth red and moist; and tightly gripping her arm, her thirty-four-year-old husband, his black hair combed forward a little over the brow and waving back across his ears, looking older and dignified because he was no longer shaving the beard which had grown during his third expedition and his year in California, walking erect and proud, his vitality evident beneath his full-dress uniform. For a moment he slipped into the spectators' seat beside the one which was reserved for Jessie and said quietly in her ear, so that no one could hear:

"After today, you won't be ashamed to be known as Mrs. Fremont. Today your name is going to be vindicated."

"Oh, darling," she murmured, "nothing that could ever happen in all this world would ever make me ashamed of my name. I carry it like that medal of honor Baron Humboldt awarded you."

"I'll confess that is what I hoped you would say," he replied with a wistful smile.

As he started to rise she took his hand and asked entreatingly, "Do be careful, dear; let General Kearny make the mistakes, let him be bitter and harsh and resentful. He had his day yesterday, today is yours: you can afford to be chivalrous."

He patted her hand.

"Trust me," he said. "My sword has such a fine edge this morning that the general won't know his throat is cut until he tries to turn his head."

It was not the answer for which she had hoped, but she had to be content with it. The court was opened, General Kearny sworn in and John rose, glanced at the papers before him, then addressed his commanding officer. Jessie was relieved to see that his voice was quiet and his manner courteous. She had been sitting tensed on the hard bench of the mustard-colored room; it was still cold and she had wrapped the coat of her green redingote over her bosom. The moment John began to speak her tension relaxed and the room felt warmer; she sat comfortably, while to her ears there came the cross-examination which seemed to her to vindicate her husband.

"General Kearny, did not William W. Russell, my secretary of state in California, come to your headquarters in Los Angeles on January 13 and tell you that I had sent him from the plains of Cahuenga where I had just accepted the surrender of the Mexican Army?"

"Yes."

"Did not Mr. Russell tell you that he had been sent for the purpose of ascertaining who was in chief command at Los Angeles, and after learning who this was, to make a report of the surrender of the Mexican Army and the armistice terms I had granted them?"

"Mr. Russell came to my headquarters on the thirteenth of January."

"Did not Mr. Russell ask you whether your arrival in the country had superseded Commodore Stockton's, who had before been recognized as chief commander?"

"He asked that question."

"Did you not tell him that Commodore Stockton was still in chief command, and tell him to make his report to the commodore?"

"Yes."

"And this was exactly four days before you ordered me to cease obeying Commodore Stockton and henceforth carry out your orders?"

"It was."

"Did you receive any orders from Washington between the fourteenth and the seventeenth of January, changing your status?"

"No dispatches reached me during that period."

A gasp went up from the audience; there came scattered applause. Jessie turned about in her seat gratefully; she saw that the spectators agreed that her husband had sincerely tried to find out who was the legal commander in chief; that General Kearny had contradicted himself. While the judge advocate threatened to clear the court, John asked that General Kearny be excused and put William W. Russell on the stand. Russell testified that he was a major in the California Battalion, had participated in the surrender of the Mexicans at Cahuenga, and had been instructed by Colonel Fremont to ride to Los Angeles and find out who was the commander in chief.

"Mr. Russell, when you talked to General Kearny at headquarters, before taking your report to Commodore Stockton, was my name mentioned?"

"It was. General Kearny expressed great pleasure at Colonel Fremont being in the country, and spoke of his eminent qualifications for the office of governor and his knowledge of the Spanish language and the manner of people. He told me that it was his intention to appoint Colonel Fremont governor of California if the instructions which he brought with him from the secretary of war were recognized in California."

"Did you then submit my reports to Commodore Stockton?"

"Yes, sir; I learned from the commodore that his relations to the territory as chief commander were in no wise changed by the arrival of General Kearny in the country."

"Did you then return to the California Battalion?"

"I did. I met Colonel Fremont at the head of his battalion on the morning of the fourteenth of January, about five miles from Los Angeles. I told him that I had had much conversation with both General Kearny and Commodore Stockton, touching their respective positions in the country; that I was satisfied, from what had occurred, that General Kearny was a better friend of his than Stockton; but, from Kearny's own admission, I regretted to have to give it as my opinion that we should have to look to Commodore Stockton still as commander in chief; that I found Stockton exercising the functions of commander in chief and submitted to implicitly, as I thought, by Kearny."

"Mr. Russell, did obedience to the command of Commodore Stockton in preference to that of General Kearny, when both were claiming the chief authority, present any advantages personal or military to Colonel Fremont?"

"I think not; General Kearny was known to have funds; and expected shortly an arrival of troops. He was, besides, known to be a warm friend of Colonel Fremont's family. I am satisfied that Colonel Fremont elected to obey Commodore Stockton alone from a conviction of duty."

Once again a murmur swept the courtroom. Jessie's spirits were rising rapidly. John then summoned General Kearny back to the stand.

"General Kearny, four days later when you ordered me to cease serving under Commodore Stockton and obey your commands, did I not inform you that Commodore Stockton had refused to cancel my appointment in the Navy and that he would consider me mutinous if I failed to recognize him as commander in chief?"

"As commander in chief of California I was not bound by Commodore Stockton's statements."

"But you knew that he threatened to use his sailors and marines to keep the California Battalion from being dismembered?"

"I was not convinced that Commodore Stockton would use his sailors against the California Battalion."

"Did you inform Commodore Stockton that he was no longer commander in chief of California, and that you were?"

"I so informed the commodore."

"And did he not refuse to step down from command?"

"He refused to acknowledge my command."

"Since I had been appointed governor of California, and was the next highest ranking officer to you and the commodore, were you not trying to use me to settle your dispute with Commodore Stockton?"

The judge advocate refused to allow the question. John turned, gazed at his wife for a long moment, then walked closer to the witness box.

"When I sent my first respectful letter declining to make any decisions until the question of rank was settled, did you not say that the man who carried my letter was a stranger to you?"

"I don't recall that I did."

"Then let me read it to you from your own testimony."

After he had read this bit from General Kearny's testimony, John continued, "That letter was brought to you at your headquarters by Christopher Carson. Did you not spend many weeks on the trail with Kit Carson, using him as your guide?"

"Mr. Carson served as our guide."

"Then how could you not recognize him a few weeks later when he brought you my letter?"

"The man who brought your letter was a stranger to me."

John Fremont called Kit Carson to the stand. Jessie exchanged a fragmentary smile with him as he came down the center aisle, having been summoned by a guard. After Carson was sworn in, John asked:

"Did you take a letter from me to General Kearny on the seventeenth of January 1847, saying that until General Kearny and Commodore Stockton adjusted between themselves the question of rank, where I thought the difficulty belonged, I should have to report and receive orders as hitherto, from the commodore?"

"I carried that letter to General Kearny."

"Did he recognize you?"

"Recognize me?" asked Carson, puzzled.

"Did he know that you were Christopher Carson?"

"We were on the trail together. How could he not know me?"

"Thank you, Mr. Carson. I should like to call General Kearny to the stand again.

"General Kearny, did you not inform the officers of your staff, immediately after my refusal of January seventeenth, that you were going to arrest me?"

"I may have mentioned it."

"When did you instruct me that I was to be placed under arrest? Was it not on the sixteenth of August, six months later, after we had reached Fort Leavenworth?"

"You were placed under arrest at Fort Leavenworth."

"Did you give me any chance to gather data for my defense in California? Was I able to inform my witnesses that I had need of them in Washington for the court-martial?"

"You were informed of your arrest in due time at Fort Leavenworth.'

"When you ordered me to return to Washington, did you not refuse me the right to go to San Francisco and collect my journals, drawings, maps and specimens of the third expedition?"

"That was government property, unfit to be trusted to an officer derelict in his duty."

"Did you not refuse me permission to take my battalion to Mexico, to serve under General Taylor, even though General Scott had asked you to extend this privilege?"

"I know of no such advice from General Scott."

"When I asked for permission to return over a new route to complete my maps for the Topographical Corps, did you not oblige me to march behind your army under guard of the Mormon Battalion?"

"You marched behind the Mormon Battalion."

"Just one last question, General Kearny. Did you not attempt to prevent Lieutenant Gillespie and Midshipmen Beale and McLane from leaving California, even though they were overdue in Washington?"

"I have no authority over naval officers."

"But did you not go to Commodore Shubrick and ask that these men not be allowed to make the overland passage?"

"I informed Commodore Shubrick that I did not think Lieutenant Gillespie a responsible man to be wandering loose in California."

It was four o'clock. The court adjourned for the day. Jessie sat happy and almost complacent in her seat, waiting for the three men to gather up their papers inside the railing and go with her to the carriage. She felt that the trial was over, that it must be obvious to everyone that General Kearny had had a sudden change of attitude, had decided to assume command after informing everyone that Commodore Stockton was the commander; that John had been justified in not being able to understand this shift, since no new orders had arrived; that he was right in refusing to be responsible for deciding which of his superior officers was the commander in chief of California. General Kearny's motives and conduct had appeared in a bad light, he had shown himself overbearing while in California, and today on the stand had displayed such vindictiveness to the younger officer as to render his testimony invalid.

Early the next morning, when she was working in the archives of the War Department, she stumbled across the original report that General Stephen Watts Kearny had filed against Colonel John Fremont. Numbly she perceived that these were not the charges on which her husband was being tried, that the final bill of particulars had been drawn up by the War Department itself.

6

HER CONFIDENCE of the day before vanished. The trial was by no means over, their gleeful confidence had been self-deception. Since the War Department had enlarged and elaborated the charges, since they had selected their own board of judges and were running the trial to suit themselves, nothing John could prove would make the slightest difference in the verdict.

She told no one of her discovery, but put on a gay face and tried to make a few jokes in the carriage when her father called for her. Her sense of impending disaster was magnified during the day when she found the court consistently ruling against her husband: refusing to allow Commodore Stockton to testify on the stand that he was the legal commander of California; refusing to admit to evidence reports of the secretary of the navy and the secretary of war which praised John's conquest of California; refusing to oblige Lieutenant Emory and Colonel Cooke to testify whether or not they were the authors of the anonymous letters in the newspapers prior to the trial; refusing to allow John to introduce material tending to prove that General Kearny had used his influence to retain on the Pacific coast all naval officers sympathetic to the defendant; refusing to allow any material to be presented which might impeach General Kearny as a witness.

The trial, which up to this point had proceeded quietly, broke into an unending series of wrangles. Every few moments the court was ordered cleared, and Jessie and the spectators were forced to stand for an hour in the vestibule, returning to the courtroom in time to hear, "the court cannot inquire into the refusal of General Kearny to grant Colonel Fremont . . . the court cannot inquire into the orders given to Colonel

Fremont at Fort Leavenworth . . . the court has read the documents submitted and finds they have nothing applicable to the case now on trial . . . the court decides that Colonel Fremont's objections to the course to be pursued cannot now be entertained . . ."

After working with John, her father and brother-in-law for five hours at night on a paper to prove that certain evidence could be introduced, she would lie wide-eyed in bed until dawn, then go up to the War or Navy Department to unearth the proper documents to buttress their brief—only to find their material challenged as irrelevant and inadmissible, to have the court cleared while she stood in the cold and drafty foyer waiting to be readmitted, and then to hear the crushing blow that the court had once again decided against them.

She was no longer able to reassure her husband that all would come out well; nor for that matter could John play the game any longer. William Carey Jones alone insisted that they were getting an unprejudiced trial, even though the judges almost never agreed with his penetrating analyses of the laws of evidence. They worked terribly hard, got along on too little sleep and too little food, lived half the time on black coffee. As their sense of frustration and injustice rose, their nerves became frayed. Jessie grew thin, dropped below a hundred pounds. She was alarmed over what was happening to her husband; her heart suffered compression pains when she saw how his black eyes were sinking deeper, becoming filled with a look of hatred and the sense of persecution. This was bad, it hurt their cause, yet when she tried to quiet him, to assure him they were getting a fair trial, she knew that within the hour a decision of the court would confound her, that they would become frenzied by learning that the questions which the judge advocate was asking General Kearny had been written beforehand by General Kearny himself!

Her father's wrath had been aroused as Jessie had never seen it during the years of his hardest battles. The attack on his son-in-law left him grieved and wildly partisan. At least half of his judgments had to be thrown out because he was indulging in illogical and violent reasoning.

Sitting beside him, emanating a chill which would have frozen any other man's turbulence, sat William Carey Jones, with cold green eyes, his light-skinned face expressionless, unruffled, dousing the fire of Tom Benton's emotions in icy legalistic thinking. Jessie frequently had to remember back to that one revealing moment when he had permitted himself to display his loyalty for the family, or she would have thought him so disinterested as to be worthless as counsel. Yet as she observed the means by which the briefs and arguments were prepared step by step so that not only before the court but in the daily press John would look his very best, she saw that the rapierlike brain of William Jones was their greatest asset.

She watched her husband at work, torn by the accusations and evidence piling up against him, realizing how much damage his enemies were doing to his reputation day by day, yet always and completely positive that he had been right, that there had been no other possible course of action for him, that General Kearny's entire motivation was one of revenge because of wounded dignity, the motivation of men like Emory and Cooke based on envy and jealousy, that of the War Department to reestablish its own pre-eminence when obliged to work in concert with the Navy.

It was neither the nerve strain nor the unceasing labor that got them down, but rather the feeling that they were batting their heads against a stone wall. The court seemed to be hearing the same words of defense that Jessie, the spectators and the newspaper reporters were hearing, yet no argument had any effect. The newspapers grew irritated with the court, asked in editorials why it was taking longer to settle their internecine squabble than to win the war in Mexico.

Thomas Hart Benton, the oldest and wisest among them, broke first under the strain. Shortly after the opening of the court one early December morning, General Kearny rose heavily to his feet and charged:

"I consider it due to the dignity of the court that I should here state that when I was answering the questions propounded to me by the court, the senior counsel of the accused, Thomas H. Benton, of Missouri, sat in his place, making mouths and grimaces at me, which I considered were intended to offend, to insult, and to overawe me."

There was a gasp in the courtroom. Jessie's cheeks flamed in embarrassment. The spectators craned to concentrate their gaze on Senator Benton. Over the sharp whisperings in the audience, Jessie heard the president of the court say that he had not observed the occurrence but regretted very much to hear of it. He then read the 76th Article of the Rules and Articles of War prohibiting the use of menacing words, signs or gestures in presence of the court-martial. There was an expectant hush when the president finished. All eyes were again turned on Senator Benton. He pulled himself to his feet, his face a dull brick red, and cried angrily:

"General Kearny fixed his eyes upon Colonel Fremont, looked insultingly and fiendishly at him. The judge advocate, by leading questions, led General Kearny into a modification of what he had previously sworn . . ."

A member of the court rose and said: "Mr. President, remarks reflecting upon the integrity of our proceedings are not, in my opinion, admissible . . ."

Tom Benton boomed out, "When General Kearny fixed his eyes on Colonel Fremont, I determined if he should attempt again to look down the prisoner, I would look at him. I did this today; and the look of today was the consequence of the looks in this court before. I did today look at General Kearny when he looked at Colonel Fremont, and I looked at him till his eyes fell—till they fell upon the floor!"

When Jessie reached home, after hearing her father reprimanded by the court, she flung herself into her big leather chair and wept unrestrainedly. This was the kind of blow for which she was not prepared. Whatever obloquy her husband might endure because of his conduct in the line of duty they could somehow face up to; but that her father should so completely forget himself . . . that he should leave himself open to bitter criticism, made her heartsick and guilty at the grief she was bringing upon him. Because of her he was profoundly hurting his name and the career he had so long cherished.

7

AT THE BEGINNING OF DECEMBER, after having awakened with nausea three mornings in a row, she knew that she was pregnant again. With the knowledge came feelings compounded of elation and misgiving. This was the first time since the birth of Lily that she had become pregnant; that this time she would have a son she had not the slightest doubt. She knew what joy the arrival of a boy would bring to her husband, how much pride and renewed ambition. For all this she was happy, and yet if her husband were convicted and discharged from the service he would be lost, not know where to go or where to turn; their delight at the birth of their child would be submerged by their misfortune.

The very moment she was convinced that she was with child, Jessie made two resolutions: that she would tell no one until the trial was over; that they simply must not lose the case. She vowed that she would work her fingers to the bone, fight every last point to its uttermost extremity and beyond, that they would never give in. The early scenes of triumph, the clear-cut justification for her husband had to be brought out of this maze of quarrels and dusty documents. Her son must not be born into a world in which his father was an outcast. He must be born into a world in which the name of Fremont was honored.

She walked to her mother's room and, being preoccupied with her own thoughts, forgot to knock. Eliza was sitting on her mother's chaise; a fragment of a sentence hung in mid-air; the two women looked guilty. Jessie closed the door and, holding the knob in her tightly clenched fist, leaned against it, crushing her fingers. The physical pain drove out the

pain of having come upon her mother and sister while they were discussing her. The three women maintained an awkward silence for a
moment while Jessie asked herself what it was that they had been talking
about. Had they been condemning her husband? Had they been criticizing her for her part in this drama? Were they ashamed of the scandal,
resentful that their names had been dragged through the gutters of public gossip?

She left the door and came forward to her mother and sister; the
intensity of her manner made them look up at her, and when she saw
their eyes, soft and solicitous, she understood that only in her overwrought condition could she have accused her mother and sister of being
disloyal. They had been pitying her, that was all; pitying her for her
troubles and her burdens. She could imagine the dialogue between them,
could hear them regretting that she had married a public figure, that
she had gotten herself immersed in these questionable courses of action,
pitying her for her misfortunes. She knew that her mother would be remembering the scene on the boat and in the carriage going to Cherry
Grove, when she had cautioned her daughter against plunging her happy
and protected life into conflict; would be remembering how positive
Jessie had been that that was what she wanted, that her mother had been
wrong to evade the important issues of life. Her mother probably thought
that now she understood what a terrible mistake she had made, and
wished that she had listened to older counsel.

She thought nothing of the sort; she did not regret her marriage or
anything that happened in it, including the events that had led up to
this trial. She was not afraid of life; she was not afraid of bold and vigorous action; she was not even afraid of this trial and its consequences.
Having endured the worst that participation could bring about, she was
qualified to speak; she wanted to cry out to her mother that she had not
changed her mind, that she still believed in a life of action and conflict,
in working by a man's side no matter how much mud splattered on the
hem of her garment.

She did not want their pity; it was unendurable to her. They did not
understand that they were pitying her for a suffering which she was not
undergoing. If it were part of her job to have the fierce white light of
publicity on her; if it were part of her job to endure public exposure as
well as public acclaim; if it were part of her job to have her husband and
her name smeared with abuse, then that was the price she would pay in
order to carry forward an important work. No, she did not want their
pity; it was misplaced. Let them rather pity weakness and withdrawal
the inability to endure the ravages of conflict and to come out of it with
a serene heart and an ever increased faith in one's destiny.

She had forgotten why she had come into the room. She smiled a little too brightly, kissed her mother and her sister on the cheek, went out again without speaking.

On the night of December eighteenth Jessie, John, Tom Benton and William Jones worked straight through until dawn organizing a bill of particulars against the conduct of the court, summing up and analyzing every adverse decision and showing how their parallels had been decided affirmatively for General Kearny. They finished work at six, after which she had a cup of coffee, bathed, and was driven to the War Department to copy a number of paragraphs needed in the brief. The work occupied her until a few minutes before noon, allowing no chance to refresh herself or even to get a bite of food. She hurried to the Arsenal to provide her husband with the needed material.

She could not see him very clearly when he arose to present his brief, but she could not decide whether this was because the now unhappy, shrunken face of John Fremont was suffused in a haze of frustration or because there was a roaring in her head. The first words were the only ones that Colonel Fremont could speak out: the judge advocate challenged the admissibility of the brief, and the court was cleared. She went out into the bitterly cold vestibule, with icy drafts blowing in through the windows and the cracks under the doors. She stood still as long as she could, then walked back and forth to generate warmth. By three o'clock she could no longer stand on her feet and had to ask an acquaintance to drive her home. She went to bed immediately. The room was swinging around, her body was burning as though a coal stove had been ignited inside her, her ears were pounding and her mouth felt filled with cotton. Only dimly did she hear her husband's words of comfort. But one word of the doctor's she heard distinctly before she lost consciousness:

"Pneumonia."

Her sister Eliza came back home to manage the household. Eliza was not very good at expressing herself in words, but when it came to expressing herself in deed, there was no one more eloquent. She kept Jessie's room at exactly the right temperature, no easy task in the middle of a raw December; either she or Maylee or a nurse was present every moment of the night and day; delicate and nutritious foods were prepared, and kept warm over a brazier at the bedside. Mrs. Benton, who had taken to her bed altogether for the past two months to avoid the storms which were rocking the Benton household, had Maylee dress her each morning and, despite the fact that the left side of her face and body still were semiparalyzed, spent many hours by her daughter's side, holding her hand and telling bright stories from her childhood.

The most stricken was John, who felt that somehow he had brought this illness upon his wife. Jessie saw that he was reproaching himself unreservedly, even though when he visited her he kept a carefree smile on his face.

Tom Benton alone did not seem alarmed: Jessie had pneumonia? Well, lots of people had pneumonia! If he had been able to conquer the tuberculosis which had carried off the rest of his family, how could anyone doubt that Jessie would very quickly throw off anything so transitory as pneumonia?

Nor had it occurred to Jessie that her life was in danger; all of her nightmares had been woven around her husband and the trial. For four days she was very ill; at three o'clock of the fifth morning the fever broke. As soon as her strength returned she demanded news of each day's proceedings. She thought it sweet of her husband and father to take a light tone, to assure her that everything was going well. They did not know that she had bribed Josheem to bring her fresh copies of the *Union* and the *National Intelligencer* at noon after the men had left the house, and that she was following the case word for word. It was not good for her to read the proceedings when they contained bad news, but the anxiety of uncertainty was worse.

She spent Christmas and New Year's in bed propped up straight against a bank of cushions. Her father set up a small Christmas tree in the corner of her bedroom, and the doctor gave permission for the family gifts to be opened in her presence on Christmas morning.

John had run wild, spending almost the last of their rapidly diminishing funds on dozens of gifts for her, ranging all the way from pearl earrings to a sea-green silk lounging robe which she had to take off hastily because it made her face seem even greener than it was.

By the end of the third week she was out of bed trying a few experimental steps around the room, her legs feeling as weak as they had the first time she had tried to walk after giving birth to Lily. She leaned heavily on her husband's arm, rubbing her toes back and forth luxuriously on the soft, thick carpet. She had thought she would like to stay up for an hour or two, but at the end of five minutes she was grateful to be helped back to bed. Each day she ate everything Maylee put before her in an effort to recover quickly, put on a little weight, so that the men would let her resume work. By the third week in January she was remaining up all day. She did her best to conceal her pregnancy from the doctor; he complied with her tacit wish to keep the matter secret for just a little longer.

The hearing already had dragged through three months, exhausting the patience of the nation. By the last days in January the end finally came into sight. Though John refused her permission to attend court for the few remaining sessions, the men could not persuade her to keep away from the drawing up of the final statement for the defense. This summation proved to be their best collaboration of the trial, each of the four contributing his own particular analysis of the events. The document began with John's arrival in California, told of the ammunition, food, money and medical supplies given him by the Navy in order to help in the conquest, related the story of the war with Mexico and the surrender in California and the events leading up to the conflict over command. The testimony and documents submitted over a period of three months were sifted and analyzed, the discrepancies and irregularities set side by side.

On the face of it Jessie felt confident that although the court might bring in a guilty verdict on the two lesser charges of disobedience and conduct to the prejudice of military discipline, there could be no real basis for sustaining the charge of mutiny.

The next morning no one worked. The family assembled for a late breakfast: Jessie and her husband, Eliza and her husband, Thomas and Elizabeth Benton, her two younger sisters and brother. They dallied over their shirred eggs and coffee cake, dressed leisurely and departed en masse for the courtroom just a few moments before noon.

Jessie was proud of John when he rose to read his final summation in a well-modulated voice. Her confidence grew as he clicked off point after point, building a solid edifice of justification. At four o'clock, when it was time to adjourn, the court granted him permission to continue his presentation, and so he carried on for another hour, his voice growing a little throaty, but more resolute all the while. At the very end she sat almost unbreathing while he made the last eloquent plea which she and her husband had written in the same collaboration with which they had created the reports of the first two expeditions.

"My acts in California have all been with high motives, and a desire for the public service. My scientific labors did something to open California to the knowledge of my countrymen. My military operations were conquests without bloodshed; my civil administration was for the public good. I offer California, during my administration, for comparison with the most tranquil portions of the United States. I prevented civil war against Commodore Stockton, by refusing to join General Kearny against him; I arrested civil war against myself, by consenting to be deposed— offering at the same time to resign my place of colonel in the Army.

"I am now ready to receive the decision of the court."

The spectators broke into applause. Even the row of judges looked satisfied, as though this had indeed been a worthy presentation of a complicated case. Jessie relaxed; their tribulations were over, they had acquitted themselves in the best possible fashion. She started to rise, as had part of the audience, when suddenly, in a hard tone, in a manner become emotional and bitter, she heard her husband exclaim:

"Mr. President, I cannot rest my case without one final statement."

O dear God, thought Jessie, what has happened? What is he going t⁻ do now?

"Certainly the difficulties in California ought to have been inqui:et into," said John loudly, "but how? Not by prosecuting the subordinate, but the principals; not by prosecuting him who prevented, but him who would have made civil war. If it was a crime in me to accept the governorship from Commodore Stockton, it was a crime in him to have bestowed it; and, in either event, crime or not, the government which knew of his intention to appoint me, and did not forbid it, has lost the right of prosecuting either of us! I consider these difficulties in California to be a comedy of three errors: first, in the faulty orders sent out from this place; next, in the unjustifiable pretensions of General Kearny; thirdly, in the conduct of the government in sustaining these pretensions. And the last of these errors I consider the greatest of the three."

When he had finished he stood by his table awkwardly. Jessie felt herself grow limp. She rose and rushed down the center aisle of the courtroom blinded by tears. All of their good work had been overthrown. The uncertainty lodged in the deepest fragment of John Charles Fremont's heart had betrayed him.

8

WHEN SHE REACHED HOME she suffered an hour of retching which produced little but yellow bile. The presence of Maylee with her strong arm clasped about her waist was all that kept her from slipping to her knees.

Maylee picked her up and put her into bed, where she lay white and weak and frightened. She pretended that she was asleep when her husband came up to the room several hours later; with her eyes shut she could see his face: dark, twisted, unhappy, ashamed of his last outburst but preferring to die before he would admit that he shouldn't have done it or that he had hurt his own chances. She lay still while he slipped into the bed beside her. She wanted to turn to him and take him in her arms, to comfort him, to kiss the unshed tears from his eyes, to smooth away the gnarled lines that slashed his face. But she dared not, for she feared she would herself break down and cry, give an indication of how tragic she thought his mistake in antagonizing the court and appearing before the nation in his last moment as an arrogant and insolent man; having built a magnificent defense to prove that he had not been guilty in Cali⁻

fornia, then in a last shattering few minutes to reveal the very temper
and manner which General Kearny and the War Department had been
prosecuting these three months long.

She did not love him the less for his outburst; she loved him the more,
as a mother loves an errant and headstrong child whom she cannot control. Nor could she reveal that she felt sorry for him and wanted to cradle
his confused, hot head on her breast. Better to let the moment go and
face the consequences than to injure their relationship by showing her
husband that she pitied him. Though he made not the slightest move,
though he lay like a man of stone at her side, she knew that he was not
asleep, and she knew the agonies he was enduring as once again he mentally recapitulated his defense. Still she gave no sign that she was awake;
better to let this cold silence lie between them.

At last she heard the slow rhythmical breathing for which she had
been listening. For another few moments she lay quietly, then she rose,
put on a quilted robe and slippers, went down to the kitchen, where she
made herself a cup of strong coffee, then went up to her father's library.
She had already participated in the writing of the defense; now she must
write the case for the prosecution, reacquaint herself with the evidence
against her husband. Once she had drawn up the most formidable bill of
particulars available, had put them all down in black and white, they
would furnish her with a means of accepting the verdict of the court-
martial, enable her to go on from there. She was frightened at what might
happen to John if a verdict of guilty on all charges was brought in; she
did not know whether he would have the stamina to keep from further
injuring himself in the intensity of his reaction. She, for the both of them,
must be prepared to accept the worst.

There were a number of glowing coals in the fireplace. She put on
some kindling from the woodbox, then added a walnut log and stood
rubbing her pale slim fingers before the flames. When they were warm
she sat in her old chair, drew her desk over her knees and began writing
rapidly.

It was not difficult to build up a formidable case against Colonel Fremont, for its particulars had been dinned into her ears in the courtroom
for three months. She recounted the twenty-two specifications, starting
with his three-day stand at Hawk's Peak, his assistance to the Americans in Mexico in their "Bear Flag Rebellion," his share in the unauthorized conquest of California, his unauthorized acceptance of Mexican surrender, through to the point where he refused to relinquish his
command to an army officer sent by the War Department.

When John C. Fremont had converted his third expedition into the
California Battalion, one of his men had refused to make the shift and

be plunged into a war. John had ordered him locked in a dungeon below Sutter's Fort overnight. By morning the man had reconsidered, joined the California Battalion. This single act of coercion constituted the blackest deed of the California exploit: John Fremont demanded absolute obedience and ironclad discipline; had he not told her stories of how he preserved this discipline on his three expeditions? Had he not clapped one of his men into prison for failure to obey an unwarranted command? Why then had he himself not accorded the same strict obedience and the same ironclad discipline to his superior officer? If discipline were imperative for those below him in rank, was it not also imperative for those above him? And if he were going to use force on a member of his exploring expedition, why was General Kearny not justified in using the same force on Colonel Fremont?

She could answer this only by concluding that John knew that under his appointment from Commodore Stockton as civil governor he would be in command of the new territory, for the Navy would not rule on shore, Commodore Stockton would set out for sea and John Fremont would be left in complete charge. Under General Kearny's appointment he always would be a subordinate: General Kearny would appoint his own staff officers with whom he had worked for years, and who were superior to him in rank. The principal appointments would go to real army men, not to a Topographical engineer; after he had done the groundwork, played the most important role in the conquest, he would be ordered to pack up his maps and journals and report back to the Topographical office in Washington, his career in California ended. He would want to write up his third expedition, make his new maps, but once that was finished, what did he do next? Having caught an image of a greater part for himself on the stage of history, the function of topographer and map maker must have seemed limited. From now on he would be a conqueror of new territory, a governor of new states. All this he stood to lose if he acknowledged General Kearny over Commodore Stockton.

Jessie laid down her pen, walked once again to the fire and threw on another log. The hours of the night slipped away and she felt forlorn; for here, hidden in the mass of detail, was the most important point of the controversy, one which had been allowed to remain obscure: John was an army man, he had always been an army man, he had attained his rank, gained his honors and done his work as an army man; the Army had financed his expeditions, won him his respect and fame. It was very well for him to be a naval officer while there was no superior army man on hand, but the very instant a superior army officer arrived on the scene there could be no question as to his obligation; under any circumstances he had no alternative, no choice. When General Kearny ordered him to obey he had but one possible answer:

"Yes, sir."

If John had made that one answer, these troubles would never have happened, there would have been no court-martial.

With equal clarity there came to her the realization that from this viewpoint the procedure of the court-martial had not been prejudiced. John had not put the Army first, above everything, and particularly above himself. Now she understood why the West Point officer did not like the volunteer officer: what the regular army man had as a part of his equipage, John did not have: the discipline that no matter how good his work, or how important he had become on the spot, he surrendered his position to a superior officer immediately that he arrived with authority to take over . . . regardless of whether the subordinate officer felt himself to be more qualified than the officer coming to supplant him. All army officers had suffered such thwarting, but they had accepted it because it was part of their tradition.

John was not and never had been an army man; he had been a topographer and engineer. Nor had she accepted the Army's iron discipline as part of her husband's unbreakable duty. Why did her father not condemn her for her mutiny, send couriers after the second expedition to bring her husband back to stand charges in Washington? Why did he allow her to send John the signal to became involved in still another mutiny?

Because we are headstrong people! Because we are driven by emotion, are certain of our superior abilities, and are unable to put ourselves aside, to make the sacrifice of pride and individuality to our government. We are all equally guilty, myself, my father and my husband, but I am the most guilty because I had no extenuating circumstances.

She went back to her desk and continued writing. When she finished, dawn was just prying up the dark flooring of the eastern sky. As she walked down the long hallway she saw a light coming from under the crack of William Carey Jones's door. She knocked lightly. After a moment her brother-in-law came to the door, a blue flannel bathrobe wrapped around his thin frame, a pen clutched in his right hand, his fingers inky.

"Haven't you been asleep, William?" she asked.

"No, I . . . I was just making a few notes."

She saw that his desk was littered with sheets of paper, and asked if she might see what he had written. When he replied that she might, she walked past him into the bedroom; Eliza was sleeping with her face turned away from the light. A glance at the small, tight, precise writing showed her that it was about the trial, but she did not gather at once what its point was. She asked in a whisper, "Why have you written down all this material?"

"A good lawyer must never be taken by surprise," he replied with a minimum of voice. "He must know everything the opposition can bring to support its contention."

Jessie smiled wanly, handing him the batch of her papers. He read two pages, then looked up at her with a startled expression.

"You've been doing exactly the same thing."

"You know the old line about great minds," she murmured, trying to force a laugh; "would you care to compare our bills of particulars?"

"Let's go into the library where we won't disturb Eliza."

He sank into his father-in-law's chair before the fire and went back to the reading of her pages. After a few moments he shook his head.

"Yes," he agreed, "Colonel Fremont's commission in the Navy was automatically canceled when General Kearny took over."

"What are our chances today in that courtroom?"

He rose, put her papers on the map table, stalked about the room holding the flannel bathrobe around his tall, skinny figure.

"Light, William, light," she murmured, "I am prepared to hear the worst."

He made the best case he could, pointing out that neither President Polk nor the Cabinet nor the majority of the Senate wanted a conviction. He spoke of her husband's long and magnificent record of service. Jessie was not convinced. She replied so softly he almost could not hear:

"William, you don't believe your own arguments. If this case had not been your brother-in-law's, you would never have pled it. You feel it the duty of the court to bring in a verdict of guilty."

He denied her accusations. She did not press him. She kissed him lightly on the cheek, thanked him for all he had done for them. Just then her child moved inside her; her heart and stomach seemed to turn over, and she began to tremble.

"Whatever the law may be, I am not able to see it that way. I am his wife, and I know how he will suffer if the court declares him guilty. I know how it will wreck his life. I want my children to have a successful father, a man who can hold his head high. Oh, William, I am responsible: I led him into his first mutiny; I urged him into the action in California which led him to believe that he could disobey General Kearny. If only I could take the blame!"

William Jones put his arm about his sister-in-law and said quietly, "Come, Jessie dear, you are overtired: you should not have worked all night. You must go to bed now and get some sleep. You will want to be strong and rested when we leave for court."

She permitted herself to be led down the long hall to her room. At the doorway he patted her shoulder with his bony fingers. Jessie crawled exhausted to bed and fell into a black sleep.

9

MAYLEE HAD TO WAKE HER at ten o'clock when she brought up a hot breakfast. Jessie heard the torrents of rain sloshing against the outside windows. It was a dark, depressing day. She put on a knitted tan wool dress with wide-bottomed sleeves over her white chemisette, and over her shoulders she gathered her new brown Cornelia wrap which she fastened in front with a cameo brooch. A last glance in the mirror showed her that her outfit looked much too somber, as though she were anticipating the worst, so she went to the top drawer of her bureau, rummaged through the jewelry and slipped a long chain of bright green beads around her neck. The beads were out of place, but they lightened her spirit.

She looked for the men and found each of them sitting alone and silent: her father in the library slumped down in his chair by the cold fireplace; her brother-in-law in his bedroom reading Plato's *Republic;* her husband in the drawing room hunched up on the divan before the bow window. She kissed him on the cheek and said, "We are all ready to go now," and gratefully took his proffered arm while he led her down to the carriage.

The courtroom was jammed with the hundreds of people come to hear the final verdict.

The judges filed in, took their places at the high tribunal. After what seemed an interminable silence, while her heart pumped hard and the child within her never stopped moving, Brigadier General George M. Brooke rose, spread out a paper before him and started to read:

"Of the first specification of first charge: Guilty. Of the second specification of first charge: Guilty. Of the third specification of first charge: Guilty."

She turned cold as he read all eleven of the first specifications, with a "Guilty" after each of them. He continued to read in a toneless voice:

"Of the first specification, second charge: Guilty. Of the second specification, second charge: Guilty," and continued to declare seven times "Guilty." Still carrying on in the clamped silence of the courtroom, he reiterated:

"Of the first specification, third charge: Guilty. Of the second specification, third charge: Guilty."

There was one last strangulating moment, and then the judge advocate rose before General Brooke and announced:

"The court finds Lieutenant Colonel Fremont guilty of mutiny; of disobedience of the lawful command of his superior officer; of conduct to the prejudice of good order and military discipline. The court does therefore sentence the said Lieutenant Colonel John C. Fremont, of the regiment of Mounted Riflemen, United States Army, to be dismissed from the service."

No one murmured or moved. Jessie did not dare to look at her husband or her father. Each sat alone, chewing the bitter herb of his thoughts. Then General Brooke once again rose and said in an easier tone: "The majority of this court after careful consideration wishes to make a final statement:

"Under the circumstances in which Lieutenant Colonel Fremont was placed between two officers of superior rank, each claiming to be commander in chief in California—circumstances in their nature calculated to embarrass the mind and excite the doubts of officers of greater experience than the accused—and in consideration of the important professional services rendered by him previous to the occurrence of those acts for which he has been tried, the undersigned, members of the court, respectfully commend Lieutenant Colonel Fremont to the lenient consideration of the President of the United States."

When they reached home John said: "You had better lie down at once, Jessie; I hope the verdict isn't going to make you ill."

She was surprised to find that instead of feeling ill she felt stronger than she had for several days; there was a time for being frightened, the waiting time, when one's fate hung in the balance and there was nothing one could do but suffer the tortures of uncertainty. Now she knew the worst; it had to be endured calmly and strongly; she had laid the groundwork for that endurance the night before when she had charted the objective case against her husband. She knew that this was the time for serenity and strength.

To her husband she replied, "Thank you, dear, but I feel all right. There is nothing those thirteen judges could have said that could have hurt me. That decision was arrived at before the case opened. Any civilian jury in a civil court would have acquitted you. I cannot be hurt by the determination of the War Department to put the Navy in its place. As the judges had the courage to say at the very end, you were the victim of a conflict over authority. I held before this trial opened, and I hold even more strongly now, that you did exactly right. If it means anything to you, my darling, I acquit you on all charges, and I say 'well done.' "

"It means a great deal to me," said John, not looking at her. "Your faith in me is the one rock that can never be shattered."

"Good then, let us go in to dinner. I am ravenous. It seems to me that I haven't eaten a hearty meal for weeks."

Later that evening she found her father in the library. She closed and locked the door behind her. He was having a difficult time repressing his anger.

"Very well," she said in a small voice. "The verdict is in. There is nothing we can do about the court-martial. Let us put all thoughts of it out of our minds. The important question now is: what will President Polk do?"

"He will overrule the decision of the court," growled Tom Benton.

"Are you certain of that?"

"He damned well better," he cried, "or I'll blast his administration. He knows that he and his Cabinet are responsible for the mess in California. They played careful and cautious; they wanted the credit for acquiring California, but they avoided the responsibility as though it were scarlet fever. They're avoiding the conflict of the Army and Navy in exactly the same fashion. If President Polk doesn't countermand that verdict, I'll start a senatorial investigation that will expose the whole regime."

Jessie felt the old sense of fear come over her. Why did men try to cover trouble with more trouble? Why didn't they know that the more deeply one became involved in exposure the more impossible it was to pull oneself up out of the morass? She did not want any more investigations; she did not want more charges and trials and hurt feelings and blasted reputations. She wanted only peace now, peace to go back to their work. She wanted her husband's hurts healed, as she knew that time alone could heal them. She wanted soft words now and quiet thinking, not threats and anger.

"I only want one thing, Father," she said. "I want President Polk to commute the sentence."

Her father sensed the tremulousness in his daughter's voice. He held out his big bearish arms to her and she sat on one knee hiding her face in his shoulder.

"I'm sorry, my little girl," he said softly. "I'm just dreadfully sorry. But don't feel too badly about it; most of the newspapers will protest the verdict, call it intergovernmental politics, nothing more."

Without lifting her head, Jessie asked in a muffled voice, "Will President Polk commute the sentence?"

"Yes. Of that I am certain. The court's recommendation for leniency makes it inevitable. That is why the judges put it in: it is their way of telling John that all is forgiven, and he can come home."

She lifted her head, speaking with all the intensity of her being:

"He must not leave the service. He has been in the Army for ten years. It's the only life he knows and the only life he loves. He has such pride in the Topographical Corps; he had plans for so many expeditions, and so much valuable work in carrying on the tasks of Nicollet and Hassler. If he must give up his uniform and his rank and his work, he will be like a man whose arms have been cut off . . ."

"I know, I know," interrupted her father sympathetically. "We cannot let him leave the Army. That is the one blow that would really cripple him. I will go to President Polk tomorrow, even though it is unnecessary. No one wants Colonel Fremont out of the service."

"If President Polk will order that the verdict be set aside, I won't regret anything that has happened or even condemn the court. We'll start fresh. I've talked to his fellow officers in the Topographical Corps; they want him back, they want him to continue his work. We'll get him sent out on another expedition, mapping the southwest trail to Los Angeles, perhaps. By the time he returns everything will be forgotten."

In her agitation she rose, walked to the long rough table and began opening atlases without seeing the maps. Her father came to her side.

"Everything you say is true, Jessie; true and sensible. Have no further fears. In another few days your husband will be back at work in the Topographical office drawing his maps of the third expedition."

Jessie turned about, a new vitality seizing her.

"That is the way it must be, Father; he must go back to work at once. I know that after he is plunged into his maps and his reports these bad memories will fade. After all, he did find a new trail to California, one which will replace the Oregon Trail. Thousands of people in the country are waiting to see his new map and read his report. And that is where he must go for his ultimate justification, to the people. They will sustain Colonel Fremont. But he must get back to his work; he must publish the results of his third expedition."

10

The next two days, while they waited for President Polk's decision, passed for Jessie in alternate rushes of hope and anxiety. She knew that when her father spoke in loud, blustering tones he could be wrong in his judgment, but he had assured her quietly that the president would commute her husband's sentence. She firmly believed this, but of it she said no word to John. She did not know what he was thinking, for he talked little, disappeared for long stretches each day, returning with his boots and the bottom of his trousers wet and mud-stained. That he had great hopes in President Polk, she knew, for had not President Polk sent him secret orders with Lieutenant Gillespie to take charge of the conquest in California? Had he not been Polk's confidential agent, superior in command to both General Kearny and Commodore Stockton? President Polk would not let him down. He would sustain Colonel Fremont, overthrow and dismiss the charges, praise him for his work in California and tell him to resume his sword. All these things Jessie learned were in her husband's mind from the scattered phrases he let drop as the weary hours spun themselves out.

At noon of the third day, just as they were about to sit down to a luncheon for which no one had any appetite, a courier arrived from the War Department. John jumped up from the luncheon table, ran into the foyer, snatched the letter when Jessie reached his side; together they read the lines that danced crazily before them:

Upon an inspection of the record, I am not satisfied that the facts proved in this case constitute the military crime of "mutiny." I am of the opinion that the second and third charges are sustained by the proof, and that the conviction upon these charges warrants the sentence of the court. The sentence of the court is therefore approved, but in consideration of the peculiar circumstances of the case, of the previous meritorious and valuable services of Lieutenant Colonel Fremont, and of the foregoing recommendations of a majority of the members of the court, the penalty of dismissal from the service is remitted.

Lieutenant Colonel Fremont will accordingly be released from arrest, will resume his sword, and report for duty.

JAMES K. POLK

Washington, February 14, 1848.

Relief and joy swept through her. President Polk had sustained her judgment, and that of the press and the people, by declaring her husband innocent of mutiny! It was unimportant that he upheld the court in decreeing that John had been guilty of conduct in the prejudice of military discipline. What was important was the fact that the president had praised her husband, spoken of his meritorious and valuable services. He had remitted the penalty of dismissal, ordered Colonel Fremont to resume his sword and report for duty.

She slid her arm about his shoulder and cried, "Oh, I am so happy, I knew it would come out all right. The president has vindicated you and praised you to the whole country."

John broke away from her embrace, stabbed her with a dark look of withdrawal, crumpled the president's paper to a pulp in his hand, flung it away from him and stormed out of her presence.

What have I done? she asked herself, numbly. Why does he behave like this?

After a moment she followed him up the stairs to their bedroom. He was standing at a window with his back to her, a back that had anger and hurt humiliation written across every hostile line. Jessie entered and stood in the center of the room.

"John," she said softly, "I'm sorry if I offended you. It was only that I was so happy and proud that President Polk had praised your work in California. It seemed to me that by praising you, he was telling the nation obliquely that this trial should never have been held."

Her words struck irresilience. Still groping in the dark, fearful lest she offend him further, she slid into a chair, was silent for a few moments, then continued:

"You see, my dear, I am being a little selfish in this affair: I know that in part they have been trying you for my act two years ago in St. Louis, when I suppressed the order summoning you back to Washington. And I sent you the first unauthorized instructions to act in California. If President Polk had declared you guilty of mutiny, he would have been convicting me as well. But the president said we are not guilty of mutiny. If he's unwilling to expose his own hand, to tell the world that he fomented the uprising in California through you, then we must suffer in silence. That is the part of the job we agreed to do when I suggested you move quickly and boldly. Who in the country is better able to vindicate you than our chief executive? The president has declared publicly how valuable you have been, and by ordering you back to your command, he is telling the country that you are indispensable."

John turned about quickly, his eyes blazing, his skin greenish beneath the black beard.

"I won't take his charity," he said in a cold, embittered voice. "He knows I'm innocent; that whole prejudiced court knows I'm innocent; but they turned against me, they slandered my character and minimized my contribution. Then they throw me a bone with a few shreds of meat on it and expect me to grovel before them in gratitude. President Polk has done a cowardly thing; he is perpetuating the injustice of the court. Why didn't he have the courage to declare me innocent . . . ?"

"He did, darling, he did," urged Jessie, trying to placate him. "Don't you see how he told the court they were wrong when they declared you guilty of mutiny?"

"Then why didn't he overthrow the other two convictions? Why does he deal in half-measures . . . ?"

She interrupted, but quietly, so as not to antagonize him:

"It wouldn't be wise to hurt the War Department too severely, John. You must be tolerant; you must understand that the president can't completely disavow the Army. That would lead to ill feelings, to conflicts within the government . . ."

"I see! It's better to commit still another injustice, to declare an innocent man guilty, rather than incur the displeasure . . ."

"It goes deeper than that, John dear. Every day of his life the president has to make a thousand compromises. In this affair he has to keep you satisfied, and the Army and the Navy satisfied as well. I think he leaned over on your side considerably; he will suffer from it, never fear."

He took several steps toward her, demanding, "Then you approve his decision? You approve his declaring me guilty of disobedience to my superior officers, of conduct prejudicial to good order and military discipline? I never thought I would live to see the day when my wife . . ."

Sick at heart, Jessie jumped up, went to him and flung her arms about his neck.

"No, no! I'm only saying that it was a sop the president had to throw to the Army."

"Yet you approve the president's confirmation of the conviction," he flung out at her. "What a miserable state of affairs this is: you say I am innocent of the charges, yet you approve the guilty verdict! Really, Jessie, I am astonished! You're taking sides against me."

"Please don't say things like that. Can't you be generous enough to allow this compromise? Then the affair will be settled to everyone's satisfaction . . ."

"To everyone's satisfaction!" he cried with irony. "To my satisfaction? After I conquered a whole new territory for them, I have to be tried like a criminal, have the court declare me guilty and the president sustain the verdict, and my wife tells me that it should be to my satisfaction! Jessie, what has come over you? How can you say these things to me?"

She realized that it would be unwise to continue. Instead she agreed that President Polk had avoided his full duty. Since her opposition seemed only to infuriate him, she understood that it would be better to go along with him and by her agreement, her love, slowly soften his harsh anger, blur the edges of his indignation, and let time come to her rescue. She must not allow him to feel that she too was against him, that she was part of the conspiracy to persecute him. Only a few days before he had told her that her faith in him was the one rock that could never be shattered. Right or wrong, she must never allow that faith in her loyalty to be dissipated.

There was a knock at the door. Jessie called, "Come in." Her father entered the room. He carried the president's paper in his hand; he had smoothed it out, read the message and come up to congratulate John on the outcome.

"I told you that President Polk would stand by the colonel!" he exclaimed happily to his daughter. He walked to his son-in-law with his hand extended. "Ah John," he said kindly, "I'm happy for all our sakes that it's over. It will be good to see you come striding down the street again with your sword clanging at your side. I know how anxious you are to get back to your work . . ."

"I am not going back to my work," broke in John, sharply.

Tom Benton's hand dropped to his side, while his big bluff face bore an expression of bewilderment.

"Not going back . . ."

"No. I am resigning from the Army."

Tom screwed up his eyes until they were reduced to narrow slits, but he could perceive the meaning no better that way. He turned to his daughter, asking, "What is the meaning of this, Jessie?"

She was passionately convinced that John must not resign, both because she felt that his resignation would be in some small measure an admission of guilt, but mostly because she was horrified at the thought of his giving up the work for which he had trained himself, which he loved so ardently, and for which he was so well equipped. What would he do? After his expeditions and years on the trail, could he become a government clerk, go to work in a shop? To what did a man of his training turn? He could get a teaching job, but he was a man of action, not a man of theory and classrooms; he would wither in such an atmosphere. She was not worried about how good a living he could earn, that was unimportant; what concerned her was how her husband was going to find another place in the world which would enable him to be valuable, to hold his head high, to keep his flaming spirit, to be a man among men and a leader among men. He had deliberately and joyously chosen his role and prepared himself for it, just as her father had, and she knew how badly it would break Thomas Hart Benton if he could no longer be the senator from Missouri.

She must not let her husband resign from the Army! Yet he was utterly confident that she would agree with him and sustain his judgment: their years of happy marriage, the complete confidence and intimacy of their every plan had made it impossible for him to imagine that she would not uphold his decision.

Faced with a painful dilemma, she had to choose between the equally desperate alternatives of permitting John to wreck his brilliant career, or herself to wreck their marriage; for she sensed that their marriage would be irrevocably injured if she inflicted upon him the blow of contesting his judgment. Before she had accepted John's proposal of marriage she had asked for the right to collaborate with her husband in his work, and he had granted that right. It was a tragic mistake for him to resign; it was arbitrary of him to take this step without consulting with her. But there had been another covenant in the marriage agreement: she had promised to cherish him in sickness and in health, in misfortune and in prosperity, to go with him whither he went. These vows left no room for indecision: she had no right to cut the fabric of their marriage. His career would shift and change and vary, rise and fall, succeed and fail many times over the years. But the marriage relationship was more tenuous, more in need of protection: it must never fail, it must never shift and change and vary, it must not endure despair and renunciation.

She thought, There are no ugly or painful memories that either of us can evoke about our marriage, nor must there be any. Marriage is not only the most important relationship, but the one which can make all the rest of life seem beautiful and worthwhile, no matter how difficult its externals. If I sustain our marriage, I sustain all; if I fail in this and yet succeed in everything else, I shall have failed in my life.

She went to her husband's side, slipped her hand into his and held herself against his shoulder.

"It's very simple, Father," she said in a quiet, almost casual tone. "John is resigning from the Army."

"But why?" thundered Tom Benton. "He's been pardoned! He's been praised! Everyone expects him to go back . . ."

"I'm not going back to an army that could declare me guilty on twenty-two specifications, not even having the decency or comradely good will to declare that I had proved my innocence on at least one of the counts."

"Of course, of course," Tom boomed, "it was a miserable show. But seven of the judges signed the affidavit asking the president to commute the order."

John picked up a copy of the document lying on his desk, folded back the first page, then pointed to a paragraph on the second.

"Did you read this?" he demanded, harshly. "Do you really advise me to return to an army which says: 'The court has found nothing conflicting in the orders and instructions of the government; nothing impeaching the testimony of the part of the prosecution; nothing, in fine, to qualify, in a legal sense, the resistance to authority of which the accused is convicted . . .' The only way I can register a full protest is to resign."

Realizing the grave consequences, but not knowing what to do next, Tom Benton turned to his daughter for the help he was certain would be forthcoming.

"What do you say to all this, Jessie?" he demanded.

For a split second Jessie thought that her breath would stop coming. Her husband had been hurt anew by her father's stand; his pride already had suffered so deeply that there was danger of injuring his very fiber. He would never recover if they stood against him. Knowing that her father was absolutely right and her husband absolutely wrong, she nevertheless understood that she must stand by her husband, by this man who had never had a sense of security, a sense of the confidence of the world and his associates. She must accept his judgment and, more important, show him by every word and gesture that she agreed with him.

She caught hold of herself, drew breath in sharply and replied, her voice under full control:

"I agree with John."

Her father's face seemed to sag.

"You agree! But Jessie, that's impos . . . Only two days ago you . . ."

"Two days ago I did not know that President Polk would not dismiss all the charges."

"But don't you realize . . ."

"I realize that an injustice has been done to my husband. It is his right to register the severest possible protest."

All of the pomp and sternness went out of Tom Benton; to Jessie's blurred eyes it seemed that her father too was trapped.

He cried in despair, "I thought I had trained you in masculine logic. I thought I had made a man of you in straight thinking. And here you are, thinking like a woman!"

Jessie smiled a little plaintively, then replied, "Yes, Father, just like a woman."

There was a finality in her voice which prevented Tom Benton from persisting. She was unhappy at hurting him, at being obliged to conceal the truth behind her motives. But her first duty was to protect her husband; in marriage there was no right or wrong, logic or illogic, reason or unreason; there was only a man's nature to work with, a man's gifts and limitations, his emotion, his temperament, his personality, his character: these and these alone were the determinants of conduct. Marriage was the rock; all else was the foam which beat against the rock.

11

SHE WENT WITH HIM to select the best black broadcloth on the market, yet the first time she saw her husband in civilian clothes Jessie's heart sank. In the eight years that she had known him she had never seen John in any apparel but his army uniform, which he had always worn handsomely and with pride. His dark suit had been well made, it fitted him nicely, but he wore it awkwardly; he who had shown infinite grace beneath his plain army blue now evidenced by every stiff, resentful movement that he knew his stature had been lessened.

Despite the fact that his notes, journals and drawings still were in San Francisco, Jessie was convinced that they had to write the memoir of his third expedition. Even if nothing appreciable came of it, the work would be the best thing conceivable for him. It would be difficult to get him to begin work; yet there were important reasons why she must bring this third report into being: his salary, never a large one, had now stopped altogether. It was the first time that she had encountered an actual need for money: while her husband's salary had been modest, their expenses in the Benton home had been small, otherwise they could not have saved the three thousand dollars which he had handed over to the American consul Larkin in Monterey to buy a ranch in the Santa Cruz mountains overlooking the Pacific Ocean. They yearned to leave Washington behind them, to go out to California, build themselves a home on their ranch, set up a little community to be called Fremontville.

But they hadn't the money to book passage to California, for the voyage was an expensive one; they had no money to build themselves a house even if they could reach their ranch; most serious of all, they had no resources with which to buy horses, farm machinery, feed and live-stock, or to pay for the necessary labor. Tom Benton had offered to lend them money; Harriet Bodisco had come to Jessie just before the trial with a jewel case of diamonds and sapphires and asked her to please sell them and use the money for their expenses; friends like James Buchanan had offered to lend them anything they might need.

She was not frightened at the lack of money, but she sensed how severely her husband might suffer if the burden of debt were added to the others. The memoir was a way out of their difficulties; it would set her husband back to work, help rid him of his concentration on himself. Its publication could perhaps earn them a sum of money adequate to get them to California and start work on their ranch. If the book were successful, then she was confident that the newspapers and magazines would buy their stories.

She worked on the assumption that eventually he would of course write his third report; she had known that he would refuse to do so, and had prepared her attack against this defeatism. It was a long, slow, uphill battle, but she was in no hurry. A good wife must be a leveler: when her husband was riding the crest it was her obligation to deflate his ego by placing his accomplishment in proper perspective, to keep him from growing inordinately fond of himself. This was a comparatively simple task for any woman who had a light touch and was gifted with humor;

the more difficult task for a wife was when her husband was discouraged, unhappy, at loose ends, without a job or a purpose or a direction. It was then that the wife had to create a healthy setting for her husband, establish the right mood, bring out the best in him, buttress his confidence by keeping in the forefront his gifts and accomplishments.

Being a good wife was probably the most difficult achievement in the human agenda.

After a few weeks, in the early days of March, she saw that she almost had him convinced; she needed only one culminating stroke. That night she confided to her husband that she was pregnant, that this time she had the utmost confidence it would be their long-desired son, and she wanted to have the report finished before young John came into the world. She determined that by the time the child was born, sometime late in July, the memoir must be completed and published, her husband once again established.

Now more than ever she was grateful for the years of intensive training she had had with her father. She worked steadily, but not too long at a stretch. She was not carrying as well as she had with Lily; her youth and health had been eaten into. However, her main concern was with her husband. Though she had succeeded in reviving his energy and health sufficiently to begin work, he would go to no dinners or parties, he took the long walks and rides so necessary to his well-being only after dark, after he had put her to bed. At the dinner table it was obvious that he was unhappy, constrained. For once she did not regret it when Congress adjourned in the spring and her father returned to St. Louis. She thought that the work and her companionship were helping her husband a little, bringing him back slowly, enabling his eyes to look at people head on. Yet no one knew better than she what a slow process his recovery would be.

Then one day, as she was sitting before her desk in the library rewriting a section of geographic description, he burst into the room with his old-time enthusiasm, embraced her and cried:

"Darling, listen to this! Your father has arranged another expedition for me!"

Her eyes crinkled as she looked at his glowing face, spots of color bringing the warm flesh tones back to his cheeks, his eyes dancing.

"Another expedition," she said slowly. "But how . . . ?"

"Some of his friends in St. Louis want to build a railroad to the Pacific coast. They have the money and the backing; all they need is a southern route that the trains will be able to run over in winter."

"They are engaging you to find a railroad pass," exclaimed Jessie.

"But of course! Whom else could they turn to to find another pass?"

He pushed aside her little table with so much vitality that it fell over

on the red carpet, the papers flying. He went on both knees before her,
slipped his hands under her arms and, gripping her shoulder blades with
powerful fingers, exclaimed in a voice she had not heard since he had left
on his third expedition almost three years before:

"They are going to finance the expedition any way I want to put it
together. And they are willing to pay me partly in railroad stock."

She gave him a kiss of affirmation.

"You see," she exclaimed, "you are going to be a railroad magnate!
And after you find a new pass you will serve as engineer, lay out the whole
route for the railroad, just as you helped Captain Williams before you
came to Washington."

"God bless your father!" exclaimed John.

Amen, said Jessie to herself; he has saved our lives.

Aloud she said, "Let me see the letter. When must you go? Are you to
buy your equipment in New York or St. Louis? How soon . . . ?"

"Not so fast, not so fast," he laughed gaily. "The details are to be
worked out later. But here, you can see by the letter it is all settled. Ah,
Jessie, I'm so happy at this chance . . ."

Jessie rubbed her cheek down the side of his soft beard.

"We must hurry and finish our report," she commented. "We must
have it ready for the printer before you have to go to St. Louis. And while
you are organizing your expedition and setting out on the trail for the
coast for the fourth time, the country will be reading of your route to
California . . . There, I'm crying all over your lovely beard. I am so
happy for all of us. And particularly for your son; when he gets himself
born his first sight of his father will be one of watching you prepare for
the trail."

He combed his fingers through her long brown hair.

"I'm so happy I'll even take a second daughter and like it."

"You'll say as Father did," replied Jessie mockingly, " 'two daughters
are a crown to any household.' But will you swear?"

"Just like General Scott," he grinned. "I thought you were so anxious
to get on with this work? Come along, then, let's gather these papers
together. I think I can dictate some good material: my mind is on fire; I
can remember whole passages I wrote in my journal."

The old John returned in full measure. They worked together vigorously and well, pleased with the way the memoir was shaping up, excited
over the early preparations he was making to assemble his comrades from
the first three expeditions. During the last two weeks of May she did an
extensive rewrite by herself to give the material greater readability. A
publisher had been found who was enthusiastic at the prospects of a
robust sale.

One evening toward the end of May when she had put in an extremely long day and had just about finished the last pages, she turned from her work and said to her husband, who was lying in front of the fire:

"John, you promised that there would be no more separations. The baby is due at the end of July. You don't expect to leave on the expedition until the end of September. I'll be strong enough by then; can't I come with you? I have always wanted to make the overland passage."

He turned over on his side, supported his head on one elbow and gazed at her admiringly.

"You have a lot of spunk, Jessie: you can sit there big with child and declare that only a few weeks after your baby is born you want to make the crossing over the Rockies in winter. No, my dear, not this time."

"But I can't bear the thought of being separated from you . . ."

He leaped to his feet, picked her out of her chair, and sat down with her on his lap.

"You're right, Jessie, no more long separations: you will come with me to the Delaware Indian Reservation on the Missouri, my last jumping-off place. While I head overland, you will return to New York and take a ship around Cape Horn. By the time I reach San Francisco you will be there with the two children. We will go to our ranch and build our home, and then we will never be separated any more."

Jessie rested securely with her head against his chest. She felt tired and weak from her labors of the day and from a sense of being stretched taut by the growing child within her.

"I suppose you're right," she said. "The boy would be too young to send with a wet nurse around the Horn. It won't be such a long time, and I'll be happy at the thought of our new home. Now, set me back in the chair so I can finish those last pages. I want you to be here when I write Finis."

He put her back in her chair, adjusted her desk, then went to the map table. After a moment or two she called:

"Don't move the lamp. It makes it too dark for me to write."

He turned swiftly.

"What did you say, Jessie?"

"I said don't move the lamp, it's growing dark. Oh, John, quick, I'm faint . . ."

He carried her to her bed, then summoned the doctor, who ordered her to remain there for the six or seven weeks until her baby should be born. She felt well again the next day, but was glad the doctor had restricted her. She would have a chance to rest and grow strong for her hour of trial. The memoir went to the printer, and in June the Senate ordered twenty thousand copies of John's map to California. The map was received with acclaim throughout the nation; this triumph, added to the fact that it was known he was organizing a fourth expedition, brought him back to himself. The bad days were behind them; they had survived and were going forward.

And so Jessie lay quietly in her blue bedroom with the windows overlooking the garden wide open, while her friends came to call, bringing her candy and light romantic novels.

At dawn of July 24, 1848, her son was born. It had taken her almost seven years to fulfill one of her husband's greatest needs, yet if she had had to wait so long, surely she could not have found a better moment to bear a male heir. Flushed with pride she said to her husband as he appeared in the doorway:

"You don't need a flag to put over my bed this time. You have a son. We're going to name him John Charles Fremont, after you."

He caressed her with the love and gratitude in his eyes, then went to her side, kissed the palm of each hand.

"Not John Charles Fremont," he said, generous in his joy. "Benton Fremont, after your father. He has done so much for us. I want my son to carry his name."

12

TOWARD THE END OF SEPTEMBER she felt sufficiently strong to make the trip to St. Louis. They traveled together as a family of four now. Lily, who was almost six, was a quiet child, matter-of-fact, without any of the impetuousness of her parents, rather like her grandmother and her aunt Eliza. They had tried to keep most of the troubles of the trial away from Lily's small world, but she had seemed to understand what was going on, and Jessie had noted that her plain-faced and mild-mannered little girl had been solicitous of them during the bad months.

Lily seemed joyous about having a baby in the family; she was more affectionate with the little one than she ever had been with her mother or father. She hovered over the child, wanting to do little duties for him. Jessie occasionally would let her select the dress or wrapper he was to wear, which made her feel important.

"When will he be old enough for me to play with him, Mother?" she would ask.

"Soon," replied Jessie with a satisfied smile.

"But how soon? When we get to St. Louis? Will you let me dress him?"

She was nursing the baby herself. It was too early to know what he would be like, but she was sometimes a little disturbed at how quietly he lay in her arms, how much she had to urge him to suck the milk from her breast. He had been born with a patch of black hair coming over his ears and straggling down the back of his neck; in his features he looked like his father, even to the dark skin. She loved him wildly.

The early parts of the trip by stagecoach and train were pleasant in the early fall weather, with the leaves turning brown and the crops in the fields half through their harvest. They stood in the prow of the little river boat *Saratoga* making its way down the Ohio. Jessie held the baby in her arms, with Lily clinging to her skirt. Though she had borne two children her figure still was lithe and girlish; her eyes were a deeper hazel and more solicitous now, for they had come to know the nature of pain, but her face was happy once again, her skin smooth, flushed with health. John was wearing a mustache, but he had had his beard cropped close before leaving Washington, and he was carrying his civilian clothes with an air of familiarity.

With a start Jessie realized that they were in much the same position as Mary Algood, the young mother with whom she had talked on the outskirts of St. Louis and who had invited her to come along to Oregon. It was now the Fremonts' turn to go west to become free again. Her brain whirled at the thought of how far they had risen in so few years, and how far they had fallen in an even shorter time.

It was particularly good to be back home in St. Louis. Everyone received them cordially. The enclosed galleries around the patio were still warm and redolent of acacias. She was happy to slip into the slow, peaceful life of the Mississippi River port, content to do little but take care of her son while John scurried about to meetings, buying his supplies and interviewing the French voyagers who wanted to accompany him. He was disconcerted that only a few of his old-time companions of the trail were available; the others were scattered all over the Pacific coast and the Southwest; for the most part he had to accept new and untried men.

Her father was entranced by his first grandson, particularly because he had been named Benton. It seemed to Jessie that everybody wanted to fondle the infant. She had been told that she would leave with her husband for the Delaware Indian Reservation in October. A competent and reliable nurse was found so that Jessie was able to spend the last few days helping John and preparing her own clothing. Two days before they were to leave, John awakened at dawn, dressed and hurried out to meet his party of frontiersmen. Jessie was lying abed, half asleep and half awake when the nurse came running in, her eyes wide with terror.

"Mrs. Fremont," she cried, "come quick! We can't wake the baby."

Springing out of bed, Jessie ran next door to the nursery. Lily, still in her nightgown, was standing over the crib frantically rubbing young Benton's hand between hers.

"Mama," she cried, "the baby won't wake up. We've been shaking him and shaking him and he won't wake up."

Jessie took a quick look at her son, saw that his face was purple. She sent for the doctor, then picked the boy up, wrapped a blanket around him, carried him into her room and took him into bed with her, clasping him fiercely against her bosom, her eyes wide and unseeing, her heart like a stone in her chest.

She did not know how much time passed. Their family doctor, who had taken care of the baby since their arrival in St. Louis, came into the room. Gently he took the child from Jessie, unwrapped the blanket and made a quick examination. He then covered the child. It was several moments before he spoke.

"I'm terribly sorry, Mrs. Fremont," he said. "The boy is dead. I've been afraid all along that he had a defective heart. He must have been born with it."

Jessie's ears were shut to words and her mind to meaning. She held the child to her, his little head on her shoulder, her cheek on his.

"The baby is dead, Miss Jessie," said the doctor. "Do let me have him."

She made no move. After several moments she looked up at the doctor with a twisted smile and said without emotion: "I have had him such a little while. Please go away, all of you. We'll wait here until my husband comes."

She remained alone, still clasping the child. After a time John came up the stairs and into their room. She saw his sharp, worried look, his first concern for her and how she might be taking the loss. He leaned over her where she lay white-faced in the bed. She was grateful for his silence, and then she was grateful that he had begun to speak. His voice was compassionate.

"I won't try to comfort you, Jessie."

"No, please don't."

"The boy is gone. We will have to get used to the idea. It will be hard, but we can do it, together."

"You may take him now," she murmured.

John lifted the paper-light body of his dead son, took a last look at the boy's face, then covered his head with the blanket, stepped outside the door and gave him to the nurse. Quickly he returned to his wife's side, and with the blankets tucked under her back and legs picked her up and carried her to a deep chair by the window, where she held herself to him with the same fierceness with which she had just a moment before held her son.

"You can cry now, my dear," he said.

And so the tears came. All the tears she had not shed when her husband had returned from California a prisoner; all the tears she had not shed during the days of the trial when the man she loved was publicly lacerated until all of his pride was stripped from him; all the tears she had not shed when the court had declared her husband a malefactor, a traitor to his service; all the tears she had not shed when she had felt it imperative to support her husband against her father, to help him resign from the service and halt his career; all the tears she had not shed when she had seen her husband that first time in civilian clothes and realized how wounded he was and how profoundly his stature had diminished.

All these things somehow had not counted when her son had been born; this good fortune had made up for all they had undergone; she no longer had any hatred for General Stephen Watts Kearny, for the judges of the tribunal. In the depths of her gratitude she had freely forgiven them all, harbored no resentment.

As the hours passed, the bitterness flooded back. If not for General Kearny there would have been no arrest, no blasting of her husband's career in California, no court-martial. Her husband's return to Washington would have been one of triumph; she could have carried her child in health and serenity. Instead they had sapped her strength, made her undergo unending torment, and as her strength had fled, so had the strength of the child she was carrying. A defective heart? No wonder! How could she have carried a normal, healthy child during those miserable months? Now she could never forgive her husband's enemies: they had robbed him of his son.

Lily was sent to the Brants' so that she would not be exposed to the grief of the household. When she was brought back Jessie asked that she come up to her room. Lily was uneasy. Jessie took her daughter on her lap.

"I have something to tell you . . . about . . . the baby. You see Lily . . . he . . ."

"I know," interrupted Lily. "He'll never grow up to play with me."

On the evening before they were scheduled to leave for the reservation, while she was mechanically chewing the food which had been brought to her on a tray, John said, "My dear, it would be better if you don't come with me. Here you will have your father to watch over you, a good doctor and a nurse. Conditions are primitive on the Indian reservation . . ."

"Please," begged Jessie, "don't make me stay here. I'm not sick in my body, only in my heart. I feel better when you're by my side."

"It's lonely on the reservation; there is only one white couple. I won't be able to be with you much during the day, I will have to be working with the men."

She slipped her hand gently into his.

"Just to know that you are close by will be enough for me. If I am with you I won't need doctors and nurses. Please let me come. I need to be near you these next weeks."

He squeezed her hand reassuringly.

"All right, I'll take you with me on one condition: that you eat your dinner. You're getting so thin, I'm frightened for you."

She took the fork of potatoes which he held to her lips.

"Don't be frightened for me, John. I'll be all right. We'll have more sons. Being with you on the reservation will help me; when the time comes for you to leave, I will return to New York and take the ship around the Horn."

13

THEY REACHED THE INDIAN RESERVATION at dusk of the second day. On the clearing were a number of tepees of the Indian colony and two rough log cabins, one occupied by Major Cummins and his wife, the other for passing trappers, guides and army officers. Major Cummins and his wife were plain but kindly people to whom hospitality was the first law of the frontier. They had had no opportunity to hear of Jessie's loss; when the cabins came in sight, Jessie asked her husband if they might omit all mention of the boy.

The Cumminses had lived at this frontier point for thirty years, on the edge of the trailless prairie. Mrs. Cummins was a woman of about fifty, with all of the independence and matter-of-factness of the wives who follow their husbands to the outposts of the world. She settled Jessie in the one-room cabin with its hard-beaten earth floor, its open fireplace for both cooking and heating, hand-hewn log table and chairs, and one shop-built piece on the reservation, the bed that had been carted on horseback from St. Louis. Jessie had no wish to appear unresponsive to Mrs. Cummins.

John rose each day at dawn to join his men at camp. At midmorning Jessie would walk a mile or so over the prairie to sit in the shade of the cottonwoods and watch them put their wagons, animals, gear, scientific implements and foodstuffs into shape. It brought her comfort to watch her husband directing his men, supervising the details of work to insure their greatest possible safety. He appeared at his best at such moments: giving his orders in a low and gentle tone of voice, yet commanding the respect and instant attention of the men. She liked to watch the rhythmical way he moved about the camp, the bright gleam of his eyes as he gave a word of approval here, corrected an error or oversight there, the ease with which he operated because of his experience and skill; the feeling he gave of assurance, of joy in a well-loved task. And Jessie was grateful to her father for having secured this chance for him, grateful that Tom Benton should have invested several thousand dollars in a venture from which he was not likely to receive any return.

She walked back to the reservation at noon; John rode in about four o'clock to have a cup of hot tea with her and to chat quietly of the simple things that had happened during the day, or to lay their plans for the house they would build in California, with its windows overlooking the Pacific, the simple log-cabin school and church they would put up, much as Grandmother Benton had in Bentonville a half-century before.

The nights should have been the easiest, for her husband was at her side, falling asleep with his arms about her, but in the darkness the images came back, images which the sparkling sun diffused. At night, lying sleepless, her thin body curled up but her mind stiff and slablike, she saw the face of her infant before her; she felt the tugging of his gums at her breast; lived again the joy of those first hours when she realized she had given her husband a son to carry his name. At such moments she knew that there was no grief that could compare with the death of a son.

When she fell into a troubled sleep she would be awakened by a swift muted cry which would rend the silence of the night air, the cry of a momentary but mortal struggle as something outside the cabin was killed by an attacker. She mentioned these ghostly noises to no one, and it was not until the fourth day that she accidentally learned what they were, by going out with John at dawn one morning to find the usually quiet-spoken Major Cummins in a torrential rage.

"That blasted wolf killed another of our sheep," he cried. "She just had a litter of cubs and she drags our sheep back there to feed 'em. We've worked so hard and so long to raise these ewes; we can hardly last out the winter without fresh meat."

The merging nights and days passed all too quickly for her. At last the hour of parting struck. John's men had moved ten miles out to the edge of the prairie, the horses being fattened against the lean months of forage in the snow-covered mountains. They were to strike camp at sunrise the next morning. As he left the cabin John called that he would be back for four o'clock tea.

At noon Major Cummins knocked at her door.

"Come along with me, Mrs. Fremont," he exclaimed, a look of resolution on his grizzled face. "I'm about to prove the old adage that revenge is sweet."

Not knowing what he meant or what he wanted of her, Jessie thought it the courteous course to go along. The major had two horses in the small corral between the cabins; he helped her into the saddle and headed sharply west to a deep-gorged ravine. He dismounted, assisted Jessie off her horse, took her by the arm and led her at so fast a pace that she would have fallen were it not for his tight grip. The trail turned sharply, and just ahead Jessie saw a clump of oaks.

"Wait here, Mrs. Fremont," said the major, "you will be able to see all right."

She watched him drop silently to the oaks, take out his revolver and fire quickly five times. When the sound of the shots died away she heard death moans similar to the ones that had interrupted her sleep in the cabin. Major Cummins came up the trail, flushed.

"That will be the end of the sheep killing," he told her with grim satisfaction. "I just killed all five of the wolf cubs."

Jessie's head throbbed. Killing and death, death and killing. That's all there was in this world. Everyone and everything kills. Men kill each other, animals kill each other, men and animals kill each other. Death and bloodshed and misery.

She whispered, "Major, I am feeling ill. You had better take me on your horse and hold me, or I'll fall off."

Anxious, though not understanding, Major Cummins lifted her to his horse and carried her quickly back to the reservation. He summoned his wife, who put her to bed and made her a strong cup of coffee. Jessie thanked the woman, said that she thought she could go to sleep.

She lay abed in the most aching misery she had ever known, worse than that hour when she had held her dead son in her arms. What was left but death, continuous and senseless death? What did life hold but ugly and senseless and tragic destruction of one's hopes and plans and ideals? She was not bitter against any one person or any one thing: wolves had to kill sheep to live; men had to kill wolves to live. But did men have to kill men to live? Did they have to destroy each other to stay alive? Did Kearny have to kill her infant son in order to survive? Was this world nothing more than a cage of snarling beasts, with the rule of dog eat dog the only one that made survival possible? If everyone and everything had to kill to live, was life worth while?

She did not hold Major Cummins responsible for what she had just gone through; she did not even hold him responsible for what she knew the wolf mother would suffer when she came back to her lair and found her five cubs dead. Major Cummins had had no way of knowing what this sight would do to her; nor had he any way of knowing what this killing would do to the wolf mother. And even if he had known, could he have refrained from the butchering? Could he let the wolf take away the meat that he and his family needed to live on when they would be snow-bound in winter?

Through all the years of her childhood, up to the last few months, she had believed that she lived in a good and beautiful world, a world in which ideals and kindness could survive, in which each person could determine the kind of life he wanted to live, where intelligence and training and industry led to accomplishment, where one could rest secure in the knowledge that he lived in an orderly universe.

What a sentimental child she had been, what a blind, stupid and misguided idiot! She had thought she could lay out the pattern of her days. She had thought she knew what she was doing, that she could control events and circumstance. She had not listened to counsel, taken the opinion or guidance of older and wiser people; she had been positive of what she wanted, of how she was going to get it; of exactly what she was going to do with her life as the accomplishments and rewards rolled up. And now the dream had given way to the reality. What was there but fire, the fire of greed and quarrelsomeness and lust for destroying?

She had thought before that her heart had been broken; now she knew that it had only been suspended, enduring in a kind of somnambulistic trance the misery of her loss. Always deep at the base of her brain had been the knowledge that time would cure this illness, that her strength would revive, that she would be able to go on, to conceive and bear more sons. She had known she could survive.

Now she felt no further chance for survival; now her heart and her brain and her spirit were truly broken by the unending, senseless and brutal tragedies of mankind.

And now she knew that she had been bitterly wrong; her mother had been right. Only a few months before when she had seen pity in her mother's eyes she had rejected it summarily, wanting and needing no pity, thinking her mother weak in failing to understand that her daughter had the stamina to brave the revolutions of fortune. But now her mind brought back line by line everything her mother had told her on her trip to Cherry Grove before her marriage:

"I like your young man, Jessie, don't misunderstand me, but he is like your father! He will always be striving and battling his way uphill, spreading about him with a vast club, just as Tom Benton always has, and for that reason he will have his enemies lurking around every corner, with daggers and foul names, ready to stab at every opportunity. You will never know quiet or tranquillity, Jessie. You will live forever in conflict and dissension, with struggle mixed into the very food you eat at your dinner table, poisoning the milk with which you feed your babies. That is not good for a woman, Jessie. It kills everything in her, destroys that inner spirit which must give her a sense of relaxation and security if she is to live happily and raise her children. A man's work is the least important part of him, the menial labor that he must do, and get done as fast as possible, in order to earn a living, and when he enters his home he should wipe off the stain of that labor as he wipes the mud from his shoes. My poor baby, how I pity you! How much misery and suffering you are rushing out to embrace."

A woman's position had truly been decreed by nature: to manage her home, bear her children, keep her house and children and husband well and cared for. Outside this realm she should never set foot. She should not go into the arenas of conflict, demand the right to work and fight by her husband's side, bear the blows and exhaustions and disillusionments of a man's world of conflict. She had been so very wrong: she should have married someone like her cousin Preston Johnson; no matter how much she had admired and loved John she should have known from what her mother had told her of the fighting and tempestuous male, she should have known from the revelations of his belligerent nature that trouble would arise, trouble so deep-cutting and critical that it would endanger them all, not only their health and position but their very lives as well.

Already it had cost the life of her son. And now it was costing her own life: for she knew that there was not the strength in her ever to believe again, ever to hope for peace or an orderly and sweet life. She was only twenty-four, but she had endured the sufferings of a hundred years; her heart had grown old and died within her breast. That breast was dead too, the milk within her had dried. Grandmother McDowell had told her that last time at Cherry Grove, "You will have your battles after you marry that young man of yours, and you will carry scars, but you will carry them the way my mother did, like medals bestowed for bravery." Grandmother McDowell had misjudged her, just as she had misjudged herself. She could endure no more battles, carry no more scars.

For all this she blamed no one but herself. She had been the aggressive woman, headstrong and determined; she had thought to change the status of a wife, to make of a wife something more than a housekeeper and a brood mare; she had thought to develop a husband's sinews and to further the world's work by the use of the training and brains that God had vouchsafed her sex. And now in seven years she had willfully and blindly destroyed them all: her son, herself, her husband. For how could John survive with a dead woman by his side, a woman whose love for him had vanished because love had been burnt out of her heart by human cruelty? She did not feel sorry for her little boy, he was dead and gone; she felt sorry only for those who were living and who would be hurt so deeply by her death: her husband, her daughter, her father and mother. If only she had not insisted upon working so hard at the trial, insisted upon going every day, exposing herself to the emotional turmoil, to the cold and fatigue, she would not have injured her baby. She had killed her son, just as deliberately as Major Cummins had killed the wolf cubs. Her husband should hate her for that. He does hate me, she thought, only he's too kind to let me see it. Why shouldn't he hate me, when I killed his career too, when I am responsible for his troubles, when I am the one who encouraged him to mutiny?

I wanted to be a good wife. I worked so hard to be a good wife; now I know that the best wife is the least wife. There can be no mixing of a man's world and a woman's world; if I had stayed out of his affairs they would not be in chaos. If only I had shown the same responsibility to the child I was carrying; if only I had said to myself, I am pregnant, I must not expose myself to this excitement . . . If only . . .

Ah yes, she thought with a terrifying clarity, if only. Two of the shortest words in the English language, and yet how long their implications. On what a long trail they have led me to this dreadful moment. A few hours ago I said that there is no grief that can compare with the death of a son. In this too I was wrong: even greater is the grief of knowing that you have come to the end of love and marriage with the man who was the fulfillment of your dreams. I cannot go out to California to meet him; I cannot endure the voyage; I cannot endure starting over again. I cannot endure the thought of making similar mistakes, of leading us both to the same unhappy ending in everything we start. I am no good for John. I have killed my love for him because I have killed everything inside me that can feel. What will living with a dead woman do to his tortured soul? Isn't it kinder to let him go to California and build a new life for himself there without me? I can only do him harm. But can I break my pledge to him, let him arrive and find that I am never coming? He called me the rock of his faith; with this last rock shattered, what will happen to him? O dear God, she murmured, what am I to do?

The long howls of the wolf, who was mourning her cubs, began to penetrate the log walls of the cabin, coming nearer and nearer until Jessie felt they were inside the cabin with her. The young dogs shut in the enclosure between the two cabins howled with fright and the prairie wind shrieked as it whipped around the lonely buildings.

She rose from the bed and began walking about the cabin, first longways, then sideways, brushing against the wooden table and benches and bed, hard bitter sobs welling in her throat with excruciating pain.

Before her rose the whipped figure of her father standing in the dark library, facing the drawn blinds of the front windows, weeping silently because his wife had been felled by paralysis. She heard his words clearly as they came to her between the howls of the she-wolf. "Jessie, you can't know what it's like not to be able to fight back. It's like being hit in the dark: you don't know who your adversary is—you don't know where to

turn, what to say or do. I've never felt helpless before, but now . . ."
Now she too had been struck in the dark; she too felt helpless because
there was no way to fight back. Who was her adversary?

She heard the sound of voices, her husband's among them. Quickly she
poured some water from the earthen bowl into an enamel pan, splashing
it into her feverish eyes and mouth, running it over her brow and into
her hair. Her King George's Mark, swollen and red, throbbed fiercely.
She dried her hands and face with a towel and ran a comb through her
hair while she heard John's rapid footsteps approaching the cabin. She
stirred the dead ashes of the fire, threw on some kindling and got the
teakettle ready.

These were her final hours with her husband. She knew that as a last
act of kindness she must not let him perceive what she was undergoing.
She must not cripple him in this expedition which was to be the most
important of them all, for he needed success most now, now that he was
discredited, a man without a career. She must somehow give him the
strength and the courage to go forward, to be successful and re-establish
himself.

She saw by his face that he grasped something of what she had been
suffering. She was relieved to learn that he misunderstood its source. He
kissed her cheek, murmuring, "Courage, little lady. This will be the shortest separation of all. In two months, three at the most, we will be in San
Francisco together. I will be showing you the beautiful strait which leads
from the Pacific to San Francisco Bay. We will be buying lumber and
furniture for our home overlooking the ocean."

Jessie smiled, then with a forced note of gaiety cried, "You came earlier
than I had thought. I must be a sight. Give me a few minutes."

She retired to the corner of the cabin beyond the fire, took a little
rouge from her handbag and applied it to her cheeks, then let down her
hair, brushed it, straightened the part in the center, pulled the long brown
strands over her ears and pinned them low and tight at her neck. She was
surprised to see how easy it was to play this game, for when all is lost what
more has one to lose; when all feeling is gone, what does it matter what
feeling one pretends?

She went to her husband and asked, "There, isn't that better?"

"Much better," he agreed. "I want my memory of you to be beautiful
and serene. And now where is that cup of tea you promised me if I would
come home early?"

She fixed a cup of hot black tea for him, pretending to drink a little of
her own, asking him questions about the last-minute arrangements for the
expedition. Major Cummins and his wife had invited them for their farewell dinner in the settlement. Mrs. Cummins put out the few pieces of

fine china that were left after her thirty years' sojourn in this wilderness. She had roasted a chicken, and there were colored candles lighted festively on the log table. The major triumphantly brought out one of his few remaining bottles of wine. Jessie talked of things of which she had no thought before, or memory after they left her lips, but the moments began to seem endless, and toward seven o'clock she thanked the Cumminses for their kindness and walked back to the cabin with her husband.

This was their last hour together. She prayed for the strength to carry it off. But when he took her in his arms, when he set her beside him on the edge of the bed, when he began speaking of how much he would miss her, of how he would think of her night and day until they could be together in San Francisco, all of the grim and sordid bleakness of death came over her again. She became pale and lifeless. Some part of her maintained its consciousness, continued to go through the motions of being kind, of pretending that nothing had happened between them, of fulfilling that moment of love so important to a couple that is to be separated by countless miles and minutes.

It was here at last that she failed, that her pretenses broke down. For her lips were dry and ashen, her body was dry and ashen. She knew that in death there could be no creating of life, not even the going through of the motions; that love can penetrate, love can be rhythmical, but in death the brain and the heart and the pulse and the womb are closed; there can be no entrance of life into death.

She lay on the bed silent, her eyes closed. He tried to talk to her: to comfort her over the loss of their child, to minimize the hardship and the extent of their coming separation, to hearten her by his enthusiasm for their fresh start in California, for the new life they would build, the new sons they would create. She heard the sound of his voice but none of the words; her strength had vanished. She was spent. This was the greatest of her failures: that she must send this unfortunate man out into the trackless snows of the Rockies, into hardship, privation and ever constant danger of death, send him out heavy of heart, beaten before he started.

She felt his kiss on her cheek, heard his murmured good-by, managed to pull herself up halfway to run her fingers down his silken beard, to wish him well. But the actual moment of his going, the closing of the door behind him, she did not know.

She was lying in a half-torpor when she heard Mrs. Cummins calling to her many times. She rose, wrapped a heavy shawl around her shoulders and opened the door. An army sergeant was standing beside Mrs. Cummins, his face caked with perspiration and dirt, his uniform crushed and ringed with sweat. While she stood staring at them blankly, she heard Mrs. Cummins say:

"This is Sergeant O'Leary, come with a message from St. Louis."

The sergeant stepped forward, opened a dispatch case at his side, and handed her a sealed letter.

"From General Kearny," he said. "I was ordered to deliver it in the fastest possible time."

She tore open the envelope, but was unable to read the message in the dark. She bade the sergeant enter. Then she went to the fire and read the message in the dying flames:

DEAR MISS JESSIE:

You were right, we cannot destroy our friends without destroying ourselves. The whole trial was a dreadful mistake. Please come back with this courier. I want to beg your forgiveness for the harm I have done you and your family. If you cannot come, won't you please send a message that you forgive me?

Your old and devoted friend,
STEPHEN WATTS KEARNY

Jessie reread the note, going from the last line to the first over and over again, uncomprehending. Why was General Kearny doing this? And why had he not done it before she left St. Louis? He had been there all the time at Jefferson Barracks, but he had sent no word, not even when her son had died. Why now . . . ?

She turned to the army officer who was standing stiffly, his cap crushed under his arm.

"Why had you to ride so hard?" she asked. "Why is General Kearny in such haste?"

The sergeant wiped the dust off his lower lip by running his left thumb roughly across it.

"The general be dying, mum. The doctor say he has only a few hours to live. The general ordered I should bring you back with me. He says he must see you before he die."

Jessie stood silently, the letter hanging loosely at her side. If only this had happened before, she thought, I could have felt there was some decency left in the world. But now it is too late. Stephen Kearny is frightened. He doesn't want to die with me on his conscience. After breaking my husband and killing my son, he wants a cheap and easy forgiveness.

To the sergeant she said, "I cannot go back with you. Tell General Kearny it is impossible."

"I don't know what's in the message, mum," he answered, "but the general told me if I couldn't bring you I was to bring an answer."

"There is no answer."

The man shifted from one foot to the other.

"Please," he said, "I been with the general many a year now. I fit with him agin the Indians, I was with him on the march to California. I been his dispatch bearer and he been my friend. He's terribly unhappy, mum, said, 'Just ask her to say those few words, O'Leary. Just ask her to say she forgive me.' "

Jessie stood cold and impassive.

"Tell the general I cannot forgive him. Tell him a grave stands between us."

The sergeant opened his mouth to speak, but the misery in her eyes stopped him. He pulled himself up slowly, awkwardly, then saluted, left the cabin.

She stood there, her brain as black as the starless night. After a time she put a log on the fire, then pulled an end of the heavy bench to the hearth and sat down, her bony elbows digging into her thighs, the palms of her hands holding her eyelids tight-closed and stretched wide apart, blotting out all memory. Here she sat while time passed, the minutes, the hours, the bleak black minutes and hours that stretched ahead endlessly.

She was aroused by the swift gallop of a horseback rider. The lightning beats thundered up to her doorstep, were pulled to an abrupt stop. There was a sound of something hitting the earth, the door of her cabin was thrown open. Jessie looked up to see John standing there, disheveled, grim. He threw the door shut hard behind him, rushed to her side, locked his arms fiercely about her.

"Jessie, I couldn't go. I couldn't leave you this way. I know how ill you are, and how wretched. You need me with you. I am not going away. I have given up the expedition. I put someone else in charge. They leave at dawn. Come, let us pack our things. We will go to St. Louis, and then on to New York. I promised you we would never be separated again, and we never will."

His voice was hoarse. She stared at him, unbelieving. This was the one sacrifice nobody could have asked or expected him to make; it left him once again without a rudder or a future. To one of his intense pride it would have been easier to throw away his life than to throw away this opportunity to re-establish himself. From the ravaged lines in his face she could tell something of the struggle he had undergone to achieve this unselfishness. But his love for her had been sufficiently strong: to save her from further suffering he had been willing to face contempt for his failure to carry through. He had known he could never explain or justify himself; he had known what his bruised pride would be forced to undergo. He was willing to face this punishment for her sake.

A little feeling crept back into her tired body and nerves.

"You would give up . . . the expedition . . . when it means so much to you?"

"It means nothing to me," he cried. "You are the only one who means anything to me. You are my love and my life. I cannot leave you alone now."

"But so much is at stake," she whispered. "If you are successful, you have a life to live again. Without it you have nothing . . ."

He ran his fingers roughly, supplicatingly over her face.

"How wrong you are, Jessie! I have you to turn to! You are my future, you are everything I want and need. With you I can rise again, I can do anything. Our love is more important than any expedition or any chance for success. Don't you understand that, darling? Don't you understand that we must go on together, always side by side?"

She took his dirt-lined hand and kissed the pocket of its warm, curved palm. If John were willing to make this sacrifice for her, then her love and marriage had not been a failure.

"You would do this for me?" she persisted. "You would give up the only thing that brought you back to life? You would let some other man command your party, find the new pass and lay out the railroad route? You would give up everything you hoped would grow out of this work because I am ill and unhappy and I need you?"

His face showed hurt astonishment.

"But of course, Jessie! How can you doubt it? Did my love seem such a shallow thing? Did you think there was any sacrifice I wouldn't gladly make to protect you? Ah, Jessie, how little you really know me! How little you have known of how much I love you, and what our marriage has meant to me."

She was crying now, she could feel the hot tears streaming down her cheeks; and these hot tears seemed like rivers of strength pouring courage and hope back into her body. She slipped off the edge of the bench onto the floor beside him. She wrapped her arms tightly and securely about his neck, her mouth clinging to his.

True love never died; it surmounted all obstacles, it was indestructible; all else perished: hopes, plans, dreams, illusions, ambition and accomplishment, kindness, good will, even sweet charity. Yet one was able to carry on because the greatest force of all survived. So often it seemed to have worn thin, to have turned sour, to have been beaten out of shape: yet, miracle of miracles, love survived; it could conquer death, achieve eternal rebirth.

"Yes, John," she murmured against his lips. "I understand. All is well. I love you too, more than I ever have before. You can go now, you can be happy and sure about me. I will be well again, quickly. I will be in St.

Louis within two days, then go on to New York and catch the first ship for California. Yes, my darling, I will be in San Francisco before you, awaiting your arrival as eagerly as any woman ever waited for her love. You still have an hour to daybreak. You can make camp in time to give the order for the march. Good-by, and may God keep you."

She stood in the open doorway watching her husband gallop off into the blackness of the night. When the last reverberation of the hoofbeats had died away she turned back to the cabin and set about packing her bags. With the first light of dawn she mounted her horse and headed east into the rising sun on the first leg of the long journey to San Francisco.

BOOK FOUR

To Consecrate a Hearth

THE MID-MARCH WINDS were icy and the wooden planks of the wharf slippery under foot when Jessie and Lily boarded the S.S. *Panama.* Tom Benton had insisted upon bringing them to New York, had filled their cabin with the newest books, fruit and flowers. They were determined to be lighthearted about the parting, hustling about the cabin unpacking valises and trying to make it seem a little like home. They spoke in quick rushes of how soon California could become a state, what John's chances were of being elected the first senator; of the possibility that there really was a large quantity of gold, and how quickly a genuine gold rush would settle the new territory. But at last there was no more time for impersonal talk, and father and daughter embraced, murmuring words of farewell.

She stood alongside of the rail while orders were shouted; there were the noises of the hauling up of the gangplank, of winches being turned. The ship pulled slowly into the bay. When she could no longer see the little wharf in the blackness, she turned and went down to her cabin. The two kerosene lamps were swinging from their hooks in the ceiling beams. Lily was in her berth, lying wide-eyed.

"Haven't you gone to sleep yet, child?" Jessie asked.

"No, Mother, I'm frightened. Won't you come in bed with me?"

"Yes, dear, I'll undress immediately."

It took only a moment to slip out of her clothes and don a warm flannel nightgown. Outside the two square portholes a gale was raging as the ship pitched its way forward. She got into the berth with Lily; they comforted each other in the darkness with talk about the future. Jessie tried to imbue the child with her own excitement and impatience to reach California.

The first three days were stormy. When she dressed and went out on deck on the fourth morning off the coast of Florida, she found the sun shining brightly and the ocean tranquil.

Captain Schenck of the S.S. *Panama* had assured Senator Benton that everything would be done to keep her comfortable. She sat on deck in a wicker lounge chair with the sun beating strong on her face, while Lily went forward to watch the sailors paint the gear. The sun had a soothing quality; so did the quiet and the blue skies, the flight of gulls out from the coast of Florida and the Bahamas. In the heat of the day she took long naps; at sunset, with the skies flaming cerise and indigo, she walked for an hour about the deck, storing up strength for the difficult days ahead when she must cross Panama.

Though she had planned to go around Cape Horn on the S.S. *Fredonia* which had left in January, her father had insisted that she have more rest before she made the journey, that John could not be in California before March, and that it would be better if he arrived there first and prepared a place for them. In addition he wanted her to wait a few months so that she could travel on the newly proposed line of government steamships. Rumors that gold had been discovered in California had reached Washington toward the beginning of 1848, but no one in the East had given them any serious credence; in December of 1848 a tea caddy filled with gold nuggets was delivered to President Polk. This first concrete evidence of gold had excited the easily inflammable and congenitally adventuresome, who prepared to get to California as fast as they could and by any means available. Though most people in the East did not consider one tea caddy of gold to be proof of a gold strike, the government used the additional inducement of gold on the west coast to establish regular steamship connections with California. The S.S. *California* left to go around the Horn and was to remain on the west coast plying between San Francisco and Panama City. The S.S. *Panama* left New York on March 13, 1849, for Chagres, the port of entry to Panama on the Atlantic coast. Jessie, Lily and the other passengers would cross the Isthmus, which had just been opened to travel, and catch the S.S. *California,* which would come down from San Francisco to pick them up.

In the evenings she read from the volumes on agriculture she had bought in Washington in order to prepare herself to be a farmer's wife. She did not think that John should become a farmer; he lacked not only the training, but the temperament as well; yet the important thing was to establish a permanent home in California. When Elizabeth Benton had heard of her daughter's plans to erect a log cabin in the Santa Cruz mountains outside of San Francisco, she had taken Jessie's hand and murmured, "Remember that you were born on land that had never been bought or sold, a crown grant for military services to my grandfather's father. Not only should your home be inherited, Jessie, but your servants and money as well. 'The gods are slow to consecrate a new hearth.' You're not strong enough to endure the hardships of wild country like California. Let John complete his railroad expedition, return to Washington and find his life here. You would be a great deal happier."

On the ride to Cherry Grove eight years before, seventeen-year-old Jessie had shrugged off her mother's warnings as unimportant. But this was a chastened Jessie who had already endured much of the worst her mother had predicted.

"Someone has to build a hearth at the beginning, Mother," she had replied, "or the rest of us wouldn't be able to inherit it."

John would eventually find other activities more interesting to him than farming, but first their home place must be established. If her mother had been right in saying that "the gods are slow to consecrate a new hearth," then the more reason to begin at once.

At the end of two weeks of sailing, when she had her first sight of palm trees and the tropical growth of Chagres, it was another wrench to know that she would have to leave Captain Schenck, her last connection with home. She awakened while it was still dark, dressed herself by candlelight in the clothes she had laid out the night before. With Lily's hand clutched tightly in hers, she went on deck in time to watch the tropical sunrise, the sun bursting above the horizon as though it were shot out of a cannon, day breaking with the same roar with which the sea was breaking on the white beach of Chagres. It was her first view of the tropics; from a distance it looked friendly enough, with the palm trees fringing the sand bar and the heavy green growth along the river. When Captain Schenck came forward, Jessie turned a smiling face toward him.

"So the voyage is ended, Captain," she said. "You have made it pleasant for me and my little girl."

Captain Schenck did not return her smile. Anxiously he said, "Then let me perform one last service for Senator Benton and Colonel Fremont. Do not attempt to cross Panama. The country is rotten with Chagres fever. People are dying in the boats and on the trails. The food is abominable, the water is poisoned. That route should never have been opened."

The unexpected opposition to her continuing onward to meet John brought sharply to her mind the scene at the Delaware Indian Reservation where she had come so close to losing her love, her husband and everything that had meaning in her life. She valued it doubly now for having so nearly lost it. Any thought that she might fail in her efforts to join her husband in San Francisco brought back the intensity of those despair-fraught hours in Major Cummins' cabin.

"I am certain I will be able to stand the passage, Captain," she answered serenely.

The ship was rolling under them and she was anxious to get ashore. She returned to her cabin for her coat and purse. Having left her door ajar, she heard the heavy stomping of a man's boots. An unfamiliar voice cried:

"I ain't taking the responsibility for any Washington fine lady across Panama. She'll object to the Indians havin' no clothes on, she'll make trouble, she'll not be able to stand it."

She hadn't heard the phrase "fine lady" since the day she had left Miss English's Academy. She gave her hat a final touch, resolutely swished her long dark skirt out behind her, opened the door and faced the stranger. The man looked at her slender, ivory-tinted face, at her fragile figure, at the burning hazel eyes, and said stumblingly, "Why, you're not a fine lady at all; you're just a poor thin woman!"

She handed Lily to a sailor who carried her down the ship's rope ladder and placed her in the tender that was bobbing on the bay. Swinging from side to side Jessie manipulated the ladder, edged herself into the tender. The little boat made its way to shore.

2

AT THE WATERFRONT she was almost overcome by the stench of stale fish, tea and cinnamon; but she felt at home with the throngs of men who were jamming the beach ready to start their journey overland, for it sounded like St. Louis in the early days, soft Spanish intermingled with the French patois, Indians and Negroes talking their own dialects, the American and English swearing at everybody in their haste to arrange for transportation. She thought with a smile, if one were going to be a world traveler, St. Louis was an ideal training ground.

Jessie and Lily and their baggage were to be transported up the first eight miles of the Chagres River in one of the deep-water boats with a number of Americans who had been wise enough to arrange for passage. Within two hours after landing she was on her way. The banks of the river were low and covered with jungle growth to the water's edge, where white and scarlet flowers rose from the tangled green. By midafternoon the chugging motor had covered the eight miles and swerved into shore; they had had no food, no tarpaulin to protect them from the fierce heat, no water which she felt safe in drinking, though they were painfully parched, no way to take care of their personal needs. She disembarked and was informed by the native boatman, in sign language, that they would be transferred to the narrow dugouts which were tied to the thick overhanging branches. Each of the dugouts was manned by naked Negroes and Indians. Jessie felt Lily's hand clutching her own.

"Don't be frightened by their noise," she reassured her, "they're laughing and yelling out of excitement. It is only a three-day voyage up the shallows, and then we will be out on the trail."

A man in uniform appeared in the clearing. He came to her and said, "I'm Captain Tucker; I received a letter that you were coming. I have the company's boat ready for you and your daughter. I'm sorry I can't go along; you will be the only woman aboard, but the native crew is reliable, they frequently carry my wife to company headquarters."

"You mean we won't have to travel in those dugouts?" asked Jessie, realizing how far her heart had sunk at the sight of the savages.

Captain Tucker laughed. "I don't blame you for your consternation. But I think we can keep you comfortable. The company has tent camps at regular intervals up the river and my carriers have informed them that you are coming. Will you get into the boat now; there is no time to lose if you are to make the first camp by nightfall."

She thanked him heartily. The Jamaica Negroes pushed out against the heavy current, poling slowly upstream while they chanted in rhythm. Sometimes they traveled in midstream where the sun was so hot it burned the skin like a fire, but more often they stayed close to the shore, gliding lazily under the arching trees and canopies of flowering vines. When they could go no further because of growths of jungle creeper, Jessie and her daughter would have to go ashore and sit in the midst of the dank green foliage while the boatmen jumped into the water and with their long knives cut a trail along the riverbank. Then they would come back for Jessie, and half pull, half push the boat through the clearing while their wild singings joined in with the screeches of the tropical jungle birds.

They made their first landing while the sun was still bright. In a small clearing a company tent with a wooden floor had been set up. She wondered why they had stopped so early, but she soon knew the answer, for night came upon them with the swiftness of a falling star. The native boys made a small fire outside the tent flaps as a protection against the animals and the deadly dews, then brought her some cooked food, but she preferred not to eat it, feeding Lily and herself a few cookies and an apple which she had brought from the ship. After the child had fallen asleep, Jessie lay awake in her narrow iron cot listening to the discordant night noises of the tropics, to what seemed an unceasing rush of sound all around the tent.

There was no sleep in her, for she was possessed by the irony that she whose husband had marked and broken more trails across the continent than any other living American should be denied the right to travel on one of them and be plunged instead into this aboriginal nightmare. All the time she had worked on the three reports, watched John's maps grow, she had had the intensest personal interest in each mile of the terrain, for she had always thought that she would one day travel these routes. She had not only been prepared over a number of years, but had been anxious to encounter the hazards of the covered wagon, the plains, the snow-bound mountain passes, the hostile Indians, the moisture-parched deserts; all these images and the attendant hardships had been part of her thoughts since she had been a child. Yet here she was set down in the midst of country and hardship which she had never anticipated, and for which she was in no way prepared. Here she was on the first real voyage of her life, traveling without husband or friend by her side, in country so fantastic that not even the Spanish explorers had done it descriptive justice. This was land upon which no one she had ever known had laid eyes or foot; for perhaps the thousandth time she recalled Mary Algood, sitting by her blue-painted Delaware wagon, about to set off on the Oregon Trail. If only John's eyes had seen this country, John's drawing pencil sketched its character, she would have felt more at home.

The next morning they were off at the crack of dawn, being poled up the stiff current. She told Lily stories of how the first white men who had invaded Peru had carried their loot down this very river on their way to the Atlantic Ocean and back to Spain. The banks were brilliant with white and scarlet perch flowers; the native boys jumped into the river to cool off or cut food from the bank, but Jessie and Lily suffered agonies of heat, hunger, thirst and the other pressures to which the body is heir.

The nights were dank with mist; the cries of sudden death in the jungle gave the journey a mortal aspect. She was grateful for the floored tents and cots; without this barest of protection she doubted their chances of continuing. Though she had sympathized with her husband's privations on the trail, she now realized that her sympathy had been cerebral; her husband had suffered from the cold while she was suffering from the heat, he had been victim to the sparseness of vegetation while she was oppressed by its lushness, yet now that she was experiencing these momentary tortures with her own flesh she at last had an intimation of the agonies that must have racked the body of John Fremont.

On the morning of the fourth day they reached Gorgona, a little settlement where they transferred from the shallow Chagres to the trail over the mountains. Though it was only eight in the morning the sun was like a knife under the eyelids. The alcalde was down at the landing beach to invite her to his home for breakfast. His house was built on stilts with a thatched roof of palm fronds and wattled sides. They had no sooner seated themselves at the rattan table than native boys brought in two big baking dishes and popped off the covers. Jessie let out an exclamation of horror, for in the big casserole there was something that resembled a child.

"Special for the honored guests," said the alcalde, his eyes gleaming while he rubbed his hands in anticipation. "Baked ring-tailed monkey and boiled iguana lizard."

Her stomach slowly seemed to rise to her throat. One look at Lily's face told her that the child would not be able to eat the monkey. They needed strength for the arduous three-day trip over the mountains. She remembered how John had preferred the pangs and weakness of hunger to eating a portion of their pet dog. She decided that her husband was more fastidious than she. To her daughter she murmured:

"Remember what Sam Weller used to say: 'Weal pie ware a good thing when you knew it waren't made of kittens.'"

They both ate a little of the monkey, but the lizard was too much for them. Then the alcalde took them to the clearing which marked the beginning of the mule track to Panama. Part of Jessie's baggage was placed on a mule, the rest of it on a cow which was to head the procession. To the chief baggageman she said, "Will you please put my daughter on a mule immediately in front of mine, and make sure the animal is kept there?"

"He stay dere, lady," laughed the baggageman. "No place to go else."

There were fifty mules, a half-dozen cows and thirty men in the caravan. The native leader gave a fierce whoop which was echoed up and down the line, the mules began to move beneath them. The track followed the contour of the mountains, up to the top of a hill and down again into the valley on the twenty-one-mile pilgrimage to Panama City. The mule steps that had been cut by hand into the mountainside were rarely more than four feet wide, and at the edge one looked down a thousand feet into jungle growth. Mango trees and alders were packed solid along the trail, topped by towering palms and cocoanuts. In spite of the intense glare of the tropical sun, it was dark under the green roof; Jessie kept looking upward to find a ray of sunlight toward the top of the branches, then a few steps more and it would be dark green again, with a sudden burst of rain falling down through the matted foliage. There were no bridges across the narrow streams; the mules jumped them, and several of the travelers were dumped head first into the water. She was thankful that both she and Lily were experienced riders, and was proud, as she rode behind the slender form of her daughter, at the way the child was withstanding their travels, the constantly changing temperatures, the strange sights, steady hours of movement, the hardships of hunger, heat and personal discomfort.

The first night they slept in a tent with a wooden floor, but on the second night there was only a filthy Indian hut. Jessie took two blankets out of her boxes, rolled Lily in one and herself in the other and slept the sleep of exhaustion, impervious to the lizards, snakes and hundreds of insects which crawled across them in the course of the night. The sunrise was glorious: from the mountain top she looked down into a sea of blossoms, and beyond she saw as Balboa had seen from this very peak before her the Pacific Ocean at her feet. She ardently wished that Tom Benton could be sharing with her this first view of the Pacific.

Several hours before the sixth nightfall they reached Panama City. The trail came out of the mountains some distance from the walled city, with its ancient cathedral. Her first sight of the cathedral roof and spire of inlaid mother-of-pearl made her think that she had fallen victim of the Chagres fever, after all. At the trail's end there were Indian carriers, one of whom took her on his back, and another Lily, and carried them over the shallow water of the bay and across the sand reef to the entrance of Panama City. She walked on the ancient roadway through the railed gate, entered the walled town with its weather-stained old houses and wide balconies leaning out so far they almost closed over the narrow passages. In the streets were trotting donkeys carrying bundles of leaves and water jars, dusky Indian women wearing a single white garment.

Instead of finding a sleepy little Spanish town with a few natives wandering the streets, she found the place a bedlam of stranded Americans, several hundred of them camping on the hillside above the city, others hustling and jostling through the streets. While waiting for the Indian carriers to bring her baggage to the Cathedral Square, from which point she would seek a hotel, she inquired of the group of Americans who were wearing the western garb she knew so well from St. Louis:

"Why are so many of you men here?"

A lean, gray-haired man in a leather jacket and buckskin pants stepped forward and said, "Ain't you heard the news, ma'am, the ship ain't coming back to Panama."

Stupefied, having visions of Lily and herself camping endlessly on the hills above Panama, she could only gasp: "Ship not coming back? But why? What do you mean?"

A young man dressed in a black business suit much the worse for wear replied, "Don't you know what's happened in California, ma'am? All the ships' crews have deserted and gone into the gold fields. The *California* was due a month ago, but it never got here."

She looked from face to face anxiously, then asked, "Deserted their ships?"

There was a moment of silence while the men looked at each other. Then everyone began talking at once. "Yes, ma'am! All the rumors was true! Millions of dollars' worth of gold! People picking it up on the mountainside in sacks! Getting rich overnight! Here we're rottin' in Panama City, and millions of dollars of gold laying all over California just waiting to be picked up."

The verification that there was gold in California meant little to her except that she and Lily would be marooned in Panama City. She asked the first man who had spoken, the gray-haired one, if he knew anything about the hotels in Panama. He assured her that they were vermin-infested, that there were no rooms anyway. Night was drawing on when she saw coming toward her a Spanish woman with white hair under a black mantilla. Trailing her were several native boys. She came to Jessie and said:

"I am Madame Arce, cousin of the American minister from New Granada, General Herran. He wrote to me that you were coming and told me of the many happy hours he had spent in your home in Washington. It is now my privilege to return that hospitality. Will you come with me, Madame Fremont?"

She followed Madame Arce across the square to a great barrack of a house with twenty-foot ceilings, and windows as big as barn doors. When she was led to her bedroom she found it furnished with a lounge covered in a blue damask, two hammocks, and crystal chandeliers with wax lights. Madame Arce made available to her a velvet-footed girl with a soft laugh, named Candelarias. Jessie's relief at being rescued was so great that she murmured to Lily, "Now I know how your father must have felt when he found that pass across the Sierras."

Madame Arce's house was a tropical version of Tom Benton's home overlooking the Mississippi, built around an enclosed patio, with the floors red-tiled. She stepped out onto the wide gallery which surrounded the house and overlooked the cathedral. A few moments later there was a knock at her door and Candelarias asked if she would like to have a bath before dinner. Jessie called to Lily and they walked to an outside bathhouse much like her father's shower on C Street, for on a high ledge there were containers, ranging from small vases to four-foot-high jars filled with water from the well. The smaller jars were dumped on them by three grinning young girls, then the larger jars were overturned as they became accustomed to the coldness of the water.

The days passed, a week, two weeks, three weeks. Jessie spent many hours with Madame Arce in the coolness of the back garden speaking in the Spanish they both loved, walking along the ramparts of the old town at sunset and watching the twenty-foot tide crashing over the reefs. In the evening she strolled about the Cathedral Square talking to the men whom she knew from her own ship and those with whom she had become acquainted during her first hour in Panama. They were growing more desperate with each passing day. There was no food to be bought, they were living on the salted foods they had carried with them, and death from disease was an everyday occurrence in the camps that dotted the hillsides.

A month passed and still there was no ship and no news of any; the men were becoming frightened that they would all die here in Panama, that there would be no chance for them to escape.

Jessie was well cared for, yet she too was growing uneasy. There had been no word from John since he had left her side that early morning on the Delaware Indian Reservation. Some five months had passed since then; if all had gone well, her husband and his party should be safely in San Francisco. He would be waiting for her, scanning the sea for her arrival. He would be fearful lest she had encountered difficulties, or had been too delicate to withstand the rigors of Panama, where strong men were stricken and died within a few hours. She knew the heartbreak of worrying about a loved one; that had been her lot over the years; she did not want her husband to undergo this slow torture. And yet there was nothing she could do but sit and wait and let the days succeed each other as painlessly as possible.

3

THE RAINY SEASON came down like a thunderclap, filling the streets of the little town as though they were shallow pools. Madame Arce's house was wet, the floors, ceilings wet; lanes of damp ooze trickled down the twenty-foot walls, while outside the rains filled the air with sickening inhalations. Jessie caught cold, and with it a racking cough. Madame Arce insisted that she remain in bed, while Candelarias kept a fire lighted in the room in a vain attempt to dry out the walls. She lay in the hammock, her dreams shattered by grotesque pictures of screaming, naked savages dancing around her, taunting her with being a fine lady, the hallucinations dissolving into pictures of the snow-locked Sierras where freezing men fell forward into the snow.

Another month passed, and then one night she was awakened by the booming of a cannon which told her, even as the noise tore her from her dream, that an American ship had arrived. She rushed out on the balcony to behold a wild scene. It was a bright moonlight night and every trail leading down from the hills was filled with singing and shouting Americans who were crying out with joy as they hurried toward the ramparts. The Indians too had been awakened, and they were singing and dancing in sympathy. On the balcony of every house were shrouded figures in their night clothes watching the scene. Even before she could return to her room to begin dressing and packing, there was another boom from a cannon; a second American ship had dropped anchor in the harbor.

Breathlessly she dressed Lily and herself, began throwing clothes into her suitcases, then went out on the balcony again to search for the ship as the light of day began to filter through. She saw a man in the uniform of the United States Navy stride across the square. She rushed down the patio stairs, across the red tile, and threw open the heavy door. With a glad cry she grasped the hand of Lieutenant Fitzhugh Beale, who had been a friend of Colonel Fremont's in California, fought with him in the conquest, testified for him at the court-martial and been their guest in the Benton home in Washington.

"Ah, Mrs. Fremont!" he cried. "I had surmised you were stranded here, waiting for the *California*. I've just come down on her, with naval dispatches and samples of gold dust."

"Have you heard news of Colonel Fremont?"

"No."

She led him to the back garden, then told him of her voyage while he sipped a warm drink. Lieutenant Beale was blue-eyed, blond, about thirty, with a long, horselike face. He loved danger and movement and an ever changing panorama: a congenital bachelor, he had been at sea since he was twelve; among his intimates he was known as "Beale of the steady hands and wandering feet." Jessie saw that he was uneasy, that he had something to tell her. He asked permission to light a cigar, gazing at the burnt match for a moment before speaking.

"I must hurry on to Chagres and deliver my papers to the next ship leaving for New York. Every possible facility has been given me to make the Panama crossing as quickly and easily as possible. Mrs. Fremont, you look ill; I don't think you should expose yourself to more hardship. I urge you to return to Chagres with me; there will be a fast ship for New York, and I will arrange for you to be taken care of."

Her thoughts colliding, she asked:

"But why should I return to New York now, when there is a ship to take me to San Francisco?"

"Mrs. Fremont, San Francisco has gone crazy wild. The original settlers have rushed off for the gold fields; the new arrivals are insane with excitement to get away and find their millions in gold. The hotels are dirty and cold and jammed, there is no help to be had except Indians and Chinese, and people will tell you that their time is worth fifty dollars a minute. San Francisco isn't a town, it isn't even a village, it's just a settlement of delirious maniacs living in shanties and knock-together cabins, waiting for the moment when they can get away to the gold fields. There is no water, no adequate food, no sanitary equipment. The streets are flowing mud streams impossible to cross. Why, I have seen men try to pave them with bales of cotton and bags of flour. There is no lumber available, no brick or stone, nothing with which you and the colonel could build a house. The shanty towns are full of fever and cholera, and the death rate is terrifying. Mrs. Fremont, I beg you not to risk arriving alone in the hysterical hamlet; there can't be more than two or three white women there."

She watched the young lieutenant puff animatedly on his cigar, feeling a familiar paralyzing fear clutch at her heart.

"Please tell me the news, Lieutenant Beale," she murmured. "You said that you had not heard from Colonel Fremont."

The lieutenant took the cigar out of his mouth. "It is true, I have not heard from him. But I have heard about him. There has been trouble, Mrs. Fremont. Your husband's expedition never got over the Rockies. The fur traders and the Indians warned them not to go in, told them that the snow and the cold had never been so intense, that it was impossible to cross the Rockies at that point. But Colonel Fremont insisted. He said there must be a pass on the thirty-eighth parallel . . . and he ran into the most impenetrable part of the Rockies, in the worst winter within the memory of anyone who knows that country."

Her body as cold as though she herself had plunged into the frozen Rockies, she asked, "My husband, is he safe?"

After a barely imperceptible pause, Lieutenant Beale replied, "We don't know. The colonel engaged Bill Williams to guide him. Williams wanted to take a southerly route, but your husband felt that would defeat the purpose of the expedition, that he had to find a central pass for the railroad. The colonel and Williams quarreled; they never found a pass. They pushed deeper and deeper into the snows until they could go no farther. Then they turned back . . . they lost their mules and supplies . . . The men began to die along the trail . . ."

"But my husband. What about Colonel Fremont?"

His head down, Lieutenant Beale repeated, "We don't know, Miss Jessie."

"Some of the party must have gotten out. Else how would you know?"

"The colonel sent out a relief party with Williams, Brackenridge, King and Creutzfeldt to get help in New Mexico and rush it back. King starved to death, but Williams, Brackenridge and Creutzfeldt got through. From them we learned about the disaster to the expedition."

Twisting her lace handkerchief between her taut fingers, Jessie cried, "If the relief party got out, then surely they must have sent back supplies. The rest of the men must be safe?"

Lieutenant Beale shook his head slowly. "The three men were almost dead before they reached a settlement. They did not have the strength to take back relief, and there was no one at the settlement who could go into the mountains. A runner carried the news to Kit Carson at Taos, but it would have taken too long for Carson to organize relief and get up into the Rockies. The rest of the expedition would have had to get out on its own resources."

"Then there is no word about Colonel Fremont?"

"None."

"He was still alive when the Williams party was sent out for relief?"

"It was the colonel who sent them."

"What was his condition then?"

"His leg was badly frozen."

"There has been no word from anybody left in the mountains?"

"None. Williams says they could not have lived more than a few days . . ."

She stalked agitatedly about the patio.

"My husband could not have perished in the snows! He faced greater hardships when he crossed the Sierras in '44. If Williams could get out with a relief party, then Colonel Fremont can get out with the rest of the expedition. Neither the snows nor the mountains could ever kill him. There is no man in the world better equipped to survive . . ."

Lieutenant Beale put his arm about her.

"The expedition is ended, Miss Jessie; the equipment was abandoned, no one got over the mountains and no one got through to California. Those who survived are returning east to St. Louis. If Colonel Fremont came out of the Rockies, he will be in St. Louis by now. I have made all arrangements to take you back across Panama. There are merchantmen in the harbor at Chagres; they will not be leaving before we reach there. Miss Jessie, I want you to pack your things and return with me. I will put you on a ship for New York."

Pale now, and coughing, she faced Lieutenant Beale determinedly. "You believe that my husband is dead?"

He did not answer.

"No, don't be afraid for me. I have gone through this before. Tell me if you think there is any chance that my husband is alive."

When Lieutenant Beale could not garner the courage to speak, she said, "Very well, you think he is dead."

He took her hand between his. "Please prepare to leave with me for Chagres. You will be in New York almost by the time your husband is in St. Louis. Within a few weeks you will be reunited."

Though he maintained that the reason he wanted her to leave was that her husband would have returned east, she knew that his real reason was that he believed she was going on to San Francisco to meet a man who was buried in the glacial snows of the highest Rockies.

"I thank you for your kindness, Lieutenant; I know how much you have my interest at heart; but you are mistaken. Colonel Fremont must be in San Francisco by now; he will be waiting; I promised I would meet him there."

He bowed. "Please think it over, Miss Jessie."

After he had left she sat rocking in a chair. So the fourth expedition had failed! For her own part she did not suffer too greatly over the failure: the men had met insuperable obstacles, that was all; they had done their best, but it had not been enough in the face of the unscalable Rockies. But how would John take it: the loss of the money that his admirers in St. Louis had invested, the loss of his opportunity to reestablish himself as an explorer and trail blazer? Would he not consider it a matter of personal inadequacy, count the failure his own, be stricken by it? Would he not fear the criticism and the disgrace of having some of the men perish under his leadership? Would this make it impossible for him ever to start out again?

And here again was the phantom of her husband's death. She could believe it this time no more than the last, but in the closeness of the warm spring morning she was gripped by the terrifying realization that John might have been seriously injured. Bill Williams had reported him suffering from a badly frozen leg. The mules had frozen to death or been killed for food; there was no way for him to come down the vastness of the Rockies except on his own feet, for his men would be too weak to carry him. What then if he could no longer drag that frozen leg? He was not stronger than the forces of nature: because he had forced the Sierras, there was no reason to believe he was an imperishable one.

Her mind would not allow her to conceive that her beloved was dead, yet there might be no way for him to get through to California. He would return to St. Louis or Washington to recoup his health. By what token should she go up to San Francisco, pestilential mudhole caught in the hysteria of the gold rush, where she had neither friend nor relative, where she would be alone with her daughter, with no place to go and nothing to do, and no husband to meet her?

She was so homesick that the tears coursed unrestrainedly down her cheeks. Would anyone blame her if she let herself be persuaded that there was no sense in going on to San Francisco? True, she had promised to meet her husband there; but if he had been unable to reach San Francisco, if he were even now on his way to St. Louis, what possible sense could there be in her going on? Why persist in this cruel voyage? They would have no way of communicating with each other, to tell whether she should once more take ship to Panama, or whether John would come overland in the summer to join her. The best that could happen would be confusion and heartbreak and more months of separation.

She got out of the chair and walked upstairs to the balcony. The cooler air refreshed her a little. The Cathedral Square was abandoned but the spire gleamed with oriental splendor. And standing there, feeling desperately alone, wanting her husband's arms about her as she had never wanted them before, not even in the darkest hours in St. Louis when everyone had thought he was dead, she knew that she could not return to New York. She had not said, "I'll meet you in San Francisco if circumstances permit," or "providing I'm sure you will be there to meet me," or "if I can make it." She had made a categorical promise, and promises were made to be kept, the hard ones as well as the easy ones. If she kept this promise, under these almost unendurable circumstances, then not only would John know that she always would keep her promises, but even more important, she herself would know that she could keep them.

4

SHE FINISHED HER PACKING. Madame Arce came to her bedroom to express her happiness that she would at last go on to her own country and her own people. Jessie embraced the older woman, murmuring softly, "If not for you I might have died here. How am I to repay your kindness?"

Madame Arce replied, smiling, "In the Spanish language we do not have the word repay."

They were still murmuring gracious words to each other when another clamor arose in the town. A new party of Americans had just come off the trail from Chagres. With them had arrived a carefully guarded United States mail sack, its destination San Francisco. A portion of the mail would surely be addressed to the Americans who had been detained in Panama City these several months.

The head baggageman turned the sack over to the American representative in Panama City, a Central American consul who had no authority to do otherwise than to deliver it to the first ship headed north for San Francisco. When the Americans learned that mail had come in they thronged the official's office demanding that he open the pouch. Jessie rushed through the courtyard to join the excited group in front of the consul's office. The consul kept repeating, "I decline to usurp functions. It is locked. It cannot be opened until it reaches San Francisco. Do you not see it is marked, 'Destination San Francisco'? I have no authority . . ."

The Americans had no intention of waiting several weeks for news of their families while the locked mail sack accompanied them to San Francisco. "We'll take the responsibility!" they shouted. "We'll sign a petition! Every last one of us will sign for his letter!"

If John had come down from the mountains alive there would be a letter from him in that sack. She was positive the letter was there, and she was determined to have it. She pushed her way through the crowd. The men cried, "Here's Mrs. Fremont! She wants news of the colonel. Open that blasted sack and give us our mail."

The consul took one last look at the men's faces, then gazed into Jessie's eyes and said quickly, "Very well, but I do not take responsibility. I do not cut open this sack! You must appoint a committee and the committee must take responsibility."

The pouch was torn open before the consul had his last words out. Someone cried, "For you, Mrs. Fremont!" With tears half blinding her, Jessie saw that she had a fat envelope from Taos addressed in her husband's handwriting, another from her father in Washington. She stumbled across the square, ran up the patio stairs, tore open John's envelope and read:

> Taos, New Mexico
> January 27, 1849

MY VERY DEAR WIFE:

I write to you from the house of our good friend Kit Carson. This morning a cup of chocolate was brought to me, while yet in bed. While in the enjoyment of this luxury, I pleased myself in imagining how gratified you would be in picturing me here in Kit's care, whom you will fancy constantly endeavoring to make me comfortable . . .

She could read no further, for tears were falling on the familiar and dearly beloved handwriting. He was safe! He had not perished in the snows! If she had yielded to her own weakness, if she had given in to the persuasiveness of Lieutenant Beale, she would have passed this mail sack on the trail to Gorgona, she would not have known that her husband was alive until she had reached New York.

She stretched out on the lounge and buried her face in the damask, unable to think or read, knowing only overwhelming relief at his safety. After some time she picked up the letter again. There were ten tightly packed pages of handwriting, for John had put them into journal form, making his letter to her serve as a record of the harrowing and tragic events of the fourth expedition. She paled as she read on: eleven men had perished out of the thirty-three, died of cold and hunger and insanity on the trail; those who had been saved had emerged as emaciated shadows, half out of their minds with grief and suffering. Everyone in the party was blaming, criticizing and hating everyone else; John blamed Williams for the tragedy; Williams blamed John for interference, for guiding the party into hopeless tracks. John was blamed for ordering the men to try to save the baggage instead of themselves, an act which had cost perhaps nine lives; Williams was accused of cannibalism while on his way out with the relief party. Both men were blamed for not having gone back to save the balance of the party after they had made their way out. John's own life had been saved only by meeting the son of an Indian chief with whom he had been friends years before. He had reached Kit Carson's home unable to drag his leg behind him, a scarecrow, sick in body and despairing of heart.

Yet in spite of his misfortunes, he ended the letter on a cheerful note, saying that he did not consider the expedition a failure, for he had learned much about that mountainous region, was convinced that a railroad pass could be found close by, and that he would one day find it under more favorable circumstances.

When I think of you, I feel a warm glow at my heart, which renovates it like a good medicine, and I forget painful feelings in strong hope for the future. We shall yet, dearest wife, enjoy quiet and happiness together —these are nearly one and the same to me now. I make frequently pleasant pictures of the happy home we are to have, and oftenest and among the pleasantest of all I see our library with its bright fire in the rainy stormy days, and the large windows looking out upon the sea in the bright weather. I have it all planned in my own mind.

She had been right, she thought exultantly. She had kept her pledge and they would meet in San Francisco!

But when? He had written this letter while in bed, unable to move about; there was no way for him to get to California except on foot or horseback, and he could not risk the hazardous journey until he was strong again. How long might that be? Perhaps months. Perhaps never! She had known frontiersmen whose legs had been frozen, and who had lost them. If John's leg did not heal he would need medical care; if it could not be provided in Taos, Kit Carson would have to take him back to St. Louis for hospitalization. Yes, she would meet her husband in San Francisco; but when?

She opened the letter from her father; in it he told her the bad news of the expedition, including an article he had written for the eastern papers. He told her how ill her husband was in Taos, how badly his leg and side had been affected. He was altogether certain there would be no way for John to make the crossing to California without seriously endangering his life. He told his daughter that he was sending dispatches to Taos urging John to return to St. Louis as fast as his health would permit; and he now urged his daughter with equal vehemence to return to New York, whence she could go to St. Louis to join her husband.

Jessie put aside the letter and stared at the high ceiling of Madame Arce's bedroom; yes, her father would urge John to return to St. Louis, just as Lieutenant Beale had urged her to return to New York. Sick as she was, she had refused to turn back; sick as he might be, John would refuse to turn back.

A sailor from the S.S. *Panama* knocked at Madame Arce's door to inform them that the captain wanted Mrs. Fremont and her daughter to come aboard. Two Indian boys carried her luggage to the waterfront. She was rowed in a small boat to the ship and then hauled up to the deck in a wooden tub suspended by ropes at the end of a boom. Captain Schenck welcomed her. The S.S. *Panama* had returned to New York after leaving Jessie at Chagres, and had now come around the Cape with another shipload of voyagers for California. As she gazed at the hundreds of Americans crowded into every spare inch, she asked, "Where will all of us stay?"

"I don't know, Madame Fremont," replied the captain, with a wistful smile. "But we dare not refuse anyone as long as there is standing room."

Within a few hours both the S.S. *Panama* and the S.S. *California* set sail for San Francisco. Jessie's ship, which had cabin accommodations for eighty passengers, carried four hundred men. There was no cabin available, but Captain Schenck put two iron cots under the spanker boom, covering the space with a large American flag. Everyone was so happy to be en route to San Francisco that no one complained, theatricals were performed on deck, Jessie and the passengers exchanged the few books in their possession, reading aloud in the clear sunshine off the coast of Mexico.

She was delighted to meet several companionable American women, chief among them Mrs. Matilda Gray, a youngish but matronly soul who was going out to San Francisco to join her husband; and Mrs. William Gwin, one of Louisiana's most famous hostesses. Her husband was

William McK. Gwin, with a leonine head topping his superb six-foot-two figure, the voice of the professional orator, the carriage of the politician. Gwin's father had fought with Tom Benton in the War of 1812 and the families had been acquainted ever since; Gwin had no hesitancy in speaking frankly to Jessie. He had a great deal of political experience, having been a congressman from Mississippi.

"I left the most lucrative political job in the United States to migrate to California," he said. "Within a year I'll be back in Washington as the first senator from the new state."

Jessie felt a sense of amused shock, as though someone had read her thoughts aloud in public meeting.

"You seem quite certain of that, Mr. Gwin."

"I am not the only one," boomed Gwin. "Before I left Washington I told Stephen A. Douglas that by this time next year I would ask him to present my credentials to the Senate. Douglas exclaimed, 'God bless you, I believe you will.'"

To herself Jessie said, I can believe that, too; but there are only two senators from a state; how many men are headed for California with that identical ambition in mind?

When the ship reached San Diego she put Lily in the care of Mrs. Gray and locked herself in the other woman's cabin, fearful of the news that was coming, unwilling to be seen when she received it. Above the noise and shouts of the passengers who were disembarking at San Diego she heard the sound of running feet, then someone pounded on her door and a man cried, "Mrs. Fremont, the colonel's safe; he's riding up to San Francisco to meet you! He didn't lose his leg, only a bad frostbite."

Jessie unlocked the door and flung it open.

"Are you sure?" she cried.

"Yes, ma'am! He was here only a few days ago."

The last two days at sea passed swiftly in the anticipation of being reunited with her husband. On the morning of June 4 the S.S. *Panama* swung eastward toward shore. As she moved through the Golden Gate Strait into the bay, with the sandy beaches of San Francisco to the south and the rocky promontories and little islands to the north, Jessie had the impression that this channel in the curvilineal coast of California was not a strait at all, but rather a canal leading into the fertile womb of the bay, with the ship carrying the seeds of men, machinery, tools and ideas to give birth to a new civilization.

Anchored in the bay were a number of ships, their wooden masts standing up bare as winter orchards, several of them abandoned. She could see a small level square flying the flag of the California Republic, and around the sides a few wooden buildings. For the rest, there was little but unpainted shacks and cabins and miners' tents dotting the hills which rose immediately back of the square. The S.S. *Panama* fired a salvo of guns to inform San Francisco that she had arrived. A heavy anchor was dropped, and Jessie watched a number of small boats being rowed out to meet them. Once again she and Lily climbed down the side of a rope ladder and were rowed to shore. Since there was no place for the small boats to dock, the sailors had to carry them over the surf. There were hundreds of men on the beach, many of them shouting words of welcome. The cold and the fog set Jessie coughing again. She was glad this was the end of the voyage: she would need the comforts of her own home and the protection of her husband to nurse her back to vigor after the grueling months.

But as she stood uncertainly at the edge of the surf and then walked up among the red-shirted, bearded men, she caught no sight of John. Once again her heart sank. He had not yet arrived in San Francisco. She was here alone. Perhaps he had not reached California at all, and the reports in San Diego had been merely encouragement by kindhearted men. As she stood on the edge of Portsmouth Square holding Lily by one hand, Mrs. Gray came to her side.

"Never you mind, dearie," she said, "the colonel's been delayed a day or two. This is my husband; Harry, meet Mrs. Fremont. Let us take you to the Parker House."

Appreciating the kindness, Jessie let Mr. and Mrs. Gray lead her to a hotel room at the Parker House and light a fire in the grate. The Grays took Lily for a walk to see the little mining village while Jessie slept soundly, awakening after dark to the clamor of men's voices. By looking out the window she saw that she was next door to the Eldorado gambling hall and that a brawl was apparently in process. She lay down on the bed again, but a few minutes later Mrs. Gray returned with Lily and a tray of food.

For five days she remained in bed, the cough she had contracted in Panama growing increasingly worse. From the conversation outside her window and from the information vouchsafed by her few visitors, she learned that San Francisco was almost deserted, that everyone had spent whatever money he had for supplies and miners' tools and rushed to the gold fields. Aside from the small amount of trade and the gambling casinos where the men spent the night in order to keep warm, there was no life in San Francisco. As a community it had hardly been born. She thought how greatly her father would have enjoyed this rawness, and was shamed that she could not be more wholeheartedly her father's daughter.

She had grown thin again, her King George's Mark throbbed unceasingly. There were several men in town who knew Colonel Fremont from Washington or his expeditions, and they made sure she had sufficient food and firewood for the grate. They kept assuring her that her husband would arrive any hour, but with the passage of the days she realized that although the trip from San Diego was a long and hard one by horseback, and the weather had been bad, if John had been there he would have had plenty of time to reach San Francisco by now.

There were days of heavy rains, converting the earthen surface of Portsmouth Square into a muddy bog. The nights were bitterly cold, for a penetrating wind came over the bay, seeping through the walls and the ill-fitted windows of the hastily constructed hotel. The brushwood fagots smoked, making her eyes smart, and she and Lily lay huddled in the narrow iron bed, comforting each other with hopeful words and bodily warmth. This cold, bare shacklike room was her first home and her first hearth in California. She wondered if her grandmother Benton had lived thus with her children when she had first reached Tennessee; she wondered if her grandmother had suffered the despair that was gnawing at her own heart. If only she could be sleeping on the hard cold ground of the Santa Cruz ranch, for that would be her own land and her home, and the open campfire would be a truer hearth than this acridly smoking grate which choked their lungs even while it warmed their flesh.

At dusk of the tenth day as she was sitting before the fire, her thin hands clasped in her lap, she heard men's voices outside her window. Someone cried, "Your wife's inside the house, Colonel." She moved out of the chair to open the door. Before she could do so, it was flung open and John had taken her in his arms and was crushing her against him.

Neither could speak. He led her back to her chair, threw some fresh fagots on the fire, then sat on the floor by her side holding her two hands in his, gazing up at her.

"You have been ill; you are ill now, my darling."

"No . . ."

The door opened and Lily entered. John embraced his daughter, then took her on his knee. Lily said, sober-faced:

"You didn't come. Mother almost died. A lady downstairs says she will die."

He rose before Jessie, put his arms about her waist and gazed into her face. His eyes were dark, self-accusing. She ran her fingers lightly through his long gray hair, then laid her cheek on his.

"In her innocence, Lily is partly right. Being away from you is a kind of a death. Only with you am I fully alive and well."

5

THE NEXT MORNING she propped a small mirror against a straight-backed chair and sat before it combing out her hair and massaging her face, interested in her appearance for the first time in months. John brought a breakfast of hot coffee and bread up to the room, then left for the office of the American consul to pick up the deed to the Santa Cruz ranch which had been deposited there by Consul Larkin of Monterey. Several hours passed before she heard his footsteps in the hall; her quick ear perceived that something was wrong: this was not the fast springy step of her husband who could not bear to move slowly; this was the plodding step of a man who had suffered a blow. She seized this last instant to tie a blue ribbon about her hair with a small bow on top and to cast a quick look at her blue quilted robe in the pocket mirror. She forced a smile to her face.

"John, what has happened?"

He did not answer for a moment, then said:

"Larkin didn't get our ranch."

She waited for him to continue, but when he did not, she demanded, "Didn't buy . . . ? But he's had a full year."

"He bought all right," John moaned, "but not the magnificent ranch with the beautiful vines and orchards that I told him to acquire; he used our three thousand dollars to buy a wild tract of land somewhere up in the mountains called the Mariposa." He took an official-looking document from his inside coat pocket and flung it angrily on the bed. "The Mariposa," he repeated, "several hundred miles from here, a hundred miles from the ocean or the nearest settlement, high up in the Sierras, impossible to farm, overrun with Indians, so we couldn't even set up a cattle ranch . . ."

She picked up the document from the bed, opened it and gazed unseeing at the title grant. "But what does it mean?" she asked. "You didn't tell Larkin to buy the Mariposa. You told him to buy the Santa Cruz ranch. Is it possible that he confused your orders?"

"No, no! When I handed him the three thousand dollars I gave him written instructions. He had been over the land with me. There was no possibility of an error." He jumped up from his chair, striding about the cramped little room. "I'll have to borrow a horse and ride down to Monterey."

"Is the Santa Cruz ranch still available?" asked Jessie. "Has no one else bought it?"

John's eyes fell. "Our consul thinks the land has been sold. He has heard . . . Jessie, it's just coming to me. Larkin must have bought that land for himself!"

"But if that's the case, John, we can sue him; we can recover, it's a fraudulent transaction."

"How? This is not the United States. This is the Republic of California. They have no courts, no legal system, no judges, no police. It's the law of the frontier. Every man for himself . . ."

Shrewdly she asked, "Who was the previous owner of the Mariposa? Did Larkin own it, or did he buy it from someone else?"

John took the deed from her hand, glanced at it and replied, "According to this paper, Larkin bought the Mariposa from former governor Alvarado of California, who had been given it in a grant from Spain. It's a vast tract of mountains and valleys, freezing cold in winter; no one can live there. What good is a lot of land if it's valueless?"

She put her fingers lightly on his shoulder.

"I shall loathe being left here alone again, but there can be no doubt that you must see Larkin. We want either our land or our three thousand dollars!"

It had always been their intention that John should play a role in making California a state. But how could he do this if he suddenly were deprived of his property, if he were without a means of livelihood or position to buttress him? She did not want him to be known as a former explorer; that would be doubly unfortunate since the failure of his fourth expedition. In order to play a full-voiced part in the forming of the state, to be elected senator, he must be important in California while the state was being founded. But what was this job to be? Even now the delegates of the Constitutional Convention were being elected; William Gwin had thrown his hat into the ring while he was still wading ashore. John would have to move fast if he wanted to be sent to Monterey as a delegate.

She was awakened one night by a clangor in front of the hotel and saw that the sky outside her window was vividly red. The warehouse on the waterfront, where her trunks and heavy boxes were stored, was in flames. It burned all night; all night she sat by the window in her robe watching the last of her possessions go up in smoke: her clothing, her linens, blankets, books, silver, ornaments, beautiful and familiar things she had brought to make herself a home in California. First they had lost the Santa Cruz ranch, and now her only possessions were those in her small suitcases in the hotel room. Fortunately she had her money box with her; these gold coins were her last link to family and security. When they were gone, they would really be pioneers, starting from scratch like everyone around them.

John returned to the hotel after five days to tell her of his interview with Larkin.

"There's something strange about the entire transaction," he said with a baffled expression. "Thomas Larkin was always straightforward and honest, a shrewd Yankee trader, but one to be trusted. Now his answers are evasive . . ."

"But does he admit he took the three thousand dollars? Does he acknowledge that you instructed him to buy the Santa Cruz ranch?"

"Yes, he acknowledges all that, but he has a hundred strange reasons for what he did; reports came to him that the Santa Cruz soil wasn't good; he didn't think I wanted to be a farmer; he had a chance to buy the Mariposa from Alvarado and thought I would prefer to live in the mountains, since I loved them so much; he thought I would rather be a cattle rancher; he felt that he had the right to use his own judgment in my best interests."

"How much does he say he paid for the Mariposa?"

"The same three thousand dollars."

"Did you tell him we want either our land or our money?"

"Yes. He said it was impossible, that I had appointed him as my agent, with discretionary powers, and I had to accept the results of his judgment. He was sorry if I was disappointed, but . . . "

They sat in silence in the mean little room, the future staring them down. She knew that John was grieving mostly over the loss of the beautiful ranch and his opportunity to earn a living as a farmer. For her the blow was of a different and more subtle nature: she had been deprived of her opportunity to create a home. Perhaps the gods were not only slow to consecrate a new hearth, but actually reluctant to see one laid. If Consul Larkin had bought any piece of land other than the Mariposa, even though it might have been inferior to the Santa Cruz ranch, she would not have felt so bad, for they still would have had their chance to make a home place. But the Mariposa was wild and frozen mountainous country, overrun by hostile Indians; it would be impossible for them to settle there.

What were they to do next? John was not the kind to grasp a pick and basin and rush to the gold fields; nor was there any business he could enter into in San Francisco. Perhaps in time he might receive a government appointment, but that was months off. She had brought with her one thousand dollars in gold loaned to her by her father to buy lumber and farm equipment, but her husband had borrowed twice that sum in Taos in order to bring the remnants of his party through to California.

"What do you think we ought to do?" she asked, curled up crossways on the bed. He too curled himself across the bed, running his fingers gently over her sunken cheeks.

"I'm sorry you got the starved-cat wife again, John."

"I'll confess I was hoping to find the bumpy one."

"Be patient, my dear."

"You asked what we should do first," he cried. "We are going to cure that cold of yours and get some weight back on you. I'm going to show you the beauties of California: all you've seen so far is this mudhole, but down on the peninsula there are bright sunshine and rolling hills and lovely valleys. I'm going to take you where it's warm and the countryside is beautiful. When we have had a month's vacation, we will face the future."

She snuggled closer into his arms, murmured, "Thank you, darling. But shouldn't you spend that month campaigning? The elected delegates are to meet in Monterey in September to adopt a constitution."

He had a way of welding firmness with tenderness. "My first task is to nurse you back to health. You are more important to me than politics. Besides, I'm not . . . I'm not a campaigner. Most of the people in the state know me, or know of me. There's little I could say from a stump that they don't already know."

Her mind went back to the spring evening in the summerhouse on C Street when Tom Benton had perceived that his daughter was in love with Lieutenant Fremont. John had said, "I am not much interested in politics."

"But surely you want to participate in the Constitutional Convention?"

"Not as a delegate. As a friend and adviser of the delegates, as an influence behind the scenes. I think I can do more good that way."

She did not see how, but she thought it wiser not to press the point. Instead she closed her eyes to embrace the vision of a month of leisure in warmth and beauty, with her husband at her side.

Gregorio, an Indian boy who had stuck with John through the worst rigors of the cold and starvation and had accompanied him from Taos, joined them on their trip down the peninsula. Also old Knight, who had been with John on an earlier expedition and was one of the sharpest frontiersmen of the West.

The following morning John disappeared early, telling her to be in front of the Parker House in an hour. Jessie dressed in her black silk, with the silk bonnet that matched. She did not think it a proper costume in which to go camping, but it was the only one she had left. After an hour she and Lily went down to the entrance of the Parker House. Within a few moments her husband came driving across Portsmouth Square in a six-seated surrey, the first she had seen in California. John whoaed the

horses, jumped out and helped his wife into the new and luxurious interior, with its upholstered cushions of Spanish leather, compartments
for storage of suitcases and foodstuffs.

"Where ever did you find this in San Francisco?" she asked in awe,
caressing the beautiful upholstery.

"I had it made for you in New Jersey before I left. It's been standing
here in a storehouse for two months. It's guaranteed to ride as smooth as
a boat, and look, it has reversible seats that make a bed. You can sleep in
here as comfortably as you would at home. Lily will have plenty of space
in this large boot to stretch out."

"Oh, darling," she murmured, "this is the first piece of good luck we've
had in California."

"There's another piece of good luck waiting around the corner, afraid
to come to you, but I have convinced him that all is forgiven."

Jessie saw Lieutenant Beale come striding toward her with a sheepish
grin on his long face. He said, "Madame Fremont, I am a fool! I do not
deserve your forgiveness! If you had followed my wretched advice you
would now be in the East while your husband would be here. When I
think how hard I tried to persuade you . . ."

"These are things that only women understand, Lieutenant," she replied gaily. "There's nothing to forgive; I was touched by your concern
for me in Panama."

"Then may we take him along on our junket?" asked her husband.
"He makes an excellent *pot-au-feu* when he doesn't throw too much
pepper into it; and he's the one who begged, borrowed or stole these
beautiful white horses."

They followed the trail down the peninsula, leaving behind the fog and
cold of San Francisco, and within a couple of hours had emerged into
warm clear sunlight, with the ripe fields of oats moving gently on the
hillsides, and the wild cattle grazing under the trees. The countryside was
like a park with mile after mile of beautiful grasses, wild flowers and
magnificent trees. When the air grew a little cool, John threw his faded
blue army cape over her shoulders.

They made camp in midafternoon by the side of a brook. While Jessie
refreshed herself and Lily in the cold water the men rode off in search of
a neighboring ranch house, returning with half a sheep and some fresh
corn which they barbecued over live coals of the fire. The Morocco
carriage cushions were piled in front of the fire for Jessie and Lily, who
ate their meat from the ends of long twigs. John had brought along claret
and tea and a box of French bonbons for Lily. Under the deepening
cloudless sky the air was soft and warm. Supper was finished by dusk.
Fresh logs were put on the fire, the men began telling stories of other

camps on the frontiers of South America, the Orient, and this wide American continent. Gregorio told of his childhood with the Indian tribe. Beale told sea stories and little jokes to make Jessie laugh. Old Knight, tall and gnarled as a mountain pine, ageless, with a long white beard which seemed somehow transplanted from his bald and shiny head, spun yarns of the days when the frontier had been only a hundred miles west of Washington.

As the night skies deepened, the campfire lighted the trees and brook, then the stars came out and to Jessie it was a scene of great beauty. This is my first hearth, she said to herself, just the kind we should have in a new country. May all of my hearths be as serene.

By nine o'clock she and Lily were comfortably settled in the carriage. The men had tied their hammocks to the trees and fallen asleep. Jessie listened to the crackling of the logs on the fire, the mules munching their wild oats, the half-muted cry of a coyote who had not the courage to come in and steal her supper. At dawn John awakened her with a cup of hot tea, then made a dressing tent for her by the side of the brook from a pair of blankets. She took her tin basin, towels, French soap and cologne to the running water, scrubbed Lily and then gave herself a leisurely bath. A doctor might have told her that bathing in a cold stream at dawn was dangerous; they had told that to her father forty years before. By the time she had dressed and returned to the campfire the carriage was ready, with most of the gear packed. After a cup of tea and a couple of old Knight's hot muffins, she said to John:

"Now what is my share of the duties?"

"To eat with all the appetite you can gather, to be happy."

"That's all, no work?"

"No work," replied the men. "This is your holiday. Women are useless on the trail, anyway."

The sun was bright and warm when they started toward San José. There weren't any roads, but the sturdily built carriage could go anywhere that wheels could go, and so they drove through the dry fertile valleys, climbed up the hills to overlook the ocean, followed bridle paths among the pines ever southward into warmer country, the men holding back the carriage with their riatas on steep grades. Knight and Gregorio would walk ahead of the two pack mules, which carried leather panniers loaded with clothing, cans and bottles of food, hammocks, pots and pans. John and Beale took turns driving the horses. At noon they stopped for luncheon and a siesta, throwing into the *pot-au-feu* large Spanish onions, sweet red peppers and whatever the men had shot that morning. They also scoured the countryside for eggs and fruits. When Jessie awakened from her nap they would drive on until time to make camp. For the first week her cough persisted; she began taking sun baths during the noon halt and by the end of the second week the pain in her chest was easing.

And so she moved through the balmy days, having no interest in time, regaining her joyousness with each passing hour. Sometimes in an inland valley behind the coast range the sun was burning hot, sometimes the air from the sea was soft and cool. When they put into a village they had their linens washed by the Indian women; sometimes they stopped at the ranches of the Californios where Jessie had proof that General Kearny's charges against her husband of maltreating the natives had been false. The Californios welcomed the party, staged fiestas in their honor, while Jessie and the women talked of clothes and babies. They had the good fortune to participate in a three-day wedding celebration, riding in the parade amidst the satin dresses and slippers of the women and the short velvet jackets and colorful velvet trousers of the men. Jessie's carriage was a matter of great interest to the Californios, who had nothing but solid wooden wheel carts pulled by oxen.

On the last night of July, while they were camped in the Santa Cruz mountains overlooking the sea, not far from the ranch which was supposed to have been their home, a sudden gust of rain swept across the ridge. John said, "I think your vacation is over, madame. We must decide now where we are going to settle down."

Jessie sighed reluctantly. "This has been a wonderful month. But I'm ready to set up our home. Where shall it be? How far are we from the Mariposa?"

"About two hundred miles, I should guess."

"Would it be difficult for us to see the land? I'm curious about it."

"It's a long journey on horseback across mountain trails and unbridged streams."

"What route would we take? Tell me how we get in."

His eyes lighted as he thought of the journey. "We'd go up the San Joaquin Valley, then straight into the Sierras."

"Would we pass the gold fields?"

"Yes, we'd go straight through the gold country."

They looked at each other, an expression of incredulity coming over their faces.

"By the Eternal, Jessie," whispered John, "I never thought of it before. We own the largest tract of mountain country in California. Men are washing out fortunes in gold dust only a hundred miles away . . ."

Her eyes wide with wonderment, she whispered too, "Darling, is it possible? Could there be gold on the Mariposa?"

He sprang to his feet. "It's the same mountain range; it would have the same rock formations, the same mineral deposits. It would have the same kind of rushing mountain streams to carry the gold dust down."

A slow, warm smile lighting her face, she said, "Could we start for San Francisco tomorrow morning? Could we buy picks and shovels and join the gold rush?"

"It's a risk, you know," said John. "Once we occupy the Mariposa, even to hunt gold on it, we will be making a legal acceptance of the land. We can never get our three thousand dollars from Larkin."

"We have no way of getting it back, anyway."

"How much cash do we have left out of your father's thousand dollars?"

"About five hundred."

"Then why don't we plunge the rest of our resources in a real gamble?"

"How do you mean?"

"While I was coming out from Taos I encountered a party of Sonorans from Mexico, en route to the gold fields. I rode with them for several days. When I was in Monterey I met them again; they were exhausted from the long march and planned to rest before starting into the mountains. I think I can make a deal with them: if I outfit them with food and tools and offer them half of all the gold they find on the Mariposa, they'll bring us down a fortune—if there is a fortune to be brought down. If there's no gold in the Mariposa, we will be broke."

"I'm not scared, John. Besides, I think it is futile to arrive in California at the height of the greatest gold strike the world has ever known and not take part in it. I'd like to wade up a mountain stream myself with a dish-pan in my hands and see if I couldn't collect some gold dust . . ."

Exhilarated, he chuckled, "That's the mercenary streak in you, Jessie; let me be the luster after wealth in this family, it doesn't become you. I'll take the Sonorans up to the Mariposa. When we return you will be a rich man's lady."

"Just so long as I'm not a Washington fine lady," she retorted.

6

THE NEXT AFTERNOON they reached the plateau above Monterey, with the little village nestling in the pines beneath them, and still farther down, the rocky shore of the crescent-curved bay. Jessie stood among the pines, watching the gulls flash white across the sun; she said to her husband, "Why couldn't we make our permanent camp here within sight and sound of all this beauty? It is warmer and quieter than San Francisco."

"Yes, I think you would be happy in Monterey. I will go into town to see if I can find us a house."

He was gone only an hour when she saw him swinging up the little trail from the village.

"There are no houses available," he announced, "but I've found two lovely rooms in the house of the wife of the Mexican general Castro, who was exiled to Mexico City after our conquest. She does not hold this against us. We will be comfortable there."

He helped her into the carriage and drove it down the winding path to the village. Madame Castro's house was the former Mexican governor's home: a huge ballroom fronted the bay, two adobe wings ran back from the water to meet a garden enclosed in soft-colored adobe walls; the roof was of rough red tile, the floors of smooth red tile, and there were hedges of pinks lining the garden walls and walks.

The ballroom was now rented as a warehouse for a flour merchant; Jessie was ushered into one of the wings which contained two rooms, high-ceilinged, the adobe walls whitewashed. They were innocent of furniture except for a wood stove in a small anteroom. Jessie presented her compliments to Madame Castro, who loaned them two cots and two chairs, several pots and pans, a few dishes and some flatware.

Leaving her to survey her new home, and to wonder how she was going to get it furnished, John went out to find his Sonorans, returning at lunchtime.

"The Mexicans have agreed to my proposition," he told her excitedly, "I must leave for San Francisco with them at once."

At her crestfallen expression, he added quickly, "I will be back in a couple of weeks, just as soon as there is news."

"Very well," said Jessie, "but since you are going up to San Francisco, you must use part of our funds to buy furniture and linens and dishes and silverware. This is the first time I shall be a housewife, and I am afraid I can't do very well with a few borrowed dishes. Let me give you a list; and you had better buy materials so that I can make some clothes for Lily and myself. Our two outfits are threadbare."

He left by midafternoon, assuring her that the first ship to reach Monterey would carry everything needed to make them happy at Madame Castro's. Jessie was delighted when Gregorio asked permission to remain behind as houseboy. She set about her duties as housewife, but the gold seekers had swept the country clean of every vestige of chicken, eggs, milk, meat, vegetables, fruits, canned goods and the wheat and grain staples. She could find little to buy but rice and beans, a little flour and sugar. She had never cooked anything more than a pot of coffee, and now she was thrust into the position of feeding herself, Lily and Gregorio on a few crude staples. Occasionally when she came back from a brisk walk in the hills with Lily she would find Gregorio squatting before the fire, a broad red sash around his waist and a red silk handkerchief tied around his jet-black hair, cooking a *guisado,* a compound of birds, squirrel, dried red peppers and rice stewed together.

Gregorio liked to picture himself in the role of houseboy, as he had been for the Mission Fathers, but he had preconceived notions of what a man might and might not do: he would light the fire in the open hearth in the living room, but a man did not chop wood, that was a squaw's work, so Jessie chopped her own firewood. Men shot food, but they did not cook over a stove, that was squaw's work, and so Jessie did the cooking.

"It's a good thing Gregorio is ornamental," she laughed to Lily, "with that red band around his straight Indian hair, because he really isn't useful. You and I do more cooking for him than he does for us."

"When he shoots a partridge or quail," answered Lily, "he cooks it over the open fire and brings it to us on a stick."

"Yes," agreed Jessie with a wry smile, "whether it's three in the afternoon or three in the morning! We have to eat it whether we're hungry or not, so that we won't offend him. I wonder if I'll ever be able to teach him the quaint American custom of cooking and serving food at mealtimes?"

"I don't think so," replied Lily, straight-faced. "You see, Mother, the Indians never had clocks and so they didn't know when it was mealtime. They ate when they got hungry, or they had shot something."

At the end of two weeks a ship arrived from San Francisco, and a number of sailors began bringing crates up to the Castro house. When everything had been assembled Jessie found that her husband had sent her two high, roomy New England bedsteads, plenty of sheets and blankets, woven East Indian wicker chairs, a beautiful inlaid teakwood table, enough Chinese matting to cover the tile floors, white lace material for curtains, Chinese satins and French damasks for draperies, two exquisitely shaped English pottery punch bowls to be used as washbasins, colorful French and Chinese satin-cushioned bamboo couches and chairs; two big grizzly-bear skins to be thrown over the matted floor in front of the fireplace; tin candlesticks and tall white spermaceti candles under whose light she and her father had worked for so many hours in their library in Washington. Wrapped as though it were the prize of the shipment, she found a copy of Lane's translation of *The Arabian Nights,* the only book in her possession.

With help from Madame Castro, and with Gregorio doing the heavy work, Jessie tacked the lovely white curtains over the windows, spread the matting on the floor, set out the beds in the rear room and the teakwood table with the wicker chair in the living room. When the place began to look warm and homelike, she had Gregorio bring in the last big package and open it in front of the fire. For a moment she believed she was dreaming, for someone had sold to her husband as "very durable for a lady's winter clothes" harsh merinos, thick muslins and cotton-back satins in loud and garish patterns. After her first shock, she had to laugh.

"It serves me right," she said to Lily, "for letting a man buy cloth for women's clothes; but never mind, we'll make the best of it. Here we go for a winter wardrobe."

She carefully ripped up her one remaining set of cambric underclothes to use as a pattern, also the one faithful black silk dress which remained of her Washington wardrobe. She did the same for Lily, laying out the patterns on the living-room floor as a guide, attempting to copy their lines in these new and strangely intractable stuffs. She pinned, measured, and remeasured herself and Lily before daring to put scissors to cloth. She had grown so thin since the black silk dress had been made that the first fitting showed the need for drastic alterations. She told her daughter the story of the old lady in St. Louis who never shaped stockings, but knitted them straight to the heel, saying, "It's a mighty poor leg that can't shape its own stocking." She built Lily's wardrobe and her own on this plan, playing a game in which she became Mrs. Abbott of London, fashionable mantua maker, and Lily her wealthy and imperious client, having elegant gowns built for Washington society. The game had added piquancy, for John had taken nearly all their money to San Francisco to outfit the Sonorans, and Jessie was getting down to her last few dollars for food. Their furnishings, she surmised with a crooked smile as she gazed about her, had been bought on credit.

With her husband away, Lily became her companion. She took her daughter for long walks among the pine-covered hills overlooking the bay, spent several hours each day teaching her arithmetic, geography and history, gave the seven-year-old a feeling of participation in their communal life by letting her do her share of the housework. Although these separations from her husband gave her the opportunity to devote herself to her daughter, they also brought Jessie closest to Lily during those periods when the light was gone from her eye and the sparkle from her brain and spirit. Lily was an observant child, she commented on what a different person her mother was when Father was present, how much more gay she was then, her step and her words fast and strong. Jessie felt conscience-stricken and redoubled her efforts to make Lily feel her love, but the light, the inner warmth and glow went out when John left, and all that was available for her daughter was the shell of a woman, wishing away her days until her husband would return.

She was perplexed by Lily's unfolding nature; by some strange twist of fate she found her daughter unimaginative in everything except this suffering of her mother's while her father was away. While she knew that the child must resent her father's dominating her mother's love and interest, yet when loneliness overcame her, it was Lily who served as comforter, stroking her hair the way John did, speaking her father's words of endearment exactly in her father's tone. She could discover no way in which Lily was like herself or John. She was a great deal like her aunt Eliza: biggish and awkward in figure, with plain features, literal-minded, practical in a way that neither Jessie nor John could ever be. Jessie had once remarked to her husband that Lily was a demon for the unvarnished truth; the daughter frequently punctured the romantic imaginings of her parents. There were occasions when Jessie was grateful, for the Fremont family had no more room for romantics, and a practical nature at the family board could be a blessing.

Late one afternoon, about a month after John had left for San Francisco, while she was sewing before the hearth in the living room, with Gregorio and Lily squatting on their haunches before the fire toasting quail, the door was thrown open and John burst into the room, his face and clothing soiled from the long ride, but a fiery glow in his eyes. He was at her side before she could rise, had laid a heavy sack at her feet. She did not open it but only gazed up at him. He quickly untied the thongs about the neck of the sack, scooped his right hand into it and with his left hand grasping her wrist tightly, poured a slow, bright stream of powder into her palm.

"Gold!" she cried.

"Yes, my darling, gold. Do you know how much gold is in this sack? One hundred pounds! Worth almost twenty-five thousand dollars!" He left her side and ran to the door, crying over his shoulder, "Wait there, don't move." In a moment he returned with another heavy sack in each hand, the weight far more than he could ordinarily have borne. He dropped the two sacks in front of her on the hearth, untied the thongs and spilled out a handful of gold from each.

"Every creek is lined with gold. The Sonorans washed out seventy-five thousand dollars' worth in three weeks!"

This turn of events was more than Jessie could comprehend. She had been reduced to her last few dollars for provisions, and now suddenly she had hundred-pound sacks of gold dust dumped at her feet. When she at last found her tongue, all she could stutter, unbelievingly, was:

"It's . . . all . . . ours?"

"No, only half is ours; you remember, I promised the Sonorans half the gold they found. But there are millions of dollars' worth of gold in there. It's richer than anything yet found in California. But that's not the

most important part: I think the Mother Lode runs through our Mariposa!"

"Mother Lode?" she repeated meaninglessly, still too stunned to think.

"Yes. While crossing our land I saw geological formations that I
thought gave promise of containing precious minerals. Then I found a
large piece of gold-bearing quartz. Do you know what that means, Jessie?
All the gold that we wash out of the rivers comes originally from the gold-
quartz rock formations. A thousand men swarming over the streams of
the Mariposa could wash out all the gold that the water has carried
down for centuries; that supply can be exhausted within a few months.
But if we have the original source, the deep layers of gold quartz that
might run across a whole mountain range, then literally there are millions
of dollars in the Mariposa!"

She didn't know whether to laugh or cry; there certainly was no dis-
puting these three heavy sacks of gold, or the piece of quartz with the
strong gold streak through it.

Money had never been important in her life, but that was because she
had never wanted for it. Having arrived in a strange country, only to find
themselves dispossessed of their ranch, several thousand dollars in debt,
and with no means of earning a livelihood, she felt this discovery to be
providential. This gold through which she ran her fingers in the open
mouths of the sacks was to her more a symbol of happiness than of
wealth, for she knew how much it could mean to her husband: in success,
in accomplishment, while at the height of his powers and in the midst of
overwhelming praise, John was modest, reserved, unassuming, warm-
hearted, generous, lovable. He was built to withstand success; the greater
the success, the finer John Fremont shone forth. But he was not equipped
to withstand failure or defeat; these brought out the very worst in him.
They made him suspicious, vindictive, intolerant, mean-spirited and
small-souled. That was why she had been so stricken in Panama at the
news of the collapse and destruction of the fourth expedition; that was
why the loss of the Santa Cruz ranch, even though she had never thought
that he should be a farmer, had been such a serious blow: she had feared
it might turn her husband bitter, start him thinking in terms of conspiracy
and persecution.

But now he would be rich. This was a kind of success everyone could
understand and no one could dispute. Even more important than being
rich, he would have become the darling of the gods: for he had discovered gold on his own land, not merely the gold that had been washed
down by the streams, but the very source of that gold. She knew that
when word of this discovery reached the East it would wipe out the
criticism of his failure to find a new railroad pass, his failure to keep his

party alive and return them all to safety. The news that John Fremont had discovered part of the Mother Lode on his Mariposa estate would sweep the East with as wild an excitement as had any of the reports of his first three expeditions—and it would do as much to intensify the ever growing migration to California! She uttered thanks to God, grateful that her man had once again been set on his feet.

7

BY THE FOLLOWING MORNING, when he had dashed off for the mines, it all seemed like a fantastic dream; every once in a while she would have to return to the sacks and run her fingers through the shining dust to reassure herself that she had not been dreaming. Yet the presence of the gold in the house brought little material change, for there was no additional food available, and there were no men left in Monterey to perform any kind of service; everyone had rushed to the gold fields, and the Indian women would do no work. One day a strapping Texan knocked at her door with a healthy young mulatto girl in tow.

"I hear you are in need of a servant, Mrs. Fremont," he said. "I come to sell you this slave girl. I'm going into the gold fields and I don't need her no more. I'll make a reasonable bargain."

"Would you allow her to work for me for wages?"

"No, ma'am," replied the Texan, "I want to sell her and get rid of her for good."

"I don't want to buy her," replied Jessie firmly.

"But why not, ma'am? I'm not even naming the price. I can collect from the colonel any time."

"I thank you for your kindness, sir," she replied, "but you don't understand. I don't believe in buying and selling persons."

"Why should you keep yourself from living in comfort?" asked the Texan. "Everybody buys and sells niggers."

"Colonel Fremont and I do not. We don't believe in slavery. We have always had colored people in our home, but they have been freemen, free to go when they wished."

And so she continued to scrub her own floors, pushing aside the gold sacks under the bed so that she could wash where they had been standing.

In addition to the gracious Spanish women with whom she could spend a neighborly hour now and then, she found that the United States Army officers were moving their headquarters to Monterey because living in San Francisco had grown too expensive. Generals James Benton Riley and P. T. Smith were there with their wives, and young William T. Sherman, with a consumptive cough but an inexhaustible supply of good stories. During August, Monterey became excited and busy, for it was to be the first state capital and within a few weeks the delegates would assemble to organize their government and draw up a constitution. Colton Hall, which the Reverend Samuel Wiley had been using as a school, was turned into a convention hall; a hotel had been started for the delegates, but since the mechanics had departed for the mines, there were few carpenters to work on it.

By the first of September the delegates began to ride into Monterey. For the most part they were a rough-hewn group of frontiersmen, all of whom carried weapons; some of them Jessie knew from Washington and St. Louis, with most of the others John was acquainted from his former stays in California. Six-foot-six Robert Semple, who had been important in forming the Bear Flag Republic, was chosen chairman; William G. Marcy, son of the secretary of war, was appointed secretary; J. Ross Browne, a traveling journalist, was made shorthand reporter; W. E. P. Hartnell, an Englishman, was engaged as interpreter for the Californios. There were early settlers, professional politicians, Englishmen, Irishmen, Frenchmen, Spaniards: America in microcosm.

Two days before the convention opened the hotel owner abandoned all hopes of getting his building completed, announcing, "The weather will hold good; the delegates can roll up in their serapes and sleep under the pine trees." However, there was not a restaurant in town; some of the men brought their own food in packs, but others came totally unprepared. Hospitality was for Jessie as natural as breathing, and she held open house every afternoon. While she could serve no varied menus, she had become good at making rice puddings, and the delegates were expert with their guns and fishing lines. Few came to dinner without a bird or a fish in hand.

She and Gregorio set up a long wooden table in the big garden. Here every afternoon ten or fifteen delegates would gather to talk politics and discuss the coming convention. Of the thirty-six American delegates, twenty-two came from the north and only fourteen from the south; nevertheless, the contest over slavery was sure to be hotly waged. There were three other American women in Monterey, Mrs. Larkin, Mrs. Riley and Mrs. Smith, all pleasant and hospitable women who did their share in entertaining the delegates; however, because Jessie and John had already been friends with some thirty out of the thirty-six delegates, their home became the informal star chamber of the convention, and here many of the issues were rehearsed. Long experience in the clash of political theories had taught Jessie how to sustain an atmosphere in which these ideas could be fought to their logical conclusions. Her two rooms were small;

the furnishings were bizarre and ill-fitted; the outdoor table was of rough wooden planks; but her warmth, her delight in participating in the creation of the new state kept the glow on her cheeks, her eyes sparkling, her tongue witty and welcoming.

As she looked about the rough board table with its covering of unbleached muslin brier-stitched with red thread, the oddly assorted silverware and unmatched Chinese and Mexican dishware; as she looked at the unshaven, roughly garbed frontiersmen eating the fish which they had caught themselves in Monterey Bay, and she had baked over the outdoor fire, with big bowls of rice pudding in the center of the table to finish off the repast, her mind went back to the highly polished mahogany table in the Benton dining room in Washington, with its shining damask cloths, gleaming silver and cut-glass bowls of fruits and candies, with Joshaam and Josheem padding about silently, passing the sides of rare roast beef, the terrapin, the roast duck and turkey, the beef and kidney pies.

Incongruous as were the furnished two rooms at Madame Castro's house, she developed a genuine love for them. Visited by men who spent most of the year sleeping on the ground or living in improvised shacks, tents or wretched boardinghouses, Jessie's rooms seemed like a breath of home. One Sunday evening when the weather suddenly turned cold, and they were eating indoors, William Gwin, John Sutter, Robert Semple, and Henry W. Halleck made an inspection of the rooms, and then Semple said: "Mrs. Fremont, we were saying among ourselves how surprising it was that you could achieve such comfort in a queer place like Monterey."

Jessie looked about her critically, trying to see the rooms with the eyes of a stranger. On the floor were the two grizzly-bear skins, their glass eyes lighted by the fire; the windows were draped with elegant Chinese brocade, the adobe walls were crudely whitewashed, and on the Chinese rattan furniture were cushions covered with exquisite French silks. The only wall decoration was a colored print of St. Francis, while on the Chinese teakwood table was the representative of another great religion, a bronze Buddha; alongside were a two-year-old copy of the London *Punch* and her Martha Washington sewing basket, the same one in which she had concealed the letter from Colonel Abert. She took the stance of a professional lecturer, raised one arm in the air for silence, and announced in her father's sometime pontifical tone:

"Gentlemen, at first glance you might think this room incongruous, but having made close study of it, I find it true to the period, Pioneer Forty-nine, worthy elements from all over the world, guarded by a California grizzly."

Her one disappointment was that her husband was not at home to join in the hospitality, the discussions, and the formulation of policy. She felt that John should have been a member of this convention, that even now he should be having serious talks with every delegate, helping to set official state policy. But word of the tremendous findings on the Mariposa had spread over central California and already several thousand prospectors were placer mining on the Fremont land. Their land grant did not give them exclusive mineral rights; anyone was entitled to wash out and pick up the gold lying in the Mariposa streams. John had felt that at that particular moment he should be with the Sonorans, helping them find the best streams in which to work, taking out their gold nuggets and gold dust before another several thousand prospectors flooded over the land. Jessie had not thought it so necessary to get out the last possible bag of gold dust; they had not come to California to be gold miners or to become rich; they had come to enter into the local politics; why then allow the accidental discovery of gold on the Mariposa to upset their plans and to keep John away from the California Constitutional Convention?

She had suggested all this to her husband, but he had declared that as long he was not a delegate there was no proper place for him; that most of the delegates knew his stand and his politics from years of contact; that no one could blame him for making gold while the sun shone. Later, when they opened their regular quartz mines, their property would be safe and he would not have to be on the ground. It was unfortunate that the convention and the Mariposa gold rush were taking place at the same moment, but he felt he owed it to all of them to get out as much gold as he could and let Jessie be his representative in Monterey as she had been in Washington.

One evening Delegate Lippincott of Philadelphia brought fifteen delegates in to dinner. They watched Jessie standing over the stove cooking the food; they watched her cover the rough planks with the strips of unbleached muslin brier-stitched together; they watched her serve, with Gregorio's help, twenty-four guests; they saw her sit at the head of the table and with high spirits guide the political discussions so that they included everyone about the table; they saw her gather up the soiled plates, then wash the dishes and silver while William Sherman, the Reverend Wiley and Robert Semple stood about drying them, everyone keeping up a rapid-fire repartee. When the work was done and they had assembled in the living room, several of the lanky frontiersmen sprawling on the floor in front of the fire, one of the delegation said:

"Mrs. Fremont, we heard in town that you were offered a young slave girl to do your work and you refused to buy her. Is that true?"

"Quite true," replied Jessie. "Neither Mr. Fremont nor I believe in buying and selling human beings. I would never consent to use or own a slave."

"Not even if it meant you would have to scrub your own floors and wash your own dishes for the rest of your life?"

"Not even," said Jessie with a quiet smile.

"The women in San Francisco are crying for suv-vents, but if you, a Washington fine lady, can get along without, they shan't have them. We'll keep clear of slave labor."

Hallelujah! thought Jessie. At last that title "fine lady" may accomplish some good. Aloud she said:

"Colonel Fremont has called California the Italy of America. Isn't it an ideal place for small homes and well-tended acreage? If we keep slave labor out, we will have the wealthy and comfortable middle class, but no poor."

"That's a fine sentiment," replied William Steuart, head of the pro-slavery leaders, "but the aristocracy will always have slaves."

"How about you joining the aristocracy of emancipators, Mr. Steuart?" she shot back. "My father freed all his slaves in St. Louis before he went to Washington twenty-five years ago."

"But who's going to do all the hard and dirty labor?"

"You are," flashed Jessie, "and I am! I am raising a child in California, and before long you men will be bringing your wives out here or marrying and raising families. It isn't a pretty sight in a free country for a child to see and hear chain gangs clanking through the streets or to watch officers chasing a fugitive slave and putting him in irons. Is that what we're founding a new state for? If so, it would be better if we all returned east and left this beautiful country alone."

On the day before the convention was to open, John rode in from the Mariposa, unable to stay away. There was a gala party in the Fremont rooms that night, with every American in Monterey assembled, even Consul Larkin, looking sheepish, but wanting to be friends again.

The next morning the convention opened. Jessie and John sat behind the rough wooden railing which had been stretched across the middle of the hall. Using the constitutions of New York and Iowa as models, the delegates pushed forward rapidly in a series of sharp discussions, debates which seemed to Jessie to be on a high plane of intelligence and integrity. She rememberd the story her father told her of the Constitutional Convention of Missouri, which much of the California procedure now duplicated.

William Gwin dominated the convention with his magnificent figure, leonine head and orator's voice. He was a sincere man, honest according to his lights, an able tactician in parliamentary procedure. Jessie saw that the delegates not only admired him but had faith in his judgment. As the days passed and Gwin directed more and more of the discussion, she became convinced that his boast in Washington would be carried out, that he would be returned by the legislature as one of the first two California senators. That left only one berth open. To whom would it go? To her husband, sitting quietly beside her, for some reason best known to himself never rising to his feet, never asking for permission to participate, content to exercise his influence at home over the dinner table in quiet and friendly chats?

After the convention had been in session for a week, and it was evident that California would become a free state, John could contain himself no longer. He rode south to buy several big cattle ranches which he had admired since he had first seen them during the conquest, then returned to San Francisco to invest some of his rapidly accumulating gold in tracts of land lying about a mile west of Portsmouth Square. He sent word not to expect him for a considerable time, as the Sonorans wanted to go home for Christmas and he thought he ought to stay on the Mariposa as long as possible. Gregorio went up to the mountains to be with him, leaving Jessie and Lily alone. With the last of the delegates gone, Monterey seemed quiet and lonely.

8

In october slashing rains were whipped against the windows by strong winds off the Pacific. The streets became the same kind of mudholes Jessie remembered from the early days of Washington, and there could be little visiting back and forth. One large window overlooked the bay, the deserted beach and the rocks beyond. She thought, With the sea one is never alone. Yet with the sea, as with everything else, its joys are enhanced a hundredfold when you have a loved one by your side to share in its rich variety. After supper Lily would get into her nightgown and then stretch out on the grizzly rug before the fire, where she would burn the resinous pine cones which crackled and made ever changing flame pictures.

The days and the nights were long, for she had too little to do, and her library consisted of exactly the one book which John had found in San Francisco while buying furniture. She read one story from *The Arabian Nights* to Lily each Sunday night, Lily calling it their Sunday dessert, for she wanted to make the book last as long as possible. Fortunately the flour merchant who had taken over the ballroom at the front of the house found five bound volumes of the London *Times* and a number of volumes of the *Merchant's Magazine,* which he gave to her. She had not much interest in commerce, but for want of something better to read she persisted and finally grew interested: for a lover of books is like a lover of women, he would rather have an interesting book than a dull one, but he would rather have a dull one than none at all. Then General Riley stumbled across a volume of Lord Byron's poems, and these brought her many hours of beauty as she sat before her fireplace while the winter surf boomed across the rocks and the night was filled with cold and rain.

Every week or two Gregorio or a trusted Sonoran would arrive with more sacks of gold dust, which she stored in trunks and boxes under the beds. One day in November, General Riley's wife was visiting when Gregorio came in with two of the heavy buckskin sacks. Mrs. Riley, who had been in the Army since she was nineteen, living on low-scale army pay, said:

"I really must congratulate you on your growing riches."

The well-meant remark, said without any apparent envy, threw Jessie's weeks of loneliness into focus. She did not enjoy being separated from her husband for the sake of making money; they had already been separated too much and too cruelly. Nor did she enjoy the thought of sitting in two rain-swept rooms with nothing to do but feed herself and her child, while the weeks and the months passed, and she had no part to play, no job to do. John would be obliged to spend a considerable portion of his time on the Mariposa; he thought it too remote and too dangerous for his wife to come there and make their home. What then was she to do? Sit here in Madame Castro's two rooms while they accumulated more and more wealth? To what end? She asked only a few simple things of life: the company and love of her husband; important work to do at his side; sons to bear his name. Turning to Mrs. Riley she murmured:

"Gold isn't much as an end, is it? It can't conjure comforts or an ounce of brain rations. I am simply famished for the taste of a good book. I'd give every last one of those buckskin sacks to have my husband here with me now."

As the long months of winter spun themselves out, and John managed to get home only for a day or two, Jessie realized that this was almost the same as his being out on another expedition. She counted back over the memories of her marriage, realizing that more than half the time she had been alone, prey to illness, anxiety and uncertainty over his welfare. She did not think that the quantity of money involved should have any influence on her feelings; she could not have felt more keenly a sense of life in abeyance if John had been earning single dollars instead of tens of thousands.

Toward the end of November she received in the mail a long envelope addressed to Colonel John C. Fremont, which proved to be a questionnaire relating to her husband's political beliefs. The committee that had written the letter wished to assure Colonel Fremont that if he would answer the questions satisfactorily, they would back him for the United States Senate.

She engaged an Indian to ride to the Mariposa and summon John, for an immediate answer was expected, and both letters would be published in the California newspapers. She made a copy of the letter to send with the messenger, so that he could be formulating his reply on the long ride home. He arrived at the end of the fourth day, tired and overwrought: there were now some three thousand prospectors pouring over the Mariposa; the Sonorans figured that they had enough money to last the rest of their lives in Mexico and would work no longer; there was no labor available at any price to take their place. Jessie saw that her husband was less than ever interested in politics. She boiled an iron tub of water over the outside fire in order that he might have a brisk scrub-up, then they had tea and biscuits.

"You see," she said, "I'm a better visionary than I am a cook: I predicted when you left on the second expedition five years ago that you would be one of the first senators from California."

He did not look as pleased at her outburst of confidence as she had hoped. His dark eyes could peer as fiercely inward as they could peer outward, and she saw that her husband had been undergoing several days of intense soul searching.

"If I am elected, Jessie," he said, "what do we do with the Mariposa and our mines? All the surface gold will be gone very shortly. We'll have to buy machinery, bring in a competent labor supply and follow the gold quartz into the sides of the mountains. If we don't start this work very soon, others will, and we will lose possession; under existing law we have no mineral rights even inside our land unless we set up permanent equipment to mine it. If I were to be elected and we left for Washington, how do we know when we would get back? Our dream of wealth will be gone; others will have pre-empted it."

She did not think this a serious problem; even after they had paid the Sonorans their half of the gold dust, there still would be about two hundred thousand dollars in gold for them. This was a great deal of money; it was a lifetime's money; why did they need millions, particularly if the cost of those millions was a seat in the United States Senate?

She knew it would not be wise to argue thus to her husband; it would seem that she was trying to force her peculiar values on him, as though she would oblige him to think that because in the Benton family a United States senator was the world's most important dignitary, John Charles Fremont, who had never shown any appetite for the Senate, should give up the opportunity to become one of the world's richest and most power-

ful men, an opportunity neither remote nor fanciful, but at his very finger tips.

"I don't want to influence you," she said—"that is, not too strongly.
I've always dreamed of seeing you in the Senate, but there's no reason
why you should shackle yourself with my ambitions. After all, it is you
who will have to do the work, and so you should decide for yourself. If
you want to go to the Senate, then we should write the strongest polemic
on your political philosophy we can create; if you would prefer to stay
here and start to mine on a big scale, then we will forget about Washington, and Lily and I will move up to the Mariposa with you and build
our home there. You say you will need labor for the mines; the best way
to attract it is to have a going community with comfortable cabins and a
store and a school for the children."

"Yes, those are our alternatives."

"Then it's purely a case of values. Which means the more to you?"

He was silent for a long time, his chin resting on his chest, his eyes
staring inward, not seeing the strained and hopeful expression on his
wife's face.

"I should like to try to do both," he finally said; "I think we can work
it out. I will stand for the election, and we will leave for Washington immediately if I am successful. When our ship arrives in New York, I will
buy the mining equipment and send it out here. I will also try to hire
mining engineers and have them accompany the equipment and install it.
At the end of the congressional session we will come back to California
for as long as we can, long enough to supervise the mines and set up a
system."

He looked toward her hopefully. "Do you think we can do them both,
Jessie, or am I being overly ambitious?"

"We can try, darling. Shall we begin work now on the answer to this
letter?"

"No, I'm too tired. I need a night's sleep; besides, though it's difficult
to keep track of time in the mountains, it seems to me that it has been a
month since I embraced my wife."

"Only a month?" she murmured. "I would say it was a year."

They spent the next day drafting his free-state, Democratic stand, and
his answer to the questions affecting California. The following day he returned to the mines, promising to be back for Christmas.

Once again Jessie was alone in her rooms overlooking the Pacific.
Christmas approached slowly through a succession of dark and wind-
swept days. Neither Jessie nor Lily could venture forth in such weather,
and so Jessie would light a half-dozen candles in the tin holders John
had sent down from San Francisco with the furnishings and go over the

pictures in an illustrated London *Times.* Just two days before the holiday her door was wrenched open, rain swept into the room, then the
door was slammed shut. She turned quickly from the fire to see John
leaning against a now wet door, panting for breath, his sombrero, face
and native jacket drenched, the water running off his high boots in rivu-
lets onto the floor.

"Jessie, I couldn't wait, I have ridden from San José to greet the first
senator's lady from California."

She cried from her chair, "John, you've been elected!"

"On the first ballot," he exulted. "I received twenty-four votes out of
thirty-six. William Gwin was elected on the third ballot. We sail for New
York on New Year's Day."

She sprang out of her chair, ran to him and flung her arms about him,
kissing him joyfully.

"You'll get wet," he laughed. "I'd better not walk across the room,
I'd make it a pool of water."

"Drop out of those clothes right where you stand, then come to the
fire and get warm. I'll have dry clothes for you in a minute. You must be
tired. It's a seventy-mile ride from San José."

After a gay supper of coffee, cold beef and bread, and a bottle of
champagne to celebrate their victory, they sprawled out on the warm
bear rugs facing the fire, their chins cupped in the palms of their hands,
their fingers framing the ovals of their excited faces.

"Ah, my dear," she murmured, "it will be a happy day for me when
I see you in the Senate. I will have that exact seat in the visitors' gallery
where Father first put me to listen to him speak when I was only eight."

"It will be a happy day for me," rejoined her husband, "when I see
Maylee serving you morning tea in bed."

Later, in the glow of the burned-down eucalyptus logs, they fell asleep
on the rugs. At dawn, after a cup of hot coffee, Jessie embraced her husband and he left to ride the seventy miles back to San José.

In festive mood she had Gregorio cut them an evergreen from the hills
above the bay and set it in a corner of her living room. Having no ornaments for the tree, she searched through her possessions until she found
some old tin foil, rolled it into soft balls and stuck them on the ends of the
branches. The tin candleholders she tied to the stronger branches, putting
in red and yellow candles. Having opened a can of sardines for lunch, she
had Gregorio cut up the tin into odd shapes and make little holes in them
so they could be strung onto the tree, then sent him out to the hotel where
she had seen pieces of sheet metal thrown down from the now finished
roof. Gregorio cut this metal roughly into shapes of stars and crescents,
which Jessie painted blue and red before hanging on the tree.

John returned on Christmas Eve with gifts for everyone, a beautiful doll just off the boat from China for his daughter, a soft red cashmere shawl for Jessie, and the first box of candy manufactured in California.

The week between Christmas and New Year's was crowded and exciting. John was busy making arrangements for agents to handle the mines. The Sonorans came down from the Mariposa and took their half of the gold. Jessie had a great deal of packing to do, the furniture had to be stored so that they could have it again when they returned to build a home on the Mariposa. She took a last sentimental walk through the empty rooms, remembering how uncertain their future had been when first they had moved in five months before.

The S.S. *Oregon* came into the harbor at Monterey on New Year's night, firing its guns to notify the passengers ashore. In the most torrential rain she had ever seen, and with the streets pouring rivers of mud down to the sea, they trudged to the waterfront followed by Gregorio and another Indian boy carrying their luggage. John lifted her into a rowboat, Gregorio carried Lily. They sat in the downpouring torrents while the two Indian boys rowed them out through the blackness of the night.

"Don't cry so hard, Gregorio," said Jessie, "you're waterlogging the boat. We promise to come back soon."

Once again she climbed up a ship's rope ladder, swaying from side to side as the wind-swept rain buffeted her. The S.S. *Oregon* stopped at Mazatlan to coal. Consul Parrott, who had fought with Colonel Fremont and the California Battalion, came aboard to invite them to his thick-walled Mexican house for dinner. The weather was warm off the coast of Mexico and Jessie had found her Monterey clothes too heavy for comfort. Searching through her bags she discovered a white, ruffled morning sacque to wear with her rough merino skirt.

By the time they returned to their ship the night air had turned cool. Jessie realized too late that she had made a serious error; her cough returned and she was confined to her bunk for the rest of the voyage to Panama. John too was stretched flat on his back, his left side and frost-bitten leg gripped with rheumatism. Both were taken off the ship on stretchers, with Lily, white-faced with worry, watching over them. Again Madame Arce came to Jessie's rescue. She took the Fremonts to her home and installed them in the same bedroom Jessie had occupied eight months before. She and her servants devoted their full time to nursing the sick couple, concealing from them the fact that Lily was down with Chagres fever, as ill as her parents.

They had been scheduled to catch the ship which left Chagres five days after they had reached Panama City. Instead they lay in their hammocks in Madame Arce's house for a month. During the last week John was able to hobble around the room, and Jessie's fever went down. John L. Stephens, who was building the Panama Railroad, came in late each afternoon, murmuring, "I have come to take my chill with you."

When the last day arrived on which they could possibly catch the next steamer to New York, Jessie insisted that she was strong enough to travel. John limped out of the room and went aboard a United States man-of-war in the harbor. When he returned he said, "We can leave in the morning; I've borrowed a ship's hammock; we'll rig an awning over it to keep out the sun, and hire Indian bearers to carry you across Panama."

The next morning John Stephens brought four of his best Indian car-riers. Jessie was taken out to her palanquin and lifted into it. Madame Arce settled a crimson silk, lace-trimmed pillow under her head and filled the flat canvas pockets with handkerchiefs and flasks of cologne. John and Lily each had a mule to ride. Lily was recovering, but all of her hair had been shaved off during the fever, and her face was pinched and white. Jessie had quite a start when she first saw her daughter, but the stolid Lily assured her that she was well again and perfectly able to ride the mule to Gorgona. As the Indian bearers moved through the streets of Panama, the natives came out from their houses to see the strange cor-tege.

After two days and nights on the trail, and two days in the boat going down the Chagres River, during which Jessie stoked herself regularly with quinine and coffee, she at last caught sight of the masts of the steamer. Once in their cabin, she sat on the edge of the berth, ran her hand over her husband's forehead with her fingers, combed the hair back from his brow. Then she lay down in the berth alongside of him, motion-ing Lily to come into her arms. She lay quietly, one arm about her hus-band, the other about her daughter; the bunk was crowded with the three of them in it, but Jessie did not care; she was happy to have them all to-gether again.

From the docks in New York they drove direct to the Irving House. The manager told them they would have the suite just vacated by Jenny Lind. They walked into the sitting room and stood in the middle of the room in front of a long French mirror in which Jessie had an opportunity to survey her family. First came Lily; she had eaten steadily for two weeks aboard ship, was now plump and red-cheeked; her brown merino dress was too small for her and she seemed to be bursting out of it both fore and aft; it was also too short, revealing the unbleached muslin pan-ties. She had on a pair of Indian buckskin shoes presented to her by Gregorio, and since her hat had blown overboard, her shaved head was wrapped in a black silk handkerchief, making her look like one of the immigrant children off the boats from Europe.

In the middle was her husband, dressed in knee-high miner's boots and his California outfit of miner's trousers, buckskin jacket, open-throated shirt and handkerchief tied around his neck, his gray-shot beard untrimmed, his hair as long as when he had come home from his expeditions. Then her eyes fell upon herself: emaciated, her pale skin made to look a jaundiced yellow by the rough-fitting, brown satin basque blouse. The dark skirt she had cut out of her riding outfit hung straight and shapeless to her ankles, and out of it peeped rusty black satin slippers, the only pair of shoes she had left; held on to her head with a China crepe scarf was a leghorn hat whose color clashed with the brown blouse and blue skirt.

To herself she murmured, The senator's lady from the Golden West! Miss English should see me now!

She had been away a year, six months of it spent in California, the rest in travel. She had made no home there, made no real indentation upon the country; she did not belong, yet she wanted to belong. In the back of her mind she knew that the reason she had failed had been that, in spite of her lifetime ambition to go west to the frontier, she had not set out for California with a wholehearted desire to settle there permanently and make it her life. She had gone with the idea that she and her husband would very soon return to Washington as Senator and Mrs. Fremont. In a sense she had been disloyal to the new land; perhaps that was why the gods had refused to consecrate her hearth. If she wanted a hearth in California, she would have to go there with the idea of remaining forever, loyal and devoted, and enduring of hardship. In spite of the battered apparition of the three of them in the glass, she knew that she did want to go back to California. Perhaps next time she could become part of the country, indigenous to its life.

9

THEY SPENT TWO DAYS getting their land legs, buying clothes, preparing for the train trip to Washington. She had been able to send a telegram to her father announcing their safe arrival in New York, a telegram over the wires that Samuel Morse had begged Congress to build for the five lean years during which he had come so often to the Bentons' to show why the telegraph was practical.

Tom Benton met them at the station, looking old and harassed but happy at welcoming them home. It was the first time she had been away from the family, and it seemed to her that the year had made more than its proportion of changes: her sisters had grown into young ladies; Randolph had developed into a tall, pleasant lad with her mother's finely chiseled features and her father's slightly hoarse voice; her mother's face and body had grown frail; her father's battle-scarred features reflected his heavy burdens.

She walked about the house enjoying the smell of rose geraniums in the drawing room, looking with joy at the damask-covered dining table and silver service set out for dinner; she moved about the library touching the leather-bound books, the arms of comfortable chairs, her writing desk in front of the fireplace.

Their friends came in to welcome them and congratulate John on his election. James Buchanan gave a formal dinner in their honor. Jessie ordered a new gown of soft brocade with lace frills. As they sat down to the table flanked by friendly cabinet officers, congressmen, army and navy officers, ambassadors and a considerable portion of Washington society, Jessie and John exchanged a meaningful glance: they remembered how Washington had treated them when they left, with few people calling, the Army wanting no part of their indicted brother, the Cabinet officers remaining away for fear of embarrassing the administration, the congressmen unwilling to take sides. Now they were the darlings of Washington society, rich with their fabulous California gold, John the first senator from what would soon be the first state of the Far West. As Jessie gazed at her husband she saw that he wore his new dinner clothes with poise and dignity but that he looked thin, his gray hair and weather-beaten face making him seem far older than his thirty-seven years. When John looked at his wife he saw a young woman of twenty-six with flashing hazel eyes, brown hair a little thinner than when he had first known her but gleaming richly as it was combed over her ears and gathered low at the back of her neck; her skin as clear as a child's in spite of the rigors of Panama and California, her delicate sloping shoulders white and firm and warm to the eye above her Empire gown of deep blue brocade. Simultaneously they recalled that moment in the Irving House when they had first seen themselves in their crude, garish and ill-fitting clothes.

Jessie was delighted to be back in cultivated society. She laughed gaily, more intoxicated by the swift flow of conversation than by the many toasts she drank to California and its admission as a state. John too had a gleam in his eye while he told about the possibility of a railroad to California, of the wealth and beauty of the state; but mostly their eyes sought each other, for they could not believe that they were back in Washington, just as though nothing had happened to them.

James Buchanan leaned over and murmured to her, "Miss Jessie, I don't think you should engage in flirtation with your husband while sitting next to me."

"Flirtation?"

"I would describe it as such," he replied, "a mental wink, a flash of the eye, a fleeting smile . . . I am beginning to suspect that your husband loves you."

"An unwarranted hypothesis," laughed Jessie. "He is so stunned at seeing me in an evening gown, after my unbleached muslins and black merinos, that he can hardly believe his eyes."

There was a week of parties and dinners and fun, and then they settled down to work. Behind the closed door of the library, Thomas Hart Benton admitted to his young daughter that his position in the Senate was in danger. His long fight to prevent the extension of slavery had consolidated the slavery men of Missouri against him, and after thirty years of service it was growing apparent that they had a chance to defeat him in the coming election. The focal center of the slavery battle was now California: since its own legislature had declared California to be a free state, the slavery men in the Congress were determined that California must not be admitted to the Union.

Tom Benton thus faced a painful dilemma: for thirty years he had been working to bring the Pacific coast into the United States; he had always been opposed to the extension of slavery beyond the existing southern states; but if he fought for the admission of California as a free state, his waging of the battle would afford the last round of ammunition needed to put him out of the United States Senate.

John was a senator-elect from California, but California was not yet a state and so actually he had no job. Officially there was little he could do to hasten the admission, but unofficially the Fremonts served as goodwill ambassadors and an information service on the topography, climate and general future of that territory. Through the Benton home on C Street moved a large section of official Washington. Many of those who had been skeptical about the distant land left at the end of the evening having caught some of their enthusiasm. Neither Jessie nor John had anticipated a serious struggle over the admission of California: Why wage a war over a territory, pour thousands of settlers into its boundaries, and then refuse to incorporate it within the nation? Nevertheless the weeks and the months passed, the beautiful spring merged into the hot summer and the hot summer spent itself into an early fall while the slavery faction maneuvered to gain ever increased concessions as the price of admitting California.

John utilized some of his leisure to buy mining equipment which he shipped out to San Francisco. After the third of his buying junkets, during which he laid out a great deal of cash, he informed Jessie that he was going to have to capitalize the Mariposa, issue leases on certain of the mines, and sell stock in them. This would provide the capital to build dams, roads and buy other expensive equipment so necessary for large-scale mining. She was disturbed at the idea, for it meant setting up in business; there would be stockholders, managers and boards, control would eventually be taken from John's hands, he would be responsible to a great many people. She asked her husband if he did not think it would be better to mine on a small scale and remain the master of his mines. He laughingly replied:

"Jessie, you sound as though you didn't want us to take too much gold out of the Mariposa. Don't you like money?"

"Yes, I love money," she exclaimed. "But like every other vice, it should be indulged in moderately. Besides, I think you're meant for more important things than just making money. Did I ever tell you what Nicollet said about money? He said that the accumulation of money was a period of affliction, like adolescence, which we had to pass through before we could reach maturity. I'd like to take just a modest amount of gold out of the Mariposa, John, enough to buy you the freedom and financing for whatever work may appeal to you: further expeditions, mapping a railroad route to California, building wagon roads to the West. I don't think the Mariposa gold should be an end, I think that it should be a means: a means of fulfilling your life and your work. Or do I sound like a moralistic schoolteacher?"

"You sound like a schoolteacher . . . and you sound right. However, one cannot fly in the teeth of fate; the gods dumped a Mother Lode into my lap; to do less than exploit it to its fullest, to refuse to extract the millions of gold from those quartz lodes would be like refusing to accept the gifts of the gods."

"Yes," she agreed thoughtfully, "I can see that point of view. But did it ever occur to you that the gods might also appreciate a bit of restraint? That it might be the better part of virtue not to gobble up their gifts? When the slavery men at Monterey told you that you could be the richest man in the world if you would use slave labor in your mines, you said that that was too high a price to pay for wealth. Then why isn't giving your own life to digging out gold too high a price to pay? I would rather have you a free workman than a bounden mine owner."

John did not agree, and so an English agent by the name of Hoffman was given the right to sell leases on the Ave Maria, West Mariposa and East Mariposa mines. The agreement signed, Hoffman took the next ship to England to set up stock companies, the proceeds of which were to be sent to John to turn the three mines into major producing units. A few weeks later she learned that her husband was dealing with a second agent by the name of Thomas Sargent, giving him the right to sell leases for half of the vast Mariposa tract. Sargent also planned to go to England to sell stock in the company. She had no wish to intrude upon her husband's business arrangements, and she was reassured by the fact that her father approved of Sargent and the granting of the additional leases.

On the morning of September 10, 1850, when John Charles Fremont was to be presented to the United States Senate, Jessie rose early, took a leisurely bath, creamed her face, dressed partially, then sat before her dressing table to brush her long brown hair and coil it low on her neck. When she tried to rise to put on her gown there swept over her the same wave of nausea that she had suffered while carrying her son. She laughed gaily to herself as she thought, California may be fertile country, but Washington is the better conceiving ground!

She rode with her husband and her father up to the Senate; they were as gay as children, laughing at silly jokes, yet there was an undertone of fatality about it, for Tom Benton knew that the South was rapidly losing its temper, growing angry and frightened, that this night well be his last session. He had always wanted to die in the seat behind his Senate desk, in the midst of a fiery debate; yet if he had to be dispossessed now, go down to defeat as one of the first casualties of the threatening conflict between the North and the South, it was a good feeling to know that his daughter's husband would take his place, that California from 1840 to 1870 would be the frontier of freedom and the capital of the West, just as Missouri had been during his thirty years from 1820 to 1850.

Jessie took her accustomed seat in the front row of the visitors' gallery across from the eagle poised on top of the canopy which covered the Speaker's chair. Below were seated the senators from thirty-one states, in their long, tight black trousers held down by straps under the heels of their boots, their long-tailed, square-cut black coats and the wide lapels which framed the bow tie and white shirt.

She believed that her husband was the youngest man on the floor. She also thought him the handsomest. She glowed with pride as she watched him being sworn in as a United States senator.

In the three weeks that remained of the session she worked hard as John's secretary. Her experiences as a traveler, housewife and mother enabled her to help her husband. Yet John needed little help: she had never seen his mind work with greater clarity or comprehensiveness. Although he was no lawyer, he dictated bills to extend the laws of the judicial system of the United States to California, bills to grant public lands for purposes of education and the building of universities, asylums for the deaf and dumb, the blind and the insane, bills to record land titles, settle land claims, to negotiate the working of mines, for a system of post roads and national roads to California. She saw that California was indeed being well represented. His eighteen bills to facilitate the migration of the people westward, and for the internal developments of California, were all passed by the Senate. At the end of the session even those southerners who had so bitterly opposed the introduction of California, Barnwell, Davis, Calhoun, Clay, congratulated Senator Fremont on his legislative program.

Jessie carried the new child well, strong and happy and hopeful about the future. She indulged herself not at all, went for long walks, danced at the frequent balls. On the afternoon that the Senate adjourned, she asked, "When is Gwin going back to California to stand for re-election?"

After a moment of hesitation John replied. "He isn't going. At least, not yet . . ."

She blinked uncomprehendingly. "He isn't going to stand for re-election? But that's not like Gwin. He told me himself he's determined to remain a senator from California."

"Yes, that's true. But you know, Jessie, we have a long term and a short term."

"You were elected to the long term. You have another five years . . ."

John shook his head. "Neither of us was elected to the long term. I know you have been assuming all along, Jessie, that I had the long term, and you were so happy about it I just hated to put any doubts in your mind."

Her cheeks flamed.

"But why should I have had any doubts? You received an overwhelming majority of votes. That makes you the man they want in the Senate, that gives you the six-year term."

"The election laws don't say so. Gwin and I have to draw lots for it."

She lost her temper.

"It's too utterly preposterous, John, that you should agree to gamble over a seat in the Senate. What about fighting for your rights? I don't understand you, this is out of character; two thirds of the people in California meant for you to have the long term. Gwin has no real stake in California: he went out there as a political adventurer, determined to pull the prize plum out of the pie! What does he know about California? What part did he play in making California an American state, except trying to get it to go proslavery at the convention? Your expeditions and reports are responsible for half the families that are now living out there. You played a critical role in the conquest of the state; kept it from falling into British hands. You know every valley and mountain range. You know what the people are like and what their needs are, they trust you to do important things for them here in Washington . . ."

She slumped down into her chair, her anger burnt out.

"I'm sorry I shouted at you, dear, but it just seems so incongruous for the first citizen of California to gamble over a senatorial seat with a political adventurer. There is no rhyme or reason in it."

He sat beside her and brushed the tears from her eyes with a hard circular motion of his palm.

"There's nothing I can do, Jessie; what you suggest would cause a scandal. People would say that it was another of John Fremont's uprisings, a mutiny against established tradition. Don't you see, there's no law to sustain me; it has always been a gentlemen's agreement that two senators elected from a new state must draw lots for the long and short terms."

His reference to another John Fremont uprising quieted her.

"Your stand against slavery has earned you powerful enemies here in Washington," she pleaded; "at the end of a six-year term you will have made friends with them, you will have done so much good work for California that you will be re-elected again and again for thirty full years, the way Father has from Missouri. But if you go back now after only three weeks in the Senate, the slavery group will fight you tooth and nail."

John's black eyes peered at her unhappily.

"We have to take our chances; we have to draw lots. Wish me luck, dear. I'm going to draw the long term."

She smiled a little wistfully, kissed the niche in the corner of his mouth.

"Of course you will," she said.

There was no need for John to tell her the next day when he returned home, his face a polite but withdrawn mask, that he had drawn the short term. The thirty-year career in the Senate had evaporated to three short weeks! Another turn of the wheel of fortune: when they were down, the wheel spun, they found gold, they were elected, they returned to Washington triumphant. Then the wheel turned again, thousands of gold seekers flooded their lands; they had to incorporate and give away control over their property; the senatorial career was ended almost as it began.

10

SHE OCCASIONALLY ACCOMPANIED John to New York to buy the modern mining equipment with which to dig their tunnels into the sides of the Mariposa. He decided to spend the New Year holiday in Washington, then take the ship that left New York on January 2, 1851.

She had a long session with herself in which she weighed the comparatives of her problem: she was six months with child; though the roughness of the sea voyage was not too formidable a danger, the crossing of

Panama might be. Having lost young Benton, this coming child meant twice as much to both of them; on the other hand she could not bear the thought of another long separation from her husband. She knew that with John to watch over her she would be well cared for on the trail across Panama; nor was there fear in her heart: this was the opportunity to demonstrate that she had the makings of the pioneer wife, that she meant to create a home and a hearth in California. This was her challenge, more serious and more important than her first lonely trip had been: to carry inside her the new generation of the frontier, to give birth to her baby in the almost unborn community.

"I won't be gone so very long, Jessie," he assured her, "just long enough to stand for re-election and to see that the mine machinery is installed. I will be back in Washington by July."

"You mean *we* will be back in Washington by July," she replied calmly. "I'm going with you."

A look of terror flashed into his eyes.

"But you can't . . . We can't risk the child. The rigors of crossing Panama . . ."

She stood resolutely before him, tossing her hair free from her head with a spirited gesture.

"We have nothing to fear," she said. "I never felt stronger, and I am positive that this is a healthy child I am carrying. If you are going to California, the children and I are going with you. Your son is going to be born in California."

"But Jessie," he protested, "the ocean is rough in winter. You have to go over the Gorgona trail by muleback . . ."

"No, no," she cried, "I will go over the trail in my palanquin. I had a comfortable ride last time. I've learned many things about Panama: I'm taking my own tea things, canned foods that are easy to prepare and digest. The passage will be swifter now, with so many thousands of Americans having made the crossing. Please, let's not discuss it. There's confidence in my heart, and that is the best protection our child could have."

They sailed on January 3 for Chagres. The first few days were rough, so Jessie stayed in her berth and slept through them. Lily kept her father company on deck. At Chagres a little wharf had been built, and she did not have to bob around in a tender. John had sent money and instructions ahead, so there was a boat to convey them up the Chagres to Gorgona. She got bumped around a little in her canopied hammock over the mountain trail, but she laughed at the hardship and felt not the slightest worry. They arrived in San Francisco early in April. When she landed at the broad wooden pier and caught her first glimpse of the town she was glad she had made her decision, for the city had grown miraculously, many homes had sprung up, hundreds of workmen were sawing and pounding, there were wooden sidewalks and Market Street was an imposing area of white-front hotels and business firms.

She did not want her child to be born in a hotel, she wanted him to be born at her own hearth, so they set out at once to buy a house. The only one they could find was an ugly wooden frame structure high up on Stockton Street overlooking the Portsmouth Square. There was no interior decoration, the walls were bare, but the rooms were large and the furnishings comfortable. They bought the house and moved in. On the morning of April 15 she gave birth to a son, whom they promptly named John Charles.

Gregorio had come running to join his family again. When the nurse announced that she would leave at the end of the first week, Gregorio said laughingly, "My mother had ten babies, I helped raise seven of them. I know everything to do. I take care of Charlie when the nurse go."

Jessie remained in bed while John went about San Francisco hiring mechanics for the mines, buying supplies, checking the homes and shops that had been built on the land he had bought before leaving for Washington. A committee of Australians who had established a colony on the Fremont holdings came to the house and presented to her a petition asking that they be allowed to buy their land so that they could feel permanently settled. She promised to urge their request on her husband. That evening she asked John to sell the Australians the property, pointing out that these people were as anxious for their own hearths as they were.

When the baby was fifteen days old, and she was rocking him in an improvised crib, she heard alarmed shouts below her. A few moments later she smelled smoke. Sending for Gregorio, she demanded to know what was happening.

"There's a fire on the south side of the square."

"Is it coming this way?"

Gregorio went to the bedroom window and called back, "I can't tell where the fire come, but the wind come this way."

At that moment John rushed in with extra blankets and a grass hammock.

"There's nothing to be alarmed about," he said reassuringly, "but we must be prepared. The houses below us on the hill are catching. If the fire rises much higher Gregorio and I will carry you and the baby to Russian Hill. The sand dunes will keep the fire from reaching there. I've already sent over our silverware and papers."

"I've ridden in hammocks before," she replied calmly; "just give me two minutes' notice to prepare Charlie."

By nightfall all of San Francisco was aglow, the air filled with smoke and flying ash. From her bed Jessie could watch the night sky grow redder and redder. Friends thronged up the hill to help John hang wet canvas and soaked carpet over the side of the house to prevent sparks from setting it aflame. Below her she could hear the shouts of the men fighting the fires; by the growing intensity and the heat she knew that the flames were coming ever higher on the hill. The sidewalks, made of wooden planks, carried the flames, and the crackling fires of the wooden houses mingled with the sounds of the fire bells and shouts of the men dashing through the streets trying to save their properties.

At midnight there was a sharp veering of the wind. The fire began racing south again across the square. Their home was saved.

The next morning, leaning on the arm of her husband, Jessie circled the house to survey the damage. Below her most of the city lay in ashes. The paint was blistered on her own home, but there was no other damage. It wasn't until she had gone back into the house and climbed into bed again that she realized her calm of the night before had been the same kind of protection with which she had insulated herself for the trip across Panama.

At the end of a month, when her strength had returned, and the machinery had arrived for the mines, John left for the Mariposa to begin the installation work. He was standing for re-election, yet he would do nothing to promote his candidacy. Jessie wondered why her husband declined to strive as mightily for the political office he wanted as he had striven to make himself a successful engineer. Electioneering demanded that a man get out on the stump, that he tour the state, speaking to every group that assembled, that he keep a steady stream of articles flowing to the press, that he treat politics as though it were a business or a profession and throw himself into it wholeheartedly if he expected to achieve the desired result. But John would not electioneer and would not campaign. As he had in Monterey, he said quietly to his wife:

"Everyone in this state knows me and knows whether or not he wants me to continue being senator. Shaking a few thousand hands won't change the results of the election; if the majority of the people in this state are in favor of slavery, then I'll be defeated; if the majority are in favor of freedom, then I'll be sent back to the Senate. No one is going to change the mind of a slavery man by making a speech at him; and besides I'm not a good speechmaker."

She respected his reticence, his refusal to fight for his seat in the Senate. Nevertheless she wished that there were some way to campaign for him. She would have been entirely willing to take her carriage and the team of horses and stump the state, speaking in every hamlet and village, debating with the slavery faction. But alas, there was nothing she could do; a wife could not campaign for her husband, and surely a wife could not urge that a man plunge himself into public conflict if it was against his temperament to do so.

And once again she was puzzled by the riddle of her husband's character. Why, under one set of circumstances, did he grasp more power and authority than he was entitled to, then in another field be modest, self-effacing, refuse to play the critical part which everyone expected of him? Was he behaving this way because the court-martial had declared him to be a usurper, a man seeking personal power and fame—and he wanted to live down the accusation? Or did this contradiction in his temperament arise from the various components within his mind: the components dealing with politics enclosing one set of attitudes; those dealing with war and the Army another and very different set? Only she knew how many dozens of separately locked compartments there were, and how divergent their contents.

She remembered how in the first days of her honeymoon she had dimly perceived that marriage might mean the spending of a lifetime trying to understand her mate, evolving the mysteries of character which even he didn't know were there. She had said to herself then, I would not want a man who would be obvious. It will be an exhilarating pursuit, trying to understand what will come next, fitting all the pieces together. And what a great hour it will be, ten years from now, fifty years from now, when I finally understand John. She had now been married for ten years, she understood many fragments of her husband's behavior, and yet she had to confess to herself that she was no closer to a solution of his character than she had been the day she married him.

San Francisco was growing at an amazing rate; she liked to walk down into the business district and shop for rare art objects or furnishings from the Orient, wines or sweets from Paris, woolens from England. On one of her trips she was delighted to find two sets of violet-colored muslin curtains, which she tied back with pink ribbons to brighten the parlor and dining room. There were a flourishing newspaper and theater; thousands of people were coming in from overland trails and by ship from Australia and the Orient. They were a conglomerate crew: along with the eastern farmers and settlers, the staid businessmen and the gold seekers, there was a large crowd of British criminals released from Botany Bay in Australia, as well as the irresponsible *Guarde Mobile* which had been shipped over from Paris for the greater safety of France; there were the wild ones, the professional adventurers and gamblers, the thieves, embezzlers, swindlers,

murderers from all over America who had thronged to this fabulously rich
and exciting frontier.

Despite the fact that Senator Fremont's bills for the setting up of courts
and a legal structure had been passed in Washington, the machinery for
these was not yet working in San Francisco. Violence flared everywhere;
bands of armed thieves roamed the streets at night, plundering and shooting. Anyone who tried to protest had his house or business set on fire;
women could not leave their homes after nightfall, and no man's property
was safe from their depredations. The respectable merchants and settlers
in San Francisco were organizing to put an end to the lawless element
which, it was claimed, had started the fire. When the citizens' committee,
who named themselves the Vigilantes, threatened to take the law into
their own hands and punish the miscreants, civil war broke out in the
town. One warm June afternoon as she was sitting in her back garden
overlooking the bay, a handbill was thrown over the fence. She read:

*If the people of San Francisco carry out their threatened intentions, we
will fire the city. We will make your wives and families suffer for your
acts.*

She knew how fast fires could carry in the wind-swept city, and she was
afraid that her own wooden structure would go up in flames before she
could get the two children out to safety. From then on she did no more
sleeping of nights, but read, wrote letters home and to her husband, kept
a vigilant eye out of the windows which faced in three directions. In the
morning, after Gregorio and his cousin, who had become Charlie's nurse-
maid, were awake, she would draw the blinds in her room and sleep until
noon.

One Sunday morning after Gregorio and his cousin had gone to
church, and just as the bells began to toll ten o'clock, the hour when the
summer winds swept across San Francisco, she saw fire break out simultaneously in several parts of the residential district below her. She picked
up little Charlie naked and wet from the bath and wrapped him in the
skirt of her dressing gown. Lily came in with her two pet hens, asking,
"Mother, could you find me ribbons to tie their legs?"

"Go up the hills to Mrs. Fourgeand's house on Clay Street and stay
there until I come for you."

Lieutenant Beale came running, bareheaded, his face already black
with soot, led her out of the house in her slippers and gown and up the
several blocks of steep rough hill to Mrs. Fourgeand's. Here she found
dozens of women and children gathered in this one spot of safety. Lily
threw herself into her mother's arms, but Lieutenant Beale relieved the
tension by exclaiming, "Look, the baby is still asleep on my shoulder."

Jessie went into the front room, which overlooked the burning city. A Frenchwoman was kneeling before the window, laughing hysterically as she watched her house go up in flames. After a few moments she turned to Jessie, recognized her and cried, "Madame Fremont! Your house goes next. Here, take my place. It is the best seat in the house, you can see your place burn up!"

Sympathetic women led the afflicted one away. Jessie stood by the window for a long time, while her heart cried out at the sight of her home, her baby's birthplace, catching like dry tinder, almost every part of it roaring into flames at once. At the end of an hour there was nothing left but the gaunt red brick chimney pointing up to the sky like an accusing finger. At dusk most of San Francisco had once again been burned to the ground. Lieutenant Beale returned to Mrs. Fourgeand's and said, "I have a place where you and the children can rest tonight; it is not very elegant, but at least we have food and blankets there. Come along, we'll pretend we're camping on the Monterey peninsula again."

That night she lay on a cot in a tent in the sand dunes, the baby sleeping in the crook of her arm, Lily and her two chickens with blue ribbons around their legs on a mattress on the floor. She spent the night alternately weeping and trembling over the loss of this first home of her own. Bitterly she remembered, "The gods are slow to consecrate a new hearth." Imaginary fire bells clanged in her ears; behind her feverish and tightly closed eyelids she once again watched the city burn, each succeeding house catching fire and going up in flames, until the whole world outside of her eyelids was blazing.

The next morning Lieutenant Beale came back to tell her that he and Gregorio had worked all night on a former army barrack several miles out in the dunes, scrubbing it and putting it in condition so that she could have a place to live until her new home could be built. Since there were no horses or carriages available, she trudged through the sand, her water-soaked slippers heavy with mud, her dressing gown trailing. When she reached the barrack she found that the men had assembled fresh clothing, some books, candles for lighting and boxes of foodstuffs. After the children fell asleep, she sat through the long night reading Donald Mitchell's *Reveries of a Bachelor* by candlelight. She was too nervous to go to bed; she had a feeling of despair at ever becoming settled in such a wild community. The baby woke at dawn, demanding its breakfast. The Indian girl announced, "Gregorio, he find a white goat with lots of milk . . ."

Jessie smiled and thanked her, but the girl did not move.

"Some people come see you," she exclaimed. "Please you talk to them?"

She washed her hands and face, combed her hair and slipped into a dress. She walked through the front room of the barrack and opened the door. Before her stood a middle-aged Australian and his wife; she recognized them as the spokesmen for the tenants who had asked for permission to buy their land. Looking over their shoulders she saw a long procession of people coming across the dunes, all of them carrying parcels and bundles and some of them pulling carts.

"What is it?" she asked, stupefied.

"It is like this, Mrs. Fremont," replied the Australian, "when the fire began on Sunday morning we decided the wind would carry it up to your house. All of us rushed up to your home to see if we couldn't save it. You and the little ones were already gone."

"We saw we couldn't save your house, Madame Fremont," broke in the wife, "so we did the next best thing: we saved everything inside your walls." She turned and indicated the trail of people. "We carried out all of your clothing, your furniture, mirrors, china, silverware and glasses, rugs, and your books. Madame Fremont, you lose the building, nothing else."

Jessie watched the tenants come up one by one to the front porch, deposit all of her valuables: her jewelry and personal effects, her dishes and perfume bottles, her dresses and lingerie, the children's clothing, and the toys they had brought from Washington, foods and cases of wine, even the violet curtains with the pink tie-backs. The Australians knocked the furniture together, set up two beds in the back room; moved the bookcase into the front room and arranged the books on its shelves; they put the curtains on the windows, hung her pictures on the walls, and on the floors laid her carpets and rugs. Within an hour the lonely barrack in the sand dunes had been transformed into the Fremont household. The leader then brought forth a heavy parcel tied in a red silk handkerchief.

"We knew the colonel was from home," he said, "and since there was a young baby in the house, we thought money might come in handy. We brought a quarter's rent in advance."

He untied the handkerchief and let fall onto a table a heap of coins. In her excitement Jessie could not control her tears. She shook hands with every last one, thanking them warmly.

Several days passed. Though she was comfortable, surrounded by her own possessions, she longed ardently to have her husband by her side. There was no regular mail service to the Mariposa and she was unwilling to send a courier after him. She would simply have to wait until he learned of the new fire that had swept the city.

It was almost a week later when, sitting on the front porch in the warm June sunshine, she saw his familiar figure trudging over the dunes. She jumped up and ran across the sand hillocks to meet him. When she could tear herself from his embrace she asked: "But how did you know where to find us?"

"I came by the night boat from Stockton," he replied. "I practically ran up the hill from the square, but when I got to our house there was nothing left but the chimney with the sun shining on it. I asked a passer-by if he knew where you were, and he replied, 'Near Grace Church.' From the front porch of the church I surveyed the landscape, and I saw this little house with violet curtains fluttering out the windows. When I saw the pink ribbons, I was sure it was you."

That afternoon Jessie sent for the Australian tenants. John had been writing busily at his desk. When they arrived he thanked them heartily, then picked up a stack of papers.

"These are your deeds of sale. You now own your land."

There was a moment of silence, during which the men looked over the deeds. Their spokesman murmured:

"Colonel Fremont, it is better than we expected. We could pay a little more."

"You have already paid that little more," he replied. "Good luck to you, and God bless you."

When each had clasped his hand and thanked him in turn, and they had left, Jessie kissed her husband sedately and said:

"Thank you, dear. That was a special gift to me."

That evening as they walked the hills above the burned city that was already again rebuilding on its ashes, John told her of his many difficulties on the Mariposa: serious quarrels had arisen with mining groups who claimed that they had located their mines before he arrived, that he had purposely staked out his boundaries to include their holdings. They had refused to abandon their mines and were threatening warfare if anybody tried to put them off. The machinery he had bought in New York was proving costly and inefficient; only a bare portion of the available gold was being secured. The mining engineers he had hired, and whose expenses he had paid to California, had left him and were staking out their own claims. In order to operate the mines he needed dams, roads, mills, but no money had arrived from England, and trouble had arisen in London over the stock companies based on the Mariposa leases. Hoffman, his first choice, had proved to be an honest and conscientious worker, but Sargent had placed fraudulent advertisements in the London newspapers, soliciting the sale of stock, and his manipulations had cut the ground out from under Hoffman's feet; banks and investors originally interested in Mariposa leases had withdrawn their subscriptions, while Sargent was collecting funds on a basis which could dispossess the Fremonts of the entire holdings.

Nor was that all. The Indians, who had not quarreled with the whites up to this time, were on the warpath because the miners had deprived them of their hunting grounds, killed and eaten their wild cattle, and driven them so deep into the mountains that the tribes could not secure enough food. They had met in common council, decided to kill and eat the white men's cattle, and then drive the white men out of the region. There had been shootings and killings; the mining on the Mariposa would have to be stopped unless the Indians could be placated. The United States commissioners had been treating with the Indians, attempting to move them out of the gold country and on to other hunting grounds; the Indians had agreed to move on, provided they would be furnished with beef during the time it would take to move their tribes and set up on the new lands. The small quantities of cattle available were being held for extortionate rates, and the commission had been unable to secure enough to guarantee the treaty. The Indians were preparing to wage open warfare in order to drive the white men out of the gold country.

"What about your cattle, John? Have you enough to take care of their needs?"

"Yes. But the commission has no funds with which to buy—hold on now! I'm perfectly willing to let them have the cattle on credit, but you know that I don't come off very well when I spend money for the government. My notes for a half-million dollars' worth of provisions taken during the conquest have never been paid . . ."

"But if you make a bona fide offer to the commission," said Jessie, "and they make a written acceptance . . . ?"

"Then when do we get our money? The commission doesn't return to Washington for a year. If the Department of the Interior refuses to believe that the Indians were in desperate straits and ready to pillage, they can disavow their own commission, just as they disavowed me. No one can sue the federal government, so I'll once again be in the awkward position of petitioning the Congress to get our money for the cattle. It isn't that I mind so much running the risk of never being repaid, or even of the trouble and weeks of work it will involve; what I don't like is being obliged to appear before the American people as someone trying to make money off the government."

"Then don't make money off them," she replied calmly. "Go down to the commission and give them an offer which will meet your costs. That will save the government money and avert warfare with the Indians. As long as you have the cattle available, can you do less?"

"No, Senator Benton, I can't do less. Confound it; it means I'll have to be away from the mines for a solid month, and then I'll probably never get my money back. But I can't do less."

The next morning he went to Commissioner Barbour and made him an offer. Barbour replied, "Your offer is the lowest and best yet made by a respectable man. I'll take it."

John reported to Jessie; she watched as he was once again in the saddle, off for Southern California to drive up the cattle himself.

11

SEPTEMBER WAS A LOVELY MONTH. The fogs disappeared, the sun came out bright and warm; each day Jessie roamed the hills and sand dunes with Lily and little Charlie, the baby carried papoose fashion by either Gregorio or his cousin. The bay and the strait sparkled in the early fall. The children thrived, grew strong and red-cheeked.

Jessie had talked to John about their home: whether they should buy one of the few remaining residences at no matter how extortionate a price, whether they should build their new house on their lot on Stockton Street, whether they should perhaps buy a farm near by on the peninsula where it would be warm. John had been uncertain. He had told her she could do anything she wanted, but had evidenced no enthusiasm for any of the alternatives. Nor had she been able to derive any idea of his plans for the future; he spoke of going back to Washington to try to push through some mining laws, returning to New York to design and build more modern ore-crushing equipment, going to London to straighten out the financial mess, of moving the entire family up to the Mariposa. As long as his mind was suspended she did not feel free to move in any direction, and so she remained in the little barrack in the dunes.

The winter before she had spent in Madame Castro's two rooms, watching the rain pour in from the sea; the November rain swept windwise across San Francisco, and once again she was isolated in two rooms. The senatorial election came and went without John uttering one word or making a single gesture toward succeeding himself. The organized groups beat the drums for their candidates; ever-growing slavery factions decried his political experience; his friends and supporters were scattered throughout the county, busy with their own affairs. There was nothing she could do with him away, apparently disinterested in the result, and so she had to sit back and watch her husband be beaten.

She had been well trained in the history and literature of exploration, but the work of exploring had worn out; she had read books on agriculture and done what she could to prepare herself to be a farmer's wife, but the farm had never materialized. She had hoped to be a senator's wife, had been equipped by both training and temperament to fill that job; now

their seat in the Senate had vanished. There was no part she could play
in gold mining, and she frankly had little interest in it.

Her mind went back as it so often did to her few moments of conversation with Mary Algood on the outskirts of St. Louis. Mary's lot was the
hard one; she had had to cross the plains in her covered wagon, break
ground in the Oregon wilds, live the life of unrelenting toil. Yet frequently
Jessie found herself envying Mary: she had been free to go to Oregon in
her covered wagon with her husband by her side; she had been free to
stumble across stubble fields behind the plow to break the Algood acres;
she had been free from public censure and the aggravations that follow
the collapse of high ambition. Jessie knew that at each point the world
would have said she was the more fortunate of the two: her husband was
the famous explorer whose map the Algoods were using in their passage
across the plains, yet being his wife meant that she had had to endure
endless months of aloneness and agony over her husband's safety; she had
a thousand times more money than Mary Algood would ever see after a
lifetime of back-breaking toil, and yet that money only meant that she was
separated from her husband for months at a time.

John seemed no longer to need her; the same accidental discovery of
gold on the Mariposa which had removed him from any field of creative
work had also removed her opportunity to collaborate with him. It
seemed to her that before long she would be in her mother's position:
mistress of a large home, children to raise, entertaining to be done, a background to be created for her husband—and nothing more. For the hun-
dredth time she wished that Larkin had kept his Mariposa and left them
in possession of the Santa Cruz ranch with its old vines and peaceful
orchards and lovely view over the sea. She remembered what Nicollet had
told her: "Any accident or scoundrel can take your money—and usually
does—but no one can deprive you of the skill to turn out good work. The
finest and most durable possession in all the world is good workmanship."

In proportion as they amassed gold, their marriage, that individual
entity which was a third being created by their union, had deteriorated
into routine. It was no longer something greater than the sum total of the
two of them, but rather something less. She sat in the forlorn barrack on
the sand dunes with her two children, prey to loneliness, while her husband remained away for months at a time extracting wealth from the
earth. Their marriage could be a beautiful thing when they were apart
for a purpose, such as an expedition; then it could glow with a sustaining
light. Geographic separation did not detract from the stature or intensity
of the marriage, but separation in ultimate desires, separation in one's
conception of the good and valuable life could slash away at the stature
of a marriage until this third being which was created by the meeting of

two minds and two hearts had died, and there was little left but a husband and a wife.

This was the reverse of the shield of her despair on the Delaware Indian Reservation, but this could be the profounder tragedy of the two: either of the two mates might die, grow weary or calloused with the ideals of their relationship, become indifferent, disillusioned. Yet even when this happened, the other could maintain the marriage by tenderness, sympathy and patience, by hanging grimly on and fighting, by enduring difficult periods; the marriage would maintain its fundamental strength, would come back to robust life when the temporary derangement had passed. One had to refuse to think in terms of disruption or defeat or possible ending: one had to forgive transgressions, have an iron-willed, incorruptible faith in the permanence of the relationship: for a marriage, like a human life, must endure all manner of vicissitude; the weak mortal, the weak relationship went down to destruction at the first ill wind; the stalwart marriage survived all gales, even though sometimes it had to plunge blindly through black and mounting seas.

But if the marriage were dead! If it had slowly crumbled into meaninglessness, then everything was gone.

She knew that her plight was no one's fault, but rather a piling up of accidental circumstance. Yet accidental circumstance must not be allowed to be the master, or their lives would be buffeted by every changing wind. She did not want these gold mines, she did not want wealth; the gold had come into their hands only by an ironic twist of fate. Was John right in saying that if fate dumped a fortune down into your lap you were a fool not to take it? Perhaps they were the more fools in the taking!

She knew she could not impose this reasoning on John, for that would be obliging him to accept her standards. He had to reach that conclusion by himself, come to the point where he realized that the mines were costing him more in companionship and love and accomplishment than they were producing in other precious metals. She did not doubt that he would one day come to this conclusion; but how long and how far away? How many weary miles would they have to retrace their steps to find again that partnership which had characterized their earlier years?

Once again she was confronted by the unsolvable character of her husband: how could a man who was so indifferent to money and its trappings, who had worked for years in a field in which he could hope to earn nothing but the most modest army salary, suddenly devote his life to making money? How did one ever come to understand the enigma of another man's soul?

Her one joy during these long and troubled days was her love for little Charlie, which was multiplied in intensity because in it there was included the love for her lost son, Benton, and her profoundest gratitude for demonstrating that she could again bear healthy children. She insisted upon bathing the boy herself, in feeding him his morning and evening meal, so that they would grow close together, know and love each other's every move. Charlie was full of laughter, and Jessie whiled away many an hour playing games to make her son giggle.

The day before Christmas she roamed the hills with Lily looking for a Christmas tree. She rolled tin foil and made spur-of-the-moment ornaments. Friends came during the afternoon to bring gifts and extend the holiday greetings: some of the delegates to the Monterey convention who had known the warmth of her fireside and the hospitality of her table; army officers and their wives to whom she had brought memories of their homes in the East; the Australians, whose property they had made available on generous terms; their old friends Beale and Knight, to whom she and her children were like family; old acquaintances from St. Louis and Washington who had come straight from the wharf to their home on Stockton Street for a welcome to California; miners whom they had grub-staked, merchants from whom they had bought even though the wares were not yet satisfactory; the son of an Indian chief whose tribe had been rescued with John's cattle; the Saunders family, Negroes who had been saved from slavery because John had taken the man up to the Mariposa with him and helped him wash out seventeen hundred dollars in gold, enough to buy his freedom.

But by dark they had all gone, gone to join their families and friends for Christmas dinner. Jessie was left alone with her two children, for Gregorio and his cousin had ridden south for the holidays. After she fed Lily and Charlie and put them to sleep, she sat in a rocker by the Christmas tree, longing for her husband, for a roaring fire, for her parents and Eliza, for her young sisters and brother and the friends and relatives who gathered in the warm and brightly lighted rooms in their home on C Street. She fell to musing about the years that had passed and the years that were to come. There was no fireplace in this little two-room barrack, no hearthstone, yet in the mellowness of spirit engendered by Christmas she perceived that a hearth is not merely a fireplace: a hearth can also be a fire kindled in the hearts of other people, a kindness done here, a service done there, a man or woman given happiness on a frontier thousands of miles from home. It was a year and a half since they had first come to California; she had been almost the first white woman to cross Panama, hers had been one of the first American homes in Monterey; by her refusal to buy or use slaves she had played a small but significant role in keeping California free; by their discovery of gold on the Mariposa and their importing of machinery to set up permanent mines, they had quick-

and the migration of easterners to California, increased the buying power abroad of the new state; by John's willingness to provide beef for the Indians they had kept peace in the mining regions; by his comprehensive program in the Senate they were slowly bringing the United States to California; by their own return to California, by their steadfastness in remaining in San Francisco after the fires and violence and destruction, they had helped create a sense that this frontier would survive and be permanent; by making the long, hazardous trip by sea, by crossing Panama while heavy with child and by giving birth to her son in the primitive conditions of San Francisco, she had created a home of flesh and blood rather than wood and glass.

It was not much to have done, she knew, and not at all what she had planned. Yet some sixty years had passed since Grandmother Benton had set out for the frontier of Tennessee; times had changed, this new frontier was unlike any other the country had known; each one played his part according to the contour of the times and the nature of the need. If she could not duplicate Grandmother Benton's performance, it was perhaps not altogether her fault; she had done the best she could, had gone through much for her efforts. She was only twenty-seven, yet at moments like these she felt as though she had lived as long as Grandmother Benton or Grandmother McDowell.

She glanced at the clock and saw that it was an hour from midnight. She decided that she would remain awake long enough to see the Christmas Day in and would then go to her cold and lonely bed. But the wish was stronger than the will, and in a few moments she fell asleep, her head on her chest, her breathing quiet in the still house. She dreamed that she heard the swift beat of a horse coming over the dunes, of a man springing from its back and rushing across the wooden porch. The image went back to that moment on the Delaware Indian Reservation when John had returned in just this fashion to offer his sacrifice, to bring her new courage and new life. She dreamed that the door was flung open, that heavy sacks were dropped on the rough wooden floor, that she was swooped up in her husband's arms, her face covered with kisses, that she was seated again in the same chair, but this time on John's lap with his arms about her and her head on his shoulder and her lips on his lips: and at last she knew it was no dream.

"My dear," she murmured, "you did come home for Christmas."

"Could you doubt it? Are you all right? Are the children well?"

He listened quietly, his dark eyes scanning her face, while she told him of the commonplaces of her routine, led him to the bedroom to show him how well his son and daughter looked. Then he brought the two sacks into the candlelight and began showing her the gifts he had managed to purchase in his hasty flight for home.

"They aren't much," he said, "most of the stores were closed. But how would you like a trip to Paris as a Christmas gift?"

"Splendid," she replied tartly; "let's also give Charlie a peep at the man in the moon."

He chuckled, took a wallet from his back trouser pocket, opened a brightly colored envelope and dangled two long steamship tickets before her unbelieving eyes, his index finger underscoring the lines.

"Read them, Miss Jessie. We're going to have a full year in Europe."

In a whisper she read, "San Francisco to Chagres. Chagres direct to Liverpool. Folkstone to Boulogne, France."

As the tears began to roll down her cheeks, he caught them in his palm and brushed them away. Her thoughts went back ten full years to the rainy afternoon when they had sat before the fire in Hassler's workroom, with Grandmother McDowell at the front window watching the funeral procession of President Harrison, and the ardent, dark-eyed young man sitting across the tea table from her had said, "I will always love you, Jessie, of that you can be sure. I may make mistakes, I may fail you in other ways, I won't come up to your expectations, but I will always love you."

How true it was that marriage required patience rather than logic, that it must not be disrupted at every unforeseen twist of fortune, but allowed time to work out its fundamental and organic pattern.

"Can you leave the mines?" she asked.

"The mines have already separated us too long. Let's spend our time and money together while we still have them, before I prove that Nicollet was right about a fool and his funds. It will be your first real vacation in ten years. The first since you spoke those fateful words, 'Whither thou goest I will go.' Do you remember, Jessie?"

BOOK FIVE

First Lady

THEY CROSSED THE ATLANTIC on the Cunard sidewheeler, the *Africa;*
since she was the only woman on board, the captain gave her the Ladies'
Parlor as her stateroom. Two sofas were bound together to make a wide
bed for herself and Charlie. Jessie and John spent the rainy gale-swept
days relaxing and reading. When the weather was fair they tied little
Charlie on a four-foot line to the pole in the center of the room, and
although Lily declared that the baby spent as much time on his head as
on his feet, he seemed to enjoy himself.

When they reached London they found everything in readiness for
them, including their hotel suite with its chintz hangings and cheery wood
fire. Mr. Abbott Lawrence, the American minister to England, had been
a friend of Tom Benton's for many years, and so the Fremonts were taken
under official chaperonage. Jessie went twice to what the English called
"authorities of toilette," where she was measured and fitted, her preference
in fabric and color noted. For each social engagement a new and beautiful outfit would be delivered to her hotel. She was haunted by the specter
of the Jessie Fremont of Monterey who had worn a cut-off, faded blue
riding skirt and an unbleached muslin sacque. It was fun to lie in bed at
the Clarendon Hotel in a violet morning robe and have breakfast served,
while one remembered rising at dawn in the two-room barrack on the
dunes of San Francisco to light a fire in a coal stove and prepare warm
cereal for one's children.

Their first night in London she and John dined at Sion House, the
town residence of the Duke of Northumberland; here she met Lady
Bulwer, whom she had known in Washington when her husband had
been minister to the United States. Lady Bulwer took Jessie and John to

an old man who was moving about the lavishly furnished rooms sunk in
thought; she murmured, "This is my uncle, the Duke of Wellington," and
speaking very distinctly, presented the Fremonts. The Iron Duke bowed
mechanically and was about to pass on when a gleam of memory came
into his watery eyes.

"I remember that name," he said. "Fremont, the great American
traveler."

He shook hands with John. Later Jessie said to her husband, "You
have shaken the hand that proved the hand of fate to Napoleon."

Her friends decreed that they would be doing less than their simple
duty if they allowed her five minutes of any day without an affair in her
honor. When Jessie remarked to the Marchioness of Wellesley, who had
been one of the Caton girls from Maryland, that she would like to visit
Westminster Abbey, her friend replied, "Monuments live forever, people
pass away."

Jessie thought how much her mother would have enjoyed the life in
London, the capital from which the traditions and ideals of Cherry Grove
had sprung. If Elizabeth McDowell could have married a member of the
English Parliament instead of the American Congress, she would have
been perfectly at home and completely happy; it was just bad luck that
she had been plunged into a raw and crude capital, creating its own history, instead of this venerable seat of tradition. But it was to her father
that her mind turned a few nights later at the opera, when she was introduced to an Englishwoman of high birth as "Mrs. Fremont from North
America." "From North America," exclaimed the woman, examining
Jessie through her lorgnette, "I thought all North Americans were Indians." Jessie laughed to herself while she thought, Thank heavens Tom
Benton wasn't here to hear that remark. He would have declared war on
the whole British Empire!

Now, at Easter, she stood before the mirror in their suite at the Clarendon in London, surveying herself in her presentation gown. The gown
itself was of lace, adorned with artificial roses, from deep red to white.
Her dark brown hair was piled on top of her head and her light hazel eyes
were glowing with excitement. She picked up her bouquet of roses and
turned to John, who was sitting in a lounging robe watching the ritual of
his wife's dressing.

"Will I do justice to California?" she asked.

"You were more indigenous in your unbleached muslins."

"I am not trying to be indigenous, dear, I am trying to appear beautiful and sophisticated."

"Let me see the curtsy that Ambassador Lawrence's wife took a week
to teach you."

"That's because Father always had an aversion to seeing a lady bow like a man or duck like a servant."

There was a knock at the door. "That must be my carriage," she exclaimed. "I'm sorry you are not a bride, or at least a lady, so that you could be presented to the queen. However, I will meet you at the Duchess of Bedford's for tea at four o'clock."

It was only a few moments before her carriage turned into the courtyard of Buckingham Palace. She was escorted directly to the room where the ladies of the diplomatic corps were waiting. Mrs. Lawrence had gone early in order to reserve a place for her in one of the deep windows where she might see the queen drive up. The royal carriage arrived at the palace for the Easter presentation drawn by cream-colored horses. After a time the doors of the throne room were opened; Mrs. Lawrence made her curtsy, then presented Jessie, who did her best not to bow like a man or duck like a servant. After she had been presented to Prince Albert and the queen's mother, she took her place in the queue and for two hours watched the procession of English noblewomen as they made obeisance, kissed the queen's hand and then backed out from the royal presence. She was struck by the contrast between this scene and the position of the First Lady in the United States, who got a four-year lease on a White House which was forever in need of repairs, and a grudging, sometime courtesy from the voters.

After tea at the Duchess of Bedford's, Jessie and John went to the home of Sir Roderick Murchison, president of the Royal Geographical Society, who was giving a dinner for John's fellow medalists. This evening, spent among the bronzed travelers and explorers, was the most enjoyable she had in London, for here John was among his own kind. These men had read with great interest all three of their reports, had studied the Fremont maps; they in turn had sent him the accounts of their travels. They were truly friends and brothers, bound by the indestructible kinship of profession. It was a joy to watch her husband in this group, for here John was at his best; his eyes flashed, he spoke with the easy charm and sure authenticity of the man who is a sound artisan. More than ever she felt that it had been a misfortune for him to withdraw from his craft, that he must get back into it, that his talents must not be wasted.

One night in April as they were about to step into a carriage to go to a dinner party being given in their honor, four constables from Bow Street surrounded them and informed John that he was under arrest.

"Under arrest?" he demanded. "What for?"

A nervous little fellow who identified himself as a clerk from a solicitor's office cried rudely, "You'll jolly soon find out! Haul him off to jail, my boys, the mighty colonel will soon learn that in England a man has to pay his drafts."

More perplexed than frightened, Jessie asked, "John, do you know what this is about?"

"Probably the Mariposa affair. Sargent sold stock. I haven't been able to locate him."

"But you're not responsible for Sargent . . ."

"Come along now, Colonel," said one of the constables.

As they started down the street, she called, "Don't worry, dear, I'll go straight to Mr. Lawrence's house; he'll get you out."

But when she reached the minister's house she learned that he had gone to the dinner party in their honor. Once again she entered her carriage. Her host was waiting for them. She explained what had caused her delay; Abbott Lawrence excused himself from the party and went with her at once to Bow Street. The police headquarters seemed dismal, but the words of the officer in charge were still less pleasant: he informed them that Colonel Fremont's bail was a high one, that he could not release the colonel without the cash being deposited. She returned with Mr. Lawrence to the dinner, but the guests did not have enough money on them to secure John's release.

It was midnight when she left the party; she knew that John would be wondering why he was still sitting in the Bow Street jail when a fair portion of the bankers and statesmen of London were at a dinner being given in his honor. The Lawrence family took her to the Clarendon, where she found that a sleepless night in a strange hotel room, with one's husband in jail, makes an excellent time for unvarnished thinking.

While she had been driven through the parks in the mornings, been entertained at luncheons and teas, John had spent his days trying to iron out the muddle created by the conflicting and sometimes fraudulent Mariposa sales companies in London. From his reluctance to discuss the London stock promotion, she suspected that he hoped to straighten matters before relating the details. The Mariposa was a rich strike, they could extract a good deal more gold from it, yet as the complexities grew she became ever more convinced that they should have mined the gold on a small scale, or sold their rights for a flat sum. The American courts had not yet confirmed purchases made from Mexican grants, and at any moment their ownership of the Mariposa might be invalidated. Her husband was no businessman: he hadn't the temperament for it. It was unlikely that a man with his particular set of gifts could also be good at business. She had no head for business either; no one in her family had had any interest in commerce, or any heart for it. Even though she was grateful for the money they had taken out of the Mariposa, she feared lest the wealth cost more than it was worth, lest it continue to put the emphasis of their lives in the wrong place. The Mariposa mines were affording them large sums of money, yet the legal situation was so tenuous that it could snap without an instant's notice, leaving them rich in little but litigation.

The next morning, when their host of the night before went bail for John and delivered him to the Clarendon, she learned that he had not been arrested for the Mariposa financing after all, but rather for four drafts amounting to nineteen thousand dollars, which he had issued during the conquest of California. Secretary of State Buchanan had been unwilling to make good these drafts on the grounds that this would give the conquest official backing; bills introduced into Congress to pay them had never passed; and now a Californian by the name of Huttman was suing John in England, hoping to recover from his personal funds.

She did not feel that her reasoning about the Mariposa of the night before had been any the less valid because this particular difficulty had a different origin; she was certain that if the confused financing were allowed to continue they could fall into serious trouble. John agreed that the English venture had come to an unfortunate impasse; by ten o'clock he had left the hotel to visit the bankers and terminate all investments in the Mariposa. She was considerably relieved, but she found herself troubled by the thought that British investors, so frequently widows and aged people living on pensions, might have lost money on the unauthorized issue. If there had been victims of Sargent's shady sales, she would have liked to repay them: some of those who had invested had doubtless done so on the strength of John Fremont's name, feeling secure because he owned the property. But to advertise for such people would bring an avalanche of claimants down upon her, many of them fraudulent; it would also convict her husband of being responsible for Sargent's acts. She shrugged her shoulders with distaste and despair.

Toward the end of April, as she walked past the desk of the Clarendon, a clerk handed her a letter from her father. She tore open the envelope and began reading phrases that made no sense. There was a line about how her brother Randolph had delivered the Kossuth oration in St. Louis and been favorably received; then suddenly she read, " . . . cholera . . . quickly set his bowels on fire with inflammation . . . delirious by the second day, died without realizing his torment . . . so young for him to die . . . we were just beginning to be friends . . ."

Like her father, she too was just beginning to be friends with her young brother. For a time she wept, then the memories of Randolph began flooding back, memories that hurt. She had made no strong effort to know the boy: her life had been dominated by her relationship with her

0

father and her husband. She had had no time or emotion or even interest for anyone else. Only her mother had given him the patient kindness he had needed.

She had known how precious every moment was in a marriage, that tomorrow was too late to be loving and kind, that the relationship must be kept at its finest pitch every moment; yet she had never understood these simple truths in her relationship with her brother or her mother. She had been a good daughter to her father; she believed she was a good wife; was she being a good mother as well? Or were the hours and the years slipping by, while she failed Lily and Charlie the way she had failed Randolph?

She had never consciously said, I put my husband above my children, yet that decision had long since been made. As much as she loved her children, they would always come after her husband in her own mind. John had had her deepest love before there had been any children; he would still be there, still have her deepest love when the children had gone their separate ways. There was no way to conceal this fundamental of her nature from herself; nor, as she was to learn, could that knowledge be withheld from her children.

When John returned at teatime and saw how red her eyes were, he picked up the letter from the bureau and scanned it quickly. He drew the blinds against the late afternoon sun, dipped a hand towel in cold water, laid it over her feverish face. Several hours later she said, "Are your affairs well enough settled for us to leave London? Do you think we could move to Paris? We'll never find any of the tranquillity we have been seeking in this social whirl."

"We can leave within a day or two," he replied. "I have stopped all exploitation of the Mariposa in England. The stock issues will be handled by a bank in San Francisco from now on. I've also succeeded in having that Huttman suit transferred back home."

They found a small place in Paris on the Champs Elysées, an elegant little house in the Italian style, with a courtyard and large garden in the rear where the ground fell away rapidly towards the Seine, giving a fine view of the dome of the Invalides on the opposite bank. They settled in the villa for what was to be the most peaceful fourteen months of their turbulent half-century of marriage.

Almost immediately upon their arrival Jessie found she was going to have another child. She thought how fine it would be to spend the time in the quiet beauty of this villa. She was feeling lazy, but John kept in shape with fencing lessons. He would sometimes ask an instructor from the school to come to the house so she could observe his progress. As she watched the fencing she recalled the description of him sent from Monterey to the New York *Herald* by Bayard Taylor: "I have seen in no other man the qualities of lightness, activity, strength and physical endurance in so perfect an equilibrium." He was also attending the school where his beloved Nicollet had taught, studying astronomy and mathematics as well as the works of the French geologists on quartz mining.

They both spoke excellent French, which helped them to feel at home in Paris. Once a week they would drive through the park of St. Cloud to Versailles, spend the day walking through the grounds and galleries, and return home the following evening. On warm afternoons they followed their own grounds down to the Seine, where they would lie on the bank with open but unread books, watching small boats sail by; in the evenings there were delicious dinners, then an hour on the balcony overlooking the city, the air beneficently soft and quiet. Half a dozen times a day she found herself rejoicing that she not only had her husband constantly by her side, but that she also had him to herself. In the early fall they bought tickets for the grand tour of Europe, packed their bags and prepared to leave, only to decide at the last moment that it was folly to wear themselves out voyaging, they who had spent so many heartbreaking months in travel.

Having had their fill of social life in London they did little entertaining until the winter season came on; then they went regularly to the Théâtre Français and to hear Rachel at the Italian Opera. Lady Bulwer came over for the Paris season and introduced them to the diplomatic corps. They were invited to a *thé dansant* at St. Cloud given by the Prince President; they spent a dramatic day watching Louis Napoleon ride into Paris to be crowned emperor; and from their own house they watched the bridal procession of the emperor and his empress as it left the Tuileries and came up the Champs Elysées. The Count de la Garde, who had been a member of the Bonaparte family, became attached to Jessie; he would stop by at eleven after his airing in the Bois de Boulogne to recount stories of French history. The Fremont salon became popular without Jessie intending that it should.

The winter months slipped by. Though her baby was due within a week or two, she decided that she wanted to give her husband a party for his fortieth birthday. John had been troubled in his mind about reaching this milepost; he had told her that a good explorer was a young explorer. She thought that the best way to ease him into the birthday would be to invite to dinner the friends they had made during their nine months' stay, in particular the French scientists, astronomers and explorers. A few days later her second daughter, Anne, was born. The attending physicians assured her that the child was sound and healthy; the Count de la Garde named her "the little Parisienne."

At John's insistence she treated herself to a leisurely recovery, for both had the feeling that their vacation was nearly over and that they soon would be returning to the United States. The exact provocation came in the form of a letter from Tom Benton, telling them that three new railroad expeditions were being organized by the government to find the pass over the Rockies which John had failed to locate on his fourth expedition. Her father told them that a number of the leading newspapers were saying that Colonel Fremont, who was the most experienced pathfinder of the West, should be in charge of an expedition.

She had had many long talks with her husband during the reposeful winter months. They agreed that even though his studies of mining in Paris had shown him how to set up the quartz mines at the Mariposa so that they could derive continuing wealth from them, this soliciting of gold from the earth could not be an end in itself, but only a means. She had persisted in her theory that their wealth should be used to implement his further exploring, mapmaking and writing of books on new wildernesses and frontiers.

"That's all very true," he had replied, his dark eyes thoughtful, "but no man can be an explorer in a void. In exploring, as in love, one wants to be the pursued as well as the pursuer; a man has to wait until a set of circumstances arise in which there is a need for him to explore. I can't just say, 'I'll now explore in Central America' or 'I'll now explore in Canada.' That kind of thinking would never bring any worth-while results."

"Your field is the western part of the United States," replied Jessie. "No one man is more closely identified with it than you. Surely there is a great deal of work still to be done there?"

"Yes, but the specific purpose has to come to a head."

Just as, after the court-martial, the arrival of Tom Benton's letter from St. Louis telling John of the proposed fourth expedition had brought her husband back to life, now once again her father's letter threw his career into focus.

"I'll return to America on the next boat," he exclaimed. "I'll wait just long enough to buy the latest scientific equipment here in Paris. You can close the house at your leisure and then come on with the children."

Her hard-won period of tranquillity between storms was over.

"Yes, you must get back to Washington as quickly as possible," she agreed. "They'll need your help in organizing the expeditions; you will want time to plan your route and collect your party."

2

WHEN SHE REACHED C Street at the end of June with her three children, she found that official Washington had passed John by. Secretary of War Jefferson Davis was determined that the first transcontinental railroad should have a southern route, whereas John had published his views on the advisability of a central route. The War Department, which hitherto had conducted all expeditions, wanted the commands to go to the young engineers of the Topographical Department.

She rented a modestly furnished bungalow close to her father's house, settled her family comfortably, then tackled the problem of what John was to do about the rebuff. To accept this ostracism was to admit that he had exhausted his usefulness, that his days as a trail blazer were over. She had watched him sketch rough maps and indicate where he was going to find the pass that he had failed to discover in 1849; she had seen him depart from Paris wild with excitement, shepherding his newly acquired instruments as his most valuable possessions. For the first time she had seen him planning to convert the wealth of the Mariposa into a creative project: once he had charted this path across the Rockies, he intended to use the gold to lay out the railroad line and build it himself, the iron road which would fulfill her father's dream.

She was relieved to find that her husband was wistful rather than angry.

"I could organize my own party," he said; "Preuss and Kern are eager to start out with me again. But it's hard to readjust . . . I had visions of an army expedition . . . I even had hopes that they would restore my commission . . ."

He ended lamely, watching her face to see if she would show astonishment or disapproval. But she had always known how terribly he wanted the Army to solicit his rejoining; for her own part she would never rest content until she saw him in uniform again, working with the service in which he had begun his professional life.

"When President Polk commissioned you a lieutenant colonel, I prophesied that you would be a general before you were forty. My chronology is off, but when the right circumstances combine, the Army will urge you back into service. In the meanwhile you are surely not going to give up your plans for a fifth expedition? That railroad pass is so important; you are the man to find it and chart it."

"You mean we ought to finance it ourselves?"

"What better use could we put our money to? You've already spent several thousand dollars for your scientific equipment; surely you didn't ever hope to get that money back from the government?"

When John grimaced she continued, "Very well then, let's use our resources to organize the men and buy supplies. If you find the pass, the country will want to help finance your railroad; if you don't find it, we've lost nothing except a lot of gold. We can still go back and build our cabin on the Mariposa. Paris was a long way from Fremontville. Or don't you want a Fremontville any more?"

His eyes gleamed. "It will be a main stop on our railroad. I'll run it right past your front door."

The next morning, when they told her father that they were going to finance an independent expedition, Tom nodded his approval, wrote out a check for his contribution, and sent letters to his friends in St. Louis. By return mail there arrived a series of modest checks, not enough to take the financial burden off the Fremonts, but by the very gesture of faith and confidence on the part of those who had lost their money on the fourth expedition, sufficient to provide the last necessary impetus for John to work with his old-time enthusiasm.

As always it felt good to Jessie to be in Washington, even though she had returned to a disappointment. She found pleasure in the companionship of her sisters. Sarah had moved to Boston with her husband, but Eliza and Susie were still in Washington. The coming of Eliza's first child had brought her not only the health she had never enjoyed, but by filling out her tall, awkward figure and heavy-featured face, had brought her a kind of attractiveness. She and William Carey Jones had built themselves a conservative brick house on H Street, only a few blocks from the Benton home; on the wings of her first real energy Eliza had begun the study of law so that she might better understand her husband's affairs.

Jessie and Eliza frequently lunched together, either at Eliza's home or at Jessie's, where they found an hour of companionship: for marriage, children and a serious interest in their husbands' careers afforded them much common ground. The most delightful hours, however, were those spent with her youngest sister, Susie, who was now twenty. Susie had abandoned the piano after years of onslaught and was devoting her time to bedeviling the young men of Washington. She had her mother's face, the delicate features, the high coloring, the sparkling blue eyes. When Jessie had last seen Susie, two and a half years before, she had been all arms and legs and high-pitched laughter; she was now beautiful in the way that Elizabeth McDowell had been beautiful in her youth, a lighthearted child who bewitched her cavaliers. She was at the center of much of the young social life of Washington, and was dangling half a dozen men at the end of her affections, unwilling to come to any serious de-

cision because she was having far too pleasant a time in the courting.
Though Jessie was only nine years older than Susie, she felt temperamen-
tally old enough to be her mother. Susie brought her the stories of her
romances, of the music and dancing and theaters and young men who
filled her life. When she was to be out late she stayed with Jessie instead
of going home and waking their parents.

She went to the funeral of Count Bodisco, returning with Harriet
to her home in Georgetown. Harriet was now twenty-eight, full blown,
with round red cheeks and a buxom figure.

"Jessie," she said with a look of affectionate bewilderment in her eyes,
"the Russians are a wonderful people. The count showed me his will a
few days before he died. He willed me every last dollar of his estate, with
the provision that I marry a young man who will give me the pleasure he
says I gave him during the twelve years of our marriage!"

The hot weather came on. Jessie put her three children in a screened
loggia just off the garden, the coolest spot in the house. Lily and Charlie
seemed to enjoy the heat; they turned on a hose in the back yard and
kept themselves wet all day, pretending the spray was one of the foun-
tains of Paris. But little Anne, now five months old, did not fare so well.
She was refusing her food, tossing fretfully at night. Jessie spent many
anxious hours in the darkness rocking the baby's crib, singing soft lulla-
bies.

An epidemic spread through Washington. Four babies died of colic
within two days. On the morning of July tenth, Anne fell ill. Once again
Jessie sent Josheem to Silver Spring to ask Francis Blair if she might have
refuge there. Blair returned with his carriage, bundled Jessie and the
baby into it and hastened them out to the coolness and isolation of his
estate. When John arrived at dinnertime, the pain around Jessie's heart
had eased a little, for the baby seemed better. The next morning while
she was holding Anne against her bosom, and her doctor was assuring
her that the child would grow well here at Silver Spring, she felt a tiny
spasm sweep over the baby. Anne grew rigid against her breast. Her second daughter was dead.

Too numb at the suddenness of the shock to feel any articulated pain,
she gazed into the child's face. Their year in Paris was over now. She
had lost young Benton because she had been exhausted and tortured
during the court-martial, but she had carried the little Parisienne in
health and calm. She had crossed Panama while carrying Charlie, borne
him without proper medical safeguards in San Francisco. Yet Charlie
was bursting with energy and health, while little Anne was gone. How
could one understand life, make any kind of recognizable sense of it?

Even before she could cry, sharp thoughts stuck into her heart like pointed knives: she had borne four children and two were dead; half of life was wasted; half of all that one tried to do failed tragically and disap-peared. It had been that way with John, too; he had been on four expe-ditions; the first two had been glorious successes, the last two had brought conflict, failure and death.

As the doctor took the baby from her she remembered that moment in St. Louis when her first son had died, when the doctor had tried to take young Benton and she had been unable to give him up. Then her grief had been more for herself and her husband than for the lost boy; but Anne had been so sweet and fragile, with such a disarming smile; she had wanted the child to grow up to be a lovely girl. Deep within her was a sorrow for the child's sake.

She was still sitting immobile in her chair, dry-eyed, feeling hard and cold, when John reached her. He buried his head on her lap and wept. The little Parisienne had meant much to him; he could not restrain his grief. Jessie thought, When young Benton died, and I could not endure my pain, he comforted me, he was calm and resolute. Now it is my turn to comfort him: I must not weep, I must not be bitter, I must help my husband. When one is weak, the other must be strong. When one is ill, the other must be well. When one is heartbroken, the other must be calm and hopeful. Neither can be the strong one, the well one, the brave one all the time; the roles must change, they must reverse as health and courage flag or revive. Living together did not mean that each mate was always at his strongest or that the two of them together were always twice as wise or resolute; but that through love, through tenderness, through sympa-thy, even through pity, their acceptance of life and their journey through the years could be enhanced. This was collaboration; this was marriage.

She lifted his head from her lap, gripped his face tightly between her fingers, kissed away the tears.

3

IT WAS ONLY A FEW DAYS after John and his party had left St. Louis that she received a telegram telling her that he was unable to hobble along on his left leg and had been obliged to return to St. Louis for medical treat-ment.

She caught the next train for St. Louis, remembering that when she and John had first made this trip ten years before, they had used stages, canal boats and steamboats, the voyage taking over two weeks. Now she made the trip in three days and nights.

He was in their old room in the Benton house overlooking the pear orchard. "They were right, the War Department, to pass me by," he growled when she came into the room. "They knew I could never drag this confounded leg over the Rockies."

She stood in the doorway, noting how the lines of his face were visible even under the dark beard.

"You didn't get that leg dancing at Washington parties," she retorted; "you got it because you tried to blaze a railroad trail over the Rockies in the dead of winter. If you can't go on, you can't go on, but don't wear that leg like a curse; wear it the way Grandmother McDowell would say you should, like a medal bestowed for bravery under fire."

Her caustic tone had its salutary effect. He limped to her side and embraced her.

"I'm sorry I barked at you, dear. It's just that I've gone soft, and I don't like it. After a year of sleeping on lace and down in Paris, I no longer find a wet saddle the most comfortable pillow." He held her at arm's length, scanning her face. "Forgive me, Jessie, for being selfish and talking about myself. You look tired."

"Yes, I am tired," she admitted. "But that's not why I look pale. I started out on my fifth expedition just about the same moment you did on yours." She threw her head back sharply. "Like you, I find a wet saddle hard to sleep on after a soft pillow; it was easy carrying Anne because Charlie was so strong and healthy. Now . . ."

He drew her close to him and, with his arms locked about her, rocked from side to side.

"I'm afraid," she admitted, "but not too much. I seem to do all right on the odd numbers. My first and third children are as strong as tigers; my second and fourth were weak and died. I am due for a healthy child again this time."

"When will you have the baby?"

"About the middle of May."

"Good. I am rejoining my party at the Saline Fork of the Kansas River. I should be on the other side of the Rockies by February; from there we'll push on to San Francisco, and I'll come back across Panama. I'll be in Washington by the beginning of May."

On the first morning after her return to Washington she had tea and rolls at six, then walked up to the house on C Street. By six-thirty she was in the library. It was not yet light out; she saw her father's shaggy head bent over the papers on his desk, the spermaceti candles taking her mind back to that morning, twelve years before, when she was carrying her first child, her husband had just left on his first expedition, and she had joined Tom Benton in the library to help him with his work. Now she was to help her seventy-two-year-old father write his memoirs, *Thirty*

Years in the United States Senate. Impulsively she went to him, leaned her head over his shoulder and kissed him on the cheek.

"It's good to be here with you again, Father," she said fondly, "working on your papers in this beautiful library as I did for so many years."

Tom Benton reached up and patted the hand resting on his shoulder.

"I've missed you, Jessie, more than you can know. This house is so empty without you. So often I needed your help, started to call out your name . . . But you had your own life to lead, your own work to do. I want you to know I'm proud of the fine things you've accomplished with John."

"Whatever I've been able to accomplish has been because of your training and help. But I think we ought not to be separated any more. I think we all ought to stay together and work out our problems together. If John and I have to go to California again, then you must come with us. How you would love the West, Papa! It is even richer and more colorful than you dared to dream."

Tom's eyes gleamed with excitement. "Yes, Jessie," he exclaimed, "next time you go to California I shall make the trip. I've wanted to for years now. It is the one last adventure I want to enjoy before I die."

Through the fall, mail from John reached her frequently, for he was on a well-traveled route; where she had once plotted his journey through sheer wilderness, twelve years of westward movement had brought hundreds of villages, farms, forts, and a two-way stream of wagons. It was not until after the turn of the year, when she had been without a letter for several months, that amorphous fears began to press upon her. On an early February afternoon as she sat in the living room of her rented cottage, with Lily and Charlie playing at her feet, she felt sudden pangs of hunger, where only an instant before she had felt no hunger at all. With this hunger gnawing at her insides as though she had not eaten for days, her formless anxieties took shape: John was starving; the last of the supplies had long since been eaten, the last of the animals killed and dispatched; the countryside was buried under snow and there was no morsel to sustain them.

That night at dinner she could not touch her food. When her father asked what the matter was, she replied, "John is starving. I can't eat with him desperately hungry."

"You didn't tell me you heard from John today!"

"I've had no communication. I just know he is hungry."

Tom Benton was thoughtful for several moments; he had no choice but to believe that his daughter was suffering from some oppressive force. He had to contend with the actuality of her pain rather than the improbability of her knowledge.

"It may be true that John is hungry," he agreed gently; "there has frequently been a shortage of food on his expeditions. But there is nothing to worry about. He has always come through."

She sat silent, her head down, all appetite gone. When the second day passed and she had had nothing but water, Tom Benton became angry.

"This is the sheerest nonsense I ever encountered. If John were starving there would be no possible way for him to communicate that information to you. Even if he could, he would refuse to do so. I will not allow you to endanger the baby you are carrying."

"You're right, Father," she whispered.

Two nights later, February 6, 1854, she was sitting in a robe before the fire in the living room, her hair down her back, her hands clasped in her lap, trying to perceive through the flames the true picture of what her husband was enduring at that moment. She heard the front door close noisily and the sound of young laughter on the staircase. Her sister Susie and a Benton cousin, who had been to a wedding at General Jessup's, came in to spend the night. She welcomed the two girls and urged them to make themselves comfortable before the fire after their drive over the rough and frozen streets. They slipped out of their ball gowns, put on loose woolen robes, then settled at her feet to tell her of the fun and gaiety of the wedding while they brushed their hair and sipped hot tea.

The fire burned down. Jessie said, "Let me get another log or two," and went into the dining room where there was a feeder box from an outside porch. She had just knelt beside the box when she heard a voice which in all the world could be only John's whisper, "Jessie."

She did not move or even breathe; half kneeling in the darkness, a wave of intense relief swept across her brain. She knew that her husband was safe.

She rose and carried the wood into the living room. Susie, who was standing with her back to the fire, met Jessie's glance as she entered the room. "Why, Jessie dear, what has happened? Your eyes are glowing as though you had received the most wonderful news."

"I have," replied Jessie serenely, "John is safe."

Tom Benton arrived late the next morning, shaking his head disapprovingly. "All this is a piece with your being so positive he was starving. I don't like it, Jessie. It's a dangerous kind of game, more dangerous than anything John himself is facing on the trail."

"Don't be frightened," she replied softly. "I'm happy now because I know John is safe. You'll have no more trouble with me, you'll see."

"Never look a gift horse in the mouth," he said *sotto voce*. "I don't like mysticism, but if it serves to restore your appetite, I'll accept it."

She was as good as her word; relieved of anxiety over her husband, she slipped quickly through the weeks. Toward the end of March she received a letter from Parowan, in Utah, brought in by a Mormon elder who had come to Washington on business. As she tore open the envelope and folded the pages upright so that she could read, one word stood out, one word repeated in nearly every line: *hunger*. Even before she saw the salutation of "My darling wife" she had seen the word hunger, and breathlessly she was reading:

Our food supplies disappeared steadily. There was no chance to replenish them with game. We could think of little else but our hunger. We lived for nearly fifty days on our horses, until the last one was killed. Three days later as I was trudging up the mountain, hunger overcame me so completely that my strength vanished and I almost fell. I told no one of my condition, but merely said that this was an excellent spot to camp, and turned in at once. The next morning I was able to continue. I called my men together, told them that a small group on my last expedition had been guilty of eating one of their number, and cried, "If we are going to die of hunger, let us die like men." Late the following day we encountered a band of Utes, one of whom remembered me from my journey through here in 1844. They gave us a dog . . .

When she had finished the letter she leaned weakly against the edge of the fireplace. Her mind flashed to another year and another house; she saw herself lying upon her four-posted cherrywood bed in the Benton home in St. Louis, with all the world thinking John dead; she recalled that one night while the cycle of dread was revolving in her mind, somehow the circuit had broken, she had fallen into an untroubled sleep, had awakened carefree, knowing that her husband was safe.

She went to her father's house to inform him joyously that all was well with John and his party. She did not mention the word hunger.

An early March spring came to Washington. Tom Benton felt tired after the intense work of the winter and visited Silver Spring to rest for a short time. Jessie planned to spend these days in the house on C Street with her mother. She took Elizabeth her tray the first night; there was nothing on it but a cup of tepid milk and a piece of buttered toast.

When she had returned from Paris she had been able to see how much her mother had faded. Yet in the day-by-day contact with her now there was little change discernible. Her eyes were withdrawn, her face white. During the last few years Elizabeth McDowell Benton had remained alive because she knew of no way to die until her time came.

Jessie ran a warm cloth over her mother's hands, dried them, brushed her hair a little. After a few moments had passed, Elizabeth said:

"Jessie, help me . . . out . . . bed."

Jessie slipped the robe around her mother's shoulders and put warm slippers on her feet.

She supported Elizabeth, with an arm around her back, down the long hallway as her mother headed for the library. She followed closely as her mother moved about the room, touching Tom's desk, the books on the shelves, the chessboard on the Duncan Phyfe table by the windows. When she came back to the door, Jessie saw that there were tears in her eyes. She half carried, half supported her mother down the broad flight of stairs. Summoning her strength, Mrs. Benton went from room to room, gazing at the portraits of her parents in the drawing room, touching one high note on Eliza's and Susie's piano, then walked across the entrance hall to the dining room, where, leaning against the table, she gazed up at the portrait of herself as a young woman painted by Samuel Morse when portrait painting had been his career. She sat down in Tom Benton's big chair at the head of the table. Across the gleaming mahogany the two women faced each other in the rapidly falling dusk. As Jessie watched her mother's face, she saw her eyes clear, a spot of color come into the white cheeks.

"I had much happiness here . . . but it was never my home . . . in the way . . . it is your home. You grew up here . . . you have roots here. You have loved it. This home will be yours . . . what Cherry Grove was to me. Your father has willed it to you . . . it will become your inherited home . . . the inherited home of your children. I am happy . . . you will have it, Jessie, you and your family . . ."

"Father said you made this home the little White House of Washington. For years everyone of importance who came to the capital sat at this table and enjoyed your hospitality. You entertained Andrew Jackson and his Rachel here the first time they came to Washington, when no one else would receive Mrs. Jackson because she had been divorced."

Elizabeth smiled faintly. Jessie knew that in her own way her mother had been a martyr to marriage; she had said, I cannot endure this kind of life so I will quietly withdraw, but I will never hurt my husband by telling him that this has always been the wrong life for me, that it was a fatal error for me to have married him. If she could not be strong enough to stand up to a life that was against her own instincts, at least she could be strong enough to protect her husband against the knowledge of what was killing her. Elizabeth Benton too had borne a King George's Mark. Another woman would have left her husband, gone back to Cherry Grove to live, renounced her marriage as a mistake. Elizabeth McDowell Benton had paid for her mistake with her life, yet no one but her daughter knew it. There had been a chasm between them, a chasm of temperament, of values, of natures; but now Jessie felt closer to Elizabeth than she ever had before.

She perceived that courage, like loneliness, has many faces; that nothing she might ever do would require more courage than had been shown by Elizabeth of the charming and amiable background.

That night her mother slipped so quietly and gently out of life that Jessie could feel almost no transition. Her eyes seemed closed only a trifle tighter, the face only a little paler, the fragile, bony hand in her hand only a little colder. When her daughter raised the blinds to let in the first light of dawn, she saw that the ordeal of Elizabeth McDowell Benton was over.

She was lunching with her children a few weeks later when Josheem came running to the house, his eyes wild, panting, "Miss Jessie, come quick—house burning down!"

She ran through the streets of Washington; from several blocks away she could see the mounting flames. She turned down C Street, stopped running; her feet began to drag. There was a crowd already assembled in front of the Benton home; firemen were working hand hoses, attempting futilely to put out the flames. Her eyes closed and behind the lids she saw again the two great fires in San Francisco, which she had blamed on the lawlessness of the frontier community. She stood on one foot, her shoulders sagging, breathing short, labored breaths, watching her home with its memories and hopes go up in flames. This then was her inheritance; a home built, a life made, then nothing left but a bare and forlorn chimney against the sky.

Her father's carriage turned in from Pennsylvania Avenue. She helped him down. They stood with arms about each other while Tom murmured:

"My manuscript of *Thirty Years in the Senate*. It's gone."

The crowds grew more dense. Sympathetic words were spoken. She heard someone say the Senate had adjourned when they heard the news, then she saw many of the senators with whom Tom Benton had spent his working years offering their condolences, the hospitality of their homes, while the roof of the Benton house caved in and the wooden walls seemed to blaze all at once.

She asked someone to help her lead her father to her own house. Here Tom Benton sank into a big chair in the living room, his head on his chest, all life gone out of him. After a few moments there was a knock on the front door. Maylee announced President Franklin Pierce. Pierce had been a congressman from New Hampshire for some twenty years before an unkind fate had precipitated him into an office for which he had neither talent nor appetite. He was a kindly man who knew the nature of suffering: his wife had lost her mind when their young son had died, and there could be no happiness for Franklin Pierce in the White House. He went up to Tom Benton, put his hand roughly on his shoulder and said, "Senator, this is a miserable piece of fortune. I was riding when the news met me. I hurried here, stopping only long enough at the White House to give the necessary orders. You will find everything ready for you; the library and the bedroom next to it. You must stay there until you rebuild your house."

Jessie recalled what her father had said about the president: "It is Pierce's head that is wrong—his heart is always right." They were touched by his kindness, but even while they thanked him they knew that Tom could not move into the White House, for it too was a house of mourning.

True to his promise, John was back in Washington by the middle of May. In the course of their quick revelations of all that had happened in the seven months they had been separated, she hesitantly told her husband of how she had known of his hunger and been unable to eat, of how he had come to her to assure her that he was well. They had never talked of these things before; she was uneasy lest he ridicule her or even reprove her for indulging in the occult. Instead he turned searching eyes upon her and asked:

"Do you happen to remember what night that was?"

"Yes, it was February sixth."

He went to the weatherproofed duffel bag and brought forth his journal. Thumbing through it, he opened to the entry of February sixth.

"That's the very night we reached Parowan," he said in a curiously hushed voice. "We were all of us so feeble we could barely drag ourselves down the trail, but the Mormons took us in, one or two of us in each house, and they fed us and nursed us back to health." He was silent for a moment, reading his notes, then looked up at her again.

"What time of the night was it that you heard me speak to you?"

"The girls came home from the wedding about one o'clock. They slipped into gowns and settled before the fire. It must have been almost an hour later when I was kneeling by that woodbox . . ."

"Listen to this entry in my journal," he said. "After those good Mormon folk had fed me and showed me to my room, I sat down at once and wrote, 'If I could only tell Jessie that I am safe now, tell her how happy I am that we have all been saved.' "

"What time did you make that entry?"

"My notes say eleven-thirty."

"Then your message reached me, but it took two and a half hours to get here. I suppose I shouldn't complain; even Samuel Morse's telegraph couldn't do better."

John took her face in his hands. "You are a good wife, but a poor astronomer. Utah is two and a half hours earlier in time than Washington. The message I wrote to you in my journal was flashed over a quicker and more accurate wire than a Samuel Morse could ever invent."

4

TWO DAYS LATER she gave birth to a boy. They named him Frank. They were happy with their son, and with the new trail over the Central Rockies where John hoped to build his railroad. Together they wrote a short account of his travels over the pass, accompanying it with a map to indicate the proposed line to California.

They now had to give much of their time to the practicalities of business: the banking house of Palmer, Cook & Company in San Francisco had successfully floated a stock issue and John had brought bank drafts which he planned to use to straighten out his affairs in Washington. The representatives from California finally put through the Congress the bills which would pay them the hundred and eighty thousand dollars they had spent in beef cattle for the Indians; Huttman won the case which John had had transferred from London, but Congress voted to pay both the principal and the interest, and so they did not have to meet the forty-three-thousand-dollar judgment with their personal funds. Huttman's success led others in California who held John's notes from the conquest to file suit. John grumbled to Jessie that affairs were getting more complicated every hour: the government would not honor the seven hundred thousand dollars' worth of drafts he had drawn, but they were apparently willing to pay all court judgments levied against him for these obligations . . . after he had spent months defending the suits and a fortune for lawyers!

While in California he had learned that several of the best sites he had staked out for quartz mining had been claim-jumped by squatters who could not be put off the Mariposa except by force. Much of his work in Washington was with the Department of the Interior, where he was attempting to get laws passed which would protect mineral rights under the still unconfirmed land grants in California. He had no success, and with each ship that reached New York there came disquieting news from Palmer, Cook and his managers on the Mariposa, telling him that if some action were not taken the squatters would be in possession of all the mines. Jessie agreed reluctantly that he would have to make another trip to California. He could then return east to begin promotion of the central railroad line for which they hoped Congress might appropriate funds. As soon as their many affairs could be settled satisfactorily in the East, the family would move on to the Mariposa.

At the moment Jessie was loath to leave her father. Tom Benton's wife was dead, his job in the Senate gone, his house burned down, and with it his manuscript and his papers; his son was dead, his three daughters were busy raising their own families and caring for their own husbands. With the house on C Street still standing he had had his work, his books, his roots, his own roof, his friends who could come to call; he could entertain, be the master of a home, a man with a place in the world. With the burning of his home the last of his possessions had gone up in smoke, and though she kept him comfortable, in his own mind he was dispossessed. She wept for him; he had lived just a little too long, everything in his life had died before him—everything except the slavery issue.

She encouraged him to begin rewriting his book, not only because she wanted the permanent record but because the work would keep him occupied. By dint of assembling a number of documents from senatorial friends and helping him sketch the early chapters, her father's energy renewed and he threw himself forcibly into the task. With the quickening of his mental strength and courage, Old Rhinoceros Hide proved that he had justly earned his title, for at seventy-two he not only began the rewriting of his book, but plunged as well into a last great struggle to keep the slavery issue from splitting the Union.

For Jessie there was no escape from the maelstrom over slavery, for she and her husband had taken a definite stand: that the extension of slavery must be prohibited. With both the northern and southern interests trying to use the federal government as an instrument to further their beliefs, Washington became a battlefield in miniature. Discussions in the Congress were no longer restrained; they were waged in bitterness; physical blows were struck. The atmosphere was poisoned with a deadly virus, for the Fugitive Slave Law had aroused the people of the North to flaming indignation, and the Kansas-Nebraska Act, which had opened to slavery new territories from which it had been prohibited since the Missouri Compromise of 1820, had given rise to civil war in Kansas. There seemed to be no other issue on all the vast American panorama except slavery: it cut across friendships, family ties, every aspect of politics, economics, religion and ideology. Their oldest friends, intimates of the Benton and McDowell families for half a century, no longer came to the house, refused to receive the Fremonts in their homes, abused them both publicly and privately. Angry letters arrived from their friends and relatives in the South with whom they had had the closest bonds. Tom Benton, his shoulders bent, his big head covered by only a few wisps of white hair, was starting out on a lecture tour to warn the public that the South was working itself toward dissolution of the Union by force, that the moderate-thinking people in every section of the land must awaken to the dangers involved, must work together to prevent disunity.

She had not realized before how southern a city Washington was; despite the fact that there were representatives from every section of the United States, the proslavery element dominated the city: its tone, its manner, its thinking, even its press. The air was filled with hatred, vituperation and impending violence; no home could be kept free from it; few discussions, no matter how peaceably they started, but ended in curses and bad blood. After a particularly harsh outburst, she held a conference with her husband.

"John, is there any particular reason why we must remain in Washington? Do you have important business here that necessitates our living in the capital?"

"On the contrary, Jessie," he replied, "it seems to me that there is no business being transacted here at all except the war over slavery."

"Then could we go somewhere else to live? A northern city, where the people feel as we do? I haven't wanted to complain, but neither the walls of this bedroom nor the walls of this little cottage have been stout enough to keep out the quarrels."

"Don't think I haven't worried about that, Jessie," he answered. "There isn't a square inch in Washington where you can avoid them. I always loved this city, but now I am uneasy here."

"We have so little left, the city is so changed, our home has burned down, so many of our old friends hate us now . . ."

"How soon do you think you could move, and where would you like to live?"

"I would like to move tomorrow, and I'd like to live in New York. That seems the most cosmopolitan of our cities; there we can be with our own kind of people and at least avoid the more personal aspects of this controversy."

She was astonished to see how few possessions they had. It took only two days to pack them in trunks and move to New York. They rented a house on Ninth Street, near Fifth Avenue. It was three stories high with a parlor overlooking the street and a good-sized dining room behind. Going up from the entrance hall was a rather narrow flight of stairs which led to three bedrooms. Jessie considered herself fortunate in the furnishings, for they were light and cheerful maple pieces, with marine oil paintings on the walls.

Lily attended the neighboring public school. Charlie, now four years old, was sent to a day nursery. Maylee came along ostensibly to cook for Jessie and John, but actually because she had lost her heart to little

Frank. Joshaam joined the family, but his twin remained with Eliza and Tom Benton in Washington. Just as she had taken special joy in Charlie because that love encompassed her love for Benton who was gone, Jessie now found that her love for hazel-eyed, robust little Frank had an added intensity because she wanted to lavish on him all the love that would have gone to the little Parisienne.

She found that New York was not as peaceful as she had expected, but at least the agitation came from people with whom she agreed. In the late spring of 1855 she took a cottage at Siasconset, Nantucket, in order to escape the summer heat of the city. John left on his trip to the Mariposa, certain that he would be back by September. Her father accepted her invitation to spend some months in the seaside cottage with his three grandchildren.

The afternoons were spent on the beach; each evening they worked together on the *Thirty Years*. But the hour Jessie found the most vital of the day was at four o'clock when Maylee served tea on the porch overlooking the road. Tom had the leading New York, Boston, Washington, St. Louis and Charleston papers delivered to the cottage; he was greatly exercised at the growth of the new Republican party, which had been started in Wisconsin almost a year before and was sweeping the country with an evangelical fervor, bringing into its midst former Whigs, whose party was now dead, as well as great blocks of northern Democrats who had watched Franklin Pierce permit the Democratic party to serve the southern slave interests.

"Why are you so incensed at the Republicans, Father?" she queried. "Our government is based on a two-party system, and everyone knows that the Whigs are completely disorganized."

"Granted, granted," boomed Tom, whose voice had not subsided with the passage of the decades. "We need a second party, but it should be national in character, not geographic and factional. The Republicans will become a purely northern party, a solidly anti-slavery party . . ."

". . . that sounds strange coming from as old an opponent of slavery as you, Papa."

". . . which will set the North and South solidly against each other. Once this split becomes political as well as geographic, nothing will stop a civil war."

Jessie poured her father a third cup of tea, but it had grown so cold that Tom took one sip and then laid down the cup. She sorted her thoughts carefully before speaking. "It will be the slavery issue that will cause the war, Papa, not the formation of the new party."

"Again granted, but you know, Jessie, it has been my lifelong hope to settle this slavery question without force or violence. The Republican party will throw the quarrel so sharply into focus that, should they win the election in 1856, the South would secede from the Union."

He rose, feeling chilled now that the sun had gone down, started for his room, his big head sunk on his chest. Before he reached the door he turned around and said with almost resigned quietness, "Ah, Jessie, we are in for bad times. My only hope is that this Republican party will die out as fast as it came in."

"Frankly, Father," she said brusquely, "I don't follow your reasoning. You know perfectly well that the Democratic party is dominated by the southern politicians. They will never nominate anyone who does not favor slavery or who will not fight for its extension."

"Then we lifetime Democrats must try to get control of the party; we must not burn down the barn just to get rid of the rats."

She smiled at the astuteness of the political phrase. "I don't think the Republicans are barn burners, Father; if they will nominate a real anti-slavery candidate, I think John will vote for him."

In August, S. N. Carvalho arrived with a present for Jessie, a copy of the book that had just come off the press about his trip with Colonel Fremont on the fifth expedition. Carvalho, the first photographer to ac-company a transcontinental expedition, had produced many wonderful and accurate plates. He stayed for luncheon, after which the talk turned to politics.

"Did you know, Mrs. Fremont," asked Carvalho, "that the men of the fifth expedition have already picked their next candidate for president?"

"Really? Who is the unfortunate man?"

"Colonel Fremont."

"Colonel Fremont!" she exclaimed in astonishment. "How ever did that happen?"

"Very simply. We were camping on the Saline Fork of the Kansas River waiting for the colonel to rejoin us after his bad leg had taken him back to St. Louis. One evening while eating buffalo steaks around the campfire, we were discussing who the next president should be; the thought suddenly came to me: Colonel Fremont! I put him in nomina-tion right then and there."

Amused, Jessie asked, "How was the nomination received?"

"With acclamation! He was the first choice of every man in that camp."

She sat up that night reading Carvalho's book, touched by the tribute paid to John:

In all the varied scenes of vicissitude, of suffering and excitement, dur-ing a voyage when the natural character of a man is sure to be developed,

Colonel Fremont never forgot he was a gentleman; not an oath, no bois-
terous ebullitions of temper . . . Calmly and collectedly he gave his
orders, and they were invariably fulfilled to the utmost of the men's abili-
ties. The greatest etiquette and deference were always paid to him, al-
though he never ostensibly required it. Yet his reserved and exceptionable
deportment demanded from us the same respect with which we were al-
ways treated and which we ever took pleasure in reciprocating.

In early September Tom Benton returned to Washington to open a
tour at the National Theatre in the capital. Some ten days later Jessie
received a telegram from John telling her that he had returned safely to
New York and would remain there only long enough to take care of imperative business.

Four months after he had left for California, she saw her husband
walking briskly up the road. She was sitting on the front porch having
midafternoon tea with her children; John stopped for a moment as
though to survey the scene, then hastened to her. From the bottom of
the five wooden steps he said, "You all make a very lovely picture; I
think I'll just gaze at it for a while and let it sink in."

But Lily and Charlie scrambled out of their chairs and down the stairs
to throw themselves upon him; he came up with one child under each
arm to embrace her. Jessie noted that there was something unusual about
his demeanor, something over and above his joy and excitement at being
home with his family again. There was a glint behind his eyes, his mouth
seemed to want to laugh. He sat bemused in his chair, answering the
children's rapid-fire questions, interweaving stories of his trip with conditions at the Mariposa.

It was almost five when they had finished tea. Lily and Charlie ran
around to the ocean side of the house to play in the sand. The words for
which Jessie had been waiting almost an hour at last came from his lips.

"Could you put on a wrap and walk with me up the beach? We might
go as far as the lighthouse."

5

THEY LEFT THE HOUSE by the back door, tried the dry sand first but
found it too yielding, then went down to the water's edge and walked
along the damp hard-packed sand from which the tide had just receded.
They were bareheaded, the offshore breeze blowing their hair. Jessie
slipped her hand into his, the hand into which hers fitted so intimately;
she could feel the thoughts pounding through his head, yet she made no

attempt to hurry him. They turned a sharp curve of the beach; the sinking sun glared full in their eyes. He chose this moment to begin.

"Jessie," he murmured, "I've been offered the nomination for the presidency."

She stopped in her tracks, feeling the dampness of the cold sand through the soles of her shoes.

"That's what Carvalho said!"

"Carvalho?"

"Yes, he was here the other day to leave a copy of his book. He told me that your men nominated you for the presidency while encamped on the Kansas River."

"This second nomination is more official; I've just come from a conference at the St. Nicholas Hotel with the recognized leaders of the Democratic party. They strongly urged me to accept the nomination, and are positive we can win the election."

Impulsively she flung her arms around her husband. When she disengaged herself her eyes were sparkling with joy and gratification.

"Would you like to be First Lady, Jessie?" he asked softly. "You would be the most charming mistress the White House has had since Dolly Madison."

"Of course I would like the opportunity," she cried. "What woman wouldn't? I'm even conceited enough to think I might fill it rather well. I have watched the White House grow from a cold, water-logged, miasmic little house in a swamp, where the president had to pay for his own heating and lights, until it has become the beautiful mansion that it is today. During the eight years that Jackson lived there we used to have dinner *en famille* and romp through the rooms playing games. When Martin Van Buren was elected I always went to his son's birthday parties and his first dances. Nancy Polk and I had been friends during all the years that her husband was a senator, and when she moved into the White House we went calling just as we had when she was in her own home."

John took a quick glance at her flushed face, then said: "We've had bad luck with our First Ladies: poor Rachel Jackson was slandered to death by Henry Clay in that filthy campaign of 1828; she never got a chance to reign over the White House; Mrs. Van Buren was so terribly formal that the White House ceased to be what Jackson called it, 'The People's House.' Nancy Polk was pleasant as First Lady, but poor Franklin Pierce's wife has been mentally ill and has never received anyone. It's high time we had a First Lady who could carry on Anne Royall's work. There is a great deal you could do for the women of this country, Jessie; fight for their causes, help them progress, fulfill the modern ideas of a woman's place."

"It is good of you to put the emphasis on me, John, but the committee is not nominating me; it is nominating you. You will make a splendid president; I can see an era of building for this country the like of which we've never had. I can see railroads pushing out to the west coast, national roads, new cities rising on the ashes of your campfires."

The sun had gone down. Darkness was falling rapidly. Up ahead they could see the revolving beam of the lighthouse which stood on the edge of a promontory.

"Yes, it would be wonderful," he agreed. "But there are costs."

"Costs?" She quickened her pace, as though this would quicken the tempo of their discussion. "What are they asking of you?"

"We must approve the Fugitive Slave Law. We have to work for the extension of the Kansas-Nebraska Act."

The wind went out of her sails; her feet began to drag along the cold sand.

"Ah," she murmured. "We must approve of slavery! We must work for the spread of slavery in what are now free states and territories!"

"The Whigs are dying on their feet; the Republicans are too new to count; the Democratic nominee must certainly win. But no man can be nominated by the Democratic party who will not protect slave interests."

It was dark now. The sea air grew cold. Jessie wrapped her coat more securely about her to lock out the chill.

"How did they happen to choose you, John? The southern Democrats know that you're a free-soiler, that you fought for the admission of California as a free state. Why do they choose you to protect their slave interests?"

"Apparently because I would be a good compromise candidate, both geographically and ideologically. You and I were born in the South, we have strong connections there. We are also well known in the West. The free-soilers and many of the Whigs would vote for me because they know I helped to get California admitted as a free state; they would assume that I would work for free soil in the new territories. At the same time, if I publicly avow the Fugitive Slave Law and the Kansas-Nebraska Act, the slavery factions have nothing to fear from me because I have committed myself to work for their interests."

"In other words, in voting for you both factions would be voting for mutually exclusive hopes."

"Quite."

They had reached the beginning of the rocky promontory; they climbed over the sharp, ragged stones and paused at the base of the lighthouse tower. Just beneath them lay the wooden hulk of a submerged wreck; above, the circular light flashed out its message to warn all seafarers. They selected two of the flatter rocks and sat huddled together, two small, quiet figures merging into the darkness and the rocks behind them. She waited for her husband to declare himself, but he remained quiet.

"How do you feel about all this, John," she asked. "The burdens of a country facing a civil war would fall on your shoulders."

He turned and smiled his wistful, poignant smile.

"I want you to be First Lady," he said. "I would like to see you mistress of the White House. It is a role for which you have been preparing all your life. There is no woman in America today so qualified to do a glorious job." He took her hand and laid it alongside his cheek. "You have gone through a great deal for me, Jessie. You have endured agonies of the mind and the flesh. I have dragged you through quarrels and scandals and disease-ridden frontiers. Always you have stood by my side, backed me even when I have been wrong. Yes, my dear, I've known for a long time how wrong I was to resign from the Army after the court-martial; now that I have the opportunity of becoming president I have the courage to confess to you how utterly headstrong I was, how dominated by false pride. But you did not fight me, you did not force me to go your way, even though it was the right way, even though you knew how much we would have to endure if I resigned. It was I who cost you your first son. I know all you endured in San Francisco in those lonely months while I left you in the sand dunes and tried to hack out enough gold from the Mariposa to give me security for the rest of my life, a security which would have defeated those promises and hopes set in motion that day in Hassler's workroom. I know that in the past few years I have been giving my time and energy to a business which you thought purposeless. Yet you've been patient, you've gone along with me when I've been wasteful of our years and our dreams . . ."

"Because I always had confidence that eventually . . ."

"Could this serve as the eventuality you've been hoping for, Jessie? I can be president of the United States and you can be First Lady. I owe you that for everything you've been through; I owe it to you for the love you've given me. I have never given you a real home; the White House could be your home. I haven't given you the position in society you deserve; this could be my way of letting the rest of the world know you are truly the first lady of your times."

She was quiet for several moments, breathing deeply, feeling unfathomable emotion, watching the slow-moving light as it illumined for a moment the succeeding spokes of dark water.

"In order to see me First Lady," she said almost hoarsely, "you would go against your lifetime principles? You would issue the orders through which runaway slaves would be dragged back in chains to their bondage? You would permit slavery to extend to free Kansas and all the thousands of miles of free land between there and southern California?"

He did not reply.

"John," she cried, "I want to be the president's wife. Looking back now, I guess I've always hoped I would be. Maybe there is some way we can work this out: if they don't nominate you, they'll nominate an out-and-out slavery man, won't they? Surely it would be better to have a free soiler in the White House, though he made temporary concessions, than to have a slavery man who will work every hour to extend the borders of slave territory."

"There is logic in what you say."

"We know how angry the North and South will grow, John, and how bitter; perhaps only a compromise candidate can keep the country from civil war. Perhaps you are the man to do that; you have friends in the South as well as the North and the West. You can pour oil on troubled waters, keep the North and South from each other's throat. Father says that no cotton can be grown in Kansas or any of the other states in the Midwest and Southwest, that the southerners who take slaves there will be obliged to send them back. As for the Fugitive Slave Law, the Underground Railroad is growing so effective that the South will find it too difficult and too expensive to retrieve its runaways. The Democrats have picked you as a compromise candidate; perhaps you too can make a compromise, John, and spend the next four years in the White House keeping the country at peace."

"You make a good case, Jessie," he said softly; "those are compromises I could make. Will you stand by that attitude? Can you continue to justify it? Your father would say that it would be the wise thing to do. Do you agree with him? Or have you built this case to make it easy for me to compromise?"

She turned full face to him; even in the darkness they could see each other plainly. Should she not sacrifice her own feelings for his sake, brave the storms of criticism and abuse which would be hurled at them by their former comrades? Would there not be compensations, advances she could make for the women of the country which would recompense for such compromises? Her main ambition had always been to help her husband achieve his highest potential; where better to achieve it than as president of the United States, a president who loved both the North and the South, who would bind up the wounds of the nation, strive for peace and friendship?

As a woman in love, she must help her man reach the uttermost peak of position and achieve the highest attainable goal. But as a wife creating a marriage which would survive even after their deaths, which would go on even longer than their children or grandchildren, must she not help her husband realize his greatest spiritual potential? Must marriage be baldly opportunistic, crawling ever upward on its hands and knees over dead rocks and dead timber, dead ideals and dead friends? Or was marriage an intense flame which devoured the dross in the husband and wife, leaving only what was pure and fine?

"I could be willing to make these compromises, John, only if you wanted them made. I won't try to conceal from you that I want to see you inaugurated president of the United States . . ."

"You scrubbed your own floors and washed your own dishes in Monterey rather than buy a slave . . ."

" . . . you refused to buy slaves to work your mines even though you could have become a millionaire by doing so and found that security you were so frantically seeking. During those early days in Monterey when the delegates were arguing slavery over our dinner table, I won sympathy for freedom by demanding how they would like to have their children watch fugitive slaves being returned in irons. Can we support a slavery law in 1856 which we utilized to support freedom in 1850?"

They sat silently in the darkness. She knew how much it meant to him to become president, for then the last would be the first, the bastard would be king. It would be a thousand times more difficult for him to give up this opportunity than for any other man. But the price he must pay to become president was critically high: for approving the Fugitive Slave Law and the Kansas-Nebraska Act the abolitionists and all those against slavery would despise him as a turncoat, one who had sold out for the highest possible offer. The Democrats would despise him as a weakling, an opportunist whom they could use for their own purposes.

She wanted to be First Lady; but even more she wanted to remain true to the fundamental beliefs and convictions of their lifetime.

She felt that John would be wrong, terribly wrong, in accepting the nomination under these conditions. Yet if he had his heart set on becoming president, how could she thwart him? He had said that he wanted her to be First Lady, that he would pay almost any price to see her mistress of the White House. But it was a price she did not want him to pay.

She knew that just as she had sustained him when he had determined to resign from the Army, she must sustain him now if he wished to resign from his fight against slavery. Resolutely she turned to her husband and said, "You must speak frankly to me. You have had many hours in which to think things over and resolve your doubts. I will approve of your decision whichever way you make it. But you must not put the burden of the decision on me. It is you who must either decide to be president or renounce the opportunity."

"Very well, Jessie, you have asked for a categorical answer, and I shall give it to you. Coming up on the train I asked myself, 'Does every man have his price? Have I reached the breaking point?' "

She watched him stare out to sea for a moment, then he said, "We have a clear choice: we can either serve as this beacon light, flashing a message of freedom to all those at sea, or we can smash our ideals against the rocks, like that battered hulk of a ship beneath us."

"Then you are willing to forego the opportunity?"

"There has never been any doubt in my mind. I would have taken the nomination for your sake, my dear, but I never wanted it."

"John," she murmured, "do you know what picture comes to my mind? It is of your second expedition, when you were trapped in the Sierras, when nothing but death awaited you, and yet you had the courage to force a passage where lesser men would have fallen. This crossing tonight was even more hazardous for you, yet you have made it safely and blazed a new trail. If you had been willing to pay the price to be president, I would have gone along with the case for compromise; but, my dear, you have been of greater value to your country in this last hour, you have done more for the cause of freedom than you could have in four years in the White House. I am proud of you, and I love you very much. I am ready now to go back to those two rooms at Madame Castro's in Monterey, or to the barrack on the sand dunes in San Francisco. I can be perfectly happy and contented."

She was cold and cramped from their awkward position. Her husband helped her along the rocks to the shore. They walked back in the soft, dry sand, slowly, not speaking, not touching, yet in complete union. Just before they reached the house, he stopped and took her in his arms.

"The Democratic chairman at the St. Nicholas Hotel said that no woman could refuse the presidency. That is why I did not want to deny it to you. But he was wrong; he didn't know my Jessie."

6

ON THE FIRST OF OCTOBER they moved back to their house on Ninth Street in New York City. The air was sharp and invigorating, but even more invigorating was the temper of the times. She was intensely interested in watching the mass meetings against slavery, the growing partisanship of the press, but above all the spontaneous growth of the Republican party in all parts of the North and West. The leaders of the

Republican party knew that they could not elect either a platform or an idea in the 1856 campaign. They would have to elect a man. Since their party was young, they wanted a young candidate; since their entrance into politics was new, they wanted a candidate new to national politics; since they were an exploring party which must blaze new trails across the wilderness of political confusion, they wanted a trail blazer; since their platform was to be based on the romantic notion of universal freedom, they needed a romantic figure; since their fight for freedom was to be heroic, they needed a heroic figure; since they were so little known, they would need a universally known figure; and finally, since this election would create in embryo a geographic and ideological war, they needed a man of indomitable courage, one whose spirit and will to conquer would not flag in the most desperate passes.

Though neither John nor Jessie had publicized their rejection of the Democratic nomination, word of this dedication to principle made its way through political circles. John was young, only forty-three. He was new to national politics; he had few passionate enemies, was not beaten and battered by years of political quarrels. He was a trail blazer, nationally known and admired, a man of superb courage, a romantic figure. Yet all these seemingly obvious virtues might have remained hidden had not the Democrats offered him the nomination first; by so doing they virtually set up their opposition: if the Democrats had been so positive that John Fremont could win, why could he not win for the Republicans as well?

The intimation that John might become the Republican nominee was first brought to them when a committee composed of Francis Blair and his son, Frank, Nathaniel P. Banks, Senator Henry Wilson of Massachusetts, Joseph Palmer, head of Palmer, Cook & Company, and Senator John P. Hale of New Hampshire called at the house on Ninth Street. While Jessie, in a violet-colored silk gown with a flattering cowled neck, served tea and cinnamon toast, the unofficial delegation urged John not to take his family to California, but to remain in New York for a series of conferences with the Republican leaders of other states who were traveling back and forth in the intense excitement surrounding the birth of a new and radical movement. When the gentlemen had finished their discussion and had left the Fremont parlor heavy with bluish cigar smoke, Jessie asked, "Can the Republicans win?"

"I didn't think so a few days ago. But if the enthusiasm of those men is indicative of the feeling in the North and West, they have a chance."

"Are you willing to take this nomination even if they have no chance?"

"I don't think we have any right to demand a guarantee of success. If this is our fight, then we must participate in it. It's the waging of the battle that is important. Even if the Republicans lose in 1856, it may be a victory for them in that they will have established their party and created a real chance to win in 1860. No battle can be viewed by itself, but only in relation to an entire campaign; sometimes battles that were lost in the beginning are the very ones which insure victory in the end. Our refusal to join battle last month when the Democrats offered us the nomination has put us in a strategic position today."

"Father always said that the office should seek the man, not the man the office. Since the nomination is seeking you, you can take it with a full heart and with full confidence. Your name would help the growth of the party. If anyone can win for the Republicans, you can."

In quiet times, party agitation began only a couple of months before the conventions; but these were troubled times, and by November of 1855, a whole year before the election, the newspapers were full of political maneuvers and potential candidates. Jessie subscribed to the newspapers of every major city in the North and the West; she was able to show her husband that the idea of his leading the Republican party was spreading like a prairie fire. Other candidates were mentioned, veterans like William H. Seward, Salmon P. Chase, Judge John McLean, who had worked long and hard against slavery; but this very fact made them unavailable: they had made too many enemies, there was too much that could be charged against them.

At a national committee meeting held at Silver Spring in December, Francis Preston Blair and such other important national figures as Charles Sumner, Preston King, Nathaniel P. Banks, Salmon Chase, Dr. Bailey and a host of others agreed that John Fremont was the one and only man who could lead the Republican party to victory. Francis Blair said that he would take full charge of the campaign if John were nominated; his dynamic son, Frank, vowed that he would organize a speakers' bureau which would carry John's name to every hamlet in America.

With the turn of the year the Fremont home on Ninth Street became the semiofficial headquarters of the Republicans in New York City; hardly a day went by but there were ten or twenty guests at luncheon, tea or dinner. Seeing Joshaam adding wooden horses and planks to the moderate-sized dinner table brought a glow to Jessie's eyes as she thought back to the best years in the Benton home, when so many of the political issues were formulated over its long mahogany dining table. This unceasing ferment in her household was meat and drink to her; she kept her thirteen-year-old daughter in the midst of things so that she would have the same training she had had in Washington. Joshaam served Lily only the tiniest portions, for the daughter, like the mother, could not eat while arguments were obscuring the beef or the chicken pies. After the last of

the company had left, Jessie and Lily would go into the kitchen, rewarm
the food that Maylee had left for them, and discuss the politics that had
been reviewed during the course of the evening.

At the end of the first week in March, after a number of confidential
meetings, John assured his wife there could be little doubt about his receiving the nomination. Jessie turned her mind to the one problem she
had been avoiding: Tom Benton was making a last-ditch stand against
the Republican party, as he had told her that he would at Siasconset the
summer before. What would he say now that it was his son-in-law who
would be named to head the new party? Surely this would make matters
appear in a different light, cause him to change his viewpoint?

She went alone to Washington to reveal the news to her father. Eliza
had made him comfortable in a combination bedroom and study, where
he was surrounded by books and papers loaned by his former colleagues.
Tom Benton was seventy-four years of age. Neither the spirit nor the
will had flagged, but his physical empire, which he had all but lost when
he was twenty, was crumbling under the ravages of time. The pleasure in
Tom Benton's face at seeing her made her errand the more difficult.

She closed the door of the library behind her and said abruptly,
"Father, John has been assured of the Republican nomination for the
presidency."

His jaw set and his face solidified into the stubborn mask she knew so
well from the days when he was fighting with all his strength against
Biddle's Bank of the United States. He walked to a leather armchair
which Eliza had bought for him, sat down heavily and shaded his eyes
with the great paw of his left hand, a hand which only lately had become
marked with brownish spots. She stood before him, uncertain.

"Aren't you glad, Father?" she asked. "You were so proud of John
when he turned down the Democratic nomination. Why aren't you proud
when he is chosen by the freedom party?"

Tom Benton dropped his hand wearily to his lap; as the daughter and
father looked deep into each other's eyes there passed before both of them
the panorama of their years together.

"I am proud that John has become one of the outstanding figures of
his time," he said hoarsely; "but he must not accept the Republican
nomination. That would be even worse than taking the Democratic
offer."

She could only exclaim, "But why, Papa? There is no one in the
country more ardently opposed to the extension of slavery than you. The
Republicans will keep slavery from spreading."

"If that were all they were going to do, I would back them with my remaining strength. But they are purely a geographical party, Jessie; they will split the nation in two."

"It is a geographical party because the slaveholding states won't join it. They'll never be anything but Democratic. New England, the East, the Middle West, and the West are against slavery; they'll vote for John and the Republican party."

"If they do, Jessie, they'll be voting not for John but for civil war. Mark my words, if John accepts the Republican nomination and is elected, he will be responsible for plunging the nation into bloodshed. I know that neither he nor you want to do this. If you were determined to become First Lady at any price, then you should have accepted the Democratic offer: you would have had to endorse slavery, perhaps even extend it a little, but you would not have caused the secession of the South."

There was a knock at the door. Josheem came in with coffee, scones and the blackberry jam which he knew Jessie liked. She shook hands with the tall and lanky Negro, glad to see him again.

"We miss you in Washington, Miss Jessie," he said with a wide grin. "When you all comin' back here to live?"

"About the fourth of next March," she replied with a half-smile as she glanced at her father.

"You goin' to take a house here, Miss Jessie?"

"I understand the White House is for rent, Josheem. But Father doesn't think I ought to take a lease on it; he says the water still gathers in the kitchen during the rainy season, and everybody who lives there gets miasma."

His eyes wide with wonder, Josheem murmured, "Why, Miss Jessie, there ain't been no water in the kitchen in the White House since President Jackson left, and the swamps was all drained years ago. If'n you got a chance to move into that White House, don't you be afeared of anything: Mammy Maylee, Joshaam and I will keep it warm and dry."

Tom Benton dismissed him with a wave of his hand.

"You are right, Jessie," he said harshly. "The White House will be filled with miasma if the Republicans get in. I most strongly advise you not to let John accept the nomination."

"And if he does accept?"

"Then I'll oppose his election. I'll stump the country warning people that they must not put a factional party into the White House."

She was aghast. "You mean you would campaign against your own son-in-law?"

"I would be obliged to. It would not be easy, Jessie, but then, not many things in my life have been easy."

She picked up her coffee cup, walked to the front window and stood staring out, not seeing the houses opposite but rather the face of her husband, visualizing how she would have to tell him that her father was renouncing him. She gulped the coffee, hot and black, and thought numbly how the tables had turned: When John resigned from the Army, Father expected my support; he had every right to expect it, but I failed to say that John must not do so. Now that I have every right to expect him to support me, he refuses to do so. I had my reasons eight years ago; Father has his reasons now; how miserable it is when a daughter and father must oppose each other.

She went to her father's chair and, with an affectionate gesture, brushed back with her fingers the remaining strands of his white hair.

"Will the country interpret this as a political gesture, Papa, or will they feel it a personal repudiation on the part of Tom Benton towards his son-in-law?"

"I long ago gave up the futile pursuit of trying to determine in advance what people will think."

"Won't the public be right in saying, 'If a man's father-in-law is against him, how can you expect strangers to be for him?' "

"Frankly I don't know," he replied with a touch of coolness. "John has had no political training aside from his three weeks in the Senate; his background has been scientific; it would be a tremendous gamble to put in the White House a man as innocent of political experience as he. I believe in his integrity; I know his capacity for work, and I am convinced there is no more courageous man in America today. I don't know whether he would make a good president in these bitterly partisan and angry times. But even if I did know, I would not vote for him or anyone else, no matter what genius he might have for the presidency, if he were running on a divisionist ticket. If John had taken the Democratic nomination, I would have campaigned for him."

"I see; even though he would be committing himself to a program in which none of us believed, you would have campaigned for him! You would have backed a man who had sold himself for a high offer."

"My dear," her father replied, shrugging, "your husband's idealism is a luxury to me. I care only about the peace of the nation, of the North and South getting along in friendship, and the Union being preserved. If John had been elected as a Democrat, there would be no fear of civil war. If he is elected as a Republican . . ."

She came behind her father's chair, put her arms about his neck, laid her cheek on the white hairs over his temple. "Father, you always said no matter what happened, we must stand together. Please don't desert me now."

Something in her voice, something overstrained, caught his ear. He reached up, took one of her hands, drew her around to him. Then he searched her face carefully, trying to read what lay behind her eyes.

"I know you're not doing all this for yourself," he said softly. "If you had wanted to be First Lady, you could have persuaded John to accept the Democratic nomination. Then why are you doing it now? What is there in the situation that goes beyond politics? You owe me full honesty, Jessie."

For a moment her eyes wavered, her head sunk down. Then she said, "I thought I would never tell this to anyone, but now I know I must. You see, Father, John is not . . . not exactly . . . like other men. He has scars across his mind. Those scars are why he sometimes does things that you cannot understand, and they are why I have sometimes agreed with his judgments even against your superior reasoning . . ."

" . . . such as the time you let him resign from the Army?"

"Yes. John's mother was married at seventeen to a man over sixty . . . After twelve years of unhappiness, she met John's father, Charles Frémon, and ran away with him. She told John there was a marriage ceremony performed, but her husband was apparently unable to secure a divorce from the Virginia legislature—and so the Frémon marriage would have been illegal in any event. John was a . . . a natural child."

Tom stared at his daughter, dumbfounded.

"Illegitimate," he murmured. "Why, I had no idea . . . Jessie, how long have you known this?"

"John told me before we were married. He thought I might want to break our engagement."

"By the Eternal," he whispered to himself. "How has this been kept from me all these years? Why has no one ever told me?"

"Because they would have been frightened for their lives."

"Does anyone else know? How common is this knowledge?"

"It's well known in the South," she replied frankly. "It would have been impossible to conceal . . . Now you can see, Father, why I don't want to inflict any more scars upon him. Another man, perhaps, might understand it as a purely political question; John may take it personally; it may embitter his relationship with you."

Tom began stalking the small, crowded room.

"Then I am a thousand times more right than before, Jessie," he exclaimed. "You must not allow John to expose himself. This campaign is going to be the bitterest and most violent since Andrew Jackson beat Henry Clay in '28. When people are on the verge of a civil war, they care nothing about personal feelings. His illegitimate birth will be spread from one end of the nation to the other; it will create a frightful scandal. Think of the slander and the mud that will be flung."

"John will know why the Democrats are slinging mud at him; he can rise above the tumult because he will understand its objective. But he has loved you and you have loved him; if you abandon him there will be no way for him to understand."

"Jessie, even if you are willing to expose yourself to this scandal, have you no consideration for your three children? Are you willing to have them go through life bearing the burden of your political ambitions?"

"I know that you love Lily and Charlie and Frank. If you are fearful lest these charges hurt their position in the world, then back John in this fight, help put him in the White House. The children of a president need never fear for their social position."

Tom Benton sat down heavily. Jessie knew that she had taken an unfair advantage. After a pause, he dropped the hand that had been veiling his eyes; she saw that he had been crying in the peculiar way in which old men cry without shedding tears.

"Jessie, my dear," he said, "nothing but the death of your mother and your brother has hurt me as much as this: but I still must turn against you. I don't have long to live now, and I can't go to my grave feeling that I played a part in bringing on civil war. You have me caught in the dilemma between loyalty to my family and loyalty to my country; it's a miserable and painful decision for any man to have to make, particularly for a man who has loved you as devotedly as I have. As deeply as I have loved you, Jessie, I also loved my seat in the United States Senate. I don't need to tell you that it was the backbone of my life, the justification of my existence. Yet I gave it up to fight for the admission of California as a free state. I can break, Jessie; I am almost at the breaking point now, but I cannot bend. I want to see you in the White House; that would bring joy and solace to my last years, seeing my little Jessie as the First Lady of the land. It's hard to give up, perhaps even harder than giving up my desk in the Senate four years ago. But I can't approve the election of John as a Republican, even though it will put you in the White House, for I know that it will disrupt the Union. Please forgive me, my dear. I am an old and stubborn man, but I must stand by my lifetime faith. You would not ask me to do otherwise."

When she returned to New York and related her father's decision to her husband, John said softly: "Your father has fought so many fights for me, he is entitled to wage one against me. I wish he hadn't chosen this particular time and issue, but Tom Benton was always one to pick his own battles."

They were pleased when the Democrats nominated James Buchanan on the seventeeth ballot: he was a northerner, had never owned a slave, never publicly favored slavery, had a superb background of training in the federal government; no one knew better than Jessie his scrupulousness of ethic. They agreed that he was a good choice, for as an experienced diplomat, a born compromiser, he would strive to find new and effective means of appeasing the firebrands of both factions.

She went alone to the Republican convention in Philadelphia because John did not consider it proper for a potential candidate to mingle with the delegates. She arrived by train on the afternoon of June 16, and was at Musical Fund Hall by eleven o'clock the next morning. As she took her seat in the front row of the visitors' gallery she was struck by the evangelical nature of the assembly, for this was no routine, prearranged party machine politicking. The thousand delegates milling about on the floor of Musical Fund Hall were dominated by a religious fervor; in their eyes was the gleam of the crusader for freedom. It was a heterogeneous throng, clothed in everything from the striped trousers of northern society to the buckskin pants of the western frontier. To Jessie it seemed nothing less than a miracle that a single idea could pervade and dominate this assemblage, yet when David Wilmot mounted the platform and enunciated the dominant issues of the Republican platform—unalterable opposition to the extension of slavery, denial of the power of Congress to legalize slavery within the new territories, the continuance of the Missouri Compromise, the admission of Kansas as a free state—the convention rose as one man, shouting its tremendous faith in freedom for all the peoples of America. As Jessie watched the newspaper reporters writing at top speed to carry the news of this revolutionary convention to the country, she remembered the reporters who had sat each day at the court-martial carrying the account of John's trial to the nation. She recognized a number of these men as the same ones who had covered the Washington assignment, and who were now going to tell the nation of the choice of the young, vigorous, progressive Republicans.

She expected that John would be unanimously nominated on the first ballot; however, he gathered only 359 votes, while Judge McLean of Ohio had 196 votes. She was astonished at the strength shown by McLean; for a moment her confidence faltered. But David Wilmot, who had won over the convention by his reading of their platform, sprang up and made a mighty plea for unanimity behind John Fremont. The pandemonium that followed almost drowned out the count of votes, but she saw by the pad in her lap that her husband now had 529 votes and was the first presidential nominee of the new party. While the band played its loudest, the thousand delegates and the visitors in the gallery roared their cheers and acclamations deafeningly. The clamor reached its height when a huge banner was strung across the platform reading:

FREE SPEECH, FREE PRESS, FREE SOIL, FREE MEN,
FREMONT AND VICTORY

She sat quietly in her seat in the midst of the impassioned ones about her who were throwing their hats and handkerchiefs and newspapers into the air, while the tears rolled down her cheeks. She supposed it was unworthy of her, but her happiness at this moment of wild acclaim bore little relation to politics, elections or even to such profound issues as slavery and the impregnability of the Union. While the thousand zealots about her saw in the nomination of John Fremont the end of slavery in the United States, Jessie Fremont could feel only as a woman and a wife. The fact that her husband was the outstanding figure in the United States justified not only her original judgment and faith in him, but the design of their marriage. In fifteen years he had risen from an obscure second lieutenant in the Topographical Corps to become the leader of the greatest movement in America since the Revolution. His prominence, his importance, his success were not due solely to his accomplishments, nor were they attributable to anything she had done to help him; they had come about as a result of their collaboration, they were symbolic of the strength and solidity and intelligence of the marriage the two of them had created. Either of them alone might have achieved interesting results; the two of them together in an ordinary marital relationship doubtless would have prospered; but it was their dedication to this marriage that had inspired them to good work, preserved them under desperate difficulties, enabled them to strive ever upward. They had made errors of overzealousness, but never had their failures or shortcomings arisen from a lack of faith or interest in each other, the task at hand, or their marriage. To her intensely feminine mind it was this marriage which was now being nominated to serve as president, to reside in the White House.

As she watched the delegates marching with frenzied joy, chanting, "Free Speech, Free Press, Free Soil, Free Men, Fremont and Victory!" she knew that by the grace of God she had succeeded far better than she had envisaged in her wildest dreams.

Only the year before, they had left Washington believing they no longer belonged there. Now they would move back with bands playing and flags flying; the hearth she had failed to create in Monterey, or in the sand dunes of San Francisco, would be lighted triumphantly in the White House.

7

SHE WAS INTERESTED to find out what kind of a campaign John planned to wage, whether he would make speeches only in the key cities or would spend the months on the long swing through the country, reaching as many people as he could with his personal message. When she returned home she glowingly related every detail of the convention to her proud family. But when she asked her husband what his plans were, he replied, "I have none."

"But don't you intend to . . . ?"

"I have nothing to tell people that they don't already know, Jessie. I am against the further extension of slavery. In those few words rests the entire campaign. The people of this country know me, they know what I think and what I stand for. There is nothing I could tell them that would bring them any more enlightenment or give them any more cause to vote for me than they have now."

"California!" exclaimed Jessie. "That's exactly what you said in California when you were running for the Senate."

"Is it?"

"I guess you must have meant it the first time, if you're still holding to it six years later."

"I didn't seek the office, Jessie; the office sought me. Then why is it either right or necessary for me to travel through the country making rash promises or inciting the people? I can't promise them anything, and I certainly can't fool them. Those who want to vote for me will vote for me; the others won't."

"Very well," she agreed resignedly. "If that's the way you feel the campaign must be waged . . ."

"Now that you've brought the subject up, I can tell you further that I don't want to become emotionally involved. I don't think that's the function of a candidate. I think it's his job to be quiet and dignified."

"If you can do that, you're a marvel," replied Jessie, laughing; "what can I do to help you accomplish it?"

"Act as my aide-de-camp, just as you always have while I was preparing the expeditions, and in Washington while I was on the trail. Be my spokesman. Interview the newspaper reporters when they come, help me write the special articles that are needed, answer the political mail . . . I'll work with the Republican board of strategy, but I'd rather not appear in public. I don't want to enter into a thousand arguments and quarrels, get the hysteria of mass meetings in my blood. I think I can make my best contribution by trying to keep tempers down, since nearly everybody else will be in a bloodthirsty mood."

Francis Blair, who was the Republican campaign chairman, yielded to Jessie's urging that he occupy the spare bedroom in her house. Blair was sixty-five years old, bald except for a fringe of black and gray hair which ran around the base of his head and stopped over his ears. He had big bushy eyebrows which hung over and concealed much of his eyes; his mouth and jowls had begun to break with age, but even at sixty-five he was a gamecock of a man, an adroit strategist and last-barricade fighter. He had been important in presidential elections ever since he had helped put Martin Van Buren into the White House in 1836. He had frequently been called a president maker; this time, he told John and Jessie, he was really going to earn the title.

His younger son Frank, who had practiced law in St. Louis as a protégé of Tom Benton's, became the roving chairman. Frank was tall, lean, fiery, smart, with a shock of black hair, a bold black mustache which he wore long and down the sides of his chin. Tom Benton had frequently said that Frank Blair was like his own son, for Frank was a man of fanatical loyalties, without a shred of fear; he had fought slavery since the day he could talk, and like his father and brother Montgomery, he had written, lectured and canvassed for the development of the West. He had served in the Missouri legislature for the past four years as a Free-Soil Democrat, working hard for the formation of the Republican party in Missouri.

There had been a time when Tom Benton had hoped that Jessie would marry Frank Blair, but Frank had been only eighteen when Jessie met John Fremont.

She was delighted with her job as aide-de-camp; it was one she had been trained to fulfill, and for which she had the greatest enthusiasm. She consulted with John constantly, doing little of importance on her own responsibility, but the major burden of the work fell on her shoulders. Mail poured in from all over the country, from individuals demanding to know how John felt about every last issue. Each letter had to be answered honestly and to the point, for when it returned to Michigan or Kentucky or California it would be shown to everyone within a radius of twenty miles and would engender countless discussions. Newspaper editors would pose a list of questions at John Fremont, challenging him to answer. A frank, direct and closely reasoned statement would have to be prepared at once, to be published in the paper within a week in order that its readers might be satisfied, and no one would have an opportunity to say that candidate Fremont was afraid or unable to meet issues.

The most pleasant part of the work was the daily interviews with women reporters, the literary descendants of Anne Royall who were now

taking a firm place in American journalism, beginning to wage their intensive campaigns for woman suffrage and equal rights. Though these
ladies were reporting for the women's magazines and the women's pages
of the newspapers, she knew the importance of the articles they would
write, for few men voted for a candidate whom their wives disliked. She
encouraged the women reporters to come in at teatime, and over her
favorite combination of sassafras tea, spice cake, scones and blackberry
jam she would answer questions about her life in California, the travels
across Panama, her early years with Senator Benton of Missouri, her stay
in Europe, how she envisaged the family life of the White House. For the
most part these tea sessions were amiable, but occasionally there was a
spirited contretemps. Unsympathetic interviewers snarled at her for serving tea in the English fashion, for wearing a loose-fitting silk housecoat
instead of a black silk dress, for having two colored servants. She turned
aside their brusqueness by telling how she had cooked over an open fire in
her rooms in Monterey, of the year when she and Lily had only unbleached muslins of their own sewing.

Across her desk came both the plans and the evidences of the Republican fervor sweeping the nation. Campaign biographies of John, written
by John Bigelow, Horace Greeley and Charles Upham, sold by the tens of
thousands and were serialized in the Republican newspapers; lithographs
showing his dark, serious, sensitive face could be seen in home and store
windows in the North and West. The northern and western newspapers
were filled with glowing accounts of the Fremont expeditions, of his
qualities as a leader, with the tributes of the men who had suffered so
greatly with him on the trail. Testimonials from every part of the Union
sang his praises as a man of courage and character, as a leader, a student,
a thinker. English and European scientists spoke of his accomplishments;
university presidents, poets, clergymen, sprang forth to battle for "Free
Speech, Free Press, Free Soil, Free Men, Fremont and Victory!"

Each day brought her fresh gratifications and fresh disappointments:
Millard Fillmore and his Free-Soilers, who had formed a third party,
were using the Republican campaign material to publicize their own
party. William L. Dayton, who had been given the vice-presidential
nomination against John's expressed wish, contributed nothing to the
campaign. The sons of Daniel Webster and Henry Clay came out against
John Fremont for fear of southern secession; important Whig leaders,
such as Rufus Choate and Caleb Cushing, campaigned arduously among
their fellow Whigs to vote for the long-detested Democrats on the grounds
that Tom Benton had been right when he told the Missouri voters that the
South would never submit to Fremont and the Republican platform. But

on the same day there arrived a poem from John G. Whittier, which read:

> *Rise up, Fremont, and go before;*
> *The hour must have its man;*
> *Put on the hunting shirt once more,*
> *And lead in Freedom's van!*

Then a poem arrived from Walt Whitman, and another from Henry W. Longfellow. Most of the literary figures of the age extolled him in public print: Washington Irving, Edward Everett Hale, Ralph Waldo Emerson. So many songs were written that two musical pamphlets were published. Many of the songs stressed the differences between the gray, aged Buchanan and the youthful Fremont. The take-off on Stephen Foster's *Camptown Races* was the most popular:

> *The Mustang Colt is strong and young, Du da, du da,*
> *His wind is sound and his knees not sprung, Du da, du da day.*
>
> Chorus: *We're bound to work all night,*
> *We're bound to work all day,*
> *I'll bet my money on the Mustang Colt,*
> *Will anybody bet on the Gray?*

There passed over their dining-room table hundreds of letters from lifetime friends and relatives in the South renouncing them forever. "Traitor" was one of the least offensive of the names called. Of these disappointments Jessie told little to John; the disavowing letters she showed him not at all. If he were to be elected, she did not want him to go into the White House with this burden of hatred and disavowal in his soul.

During the weeks of July, while the campaign machinery was beginning to roll, the opposition press restrained itself. Then, about the first of August, the one story appeared which she knew must come; it was published simultaneously in almost every Democratic paper in the country: John was publicly labeled a "French bastard." The story of his illegitimacy was spread over hundreds of columns. She would have found it bad enough had the papers been content to tell the truth, but ever new fodder was needed, and so the facts of his birth were cruelly distorted, his mother's character and life made scandalous, his father described as a French pseudo-artist and adventurer. The fury of the charges mounted day by day; the country was asked by the Democratic press if it wanted a bastard ruling over the White House; it was asked what would happen to the morals and family life of America if this tragedy should befall them, declaring that the United States would become the butt of obscene

European laughter. As a climax the press suggested that the kindest thing that could be done for John Fremont would be to ship him, along with his ridiculous French beard, back to the gutters of Paris where he belonged.

Frantic at the intensity of this attack, she did her best to conceal the papers from John's eyes. When Francis Blair or his son Frank came in waving the sheets with murderous expressions on their faces, Jessie persuaded them not to discuss the matter with John, but to ignore the mudslinging. She remembered only too well her father's warning as the Democrats appeared momentarily to have abandoned the issue of slavery and to have determined to settle the election on the basis of John's paternity. She suffered most keenly over what Lily and Charlie would think when they saw the charges, for it was impossible to keep them from seeing the newspapers, and she did not feel that she could deceive them by denying the story. For a few days she thought she saw a look of reproach and unhappiness in her daughter's eyes, yet it was not long before the hardheaded and capable Lily somehow settled the matter to her own satisfaction and to her brother's. To Jessie's intense relief, neither child ever mentioned the matter to her.

One afternoon John returned from a walk with copies of several southern newspapers he had picked up on a Broadway newsstand. Her heart sank at the sight of him; though it was fifteen years later, the expression on his face was the same as he had worn when he had first told her of this illegitimacy. His skin was dark, his eyes small and hurt and withdrawn, his gestures were fraught with pain and awkward as he moved about the room; this was how he had carried himself when he had returned from California under arrest, for his torso was twisted at an ugly angle, his arms did not seem to fit their sockets.

She said in as quiet a tone as she could muster, "Surely this doesn't take you by surprise? You knew that the Democrats were desperate, that they would utilize any means at hand . . ."

"I know who started this," he replied fiercely. "It was the editor of the Charleston paper. He has provided the others with the material. Jessie, I'm going to put an end to this campaign of slander, not for my sake but for yours and the children."

"That's what they're trying to do, dear, get you so wrought up that you'll be indiscreet and provide them with more campaign ammunition. But they don't know you, John; they don't know that you're above vicious backbiting."

"I'm used to a fight in the open," he replied, partially mollified, "not one filled with innuendo and recrimination. I'll meet them on any grounds if they'll stand up and be men."

"You know, John," she continued in an impersonal tone, "I couldn't fully understand why it was that you wanted to remain aloof from the campaign; I am not sure that in the beginning I altogether approved. But now I see how completely right you were. You have the surest method of defeating them: let them expose themselves to the country in their full venality; every time they do so, they make votes for us."

His tenseness eased, the hate faded from his eyes. He sank into a chair, motioning for her to come to him.

"I've frequently heard that the aide-de-camp was a more capable strategist than his commanding officer. It's a fortunate thing that I encountered you first, Jessie, and not a southern editor . . ."

"The fault is partly yours, for you disobeyed your own orders. Why did you buy those southern papers? They won't publish your answers, and nothing you could say would change a slave vote anyway. Since there is nothing to be gained, why don't you avoid the campaign material?"

"Heaven knows I'm willing," he groaned. "I don't want to see another newspaper for a year."

"As aide-de-camp," she replied, "I will blue-pencil the newspapers, giving you only the genuinely important material. Then you can preserve your full energy for the work that needs doing."

He looked up at his wife, shaking his head in affectionate amazement.

"Do you realize what punishment you're going to take?" he asked. "In order to blue-pencil the vicious material you have to read it all first. Once those lines get into your head you can never get them out. Since when are you stronger than I, more able to endure a whipping?"

"I am not stronger, John; I'm just better able to relegate personal attacks on you to their proper place. I know they're false, I know they are intended solely to turn people against you; I will not react to them emotionally, I will be objective about their vituperation, and the wilder they grow the more frightened I will know they are becoming."

"Very well then, I will go back to my original conception: I shall read nothing except what you have edited. I shall remain calm and aloof and dignified"—he gave her a wistful smile—"even if it kills you!"

8

As IN THE BENTON HOME IN WASHINGTON, they occupied the back bedroom overlooking a small garden, where they occasionally found an hour of quiet and privacy. John took the front room on the second floor for his study. Three times a week a fencing master came in; the books and furniture were moved to one side and here he kept in physical form by matching rapiers with the instructors.

Instead of spending his days and weeks making campaign speeches, he assembled an extensive library on American government: there were books on the constitutional powers of the three branches, accounts of the Revolution and the convention that followed, George Bancroft's histories, biographies of the men who had played key parts in the formation of the government. He told Jessie that he needed this study to compensate for Buchanan's long experience. In the evening, if there were no guests, a big lamp would be placed in the center of the table after the dishes had been cleared, and under its light John and Lily would study their books, John annotating the margins, while Jessie answered personal letters and supplied information to newspaper editors, her pen, scratching through the hours, dipping into the inkwell with a steady motion, filling the pages of foolscap.

With the passing of the weeks the Republican cause gained momentum. Abraham Lincoln sang John's praises to ten thousand enthusiasts at Princeton and to thirty thousand at the State Fair at Alton. Demonstrations gathered: twenty-five thousand at Massillon, thirty thousand at Kalamazoo, thirty thousand at Beloit. The Tabernacle in New York was rocked by the oratory of William Cullen Bryant, Carl Schurz, Charles A. Dana, Horace Greeley, Hannibal Hamlin, Franz Sigel. Gigantic mass meetings in every city roared their approval of "Free Speech, Free Press, Free Soil, Free Men, Fremont and Victory!" Torchlight processions fired the nights, the men wearing black oilcloth hats and raincapes to catch the running paraffin of their candle lamps. Bands and military parades stretched for miles, almost a hundred thousand people marching in a Fremont parade in Indianapolis, kept in time by the blaring of fifty bands. Hundreds of orators toured the country, and many others who had never been speakers before and never would be again.

Early tests indicated that Francis Blair had been right, that given the proper man to head the movement, the Republicans could sweep the nation. However, as the Republican forces gathered strength, the southern Democrats became more desperate; Jessie was sickened by the intensity of the personal vilification. John was declared to be an habitual drunkard, to have been seen sprawling in the gutters; of being not only a slaveowner but a slave merchant, buying and selling slaves on a commercial basis for profit; of carrying on a clandestine affair with the maid in his household; of making himself a millionaire during the California conquest by buying great blocks of land, thousands of horses and cattle with government notes; of defrauding the English public through his agent Sargent; of working secretly with Palmer, Cook & Company, the San Francisco bankers, to leave Americans holding worthless mining stock.

Day by day the violence mounted. Jessie saw that there was almost no name in the language too foul to be levied against her husband. He was called a brigand, a horse thief, a despoiler of innocent Spanish women, a braggart, a cheat, a hypocrite. All the material of the court-martial supplied by General Kearny, Colonel Cooke and Lieutenant Emory was divorced from its text and spread throughout the land in anonymously printed brochures. Putting together the body of accusation, there could be little doubt that John Fremont was the lowest human creature ever spawned.

Fifteen years before, when her mother had told her on their ride to Cherry Grove how wretched it was to live in the midst of incessant public name calling, Jessie had assured her that this practice was an innocent part of the game of politics and could do no real harm. Now that her husband was being administered a more severe lashing than even her father had been obliged to endure, she realized how much truth there had been in her mother's observations. Slowly she came to perceive that one of the greatest accomplishments of the democratic form of government, the freedom of the press, was in process of destroying democracy because it was destroying the validity of popular elections. The press was misnamed; these scandalmongering sheets were not newspapers, they were prejudice papers, political lie factories. They cared less about the news than an incendiary does about the house he burns down; news was something to be thrown into the wastebasket if it hurt the paper's cause, something to be twisted and perverted to keep a political party and a special group of interests in power. The Republican press, she knew, was as bad; it was not slandering Buchanan's personal character, but it was inciting the North and the West to sectional hatred and violence. She posed this dilemma to Francis Blair, commenting that although the elimination of the freedom of the press would destroy democracy, the press was doing its best to destroy democracy anyhow. Blair, who had started one of the nation's earliest newspapers, replied quietly:

"Very few of our papers were begun to disseminate the news, Jessie. They were begun to promote a political party or a political candidate, and they have never changed their character. Some day, if elections become quieter and more civilized, papers will content themselves with reporting the news and leave the hysteria to the voters. Right now, however, the main task is to defeat their opponent at any cost."

"Yes," she agreed bitterly, pushing a batch of clippings across the table toward him. "At any cost . . . to the nation."

It was not until late September that the most devious blow of all was struck: John Fremont was charged with being a Catholic. The Know-Nothing or anti-Catholic party was strong, and had been for a number of years; anti-Catholicism was one of the most dangerous political issues of the day, filling the air with almost as much poison as the slavery issue. Now all of the incipient tragedy of religious intolerance was dragged into the campaign by the simple device of labeling John Fremont a Catholic; for once it had been established that he was a Catholic, all the anti-Catholic charges that had been circulating underground for the past twenty years could be brought into the open and made public. If John Fremont were an emissary of the Pope and were put in the White House, Catholicism would dominate American life, all Protestants would be obliterated by fire and the sword, the United States would become a Catholic country, the Pope would move the Vatican to Washington!

It was claimed that John's father was a French Catholic; that John had lived in a monastery in Baltimore; that he had carved a cross upon Rock Independence on his first expedition. To buttress the charge, documents were published showing that John Fremont and Jessie Benton had been married by a Catholic priest. Upon this one fragment of meaningless truth, the Democrats were arousing the hatred of anti-Catholics throughout the country. Jessie felt bad about this because it was her fault: if she had been willing to wait for her parents' consent, they could have been married by a Presbyterian or Episcopalian minister, and this most dangerous of all issues, that of religious intolerance, might never have been raised.

Nor was it possible to keep this conflagration from John, for an important Republican committee arrived at the Fremont home to settle the matter. Francis Blair said, "John, we know that you are an Episcopalian. The charge that you are a Catholic is costing us vast blocks of votes. You will have to publish a denial; we will have to prove that you have always been an Episcopalian."

Jessie wached her husband while he sat in the armchair by the front window overlooking the street. Since the day when she had quieted him over the attack on his parentage, he had preserved his calm and dignity, had met everyone who came to him with courtesy; and he had never uttered or written one word of anger or vilification. He looked from face to face of the committeemen and then said resolutely:

"No, gentlemen; I shall make no denial."

Everyone began talking at once.

"No denial? But you must! Silence gives assent. People will think . . . You'll convict yourself . . ."

"All of what you say is true," he replied. "They are hurting us greatly. But if I acknowledge the attack by denying it, I thereby admit that religion is a matter of political issue in this country, that people have a right to quarrel about it and refuse office to one religion or another. If I publicly deny that I am a Catholic, it will appear that I am repudiating the Catholics, that I am agreeing that no Catholic can become president of this country, that I am indifferent to the venal slanders that are being told about them. I will not dignify their campaign by participating in it. We have religious tolerance in this country. A man's religion is his private affair. My religion is my own, and I shall make no public statement on it."

He had spoken gently but his voice rang true. There was a moment of silence while the committeemen examined the floor, their shoes, the walls and the ceilings. James Gordon Bennett of the New York *Herald* finally rose and exclaimed, "Follow those convictions, Colonel, and I will sustain you." The other committee members accepted his decision, some of them with misgivings, others with pride in their candidate.

To Jessie it seemed that her husband had achieved at this moment a greatness equal to his rejection of the Democratic nomination. In his refusal to allow Catholicism to enter the campaign as an issue, she saw another instance of his philosophy of *noblesse oblige*.

Her months of thoughtful labors were having their effect. Magazines and newspapers began to run sympathetic articles about her; stories of her courtesy and hospitality began to circle the country. She was declared to be the most fitting First Lady the White House would have had since Dolly Madison; stories of her intelligence and integrity were told to the country in terms of her collaboration with her husband. As a result the Republican ticket was slowly changed to read: FREMONT AND JESSIE rather than FREMONT AND DAYTON. By October the Republicans had become as proud of Jessie as they were of John, and had jettisoned their vice-presidential candidate.

For the first time in American history a political party was bragging about their candidate's wife, intimating to the voters that the First Lady was important to the welfare of the people. The Democratic nominee's bachelordom was cited as a liability, an idea which James Buchanan sustained by making a surprise visit to the house on Ninth Street. It was eleven in the morning, and the house was empty except for the servants. Even before she could express her surprise at the visit, Jessie noted how old and puffy James Buchanan looked, as though he were unhappy at the thought that he might be elected. The white powder which seemed to cover the exposed half of his underlip had spread over his face, leaving nothing alive but the round virginal eyes.

"Why, Mr. Buchanan!" she exclaimed. "What a wonderful treat to see you in the midst of battle!"

"Ah well, Jessie," murmured Buchanan, "there is little we can do to stop them from fighting. John and I are the innocent bystanders . . .

I had a spare hour during my New York visit, and so I have come to tell you that you should be First Lady."

Astonished, Jessie laughed, "Does that mean that you are going to vote for us, Mr. Buchanan?"

"Much as I don't think John ought to be president," he replied with a twinkle, "I am sorely tempted to vote for him just to get you into the White House."

"That, Mr. Buchanan, is about the sweetest compliment anyone ever paid me. I am going to feel very badly at defeating you, after you have been so nice."

Buchanan took the chair by the window which Jessie indicated for him. "You can't defeat me, Jessie, because too many people in this country know that the election of a Republican will bring on civil war. You will recall how I worked for peace with England over the Canadian-boundary dispute, and how I tried my utmost to keep us out of war with Mexico . . ."

" . . . while Mr. Fremont and I did our best to get us into a war."

James Buchanan smiled. "Quite so. The American people know that I won't be particularly ornamental in the White House, they know I can't bring a Miss Jessie with me, but they believe that I will work for peace, peace at any price. Please believe me, Miss Jessie, any price is a good price to pay for peace. That's why I can't vote for John, even to see you First Lady: he would use force to restrain the South, and that would precipitate a war almost immediately."

"You are too good a candidate for your party, Mr. Buchanan; just as you are tempted to vote for me, my admiration might very well tempt me to vote for you. In the remote possibility that you should beat John," she continued, "your niece will make a charming mistress for the White House."

Buchanan rose, picked up his hat, made his way toward the front door. "Quite so, Miss Jessie," he said, "but the White House needs more than a charming mistress. Next time I run for president I'm going to have you nominated as my running mate. My compliments to your good husband."

In spite of the tremendous amount of work to be done and the excitement and pressure surrounding it, she had the time of her life. It was like that period when she had been at the core of American-Mexican relations, with material flowing in to her from every source, making her a kind of editor in chief of the impending war. In her position in the dining room on Ninth Street where she worked she was a kind of editor in chief of the campaign, for into this room all the information flowed, and out of it went many of the major articles and decisions of the hectic months. As the campaign gained momentum John began to make brief, friendly speeches to the crowds which assembled outside their house nearly every afternoon at five o'clock; he wrote many of the important letters himself and began to lay out the newspaper articles with her.

When the people in front of the Fremont house, after calling for John and listening to his short speech, would cry, "Fremont and Jessie!" she became uneasy lest he conclude that this was something of her doing, lest he suspect that she was unwilling to play a secondary role, that she wanted to be the equal of the presidential nominee. She began concealing some of the articles in which she was the main topic. She had exercised the utmost tact in all of her interviews and writing to play down her own part in her husband's life, to show that it had always been subsidiary. When John had proposed to her at Hassler's, she had promised, "I will never embarrass you, I want no credit or public acclaim; I will never stalk the street with a bundle of causes in my arm so that my friends will duck down side alleys when they see me coming." She was relieved to find that no one knew of her collaboration on the three Fremont reports, of the part she had played in the preparation of the court-martial defense, or of her political sessions in Monterey while John was on the Mariposa. It would take only one hint of all this to start the Democratic press crying that John Fremont was led by his wife; she was uneasy at what such a barb might do to their collaboration.

Walking up Broadway one morning she heard a group of young men singing lustily, "We go for our country and Union, and brave little Jessie forever." Soon copies of other campaign songs began arriving in the mails. There was one that was sung to the tune of "Comin' through the Rye," which was called, "O, Jessie is a Sweet Bright Lady" and went:

> *We'll with Johnny, give 'em Jessie,*
> *'Neath the White House roof;*
> *From brave Johnny and sweet Jessie,*
> *Need Southron hold aloof?*

Then there was another which made it seem that, if she were not running for vice-president, most surely she must have been running for assistant president:

> *She's wise and she's prudent; she's good as she's bonnie;*
> *For virtue and Freedom she takes a brave stand;*
> *For the Chieftain's White Mansion she's better than onie;*
> *So give her "God speed!" there, the flower o' the land.*

Francis Blair was delighted with her services: he felt that she was playing an important part in enlisting the aid of northern and western women in the Republican party. He told her that up to this time women's influence in politics had been negligible, but that his son Frank's letters, coming in from every important station in the Republican campaign, indicated that women were pleased and excited at the prospect of having a representative in the White House, that their political excitement was having a strong effect on their men. He urged Jessie to redouble her efforts. When she protested that she had to be discreet, that some people might not think it seeming for a woman to play too active a part in a national election, Francis Blair expressed astonishment at what he called her sudden reversal of a lifetime philosophy, generously confiding that if John were elected, an important portion of the credit must go to her.

"Wait until you see the new banners that are being made for our big parades," he told her with his eyes twinkling; "they read: JESSIE BENT-ON BEING FREE. It will make every woman in the North insist that she too is Bent-On being free."

It was Lily who finally got her into difficulty, but at the same time allayed her fears. Lily found a batch of suppressed articles and songs about her mother in a desk drawer. Pleased, she took them to her father. John asked his wife why she hadn't shown them to him. Jessie blushed, said with a sideward toss of her head, "Oh, they're just trivia from the women's papers, gossip about what kind of food I would serve in the White House if you were elected. They have nothing to do with the campaign."

John laid out the articles on the dining-room table, read bits of them here and there, hummed aloud a song:

> *Freedom's star shall brightly shine,*
> *And Plenty's horn shall bless ye,*
> *When in the White House we enshrine*
> *Fremont and gentle Jessie.*

When he had finished, he looked into his wife's embarrassed face. "They have a great deal to do with the election," he answered. "There are a lot of people who are going to vote for you who wouldn't vote for me. It's the first time in the history of our nation that a candidate's wife has been of importance in the election. People know you and like you, Jessie. They know how hard you've worked for me for fifteen years. They admire you for that, and they'll vote for you . . ."

"Really, John . . ."

"So take the tribute as an indication of how successful our marriage has been. People know that you are my full partner, that by electing me they'll be getting two Fremonts for the price of one. You told me in Hassler's workroom the day I asked you to marry me that the one thing you wanted in life was a good marriage collaboration; you've achieved it so well that you will be the first First Lady to be elected by popular ballot."

9

WITH THE MOUNTING ENTHUSIASM of the Republicans, the steady growth in the party's strength and the rapidity with which it absorbed segments of the old Whig party, it became evident that John Fremont had an excellent possibility of becoming the fifteenth president of the United States. The Free-Soil party was a small cloud on the horizon which might cut into John's freedom vote, but Millard Fillmore did not seem a strong candidate, and the Republicans were not much concerned. With the rise in optimism Jessie found herself unable to refrain from planning the redecoration of certain portions of the White House, in particular the old-fashioned bedrooms, the rather darkish family dining room, and the nursery, which had not heard childish laughter for far too many years. She decided to reintroduce some of the informal customs of Andrew Jackson's regime; she would abolish the formal receiving lines and the rigid dinner parties to which only those who were invited might come; the line of formally gowned ladies who assisted at receptions would be replaced by an open door. Dinner would be served *en famille;* their friends could drop in any night, those who were going through Washington would always be welcome. The White House dinner table would become an elaborate version of the Benton dinner table, where all of national politics would be rehearsed. She remembered the first time she had ever seen the White House; her father had taken her there just before a big reception and supper. The wood fires flamed brightly in each room, the wax lights burned in soft profusion, the rooms were decorated with rows of camellias and laurestinus. In the state dining room the horseshoe-shaped table, covered in the center with berries, candies, nuts and fruits, groaned under every kind of delicious food the French chef could conjure, climaxed at either end by her father's favorite Sunday dish, whole iced salmons lying in waves of meat jelly.

She would bring those days back to the White House. Every American would feel it was his second home.

The campaign was fraught with a thousand implications, yet it became evident by October that it would be decided on one fundamental: would the election of John Fremont cause the South to secede? From a hundred stumps in Missouri, Tom Benton was proclaiming that the South would secede immediately if a "Black Republican" were elected. Voters in the North began to ask, "What good will it do to elect John Fremont if it is going to cost us a civil war?"

Election day dawned sharp and clear. The Fremont family rose early, put on their best clothes, and Jessie, Lily and Charlie accompanied John while he cast his ballot. Then they went to campaign headquarters on Broadway, where by noon the election results were already coming in over Samuel Morse's telegraph. By dinnertime it became evident that John was carrying majorities in New York, Ohio, Michigan, Wisconsin, Iowa, Connecticut, Maine, Massachusetts, New Hampshire, Rhode Island and Vermont. He began to fall behind in Pennsylvania, Illinois and Indiana, all three of which states the Blairs and the Fremonts had expected to go Republican. The severest personal blow to Jessie was that Missouri yielded to Tom Benton's arguments and voted Democratic. Little Charlie and John did well by the dinner that was brought in on trays, but neither Jessie nor Lily could touch a bite: it was becoming evident that Millard Fillmore and his Free-Soilers were taking enough Republican votes to swing doubtful states into the Democratic camp.

For Jessie the excitements of the day were framed in gratifications as well as disappointments: the loyalty of the volunteer campaign workers around her, most of them young and fired by the cause of freedom; their unwillingness to concede defeat until the last possible moment, and the courage with which they kept repeating, "We may be beaten this time, but we'll elect John Fremont in 1860"; the disappointment of such men as Dana and Greeley, who came in during the evening to shake hands with them and tell them they had put up a magnificent fight; John's reserved, unemotional reaction to the growing indications of defeat; all these were compensations for the fact that they had run almost half a million votes behind James Buchanan.

They remained at headquarters until dawn, shaking hands with each departing campaigner, then dissecting the election results scientifically with Francis and Frank Blair: Fillmore and his Free-Soilers had drawn eight hundred thousand ballots, votes which would have been Republican if the North had not been split. Three hundred thousand Whigs had voted for Buchanan to avoid secession, rather than for Fremont and the party which more closely represented their own convictions. Jessie thought, If only those Whigs and northern Democrats who believed in the Republican cause had not been frightened by the threats of southern secession, John would have been elected; if only the Republicans had selected the man from Pennsylvania whom they had originally wanted for vice-president, he might have defeated Buchanan in his own state; if only Tom Benton hadn't come out against his son-in-law; if only the new party had had campaign funds to match their youthful enthusiasm; if only . . .

Ah yes, she whispered to herself as the first rays of the sun came into the now cold and forlorn campaign headquarters, if only . . .

They walked home through the deserted streets. Jessie and her daughter went into the kitchen to fry eggs and ham steaks. She served breakfast on the dining-room table across which the material of the campaign had flowed for almost five months. In the middle of his meal Francis Blair suddenly broke down; the tears began dropping into his plate.

"Forgive an old man," he said, "but I cannot contain my disappointment. I was so sure we were making a new political party, a new president and a new era. Now that it is all over we have accomplished nothing . . . nothing . . . We also ran!"

Encouraged by this breakdown, Lily began to whimper. "I had so many plans made to spend the next four years in the White House. I was going to give a lot of wonderful parties and all the boys and girls in Washington would be my friends . . ."

"I had even redecorated the White House," said Jessie with a wry smile, "put new French wallpaper in the reception room. I had set up buffet suppers for a thousand guests. Lily, stop that blubbering. Go put on your coat and walk around Washington Square until you can control yourself. If you can't take disappointments better than this, you're going to make yourself miserable through half your life."

Lily put on her coat and went out the front door. Francis Blair excused himself and went up to his bedroom. Their appetites gone, Jessie and John sat looking at each other across the table.

"Don't you think we ought to try to get some rest?" she asked.

"Yes, we should try."

They trudged wearily upstairs to their bedroom. Jessie turned down the candlewick cover. They did not undress, but slipped out of their heavy outer garments and put on robes. They were too tired to talk and too tired to sleep; they lay rigidly side by side, each thinking his own thoughts.

For the first time since she had spent the lonely and meaningless months in the sand dunes of San Francisco, five years before, she was overcome by despondency. She had always had the utmost faith in their accomplishments, yet she now had to admit that their career could best be described by what the French so aptly called *génie manqué:* they almost achieved so many magnificent results, but nothing actually came to its final and complete fruition. They started upward on so many promising cycles, rode superbly to the top—and immediately began sliding down the other side. They could not seem to make anything last, to continue in a straight line of achievement. Where did they go next, and what did they do? Would they be able to sustain the next role? Or would they once again rise to great heights, only to fall and be cast out?

She realized that this was hardly fair: John had achieved greatly as an explorer, had played a critical role in the settling of the West, had done good work as a conqueror, a civil governor, a senator, a presidential candidate. But in none of them had he been anything more than momentarily successful; the roles changed so fast as to make one dizzy! What was the matter with her husband, that this should happen? What was the matter with her? What was the matter with their marriage? She had so often concerned herself with the enigma of John Fremont, but now she saw that it was the riddle of their marriage that was truly perplexing. She found herself wondering why it was that no matter how great the difficulty or the crisis, neither of them failed in their personal relationship to each other, and yet this solid and successful marriage encountered defeat at almost every turn of its external and worldly career. Why did not a good marriage lead to an equally good career? Was there something in the one which excluded the other? Or were those gifts which enabled a man and woman to live together in love and harmony the very attributes which precluded worldly success? They failed for valid reasons, sometimes even for heroic reasons, but always in the last analysis they had failed.

Or had they? Was it because she was thinking of the end as more important than the means? Actually John had been wonderfully successful as a presidential candidate. He had been faithful to the finest elements in his own character and to the finest traditions of American statesmanship. Only she and her husband would know that; the rest of the country would consider them as having failed; but since when had this kind of knowledge between them been insufficient? Had they not been willing to risk censure and ostracism for the conquest of California? Though this eventuality had not materialized in precisely the form for which they had been prepared, had they not suffered because they could not reveal the complete picture to the nation? This time they had been working under their own secret orders: refusal to accept the Democratic nomination; refusal to order a campaign of viciousness, to enter a campaign of religious intolerance. They could not go to the public and cry, "We insisted upon winning under ideal conditions!"

No, they could not parade their virtue. They had lost, and that was the end. But between them, between man and wife, they would always know they could have been president and First Lady had they been willing to pay the price. Such confidences were good for a marriage: they gave it meaning, they gave it dimension.

John got out of bed and went into his study. She heard him opening and closing books, moving furniture around. She rose, went to his doorway and saw him standing among his papers and notes, gazing down at them with a surfeited expression. He looked up, said over his shoulder, without moving, only his dark, withdrawn eyes seeming alive:

"Can you keep a secret?"

"Now that the newspaper reporters have evaporated, I daresay I can."

"Then I will have to confess that I regret deeply having thought it necessary to be so confounded noble. I should never have turned down the Democratic nomination! Or, having taken the Republican nomination, I should have campaigned wildly, threatened civil war if I weren't elected, allowed the religious issue to be introduced. Yesterday there were thousands of people thronging in front of our house; today we are alone, not even one newspaper reporter to find out how a loser feels. I tell you, Jessie, we were idiots! We should have played the game according to the rules of politics! The rules were made for us, years ago. If we had been sensible and practical, you could be out this morning buying violet-colored curtains with pink tie-backs for the White House, instead of talking alone with your husband in a cheerless room full of useless memories!"

Having gone through her own peculiar form of despondence, she was better able to understand her husband's regrets.

"You're entitled to grumble, John," she said sympathetically; "an overdose of idealism, like a too-rich pastry, leaves a slightly sickish-sweet taste in one's mouth. But you couldn't have done otherwise, my dear, and I'm proud of you. I prefer being alone in this little room with you, in the midst of all the work and the memories that now seem useless, to buying violet-colored curtains with pink tie-backs, if I had to prostrate myself to get them. You remember what you told me that night when we first knew it was possible for you to have the Republican nomination: sometimes a lost battle contributes to the winning of a campaign. You and the Republican party have been defeated in your first national election, but you have both conducted yourself so well that it must inevitably lead to victory. Perhaps that victory will be under you in 1860; perhaps it will be under some other Republican; but whoever may win will owe you a great debt. Your candidacy brought to the Republican party almost a million and a half votes; it has established the Republicans as the permanent second party. You have preserved the dignity of the electoral process in a year of blood and passion when you could have easily inflamed your followers. This was your contribution, my dear, as important as any that James Buchanan will be able to make in the White House."

They stood looking at each other in the dark room, with the world very quiet and shut out, two forlorn figures who had been rejected, yet not disgraced; who had lost everything and yet lost nothing; to whom the cost had been tremendous, yet who now had more than they had started with. A few hours before they had been two of the three most important individuals in their nation; today, they felt like the least important within its borders, with little to do but lick their wounds.

She did not know who made the first move, or whether either of them spoke, or how they reached each other, yet like that first embrace in the foyer of her home in Washington, they were suddenly and miraculously in each other's arms. Words, almost any words at this moment, could have lied, lied tenderly, pityingly; but this kiss could not lie, it told them both that there was neither failure nor unhappiness in their world, whatever might happen, so long as they loved and worked together.

From the fullness of her heart, she murmured:

"Story writers say that love is concerned only with young people, that the excitement and glamor of romance end at the altar. How blind they are; the best romance is inside marriage; the finest love stories come after the wedding, not before."

BOOK SIX

General Jessie

THEIR COTTAGE WAS LOCATED in the center of twelve parklike acres which their manager had fenced in several years before, surrounded by white oaks and colorful California mountain shrubbery. There was a mining village named Bear Valley eleven miles away, but for the most part Fremontville had to be self-sufficient. Their meat and vegetables, eggs and milk had to be imported from San Francisco, for the miners were content with canned food and rice. Jessie brought up the two rooms of furnishings which had been stored by the flour merchant at Madame Castro's in Monterey. She missed the outlook on the sea, but the mountains were covered with a compensating carpet of golden poppies. By climbing to the crest above them they could see for a hundred miles in all directions, the San Joaquin River with its broad belt of trees, the Stanislaus and Tuolumne rivers flashing across the broad plain like metallic ribbons.

Jessie, John and their three children had driven eighty miles from Stockton in an open carriage to settle on the Mariposa. They found a number of small wooden buildings inside their enclosure; a barn was converted into a storeroom, a lean-to into a kitchen. Jessie gave their cabin a coat of whitewash on the outside, put up plank walls on the inside. When the furniture arrived from Monterey she put the white lace curtains on the windows, the Chinese matting on the floor, the high New England bedsteads in the bedroom. In the living room she laid the grizzly-bear skins before the fireplace, then placed the East India wicker chairs and the Chinese satin-cushioned bamboo couches. Lily put in a yard of chickens, geese and ducks. An Italian neighbor who was struggling to raise a vegetable garden was given the overflow supply of water from John's mines, in return for which he shared his precious crop.

The mail steamer arrived in San Francisco every two weeks, and the mail was delivered by wagon to the village of Bear Valley. When Lily rode to town on horseback she would return with panniers loaded with letters, canned goods, packages of books and magazines, fresh food and candy from San Francisco. Bear Valley was a typical Sierra mining village, with one block of saloons and general stores on either side of a deeply rutted dirt road. Miners' cabins dotted the hills behind it. There were a number of respectable and congenial families here with young wives and children, but much of the town was made up of adventurers. They made their living by claim jumping, having banded together for this purpose into what they called the Hornitas League.

John now had some forty men working for him. At the Princeton mine he had set up twenty-four stamps and a mill driven by steam which enabled him to get seventy dollars' worth of gold out of each ton of rock. The Pine Tree and Josephine mines were being tunneled and were yielding around seventy thousand dollars' worth of gold a year; the Mariposa mine was the richest, with rock of white ribbon quartz. Most of John's workers had cabins in Bear Valley or immediately around the Fremont enclosure. There were Cornish families whom he had sent over when he was in England, a number of southerners who had come in to make their fortune but had gone to work at good wages instead, drifters of all kinds who worked for a week or a month and disappeared.

Jessie set out to make the acquaintance of her neighbors: her store-room, in which she kept the foodstuffs that were brought from Stockton by wagon, became an emergency larder for the district; she found herself summoned as an emergency doctor when the Calhoun baby had a fit because he had swallowed a piece of salt pork. Their former manager had left behind some memoirs on the French Revolution, an illustrated set of Shakespeare, three volumes of medical jurisprudence. In the months before Jessie's cases of books reached her from the East, she used the texts on hand to train her little brood.

"It's going to be an irregular course," she told John. "Just what use they will be able to make of medical jurisprudence I don't know, but any study is good for their minds."

With the nucleus of her own three children, she soon found that she was conducting a school, for a half-dozen of John's miners' wives, as well as others among their Sierra neighbors, brought in their children several times a week to participate.

And so at last Fremontville came into existence. They had a store and a school. They built log cabins for the miners who came to work, and enjoyed a kind of community life. There was no church as yet; Jessie had always envisaged a log-cabin church, but somehow they did not get around to building it.

Her only real disappointment was in not having her father at Fremont-ville. Tom Benton had planned for more than a year to come with them, but almost at the last moment he had begged off: there was still so much work to be done in the East; he wanted to finish the second volume of his *Thirty Years' View;* he could not desert his fight against the break in the Union. He promised to come out later, when the second volume was finished, when he had completed his lecture series. She had tried to convince him that he had already done several lifetimes of work, that a year in the out of doors of the West would renew his strength. She was never really convinced of the validity of his reasons for staying. She wrote to him on every mail that went east, long letters describing their life in the mountains. Tom Benton never failed to send her several packets of news, as well as the newest books being published on the Atlantic seaboard.

Lily, who was now a tall sturdy girl of fifteen, liked best to roam the mountains. Her father gave her a pale cream-colored horse with a silver mane and tail whom she named Chiquita; she spent the major part of her day, when Jessie was not training her in history and poetry and reading, riding the trails and valleys of the Sierras, bringing home great armfuls of wild flowers. She frequently rode to the various mines with her father, standing in the entrance to watch the liquid gold pour from the retorts.

Jessie was fortunate in securing the services of an Irishwoman by the name of Rose, whom they quickly dubbed Irish Rose, to do the cooking; and a gnarled, bitter, mountain man by the name of Isaac, part Indian and part Negro, to take care of the horses, the grounds, and to drive the carriage. Isaac was small, dark, silent as deep night and distrustful of all the world. Neither Jessie nor John could understand why he was willing to work for them, but they soon found the answer in the manner in which Isaac lavished his love on Charlie and three-year-old Frank, teaching them to ride and handle guns.

The Sierras were full of Indian settlements; there were constant quarrels and killings between the wandering miners and the tribes. However, John had a genius with Indians: his Delaware scouts had accompanied him on four of his expeditions; the delivery of his cattle five years before to the Sierra Indians had kept them from starvation and won their gratitude; he saw to it that they were not disturbed at the springs or in their settlements. The Indian women, returning to their camps from their berry and faggot gathering, would squat under the shade of a tall pine tree that stood in front of Jessie's cottage. Since their favorite repast was a helping of turnip peelings and suet between two pieces of bread, Irish Rose saved her scraps for them, and Charlie and Frank would play with the Indian children while the squaws ate. The Indian men returning from a hunt would drop off fresh meat.

Jessie began to notice that the Indians had a name for her house. When she asked what it meant they told her: "White House." Standing under the pine tree with a group of squaws, their papooses lashed to their backs in woven baskets, Jessie turned to look at her two-room whitewashed cabin.

It's a bit different from that other White House, she thought. That evening she told her husband of the name their house had earned. John replied, "Everyone in this part of the mountains calls it that."

"Do they mean it ironically?"

"I don't think so. It's just that a coat of paint is so rare in the Sierras."

"Do you ever have any regrets, John?" she asked softly. "We would have been entertaining ambassadors instead of Indian squaws . . ."

"I don't believe in mourning the gold ore that escapes through the slough," he replied. "This is what we have."

Though he did his best to conceal his business worries from her, she knew that he had ample cause to be disturbed. According to the ruling just handed down by a California court, anyone could enter and take possession of an unoccupied mine, even though it had been occupied five minutes before, and thousands of dollars had been invested in it. John had put almost thirty thousand dollars in the Pine Tree mine, only to have his guard bribed while the miners were home in their beds. When John arrived the next morning the Hornitas League was working his mine and was legally entitled to keep it. There was no way to recover the thirty thousand dollars he had invested or to claim any part of the gold they were gathering with his equipment.

When Jessie and John had returned to Mariposa after their two years' absence, the mines were almost a half a million dollars in debt. At first she tried to understand how the mines could have run so deeply in debt when so much gold was being taken out. John assured her that the business was on a sound basis because the half-million dollars represented investments in heavy machinery, stamping mills, smelters, roads, which cost a great deal to install but would pay back their costs many times over.

With her husband taking full charge she imagined that the debts would be paid off. Instead they continued to grow. John was a good engineer and had a daring mind: he built a huge storage dam on the Merced River to give them water power, probably the first power dam built in California. He imported hundreds of Chinese workmen from San Francisco to build a railroad around the contour of the mountain so that the ore could be brought down speedily to the smelters in town. He installed new ore-crushing apparatus at the Benton Mills, where twelve stamps were in continuous operation. All this cost large sums of money, but he was confident that he would have a hundred stamps in operation in another year or so; by that time they would be clearing ten thousand dollars a week and could easily meet their obligations.

Despite his assurance, Jessie knew that he was restless. He rose while it was still dark and left for the mines, returning after the sun had gone down. Every week he was off to Stockton or Sacramento or San Francisco to see his lawyers, to try to buy new equipment, to hunt for respectable miners. He was constantly making plans for a quick trip to New York, to cross to Europe for more modern equipment, to float new stock issues, engage more Cornish miners. She knew that for some of these things there was a need, but for the most part his desire for locomotion was mental. None of his plans for a railroad to the West had yet materialized; he was now a gold miner and nothing more. There was really little else on hand for him to do: a man is not always master of his fate; there were frequent fill-in periods, hiatuses, years when he could only do what was at hand.

For her own part the founding of Fremontville had come almost a decade too late, catching her at a time when she would have preferred the cosmopolitan life of New York or San Francisco. The years since she had first arrived in San Francisco aboard the S.S. *Panama,* afire to create her own hearth, had brought deep-lying changes. The naïveté was gone from her concept of building a township. What at twenty-five years of age would have been a gay adventure had to be accomplished at thirty-three by a conscious effort. After almost having been First Lady of the United States it was difficult to throw oneself heartily into being First Lady of Fremontville. Under her guidance the settlement on the Mariposa became homelike and enjoyable for her husband and her children and her neighbors, but for Jessie Benton Fremont the ambition to pioneer had been achieved too late to vouchsafe its full flavor.

They had arrived on the Mariposa in the spring, the most beautiful time of the year in the Sierras, when the air is crystal clear and tangy with the perfume of pine, oak and chaparral. Though John was away much of the time, she was not too lonely, for a stagecoach line had been established between St. Louis and San Francisco which took only three weeks to complete the journey, and there were frequent visitors at Fremontville. A number of their old friends from San Francisco came through on hunting and prospecting trips, including Fitzhugh Beale and old Knight. An English family they had known in London sent out their seventeen-year-old son Douglass, a six-foot, spindly, towheaded boy who had been studying too hard and who needed a spell of outdoor life. Richard Henry Dana, who had seen California ten years before John first reached there, and whose book, *Two Years Before the Mast,* had made him famous, arrived for what developed into an exhilarating visit.

Then summer came. The sun beat down into Bear Valley all day, the surrounding ravines and mountains holding the heat in, clamping it down like an iron roof upon the Fremont cottage. The dust made the air almost unbearable; the ground was so burnt that the children had to make leather shoes for the dogs to keep their feet from blistering.

She was awakened early one morning by a knock at the door. A man's voice called, "Colonel, the Hornitas League has jumped the Black Drift."

As John quickly got out of bed she asked, "What does that mean?"

"Only mine work," he replied.

She lay awake for a few moments enjoying the brief coolness which came before dawn. When she rose the sun was up, hot and fiery. She had breakfast with Lily and Douglass, after which they devoted an hour to reading about the French Revolution. Ordinarily Isaac took Charlie and Frank to the barn for their play hours because it was cooler there, but today he would not let them out of the cottage. Jessie noticed that neither Lily nor Douglass had any interest in their lesson, that everybody about the place seemed jumpy. It did not take her long to conclude that the predawn visitor had brought bad news. When she demanded of Isaac what had happened, he told her plainly that the Hornitas League was attempting to take possession of their Black Drift mine. Six of John's Cornish miners were at work inside, a fact which the League had not known. Since they could not take immediate possession, the mine jumpers decided to starve the men out. If they could force the miners from the Black Drift, within a few weeks they would have taken possession of every mine on the Mariposa.

The boys climbed into an oak from where they could see past the steam mill and up the yellow road which glared in the hot sunshine. Jessie took her usual place at the front-room window. Just as the sunset sky was flaming crimson the boys caught sight of their father, his horse showing black against the sky. "Father's coming!" shouted Charlie.

"Have they got into the Black Drift?" she demanded at once.

"No," replied John, unbuckling his revolver belts, "and they're not going to. Those six Cornish miners will never be frightened out."

"John, we've got to get a message down to the governor."

"They have every pass and road blocked off with armed men. I tried to send three different expresses through today, but they were all shot at."

They did not sleep much that night, preferring to talk in the coolness of possible ways of ending this blight on the mining region. John vowed that once he got rid of the Hornitas crowd he would go to San Francisco and have his lawyers appeal the claim-jumping law.

He left at four in the morning for the Black Drift. Jessie rose when the sun came up, to find Lily missing. No one knew where she had gone. An hour later Douglass returned to tell them that Lily was riding to the governor, that she had made her way up dry creek beds and through thickets of manzanita and chaparral which concealed her horse until she got across the summit, and was already down the opposite side of the range, having eluded the Hornitas guards. Jessie flushed with pride in her daughter's courage.

Shortly before noon, Mrs. Caton, wife of the foreman in the Black Drift mine, arrived from her cabin about a mile beyond the clearing. She had a luncheon basket on her arm.

"I'm taking Caton's dinner in to him, Mrs. Fremont."

"The Hornitas League will never let you through."

"I've got Caton's revolvers strapped under my dress," the woman replied grimly. "I wish I could wear one of your Paris crinolines, then I could take in a whole arsenal."

Since she could not dissuade Mrs. Caton, Jessie decided to go with her. Mrs. Caton unstrapped one of her revolvers and put it under the napkin which covered the luncheon basket; then they walked the two miles up the narrow trail leading to the Black Drift. As they came to the sharp bend, Mrs. Caton said, "Wait here, Mrs. Fremont, where the Leaguers can't see you."

Jessie concealed herself behind a rock and watched her storm up to the entrance of the mine. The Leaguers blocked her way. Mrs. Caton reached into her basket, took out her revolver and exclaimed, "You wouldn't like to be shot by a woman! You've just got to let me carry his supper in to Caton. You have your quarrel with the colonel about mines and lands and you can fight that out with him. But I'm a poor woman that's got only my husband, and five children for him to work for. I stand by Caton."

Her uplifted revolver waved like a fan toward one and then another; they fell back and let her enter the mine. A few moments later Jessie saw her emerge from the tunnel.

"They didn't dare to shoot a woman," she said with a quick laugh when she had rejoined Jessie. "I put enough food in the basket for all six of the men in there."

When John returned that afternoon Jessie informed him of Lily's exploit. She also told him about Mrs. Caton. "She was superb, John: the picture of everlasting woman, determined to feed her man or die in the attempt! I don't know where she got the courage."

"Each of us has his own way of showing courage," replied John with a half-smile; "look at Lily. I think we've got them licked, Jessie. The hundred-degree heat up at the tunnel opening is burning out their enthusiasm. If we could hold them off for another day . . .''

Early the next morning a message was brought to Jessie which read:

Resolved at Bates Tavern that Mrs. Fremont be allowed twenty-four hours to leave her house. An escort will see you across the mountain and down to the plain. You can take your children and clothes, no harm will be done to you. If you are not gone within twenty-four hours, the house will be burned and you must take the consequences. We will kill the colonel. Signed for all present.

DENNIS O'BRIEN, President.

She thought quickly, If the men at the Bates Tavern start drinking they will never allow us the twenty-four hours' grace, but will fire our house just as they twice fired San Francisco. Going to her closet she selected her prettiest Paris muslin, with gay ribbons, and summoned Isaac to drive her to the Bates Tavern in Bear Valley. A number of the Hornitas Leaguers were lounging on the front veranda. Isaac drove up to the front steps.

Jessie rose to her feet and eyed the men in cold silence. After a moment she exclaimed in Tom Benton's senatorial voice:

"The White House and the land it stands on is ours. We intend to remain upon it. If you burn the house, we will camp there in tents. If you kill the colonel, you will have to kill me too and my three children. You are a pack of worthless cowards! If there was a real man among you, he would be out finding his own gold instead of trying to steal from others. Good day to you all."

With this she sat down, crying in the same tone she had used so many times in Washington, Paris and London, "Home, Isaac!"

When John returned at noon and learned what she had done, he whispered against her ear, "I'm a poor woman that's got only my husband and five children for him to work for. I stand by Caton!"

By this time they were seriously concerned about Lily, for if she had gotten through safely, she should have been home by now. An hour later the boys, who were holding down their observation post in the oak tree, shouted, "Here she comes!"

Lily was tired but calm. She couldn't understand why everyone was making such a fuss over her, or why Mama should shed tears of relief. She had followed a steep descent to the river, along which she had ridden behind granite boulders, then guided herself by the stars until she reached a rope ferry, where she found an old friend of Colonel Fremont's. He had dashed off for Stockton to send the alarm.

All night Jessie heard the sound of shots reverberating in the hills and the wild gallop of horses' hooves, but no one came near the White House. By noon a hundred men of the Coulterville Home Guard had arrived and were scattering through the mountains. At nightfall five hundred troops arrived under the state marshal, accompanied by a convoy of twenty-mule teams from Stockton, carrying arms and ammunition. The troops were bivouacked on the twelve acres surrounding the White House, and by the following day the Hornitas League had vanished from the Sierras.

Late that afternoon Jessie received a delegation of wives who lived in the mountains between the White House and Bear Valley. She invited them to stay for tea. The women were picturesque in their blue merino dresses, wide knitted collars and hats loaded down with flowers and ribbons. The storeroom, which had been all but exhausted by the state troops and the Coulterville Guard, was ransacked for boxed cookies, candy and Chinese tea. One of the women announced, "Had you left the cottage, Mrs. Fremont, our hills would have run blood."

A second woman, young and with golden hair, who reminded Jessie of Mary Algood, exclaimed enthusiastically, "We're going to celebrate the defeat of the Hornitas League with a regular ball: printed invitations and a ball committee and dancing in the Odd Fellows Hall."

A week later Jessie, John and Lily drove into Bear Valley to attend the first formal affair of the Sierras. The women were excited and happy-faced, the men dressed in their Sunday-best. Behind the ballroom was a room with two beds in which were put the half-dozen young babies who had to be brought. The hall was decorated with native evergreens and well lighted with candles, the fiddler and guitar player sitting back to back in the center of the room. Jessie danced twice with John, then watched her daughter be the belle of the ball, for Lily's feat was known throughout the mountains. Bemused, she remembered that she had been only a year older than Lily when she had danced at Harriet Bodisco's state wedding with young Lieutenant Fremont, amidst the jewels and lace gowns, the gold braid and thousand lighted candles, with the European orchestra playing behind its screen of palms in the ballroom.

Toward the end of the evening Lily came to her with two high points of color in her cheeks to confess that she had just received a proposal of marriage. Jessie was shocked, for she still thought of Lily as a child. For the first time in sixteen years she understood why her father had fought so hard against her precipitate marriage to Lieutenant Fremont when she had been only seventeen.

Poor Father, she mused. I surely gave him a difficult time. But even so, I was right. If Lily finds a nice young man in these mountains, I shan't stand in her way.

2

Now THAT PEACE DESCENDED upon the Sierras, Jessie asked if they might not build themselves a more adequate home.

"You know, John," she said, "you can calculate to a fraction the displacement caused by a man-of-war, but there is no calculating the displacement caused by two small boys."

John laughed at the phrase. "You won't find it easy building up here. It's a long haul for materials from San Francisco and Stockton."

"I have no intention of erecting a two-story brick house."

"Then go ahead, but don't spend more than five thousand dollars. That is all the cash we can spare now. I have to go down to San Francisco; are there some things I could order for you and bring back with me?"

"No," she replied with an enigmatic smile. "I can handle everything from here. You'll be back for Christmas Eve, of course?"

"Of course."

As soon as her husband left, Jessie set about bringing her new house into being: several pine trees were cut down and the trunks trimmed so that they made smooth rollers. The five detached buildings on the twelve acres, including the barn, storeroom, kitchen, office and a far cottage were hoisted onto the rollers by a grizzled old man from Maine and his three sons, who had done all the hauling of the logs to make John's mills and dams. Ox teams pulled them to the White House, where they were joined together.

She spread word throughout Bear Valley that she wanted to have her home completed in two weeks, in time for Christmas Eve; because the countryside had just come through a harrowing time together, the men and their wives laid aside more pressing tasks to help her. Carpenters joined the six buildings together and built a broad veranda across the full length of the house. The roof was covered with uniform shingles, the front with neat planking. A competent bricklayer came for three days to the White House to build a sturdy chimney. She scoured the countryside for all the windowpanes she could find, running them in a solid line across the front and back of the rooms and achieving a Queen Anne effect, with a magnificent view of Bear Valley.

At the end of the first week the house had been put together, the wide veranda built, the heavy mechanical work completed; she now had another week in which to finish the interior. On no other frontier could she have found the luxurious furnishings that were available in Bear

Valley, for miners made their money unexpectedly and fast, and when they had it to spend they wanted the world's finest goods. In the crude, unpainted plank stores of Bear Valley she discovered imported French wallpapers, as lovely as any she had seen in Paris, the most expensive carpeting and rugs imported from the Orient and Europe, rolls of Chinese silks from which to make curtains. She bought matting for the wide veranda, cane furniture and hammocks, then enclosed it with green Venetian blinds. She framed the windows with full straight woolen draperies with a deep frill atop; they could be closed at night to shut out the darkness and give a sense of intimacy to those sitting before a wood fire reading or chatting by waxlight.

One of the miners had been a scene painter for the St. Charles Theatre in New Orleans; he took charge of the delicate wallpapers. The parlor was done in cream-white and gold with deep borders of dull red, Jessie's bedroom in pale blue with white roses. The dining room was made the formal chamber of the house, being hung with walnut and oak papers, which gave it the air of a great house in the East. The men who sewed sacks for the ore of the mines came down with their needles and thread to sew the carpeting. An old piano was found in Stockton and brought up by twenty-mule team; Jessie located some strings in the store at Bear Valley and summoned the blacksmith, Manuel, a Virginia Negro, who wound on the new strings with a winch, tightening them until Jessie, who was tapping at the keyboard, would exclaim, "Stop!"

By the end of the tenth day the fireplace was finished and she lit a fire in the hearth. It drew perfectly. On the twelfth day the painters finished giving the outside and the roof a coat of white paint, for she was unwilling to give up the name by which the Fremont home was known throughout the mountains.

Charlie and Frank were sent with Isaac up the side of the mountain to select a fir tree. Jessie trimmed it to the right size, then brought it into the dining room. She and Lily brushed the long cones with glue and covered them with gilt paper. The tree was set in the corner by the brick fireplace with a gold star resting on the top dark green spire. A Vienna baker who had recently opened his shop in Bear Valley made candles of beeswax for her, coloring them with gold leaf. For a month she had been ordering her Christmas candies, fruits, picture books, toys and games, as well as inexpensive colored jewelry for the Indians; the gifts were now wrapped separately and placed beneath the tree. The boys distributed wreaths of ground pine about the house and hung up the wild-rose haws which had to take the place of holly berries.

A heavy mist rolled down the mountains before dusk on Christmas Eve, a mist which Jessie knew would delay John. Lily and Douglass were sent down the trail on their horses with lighted torches to cheer him on the last few miles. By dark she saw the torches coming back toward the house; she refreshed the lights in the Queen Anne windows. When John dismounted, walked through the wide veranda and into a house that had not been there two weeks before, he was stupefied. Jessie led him in this dazed condition from room to room, while she pelted his unhearing ears with descriptions of the scene painter who had hung the wallpapers, the blacksmith who had tuned the piano, the sack sewers who had laid the carpets. At the end of the tour she exclaimed in final triumph, "And it cost me only one fifth of what you said I might spend."

She had invited everyone who had worked on the house to see the tree on Christmas Day, and to receive their gifts of appreciation. They came on horseback, in carriages and prairie schooners all during the afternoon, but the guests were by no means confined to those who had thrown up her house and painted and decorated it. Wives and mothers who had been in the Sierras for almost ten years without having seen a Christmas tree came with their husbands and children to ask if they could not have just one look. The Bear Valley committee arrived, bringing their husbands, and along with them many of the wives and mothers who had been at the Odd Fellows ball, wanting nothing more than to see a lighted Christmas tree again. The miners came in from the Fremont mines, the bachelors in groups, the married men with their families. The Indian women arrived with their papooses; they could not be persuaded to come indoors, but sat in their regular seats under the trees gazing through the windows.

By dusk Jessie began to count noses and saw that she had almost a hundred friends and neighbors thronging her home. Many of these people, who had ridden for hours to get to the White House, had had no food since morning. Irish Rose was equal to the task: platters of cold meats and hard-boiled eggs, crackers and rolls and cakes were circulated among the guests; even Isaac thawed out for the occasion and consented to pass the glasses of wine. There were beads and necklaces for the Indians, toys for each of the mining children. At seven o'clock, when everyone had crowded into the parlor and the adjoining dining room, Jessie lit the candles on the tree.

A hush fell over the group. There were tears in many eyes. The old father from Maine, whom Jessie had named Kriss Kringle, fell to his knees before the tree, offering up a fervent prayer of thankfulness to God. One by one the miners, their wives and their children went on their knees and joined in the prayer. Jessie and John knelt with Lily at their side and their two sons before them. When the old man's prayer came to an end there was a moment of silence; John whispered to his wife: "You told me that if only we had a church, Fremontville would be complete. Here is your church."

3

THE BOYS PLAYED in the winter snows and came in bright-eyed and rosy-cheeked. An old friend from New York, Hannah Kirsten, who had come out to visit her brother in San Francisco, journeyed up to the Mariposa for a month's visit with Jessie. Hannah was young, with a happy disposition and a fine musical talent. The White House was filled with the beautiful music of her songs and piano playing.

One day when Jessie and Hannah were sitting on the veranda facing the long draw up Bear Valley, they saw a strange-looking creature coming along the trail, wobbling from side to side on a small horse, his feet almost touching the ground.

"By the Eternal," exclaimed Jessie, "it's Horace Greeley!"

Greeley, founder of the New York *Tribune,* was tall, skinny, angular; neither his head, torso nor limbs seemed to bear much relation to each other, as though all three had been sired by different parents and stuck together with mucilage. His head was round, with a bulging forehead, his hair worn long and around his face. One trouser leg was stuffed inside his high boot, the other was hanging out. The rest of his costume consisted of a string necktie which hung over one shoulder, a white linen suit, a tall white hat and a bulging umbrella.

After three weeks of being bumped around in a stagecoach, of putting up in frontier cabins and inns, Horace Greeley was as dumbfounded at Jessie's home as John had been. That evening as they lingered late over dinner in the oak-and-walnut-papered dining room, he complimented Jessie on her gift for getting things done.

"You have executive ability, Jessie," he said wistfully; "my wife has none at all. Our servants come in the front door and go out the back. For years now I have really had no home. My wife cares nothing about food; the rooms are a boar's nest of confusion and discomfort. It's impossible for me to bring friends home. When she grows angry at my preoccupation she will seize the manuscript on which I am working and fling it into the fire. Ah well, I love my Mary, but if only she had a little executive ability . . ."

Jessie and John had talked little national politics since their arrival at Mariposa, for John had no intention of going through another presidential campaign. Greeley, whose trip west had been prompted by his desire to test the political temper of the times, gave them a brilliant survey of the increasing struggle between the North and the South. He was in·

censed at President James Buchanan, speaking of the "curse of the good man, the honest man, the man who compromises for peace at any price"; for Buchanan was permitting the South to arm itself, to deplete the northern store of munitions, to talk openly of rebellion, while at the same time he kept the North from preparing for war by decrying preparedness as an attitude which might provoke the South to rebellion. Greeley insisted that if John had been elected he would have thrown cold water on talk of rebellion by arming the North, by strengthening national forts and garrisons in the South, by allowing the South no opportunity to prepare itself for a conflict.

Jessie asked, "Can we use force to keep the South in the Union?"

"Yes," replied John. "Just as we use force to keep one man from murdering another; or, more apposite, from committing suicide."

It was only a few days after Greeley's departure that Jessie received a letter from Eliza telling her of her father's death in Washington. She was totally unprepared for the blow; though Tom Benton's strength had been failing, he had seemed hardy when she left him a year before. He had been promising to come out to California that spring.

When John returned from the mines, he explained that Tom Benton had died of cancer; that her father had known of his sickness when he bade her farewell the year before. That was why he had not come out to California with them.

"Your father swore me to secrecy; he said he didn't want you grieving or spending your days with the anxiety of his death hanging over you. Now you know how hard it was for him to let you go . . . He went to bed the day we left, and he never got up again."

Through her tears Jessie said, "He wanted to die with his hand in mine; he told me that after Mother's death. Yet he let me go, knowing that he would never see me again . . ."

By June the fierce summer heat came again to Bear Valley; there was no breath of air, nor were the nights long enough for the hotness to rise out of the valley. John had been going into San Francisco every few weeks. In the middle of July he suggested that she accompany him, for it was cool in the city. They crossed the Tuolumne and Stanislaus rivers by ferry, then took the night boat from Stockton, putting their carriage and horses on board. In the morning John drove her along Golden Gate strait, stopping the horses before a promontory which projected out into the bay, pointing straight at Alcatraz Island. A house sat primly in the midst of mountain laurel and small trees whipped by the ocean winds. Standing on the edge of the bluff, with the bay and the strait just ahead of her, the mountains of Contra Costa beyond and the blue Pacific to the west, Jessie exclaimed, "What a heavenly spot. Whose is it?"

"Yours."

It was now her turn to be speechless.

"I bought the house and twelve acres from a San Francisco banker for forty-two thousand dollars. We always said our California home must overlook the Pacific. Do you like it? It's called Black Point. We can spend as much of the year as we want here, and go up to the White House for the spring and fall months. I've deeded it in your name, Jessie. It will always belong to you and the children."

Breathlessly happy and excited, she cried, "May I see the inside of the cottage?"

The house was simple but sturdily built. As she walked through the empty rooms she exclaimed, "We'll build a glass veranda all around the seaside: that'll cut off the winds and leave us free to watch the ships go in and out at all seasons of the year. I'll build a summer house 'way out there on the edge of the bluff for the warm weather. We'll bring in paint and wallpaper and within a few weeks you won't recognize the place."

She spent an active month redecorating and furnishing her new home, surrounding it on three sides with a glass veranda on which she placed lounging chairs and writing tables, enlarging the parlor to twice its size, with a native stone fireplace filling one whole wall. She laid out paths among the roses and fuchsia, while John built a stable for their horses and carriages. She knew it was extravagant to buy all new furniture, rugs and draperies when she had so many beautiful things in the White House, but they would spend many months of the year at the mines and she did not have the heart to upset it in any way.

When the children's bedrooms had been freshly wallpapered and carpeted she sent a message to the Mariposa. Irish Rose and Isaac brought the two small boys and Lily down in safety.

It was nine years since she had climbed down the sides of the S.S. *Panama* and been carried over the shallow surf by a sailor. Then there had been only a few crude buildings bordering Portsmouth Square; today San Francisco was a city with rows of well-built homes, a prosperous business district and small factories springing up on the outskirts. Trade with the Orient kept the harbor full of ships, while the overland stage and the pony express were bringing in settlers and mail across the mountains and plains in thirteen days from New York and ten days from St. Louis. Samuel Morse's telegraph had been completed to San Francisco; there was a steam railroad on Market Street, omnibuses to the Presidio, horsecars in the business district. A literary magazine, the *Golden Era*, had been established to serve as the counterpart of Boston's *Atlantic Monthly*. The best plays and concert artists included San Francisco in their itineraries; there was a full season of opera.

Jessie enjoyed San Francisco: it was young enough to be awkward in its growing pains, yet full of an impetuous vitality which kept events so rapidly on the march that each day the city was born anew. Her big parlor and glassed-in porch, overlooking the strait, the ocean and the bay, became San Francisco's first literary and political salon. With her father dead, she had no desire to return east to live. The children loved Black Point, they found playmates on the settlement overlooking the strait and spent their hours wandering the dunes and the beaches below. The fog bell clanged in a low friendly tone, the circular light on Alcatraz Island reminded her of the lighthouse at Siasconset.

She was now thirty-four, no longer young, but maturity had brought its own kind of beauty. Her hazel eyes seemed deeper in color and more compassionate; her mouth was more understanding than resolute. A touch of gray was beginning to show at the center part in her hair. The fragile oval had filled out a little. There were adaptations too in her temperament: she no longer fought so hard for every next hour, every next month; she had developed a kind of rugged acceptance, if not of every twist and turn of their fortune, at least of their over-all pattern. She no longer was so determined to rush out and confront fate in its lair; she was willing to wait a little, to let fate meet her halfway. Nor did she feel that every hour not spent in the pursuit of one's major aim was an hour wasted; she had come to accept the fact that their professional career, like their marriage, had its own pace and rhythm; now it moved slowly, seemed mired in the morass of petty activity; now it rushed forward to some momentous achievement. She no longer had the desire to be forever rushing forward; it was good to renew one's strength, to evaluate the past, gain perspective.

Yet if she were maturing in some ways, in others she could not feel that she was a day older than when she had driven to Mrs. Crittenden's house to be married by Father Van Horseigh. Her external life might wear a little thin, sometimes pull at the seams, but the miracle of her marriage never faded. Even after seventeen years, her sense of excitement at John's physical presence had not abated. The touch of his hand, his kiss, his embrace were as magically joyous and delightful as they had been in those early weeks of their honeymoon in the back bedroom of the house on C Street. On the Mariposa she had been obliged to use the twin New England bedsteads which had been stored in Monterey all these years; there had been no chance to reach out a hand for the reassuring touch of his presence should she awaken during the night. Now in San Francisco she bought a big cherrywood bed similar to the one they had had in St. Louis, and here, during the long cool nights, they listened to the fog bell and the gentle lapping of the waters at the base of the cliff, talking of their plans.

After nearly two decades of marriage, and the bearing of five children, her passion for her husband ran as strong as in the earliest days. Before she had met John she had gathered that the physical side of marriage was a burden women carried in order to bear children, and to accommodate their husbands. Any concept of fulfillment was unthinkable to a respectable wife. Jessie had known this to be a monstrous lie from the first moment she had encountered John Fremont; it had proved to be a lie during the rapturous days of their honeymoon; and it was more than ever a lie today. The years might grow old, and the world, but never a good marriage.

And now, even as on that New Year's morning of 1842, she lay by her husband's side, listening to his steady breathing, ruminating over the enigma of John Fremont which she had never solved: she felt in him an aloneness, a seeking for something that can never be found, a last hidden rampart of self-defense. His life had fallen from its sublime heights to mediocre routine; at the back of his brain was the compulsion to unceasing expedition, though it might be only up to the Mariposa. Dimly she perceived that he was longing for that ultimate moment of triumph, that single greatest moment of his life, from which all the rest had been a falling away: when he had so divinely risen above human strength and forced the crossing of the Sierras. In her love for him there was mixed this fine leaven of pity, pity at the unceasing urges that pushed him forward and made no place his home, no hearth his undying fire. Nothing that could ever happen to John could make him secure: all his life he would be the pursuer and the pursued, pursuing legitimacy, pursued by all the phantoms to which the insecure mind falls prey.

For herself she had learned that the future must inevitably arrive, that they were not likely to pass the rest of their lives serenely in some uneventful corner; that was neither in their own character nor in the character of the times. Even here, living in her lovely and secluded home, several thousand miles from the core of the slavery controversy, they had been caught up in the struggle that was being waged to take California out of the Union in the event of secession.

Their companion in the fight against the growing number of slavery sympathizers in California was the Reverend Thomas Starr King. Former minister of the Hollis Street Church in Boston, King had come to San Francisco to be pastor of the Unitarian church. He was a man of wide learning, a passionate warrior for freedom and a mesmeric speaker in the manner of Henry Ward Beecher and Theodore Parker. He was young, slender, beardless, with yellow hair which hung down over his collar.

and a powerful, open face, with great burning eyes. Jessie and King became friends, for they had much in common: the love of liberty, books and writing, the exciting march of ideas. They differed only in one particular, their devotion to San Francisco. King never got over being astonished at the lack of grace and elegance of the frontier, the houses which seemed to be chasing each other up hill and down dale, the throngs of Chinamen on the streets.

One Sunday he complained that it was impossible for him to get his work done because all San Francisco thought it could walk up to his front door, knock, and spend the rest of the day discussing politics or religion with him. "I can't even salvage sufficient time or privacy to write my sermons, Mrs. Fremont. I declare, I shall have to take pencil and paper and hide in the dunes."

"Why not use the little summerhouse we've built on the bluff?" asked Jessie. "No one need know you're working there."

He accepted with alacrity. Each day at one o'clock he arrived with his papers and set himself up in the arbor to read, study and write the articles which appeared in the Boston *Transcript* and the *Atlantic Monthly*. By late afternoon he came up the trail, his tawny hair blowing in the breeze, his slender body swinging along jerkily. Over his several cups of tea he would read Jessie the sermons, articles and stories he had written, ask for her criticism, defend volcanically everything he had done, only to incorporate many of her suggestions in his work the following day. Once in passing he mentioned the name of Bret Harte.

"Bret Harte," murmured Jessie. "Isn't he the one whose stories I read in the *Golden Era?*"

"Yes, he's a printer on the *Golden Era*. He writes his pieces in the composing room, not with pencil but with galley type."

"Think how strong the writing force must be within him if he can set up whole stories in type! I should like to meet him. Won't you bring him here sometime?"

King said hesitantly, "He's so dreadfully shy . . . he won't go anywhere . . . particularly when there are ladies present. Among other reasons, he's poor; he has only that miserable printer's wage; his clothes are worn thin."

"Very well," she replied, "if he is too proud to come to me, I am not too proud to go to him. We need vigorous young writers who can dramatize the West."

The next afternoon she went to the office of the *Golden Era* and asked if she might speak to Mr. Bret Harte. After ten minutes a young man of about twenty-four came down. He was of medium height, slight of build, with a black mustache and a thatch of intensely black hair parted sharply on the left side. He was dark-complexioned, one eye seemed larger than the other; he gave the impression of a turbulent young man, wanting to be pleasant, yet not knowing how.

"Forgive me for intruding upon you, but the Reverend Thomas King has talked of you and I have read several of your stories in the *Golden Era*. I liked them very much, in particular one in which your central character was like an old innkeeper Colonel Fremont knows in Tuolumne, who has good within him, behind a perfectly abominable front."

Bret Harte relaxed a little.

"Won't you come to dinner this Sunday? We should all be friends."

On Sunday he appeared in a long cutaway black coat, wide gray trousers, a low-fitting wide collar and a beautiful gray cravat.

He has spent his last dollar for a new outfit, mused Jessie; but it will do him good, for it will make him feel more at ease.

She led him out to the glass-enclosed veranda. Of his own writing he would say nothing. However, by the end of the afternoon, after John had told him stories of the Hornitas League, young Harte lost a little of his self-consciousness. He even seemed to accept with eagerness John's invitation to dinner the following Sunday.

During the week she had a note asking if he might come an hour earlier to discuss a story. She walked with him along the cliff, with the sun sparkling on the water. He talked about the character of the miners he was describing. She told him of her husband's experiences. He dropped in unexpectedly the following Thursday to read her the new story and to ask for her criticism. When she had finished he sat staring down at the carpet.

"Do you know, Mrs. Fremont," he said, "this is the first constructive criticism I have had. I find it very good to be able to talk about my stories, to treat my characters as living beings, capable of modification and change."

From then on Bret Harte came every Sunday to dinner, reading them the result of his week's work. She thought the stories imitative and precious, but they showed a constantly growing power. She and Thomas King sent his stories east with recommendations to the newspaper and magazine editors.

One rainy afternoon, when the rest of the company was late in arriving, Jessie said, "You have told me so little about yourself, Mr. Harte. Where did you come from? What brought you to San Francisco?"

There was an awkward silence before Harte began in a constrained voice to tell how his widowed mother had come to California to marry a Colonel Williams in Oakland; how he had followed her when he was eighteen; worked in apothecary shops, been a private tutor, an expressman, taught school in a small town and worked on mining-camp newspapers. He was now twenty-four, determined to have a literary career, but with no idea of how he could earn his bread and at the same time keep enough free time to write his stories.

"What is the name Harte?" she asked. "We knew a family of Hartes in London, but you don't look English. You look more like one of the Latin races, Spanish perhaps?"

His skin became darker than she had seen it before.

". . . Harte is not really my name; the *e* on the end was placed there accidentally by a printer, and I've never had the courage to take it off. You see, Mrs. Fremont . . . my name is Hart; my grandfather was a Jewish merchant in New York. I've never concealed the fact that I was a Jew, but that accidental *e* on the end of my name enabled me to find a job with the *Golden Era* . . . and to have my stories published."

He leaned toward her, exclaiming, "Mrs. Fremont, you can't understand what it is to be a minority of one, to be despised, not because you are inferior but because you are different."

Jessie's heart ached for the young man.

"My dear Mr. Harte, since I first met Mr. Fremont I have known that everybody is a minority of one, that nobody truly belongs and that every human soul is a lonely stranger."

"But how could you know that?" Harte exclaimed. "You who come from one of the most prominent families in America?"

She told him the story of her mother, who had been a tragic minority of one, living in a world which everyone else had thought magnificent; of her husband who had first revealed to her the terrors of insecurity; and finally something about herself, how in trying to follow the implications of Anne Royall's philosophy, she had so often stood alone.

"I take courage from what you have told me, Mrs. Fremont, and I thank you," said Harte. "If it is my lot to bear intolerance, then it is different in detail from every other man's burden, but no different in degree."

"Continue to write your stories, Mr. Harte," she urged. "Perfect your craft, make our West known to all the world."

Hesitantly he replied, "That is not so easy to do. My work as a printer leaves me little time to write. I have agreed to take a job on an Oregon newspaper; the wage is higher . . ."

Charlie and Frank were attending public school, in addition to which Jessie gave poetry and literature classes for the youngsters of the neighborhood three afternoons a week in her parlor. Lily had no interest in Jessie's poetry, nor did she care for the theater or opera, but at seventeen she was slowly taking over the management of the household. She liked to do the shopping, the paying of the bills and balancing of the books. She began edging her way into John's confidence about the mines and Mariposa business, trying to understand what was going on, proclaiming that if she were a man she would become a mining engineer and run the Mariposa for her father.

Even as Lily was making a stubborn effort to understand her father's business, its status and logic were growing more obscure to Jessie with each passing day. She knew that they had made a good deal of money from the increased values of their San Francisco real estate and the cattle ranches in southern California; she also knew that the mines were turning out some twenty thousand dollars' worth of gold dust a week. She was therefore taken by surprise when John told her that he was obliged to sell half of the Mariposa. To her startled inquiries he explained that the Mariposa was in debt for one million two hundred thousand dollars; that they had solid assets to show for this indebtedness, but that they could never pay it off from current income. When he explained that it would be a load off his mind if he could sell half of their holdings, pay their debts and be out in the clear, she agreed that it was wise to buy such freedom from worry. He thought that the best way to sell would be by floating stock issues in France, and told her that after the presidential election in November they would go to France to complete the arrangements, then take the grand tour of Europe for which they had made plans while Jessie was carrying the little Parisienne.

The Fremonts played a quiet but determined part in the election of Abraham Lincoln. They had never met him, but they had followed his debates with Stephen A. Douglas on the slavery issue two years before with intense interest, and had felt that Mr. Lincoln had the best of the argument. Jessie spent the months between the nomination and the election writing articles for the California newspapers, holding meetings in her home to establish Republican clubs. She organized mass rallies and parades and sometimes spoke with Thomas King to audiences of several thousand people. John made no public appearances, but devoted his time to combating a plot to force California to secede if Lincoln were elected.

When the final count was taken, Jessie saw that Abraham Lincoln had better fortune than they had had four years before. Douglas and Breckinridge were Democrats who split their party even as the Free-Soil Party had split the Republicans in 1856. Had there been but one Democrat running, Mr. Lincoln would have been hopelessly swamped. He had received a million votes less than a majority; comparatively, John had done better against Buchanan than Lincoln had done against Douglas and Breckinridge. She was struck by the twist of fate which placed one man in the White House in Washington, D.C., and another man in the White House in Bear Valley, California.

With the election over, and a loyal Union general arrived from Washington to command the strengthened federal garrisons, California was safe. John completed their preparations for the journey. The steamship tickets were purchased, plans were made to leave the children with Eliza and Susie. Everything was in readiness for what was to be a combination business and pleasure trip. Jessie was looking forward to the days of uninterrupted companionship with her husband.

Three days before they were to sail she had to make a hurried trip to Palmer, Cook & Company. She had always been terrorized by the steepness of the San Francisco hills and avoided them whenever possible. This day she told Isaac to follow the most direct route. Isaac had taken horses and carriages down far steeper hills in the Sierras, but he had no understanding of paved streets; in the middle of Russian Hill one of the horses fell to its knees and the carriage overturned. Jessie was thrown out. When she awakened in her own bed at home she found that her left arm had been broken. John prepared to cancel their trip until she was well, but Jessie knew that the business plans were arranged for immediate negotiation, that if they were set aside now they might never go through as he wanted them.

"You go ahead, John," she urged. "Take care of your business and come back as fast as you can."

He waited for two days before making up his mind. At the last moment he yielded to her persuasions, hurriedly packed his suitcases and sailed for Panama.

Lily was an excellent nurse; the girl was so delighted at not having to leave San Francisco that Jessie sometimes thought her daughter believed the carriage accident to have been the working of divine providence. She drifted through the days, missing her husband but not too unhappy, content to read, to visit with her friends, to gaze out over the waters. When Fitzhugh Beale was installed as surveyor general of the Land Office she persuaded him to appoint Bret Harte as a clerk at one hundred dollars a month. Beale did not take to the idea of having a writer use the Land Office for his private Bohemia, but she assured him that Harte would do his full share of the work and still have time and energy for his writing. In gratitude Bret Harte exclaimed, "If I were to be cast away on a desert island, I should expect a savage to come forward with a three-cornered note from you to tell me that, at your request, I had been appointed governor of the island at a salary of two thousand four hundred dollars."

She had a letter from John telling her that he had spent an hour with

Abraham Lincoln at the Astor House in New York. Mr. Lincoln still had strong hopes that all differences could be settled without reverting to war, but John wrote to his wife in confidence, "With the inflammatory press and inflammatory conversations on every hand, I am convinced that actual war is not far off." He had offered his services to Mr. Lincoln, and the president-elect had assured him that if war should break out, he would be named to an important command.

In her enforced leisure Jessie had time to wonder why John couldn't have sold half of the Mariposa right here in San Francisco, or in St. Louis, Washington or New York. Why must he go to the farthest possible place to float a stock issue? Why France, of all places? Was it because the farthest place took the longest to reach, and it was the journey rather than the arrival that he wanted?

She did not hear from him again until the end of March, at which time she received a discouraging note telling her that the French were so frightened at the impending war in the United States that it was impossible to sell half of the Mariposa. He did not know what he was going to do next, but he promised to write in a few days and tell her of his decision.

Then things began to happen so fast that she was hardly able to keep them in proper sequence. On April 12 Fort Sumter was fired on. President Lincoln immediately called for volunteers. Next she heard from Postmaster General Montgomery Blair that John had been commissioned a major general. He was to be one of the four major generals of the regular army, the highest post available in the United States. His headquarters were to be in St. Louis, where his command would include not only Illinois and Missouri but all the states and territories between the Mississippi River and the Rockies, that vast expanse which John Fremont had been the first to map and open to organized immigration. Both the press and the public received the announcement with jubilation, for no man in America knew this country, foot by foot and trail by trail, as well as General Fremont.

With a quick rush of joy she realized that John once again would be back in the uniform he loved. He had passed twelve years as a civilian, and now that they were over she could admit how directionless those years had been. It was tragic that it had taken a civil war to fulfill her prediction that John would one day be a general, but when the war was over he would remain in the Army, perhaps in command of the Presidio right here in San Francisco!

In an astonishingly quick time she received a letter from her husband to the effect that he was buying arms and guns as wildly as his own credit and the backing of Ambassador Adams in England would permit; that

Barracks, Sarah Brant was on her way north and Jessie had begun to move the Brant furniture out of the two lower floors.

With a company of soldiers delegated to work under her orders, she set up the printing press, telegraph office and an emergency arsenal in the basement, as well as a room for the newspaper correspondents. The first-floor foyer she turned into a reception room; in the spacious drawing room and dining room desks were arranged for the lower-ranking officers who would have to interview the hundreds of visitors. The large front bedroom on the second floor she made into John's office; the two bedrooms adjoining it were stripped of furniture, and long plank-surfaced tables set up on horses for maps and diagrams. She then moved three desks into the second-floor hallway, one for herself in an alcove just outside John's door, the other two for Lieutenants John Howard and William Dorsheimer, John's young aides-de-camp. On the third floor there were a number of small dormer-window bedrooms which had formerly been used by the governess, tutor and bookkeeper of the Brant family. Jessie took the smallest of the rooms for herself, with John on one side and Lieutenants Howard and Dorsheimer, who were routed out of bed at all hours of the night, on the other.

The first to arrive for a conference was young Frank Blair, flaming with eagerness to help the Union gain control of Missouri. In the five years since Frank had stumped the country campaigning for John and Jessie, he had made important strides toward achieving his father's ambition of seeing him in the White House. Elected to Congress from Missouri, he had taken his place as one of the most intelligent and dynamic of the young legislators. Frank had especially endeared himself to the North for his superb daring and almost fanatical loyalty during the past troubled months: helping to form home-guard companies out of the Republican Wide Awake clubs; harassing the War Department to send in loyal troops in charge of Captain Nathaniel Lyon; working with Lyon to muster four regiments of loyal citizens into the Missouri volunteers; preserving the arsenal for the North and capturing Camp Jackson.

Jessie was alone in John's front office, tacking up regional maps, when a sentry ushered Frank in. He approved of her establishment of general headquarters; in return she thanked him for the Blair family's efforts in securing John's appointment as commander of the West.

"He was a natural selection," replied Frank quickly. "His knowledge of the West, its people and terrain, the fact that the inhabitants know and respect him, will be of great advantage to the Union cause. But I must tell you quite frankly, Jessie, that I tried to get Nathaniel Lyon appointed because I believe that he is going to become the greatest of all the Union generals in the field. However, I quickly came to see that Father and my

brother Montgomery were right: General Lyon's place is not at headquarters, but on the battlefront; General Fremont is by far the wisest
choice for commanding officer."

John came in, the two men clasped hands fervently, then plunged at
once into a discussion of strategy, working with the maps that lay strewn
over the rough plank tables. Jessie listened carefully while Frank urged
that John reinforce General Lyon immediately, and John informed him
that he had orders from President Lincoln and Secretary of War Cameron
to use all available troops to hold Cairo. John turned the conversation
from strategy to supply, urging Frank to send him the best supply merchants in St. Louis, in particular the men whom he knew to be trust-
worthy.

Jessie rose at dawn of her second day in St. Louis and rode out to the
Jefferson Barracks, where the fever patients and the wounded were quar-
tered. The Union Sanitary Commission was in process of formation, but
it had not yet begun to function in the West. As she walked down the
long barrack aisles she saw that there were no shades on the windows to
keep the blazing sun off the sick men, no nurses to tend them, no tables
or medical accessories. Mugs of black coffee and pieces of salt pork were
laid on the chests of the sick and dying men, but most of them were too ill
to raise the food to their lips.

Horrified, she returned to St. Louis and made a round of the stores,
banging her fist on the locked doors until her flesh was bruised, begging,
pleading, demanding supplies for the boys in the hospital. The Union
sympathizers gave freely; those sympathetic to the Confederacy were determined to give her nothing. Jessie cried at the owner of one store, whom
she had known for years: "If you want to abandon the Union, that's
your own business, but you cannot take it out on a sick boy who has
probably been in and out of your store since he was a child. Once a
soldier is wounded he ceases to be a Yankee or a Rebel, he's just a sick
boy who will die if you don't help him."

"Very well," replied the storekeeper, "I'll give you what you ask, but
remember—I'm doing this for Senator Benton's daughter, not General
Fremont's wife."

By noon she had assembled blinds, pillows, mattresses, blankets, dishware, tables, soap, disinfectants, paint. She rode on the seat of the lead
supply wagon, anxious to convert the ugly barracks into a hospital before
another day dawned.

She had no authority to issue orders to the wagon drivers or their
helpers, yet she pressed them into service, charging about the building like
one possessed, supervising a hundred tasks at once: the scrubbing of

floors, whitewashing of walls, installation of window coverings, putting the sick men between white sheets, with tables to hold their food and medicine. At first the soldiers demurred: they were afraid of the disease inside the hospital.

"She's got no right to give us orders," she heard one soldier mumble. "Who does she think she is, anyway?"

"She's the general's Jessie."

"Well . . . something tells me we'd better do what General Jessie says."

In the cool of evening, after they had had a light supper, Jessie and John went to his office, lit the lamps and settled down to a five-hour stretch of work. As the hours passed and John's plans became clear to her, she was thrilled by the bold stratagems which had taken shape in his mind. He had established a Union depot which combined all of the outlying railroad stations, saving countless hours in the moving of troops in and out of the city; he had ordered five river boats converted into mortar boats, assigning to army engineers the task of iron-plating the ships; ordered a fortification of St. Louis which would relieve forty thousand men for the battlefield; declared martial law in the city, putting an end to Confederate recruiting. Because his ninety-day volunteers had threatened to leave for want of their pay, he seized one hundred and fifty thousand dollars which the quartermaster had refused to relinquish; he commissioned foreign officers available in St. Louis, delegating them to train their own regiments for immediate battle service; laid out a campaign which would clear the Mississippi all the way to New Orleans.

At one in the morning John went to bed, asking Jessie to finish the written orders by the time he got up at five. She found it pleasant to work in the cool stillness of the night, with no sound to be heard except the slow movement of the sentries on guard below. Shortly after four in the morning she finished the orders, then went up to her room under the eaves and unpacked the simple clothes she had brought with her. As she lay in her narrow cot her mind went back to those wondrous, untroubled days when she was first married and had worked with her husband on the reports of the early expeditions.

5

WITHIN A WEEK after John's arrival some of the confusion had been eradicated, and results were beginning to show: St. Louis was now a Union city, the crescent-shaped fortifications were going up fast, Frank Blair's supply merchants were beginning to deliver food and clothing, a

spirit of hopefulness and faith had been instilled into the troops, the officers were studying books on military science, such foreign officers as
Zagonyi had trained several companies to a fighting pitch, the five gunboats had been completed.

But to Jessie conditions still seemed desperate: General Lyon was sending daily telegraphic messages for reinforcements. General Prentiss was
making frantic appeals for fresh troops at Cairo. The War Department
in Washington was not only unable to provide money or arms or men,
but was insisting that General Fremont dispatch his trained companies to
protect the capital. No part of the arms he had so farsightedly bought in
France or England had been shipped to his command.

On August first General Fremont took his gunboat flotilla down the
river to save Cairo from Confederate General Pope, who was advancing
on it from the south. The next morning Dorothea Dix arrived in St. Louis.
Jessie spent the following days working with the Union superintendent
of women nurses, signing up women from the city and its environs for
hospital work.

At the end of five days she received a telegram from John that he had
beaten General Pope to Cairo, had relieved General Prentiss' depleted
troops, moved the sick onto the gunboats. Jessie released the dispatch to
the newspaper reporters; General Fremont's gunboat flotilla and relief
of Cairo were acclaimed by a victory-starved North.

But when John returned to St. Louis she had no opportunity either to
welcome or congratulate him, for Frank Blair had been waiting impatiently for hours, waving distress telegrams from General Nathaniel
Lyon, who had fallen back almost as far as he could go and was now sup-
plicating John for reinforcements. Frank was pleased with the success of
the Cairo flotilla, but he was bitterly unhappy over General Lyon's plight,
feeling that the failure was his own, for he had promised his friend that
once General Fremont was in command there would be well-trained
troops forthcoming.

John listened attentively to Frank's passionate pleas, studied the latest
reports on his desk, and finally said, "Frank, I will send instructions to
General Lyon at once. It is clear to me now what he must do, and I am
sure he will do it skillfully and with success."

"Thank you!" exclaimed Frank heartily. "I knew you would not fail
me."

When Frank Blair had departed, Jessie murmured, "I don't understand; how are you going to reinforce Lyon? You have no available
troops."

"Quite so. It is impossible for me to reinforce him. Instead I shall order
him to continue to fall back. That will extend the Rebel supply lines and

make them more vulnerable. The delay will give me time to train the necessary troops; perhaps the Zagonyi Guard will be ready . . . When I order Lyon to fight, he will have an adequate army, he will defeat the Rebels and chase them out of Missouri."

Misgivings arose at once in Jessie's mind. Frank would feel that he had been misled; he would become angry when he learned that he had been put off with an oblique promise. She started to say as much, then decided that it was not part of her function to contest her husband's judgment.

She found that her work increased with each passing day, for St. Louis was one of the most feverish war centers in America. No matter how often John instructed her to write or telegraph to President Lincoln, Secretary of War Cameron or Postmaster General Montgomery Blair for "money and arms without delay and by the quickest conveyance," the best that Montgomery could answer was, "I find it impossible now to get any attention to Missouri or western matters from the authorities here. You will have to do the best you can and take all needful responsibility to defend and protect the people over whom you are specially set." John was on his own, he had to raise food and equipment from the surrounding country, enlist the men of the neighboring territories, somehow get them armed, trained, put into uniform and equipped to fight a war. To Jessie's eyes it seemed an impossible feat, and since she was unofficial chief of staff for supply, she worried over the fact that General Lyon's men had never been paid, were traveling on inadequate rations, without the proper clothing or tents or replacements for their horses or arms.

Hundreds of men thronged in and out of general headquarters each day, all wanting something: contracts, commissions, information, favors. To her dismay Jessie found that every last word, decision or act made enemies at the same time that it accomplished results. When she set up a guard system to keep out the hordes of visitors who wanted to see John each day, she heard complaints that General Jessie was being autocratic and keeping people away; yet John had begged her to keep his working hours free at any cost. When Jessie and John found that many of the contractors recommended by Frank Blair were victimizing the Union soldiers, that the guns didn't shoot, the supply wagons broke down on the road because the wood in them had rotted, that the soldiers' shoes lasted only a week because they were made of paper, that some of the canned food was poisoned and the critically needed horses fell lame a few days after being delivered, they lost faith in Frank's friends and gave out supply contracts to their own friends from the West whom they had known to be honest men. Men who were refused an audience became their personal enemies. Missourians who were refused contracts began working for John's removal by the time they had reached the bottom step of the Brant house. She was accused of having paid an exorbitant rental for the Brant house, of living in luxury and splendor, amidst fine furnishings, silver and linens. When John used his Zagonyi Guard to impress upon belligerent Missouri the fact that he had a well-organized fighting force, criticism arose on the grounds that he was acting like a European monarch.

However, these troubles became as nothing when their first real blow fell. General Lyon, fearful lest his harrowed army be disorganized and destroyed in its retreat, made a heroic attack against McCulloch's vastly superior forces at Wilson's Creek. His troops were defeated. General Lyon was shot through the breast and killed.

Headquarters was stunned by the news; where battles are fought, men die, but John had issued orders to General Lyon not to fight. The Union needed generals, particularly a general of Lyon's long experience; they needed victories, not defeats. And now John would be responsible for this serious setback.

When the first shock had passed, Jessie asked, "Perhaps General Lyon didn't get your orders?"

"He received them," answered John quietly. "But he thought I was wrong. He thought it would be irreparable to give up that part of Missouri; he reasoned that I couldn't know the full facts sitting here at headquarters."

"But in a war, can every officer make his own decisions? Musn't he obey orders and fit into a major campaign?"

"You and I are not the right ones to ask that question, Jessie," said John ruefully. "Have you forgotten about Lord Nelson and his blind eye? From our point of view, sitting here at headquarters, trying to evolve an over-all strategy, Lyon was wrong; from his point of view, urged to retreat from a battlefield which he felt he could not spare, General Lyon thought he was right. And there the case will have to rest."

"But at least the country will not blame you for Lyon's death. You did order him to fall back."

"No one will ever know that."

"What do you mean?"

"Lyon died a hero's death. Nothing must be said or done to detract from it."

"But you know what the press will say, the War Department . . ."

"Nothing must detract from General Lyon's heroic death."

She left her husband's office and made arrangements for the body to lie in state on the side veranda, putting up the flags and arranging the flowers herself. When Lyon was brought in, she had the plain wooden coffin placed in the center of the room and draped it with his regimental colors.

At five the next morning, while she was having coffee with John at his desk, an orderly announced that Frank Blair was downstairs. Jessie and John went quickly to the veranda. Frank came in, his face sallow with grief. He walked to the head of the coffin and stood staring down into his friend's face. After a moment he looked up, took in the flowers and flags; to Jessie he said, "I thank you for these last kindnesses to my friend."

Jessie did not answer. She stood quietly, uneasily, while Frank and John gazed at each other.

"He was a good general and a good friend," Frank murmured softly. "It's tragically cruel that he should have died before he had a chance to engage in a major campaign."

There was no criticism in his voice, only grief. John said, "I am sorry, Frank. I did what I could, but there was so little time . . ."

"It is not your fault, John. I only say that it would have been better in the long run to lose Cairo than to lose Lyon. We could retake Cairo, but we can never find another General Lyon."

John put his hand on Frank's shoulder. "I know that you have lost one of your dearest friends, Frank, but I have also lost my ablest commanding officer. We will miss him sorely, but you will see, his heroic death will thrill and unite the North."

Frank did not answer. John excused himself, went back to his office. Frank took a last look at his friend's face, then left the veranda, his head down.

Two days later he arrived in midafternoon with a friend whom he introduced as a clothing manufacturer, assuring John that his products would be good, then drawing forth from his pocket a contract which he put on John's desk for his signature. John had several times been criticized for signing contracts without reading or fully understanding them. As he had once explained to Jessie, he could either read the legal contracts or fight a war, but it was impossible to do both. As he sat looking blankly at the closely filled pages, Jessie asked quietly:

"How many outfits is this for, Frank?"

"Forty thousand."

Still trying to read the contract, John asked, "Forty thousand? When we have fewer than ten thousand troops in all Missouri?"

Frank's face reddened.

"Of course," he said coldly, "if you'd rather give the contracts to your California friends . . . They're the only ones who are permitted to provide for your army now. All the men in Missouri who fought this war before you ever got here aren't good enough to get contracts any more!"

"Now, Frank," pleaded Jessie. "John didn't say any such thing. He only said the number was too high . . ."

"Make the contract for ten thousand, Frank," said John; "that's all we'll need for the time being, and I'll be hard pressed to scrape together the money even for that amount."

He rose, excused himself on the basis of urgent business, and left his office. The clothing manufacturer walked out behind him. Jessie watched Frank's face to see whether the offer of a compromise had mollified him, but the young man began a passionate tirade which included all the criticism that had been levied against John since their second week in St. Louis. Keeping her temper under control, she replied, "Frank, you know perfectly well why he had to do these things. You and John must not quarrel; you have too important a job to do together."

"That's not what the high and mighty general thinks," cried Frank. "He thinks he doesn't need me any more now that I got him his command. He wants to get rid of me, me and all my friends who fought for months to keep Missouri in the Union. Once he gets rid of all of us there will be no one here to challenge his power. Then he can go on holding military parades and dazzling the city with his European uniforms . . ."

Sadly, Jessie answered, "You don't mean all these things, Frank. You wouldn't be saying them if it were not for the death of Nathaniel Lyon. You mustn't let Lyon's death warp your judgment."

"Lyon's death," exclaimed Frank. "You mean Lyon's murder! Your husband had plenty of troops and plenty of arms; he could have reinforced Lyon at any time he had wanted to—but he was afraid of Lyon, afraid Lyon would win brilliant victories, be given John Fremont's command!"

Aghast at these accusations, Jessie could only cry, "Frank, you must not say these horrible things! You will do everyone terrible harm. I will not allow you to start circulating this kind of rumor."

"You won't allow," snorted Frank, his face contorted with rage, "General Jessie will not allow! Don't you know what a ridiculous figure you are making of yourself? Don't you know how everyone resents your intrusion and wants you to go home, get out of a man's war? Don't you know how ridiculous you're making your husband look, with people saying that you wear the stars in the family and your husband takes the orders?"

She somehow managed to say, "Please go away. You've said enough."

Frank Blair replied, "Almost enough, but not quite: until John arrived here, I was the political commander of the state. But your husband decided that Missouri was too small for two commanders, that one of us had to be driven out. He thought that one was going to be me, but that's where he made his mistake. He is the one who is going to be driven out, and I am the one who is going to do the driving."

She left the office and slowly climbed the narrow stairs to her little bedroom, gazing out the dormer window over the roofs of St. Louis, seeing nothing, feeling deeply this moment of decision. Had she made a mistake in coming to St. Louis with John? Was Frank Blair right in charging that she had made both herself and her husband ridiculous in the eyes of the world? Was she exaggerating the worth of her contribution, doing more harm than good by being here? How would John react to the charge that she wore the stars?

For the first time she realized that in war no one achieves a quick and easy success. There would be many failures before a victory was achieved, there would be dreadful quarrels; everyone engaged in the fight would suffer from the quarrels, would fight two wars instead of one.

If she returned home now, if she stepped down from the work and responsibility, then no matter what happened in the war and the Department of the West, it could not be her fault, it could not hurt her marriage. Once before she had learned that the best wife was the least wife, yet here she was immersing herself in fields where a woman did not belong. She sensed from Frank's attack the intensity of the campaign that would be waged against her. She knew that, working in confusion, she must inevitably make errors, mistakes. Suppose these had serious consequences? Suppose they hurt her husband, his position, his status, his hold on his command? Would he not charge this against her; would it not cause a strain on their marriage? She had almost ruined him once before by this kind of participation. She knew that she was impulsive, strong-willed, disliking authority or restraint. Might she not do something that once again would lead to disgrace, court-martial? They were older now; they would not be able to endure trouble as they had when they were young. Would it not be the better part of wisdom to go away, to Washington perhaps, as Francis Blair originally had suggested, and let her husband fight this war without her?

In her most fanciful dreams she had never anticipated that their collaboration would involve co-operation in a war; yet that was the way it had worked out, and, startling as it seemed, now that she stopped and saw it through Frank Blair's eyes, she knew that she could not abandon her work merely because it was a war which was calling forth this collaboration. She was aware of the fact that she could get hurt, seriously hurt, just as she had been hurt after the conquest of California. She could go back to New York or Siasconset, but John had said he needed her. She thought, If my reasoning is good and my organizational work sound, if they help to win battles and end the war, who is going to say later that the work was invalid and objectionable because it stemmed from a woman rather than a man, from a marriage relationship rather than that of officer and subordinate?

How then could she run away? These were the hours and the periods for which she lived, the hours of crisis and extreme effort. These were the periods for which she enjoyed months of calm and quiet such as she had spent on the Mariposa and in the house at Black Point, resting, storing up her strength.

She walked to the chiffonier to gaze at herself in the mirror. What she saw reflected there was not the gentle face she had known. All beauty was gone, and all softness. It was impersonal, hard-set, with nothing feminine about it. Her King George's Mark had already begun to show beneath the left corner of her mouth. This was a mask that could have been fitted onto a soldier and not have seemed incongruous; the harsh black dress she wore day after day might easily be a uniform.

Resolutely she patted her hair into place, kicked out her skirt behind her, and left the room for her next conference with General Fremont.

6

JOHN HAD LITTLE TIME to deal with anything but military strategy and policy making; it was up to her to fill in the vast gaps with detail. Horace Greeley had complimented her on being an executive housewife. In this emergency, general headquarters was not unlike a home, and the plans for military supply an elaboration of the countless details one had to fulfill in order to keep a home and family functioning successfully.

Her attitude involved only a desire to extend her husband. She was proud of the manner in which he instilled a fighting spirit into the troops and prepared them for battle. She marveled at how he kept his poise and patience when Washington commandeered the arms he had bought in Europe, refusing to send any part of them to the Western Command, when General Meigs canceled his order for Canadian horses without even informing him of the cancellation. To her ever watchful eyes he showed no lessening of spirit in the chaos that surrounded him.

The days were full of worries and frustrations, for the worst blight of all had descended upon the Department of the West: southern guerrilla forces were laying waste Missouri, burning the farms and the homes and driving the Union supporters out of the state. The guerrillas operated in small bands, apparently unorganized, yet striking so suddenly and doing so much quick damage in the night that they had the effectiveness of an army. John sent out heavily armed parties in search of the guerrillas; they could not be found, let alone stopped. But one thing he did learn: the bands were composed of men from plantations who were able to leave their homes because their Negro slaves remained behind to do the work.

After battering his head against this problem through the hot days of August, he commented to Jessie, "There is only one way to beat these guerrillas, but it's a drastic action . . ."

"What is it?"

"I can liberate the slaves in my department."

"Emancipation! But, John, have you the power? Have you the right?"

"You're asking two questions in one, Jessie. As military commander, I have the power; as to whether or not I have the moral right, that is something every man will have to decide for himself. If I issue an emancipation proclamation for all slaves whose owners have gone to war against us, it will serve two important purposes: it will send these guerrilla plantation owners scurrying back to their homes to protect their property; and it will make them unwilling to risk the loss of their slaves. If they persist in fighting, they will release thousands of Negroes to the Union forces."

"It will change the nature of the war," cried Jessie. "Up to now we've been fighting to keep the South from dissolving the Union; too many people in the North think we ought to let the southern states go, that they are only a source of trouble anyway. But this proclamation would convert the war into a crusade for freedom."

He ran his hands wearily over his eyes. "I don't know," he mumbled. "When I think of this emancipation from a military point of view it looks clear and logical; then when I start thinking of the political implications . . . I am no politician, Jessie; all I want to do is defeat the secessionists in the Western Command. The closer I get to the war the less I understand what the North is fighting for. Is it to punish the South for firing on Sumter? To force them back into the Union? Or to abolish slavery, so that the nation will be able to think about something else?"

"Each group in the country has its particular reason, depending on where the people live and what they believe."

"And may I ask why you are fighting the war, Mrs. Fremont?"

"I can answer that simply and directly: to abolish slavery." She came to her husband's side. "Don't you think we should talk it over with Frank Blair?" she asked. "He will understand the political implications . . ."

"No, no!" broke in John. "This issue must be settled on its military necessity, not politically. Frank would begin to talk about its effect on the doubtful border states, whether it might not drive some of them into the Confederacy, and what its effect would be in official Washington. I would want it to be a local military maneuver, applicable to Missouri alone. Its effectiveness will depend upon its suddenness and surprise; Frank would have it in the newspapers by the next day."

There was silence in the room while they both carried forward the train of thought. Jessie found herself studying her husband. He no longer parted his hair in the middle, but wore it brushed forward in rather a short and flat line, still moderately curly. His hair and beard were more gray than black, his forehead higher because of the receding hairline; his expression was the strongest and most positive she had seen it since the days of the earliest expeditions: his eyes large, boldly analytical, determined to action. Conscious of the two stars of the major general in the epaulets on either shoulder, he gave the impression of a man of vigor and action, entirely able to emerge victorious.

Aware of her searching scrutiny, he said quietly, "What do you say, Chief of Staff? Would you approve?"

Jessie threw back her head with a defiant gesture.

"Yes, General, I approve heartily: it will show the South that we mean business, it will keep many slaveholders from waging war against us."

The next morning she was awakened at dawn by a sharp knock at her door. When she answered, the voice of an orderly called out, "Mrs. Fremont, the general wants you at his desk immediately." She dressed as quickly as she could and went down the stairs to John's office on the second floor. She did not speak, but one look at her husband showed her that he had done little sleeping, if any, that night.

"Jessie, I have decided that there is no time to be lost. We must clear Missouri of the guerrillas. This order will do it."

He picked up the sheet of tight handwriting, gave it to his wife and asked her to read it aloud. She read:

In order to suppress disorder, to maintain the public peace, and to give security and protection to the persons and property of loyal citizens, I do hereby extend and declare established martial law throughout the state of Missouri. The property, real and personal, of all persons in the state of Missouri who shall take up arms against the United States, or who shall be directly proven to have taken an active part with their enemies in the field, is declared to be confiscated to the public use, and their slaves, if any they have, are hereby declared freemen.

When she had finished she was breathing hard. John said firmly, "The time has come for decisive action. I have been given the power to crush rebellion in the department, and I will bring the penalty of rebellion home to every man striving against the Union."

She laid the order down on the desk, saying excitedly, "This is the most important document that has yet appeared in the war; giving freedom to the slaves of the Rebels will make it impossible for the South to continue fighting."

He asked her to transcribe his order so that it would be legible for the printer, and then have it set up on the press. After taking it down to the printer in the basement, she stood by his side while he ran proof. She then took a copy over to the St. Louis *Democrat,* and returned to the newspapermen's quarters to give them the full story.

Neither she nor John was prepared for the enthusiasm and almost hysterical acclaim with which his emancipation proclamation was greeted in the North. Jubilant crowds marched and sang in the streets of New England; young men who had been holding back in uncertainty as to what the war was about rushed to the recruiting offices. A member of Congress announced that "it stirred and united the people of the loyal states far more than any other event of the war." The great newspapers of the North, including the New York *Herald* and the Chicago *Times,* which had been sympathetic toward the South, joined in the praise. The emancipation proclamation, with accompanying editorials, was splashed across the front pages of the New York *Times* and *Tribune,* the Washington *National Intelligencer,* the Boston *Post,* the Chicago *Tribune. Harper's Weekly* declared it "the beginning of the end," a feeling shared by a majority of those in the loyal states. In the Midwest people cried, "At last we know what we're fighting for, and now we'll get it over with fast."

While sitting in the basement telegraph office, organizing the hundreds of congratulatory messages that were pouring in, Jessie found one from Secretary of War Cameron. She rushed it upstairs to John, for this constituted official administrative approval of his action.

But on the morning of September first, Frank Blair arrived at headquarters. John received him courteously; Jessie exchanged only a quick piercing glance. They had been careful to give him no further affront, had leaned over backwards to grant contracts of supply to several of his less unreliable friends, but the chasm between them had grown wider over conflicts in authority. Although they had had no further personal differences, their quarrel had been carried on with ever mounting intensity in the press. The *Democrat* was lavishing praise on John for his swift organization of the department; where once it had lauded Frank Blair for saving Missouri, it now urged him to go back to Washington and leave the West in the more capable hands of General Fremont. Outraged, Frank launched a violent counteroffensive in the St. Louis *Evening News,* with scathing articles on the failure of General Fremont to carry through any of the preparations so carefully laid by Blair and Lyon.

Coming into their presence now, he castigated John roundly for having usurped his authority, for having done something which would embarrass President Lincoln, the administration and the northern cause.

"This act was done behind my back!" he declared vehemently. "You had no right to make such a move without my knowledge and consent. I am the political leader here and am responsible for Missouri. Our political war is as important as the military! Had you consulted with me, I could have shown you the folly of your act."

Jessie was glad that she had not revealed to her husband Frank's quarrel with her: It would make it easier for John to keep his temper. When he denied that he was obliged to consult Frank, or get his consent before making a military move, Jessie was reassured to find his voice not only courteous but friendly.

"Then you repudiate my authority in Missouri?" Frank demanded.

"No," replied John, "I recognize your political leadership. But I am the military leader, and the emancipation proclamation was a military measure."

Outraged, Frank leaned over John's desk and said in a hoarse but intense tone, "I was grossly deceived about your capabilities. You issued your emancipation proclamation, not for military purposes, but as a political maneuver to regain the confidence of the North which you lost because of your failure to reinforce Lyon. You have made a hopeless failure and confusion of your command. I am going to admit my mistake in recommending you by filing charges with President Lincoln, asking for your recall."

He stormed out of the office. Jessie sprang up and followed, overtaking him on the broad staircase leading to the foyer.

"Frank," she said quietly, so that no one in the downstairs offices might hear, "do you realize that you've accused John of issuing his emancipation proclamation as a charlatan would, seeking political support at any cost? I know you couldn't believe that possible of John, but if you make the accusation it is going to have unfortunate implications. For the sake of our friendship, and the friendship of our families, don't let us come to a breaking point. If you disagree with the wisdom or effectiveness of the emancipation proclamation, that is your privilege, but please come back with me and tell John that you don't think him a political adventurer, endangering the cause of the Union and the war for his private purpose."

With his eyes flashing, his body taut, Frank replied, "That is precisely what I do mean. That's exactly what John Fremont is. He has failed and weakened our position in the West; now he is using the most dangerous weapon within his reach to pull himself out of the chaos. But he shan't get away with it, Jessie; I'll convict him before the world for the bungler he is."

The anxiety and tremulousness within her died. She could see no further hope in placation. In a voice as furious as Frank's she said, "Very well, Frank, if it is your purpose to declare war on us, we will treat you as we would treat a Rebel caught within the lines with a gun in his hand. If you want us for enemies, you shall have us!"

The encounter with Frank should have warned them that they might not face as clear sailing as the first outbursts of enthusiasm had indicated, but they were completely unprepared when a letter arrived by special messenger from Abraham Lincoln, six days after the publication of the emancipation proclamation, requesting that General Fremont withdraw it. They were stunned and a little ill.

"But why has President Lincoln done this," exclaimed Jessie, "when the North has approved so heartily?"

"Francis and Montgomery Blair have gotten to him: Lincoln says that the emancipation proclamation will alarm our southern Union friends and ruin our prospects in Kentucky . . ."

"And you are ordered to revoke the emancipation proclamation!"

"Yes. But it is suggested that I do it on my own authority, so that it will not appear that I have been rebuked."

"What do you intend to do? In only six days we have seen important progress against the guerrillas . . ."

"I must either admit I was wrong . . . or refuse the president's suggestion."

"Why not write Mr. Lincoln as strong a letter as you can, explaining the reasons for your action and the good it is already accomplishing?"

"First I must dictate my official reply and give it to the dispatch bearer. I am not going to take Mr. Lincoln's suggestion. If he wants the emancipation rescinded, he will have to do it by his own order. However, in a personal letter I think I can convince him to let the order stand."

He rose from his desk and paced the room. "If only I could speak to Mr. Lincoln, I could show him the merciful nature of our measure. Letters are cold things at best; Mr. Lincoln may be too busy or involved to read ours carefully, there will be no one on hand to interpret or answer questions. I wish I could go to Washington and explain the situation, but it is impossible for me to leave here."

"Isn't there anyone on your staff whom you could trust to speak for you?"

"Yes, there is one."

"Who?"

"You. You were my representative in Washington during the years I was away. You'll have to take that job again."

The request came as a surprise, yet never for an instant did she doubt that she would be received at the White House as one qualified to speak for her husband. Former presidents had always received her in this capacity; certainly Mr. Lincoln would be the more friendly, since he had campaigned so arduously for Fremont and Jessie in 1856 and they had helped win California for him in the election of 1860.

John walked to the window, raised the green blind and stood staring down into the glare of the street below. She noted how sharp and precise his profile was, how white his trim, close-cropped beard had become. He turned to her, his eyes grave, almost brooding.

"We must reach Mr. Lincoln with our private letter first and with your interpretation and presentation of the full case. That is the most important thing, Jessie, do you understand? You must get to him with this informal letter before he has had a chance to see my official dispatch or write the rescinding order. A matter of a few minutes one way or the other may make all the difference. The dispatch bearer will be on the same train . . ."

"Trust me," replied Jessie. "I know the shortest cut to the White House from any given point in Washington. It's a good deal like Colonel Abert's letter: if I had waited until the next morning, or even nightfall, a duplicate letter would have reached you by the mail boat, before DeRosier could have covered the ground on horseback."

A sudden despair came over her when she realized what she had said. Quickly she murmured, "John, have you ever regretted my decision at that moment? If I had not withheld that order there never would have been a court-martial."

"Nor would there have been a second or third expedition," he replied in a dry voice, without smiling. "We would have been robbed of our most important opportunity and would have failed to make our most important contribution. I regret nothing from those years, Jessie, except my personal quarrel with General Kearny. I don't say I was wrong in what I did, but only that I wish it could have been avoided."

"I never told you," she murmured; "after you left the Delaware Indian Reservation, an aide reached me from General Kearny begging me to come to him with my forgiveness before he died. I sent the courier back with a message that I could not forgive him, that a grave stood between us. General Kearny died the next day. I was wrong, John, I should have forgiven him . . ."

The memories of the Delaware Indian Reservation, of the loss of their first son and the tragedy that almost engulfed their marriage, swept over them both. They were quiet in the hot, bare room, reliving for a swift instant the pain of that difficult time, yet rejoicing that they had come through it unscathed, that they had other sons, that John was now a general as she had predicted he would be on the day that he was appointed a lieutenant colonel. For a moment there fell away from them their burdens, their responsibilities, their labors, the ominously threatening future, and they were cut out of time and place and crisis, were once again a husband and wife whose chief sustainer, the only thing that never failed them, was their love. For this one brief instant, cut out of a world at war, a world in flames, they were locked in embrace.

Then Jessie thanked John for his confidence, told him that she would prepare to leave on the night train and that she would do her best to represent him in Washington.

With a fragment of a smile John replied, "I am sure your campaign will be successful, General Jessie."

She reddened, not having realized that John knew of the title. He touched her shoulder reassuringly, said, "I will want to know the results of your interview at the earliest possible moment. However, you had best not send it on the regular telegraph routes, as the Blair faction undoubtedly have spies here at headquarters. Take along this cipher code and send a message to Lieutenant Howard, signing the name of his fiancée."

Jessie picked up the code book. "I'll telegraph immediately after my first interview with the president. I will do my best to make it good news."

7

AT SIX O'CLOCK THAT NIGHT she left the Union Depot. The train was jammed with soldiers, with civilians on private and governmental business, and with families from the interior of Missouri fleeing northward from the guerrillas. Though the war was only five months old the rolling stock was already deteriorating, carrying three times its normal capacity on each journey. She found a seat in one of the coaches. It was a hot September night, and by the time the train pulled out the aisles and platforms were filled with standing men, with women sitting on their suitcases.

She did not close her eyes all night: the heat, the noise of the wheels beneath her, the swaying and jostling of the train, made sleep impossible. Knowing that there would be little food available, she had packed an oilcloth bag of victuals. There was no chance to wash or change her clothing, the few facilities being overtaxed and rapidly going out of commission. She passed the hours as best she could, dropping off to sleep now and then when exhaustion overcame her, awakening stiff and sore from the hard wooden bench.

The train reached Washington a little before eight o'clock on the evening of the second day. She was met by Judge Coles, an old friend from New York, who had worked with them during the 1856 campaign. He had a carriage waiting and a room reserved for her at the Willard Hotel.

Two hours before completing the journey she had felt at the end of her strength, but now that she was in Washington, so close to the task on hand, she had no patience with her own fatigue, but only a desire to accomplish what she had planned minutely a thousand times during the fifty hours on the train.

When they reached the hotel, and Jessie had washed her hands and face, she said to Judge Coles, "I must send a message to Mr. Lincoln, urging an immediate audience."

"But surely you don't intend to go to the White House this evening?"

"Yes. It is urgent that I see the president at once."

Quietly he suggested, "Wouldn't it be better if you had a night's sleep first? You must be exhausted from your train trip. In the morning you will be refreshed, your suitcase will be here and you will be able to dress . . ."

"No, no," she interrupted. "Tomorrow morning may be too late."

Judge Coles stared at her steadfastly for a moment. "As an old friend, may I ask why? What can you possibly accomplish tonight in your exhausted condition that can't be better done tomorrow morning?"

"There was a courier on my train with a dispatch for the president. It is part of my purpose in coming here to reach the president before he acts on the basis of that dispatch."

"Mr. Lincoln may not receive your message this evening. He is harassed and overworked; it may be sometime tomorrow before he will summon you."

"I will ask him to see me at once," replied Jessie; "if the message reaches him, I think he will grant my wish."

"As you see fit, Mrs. Fremont," replied the judge rather formally. "I will find a reliable messenger while you write the note."

It seemed to Jessie that the messenger had hardly had time to reach the White House, when he was back and delivered a card. It read:

A. LINCOLN

Now

Before leaving the hotel room Jessie took a quick glance in the dresser mirror. She noted that her hair was dusty from the long train ride and that it made her seem older. She noted too that her white collar was considerably more soiled than the rest of the white lawn gown, which was badly rumpled and discolored from the train. An image replaced that in the glass, the picture of herself in her court gown standing before the dresser mirror at the Clarendon Hotel in London, her hair piled on top of her head in the nine braids of the Polish fashion, her face aglow with the excitement of the Easter presentation to the queen. Dimly, at the back of her mind, she realized that it was neither good taste nor good manners to go to the president looking so soiled and worn, yet surely the kindhearted and simple-mannered Abraham Lincoln would not take offense, any more than he would take offense at any other soldier-courier being ushered into his presence with dispatches from the front lines.

She asked Judge Coles to accompany her to the interview, then took the short cut from the Willard to the White House. As she entered the front door she said to herself, All my life I've been at home in the president's house; but now most of all I must be received well.

They were ushered into the red parlor. The page told them that the president would be there shortly. She stood awaiting President Lincoln's entrance, not wanting to be seated when he entered the room. However, the moments passed in an agony of suspense and fatigue; it seemed to her a very long time before the far door was opened and Abraham Lincoln appeared against the brighter kerosene lamps of the dining room. He stopped for an instant to close the dining-room door behind him, but as he advanced slowly toward her Jessie saw the door opened again, and behind it she caught a glimpse of Mary Todd Lincoln.

She searched the president's face intently for a clue to her reception. Mr. Lincoln's expression was noncommittal. He did not speak but only bowed slightly. After Jessie had thanked him for receiving her, she introduced Judge Coles as a member of the New York Bar. President Lincoln said nothing, nor did the expression on his face change. Upset by the coolness, she reached into her bag, drew forth John's sealed letter and said:

"General Fremont asked me to deliver this letter into your hands, Mr. President. The general felt the subject to be of so much importance that he sent me to answer any points on which you might want further information."

President Lincoln held out his hand for the letter. As he broke open the seal and moved closer to the light of the chandelier, Jessie thought in terror, His mind is already turned against John; he has been listening to our enemies. That is why he has given me such a cold reception, why he is so neglectful of me. Why has he not offered me a seat, when I must look as tired as I feel? Mr. Lincoln has already decided to discourage me and to take a stand against John. I must do my best to change his mind. I must not appear nervous or overwrought. I must sit down, the better to conceal my feelings, even though the president has not offered me a chair.

Judge Coles had discreetly withdrawn to the blue parlor, where Jessie occasionally caught a glimpse of him walking up and down before the open doorway. For a moment she watched the president while he stood beneath the chandelier reading the long letter; then she drew out one of the row of chairs and seated herself.

After a time President Lincoln finished his reading of the letter. He came to her side, pulled a second chair out of the row along the wall and sat at an angle, facing her. The long arm which held the letter seemed to be resting the sheet on the red carpet.

"Mrs. Fremont," he said, "I have written to the general and he knows what I want done."

"Mr. Lincoln, may I ask if you have revoked the general's emancipation proclamation?"

"Yes, I have just finished writing a draft of the order. It will be copied and sent tomorrow morning."

"Mr. President," she cried, "before that message is sent out, before it is too late, let me give you a full picture of what is happening in Missouri, let me show you why the general's emancipation proclamation can help materially in winning the war."

When she saw a frown come over the president's face, she continued more quickly. "That is why I have come, Mr. President, because General Fremont thought it would be advantageous if I could explain fully. The general feels that he is at the great disadvantage of being opposed by people in whom you have every confidence."

"Whom do you mean," demanded President Lincoln, "persons of different view?"

Jessie knew that she had been rebuked. She said, "The general's conviction is that it will be long and dreadful work to conquer by arms alone, that there must be other considerations to get us the support of the West. An idea sometimes can be as effective as a gun: if we convince the South that every Rebel will lose his slaves, the secessionist leaders will have an internal war on their hands, and that will seriously hamper their efforts to recruit and fight . . ."

"You are quite a female politician," remarked the president.

Jessie recoiled as though she had been struck. In the few seconds that passed as she sat in silence before the president, she reflected that he had not heard what she had said; he had rejected her reasoning summarily because she was a woman. As General Kearny had told her, women could do no good in a man's world; they would only make for chaos. And now here was Abraham Lincoln, who had campaigned so ardently for FREMONT AND JESSIE, this man who had every reason to be her friend and admirer, looking down upon her and despising her, calling her a female politician.

Her eyes reflected some of her hurt; President Lincoln's expression softened and he said in a firm but kindly manner, "The general ought not to have done it; he never would have done it if he had consulted Frank Blair. I sent Frank there to advise him and to keep me advised about the work, the true condition of things there, and how they were going."

"But, Mr. President, you gave the general *carte blanche* in the Western Department. You told him to do whatever he thought necessary for victory."

"Military victory, Mrs. Fremont." The president went on in a tone which she could only interpret as angry. "The general should never have dragged the Negro into the war! It is a war for a great national object. The Negro has nothing to do with it."

"General Fremont has strong influence and followers in Missouri; if it was his determination to carry through the emancipation order, he could do so . . ."

Mr. Lincoln frowned, said, "Mrs. Fremont, we have no independent commanders in the Union army; they are all under the command of the War Department."

She knew that the time of her interview was short, and she pushed forward to another phase of the problem.

"We were not aware that Frank Blair represented you," she said. "He did not do so openly. We had been led to believe that General Fremont was the sole commander of his department."

"Nothing has been done to limit or contravene the general's authority. Quarrels do our cause much injury, Mrs. Fremont; they should not be permitted."

He rose. Jessie looked up to where he towered above her. She saw that she had been dismissed without accomplishing any portion of the task for which she had been sent. The president had not once referred to John's long letter or asked for any further information. Apparently his mind was made up about General Fremont and the emancipation proclamation. She must make one last effort to persuade him.

She rose and began talking, swiftly. She reviewed the full history of the Western Command, the chaos in which John had found it, his work to protect St. Louis, to drill the troops, to find equipment on his own account when it could not be provided by Washington; how he had saved Cairo, inspired confidence in the men. She outlined the guerrilla warfare, the hundreds of interlocking problems and how the emancipation proclamation would settle so many of them. She made the point of which she was profoundly convinced, that this was not a war of defense on the part of the North, or a war of revenge for firing on Sumter, or even a war to force the South back into the Union. It was a war to end slavery, and if it did not end slavery, even though the southern states might be whipped back into the Union, this war would rise again and again.

She was thinking and speaking at top speed and with the utmost precision now, but at the same time her mind took in all of the externals: President Lincoln's wife was listening at the door of the dining room; Judge Coles was listening at the door of the blue room; Abraham Lincoln was towering above her, dark, brooding, wanting to stop her and not knowing how. She did not know how long she spoke, ten minutes, perhaps fifteen; she did not even know all the things she said, for her mind was racing ahead wildly, trying to use these last few precious seconds to turn the tide of the president's repudiation of her husband. She stated the full and imposing case of all that John Fremont had done, beseeching the president not to listen to John's enemies, not to withdraw his confidence, not to undermine his position by rebuking him before the nation as an impetuous and headstrong man, one who took authority into his own hands.

But suddenly her voice and her mind stopped in mid-sentence, for she perceived that Mr. Lincoln was offended: offended at her coming to the White House in her soiled gown, her hair dusty with the soot of the train and the road; offended that she had not accepted her dismissal when she had been dismissed, offended because she was intruding into a man's world where she did not belong, offended that she was trying to force her judgment upon him when the results of any serious action must be his responsibility, and his alone.

There was a harsh silence while she and the president stood looking at each other. Then, in a voice so soft she hardly knew whether the words could be heard, she thanked him for his kindness in receiving her. He did not reply.

"When could I have the answer to General Fremont's letter?" she asked.

"I have a great deal to do. Tomorrow, if possible, or the next day."

"Thank you, Mr. President. I will come for it."

"No, I will send it to you tomorrow or the day after. Where are you staying?"

"At Willard's, Mr. President. I shall wait there for your answer. Good night, sir, and thank you."

As they walked through the grounds, Judge Coles said, "Mrs. Fremont, the general will be deprived of all his part in the war; there is a faction which plans the affairs of the North, and they are against the general."

Too crushed and despondent to answer, Jessie bade the judge good night at the entrance to the hotel, went to her room and wrote out a cipher message to John. She gave him the tone of what had happened, but did not allow herself to appear too pessimistic, telling him instead that she would stay in Washington until she had fulfilled her mission. Almost ill with fatigue now, she fell out of her soiled clothes and into bed. Deep in her heart was the crushing knowledge that she had bungled, done everything exactly wrong, so thoroughly antagonized the president that there could be no possible hope of winning him back to their side.

She had wanted to be the strongest possible wife; now that it was too late, she realized that General Kearny, Frank Blair and President Lincoln had been right: the least wife is the best wife.

8

SHE SLEPT LATE the next morning, awakening after eight o'clock, took a hot bath, washed her hair carefully, and was greatly relieved to be able to don clean linens and a fresh gown. She had no sooner dressed than Francis Blair knocked sharply at the door. Five years had elapsed since he had campaigned for the Fremonts; even the fringe of hair around his bald head had now disappeared, and his eyes seemed only half open. They embraced in the manner of people acknowledging the past, yet angry and ready to fight about the future.

"Well," said Francis Blair, "who would have expected you to do such a thing as this, to come here and find fault with the president? What sense was there in antagonizing Mr. Lincoln?"

"I didn't antagonize him. On the contrary, the president was hard and cold to me. He had made up his mind against me before I got there, and did not even pay me ordinary courtesy."

"Don't you understand the staggering burden the president is laboring under?" exclaimed Blair. "You had no right to take a belligerent tone towards him; no man would have presumed to do so. If you want to play a man's game, you should not lean on your prerogatives as a woman to break the rules."

Thoroughly alarmed, she asked faintly, "Why do you charge me with these things?"

"Because the president says you taxed him so violently that he had to exercise all his tact to avoid quarreling with you. He also said you intimated that if General Fremont should decide to try conclusions with him, he could set up for himself."

Jessie was struck dumb at the last accusation. She sat down abruptly on the edge of a chair. "Try conclusions with the president! But I said no such . . . What led Mr. Lincoln to believe . . . ?"

"Didn't you tell the president that if General Fremont determined to carry through the emancipation order, he could do it without . . ."

Her heart sinking, Jessie exclaimed, "So that was why Mr. Lincoln said what he did about independent commanders! But I didn't mean that John could set himself up against the president! I only meant that Mr. Lincoln need not be afraid of John's success with the emancipation order in Missouri."

"Why did you have to come to Washington at all? Why couldn't you let Frank handle things in St. Louis, with Montgomery handling them here at the capital? Why do you have to quarrel with Frank, try to push him out of the picture in Missouri?"

Summoning her strength, Jessie replied, "We tried our best not to quarrel with Frank. We tried in every way to propitiate him. But from the moment of Nathaniel Lyon's death he seemed to lose confidence in us."

"Frank told me the very opposite. He wrote me that he was trying to avoid quarreling with you, but that you seemed to want to quarrel as an excuse to get rid of him."

"No, no! That isn't true, Mr. Blair, you know we have always loved Frank."

"Before you went to St. Louis I urged you to come to Washington, I showed you how you could help your husband here—told you that it was not fitting for a woman to go with an army. If you had stayed in Washington you could have had everything you wanted. But you disregarded me, and now, of all times that you should not have come, you go into the presence of the president in an unkempt condition . . ."

"There were reasons for my going to the president at the first possible moment, and my fresh linens had not arrived from the depot. We know that Frank sent the president an angry letter filing charges against John. That's true, isn't it?"

"Frank wrote to Mr. Lincoln," admitted Blair, "but it was not an angry letter. It merely surveyed the situation in the West."

". . . and asked for John's recall?"

"The president is going to give John every opportunity; he has faith in John's impulses and integrity, but no faith in him as a military leader. After all, John was a topographical engineer, not a military man. That is why the president has sent Montgomery and General Meigs to investigate the Western Command."

Jessie sprang up to confront Blair.

"John has accomplished miracles in Missouri in the six weeks of his command. Show me one Union general who has done better! His men are fighting every day, fighting without food, without supply wagons, without artillery . . ."

"You have done John no good. We've heard reverberations about General Jessie . . ."

"Have you heard the term used disparagingly?"

Blair took a gentler tack. "There has been no severe criticism, in fact Dorothea Dix has complimented you on your work with the sick. But the fact that the name is used is a criticism in itself. Can't you see how incongruous it is? Are you an amazon, a leader of a woman's army, that you should be called General Jessie? Since when do women become generals? It's bad taste, Jessie; it's pushing oneself in where a woman doesn't belong, no matter how good a job she may do."

"That is the sheerest sophistry, Mr. Blair. It was only five years ago that you complimented me on the part I was playing in the election, making the women of America interested in politics, helping to bring in the family vote. When a woman is serving your purpose, you approve her activities; when what she is doing seems to conflict with your interests, then you drag in the extraneous matter of sex. That's not consistent, Mr. Blair, and inconsistency is reputed to be a feminine attribute."

Francis Blair picked up his hat from the chiffonier, then put his hands on her shoulders. "Jessie, I'm too old a man now to quarrel with the children I helped raise. You know how deeply I love Frank, you know what high ambitions I hold for him. That is why it racks me so to have you two quarrel. But whatever happens, you and I must not cease loving each other: Tom Benton would insist on that, Jessie."

She kissed his leathery cheek. Blair went out, closing the door behind him. She thought how like her meeting with General Kearny over the howitzer this meeting with Francis Blair had been; she recalled what tragic results had evolved from her contretemps with Kearny, and had the gravest misgivings lest the parallel be carried out.

She waited through the hours for Mr. Lincoln's letter, hoping against hope that it would be friendly and reassuring. As she passed the small mirror she noted to her surprise that, though she had washed her hair early that morning, the dust of the train trip was still sprinkled through it. She leaned closer to the mirror and took a carefully scrutinizing look.

It isn't dust at all, she murmured, half aloud. My hair has turned gray. It must have happened last night.

For a moment she was stunned, then her eyes filled with tears.

At five in the afternoon, no longer able to endure the cramped hotel room, feeling that she would go out of her mind with anxiety if she did not get an hour's release, she put on her hat and left the hotel. She did not know where she was going, but she soon found herself turning into C Street. She stood in front of the Benton lot, which was still owned by the family, though no one had built on it. The brick chimney had been pulled down, the ground was overgrown with weeds. As she stood there, it came over her how alone she was in Washington now, and how hostile a city it had become. Eliza was away with her husband on war business. Her two younger sisters lived elsewhere, the great host of southern cousins and friends had gone home, hating the Fremont name. She had known every house and stile and meadow and stream, and nearly every face that walked the streets of the capital; now she knew no one. The city had grown past her and beyond her, she was no longer wanted here; for the first time she had been unwelcome in the White House.

Above all of her heartbreak and anxiety there was one emotion which engulfed her: if only her father could be here, if only Senator Thomas Hart Benton of Missouri had taken her arm as they mounted the steps of the White House, everything would have worked out well. But Tom Benton had lived his life, conducted his campaign, and now he was gone; she would have to fight her own battles. She recalled the words that Thomas Starr King had written to a friend about her: "Jessie Fremont carries guns enough to be formidable to a whole Cabinet: she is a she-*Merrimac,* thoroughly sheathed and carrying fire in the genuine Benton furnaces."

At this moment, tired, discouraged, uneasy at the president's long silence, her King George's Mark throbbing painfully, not knowing what to do next or where to turn, she did not feel like a she-*Merrimac;* the fires had been pretty well banked by her meetings with Mr. Lincoln and Mr. Blair. At the moment she felt only one desire, to be able to run, to run fast and far away from these scenes of conflict in Washington and St. Louis, to go back to her cottage on Black Point overlooking San Francisco Bay and the strait, where she could hear the sails flapping in the wind as the ships came into the harbor.

Early the second morning, after passing a sleepless night, she wrote Mr. Lincoln a letter:

To the President of the United States:

I was told yesterday by Mr. Francis Blair that five days since, a letter was received from his son Frank Blair, and laid before you by his son Postmaster Montgomery Blair, containing certain statements respecting General Fremont and his military command in the Western Department.

I was further told by Mr. Blair that on the basis of that letter, you sent Postmaster Blair and General Meigs to St. Louis to examine into that Department, and report.

On behalf of, and as representing General Fremont I have to request that I be furnished with copies of that letter, and any other communica-

*tions, if any, which in your judgment have made that investigation neces-
sary.*

I have the honor to be

Yours very respectfully,
JESSIE BENTON FREMONT.

By midafternoon she had a reply from the president.

MRS. GENERAL FREMONT.
MY DEAR MADAM:

*I answered the letter you bore me from General Fremont, on yesterday,
and not hearing from you during the day, I sent the answer to him by
mail. I do not feel authorized to furnish you with copies of letters in my
possession, without the consent of the writers. No impression has been
made on my mind against the honor or integrity of General Fremont,
and I now enter my protest against being understood as acting in any
hostility towards him. Your obedient servant,*

A. LINCOLN.

Seeing that there was nothing further she could do in Washington,
she took the night train back to St. Louis. The following morning, as the
train was leaving Harrisburg, a middle-aged gentleman who had been
sitting opposite her with his wife rose, came to her side, bowed respectfully, and said, "Madame Fremont, I am going to ask you a question;
my wife and I want the answer to it. Is it true that the president is going
to refuse to use emancipation as a weapon in the war?"

"It is true."

The woman threw up her hands and cried, "Oh, my son! My son! I
had given him willingly! I gave him to the Lord, but now it's for nothing."

Upon her return to St. Louis she found that John had achieved a
strategic victory: two weeks before he had appointed Ulysses S. Grant
a brigadier general, putting him in charge of southeastern Missouri and
southern Illinois, with headquarters at Cairo. General Grant had acted
with speed and vigor, moving into Paducah just ahead of the Confederate
General Polk, thus insuring to federal troops passage down the Mississippi
when the major campaign began. Grant had waited in General McClellan's outer office for four days, hoping for an appointment, and had been
ignored; John had selected him, as he told Jessie, for "qualities I could
not find combined in any other man, for General Grant has dogged per-
sistence and an iron will."

She determined to forget about the unfortunate episode in Washington,
confident that the means would soon be available for John to start on his

full-strength campaign. The reaction in the newspapers and among the public, when President Lincoln rescinded John's emancipation proclamation, was almost as intense as it had been ten days before when they had news of it: enlistments fell off, people declared themselves no longer interested in the war, the outcry in such states as Indiana and Illinois was so pain-fraught that the war effort was seriously injured.

She found it increasingly difficult to make any progress in the field of supply; Frank Blair had been provided with a complete account of her meetings in Washington with Mr. Lincoln and with his father, and was more determined than ever to secure John's removal. He organized the dissident elements in Missouri, waged a campaign against John in the *Evening News,* began spreading the impression throughout the West that since General Fremont must very soon be deposed there was consequently little sense in helping to fulfill his purposes or obeying his commands. John's former imperturbable poise was slowly being shattered by the effectiveness of Frank's campaign.

"Now I know what General Winfield Scott meant in the Mexican War," he commented, "when he complained about 'a fire in front from the Mexicans, and a fire upon my rear from Washington.' "

Jessie was no longer capable of judicious thinking about the youngest of the Blair family. "Doesn't Frank's conduct amount to treason?" she asked. "If he is doing everything in his power to obstruct the formation and supply of your army, then surely that is giving aid and comfort to the enemy? If you caught anyone else giving aid and comfort to the enemy, you'd soon put an end to his activities. Then why can't you stop Frank?"

"Because I don't know what to do with him."

During the next few days Blair's campaign for the removal of General Fremont broke into the open and was published in the northern press as well as the local western papers. The results were nearly disastrous to John's preparations. Once again husband and wife went into conference. As they sat in the bare front office, the light of the kerosene lamps flickering on the wall maps, regarding each other in gloom and misgiving, John's skin darkened, his eyes became angry. He muttered, "The simplest solution would be to shoot him; the next best thing would be to lock him in jail."

"You can't shoot him," she replied, coldly, "but you certainly can lock him up. It would be the greatest service you could perform for the northern cause."

"He belongs in jail, but . . ."

"Then put him there! You are hoping to leave for the southern battle front in a week or two. You will have no chance to be equipped if he is allowed to remain loose and oppose you. Lock him up; at least until you have won your victory in the south."

"Yes," replied John, "I think I'll do it."

He wrote out an order for the arrest, summoned the guard and sent it to Blair's home. They sat up until late that night drawing the formal charges. The next day Jessie learned that the nation was aghast at the arrest, for to the North it meant dissension and disunity and the weakening of the Union forces. A telegram arrived from Montgomery Blair which read, "I will send Frank's letter. It is not unfriendly, release him. This is no time for strife except with the enemies of the country."

The furor in the northern press shook her; she regretted their action, not because Frank had not deserved imprisonment at the Jefferson Barracks, but because John already had a sufficient number of wars on his hands. She considered the blunder to have been hers. Instead of keeping John's judgment calm in the midst of the furies, she had betrayed him, doubled his weakness by doubling his anger and counseling him to rash action. Twice within one week she had made serious errors, not only of judgment but of taste. Instead of helping her husband, she was hurting him immeasurably: she overheard one angry officer exclaim about the now notorious Blair Case: "That was General Jessie's doing!" Her husband had not reproved her for the fiasco in Washington; he had assured her that she had done her best. Yet encouraging him to imprison Frank Blair was inexcusable.

She locked herself in her bedroom to gain a few uninterrupted moments in which to think. She sat down heavily on the corner of her army cot. Didn't these two ghastly failures mean that she had exhausted her usefulness? Wouldn't it be the better part of kindness to go away now, to leave John alone to fight his war? Wouldn't it have been far better if she had accepted Frank Blair's first angry dictum that she would hurt her husband and make him ridiculous? No matter how many details she had taken off John's shoulders in the past two months, no matter how many supply trains had reached the battle fronts, no matter how many wounded had been routed to newly organized hospitals, how could these accomplishments compensate for her overzealousness?

She went out onto the tiny balcony and stood looking down into the street, watching the movement of the Zagonyi Guard on its way to the parade grounds. It was not only that she could not admit how sadly she had failed her husband, but that she must not demonstrate by public flight how misguided General Fremont had been in bringing his wife to the war. No, she must stand her ground, continue with her work, wait for the opportunity to make good her failures.

9

HER FIRST ACT was to ask John to release Frank, but Blair refused his freedom, demanding a public trial and preferring formal charges against General Fremont with the War Department. However, within a few days, despite the condemnation of the North, the imprisonment began to have beneficial results. The general staff was co-operating more heartily, supplies and equipment were coming in faster, a new vitality spread through the troops. She was beginning to breathe easier when Colonel James A. Mulligan, who was being pursued by a superior Confederate force under General Price, determined to make a stand at Lexington, threw up hasty fortifications and sent urgent telegrams to General Fremont asking for reinforcements. Though the newspapers were saying that John had forty thousand trained troops available, Jessie knew that there were at his disposal something under seven thousand men, including the Home Guard, barely enough to defend St. Louis. Yet she also knew that if Colonel Mulligan suffered a severe defeat, this last blow might be the culminating stroke against John's command. When she went to his office to urge him to send Colonel Mulligan every last man available, John handed her two telegrams. The first from Secretary of War Cameron read:

THE PRESIDENT ORDERS 5000 WELL ARMED INFANTRY TO BE SENT HERE WITHOUT A MOMENT'S DELAY.

The second was from General Winfield Scott:

DETACH 5000 INFANTRY FROM YOUR DEPARTMENT TO COME HERE WITH-OUT DELAY.   THE PRESIDENT DICTATES.

"But can't you expostulate with them?" Jessie demanded. "Can't you telegraph and tell them you need the men to reinforce Colonel Mulligan?"

For the first time in many years she saw that there were tears in his eyes. "No," he said, "that would be insubordination, with which I have been unjustly charged. The capital must be again in danger, and must be saved, even if Missouri falls and I sacrifice myself."

Three days later Colonel Mulligan suffered the worst defeat the Western Command had yet known, with three thousand, five hundred men captured, as well as large quantities of munitions and commissary stores. The North went into mourning, for Missouri was supposed to be a loyal state, controlled by General Fremont, and here they were still suffering major setbacks. Jessie was obliged to report to her husband that the chief complaint of the northern press was that General Fremont was steadily losing battles and had still to win his first major victory. Many of the papers called for a new general, one who could win.

"This simply means that you must hasten your plans, John," she said. "You will have to strike before your preparations are complete. No one ever is going to reach any degree of perfection in this war: battles will have to be fought without sufficient men, guns or supplies. They'll have to be won with substitutes like daring and courage."

". . . which the South has in equal measure. I had hoped to wait until we had a superior quantity of guns, since the North obviously has greater resources for supply. But if the North is starved for victories, if it needs them for morale, then I shall have to get a victory at any price."

Within a few days he had moved out at the head of his troops. Jessie remained behind to serve as liaison officer for supply. A continuous stream of messages came in by courier making known John's wants: "Tell the Sanitary Committee that the whole surgical department here is in a very bad condition, and gives me great anxiety . . . Our difficulty consists absolutely and only in the want of transportation; ask Captain McKeever to do all that is humanly possible to get wagons, mules, harness and drivers sent forward . . . We must have sabers and guns; send such things forward as best you can . . . Hurry up Constable's Battery if it is in any way possible to get him, and a thousand of the Austrian altered muskets would be most acceptable if we could have them sent at once . . . We want all the revolvers that can be spared . . . Hurry up the Guards and have the requisition for their clothing filled . . . Have Captain McKeever send up the Fitz H. Warren Regiment to me, all of it if possible . . . Order up instantly Colonel Crafts-Wright's Regiment . . ."

There were few officers left in St. Louis, and most of those on hand were sick. Jessie had no authority to sign orders or requisition goods; she spent half her time trying to locate the arms and supplies, the other half trying to get officers to sign the requisitions so that they would be legal. She worked with a demoniacal intensity which surpassed her own strength and abilities; for she knew how hard pressed John was, and how dangerous his position. She let no slight possibility escape her to send him a word of encouragement: to tell him how loyal the people of St. Louis were to him, of how certain they were of a smashing victory; of the tribute that Horace Greeley had paid him in the New York *Tribune,* of what a congressman had said on the floor the day before about the energy and the determination of General Fremont. She kept her letters cheerful, confident, loving; and always there would come back the reply, "I read your note to get its good, bright color."

On September twenty-ninth she received a telegram telling her that since he would be obliged to remain for a number of days in Jefferson City, she was to leave at once for his camp. She knew there was no special work for which she was wanted in Jefferson City; in addition to wanting to see her one last time before going into battle, this telegram-summons was a gesture of love and affirmation.

John met her at the railroad station in Jefferson City. She spent five days watching him whip the army into its final fighting form. There were still many things lacking: several of his officers had failed to bring up their regiments from other parts of Missouri; it was impossible to keep a continuous chain of supply wagons flowing to the camps. Yet she saw that none of these difficulties deterred John or his men: they were living off the countryside, were in the highest health and spirits and spoiling for the battle which would establish the Army of the West as one of the great fighting forces of the nation.

On the day before they were to break camp and move southward in pursuit of Confederate General Price, Secretary of War Simon Cameron arrived in camp unannounced. Secretary Cameron had long been an admirer of the Fremonts, had campaigned for them in 1856 and had supported their emancipation proclamation before Lincoln had turned the administration against it. Simon Cameron was tall, slender, with friendly gray eyes, a high brow, a magnificent stand of hair, and an ever youthful manner. He had been a newspaper editor as a youth, had joined journalism to politics, made a fortune out of state printing, gone on to railroad building and banking. Enormously successful as a businessman and a boss politician in Pennsylvania, he had scrambled for the Republican nomination in 1860, withdrawing in favor of Abraham Lincoln after Lincoln's manager had promised him the office of secretary of war. He gave war contracts only to his friends, and then blinked at their defrauding of the Union armies, a condition which had brought such an avalanche of criticism that President Lincoln was already casting about for a European appointment with which to get rid of him.

He said as bluntly as his genial manner would permit, "General, I have taken the liberty of inspecting your camp. I find things in confusion: the organization of the companies is bad, the troops are in need of clothing . . ."

"We are in need of many things, Secretary Cameron," replied John. "Supplies for which we have been begging Washington frantically for two months, and no part of which we have received. Though the men's uniforms may not be in fighting trim, their hands and hearts are."

"Please understand me, General," cried Secretary Cameron. "This investigation is not of my choosing."

"Then may we ask of whose choosing it is?" said Jessie.

"President Lincoln ordered me to investigate the general's department."

"Did you confer with Blair in St. Louis?"

"Yes, Mrs. Fremont, I went over the affairs of the department with Frank Blair."

There was an awkward moment of quiet, during which Jessie almost had to bite her tongue to keep from replying; but she had learned a bitter lesson in the past months, and so she kept silent, waiting for John to speak. It was Secretary Cameron who broke the silence.

"I have in my pocket a recall order signed by President Lincoln. He asked me to use my own judgment: if I did not find you ready to open the long-awaited campaign, I was to relieve you of your command."

Jessie had to admire the courtesy of John's manner.

"Secretary Cameron," he said, "let us not waste our time discussing Frank Blair or his charges against me in St. Louis. May I show you our plans for the offensive? We are ready to strike. In another thirty to sixty days we will have swept the Confederates out of Missouri, and our gunboat flotilla will have opened the Mississippi River all the way to New Orleans."

He launched into a vigorously detailed presentation of his campaign plans. Jessie watched Secretary Cameron; she was relieved to see the grimness ease out of his face as he became interested in John's swift maneuvers on the strategy maps before them. The sun had sunk behind the western hills and long shadows were creeping into the tent. An officer entered, saluted and said, "The troops are ready for the evening service, sir."

John looked up from his maps. "Mr. Secretary, would you pay us the honor of attending our last services?"

Secretary Cameron nodded, took Jessie's arm, went out of the tent and into the large open square. The Zagonyi Guard in its dark blue uniforms was drawn up at attention before the flag bearer, with troops solidly banking the square. The band played the hymn "Old Hundred" while the several thousand young soldiers sang the words of the simple prayer. To Jessie it was a beautiful and stirring sight, this army standing bareheaded against the setting sun as the chaplain gave the benediction. Then she heard the drumbeat which sent the companies back to their camps; as darkness overcame the square the fires were lighted on the hillsides, and they could hear the soldiers singing.

Jessie, John and Secretary Cameron stood quietly in the now deserted square until John finally said, "You have seen the Army of the West; you can see that there is no confusion in their hearts. They are ready and eager to fight for the Union."

Secretary Cameron turned to Jessie. "I will admit that Mrs. Fremont was right in her deduction. After my visit with Frank Blair in St. Louis I had decided to serve President Lincoln's removal order. But now I have changed my mind: I have seen your plans, I am impressed by your vitality, and if ever I have seen a unified body of men, ready to fight, this army which received its benediction tonight is ready. I am going to withhold the recall order until my return to Washington; this will give you a chance, General, to fulfill your hopes of routing the enemy."

"How much time will I have?"

"As much as I can earn for you. Strike hard and fast, let nothing deter you. We are starved for a victory: northern morale is shattered. Enlistments have fallen off, the administration is losing the confidence and support of the people, England and Europe expect our defeat and are planning to support the Confederacy. If you give us a victory now, at no matter what immediate cost, you may save the Union cause."

John's eyes flashed as he said, "You shall have your victory."

"Believe me, General Fremont, I myself would put no time limit on you, but your enemies in Washington are hounding Mr. Lincoln, giving him no peace, trying to force his hand . . . I can hold them off for only a few more weeks. Should you have failed by that time, you can understand that you must give place to some other officer."

"Should I fail," replied John gravely, "I will resign at once."

The next morning Jessie returned to general headquarters in St. Louis. On her maps, during the weeks following, she watched her husband push ever deeper south in pursuit of the enemy, Tipton, Warsaw, the Osage River, while General Price retreated, burning everything behind him. John had confided to her in code message that the enemy could not fall back farther than Springfield; he was confident that he could overtake them there and inflict a defeat.

Then on October twenty-sixth came news which thrilled both her and the nation: the Zagonyi Guard, numbering only one hundred and fifty men, had attacked and routed General Price's garrison of two thousand men at Springfield. This heroic action disproved the months of charges against John and the Zagonyi Guard: that they were bedecked autocrats whose only function it was to serve as a staff of honor to their general. It was the first good news Jessie had had in weeks, and she blessed the foolhardy, valiant men who had achieved the victory.

The next day, though the press still rang with praise of the Zagonyi charge, a secret message reached her from Washington. John's weeks of grace were up: President Lincoln had recalled him. The official order had already been dispatched by courier to General Hunter, in St. Louis. General Hunter was to relieve General Fremont, taking over his army and his command. After all John's work and plans, now, on the eve of his major attack, he was to be relieved, under conditions which implied that all charges against him were true.

She sat bolt upright in her chair: General Hunter was here in St. Louis. It would take two full days for President Lincoln's dispatch bearer to reach St. Louis by train. Her telegraphic message would have given her a day's start. What then, if she beat General Hunter to John's camp, gave him the word which would send him into action and bring about such a decisive victory that the recall order could never be served?

This was the opportunity she had been awaiting so eagerly, the chance to do John a service over and above the line of duty, of such outstanding importance that it would compensate for her failing with Abraham Lincoln and Frank Blair.

10

SHE SPRANG UP and went to the map of Missouri hanging on the wall. John was camped just south of Springfield, about two hundred and fifty miles away. A train was due to leave for Rolla in two hours. Rolla was halfway to Springfield; from there she could hire fast carriages, and when these failed, saddle horses. That would still give her several hours' lead on General Hunter. She quickly packed a few toilet articles in a small handbag and by four o'clock was on the train that left the Union Station. The cars were crowded with troops, the roadbed was bad, the train made long stops every few miles for purposes which the passengers never ascertained.

She rode all night in the dark, cold car, almost beside herself with impatience at the fact that the train stood still in the middle of prairie darkness as often as it moved forward. She sat with her eyes closed, but her thoughts were racing at tremendous speed, recapitulating everything they had done since the first hour they reached St. Louis, all that could be done in the future if only John's drive to the south were successful.

She relived the agonies she had endured while waiting for DeRosier's brother to return from Kaw's Landing with word from John that he had started on the trail with his second expedition before Colonel Abert's recall order could reach him. Then, she had just turned nineteen; today she was going on thirty-eight; then she had stood up against Colonel Stephen Watts Kearny; today she had stood up against Abraham Lincoln. She knew that reverberations of her session with the president had done her serious injury, that Mr. Lincoln's closest friends were publicly labeling her a virago and a fishwife, calling her a dangerous woman because of her fanatical loyalty to her husband. Was there any other kind of loyalty? If she were not passionately prejudiced in her husband's favor, what kind of a wife was she, what kind of a marriage had she created? If a wife were unwilling to dash through the night to save her husband, even though she knew from years of deep-bitten experience the suffering and hardship which might ensue, was she being the most possible wife?

At six in the morning she had coffee and a roll in the station at Rolla, then found a livery stable, engaged a carriage and two horses. The driver was old and unused to hurrying, but something in her manner persuaded him to urgency. During the long hours of the morning she was jostled and bumped along the stagecoach road; at noon they exchanged horses at an inn where she was able to get a hot meal; within the hour they were on their way again. The driver knew his road, but in the failing light of dusk, outside Lebanon, one of the wheels struck a deep rut, broke and threw the carriage over on its side. Jessie crawled out unhurt, but she could not persuade the tired driver to do anything about getting a new wheel or patching the carriage.

Leaving her suitcase behind, she walked the seven miles to Lebanon as fast as she could. She had not slept for almost forty-eight hours, she had been jostled and scrambled and thrown out on the road and was near exhaustion, but her driving will pushed her forward. In Lebanon she hoped to find a fresh carriage.

It was dark by the time she reached the public square. The town was locked up for the night. She saw that it would be almost impossible to get even a saddle horse at this hour; simultaneously she realized that she was spent, that she would not be able to ride the remaining fifty miles to John's camp without a few hours of rest. Three men were talking at one side of the square; she went to them and asked if they could direct her to an inn. An elderly man studied her carefully, then motioned for her to follow him. He led her up the hill to a large house, opened the door and showed her in. His wife and daughters took her into a large family room; she saw at once from their faces, the violins and guitars, the high pile of music books, the too tightly plaited light hair of the women, that this was a bit of Germany transplanted to Missouri.

She explained that she wanted a room in which to rest for a few hours, and some kind of conveyance to take her to Springfield. The mother showed her to a small bedroom. She slept until she heard the sound of a cart coming up the hill. She dressed quickly, found that it was four in the morning and that her hosts could locate only a plow horse and a country cart without springs. The young son went along to drive for her, but the progress was so slow that she seized the first opportunity to rent a riding horse from a farmer along the road.

It was night when she reached John's camp. The sentry took her quickly to the general's tent, before which a fire was burning. As she opened the flap and stepped in, she saw John sitting at the end of a long wooden table, poring over his maps. He sprang up, an alarmed expression on his face, asked her a hundred questions, why she had come, how she had gotten there, what had happened. It was not until she had bathed her hands and face in cold water and rested for a few moments that she could speak.

"John," she said, "President Lincoln has recalled you. General Hunter is on his way here to take over your command."

His face became a polite mask of withdrawal as he asked, "When will General Hunter arrive?"

"I don't know. I have been dreading all along that I would be too late, that he would get here before me."

"We are attacking at dawn," he said quickly. "All the plans have been laid. The Rebels are determined to make their stand at Wilson's Creek. In another few hours we will reach the culmination of our month's work . . . and avenge Nathaniel Lyon's death."

"General Hunter may be only an hour or two away."

"I will double the guard." He summoned an officer, issuing orders that no one was to be admitted through the lines for any reason whatever. When the officer had left, John said, "Come, sit here with me at the table." She sat quietly while he sketched for her with darting fingers the strategy by means of which he intended to defeat General Price's army and drive it before him. She heard little of what he said. She knew that he would lead his troops into action, that what had happened to Nathaniel Lyon at Wilson's Creek could happen to John Fremont, that many men must fall. He might be one of them. After a time John saw that she was not listening. He studied the anxiety in her eyes, then pushed aside his papers and maps, taking her hand in his.

"You would not have me be a haystack general?"

"I was just thinking: we had a twentieth anniversary a few days ago. You were in camp near the Osage River. Neither of us thought of it. We were too busy and preoccupied. So, my darling, this is a kind of anniversary party for us."

John held the palm of her hand to his cheek, saying, "We will have a celebration tomorrow—when the battle is over and the victory is won. But you have brought me a real anniversary present, Jessie: a chance to make good before it is too late. You have always given me my chance to make good, and always it has been at some critical moment like this."

They sat in the cool quiet of the tent, on either side of a corner of the rough table, while their minds went back over the twenty years; each knew that this might be the end. The tent was filled with their unspoken thoughts, their recollections of their happy years as well as the trials and difficulties they had come through. Slowly, almost painfully, Jessie said: "It's easy to speak of love in ordinary times—when there is no crisis at hand. But now, when your life is in danger, when we face a possible separation, I am so filled with gratitude for our twenty years of companionship that I have almost nothing to tell you; nothing but what I have told you so many times before: that I love you, that I loved you from the first moment you stepped from behind Father's chair at Miss English's Academy and took my hand, that you have been my whole life, and you have made my life beautiful and happy."

He did not move, but only watched her.

"I promised you that rainy afternoon, when we sat over the tea table before the blazing fire, that I would always love you. It is that love that has kept me ever striving to meet your hopes. I don't know what will happen tomorrow, Jessie; war is uncertain. A hundred unforeseen things can take place which will keep us from a real victory. But I will go onto that battlefield at dawn knowing that I must win . . ."

There was a sharp rap on the outside supporting pole of the tent. A courier pushed aside one flap and stepped in, his face streaked where the lines of perspiration had cut through the dust of the road. He saluted, asked, "General Fremont?" then ripped open his coat lining, took out a document that had been sewed in, and handed it to John.

John slammed the paper down on the table and cried, "Sir, how did you get admission into my lines?"

"I was ordered by General Hunter to deliver this message to you, sir." He saluted and disappeared.

II

JESSIE studied her husband's face anxiously while he looked first at the superscription, then at the signature at the bottom of the page. He then handed her the dispatch. She read the order, signed by President Lincoln, relieving General Fremont of his command. They sat in bitter silence for several moments, until John said, "The attack cannot be made at dawn. Everything that has been planned must be thrown aside."

"What is the hour now?"

"Almost midnight."

"Aren't you in command here until General Hunter arrives to supersede you?"

"Technically, yes."

"Then if General Hunter does not arrive by dawn, are you obliged to countermand your orders to this army? Everything has been prepared for a great victory. The Army of the West has the right to prove that it

can fight and play its part in this war. You have that right too, John. If
that messenger had been held outside the lines until morning . . ."

Seeming small and disheartened now, he could only reply, "You are
right, Jessie, the attack should be made. This order will cost the North
an important victory. Tomorrow will be a hundred days since we arrived
in St. Louis; everything we have done since then, every move that has
been made, has been pointed to this moment. It would be cruel to the
northern cause to throw away this opportunity . . ."

"Then you will attack?"

"No, I cannot. Any other officer might—any other officer should. With
my background, I cannot."

"But why, John?"

"I cannot commit mutiny."

Her thoughts stopped dead, for here was the enemy, their ever present
companion, the one word in all the world which paralyzed their brain
and courage as well, the symbol of their unhappiness. She walked quickly
to her husband's side. They must not be defeated now by torturous shadows from the past. She knew the chagrin that lay in store for him if he
were deposed now, at this very instant of climactic action; if only she
could persuade him to take the bold and brave course, her mission would
be fulfilled. In the aftermath of John's great victory she would be able to
step down with dignity, return north to her children because her task had
been completed. John would go on to greater victories. She faced her
husband resolutely.

"That is what you said when I urged you to send your troops to reinforce Colonel Mulligan, instead of obeying orders and sending your five
thousand men to Washington so that General McClellan could parade
them up and down Pennsylvania Avenue. Everything you've achieved,
John, has come through independent action rather than blind obedience.
It is the word we are afraid of, and not the act, for that cursed word
mutiny has come to haunt our dreams. When you needed money to pay the
troops, troops that were about to leave at the end of their ninety-day
enlistment, you seized the necessary money from the quartermaster. That
was illegal, but even the president approved of it. It may be illegal to start
such a battle at dawn, but to end it victoriously would never be considered
mutinous."

He shook his head despairingly.

"Ah, Jessie, the Army has a long memory: if I make a charge in the
morning and the enemy is not there, or they flee and refuse to fight, or if
they stand up and fight and we do not achieve an outstanding victory,
there will be a frightful hue and cry. It will be 'Fremont the Mutineer'
once again, the man who refuses to acknowledge authority, who is ruin-

ing the discipline of the Army, who leads his troops into battle not to help the Union but to save his own command and commission."

"Secretary Cameron told you how desperately a victory was needed; he ordered you to secure it at any cost . . ."

"Mr. Lincoln is commander in chief. His recall order supersedes Secretary Cameron's instructions."

"John, did you ever regret that I suppressed the order from Colonel Abert and sent you word which started you out on the second expedition?"

"No, Jessie, the result justified the act."

"Then why is that reasoning not equally valid now? You have reached the critical hour, the hour toward which you have been working for a hundred days. You have a decisive victory within your grasp. Will General Hunter be able to carry out your plans?"

"He will want to lay his own plans and determine his own campaign. This expedition will have been wasted."

"No victory is illegal, John, only defeats are illegal. Don't you owe it to the preparations you have made to fight this battle in the morning? You have never refused to accept the implications of bold and independent action. Is it fear of another court-martial? We have endured one such trial, we can endure another."

He sat at the end of the long wooden table, holding his face in his hands.

"I can't do it, Jessie," he murmured. "Your father once said that a little mutiny is the sometime genius of democracy. I have already indulged in that sometime genius. To that extent General Kearny was right. Consistent mutiny is more dangerous than any beneficial result it may achieve. I cannot make myself out an habitual mutineer."

She did not have the right to push him further. For herself, she was not afraid of the consequences; whether it were called mutiny, or any one of a hundred other names, she would have attacked at dawn. She had seen the men turn from raw recruits into a finely organized fighting unit; she had watched the laborious methods by means of which John had assembled sufficient guns and artillery to make this attack possible. Like Napoleon, they had spent one hundred days in a great campaign. But now it was all over, their efforts were for nothing, they would be denied any further place in this cause and this war for freedom for which they had long been preparing and had already made many sacrifices.

She knew that if the attack failed in the morning, Jessie and John Fremont would be called the "congenital mutineer and the female politician." She wondered why she, who once had been convinced by General Kearny that one cannot rise against one's own government, should now be willing to start on that rocky road all over again.

There was the sound of voices in the distance; they grew stronger by the moment and seemed to be converging from many directions. Jessie and John stepped outside the tent to learn the cause of the commotion. Word of John's removal had reached the officers' mess, and they had come to inquire. They stood about the tent in a semicircle, six deep; then there came a second movement of sound, of running feet and excited voices, and the soldiers began to pour into the open square until, in the quarter light of the moon, it seemed to Jessie that there were thousands of them stretching back to the very edge of the darkness.

One officer cried out, "Is it true, General Fremont, that you have been removed?"

"Yes," replied John quietly, "it is true." After a time he continued, "We have grown up together as an army. I have become familiar with the brave and generous spirit which you bring to the defense of your country. Continue as you have begun, and give to my successor the same cordial and enthusiastic support with which you have encouraged me. Soldiers, I regret to leave you."

There was a sharp cry of protest from the front rank of the officers. As Jessie stood to one side, she heard a unified wave of protest arise from the men, each saying something different, but each meaning the same. She could hear the officers threatening to resign, the soldiers demanding that he remain in charge, swearing that they would fight under no one else, that they would throw away their guns, that they had a right to fight as they had so long planned and been promised.

The men quieted. Everyone looked to John for his answer. He told them that no one could protest the act of the president, that it was a soldier's first duty to obey orders, that he was no longer their commanding officer, that they were not fighting for any one officer but for the great Union cause.

He asked the soldiers to return to their quarters. No one moved; this was not the answer they wanted or would accept. He turned and gazed at his wife. The air was charged with tension. She saw that he was undergoing a difficult struggle. She did not speak. It was now up to John, facing the army he had brought into existence, to make his final decision. He turned back to his men.

"Prepare for the attack!"

There was a spontaneous cry of joy; officers and men dispersed at once, shouting and singing in the wildest of enthusiasm. Jessie went inside the tent and sat at the long wooden table. After a few moments John came in and dropped down beside her. They sat with an arm about each other, these two companions of the Hundred Days. They had been plunged into a maelstrom of confusion and chaos, they had worked like people possessed, they had given the very best of their hearts and their brains to the cause they had loved for so many years. True, they had made mistakes: they had tried to fight the war, not the least expensively in dollars, but the least expensively in men. They had been fooled, cheated, defrauded—but always by northerners who were enriching themselves off war contracts. Combined with John's daring in the realm of military strategy, they had tried to utilize equal daring in the field of political maneuver, but President Lincoln had not been willing to emancipate the slaves, and so their independent action had been charged up to their record of impetuousness, to the uncontrollable passion to exceed their own authority. They still thought they were right about the emancipation of the Negroes; they still thought that that was what the war was about; they still thought that the slaves would have to be emancipated before the war could be ended, and they took comfort from the fact that half of the North sustained them in this belief. Yet here they were after only a hundred days, already disavowed and recalled. Only two or three hours, and then they must strike once again, without the legal right to do so, but with every need of their nature and of their cause crying out, even as it had in the second expedition and the California conquest, for bold and decisive action.

Once again their silence and their resolution were shattered: horses' hooves pounded in the distance, growing louder by the moment. While Jessie and John sat looking at each other in the darkness, their hands clasped, the horses galloped up to the front of the tent. The riders quickly dismounted. There was the sound of boots on the small wooden platform outside the tent. Jessie and John rose as General Hunter entered, presented his compliments to General Fremont, and took command of the Army of the West.

Their train was due in St. Louis at nine in the morning, but it did not get in until nine in the evening. When they reached the Brant house they found the street and all the open space around the house filled with women and children, with young boys and old men who had been standing there since early morning. When they got out of their carriage they heard cheers and shouts. As the crowd opened to let them through, she saw that their doorposts were garlanded and the steps covered with flowers. The wives and children of their soldiers in Springfield spoke to them as they went by, words of encouragement and praise and love. One old woman said resolutely as they passed:

"Never you mind, General Fremont and Jessie, we stand by you in your hour of disgrace."

John stood in the doorway facing the crowd below him, trying to speak, to express some word of gratitude or encouragement. Jessie did not want all these good people to see her crying; she went into the house and climbed resolutely to her tiny bedroom where, from the dormer balcony, she could gaze on the scene below. Far down the side street she saw the crowds part and horsemen come through, carrying torches. It was the Zagonyi Guard, many of them bandaged, their horses and their uniforms bullet-torn. They halted before the Brant house, wheeled front, drew their sabers and gave their last salute to their commander.

For Jessie it was such a moving sight that the tears streamed down her cheeks: these officers of the Zagonyi Guard had been dismissed from the service with John, their commissions nullified; the wounded and dead among them had been repudiated, the dead who had fought so valiantly at Springfield had died in vain.

A feeling much like the one at the Delaware Indian Reservation came over here. She sat down on the edge of her iron bed and buried her face in her hands. She knew that the war, which had hardly begun, was already over for them. All that would be left would be investigations and trials, charges and accusations, the bitterness of frustration and defeat. Yet in a sudden flash of clarity she saw that this would be true for everyone involved in this dreadful war, that few would achieve more than defeat, despair and death.

She heard the last round of cheers from the crowd below; she heard the horses wheel and go down the long cobbled street; she heard the people move away and the night grow silent; she heard her husband's weary footsteps on the stairs.

What did they do now? Where did they turn? How did they face the days ahead?

Standing there, suffering mutely, her heart hurting, scarcely able to breathe, she remembered a moment twenty years before: she was carrying her first child, and John had left that very morning on his first great expedition to the West. She would have to live without him for the next six months. She had gone very early into her father's library to help with some work. When they had organized their tasks, and her father had departed for the Senate, an overwhelming loneliness had risen out of the early morning darkness, just as now. And then she had seen that her father had left a note on her desk with a quotation from Marcus Aurelius:

Be not disturbed about the future, for if you ever come to it, you will have the same reason for your guide which preserves you at present.

She heard John's steps coming up the last few stairs. She turned from the window, a slow smile on her lips, and crossed the room quickly to throw open the door for her husband.

BOOK SEVEN

Good Times Will Come Again

WHEN SHE COULD ENDURE NO LONGER the pain of war, when death was all about her, death of their former comrades on the battlefield, death of the sons of their closest friends, when it seemed as though the whole nation would destroy itself, her mind turned for asylum to the little cottage at Black Point, so simple, so clean with the wind and the sun and the rain of the West keeping everything fresh and alive. She had three enthusiastic allies, Lily, Charlie and Frank, who were more homesick than she for San Francisco. Yet she knew that they could not go home: they had to defend themselves before a congressional investigating committee; once exonerated, there might be another command or an important position inside the government, where John could use his skill and experience to help put an end to the hostilities.

She tried to rent a furnished home in New York, but the city was crowded with war activities and the thousands of people who had flocked there from all over the North. She could find nothing livable and so, to rescue her family from hotels and to get them all under one roof again, she bought a furnished house on Nineteenth Street. John moved his papers into a small downstairs study where he devoted the days to working on his defense. Jessie spent her mornings helping to write his brief, assembling the documents that he needed to substantiate his case. They both worked hard and earnestly, discussing little else when they were in each other's presence; but John was frequently summoned to Washington to provide the investigators with information, and so part of Jessie's time was released for the task that touched her the most deeply. The sick and wounded of the Union armies were streaming into the big cities, where there were inadequate facilities to care for them. The Sanitary

Commission was doing what it could, but just as on that first day at the Jefferson Barracks, when she had found men lying mortally ill with cups of coffee and slabs of salt pork resting on their chests, so now there were insufficient hospitals to provide beds for the wounded, a dire lack of doctors, nurses, medical and sanitary supplies: the government had money on hand to buy the implements of war with which to injure men, but rarely enough to buy the remedies with which to make them well again.

After settling her family in the house on Nineteenth Street and putting the children into their various schools, she gave her afternoons and evenings to the task of raising funds. From old friends she elicited money by loving means; from others she extracted by any method she could contrive: persuasion or flattery, by shaming some, as she had in St. Louis, or conveying to others who had seen no part of the war, who had never clapped eyes on a stricken soldier, the greatness of the need and the value of the contribution. Between fund-raising campaigns she began one of the first drives to stock the hospitals with books and magazines; persuaded women to go into the sickrooms each day to write letters for the wounded; kept the wards brightened by the color and fragrance of home-grown flowers. Any day which gave one moment of happiness to a stricken man or brought him one step closer to recovery was a day superbly spent. There were letters from nearly every state in the North and West, letters from mothers thanking her for a last kindness to a boy, far away from home, before he died; letters from wives and sisters whose young men had returned to them because of an arrangement she had made for their medical care; letters from the men now back in service with the Army who had not forgotten the hour of kindly talk, the bringing of a specialist who was able to save an arm or an eye.

One of her greatest heartbreaks was the sorry condition of the wounded officers of the former Zagonyi Guard. Ill, destitute, not even entitled to government hospitalization, the plight of these men and their families was a desperate one. To Jessie's mind they had not only earned full hospitalization and financial help until they could get on their feet again, but were entitled to credit for one of the great charges of the war. One day she perceived a way to achieve both of these ends: she went to Boston to see Ticknor & Fields, a publishing company, and suggested that she write a book called *The Story of the Guard*. Mr. Ticknor advanced her six hundred dollars on the idea, all of which she spent on medical care for the suffering officers. She then settled herself in the dining room of her home with the correspondence from the Guard while they were en route to Springfield, and John's records of their early formation. She worked for eleven consecutive days, from seven in the morning until it was time to clear away her papers for dinner. Ticknor & Fields rushed *The Story of*

the Guard into print. It sold widely among a northern public avid for
stories of heroism and victory. Jessie earned several thousand dollars with
which to aid the Zagonyi officers.

She found it salutary to be doing a non-controversial labor of love: on
the political front there were no hospitals, no doctors or nurses, no books,
flowers or acts of mercy. Her reputation was now at as low a point as it
had been at a high in 1856, when almost half of the nation had cried out
for "Fremont and Jessie." Her interview with President Lincoln had
been spread abroad, without any of its extenuating circumstances. People
only knew that she had come into the presence of Mr. Lincoln soiled and
unkempt, that Mr. Lincoln had said, "She taxed me so violently that I
had to exercise all my clumsy tact to avoid quarreling with her"; that
she had belligerently told Frank Blair that she had just as much right at
the war front as any man. The Army was criticizing her for having
usurped the position of chief of staff; the echoes of the unfortunate forty-
eight hours in Washington were being repeated from mouth to mouth,
altered with each telling, exaggerated, twisted and sometimes even perverted; and this picture of herself as an ambitious, pushing, dictatorial,
vainglorious and unnatural female was something that shocked her to the
very core. How much finer and sweeter to walk into a hospital room with
a gift for a sick boy than to walk into general headquarters and be
plunged into a quarrel over the military power versus the political.

With spring, Jessie and John went down to Washington for the formal
hearing before the joint committee of both houses of Congress. Once
again, as with the court-martial ten years before, their reputation and
personal standing were at stake. Yet this could not be a scientific trial:
it was to be conducted by civilians who would be obliged to form opinions about elements of battle strategy which General Fremont had not
been given sufficient time to bring to completion. General Jessie too
would be on trial here, for although she had no official standing or commission of which she might be deprived, the investigation had the power
to condemn both her presence and her activities in St. Louis, and to convict her husband on the basis of her performance.

Instead of being uneasy and worried at the frequent postponements of
the hearing, Jessie did what she could to delay further the opening of the
investigation. True, John was being held inactive, he was spoiling for the
fight with his adversaries in the War Department, but a cooler judgment
showed her that every passing day brought them closer to vindication;
the ever onrushing failures and tragedies of the war had already enveloped so many other departments and commanders that her husband
was no longer the most important general to have been broken. Had not
President Lincoln removed General George B. McClellan as commander

of the Army of the Potomac because he was impotent to give the order which would send his superbly trained and equipped army into action? The North was coming to understand the complexity of waging a war without trained soldiers, without rifles or artillery, without food or clothing, and she saw that public sympathy was slowly swinging back to General Fremont, that the obloquy which had blanketed them when they first had reached New York was lightening, withdrawing to cover other Union commanders, continuing defeats and political frustrations in Washington.

Jessie and John stayed at the home of Eliza and William Carey Jones during the weeks of the hearing. Though no one referred back to the burdened days of the court-martial, the memory of those sorely troubled times was heavy upon them when John asked William Carey Jones for a few suggestions as to proper procedure before the Committee on the Conduct of the War.

Late in March, Jessie, Eliza and John walked up Pennsylvania Avenue in the cool spring sunlight, standing for a moment on the steps of the Congressional Building before going into the committee room. When the investigators filed in and took their places around a long table, she was relieved to find that for the most part they were men who had been sympathetic to the Fremont cause: Ben Wade of Ohio, Zachariah Chandler of Michigan, John Covode of Pennsylvania and George W. Julian of Indiana.

By checking the more important northern newspapers she saw that they were reproducing the solicitor general's charges in full, but that their sting was being pulled by accompanying editorials which pictured the chaos into which the Fremonts had been plunged in July, and told of how much more they had accomplished, under incredible hardships, than had been accomplished in most other fields of operation.

When John rose to face the commission it was with quiet assurance; his voice as he began to read his prepared defense was calm. She made no attempt to follow his argument point by point; she had been over this manuscript countless times. Instead her mind wandered back to the court-martial of fourteen years before. This too was a court-martial, though it was being held under more polite guise: what good to try a man after he had already been publicly condemned and punished? The court-martial had terminated John's career in the Topographical Corps, rung down the curtain on the first half of his professional life. Was this committee meeting then the final act in their drama? Would this investigation terminate the second half of their career, send them out to face another thirteen or twenty-three years of wandering?

She was awakened from her reverie by the mention of her own name and the revelation of material which her husband had put in the brief without her knowledge: stories of her service in St. Louis, affidavits from his general staff on her success in assembling supplies when there were simply no supplies to be had; the tribute paid to her by Dorothea Dix for setting up the hospital at Jefferson Barracks, testimonials from the Sanitary Commission which praised her work in gathering nurses and medical equipment. He testified that he had sent her to Washington, instructed her to go straight to the White House from the railroad station, that she not leave until Mr. Lincoln had a full accounting of the Western Command. She was grateful and touched when John apologized to the president by assuring Mr. Lincoln that his wife had gone to him with the fullest respect for his person and his office, that any untoward word that had been uttered had come as the result of great tension and fatigue for which he, General Fremont, alone was responsible.

It took him two and a half days to present his case; it then took the commission another two and a half days to reach its decision. Generals Fremont and Jessie were not only cleared, but given high praise for their conduct of the war. Their mistakes and failures were not glossed over, but were set down as the results of energy and purpose in trying to accomplish in a few months what would have required a year in the careful doing. John was commended for the gunboat flotilla, the Unionizing of St. Louis, the warfare against the guerrillas, the appointment and instructions to General Grant, the building of fighting morale into the Army of the West, the pursuit of General Price, who had been determined even in the face of impending defeat to take a stand against General Fremont's superior forces beyond Springfield at the dawn of the day that General Hunter took over the command.

The newspapers of the East and West were almost unanimous in their praise of the commission's decision, agreeing with its final statement that John Fremont's command of the West "was eminently characterized by earnestness, ability, and the most unquestionable loyalty." At a giant meeting at the Cooper Institute some of the North's best loved leaders, Charles Sumner, Schuyler Colfax, David Dudley Field, Charles King, William Evarts endorsed John's now repudiated doctrine of emancipation. Henry Ward Beecher urged them to come to his Plymouth Church one Sunday morning, and in his sermon contrasted John with Daniel Webster, saying that Webster had died and would remain dead because he had compromised with slavery, but that John Fremont's name would live and forever be remembered when the United States was a nation of free men. Reports came in from Cincinnati, Andover, Gallipolis and from the farm lands of Iowa that among the families who were fighting the war, the love of John Fremont and his emancipation proclamation remained deep and constant, that his removal had undermined the people's faith in their government.

She was happy that they had been exonerated, yet it was the happiness of relief and thanksgiving rather than of promise for the future. These public avowals of faith could not bring back those hours just before the dawn of November third when John and his army stood ready to score one of the first major victories for the North. The commission had justified John Fremont, the country's faith in him had been reborn, yet there were other men, younger men who would come up to take his place, men who were fresh and enthusiastic and full of fight, men with confidence because the war in all its ramifications had not yet rolled over them. They had had their chance to make a contribution to the Union cause and had somehow failed; failed, as always, for good reasons, even for heroic reasons, but nonetheless failed.

2

THE WAR YEARS had a special quality for Jessie: an ever present nervous tautness, a lean brittle hardness, the sense of living not in the hateful present, which one repudiated with each battle, but in the passionately desired and far away future.

The year 1863 opened so auspiciously that she genuinely believed its end might also see the end of the war: for on New Year's Day Abraham Lincoln gave the country an emancipation proclamation. Only fifteen months before he had cried at her, "The general should never have dragged the Negro into the war. The Negro had nothing to do with it." Now Mr. Lincoln's acceptance of emancipation had vindicated them politically, as the congressional investigators had vindicated them militarily.

Her work with the Sanitary Commission was almost done, for there was an adequate supply of nurses and hospitals, and the country had been awakened to the need of supplying funds for the wounded soldiers. Just as on that unhappy night in Washington when she had stood before the weed-grown Benton lot and yearned to be back in her home at Black Point, away from the strife and warfare which were tearing her apart, so now her thoughts went with increasing frequency to their glassed-in gallery where they watched the ships in the Golden Gate strait, where she rode horseback over the dunes with her three children and sailed the bay with them in an open boat. She yearned for peace and privacy, for the touch of her intimate possessions, for the literary discussions with Thomas Starr King and Bret Harte, for the sense of living on a frontier where people were too busy growing and building to participate in personal feuds or political vendettas. With a start she realized that she was longing for the amiable and tranquil life; if she was not yearning for the stately traditions of Cherry Grove she was at least hungering for the security and tradition of Black Point, more fitted to her own temperament than Cherry Grove, but nonetheless the beautiful refuge against controversy for which Elizabeth McDowell Benton had yearned so many years.

"I know how terribly you want to go home, Jessie," John said sympathetically, "but there would be nothing for me to do in San Francisco."

" . . . Not even your plans for the transcontinental railroad?"

"All railroad projects originate here, in the East. I'm beginning to feel my way about; the prospects look good . . . Patience, my dear, and courage," he murmured, as he kissed her cheek. "In a few years you will have your own private railroad car, and you will travel between your New York and San Francisco homes every month."

She returned his kiss, then cried, "Of course! I am trying to chase a rainbow across a whole continent. Home is where your work lies! Could anyone know that better than I?" She paused pensively. "It's only that those months at Black Point were so beautiful; they stay as vivid in my memory as though they happened yesterday. When your railroad is built, we will go back home."

Suspended in mid-air, with no real job or desire but to see this horrible war ended, she carried on a correspondence with Thomas Starr King, exchanging news of the East for King's reportage of the spirit and temper of San Francisco; she succeeded in getting one of Bret Harte's poems in the *Atlantic Monthly;* and she and John became the close friends and confidants of the poet, John Greenleaf Whittier, who had written during their presidential campaign, "Rise up, Fremont, and go before; the hour must have its man"; who had given the Fremont supporters throughout the nation a rallying point when he had written, after John's removal, "Thy error, Fremont, simply was to act a brave man's part, without the statesman's tact." John clung to Whittier's judgment and friendship because of what he described to Jessie as the poet's spiritual incorruptibility. Seeing how much of insight and perspective Whittier was able to bring to her husband, she frequently invited the poet to their home for a several days' visit; she and John went to Amesbury to spend the week end with Whittier among his flowers and books.

Then the war struck at her from yet another angle: she received a telegram from the War Department informing her that the government had taken over Black Point, that a fort was to be built on the site of her home. She read the telegram several times, unable to grasp its meaning. Why should the government want Black Point? Why must they have this particular tiny piece of land? They could not take away a family's home. A home was private property!

But when she showed the telegram to her husband, he stumblingly told her that her deductions were wrong: the government could confiscate any property it needed for the national safety. Black Point was only a mile away from Alcatraz; with cannons mounted at both these points, nc enemy ship could enter San Francisco Bay. It was cruel, it blasted their dream of returning to Black Point, but he could see the War Department's justification. No, there was nothing they could do about it except send on their title and receipt for payment, and wait for the government to return the cost of their land.

Her eyes swimming in tears, Jessie asked, "But what about our house? They have no need for our cottage."

"It's too big to be moved, and the War Department is in too much of a hurry. They'll tear it down to make way for gun emplacements."

"Tear it down!" she cried in agony. "Why do other people have the right to tear down our possessions and our lives? Why did they have the right to tear us down in St. Louis and dismiss you from your command, only to have the investigating committee and now President Lincoln acknowledge that you were right all the time? Why do they have the right to tear down our home on Black Point and then in a year or two acknowledge apologetically that they were wrong, that they didn't need the land after all? Aren't we human beings, with hearts and souls and feelings? Don't we have any rights? Can we be stripped of everything we own and everything we hold sacred? Have we no defense against them . . . ?"

"I can't answer your questions, my dear," he said, heavyhearted, "for there is no 'them.' Today it's the War Department that has deprived us of our home; yesterday it was the Blairs and Mr. Lincoln who deprived us of our command; the day before that it was the venality of the press and lack of restraint in the slanderings of a political party that lost us the presidency and the White House; the day before that it was the negligence of an election law which did not guarantee to the most widely desired senator the long term, which deprived us of our career in the Senate; the day before that it was General Kearny, Colonel Cooke and Lieutenant Emory who robbed us of our commission. You see, my dear, there is no 'them': with each turn of fortune it's another person, another reason, another force."

"Then there is nothing we can do—no protest we can make . . . ?"

"None. This telegram from the War Department does not ask your permission to take over Black Point; its purpose is to inform you that they have already done so. Now listen to me, my darling; no, no, don't turn your head away. Let me see your face. Yes, I know you're crying and that you don't like me to see you when your eyes are red; I'm even foolish enough to think that you're beautiful when you're crying, for you always cry for the right reasons. I know that San Francisco and the cottage on Black Point have been your mind's haven. We must simply find another haven . . ."

She shook her head sadly.

"It was our first real home and hearth, a way of life, a tradition to go back to. Our last refuge has been taken from us."

But she was wrong: there were other refuges, refuges of the mind, deep recesses of comfort and faith that could be stripped from her. The first came in the news of the Reverend King's death in San Francisco, death from overwork and exhaustion, from the burning out of his flaming spirit for the Union cause. On the heels of this blow, Eliza died suddenly in Washington, died from the illnesses that had plagued her during her youth. William Jones was in California on a war mission, and so Jessie went to Washington to bury her older sister in the Benton plot, at the foot of her mother and father. Along with her grief at the early passing of Eliza, who was forty-one, Jessie was stricken at how fast the Benton family was disappearing. She was only thirty-nine, and yet she had already lost her mother and her father, her brother and her sister. Now there were only herself and the two younger girls left.

Death must be my friend, she thought; he so rarely leaves my side.

She was sitting in the window of her home on Nineteenth Street one midafternoon of June 1863 when she saw John come bounding up the steps, his face wreathed in smiles. Proudly he thrust a copy of the New York *Tribune* into her hand, his eager finger circling an announcement that he had formed a partnership with Samuel Hallet, a respected promoter, and had been elected president of a proposed railroad which they were going to build across the state of Kansas. She tried to continue reading the article, which told of how General Fremont had opened offices on Beaver Street, but John was too impatient to let her finish; he took the paper from her, noisily turned the page and showed her his advertisement, which asked for bids on several thousand tons of iron rails to be delivered to Kansas City, the Kaw's Landing of his early expeditions. Even in the excitement her eyes caught the accompanying diagram and she saw that the route he had laid out for his railroad followed very closely the original trail he had mapped through the mountains and plains, that his major stations were to be built at towns which had grown up on the ashes of his early campfires.

They had lived largely on the hopes of starting their railroad, but up to this moment there had been nothing but disappointment. The blows had fallen from every side: they had necessarily neglected the Mariposa and it was sold out from under them, with John losing both ownership and control, but still holding three eighths of the profits; the federal government was disinterested in railroading and would give them no assistance; their opponents in Washington, in particular the Blair family, still made it impossible for John to secure any co-operation from the administration. He complained to Jessie, "I am completely *persona non grata* in the capital; you would think I was a fire-eating Democrat who had opposed their election. I can't build my railroad without a right of way and land grants. As Tom Benton could have told you, you can't get a right of way through Congress without being a tactical politician."

"And Lord knows we've had enough politics," she sympathized.

But now the difficult days were over: John was on the main track again, fulfilling a lifetime ambition of their family. His eyes sparkled and his proper love of self seemed to have been born again with the setting up of the new project. The newspapers carried thrilling accounts of his plans for an iron road to California; the country became railroad conscious and even the reluctant Congress began to see that they would eventually have to play some part in this expansion to the west. Taking his position as a bold and resourceful railroad builder, a man fulfilling still another dream of western expansion, John rose rapidly in favor and was restored to the position of respect he had so long enjoyed.

Once again they would be able to start a new life and work at a valuable job; all that had gone before would be forgotten in the vigor and joy of accomplishment. For the first time since General Hunter had taken over their command in the lamp-lit tent beyond Springfield, eighteen months before, she felt the promise of personal happiness and security.

3

SHE HAD INTIMATED to her husband that she was through with politics, but she soon learned that politics was not through with her. Though she no longer visited Washington, much of official Washington was in and out of her home in New York. Over her dinner table Richard Henry Dana told them that it was almost impossible to find loyalty to the president in Washington, that the general conviction of Lincoln's incompetence had taken such a firm hold that if a convention were to be held that night he could not be renominated. It was reported that only two members of the Thirty-Seventh Congress supported Mr. Lincoln, that no one in Washington except Lincoln's inner group wanted his renomination. William P. Fessenden wrote in a letter, "Never was such a shambling set of incapables collected in one government; we went in for a rail-splitter, and we have got one." Senator Sherman of Ohio charged Lincoln with responsibility for the war chaos. Reverberations came of a movement in New York to force the president to resign because he was "fickle, careless and totally unqualified."

For a long while Jessie followed the political furor simply as part of the war scene, but by the time 1863 was half over she was obliged to report to her husband that the critics of Mr. Lincoln were not baying in a hollow: they wanted Abraham Lincoln replaced by General John C. Fremont. They went to hear Wendell Phillips tell an audience of abolitionists jammed into the Cooper Institute that peace could not be restored until General Fremont manned the guns. She showed her husband cuttings from the Boston *Pioneer,* which proclaimed him to be the imperative candidate for the presidency in '64, and supporting editorials from such German newspapers as the Springfield *Staats Anzeiger* and the Mississippi *Blatter* which had begun a campaign for Fremont for president. Fremont clubs were formed in Illinois, Ohio, Wisconsin and New York. By the end of the year, as faith in President Lincoln declined, confidence in the ability and character of John Fremont began to rise to the fervor which had earned him the nomination in 1856.

Jessie did not know whether to be alarmed or pleased at these developments. Her thoughts raced on in confusion, for whenever she felt a twinge of regret that this deplorable criticism of the president was impeding the war effort, she would remember in the very same sentence the humiliation her husband had suffered at the hands of the administration. How magnificent it would be for John to replace Lincoln as the Republican nominee, to be elected to the presidency on a wave of popular acclaim— but how distasteful to go through another presidential campaign, to endure the insults and venom that had darkened their days in 1856!

But if there was uncertainty in her mind, she soon saw that there was none in her husband's: he wanted the nomination, he wanted the campaign, he wanted the election and the presidency and the White House. The slights and injustices he had suffered since the day of his appointment to the Western Command could be wiped out in one bold stroke: he would become commander in chief. He would dispossess his adversaries, the self-seeking men who had locked the borders of Washington against him; he would wage the war efficiently and decisively, end it quickly, then bend every effort of the government toward the rehabilitation of the South.

All of these things he told her, the secret hopes, revenges and gratifications which a husband confides only to a wife. When she saw how strongly he felt, how overwhelmingly he wanted the presidency, a thousand times more now than he had in 1856, she silenced the doubts and confusion in her own mind.

"Apparently you can once again have the Democratic nomination, if you want it," she commented, as she handed him a batch of clippings. "New York elected a Democratic governor in Horatio Seymour last year, and seven of the northern states went Democratic in Congress. If the temper of the people is the same in November 1864 as it is today, you could defeat Mr. Lincoln."

"No," replied John firmly, "we cannot injure the party we helped form. I am a Republican. I will never be anything else. If the war is still dragging on next spring, and I am offered the nomination of our own party . . ."

By a close survey of the newspapers in the early months of 1864, she was able to assure her husband that the popular swing to his support was gaining momentum. There was hardly a city in the North or West that did not have a Fremont club or a Fremont paper. The *New Nation* was founded to advance his candidacy. A convention of radical Republicans was called in Cleveland on May thirty-first, backed by the Fremont clubs and the many newspapers which supported him. When Jessie went to Cleveland, as she had gone to Philadelphia eight years before, she found some four hundred delegates gathered, representing practically all of the states of the North. The convention criticized President Lincoln for suspending the freedom of the press and freedom of speech, as well as the writ of habeas corpus, for being too lenient toward the South and, most important, of being incapable of terminating the conflict. While she sat, small and disheartened at the rear of the hall, convinced that John should not traffic with these malcontents and divisionists, she heard her husband nominated for the presidency.

When she had returned home from the Philadelphia convention in 1856 she had come back to her husband bursting with pride; this time she returned a little sick at her stomach. She had not been back in the house on Nineteenth Street for more than a day before she learned that John's nomination by the radical Republicans had become a serious threat to the Lincoln administration and that powerful weapons were being forged against him. Those portions of the Republican press which had been lukewarm toward Mr. Lincoln struck out boldly because their candidate had been put in jeopardy. The Cleveland *Herald* declared that the Cleveland nominating convention had been made up of "sly politicians from New York, impetuous hare-brained Germans from St. Louis, abolitionists, and personal friends and parasites of Fremont." She was further concerned to find that John's nomination greatly encouraged the South by evidencing a split in the Republican ranks; that the New York *Times* and other solidly Union papers were declaring that Mr. Lincoln had to be re-elected because any defeat now would be an admission that he should not have been elected in the first place.

Jessie found the campaign of 1864 to be even more maleficent than the one of 1856; for now, with the actualities of war, death and destruction everywhere, the voters and their press went berserk, reaching heights of name calling and personal vilification never before known. Few of the leading Republicans believed Lincoln could defeat the Democratic nominee, General George B. McClellan; his campaign managers lost all hope. Mr. Lincoln himself was resigned to defeat. It was then that the administration supporters began filing through the Fremont home to persuade John to step out of the race, offering him, through his wife, an important command in the war, the unseating of his enemies.

Jessie saw that her husband was adamant. He would not withdraw; he would strike no bargain. He told her a hundred times over that he was certain he could win. She knew that he had sufficient provocation to be sickened with idealism and to feel that the end justified the means, yet she found herself in the same position she had occupied in 1856 when John had told her about the Democratic nomination: she had wanted to become First Lady, but not at the cost of endorsing slavery. Now more than ever, after the harsh criticism that had been levied against her, she wanted to move into the White House. But if she had to risk destroying the Republican party, put a Democrat into the presidency, end the war by appeasement, with slavery still intact, was that not too high a price to pay for the chance of success? They had won two victories for idealism in 1856; for her part they must now somehow win another.

Toward the beginning of September she packed a bag and went to see John Whittier at Amesbury. Now fifty-seven, tall, with dark eyes that pierced one's intent, Whittier had suffered both physically and mentally at the hands of organized mobs that had pursued him for his fanatical loyalty to abolition. Though his poetry had a strong religious conviction, he did not hesitate to fall back on his practical experience as a political campaigner and founder of the Republican party. Jessie knew that the man who had edited anti-slavery newspapers throughout the forties and published the stirring *Voices of Freedom* poems in 1846 would give her advice that would be in season. Whittier lived alone in a small ivy-covered house, a bachelor, working as steadily as his ill health would permit at the three loves of his life: poetry, politics and freedom.

"I have come to ask what you think about the political situation, Mr. Whittier," she said. "I know how long and ardently you have supported General Fremont."

Whittier was thoughtful for a moment as he cleared away stacks of old newspapers and magazines, making room for Jessie on a wicker chair before a fireplace stuffed with discarded manuscripts. After pouring two glasses of sherry and seating himself on a hassock at her feet, he answered,

"I still support the general, but I feel that his candidacy on the third party is a tragic error."

"Why do you think so?"

"Because its sole effect will be to elect General McClellan and bring about a compromise peace with the South; the rebellion will not have been put down, slavery will not have been affected, and all those thousands of young men who died will have died for no purpose and for no accomplishment."

"My husband thinks he can win . . ."

Whittier shook his head violently. He rose and gazed at her with kindly but stubborn eyes.

"No, no, my dear Mrs. Fremont, please believe me. I would be the first to plead his cause if I thought he had a chance. But he has none. If the general persists in his candidacy and helps McClellan defeat the Republicans, his motives will be charged to personal anger against Mr. Lincoln and a desire for revenge. The effect will be disastrous for our nation. Mr. Lincoln is so tied into the secession, the war, the fight for the Union and for freedom that we cannot change horses in midstream. No one knows better than I General Fremont's magnificent faith in the cause of Union and Freedom, and how much he has already suffered for it. He must make one more sacrifice, then; he must withdraw and help Mr. Lincoln be re-elected."

"That will be bitter medicine."

"He has swallowed bitter medicine before. You came to me for an honest opinion: the people want Mr. Lincoln re-elected."

"Then you are not afraid that General McClellan will win?"

"Not if General Fremont withdraws."

Jessie smoothed the folds of her long velvet dress, then unconsciously fingered the recalcitrant strand of hair from her brow.

"Thank you, Mr. Whittier, for telling me the truth. You have given me the means to persuade General Fremont to withdraw."

The old man's eyes flashed approval.

"You will be doing your country a great service, Mrs. Fremont."

She returned to New York. When she told John the result of her interview with John Greenleaf Whittier, he asked darkly, "Then you are both convinced that I have no chance?"

" . . . You have a great chance: you can prove your faith in the Republican party by refusing to help it be defeated; you can prove that your objective is and always has been the Union cause."

"But don't you see," exclaimed John, "that by withdrawing now I maintain in office the man who relieved me of my command, who has kept me out of an important position either in the Army or the government? . . . And you are asking me to turn the other cheek!"

She cast about in her mind for the most subtle approach.

"Aren't you the one who taught me that a battle lost in the beginning may win the campaign in the end? You lost the immediate battle for the White House in 1856, but you helped create a victorious Republican party. You lost the Hundred Days in Missouri, but you contributed to the winning of the war. By stepping down from your nomination and helping Mr. Lincoln to win you will be losing still another battle, but your candidacy has already achieved important results: Mr. Lincoln has been forced to take a stronger stand against slavery; he has called for the resignation of Montgomery Blair and put the southern appeasers out of his Cabinet; the regular Republican platform was practically copied from the platform you endorsed when you accepted the nomination of the radicals."

She poured herself a glass of water from the decanter on the sideboard. Her voice, when she resumed, was low and resonant.

"I believe, John, that by refusing to accept the Democratic nomination you brought the Republican party into existence, and that that was more valuable than anything James Buchanan did in the White House from 1856 to 1860. Your emancipation proclamation created such a public demand for emancipation that Mr. Lincoln was finally forced to the point last year; your demand today for the freedom of all Negroes and a more powerful prosecution of the war will help bring them about. You have already achieved magnificent results, my dear, and they may be more important than anything Mr. Lincoln will do in Washington in the next four years. Perhaps that is your role in life, John, always to lose the opening battle, thereby laying the stage for the ultimate triumph of your cause."

John stood in hostile silence for several moments, then put his hands on her shoulders and shook her a little. He growled with affectionate gruffness, "Now that you have made me out such a hero, how can I refuse to step down? Get a pencil and paper, we'll write out a statement for the press announcing my withdrawal."

4

GENERALS GRANT, SHERMAN AND SHERIDAN finally brought in smashing victories for the Union cause; President Lincoln was re-elected. In the early spring of 1865 Generals Lee and Johnston surrendered to Grant, and the war was over.

Now that the restraints against railroad building were lifted, Jessie warmly approved the investment of their resources, some two hundred thousand dollars in savings, in the construction of the Kansas Pacific and the Missouri Pacific railroads. Always with his eye on the California terminus, John sold his interest in the two lines after they were partly constructed and bought the proposed Memphis & El Paso Railroad, which brought with its charter from the Texas legislature some eighteen million acres of land along the right of way. He next purchased land for a terminal in San Diego and drew up plans for the San Diego-Fort Yuma Railroad. For Jessie there was the old-time thrill in watching her husband function at the top of his form: bold and daring in his schemes to push the iron rails across the Rockies. At fifty-two John had a white beard and a head of white hair, but he was still as exciting as he had been in the days before their marriage, when Mrs. Crittenden had called him "the handsomest officer to walk the streets of Washington."

As the four war years had been taut, so now the years from 1865 to 1870 were wondrously slack, the most delightful period she had yet known. She decided that she must be growing old, for she was content to live peacefully, providing a gracious home and a cultivated life for her family and friends. She thought how amused her mother would be if she could see her now, living much in the manner of Cherry Grove, at long last the "fine lady" that Miss English had been so intent upon making her. Because she had never ceased to grieve over the loss of Black Point, John had insisted that in addition to their town house they should have a country place where they would find the natural beauty they had loved so much in San Francisco. The government had not yet returned the forty-two-thousand-dollar purchase price of the San Francisco property, but they were in no hurry, for it was now true that Jessie and John Fremont were millionaires.

They bought a magnificent estate of a hundred rolling acres and a gray stone mansion on the hills above the Hudson, called Pocaho. Into a mahogany-lined library, which gave a superb view of the Tappan Zee, Jessie placed the library they had bought from the Humboldts after the baron's death. Here too she assembled John's collection on military science and on political government, as well as all the books she had loved through her life, from the early Audubon volumes in the Library of Congress through the latest fiction pouring off the Boston and New York presses. The dining room, which overlooked the flower garden, and where Jessie served the finest foods her French chef could concoct, was always filled with guests. The broad, forty-foot living room which stood across the hall from the library was gay with the music and laughter of her three children and their friends. There were fine riding horses, and a handsome sailing boat for Charlie, now a young man with his father's dark, grave eyes and black hair parted in the center. Charlie was eighteen and wanted to become an admiral; he was entering Annapolis in the fall. For young Frank, now fifteen, with his mother's warm hazel eyes, slender sensitive face and brown hair, there was a grand piano which the boy often played at one and two in the morning. She educated her children by exposing them to all kinds of people, philosophies, books and the various arts, but she did not take advantage of her position by forcing them into fields for which they had neither interest nor liking. She said in effect, Here is the world; take from it what you will. My job is to open doors for you, not to push you into cold, dark rooms. Later you will decide for yourself which of the ideas and arts you wish to discard, and which you want for your lifetime friends.

She was constantly baffled by the differences in her three children, by the startling contrasts, not only between Lily and her two volatile brothers, but between the boys themselves. Charlie, open-faced, candid, was not happy unless he was on or near the water; the only books he cared for were those on travel and science. Frank was quiet and moody, uninterested in the out of doors, not seeming to come alive until darkness fell, and then spending his hours reading novels and poetry and playing the piano. She thought it odd that neither boy had as yet evidenced personal ambition.

These were years without uncertainties. They knew all the world, and all the world seemed to know and like them. There were luxurious trips to Europe, where she was presented to Queen Louisa of Denmark and became friends with Hans Christian Andersen. Her salon, which she built around the quiet but commanding personality of her husband, not only attracted the finest minds and talents in the country but served as an introduction to America for their many European friends.

She still felt that she was only the chatelaine of her wealth, supporting generously the charities of the day, in particular the funds to help the wounded soldiers of the war. At one time, in 1868, she was putting thirteen young people through college, nine young men and four young ladies. Everyone came to her for help: scientists, inventors, explorers, writers, painters, all those who needed money for any reason whatsoever. She contributed to university endowments, symphony-concert funds, art collections. She kept no track of how much money she gave away, for she had learned that John was making no attempt to keep track of how much was coming in; there was just too inexhaustible a supply to spend one's days in bookkeeping.

For their own part she and John lived unostentatiously; their clothes and pleasures were simple, Jessie wore no jewelry or furs. Aside from their travels, their money was spent in their two homes, entertaining their friends. Thirty years of marriage had deepened rather than exhausted their sense of pleasure in each other: the delight at a new hair style, the way a dress or suit fitted, the adroit expression of an idea, the slow, warm, approving smile on a face whose every expression was better known than one's own image in the mirror. In three decades of marriage they had gone through so much together, both of success and failure, that they were carved into each other's memory; there was gratitude here, but gratitude would not have been enough to engender the closeness and delight of their spirits. During the harassed and unhappy war years they had relearned that trouble and passion are poor bedfellows; now, in the easy, joyful comfort of creative years, when their last ambitions were pushing forward toward completion, their physical love flared anew.

John persuaded her to let Fagnani paint her portrait; when after many sittings the artist permitted her to gaze at the canvas she saw reflected the interesting things that had happened to her in these last years, of which she herself had been but dimly aware. She had filled out, so that her always delicate shoulders were now rounded and firm, her bosom deep. She wore her graying hair still parted in the center, but instead of combing it low at the back of her neck she let it fall in two long rich curls down the side of her head and shoulders. Her eyes seemed larger than in her early years, a far darker hazel, mellow, accepting, at peace with the world. Her mouth, always rich and red, had deepened and widened, which made her long Roman nose seem shorter and more delicate. In the painter's objective portrait she was no longer a young woman: at forty-five she was a matron, the most active part of her life behind her, but with long years to enjoy the tranquillity of middle life.

Gazing at herself as the artist Fagnani saw her, she thought about the oddness of perspective. When she stood on a hilltop overlooking a valley, the immediate foreground, the first few miles of ranches, orchards, houses and plowed fields were seen in the most vivid detail; but beyond them the landscape ran together, so that nothing was seen clearly and in detail, but rather was merged in an obscuring haze. With the years of their marriage it was the early ones that stood out now in her mind with the starkest of clarity: she could recall every hour, every ache of loneliness, every pain of disappointment and failure, every aspiration, every moment of work, every tiny, joyous success. But these later years, these years far away from youth, from the freshness of beginning, the haze of long-range perspective had covered with an obscuring veil. She could not recall or even feel the separate hours and days now: they merged into each other, grouped themselves so closely and genially that there were no sharp divisions in time. Everything passed so quickly, the months, the years, so quickly that there was no way of counting them, let alone holding them back.

She hoped that they would be able to live out their lives in this pastoral, in which they used their money for good and generous purposes while John helped lay the trails for transcontinental railroads. Yet deep in her heart she had a prescience that this could not last; nothing so far had lasted, nothing had been permanent, secure or unchangeable; they had gone through many and violent cycles. She sensed storms ahead, but she did not let this intuition detract from her enjoyment and happiness of the good years. Instead she used them, as she had always used the tranquil periods, to fortify herself against the day when they would be obliged to go to the wars again. The thought sometimes came to her that she should not spend money so lavishly, but should try to save some portion of it, invest it in land or stocks or bank vaults. And yet she had an even stronger certainty that this subterfuge could do no possible good: when the change of circumstances came, all of these thousands that she was spending now would inevitably have been lost with everything else. Better to use them, to make them serve high purposes.

The happiest day of these years of contentment was when she and John went to St. Louis to participate in the unveiling of a statue of Senator Thomas Hart Benton. Forty thousand spectators crowded into Lafayette Park to witness the ceremony, while school children in white stood about the pedestal, a band played martial music, and the westbound train stopped on the Pacific railroad tracks to blow its whistles. As Jessie pulled a cord and the white drapery slipped down from the bronze statue, there stood the Old Roman, facing westward, his slightly hoarse voice seeming to cry out the lines which were inscribed at the base: *"There is the East. There lies the road to India."* A salute of thirty guns, one for each year of his service in the Senate, was fired by order of the secretary of war. While the Missouri dignitaries were making fine speeches about Thomas Hart Benton's life and work and the things he had done for education and freedom, Jessie turned to her husband with tears in her eyes and whispered, "What a shame that Father couldn't be here for the unveiling. He would have enjoyed it so."

Her one disquietude was centered around Lily. Her daughter was now twenty-six years old; to the best of Jessie's knowledge the girl had never been in love. She had countless friends, was well liked, she would ride, hunt, fish, sail or work for a worth-while cause with the young sons of their friends and their neighbors at Pocaho or in New York. Yet she rarely accepted invitations to mixed parties, cared little for dancing, preferred the company of her family. Jessie was not able to tell whether any young men had fallen in love with her daughter, for Lily was completely

uncommunicative on the subject. On numerous occasions she had tried
to draw her out. She was able to learn that at least Lily was not pining
over an unrequited love; and she came to the conclusion that Lily had no
intention of ever falling in love! Up to this point Jessie had thought her
daughter might be maturing late, that like her aunt Eliza she was waiting
for precisely the right man to come along. Now she saw that Lily did not
believe in such romantic notions as the right man, that instead of giving
him a chance to fall in love, should he come along, Lily would ride him
half to death up the valley of the Hudson, or involve him in a fund-raising
campaign for a new clinic which would wear out his energy even as it
burned out his romantic interest.

Unable to bear the uncertainty any longer, she determined to have
matters out with Lily. It took a lot of doing, for Lily was either disinterested or elusive. Jessie cornered her one wintry night in the mahogany-
lined library and locked the door behind them. Standing with her back to
the fire she gazed at Lily's heavy brows and jaw and the resolute cast of
her features.

"Lily," she said, "you'll have to forgive me for intruding where I'm
obviously not wanted, but I am seriously upset about you."

"Why so, Mother?" Lily asked, "I'm in perfect health, I eat three wonderful meals a day, I'm out in the air in the roughest weather . . ."

"I think you know that I did not mean it literally, Lily," replied Jessie
engagingly. "I am not talking about your creature comforts, nor am I discussing the state of your health."

Her gray eyes unemotional, Lily replied, "I'm perfectly happy. You're
perfectly happy . . ."

Jessie pulled up a small wooden chair beside her daughter. She said in
a firmer tone, "No, my dear, I am not perfectly happy, because I see the
years going on, and I find you growing farther and farther away from the
most important thing in a woman's life: marriage."

"Why is it the most important, Mother?" asked Lily, with equal
firmness. "Merely because you find it so? Isn't there room for difference
of opinion on that subject?"

Jessie shook her head several times as though she could not believe
what she had just heard.

"Difference of opin . . . What are you talking about, child? What is
there in life for a woman if she doesn't have a husband and children and
a home?"

"Many, many things, Mother dear. Your belief that an unmarried
woman is a tragic and useless figure is old-fashioned. The Lord only
knows how many females were bullied into marriages they didn't want,

on those very grounds. There are lots of young women who don't want to marry, who want to live a different kind of life . . ."

"The life of a spinster?" demanded Jessie, horror-stricken.

"Don't make the word sound so ugly, darling. Don't you see, my heart is so full of love for you and Father and the boys that there just isn't room for anyone else."

"Then in your own best interests," cried Jessie, "I think your father and I ought to pack your belongings and put you out of the house. We could never forgive ourselves if we thought that you loved us so much . . ."

Lily rose from her deep chair and began striding about the room, energetically picking up objects and putting them down again; Jessie's mind flashed across the years to her meeting with George Bancroft in her sitting room at the rear of the Benton home. Lily came back and stood towering over her mother, looking down at her with assured and fearless eyes.

"Very well, Mother, you shall have blunt speaking. I shall never marry for the very simple reason that I dislike heartily the whole idea of marriage."

Aghast, Jessie could only whisper, "You dislike . . . ? But why? It isn't normal to dislike marriage. How can you possibly feel that way when you've grown up with your father and me, when you've seen how much we have loved each other over the years, when you've seen how much we have suffered and struggled, yes, and achieved too, for our marriage?"

"That is exactly what I am talking about," said Lily in a plain voice.

Coldly Jessie asked, "What are you trying to tell me, Lily?"

"I am trying to tell you, Mother dear—and apparently you will give me no peace until I do—that for twenty years I have seen what marriage has done to you and Father. I have seen how dreadfully your ambitions for that marriage have made you suffer. I was too young to understand much about the court-martial, but even at the age of six I could see the agonies you endured. I don't want to endure such things, or expose myself to them. For years, in Monterey and on the sand dunes of San Francisco, I watched you creep about the house like a stricken creature because you could not have your husband by your side. In the years when Father was away on his expeditions your existence became a still-life; when he was reported dead, I saw how near dead you were at the prospect, and how completely you would have been killed had the news been true. I don't want to be stricken that way. I don't want to be dependent on any other human being for my happiness, and my very life as well. I know what you underwent during the years of the Civil War after Father was deprived of his command; I know how many evil tongues there are in this country calling you unfortunate names because you dared to battle with President Lincoln for your husband's sake. I don't want to battle with people; I don't want to grow angry and wage wars and violate my own character for the sake of a man. I want to live on my own two feet, complete inside my own body and my own brain. To you and to Father your love and marriage are great and beautiful. But that way of life is not for me."

She paused for a moment, her voice growing quiet.

"Perhaps if I had grown up in the midst of a mild or mediocre marriage, I could have accepted the idea. The intensity of my reaction is in direct proportion to the intensity of your relationship. Please believe me, dear, and please leave me in peace on the subject: I shall never marry."

For a long time there was no sound in the room but that of the rain slashing across the library windows. Jessie made no attempt to hide or restrain the tears that coursed down her cheeks. This then was the failure of her marriage: that she had created an antipathy for it in her daughter. Now the cycle was complete. Her philosophy of marriage had been formulated as a reaction to her mother's concept of the "least marriage"; now, twenty-eight years later, in a new time and a new generation, her daughter was reacting even more violently than had she: the daughter had seen so much of the "most marriage" that she wanted no part of it for herself.

As wrong as she thought Lily was, as desperately as she regretted her daughter's decision, she knew that she could do nothing to oppose it. Time would work out its pattern. Perhaps circumstance would change Lily's mind; but in any event her daughter had a right to live her own life, free of her mother's interference and direction, just as she herself had insisted with Elizabeth McDowell Benton that, wrong, desperately wrong as her mother might believe her to be, she had the right to marry Lieutenant John C. Fremont and fulfill her own destiny.

She rose, kissed Lily lightly on the forehead and said, "At the opening of this discussion I asked you to forgive me for intruding, but that was merely a politeness. Now, at the end, I urge you most deeply to forgive me for trespassing upon your private life and your private convictions. I will never bring up the subject again. I think you are wrong, but that is apparently the prerogative of mothers. Go your own way, my dear; your father and I want only one thing for you: that you be happy. I shall make no further attempt to influence you to be happy according to my definition of the term. Good night, Lily."

5

THOUGH JOHN TOLD HER LITTLE about the complicated financing of his railroad structures, she knew that his ten-million-dollar bond issue had sold well, providing money to order locomotives, grade many miles of track in Texas, and send surveyors into New Mexico to stake out the Rocky Mountain pass. However, the money from American investors came in too slowly to suit his purposes, and in the summer of 1869 he confided to Jessie that he was at last going to achieve his plan of almost ten years before: instead of floating a stock issue for the sale of the Mariposa, which had been prevented at the last moment by the threat of civil war in the United States, he was now going to put through a bond issue in France for his Memphis & El Paso Railroad. This time his idea was eagerly seized upon, and more than five million dollars' worth of securities were sold to French investors, many of whom bought because of their faith in General Fremont.

The five-year period of tranquillity and prosperity drew to its close. She began to notice that her husband was growing worried, that his absences were longer than usual, that when he returned he was jumpy and taut once again. She had to piece together the fragments to learn that his difficulties were compounded of the mechanical and the financial: the House of Representatives had given his railroad a right of way through the territories, but the Senate defeated the bill, and without this grant there would be no way of connecting the eastern and western halves of his line. The cost of grading the land on which to lay track was everywhere higher than had been anticipated; his engineers were having recurrent troubles in the mountains due to landslides, washouts and unexpected steepness of grades; materials could not be transported to points of construction because rivers overflowed and the boats carrying railroad equipment were tied up. Nowhere was the task of building a railroad across wild and virgin territory easier or less expensive than had been anticipated; often the cost rose to three and four times its estimate. As for the financial upsets, too large a percentage of the money from French investors had been taken by the Paris banks for floating the loan; the balance of the money was provided not in cash but in supplies and rolling stock. When the equipment reached the United States from France there was no grading or roadbed ready to use it.

But the most serious blow, which came late in 1869, was a close repetition of the Sargent affair in London. John had worked through the French consul general at New York, who had introduced him to reputable

French financiers and engineers; however, when the bond issue was put through the Paris Bourse, the bonds stated that they were guaranteed by the United States government in terms of munificent land grants. When John went on record to the French public with the true facts, the sale of bonds stopped immediately and a series of civil and criminal law suits were instituted. Charges were brought in Paris against General John C. Fremont as a participant in the fraud. Senator Howard of Michigan, who originally had defeated the bill to grant the railroad right of way across the territories, used the French scandal to block John's further attempts to secure federal co-operation.

After a three-week business trip, during which she received only the barest hurried notes from him, he arrived at Pocaho one evening looking pale and ill. Jessie's heart sank at the sight of him. She had a bath prepared for him, laid out a fresh suit and then had a supper tray brought to the library. John sank into a low-lying leather seat facing the Hudson. Jessie sat quietly on the arm of his chair, her hand lightly on his shoulder. When at last he could bring himself to speak she surmised the enormity of the misfortune he had suffered by the hoarse and twisted quality of his voice.

"It's gone, Jessie, everything's gone. I came to the very end of our funds three weeks ago . . . I have been rushing about frantically trying to raise money . . . They gave me one small extension . . . Now we're through . . . I couldn't meet the payments. The mortgage holders have taken over our railroad, Jessie—we have been thrown into receivership."

She hesitated for a moment to make sure that her voice would be calm: her main concern now was to make certain that their loss be confined to metallic dollars and rails.

"But how can they take over your railroad, John? It's yours, isn't it? Your money and ability went into building it . . . Five years of your life . . . thousands of your dollars . . ."

Staring out unseeing over the river, he replied, "All of that is gone, it was swept away by floods and washouts, by hard grades and harder rock; I took tools and equipment and rails from manufacturers on credit; they have to be paid. If I can't give them the cash, I must give them the railroad."

"Surely they're not entitled to more than is owed to them? After they have been paid their debts, what is left belongs to you."

John shook his head wearily, trying to rub the exhaustion out of his eyes.

"There will be nothing left over, Jessie. As it stands now, only one-quarter laid, the line is useless—no money can be earned on it until it is completed." He looked up at her, his eyes small, dark and hurt. "Don't you understand, Jessie, we're wiped out! I've lost not only the physical property, but the control of the railroad as well."

As he poured out in an almost inarticulate rush of broken words the story of deception and betrayed friendship which were the underlying cause of his troubles, she slowly fitted together the pattern of misplaced confidence and financial intrigue with which the business end of his venture had been honeycombed. Once again, as she had that night in the Clarendon Hotel, with John in jail, she saw that neither of them had any business sense, that they were trusting souls who had never defrauded anyone and consequently knew little of how money can persuade old companions to lie and cheat and work at cross-purposes behind one's back. John was an engineer and a visionary, a rare combination of talents that had enabled him to break and map trails to the West, and now to lay iron rails along these former paths through the wilderness. Could he also be a sharp and shrewd businessman?

She was certain that her husband had done the best he could. She was equally certain that there was nothing she could have done that would have changed matters, even if she had been as close to his business transactions as she had been to his early exploring expeditions. Nor, as in the days of the court-martial, did she think it loyal or decent of her to try to postguess her husband. John had had to carry the burden of heavy responsibility in a difficult and pioneering field. What he had done had seemed the right and necessary thing to do at that moment, and so she would accept it as having been right. If one benefited from a man's accomplishments over a long period of years, it was fair play to accept philosophically the results of those judgments which turned out badly. That was what was meant by partnership; no partnership could survive on any other basis.

She kissed the corner of his mouth.

"You ran into difficulties and complications that were impossible to foresee. Who should know better than you that the pioneer in any field, the one who has the courage to fight the obstacles and hardships, is never the one to reap the benefits? Let them have this railroad; you will plan another; next time we'll get government help . . ."

"People are saying that a transcontinental railroad is an impossible dream," he broke in harshly, "that the idea should be abandoned."

" . . . We'll use the rest of our assets to get started again. You can't let yourself be discouraged by a first failure."

His eyes held hers steadily.

"Assets?" he asked dully. "What assets?"

"Our interest in the Mariposa. Our lands and ranches in California. The house in New York . . ."

A convulsion swept over John as he told her in broken phrases, " . . . You haven't really understood. I borrowed up to the hilt on the Mariposa . . . It's gone . . . Our gold mines are gone. So is our property in California . . . I mortgaged it all to push ahead with the railroad."

Aghast, she could only cry, "But not our homes, John? Not the New York house? Not Pocaho?"

" . . . The New York house, but not Pocaho; that is in your name. Everything in it belongs to you. Thank God I could not mortgage it; we have this, our home—nothing more, nothing, darling—not a cent."

He rose, walked to a far corner of the library and stood by Baron Humboldt's books. He had aged ten years in the past six months; she had seen him angry, bitter, resentful, vengeful, fighting mad, but never before had he been as crushed as he looked now, his shoulders bent over, the white hair on his bowed head standing out against the dark leather bindings.

For herself, she was momentarily disheartened, but neither stunned nor broken by these developments. Had John not been the conqueror and governor of California, only to be dragged across the continent like a criminal; had he not been America's most valuable trail blazer, map maker and opener of the West, only to be court-martialed and cast out of the Army in disgrace; had he not been the standard bearer of a new and great political movement, only to be defeated and forgotten; had he not been the commander of the Army of the West, only to be ignominiously removed without an opportunity to prove his worth? For five years they had been among the world's richest people, had been pushing through the most valuable contribution to western expansion since the Oregon Trail; now they were penniless, their railroad bankrupt, the idea of a transcontinental line proven impractical. Everything they touched they built almost to a pinnacle, then the hand of fate or the hand of man brushed them aside. Their projects went on; their ideas matured and flourished; their conquests became part of the main stream of American life; but they, the pioneers, were deprived of participation or recompense.

Very well, then, if this were their pattern, if this were their life, there was little they could do but put up with it. She was not frightened about their living, even though she had two sons to educate. Nor was she disturbed over the prospect of returning to an austere life; she would not mind cooking and cleaning in Madame Castro's rooms in Monterey or in the sand dunes of San Francisco, providing her husband were by her side. She could go back to that life, or forward to any other life that might lie ahead; recurrent adversity and disappointment had not weakened her fiber, for Jessie Benton Fremont was like a deeply built ship that drove best under a stormy wind. She had only one problem, to safeguard her husband's health and peace of mind, reconcile him to his losses, help him make his adjustments, plan with him for new directions, new activities, a new start. Surely, at fifty-seven, he was not finished? Six months before he had been at the height of his powers; today he was saddened, bewildered. Tomorrow he would rest, recoup his strength and confidence, and the day after tomorrow they would begin anew.

6

SHE DISMISSED ALL THE SERVANTS except one general maid. Lily helped with the housework, young Frank took over the gardening. In her safe-deposit vault in New York she had some stocks and bonds which John had given her as gifts; these were cashed and used for living expenses. Baron Humboldt's former library sold for a substantial sum; their horses and carriages and Charlie's sailboat brought sufficient to pay the more pressing debts. Part of the big house was closed off; all entertaining was stopped, except for their few intimate friends, chiefly Hannah Kirsten.

Jessie worked constantly, with a desperation she had never been conscious of before, sending out letters and petitions to get Congress to return the forty-two-thousand-dollar purchase price of their confiscated Black Point; to secure for John a government appointment which would afford them a modest living. Although the passing of the months lessened his bitterness, though he was able to busy himself for some little time in straightening out the tangled accounts of the Memphis & El Paso Railroad, actually there was no work for him to do, no position for him to occupy. She watched as he chafed at idleness, yet something inside him seemed to have died, and try as she might, with every means she had developed in thirty years of a loving marriage, she could not bring back to life his inner flame.

The years of opulence and Mariposa gold had weakened her habits of thrift. She became confused because the bills were still large, though they appeared to be living at a minimum, and there just was no cash with which to meet them. Without telling her family about it, she took a substantial bank loan on Pocaho, thinking that the money would earn them the months necessary to bring John a business opening, a government appointment perhaps. The stratagem was only a half-success; a personal note of John's came due, one he had forgotten in the collapse of his affairs; he was so despondent at not being able to meet the payment that Jessie handed over her bank loan, telling him that she had had the money hidden in her vault for just such an emergency.

They were without funds for the simple necessities. It was at this point that Lily took over, decided which paintings and *objets d'art* should be sold, began collecting a few of the sums owed to them. She handled their slim and often disappearing bank account, purchased the supplies, paid the bills, judged which part of the grounds should be allowed to run to weeds and which part kept up.

Jessie was grateful to her daughter for taking this burden off her shoulders; it released her full time and energies for John. They took long walks along the river; they spent the wintry nights before the log fire in the library; they made their plans to move back to San Francisco as soon as Congress paid for Black Point, and to build a little cottage overlooking the strait. She kept him encouraged by news from friends in Washington who were confident that the Black Point bill would go through, who had assured her that General Fremont was sorely needed at this post or in that position in the West, that the appointment would soon be made by President Grant or the War Department. Yet nothing came through, nothing; Congress would not pay for Black Point; President Grant ignored all requests to help his former commander.

Between them, Jessie and Lily managed the miracle of hanging on at Pocaho for almost two years. The women had a tacit agreement never to tell John what had been sold or how straitened were their circumstances. But at length the time came when Lily had to confide to her mother that there was no more money or salable assets, that in order to buy food, in order to keep Charlie at Annapolis and Frank at West Point, they would have to borrow still further on Pocaho. They knew that this was the beginning of the end, for they had been unable to meet the interest payments on the first loan; if they did not meet the new indebtedness they would lose Pocaho and be without a roof over their heads.

"I don't think we should do it that way, Mother," said Lily. "Father would be terribly distressed if we lost the house. I have one alternative, but I am not sure you will approve . . ."

"What do you suggest, Lily?"

"That I find a position in New York. A lot of girls are going into business today who never did before. I am good at business, you know, or at least Father always says I am. Then why can't I take a job in some office?"

Something in her mother's eyes stopped her.

"You are good and you are brave, Lily," she murmured. "But don't you see, we can't do this to Father. As long as we live here at Pocaho quietly, the world knows nothing of our affairs. But once you take a job we publish to all the world that we are destitute, that our daughter must support us. I would like to take a job at a desk beside you, but you know how proud your father is; he would take it as a personal token of failure. We must spare him that humiliation. Give me a little more time; something is certain to come through, an appointment, some money for Black Point . . ."

"I understand, Mother," replied Lily, her face somber.

And so they borrowed again on Pocaho. There were unexpectedly heavy expenses in the winter of '73; new debts had a way of popping up, debts of several years' standing which Jessie and Lily had not known about, but which John said had to be acknowledged. Fighting against time, fighting against hope, they fell further and further behind in their interest, and at last, toward the end of 1873, the bank foreclosed the mortgage and took over the house.

Her courage unfailing, but her heart almost broken at what this was doing to her now white-faced husband, Jessie packed their clothes and moved into New York. With their few remaining dollars they rented a small, ugly frame house on Eighth Street, the paint coming off the outside walls, the inside shabby and dirty. Jessie and Lily worked frantically for four days, painting and redecorating, while John stayed with a friend. When he came home the cramped and dark rooms were at least clean.

Their rent was paid for two months in advance. Jessie had enough cash to buy food for approximately the same period. She redoubled her efforts during the weeks, writing dozens of letters to congressmen, to their old friends in the Army and in the Cabinet, setting up ever new plans and schemes to secure for John even the simplest kind of appointment, to help push through Congress the bill necessary to repay them for Black Point. Several times it seemed as though she were to have success: John was proposed as governor for various territories, as Indian commissioner for one of the western districts, as collector or commissioner of the Land Office in San Francisco. The House of Representatives passed a bill appropriating money for Black Point, but at the last moment it was defeated in the Senate.

The two months drew to a close. Jessie was at her wit's end. Only once before had she had to think about money, after their court-martial, when they had had to borrow from Tom Benton in order to start a home in California. Jessie knew that if she appealed to her sisters or to their many friends she could borrow money. But how could she ever repay it? Although she had a fine gift for giving, she had no whit of talent for asking in return. She would have preferred to die in their shabby and cramped house on Eighth Street, die quietly and respectably, than go out and ask for alms.

Lily began disappearing shortly after luncheon each day, returning at five, with her hands looking smudgy. Jessie asked only if she was working somewhere, and was satisfied with Lily's denial. After a couple of weeks, when Lily brought an old typewriter into the house and spent several hours at it each morning, Jessie realized that her daughter was attending a secretarial school. She was proud of the matter-of-fact way in which Lily was going about the task of preparing herself for any eventuality.

At the end of the two months she knew they would have to move out of even this sordid little shelter. Where were they to go? How was she to break the news to John? How was she to keep from the world the fact that General John C. Fremont was destitute? In Monterey she had been distressed because it was the accumulation of gold that had separated them; now it was the lack of gold that would tear them apart.

As always, she contrived a way. Hannah Kirsten had been urging her to come for a visit to her home in upstate New York. John had a long-standing invitation from one of his officers of the Western Command to visit in Staten Island and talk over old army days. Lily was always welcome at her aunt Susie's in Boston.

As they sat over their last meager supper in the dark dining room, Jessie at last found the courage to say, "John, why don't we accept these invitations? Hannah has stayed with us so many times and is eager to have me visit her. You know how often Colonel Wadsworth has pleaded for you to pay him a visit. I think it would be good for you to be among old army friends again. Don't you think you might enjoy that for a time?"

John pushed aside his plate and reached for her hand across the table.

"Don't think I don't know what you've been doing, Jessie dear, or how desperately you've been trying. I have said little . . . for what could I say? I have brought us to this desperate situation, I alone . . . and yet I can see no way out of it . . . no possible help for us . . ."

She rose quickly, went to his side and kissed his eyelids.

"Now, darling," she cried, "it's only for a few weeks, then we'll be together again. An appointment will come through. Good times will come back, you will see. Haven't they always? Think how often we have reached bottom, only to begin the long climb up again. We have had so much from the world, John, so much happiness and success. Surely they have inured us to times of difficulty?"

He sat with his head down, gripping her hand tightly, unable to speak.

The next morning at a very early hour they walked down the three unpainted steps of their house, each with a suitcase in hand. At the bottom of the steps they turned to each other, mutely. To Jessie it seemed that nothing she had endured before, not even the death of young Benton, was as heartbreaking as this moment of separation. Her husband needed her now more desperately than he ever had before, yet of all the millions of dollars they had extracted from the Mariposa, she could not command a sufficient sum to stay by her husband's side, remain with him when he was crushed, ill and old-looking, suffering as only the fiercely proud man

suffers. They had been separated on their twentieth anniversary because
John had been at the head of his army, pursuing General Price, and she
had been working at headquarters in St. Louis. In a few days they would
be celebrating their thirty-second anniversary, but once again they would
be apart.

"My dear," she murmured softly, "I was just thinking of what we told
each other that night in the tent before Springfield. It's easy to speak of
love in good times, in the wonderful years such as we had on the Mariposa and at Black Point and Pocaho. But now that we are to be separated
I can think of nothing to say but that I love you, darling; I have loved
you every hour, every day, in good times and bad. You have always made
my life happy and beautiful; it is beautiful even now because I love you
and because you love me. Be of good heart, think of me every moment,
write to me every day; we will find a way, John. Haven't we always?"

The early-morning streets were deserted. The air was quiet. Behind the
closed doors and shuttered windows of the houses the world still slept.
They were alone, two little figures, old, white-haired, alone in the universe. Then suddenly they were locked securely in each other's arms, lips
to lips, two tiny, forlorn figures which now, merged into one, made a
large and great figure: the figure of love: indestructible: immortal.

7

SHE REMAINED at Hannah Kirsten's for two months, walking a little in
the afternoons along the river, listening to Hannah play the piano and
sing. She had hoped that the rest and distance from the ordeal of watching the last dollars disappear might bring fresh ideas and fresh energy
which would enable her to find some solution. At the end of two months
she was further away than ever from an understanding of what to do,
with a new despair because the passing hours had brought nothing but
blankness. The deeply built ship that drove best under a stormy wind had
lost its compass and rudder, was adrift, pounded by the ever mounting
seas. John was not unhappy with his friend in Staten Island, yet he was
growing restive as a guest. Many times she thought how senseless and
chaotic was the pattern of social responsibility when a man like John
Fremont, now in his sixties, who had contributed so much to the development of his country could be destitute, without being compensated for
property that had been pre-empted, without the saving graciousness of a
minor government job, without even a modest pension from the War
Department which he had served so well for so many years.

She knew that a disinterested party might well say it was their own
fault: they had made millions of dollars from the Mariposa, they had

been among the powerful and wealthy ones of the earth, but they had been improvident. They had let the money slip through their hands, they had not protected themselves against age and vicissitude. What use to tell these people that if they had been content to live on the outpourings of the Mariposa their money would still be intact? What use to protest that their wealth had been poured into the radical though imperative idea of a transcontinental railroad, where it had vanished as so many other fortunes had and would vanish, to form a roadbed upon which ultimately a transcontinental railroad would be erected? What use to publicize the tens of thousands they had poured into public funds, worthwhile movements and causes, money that had been given to individuals to help them out of difficulties or to achieve success? What use to cry out in anguish, If only we could get back a tithe of what we have given away, and what has been taken from us, we could live out the rest of our lives in decent comfort and self-respect?

Tired, discouraged, weak in spirit and body, she wondered what would happen to them if she continued in this state of lassitude. Her father had taught her that one must not worry about the future, for if it ever arrived one could face it with the same good judgment as in the past. That had held true for some thirty-two years of marriage; now her ability to face up to a situation had collapsed.

She had no way of knowing how long she might have remained in stunned apathy had not a telegram reached her from Staten Island with the information that John was ill with pneumonia. Instantly her mind flashed back to her own siege of pneumonia during the court-martial; she knew how easy it was to die in the grip of this malady. Without railroad tickets, without money, without plans, without anything except the knowledge that she must get to her husband at once, she began crushing her few clothes into a suitcase.

Hannah Kirsten was not the kind who comforted in words only: in a few moments Jessie found herself in the Kirsten carriage. Soon she and Hannah were in Colonel Wadsworth's home standing by the side of John's bed while the Staten Island physician explained that her husband's condition was delicate, that as soon as possible he should be taken to a mild climate for the winter, to some place like Nassau where he could recoup his strength.

Even as she stood by John's bedside gazing down into the thin, pale face of her husband, she knew what she would do to meet this situation. It was not something she had to think about; it did not take an hour or a day of sorting out plans and choosing the best; the precise knowledge of what she could and must do was suddenly there, alive and whole and ready to act upon. She told Hannah that she had to go to New York at once. In a few moments Hannah had put her on a ferry, assured her that she would remain in Staten Island to nurse John until she returned. She also promised to send Jessie a telegram at the Astor House each morning and evening.

Jessie's ferry reached New York at seven o'clock of a cold winter evening. The carriage sloshed its way through the snow-covered streets to the Astor House. She ate no supper, but undressed the moment she reached her room, stretched out in bed as cold and still as a corpse and fell asleep. She awakened at seven, bathed, creamed her face and combed her hair with the utmost care, then summoned the housekeeper and had her one purple silk dress sponged and ironed. At nine she had breakfast in the Astor House restaurant and rode to the office of the New York *Ledger*. She waited only an instant after her card had been sent in; Robert Bonner, the red-bearded Irishman who owned the *Ledger*, came out of his office, beamed at her while he wrung her hand, and then ushered her into a wood-panelled office with its great desk littered with scrambled manuscripts and a succession of evil-smelling pipes. Bonner's two passions were fast horses and provocative advertising copy; he and Lily had frequently raced the Fremont horses along the ridge above the Hudson.

In a voice well masked with confidence Jessie said, "Mr. Bonner, I have been thinking that some of my early experiences with Mr. Fremont, and some of my early travels, would make excellent articles for your readers."

Bonner nodded his head in a vigorous affirmative.

"Indeed I should think they would, Mrs. Fremont. What precisely did you have in mind?"

"Well, stories like my first crossing of Panama, when the route had just been opened and hundreds of Americans were stranded in Panama City; stories from our life in Monterey when California was being made into a state; the great fires and action of the Vigilantes in San Francisco; stories of how we were besieged by the Hornitas League in the Sierras. Or, in a different direction, my early memories of the White House, of the family life of the early presidents and their First Ladies."

"That material sounds fascinating, Mrs. Fremont."

Brusquely she asked, "How much will you pay for each story?"

Mr. Bonner was somewhat startled by this quick transition to the commercial aspect of their discussion.

"Why . . . ah . . . we can pay one hundred dollars apiece, Mrs. Fremont, always providing, of course, that the material works out well."

"Of course," agreed Jessie, standing up. "The stories will come out exceedingly well. Thank you, Mr. Bonner, and good day."

On the way back to the hotel she stopped at a stationery store where she bought pencils, erasers, pens, ink and many tablets of paper. By the time she reached her room she had reasoned that putting together the cost of steamship tickets to Nassau, hotel accommodations there, as well as medical care, the expenses would be at least a thousand dollars. In order to earn this much money she must write ten stories.

It was almost noon when she took off her hat and coat and spread out her writing materials on the desk. By six o'clock she had the first article, "Panama," complete and recopied. Hungry now, remembering that she had had nothing since breakfast, she had a light supper brought up to her room, then rested for an hour. Shortly before eight o'clock she sat down at her desk and began working on her second story. She was getting into the swing of it now and the writing came a little easier. By two in the morning "Besieged," the story of the Hornitas League, was completed and neatly recopied.

She slept from two-thirty until five-thirty. By the time she sent down for breakfast at eight-thirty she already had a rough draft of her third story. A telegram arrived from Hannah saying that John was making satisfactory progress. By one o'clock that night she had three more stories to add to the two she had done the day before. The following day she did another three, giving her a total of eight. She had had only a little over three hours' sleep the night before, so she slept from one until six in the morning. She awakened thinking, Only two more stories to go and then I'll have my thousand dollars. A reassuring telegram from Hannah cleared her mind for action.

When night fell, and she had her ten stories completed, she thought suddenly, I must not stop now; the thousand dollars may not be quite enough, I must give myself a little latitude. If I write one more . . .

The eleventh story came hard, not because her will was wearing out, but because the first great rush of material was beginning to slacken and she was growing a little hard pressed to think of a new subject. She finally decided upon "Family Life in the White House" and wrote it quickly, almost in a breath, completing it at midnight.

She stretched out fully dressed on the bed to rest for a few minutes; the next thing she knew it was morning. Once again she bathed, combed her hair, put on her purple dress and took a carriage up to the office of the *Ledger*. Mr. Bonner was a little puzzled at the purpose of her call. When she unwrapped the package she had been clutching under her arm, saying, "I have completed eleven stories," his eyes were wide with astonishment.

"Eleven stor . . . Why, Mrs. Fremont, I thought you would be weeks, even months, in the writing."

Realizing for the first time that an editor had every reason to be astonished at her procedure, Jessie asked in alarm, "But surely that will make

no difference to you? You will find these stories well done . . . they revolve about the early frontier and pioneer periods . . ."

Bonner chuckled as he replied, "It's just that I'm overcome by your
productivity. I have to browbeat most of my authors to get one story from
them in five days, let alone eleven."

"Then could I have the money right away, Mr. Bonner? One hundred
dollars a story, eleven hundred in all."

Mr. Bonner gaped at her. "Eleven hundred dollars," he murmured.
"That's a lot of money."

"It's also a lot of stories."

"But you don't object if I read them?"

"Most assuredly not; go right ahead."

The editor, who had had no intention of reading manuscript with the
author watching his every expression, gave a little sigh, picked up the first
story. He scanned five of the articles in quick succession, making a cor-
recting flick with his pencil here and there, lighting several half-smoked
pipes in the process and giving out only an occasional grunt of satisfaction. At the end of the fifth manuscript he looked up and said, "Yes, these
are well done; our subscribers will like them. Suppose I give you a check
for five hundred dollars now, and the balance in a few days after I've had
a chance to read the rest of the stories?"

"Excellent," she replied. "That will enable me to take General Fremont to Nassau. He is ill with pneumonia."

Robert Bonner rose, requested his bookkeeper to give Jessie a check,
told her that he was certain the general would get well, and suggested
that when she returned she come in to see him about further stories.

Walking quickly to the steamship offices, Jessie purchased her tickets
for Nassau, then once again boarded the ferry for Staten Island.

8

JOHN HEALED in the warmth of the Nassau sun. Jessie was so happy to
be reunited with her husband that she almost believed the illness had been
designed to bring them together again. When she thought back to the two
terror-stricken months at Hannah's she could only imagine that she must
have been as ill as John had been, and that now she had recovered from
her mental and spiritual pneumonia. She knew that she had found a way
for them to live again: after recovering from her fatigue of the four-day
effort, hundreds of stories had come to mind.

She uttered thanks to Tom Benton for once again having saved their
lives. Though she had been grateful for the editorial training he had given

her from the age of twelve, she had never imagined that she would one day use this skill for making a living; now it had not only enabled her to save her husband's life but would make it possible for them to live on together through the years. A hundred times a day she blessed her father's memory, silently blessed her husband for having been willing to let her collaborate with him on the reports, thus giving her a trade which had rescued them both.

They took leisurely walks along the white beach, gathering shells and reminiscing of other days and other beaches: Siasconset, where they had refused the Democratic nomination, Black Point, where they had walked along the sands at the base of their cottage and watched the sun plunge into the Pacific. These good memories were as healing as the clear air and the bright sunshine; soon they were going out in a little boat for a day's fishing. Flesh came back to John's emaciated frame, color to his cheeks and a renewed sparkle to his eyes. It was then she had the courage to talk to him about their future.

"John, when I think back over our years it appears to me that our best hours and our best memories are tied up with the work we did together."

He stretched out lazily on the cushions on the bottom of the boat, adjusted the parasol to keep the sun off his face, then answered slowly, "Yes, the months when we collaborated on the reports . . . the campaign of 1856 . . . the Hundred Days in Missouri . . . they stand out in my mind like great peaks in the Rockies."

"Then, as soon as you feel strong enough, why couldn't we continue our collaboration? The editor wants more stories, and we write well together—at least you always said we did. You've had sufficient adventures and experience to provide the material for a hundred books, books I always thought you should write . . ."

"I'm no author, Jessie. Have you forgotten my nosebleed in the house on C Street?"

"Neither am I! But together we have always done good work. You supply the material, I'll set down the stories. Isn't that a fair arrangement?"

In the spring they returned to New York. Jessie located a modest cottage on Staten Island, right on the waterfront, and Lily was called home.

The series of articles in the *Ledger* had been well received. Robert Bonner asked for more, "Though not eleven at a time, my dear Mrs. Fremont, I beg of you!" Since she could write them far faster than the *Ledger* could use them, she went to visit the editors of *Harper's, Century* and *Wide Awake;* they had seen the stories in the *Ledger,* so it was not difficult to sell them.

The summer and fall months passed quickly and happily, with all three of the family sharing the work. John wrote out many pages of notes about the trails and the mountains and his early expeditions for Jessie's reference. She then wrote her stories in pencil. When she had finished a rough draft Lily transferred the material to the typewriter. They made only a modest living, but they were intensely happy, for they were all busy; Charlie had completed his first cruise successfully, and Frank was doing well in his studies at West Point. Lily assumed the management of the house and the family funds, and so Jessie was relieved of a task for which she cared little, freed to work three or four hours in the morning, to take long walks with John over the Island in the afternoons, watching the ships come in and out of New York Harbor as they had watched from their glassed-in porch at Black Point.

And at last, in 1878, President Hayes appointed John to be governor of the Territory of Arizona. The salary was only two thousand dollars a year, but there was great rejoicing in Jessie's heart, for it meant that once again John would be in the service of his country, that he would be restored to activity and position.

They made the trip overland to San Francisco in seven days, riding the railroad that had risen on the ashes of John Fremont's first effort. It was seventeen years since she had sailed out of the Golden Gate strait to join her husband who had just been appointed major general of the Western Command. San Francisco was now a thriving metropolis; there was little left to remind her of her first view of the city when she clambered down the side of the S.S. *Panama* in 1849 and was carried through the surf by a sailor. Knowing that their home on Black Point had been torn down, she refused John's offer to take her there.

They stayed in San Francisco only long enough to regain their land legs, then boarded the Southern Pacific train for Los Angeles. John insisted upon riding his wife up to Fort Hill, where he could show her the emplacement and the remains of the battery which he had erected to defend the Pueblo of Los Angeles in 1847. The train carried them from Los Angeles to Yuma, where they were met by three army ambulances, each drawn by six mules. Jessie, John and Lily rode in the first ambulance, crossing the Gila River with the water up to the hubs and camping the first night on the bank of the Colorado River. For Jessie this was like the early days in California; she only wished she could see Beale and old Knight come galloping across the desert.

Jessie and Lily went house hunting in Prescott, renting one made of pine and juniper planks, covered only by cotton sheets. The wood proved to be infested with vermin, so the two women removed the sheets and scoured the planks with boiling lye. Lily kept the house filled with wild flowers in the wet season, and yellow and dark red cactus blossoms in the dry. Jessie gave history classes to the school children every Friday; she took pride in watching Prescott grow into a fair-sized village with the erection of churches, a hospital and a few plastered homes. If the hamlet was crude, with wooden sidewalks lashed by dust storms, its adobe houses sometimes melting down in the fierce rainstorms, if it was a town just being born in a wild country in process of being converted from a territory to a state, had not all her life and her family's life been spent in just such surroundings? Was it not their pattern to live with such young towns as St. Louis, Washington, Monterey, San Francisco, Mariposa and now Prescott?

John's duties were light, more a matter of keeping good will than law and order, but unfortunately their house cost ninety dollars a month, the Chinese cook provided by a sympathetic aunt in Los Angeles cost forty dollars a month, and foods were three times as high as in New York or San Francisco. Jessie continued her writing, for the two-thousand-dollar salary barely covered their food and rent. They could not keep saddle horses, for hay was fifty dollars a ton, but the army post made their stables available to the governor. John and Lily spent their days in the saddle, riding across the desert. The high altitude did not agree with Jessie. She found it difficult to work, was frequently short of breath, and when she came in from a walk she would have to lie down at once. She did not tell them that her heart and lungs were acting strangely in this new country, or that the lassitude which prevented her from continuing her writing was caused by anything more than laziness or contentment.

She stood this sapping of her energies in silence for a full year, determined neither to give in nor to worry her family. Then one day John and Lily returned from a horseback ride to find her lying face down on the floor. When they had revived her and demanded to know what had happened, she did not feel that she could conceal her ailment any longer. John announced quickly that he would resign his governorship and take her back to Staten Island. Jessie glanced at her husband's sunburned face, radiating good health. She could not let him go back to hateful idleness and obscurity.

That evening she effected a compromise: she would return east; Lily would remain in Prescott to keep her father company. They would come east for vacations, and she would visit them in Prescott during the more favorable weather. Neither her husband nor her daughter wanted to let her go, but she convinced them that it was the best way out of a difficult situation.

It was the last she was to see of her husband or daughter for three solid years, for they never garnered sufficient spare cash for traveling or visits.

Jessie lived alone in the cottage they had formerly occupied on Staten Island, writing stories and essays which were collected in book form under such titles as *Far West Sketches, A Year of American Travel, The Will and Way Stories, Souvenirs of My Time*. Her writings sold fairly well, not enough to give her any assurance for the future, but enough to make her life secure in the Staten Island bungalow and enable her to send a few dollars each month to Lily for the management of the Prescott house. She kept her living expenses low, wearing her old dresses until they were threadbare, rarely going to New York, avoiding all social affairs. Occasionally she was visited by Charlie, when he was in from a cruise, or by Frank, who was now a second lieutenant in the Army. Hannah Kirsten and others of her old friends came for several days at a time to keep her company.

Yet she was alone, always terribly alone. She recalled what Lily had said in their library at Pocaho about watching her mother crawl about the house like a stricken creature when her husband was away. In her mind she went back again and again to those years when John had been gone on his expeditions, when she had spent six months, a year, two years without him. When she struck a balance in the account books of her memory she saw that half of her married life had been spent in separatior from her husband. These separations had been necessary, sometimes to their career, sometimes to the demands of John's roving nature; yet they had never been necessary to her. Having been separated from her husband for half her life was like having been married only half as long; and it was too late now to recapture those lost years, to live still again that half of the marriage that had been so cruelly wasted. She had been through so much, she was so much older that she imagined the ache would be less and the torture less. Yet the passage of the years had not made her better able to endure separation.

Time and again she decided to return to Arizona: better to be ill at John's side than to be in the best of physical health but spiritually half alive without him. At other times she determined to ask John to come back to Staten Island, but she remembered how happy he was as governor and knew she could not do it.

More severely than anything that had happened in the three years of working alone and thinking alone, she was distressed at being by herself on her fifty-eighth birthday. She somehow felt sentimental about the occasion; she remembered how John had resisted his fortieth birthday in Paris, feeling that it was the fatal milestone to an explorer and trail blazer. It had taken her eighteen years longer to reach this frame of mind; up to this moment she had felt old only a few times in her life: at the Delaware Indian Reservation, on the sand dunes of San Francisco, in

St. Louis after they had relinquished their command to General Hunter, during the two months she had visited Hannah Kirsten. But now, going into her fifty-eighth year, sitting despondently in her little cottage, her hair snow white even though her eyebrows were still thick and black, her face fuller than when she had been young, her skin lined, the hazel in her eyes having turned to a deep brown, her once full mouth drawn taut, all these told her that she had at last grown old.

In the spring of 1883 she received a telegram from John saying that he had resigned his position and was returning to Staten Island to be with her. Her eyes lighted with happiness, but at the same moment she began to worry about their finances. She was not able to write as consistently as she had over the years: she had poured out most of her experiences and the editors were now frequently rejecting the stories. She told herself that the return of her husband would bring her new strength and spirit, that they would somehow get on.

When John came home he seemed to her as young and handsome as she had known him in his youth. He had many business hopes: the development of mines in Arizona, the promoting of a short railroad to take the place of the stagecoaches, the irrigation of Imperial Valley in California for farm lands. He spent a number of weeks trying to promote his ventures in New York, but the eastern financial magnates were not interested; they had no desire to start pioneering enterprises with a seventy-year-old man; and so within a few months his enthusiasm for being back in the East had burned out.

For the next few years they were hard put to it for funds. There was little left in their modest cottage to suggest the grandeur of bygone days; a very few precious books, one or two paintings, souvenirs from the early expeditions, the presidential campaign of 1856, the Hundred Days. Jessie did not always know how Lily managed to secure enough money to meet their ordinary needs. From the amount of time she spent in her bedroom behind the closed door, working at the heavy typewriter, Jessie sometimes suspected that her daughter was doing outside typing jobs.

They were sitting before the living-room fireplace, reading Ulysses S. Grant's *Personal Memoirs,* when Jessie exclaimed:

"You know, John, these memoirs of Grant's are popular; they've sold a great many copies. Why don't you write your memoirs? If you could put down the full story of your expeditions and everything that you have done since 1840—what a magnificent story that would make!"

John's eyes gleamed, but he did not answer.

"Who but you can pick up all the countless fragments and tell the full truth, as Father did in his *Thirty Years in the United States Senate?*"

"Yes, I should like that," replied John slowly. "Do you think we can find a publisher?"

"I am certain we can. I will go into New York tomorrow and make the arrangements."

"We would have to go to Washington to live, you know. All of the documents are there, in the Library of Congress."

"We'll manage it. You will find it stimulating to be back in Washington again. It will help you to write the book."

The next morning she found that the publishers were not overly excited about the idea. They said they would like to see the manuscript when it was completed, but they would advance no money to get it written. The firm of Belford & Clarke seemed more enthusiastic about the venture; while they too refused to advance any money they were willing to sign a generous contract and publish the manuscript immediately upon completion. Jessie was relieved that she could take at least this much good news back to her husband. Yet how were they to live in Washington for the year that would be required to write the book? As she stood at the stub-nosed prow of the Staten Island ferryboat she knew that the answer was up to her. She must become fruitful once again.

A picture arose behind her eyes: she was in the library of the home on C Street on the morning that her husband had left on his first expedition. Tom Benton was saying, "No one has ever put together a story of American exploration . . . I think our people would enjoy that story, Jessie." She had been carrying Lily when her father had first put that idea in her mind; though forty-four years had passed since then, no one had yet popularized the full story of western exploration. Here it was, ready-made for her purposes!

She told John of the contract that was being written up, putting the best face she could upon the discouraging fact that no one would advance any money against royalties, and then sat down to earn the funds they would need for the year in Washington. She made a number of false starts, but by the second week she was writing easily and steadily, evolving twenty articles about American exploration and the lives of the explorers. Four of these the New York editors rejected. The other sixteen were sold. With this money she moved her family to Washington where they rented a house on Dupont Circle overlooking the parklike grounds of the British Legation.

She turned the front room of the second floor into a workroom, for there was a bow window facing east in which she placed John's desk and across from it a green leather table for herself. Lily set up her typewriter in an alcove. Jessie found it good to be hard at work with John again, rising at seven for tea and a roll, then writing until noon, stopping for a light meal, going back to her desk at one o'clock and not stopping until six. At John's request she wrote a short biography of her father to serve as an introduction, but for the main body of the long memoir she merely took dictation from John, content to make an occasional suggestion about material that should be included. As she finished the handwritten pages, Lily took them to her adjoining alcove where she typed them. A reporter from the Washington *Star* reported to his paper:

General Fremont is now seventy-four years old, but looks scarce sixty. His hair, short beard, and mustache are white, but his brown eyes are clear and bright as stars, and his complexion has the ruddy, healthy glow of childhood.

The year passed swiftly and happily, for they were enjoying this voyage backward into their glorious past. The present existed hardly at all for them. They could not get used to the changes in Washington. What Tom Benton had found to be a miasmic mudhole in 1820 had, in 1886, grown into a world metropolis with thousands of beautiful homes, parks and government buildings. Practically all the landmarks so dear to their early years were gone: the Benton home, Hassler's house with its observatory, the glassworks and the fields across which they had walked in the days before their marriage. Gone too were most of their friends, and Tom Benton's comrades of the Senate.

They planned to do the work in two volumes. The publishers had their agents in the field taking subscriptions, but few buyers were willing to part with twelve dollars in advance of publication. Jessie was confident that once the book was released, once it had been enthusiastically reviewed in the press, it would sell well.

The book was issued, but it did not sell at all. Jessie was hard pressed to understand why: she knew that it was too expensive, that much of the material had already been published in their earlier reports and was widely known, that the publishers were new in the field and not particularly astute; but all these things put together did not explain to her satisfaction why John Fremont's *Memoirs* did not sell. Somewhere in the back of her mind was the knowledge that the book had failed because history had passed John C. Fremont by; because he had lived beyond his times, even as her father had before him; that this was a new and young world, interested in other people and other things.

For their solid year of work they received nothing; the publishers lost money on the bulky, well-illustrated book, and Jessie learned too late that their contract paid no royalties until the publisher had taken out his costs. All during the year she had watched John working happily, often brilliant in his analysis of historical forces, a man as young and vital at seventy-four as he had been in the accomplishing at thirty-four. Now, with the volume a failure, earning them not a dollar for their long labors, making it impossible for them to carry on with the proposed second volume, John became ill. When the doctor told her that she must take him at once to a country where the climate was warmer and milder, she was faced with the same problem that she had met thirteen years before. But now there was no way to earn quickly the money to take him to Nassau. She must do something the Fremonts had never done before: she went to Collis P. Huntington, who was in Washington on business for his Southern Pacific Railroad. When she had told Huntington the circumstances he said at once:

"It must be California. You should have my private car, but it is already lent. I will come to your house this evening with the railroad tickets and the necessary letters to insure you a pleasant journey."

When Jessie showed Collis Huntington into John's bedroom that evening, and her husband learned the purpose of the visit, he became angry.

"You had no right to do this, Jessie," he said with tears in his eyes. "We have no way of paying Mr. Huntington back . . ."

Huntington said quietly, "General, aren't you forgetting that our railroad goes over your buried campfires and climbs many a grade you jogged over on a mule? I think we rather owe you this."

9

SHE RENTED a vine-covered redwood house on Oak Street in Los Angeles, set in the midst of a broad lawn with flowering shrubs. Here in the warmth of the California sunshine John recovered his health. They lived quietly, rarely leaving their own grounds, welcoming old friends who came each afternoon to tea. Jessie did no more writing, for she felt that she had told all of her stories; but when young historians such as Josiah Royce attacked John, calling him a political adventurer in California who had had no secret orders, branding him as a routine trail marker who had never done any exploring, she wrote passionate articles of defense which such magazines as *Century* published.

A little money came in from these articles; each of her two sons now sent a small monthly check; they lived in modest comfort. She never relaxed her efforts to push through Congress the bill for compensation for Black Point; and here in the quiet warmth of southern California she began her last campaign: to have John put on the Army's pension list in return for his years of service. Her new efforts seemed more promising than any had been before: a bill again passed the House to return them the purchase price of Black Point, the movement to grant John a major general's pension was meeting with favor.

John was growing increasingly restless. He had been evolving promotional schemes that he wanted to talk over with former business associates in New York; his presence in Washington would be helpful in having him put on the pension list and in getting the Black Point bill through the Senate. In the winter of 1889 Jessie reluctantly agreed that he should go east. She had watched his strength ebb away, for though at seventy-seven his mind seemed as vigorous as it always had been, she knew that his physical strength was brittle. She was uneasy at letting him out of her ministering hands, away from the brusque, efficient care of Lily, but to hold him against his wishes when he so urgently needed a sense of motion would hurt him more than the separation. He planned to be gone for two months; Jessie could not spare the money to accompany him.

She remained quietly in the little cottage, waiting for the mailman to come swinging down Oak Street, a tan leather pouch at his side, bringing her the daily packet of news from John. Though he was staying at a cheap boardinghouse in a run-down part of town instead of going to the Astor House or to the home of a friend, he was feeling well, was excited and pleased to be active again. At last in April, after he had been gone for five months, she received a letter telling her that Congress had granted him a lifetime pension of six thousand dollars a year, "in view of the services to his country rendered by John C. Fremont, administrator and soldier."

Jessie hugged the letter to her, reading it again and again. This was the best news she had received for a long time. The government was at last acknowledging its debt to John Fremont. Now they could spend their remaining years in peace and contentment, unharassed by financial worries. She saw from John's letter how much it had meant to him, how pleased he was at this avowal of the value of his services and the unanimous praise which the bill received in the nation's press. He was going to wind up some business affairs, then he would return to Los Angeles and his Jessie, and they never would be parted again.

But the weeks dragged on and still John did not come home. While she did not like to urge him too strongly to return so long as he felt he had things to do in New York, she grew uneasy.

Then suddenly, without warning, on a suffocatingly hot July morning, she received a telegram from Charlie who was on shore leave in Washington. It read:

FATHER IS ILL

She sat in a rocker under a live-oak tree in her front yard, unmoving, almost unbreathing. That he should be stricken in a bleak bedroom of a strange rooming house, without his wife to take care of him, without the family he had raised, the few beloved souvenirs of his life, this brought anguish.

Three hours later, just as the bells of a near-by church began to chime of noon, a second telegram was delivered from Charlie. It said:

FATHER IS DEAD

After a time she walked slowly into the house and sat down at her desk in the corner of the little living room, above which was the portrait of General John C. Fremont made during the Hundred Days. On the side wall above her chair was the oil portrait of herself, painted shortly after her marriage. She sat looking up at the two pictures, somehow unable to feel that John Fremont was dead at seventy-eight, while she was still alive. She was heartbroken that he had died away from her, alone, without the last comfort of his hand in hers.

When night came, when some of the numbness of grief had eased, she understood that this was no accident: this was the way John Fremont had wanted to die, alone, as he had somehow always been alone, this shy, reserved little man who for forty-five years had been seeking, through the blinding snows of the high Sierras, to find that uncharted pass. He had known during these past weeks that he was going to die; much as he had loved her for fifty years he had wanted to die alone, alone in a drab rooming-house bed, die as he had been born, an outcast, an illegitimate one . . .

And now, at last, she knew that she would never accomplish the task on which she had set out as a girl of seventeen. Married half a century, she still had not solved the enigma of John Fremont. In her love, in her devotion she had perhaps come closer than any other woman could have; and yet how much there was which would go down to the grave with him, unexplained.

She had thought of this as a failure in her marriage. Now she realized that no one can ever completely understand another human soul. What was important was not the whole and total finding, but the search, the sympathy, the ever present and loving desire to understand. That, in its last analysis, was what love was, when viewed over half a century: at first it was lighthearted romance, then it was physical mating, then it was ambition and work together, then it was raising a family and creating a home, then it was service in good and various causes, then it was a mature partnership in progress and accomplishment, failure and hardship. Yes, love changed subtly with the passage of the years, but lasting longest and having the deepest meaning, creating the finest hours and the finest years, was the search for understanding, the full and sympathetic understanding of another being, the most elusive and at the same time the most beautiful of all human accomplishments. This was marriage.

The ensuing days were difficult. It was not possible to bring John's body to California for burial, nor could she reach New York in time for the funeral. She sat quietly in her chair in the corner of the living room, rereading her husband's last loving messages to her while his son buried him on a hill overlooking the Hudson River and Pocaho. She had a sense of Lily hovering over her to protect her, masking her own grief, ˜eping at a distance, not wishing to intrude yet wanting to be at her elbow for the word of comfort or the helping hand whenever it might be needed.

She shed no tears, for she had no regrets; there was nothing she had left undone, no kindness, no act of love or faith or loyalty that had been lacking. There was nothing with which to reprove herself, nothing she would have done differently. She had given John Fremont all of her love and all of her life; she could now live serenely until it was her time to go. Their lives together had passed so quickly, there had been no time to pause, to linger over the moments as they went by. Now there would be time. She was glad there would be time to relive all her memories, to watch her life pass in review, to understand it more fully now that she could hold back the hours. She had lived with John a life of tumultuous action; now she would be able to relive it quietly, savoring the best that was in it.

She picked up a letter which Charlie had written to Lily, telling his sister how painless her father's last hours had been and how thankful they should be that his last few months were happy ones. Then, at the end of the letter, she saw something which held her eye:

Of what the effect is going to be on Mother, I don't dare think. And when I do think, I doubt whether the cruelest result would not be the kindest. They lived in each other, so that I don't think there is any life for the one left.

No, Charlie, she thought, you are wrong. I won't be unhappy. Your father is safe. There is no more poverty or uncertainty for him, no more humiliation or disappointment or change of fortune. Ah, Charlie, we have lived so long together—a full half-century; we have been so close that nothing can separate us now: surely nothing so inconclusive as death. Do you imagine that merely by leaving my side your father leaves me alone? How can I ever be alone, Charlie, I who have worked and loved and suffered and rejoiced with him through all the years? You are too young to know the value of memories, my son; memories are stronger than the living flesh. Your father has died, but not in me; as long as I remain on this earth he will never die. I have him with me as surely and as vividly as I had him sitting beside me at that first musicale at Miss English's Academy, or holding me in his arms at Harriet Bodisco's wedding; just as surely as I had him with me during all those long hard months when he was away on his expeditions. True, I suffered then, for I too was young, I had no way of knowing how long and good our life together would be. But now I know it in its full length and its full goodness; I have had the greatest happiness available to a woman: I have loved my husband always and unfailingly; my husband has loved me; and our marriage has remained firm and beautiful. Do you think that these things can be taken away from a woman of sixty-six, Charlie? Do you think that, no matter how long I live, there can conceivably be time enough to relive in memory all our wonderful years together?

Nor is my work done even yet, Charlie; already the critics are hovering over your father's accomplishments, waiting to attack him. But so long as I remain alive, Charlie—and that will be for many years—your father will never go undefended. I fought for him while he was alive, and I will fight for him a thousand times harder now.

Do not grieve for me, Charlie, any more than you would grieve for your father, who had a long and magnificent life. I will know what to do with my days; a good marriage never ends; it will fill my life just as beautifully as it has for the past fifty years, fill it until the day I die.

Note on Sources

THE READER may have asked himself, "How much of this story is true?" Much of the dialogue had to be reimagined; in one or two instances I have portrayed an incident where I was convinced of its probability even though I could not document it, for example, the meeting of Jessie Fremont and Secretary George Bancroft in the Benton home before the conquest of California; I have taken an occasional minor liberty with time where the change could have no significance in history, for example, staging Harriet Williams' wedding a year later than it actually happened, in order that Jessie might attend it with Lieutenant Fremont; and I have omitted several unimportant fragments of the complete story. Aside from these technical liberties the book is true.

My main source was the writings of Jessie Fremont: her unpublished memoirs in the Bancroft Library of the University of California at Berkeley; her unpublished letters, as well as those of her father, her husband and her friends; her published books: *Souvenirs of My Time, Far West Sketches, A Year of American Travel, The Story of the Guard, The Will and the Way Stories;* and her many uncollected magazine articles. Her daughter's book, *Recollections of Elizabeth Benton Fremont,* gives many colorful pictures of their later life. Thomas Hart Benton's *Thirty Years in the United States Senate* provides rich source material for the political history of the times; of the three biographies already published about him, the ones by Theodore Roosevelt and Joseph M. Rogers are fragments; the one by William M. Meigs is a complete political biography but contains nothing of his personal life. Jessie Fremont's short biography of her father, which serves as a prologue to John C. Fremont's *Memoirs,* is sensitively done.

John C. Fremont, in addition to the reports of his expeditions, published *Memoirs of My Life.* Six biographies have been written about him; of these, three were campaign biographies written in 1856: *The Life, Explorations and Public Services of John Charles Fremont*, by Charles W. Upham; *The Life of Colonel John Charles Fremont*, by Samuel M. Smucker; *Memoir of the Life and Public Services of John Charles Fremont*, by John Bigelow, assisted by Jessie Fremont. The fourth campaign biography appeared serially in the New York *Tribune*, and then in pamphlet form, written by Horace Greeley and Thomas McElrath. Frederick S. Dellenbaugh's *Fremont and '49*, 1914, is an excellent account of the expeditions. *A Man Unafraid*, by Herbert Bashford and Harry Wagner, 1927, is eulogistic, while *John Charles Fremont*, 1930, by Cardinal Goodwin, is quarrelsome. Allan Nevins' *Fremont, Pathmarker of the West*, 1939, is complete, authentic and highly readable.

The only previous study of Jessie Fremont is *Jessie Benton Fremont*, by Catherine Coffin Phillips, privately printed by the John Henry Nash Press in San Francisco in 1935. Mrs. Phillips' book contains invaluable source material, for she knew Jessie Fremont during the latter years of Mrs. Fremont's life and collected a fine store of anecdotes. She also had access to a group of one hundred letters written by Jessie Fremont to Nellie Haskell Browne, which have now disappeared.

The article which first awakened my interest in Jessie Fremont was "Fremont and Jessie," by Robert L. Duffus in the *American Mercury* of November 1925.

A book of this type would be difficult to write were it not for the many fine volumes that have already been published by my fellow biographers. I take this means of expressing my gratitude and sincere admiration for their research:

The Life and Letters of George Bancroft, M. A. DeWolfe Howe.
The Francis Preston Blair Family in Politics, W. E. Smith.
The Life of James Buchanan, G. Ticknor Curtis.
Kit Carson, Stanley Vestal.
Horace Greeley, Don C. Seitz.
Bret Harte, Henry C. Merwin.
Bret Harte of the Old West, Alvin F. Harlow.
General Phillip Kearny, Thomas Kearny.
Thomas Starr King, C. W. Wendte.
Abraham Lincoln: A History, Volume IV, Nicolay and Hay.
The American Leonardo: The Life of Samuel F. B. Morse, Carleton Mabee.
Little Mac: The Life of General George B. McClellan, Clarence Edward Macartney.
Franklin Pierce, Roy Franklin Nichols.
James K. Polk, Andrew C. McLaughlin.
Winfield Scott, Charles Winslow Elliott.
Whittier, Bard of Freedom, Whitman Bennett.

Among the more important general books used were:

The Truth About Fremont, Ernest A. Wiltsee.
Fremont's Hundred Days, M. F. Hixon. (Photostatic copy of manuscript in New York Public Library.)
Thirty-First Star, James A. B. Scherer.

Note on Sources

The Year of Decision, Bernard DeVoto.
A History of the Presidency, Edward Stanwood.
Senate Executive Document, No. 33, First Session, Vol. 5, which is the complete story of the court-martial.
History of California, H. H. Bancroft.
Incidents of Travel and Adventure in the Far West with Colonel Fremont's Last Expedition, S. N. Carvalho.
John C. Fremont and the Republican Party, Ruhl Jacob Bartlett.
The Eve of Conflict, George Fort Milton.
Reveille in Washington, Margaret Leech.

Among the source books used on early western exploring were:

The Adventures of Captain Bonneville, U.S.A., Washington Irving.
Journals, Lewis and Clark.
An Account of the Expeditions to the Sources of the Mississippi, Zebulon Pike.
Expedition through the Upper Mississippi, Henry Schoolcraft.

General survey books in the field include:

Southern Trails to California in 1849, Ralph Bieber.
The Ashley-Smith Explorations and the Discovery of a Central Route to the Pacific, H. C. Dale.
Breaking the Wilderness, Frederick Dellenbaugh.
The Road to Oregon, W. J. Ghent.
Wagons West, a Story of the Oregon Trail, Elizabeth Page.

A complete Fremont biography follows:

Decision of California Supreme Court—Fremont vs. Fowler.
"Origin of the Fremont Exploration," Jessie Fremont. *Century,* March 1891.
"How a Woman's Wit Saved California," J. Moody. *Hist. Soc. of So. Calif.,* Pub., Vol. 4, 1899.
The Daring Adventures of Kit Carson and Fremont—Diary. N.Y.: Hurst & Co., 1885.
The Life and Love of J. C. Fremont, Samuel M. Smucker. N.Y.: Muller, Orton & Mulligan, 1856.
The Mariposa Estate, John C. Fremont. London: 1861, Whittingham & Wilkins.
Fremont's memorial to Congress for his claim for reimbursement for beef cattle.
"Fremont in the Conquest of California," John Bidwell. *Century,* February 1891.
Biographical Sketch of Colonel Fremont. Anonymous.
"Fremont Anecdotes," George R. Stewart. Typewritten item, Bancroft Library.
"The Opening of the Mariposa Mining Region," C. G. Campton. Ph.D. thesis, Berkeley.
Sons of the Eagle, George Creel.
Life of J. C. Fremont, Greeley and McElrath.
Life of Major-General J. C. Fremont, James Magoon. London: Beadle & Co., 1863.
"Montgomery and Fremont," Josiah Royce. *Century,* March 1891.
"Fremont Had No Secret Instructions," George Tays. Typewritten item, Bancroft Library.
"Senator Benton Lays His Plans," Thomas Drew. *Calif. Hist. Soc.,* Vol. 13, No. 2.
Fremont Songs for the People, 1856.

The Fremont Songster, 1856.
Defence of Lieutenant Colonel J. C. Fremont before the Military Court-Martial, Washington, January, 1848. (Pamphlet.)
Fremont, the West's Greatest Adventurer, Allan Nevins.
Fremont, Pathmarker of the West, Allan Nevins.
Letters to the Editors of the *National Intelligencer,* J. C. Fremont.
Colonel Fremont's Private and Public Character Vindicated, James Buchanan.
Colonel Fremont's Religion. Anonymous.
McClellan and Fremont, Antietam.
Fremont's Hundred Days in Missouri, Francis Preston Blair.
General Fremont and the Injustice Done Him, W. Brotherhead.
Colonel Fremont not a Roman Catholic. Anonymous.
Fremont and McClellan, V. B. Denslow.
Facts and Figures for Fremont and Freedom. Anonymous.
Fremont: His Supporters and Their Record. Anonymous.
"Fremont and the North Americans," F. H. Harrington. *Am. Hist. Rev.,* 1939, Vol. 44.
The Fremont Estate, David Hoffman.
J. C. Fremont's Record: Proof of His Romanism, Proof of His Pro-slavery Acts. Anonymous.
"Some of the Romance of Fremont," E. M. James. *Overland,* 1931, Vol. 89.
"Concerning Fremont," Thomas Kearny. *Argonaut,* 1931, Vol. 109.
Reminiscences of the Fremont Campaign, E. P. Powell.
"The Blairs and Fremont," W. F. Smith. *Missouri Hist. Rev.,* 1929, Vol. 23.
"Polk and Fremont," R. R. Stenberg. *Pac. Hist. Rev.,* 1938, Vol. 7.
Case of General Fremont, J. Thomas.
Report on Memorial of John C. Fremont.
U. S. Senate Res. of Senate Pub. Rep. of J. C. Fremont.
U. S. War Claims at St. Louis Comm. on J. C. Fremont.
Who Is John C. Fremont? Anonymous.

Manuscripts in the Bancroft Library:

Narrative of J. C. Fremont's Expedition to California in 1845–46, and Subsequent Events in California Down to 1853, Thomas B. Martin.
History of California as Dictated by Major Salvador Vallejo.
New Helvetia Diary of Events from 1845 to 1848, Swasey, Bidwell, Tooker, Sutter.
California, 1841–48, an Immigrant's Recollection of a Trip Across the Plains, John Bidwell.
Personal Reminiscences, General John A. Sutter.
Papers on the Bear Flag, Jacob P. Leese.
The Days of 1846, William Buldridge.
California in 1846, William Hargrave.
The Bear Flag Revolt, John Fowler.
Official Correspondence, Thomas S. Larkin.
Senator William Gwin's Manuscripts.
William M. Gwin, Expansionist, Hallie McPherson (in possession of Stanford Gwin of San Francisco).
Original Study of Albert Sidney Johnston, Henry Duque.
Life of Larkin, R. L. Underhill of Berkeley (unpublished manuscript in possession of author).

Letters of Thomas Hart Benton to His Daughters.
Letters and Autobiographical Writings of Jessie Fremont.
Letters and Memoranda, John C. Fremont.
Memoires, Jessie Fremont.
Statement of William F. Swasey (Cals. manuscripts D. 200).
Statement on Conditions in 1848, Charles V. Gillespie.

Manuscripts in the Huntington Library:

The Leidesdorff Papers.
Fremont and the Conquest of California, Henry L. Oak.
Unpublished Notebook of 1848–1851 (7 vols.), Edward M. Kern.
Secret Affairs of the Mexican War, Jessie Fremont.
Fort Sutter Papers, Edward Kern.
Jessie Fremont (pamphlet), Thomas R. Bard.